MICHAEL CONN

The

A former police reporter for the *Los Angeles Times*, Michael Connelly is the author of 18 acclaimed and best-selling novels. His books have been translated into 31 languages and have won awards all over the world. He lives in Florida with his wife and daughter.

Also by Michael Connelly

Fiction

The Black Echo
The Black Ice
The Concrete Blonde
The Last Coyote
The Poet
Trunk Music
Blood Work
Angels Flight
Void Moon
Chasing the Dime
The Narrows
The Closers
The Lincoln Lawyer
Echo Park
The Overlook

Non-Fiction

Crime Beat

Michael Connelly

The Harry Bosch Novels

A Darkness More Than Night

City of Bones

Lost Light

First published in Great Britain in 2008 by Orion Books,
an imprint of The Orion Publishing Group Ltd
Orion House, 5 Upper Saint Martin's Lane
London WC2H 9EA

An Hachette Livre UK Company

1 3 5 7 9 10 8 6 4 2

A CIP catalogue record for this book is
available from the British Library.

ISBN (Trade Paperback) 978 1 4091 0026 3

Typeset by Deltatype Ltd, Birkenhead, Merseyside
Printed in Great Britain by Clays Ltd, St Ives plc

The Orion Publishing Group's policy is to use papers that are natural,
renewable and recyclable products and made from wood grown in sustainable
forests. The logging and manufacturing processes are expected to
conform to the environmental regulations of the country of origin.

www.orionbooks.co.uk

Contents

A Darkness More Than Night

This is for Mary and Jack Lavelle,
who proved there are second acts

Prologue

Bosch looked through the small square of glass and saw that the man was alone in the tank. He took his gun out of its holster and handed it to the watch sergeant. Standard procedure. The steel door was unlocked and slid open. Immediately the smell of sweat and vomit stung Bosch's nostrils.

'How long's he been in here?'

'About three hours,' said the sergeant. 'He blew a one-eight, so I don't know what you're going to get.'

Bosch stepped into the holding tank and kept his eyes on the prone form on the floor.

'All right, you can close it.'

'Let me know.'

The door slid closed with a jarring bang and jolt. The man on the floor groaned and moved only slightly. Bosch walked over and sat down on the bench nearest to him. He took the tape recorder out of his jacket pocket and put it down on the bench. Glancing up at the glass window he saw the sergeant's face move away. He used the toe of his shoe to probe the man's side. The man groaned again.

'Wake up, you piece of shit.'

The man on the floor of the tank slowly rolled his head and then lifted it. Paint flecked his hair and vomit had caked on the front of his shirt and neck. He opened his eyes and immediately closed them against the harsh overhead lighting of the holding tank. His voice came out in a hoarse whisper.

'You again.'

Bosch nodded.

'Yeah. Me.'

'Our little dance.'

A smile cut across the three-day-old whiskers on the drunk's face. Bosch saw that he was missing a tooth he hadn't been missing last time. He reached down and put his hand on the recorder but did not turn it on yet.

'Get up. It's time to talk.'

'Forget it, man. I don't want—'

'You're running out of time. Talk to me.'

'Leave me the fuck alone.'

Bosch looked up at the window. It was clear. He looked back down at the man on the floor.

'Your salvation is in the truth. Now more than ever. I can't help you without the truth.'

'What're you, a priest now? You here to take my confession?'

'You here to give it?'

The man on the floor said nothing. After a while Bosch thought he might have fallen back asleep. He pushed the toe of his shoe into the man's side again, into the kidney. The man erupted in movement, flailing his arms and legs.

'Fuck you!' he yelled. 'I don't want you. I want a lawyer.'

Bosch was silent a moment. He picked up the recorder and slid it back into his pocket. He then leaned forward, elbows on his knees, and clasped his hands together. He looked at the drunk and slowly shook his head.

'Then I guess I can't help you,' he said.

He stood up and knocked on the window for the watch sergeant. He left the man lying on the floor.

1

'Someone's coming.'

Terry McCaleb looked at his wife and then followed her eyes down to the winding road below. He could see the golf cart making its way up the steep and winding road to the house. The driver was obscured by the roof of the cart.

They were sitting on the back deck of the house he and Graciela had rented up on La Mesa Avenue. The view ranged from the narrow winding road below the house to the whole of Avalon and its harbor, and then out across the Santa Monica Bay to the haze of smog that marked overtown. The view was the reason they had chosen this house to make their new home on the island. But at the moment his wife spoke, his gaze had been on the baby in his arms, not the view. He could look no farther than his daughter's wide blue and trusting eyes.

McCaleb saw the rental number on the side of the golf cart passing below. It wasn't a local coming. It was somebody who had probably come from overtown on the *Catalina Express.* Still, he wondered how Graciela knew that the visitor was coming to their house and not any of the others on La Mesa.

He didn't ask about this – she'd had premonitions before. He just waited and soon after the golf cart disappeared from sight, there was a knock at the front door. Graciela went to answer it and soon came back to the deck with a woman McCaleb had not seen in three years.

Sheriff's detective Jaye Winston smiled when she saw the child in his arms. It was genuine, but at the same time it was the distracted smile of someone who wasn't there to admire a new baby. McCaleb knew the thick green binder she carried in one hand and the videocassette in the other meant Winston was there on business. Death business.

'Terry, howya been?' she asked.

'Couldn't be better. You remember Graciela?'

'Of course. And who is this?'

'This is CiCi.'

McCaleb never used the baby's formal name around others. He only liked to call her Cielo when he was alone with her.

'CiCi,' Winston said, and hesitated as if waiting for an explanation of the name. When none came, she said, 'How old?'

'Almost four months. She's big.'

'Wow, yeah, I can see . . . And the boy . . . where's he?'

'Raymond,' Graciela said. 'He's with some friends today. Terry had a charter and so he went with friends to the park to play softball.'

The conversation was halting and strange. Winston either wasn't really interested or was unused to such banal talk.

'Would you like something to drink?' McCaleb offered as he passed the baby to Graciela.

'No, I'm fine. I had a Coke on the boat.'

As if on cue, or perhaps indignant about being passed from one set of hands to another, the baby started to fuss and Graciela said she would take her inside. She left them standing on the porch. McCaleb pointed to the round table and chairs where they ate most nights while the baby slept.

'Let's sit down.'

He pointed Winston to the chair that would give her the best view of the harbor. She put the green binder, which McCaleb recognized as a murder book, on the table and the video on top of it.

'Beautiful,' she said.

'Yeah, she's amazing. I could watch her all—'

He stopped and smiled when he realized she was talking about the view, not his child. Winston smiled, too.

'She's beautiful, Terry. She really is. You look good, too, so tan and all.'

'I've been going out on the boat.'

'And your health is good?'

'Can't complain about anything other than all the meds they make me take. But I'm three years in now and no problems. I think I'm in the clear, Jaye. I just have to keep taking the damn pills and it should stay that way.'

He smiled and he did appear to be the picture of health. As the sun had turned his skin dark, it had worked to the opposite effect on his hair. Close cropped and neat, it was almost blond now. Working on the boat had also defined the muscles of his arms and shoulders. The only giveaway was hidden under his shirt, the ten-inch scar left by transplantation surgery.

'That's great,' Winston said. 'It looks like you have a wonderful setup here. New family, new home . . . away from everything.'

She was silent a moment, turning her head as if to take in all of the view and the island and McCaleb's life at once. McCaleb had always thought Jaye Winston was attractive in a tomboyish way. She had loose sandy-blond hair that she kept shoulder length. She had never worn makeup back when he worked with her. But she had sharp, knowing eyes and an easy and somewhat sad smile, as if she saw the humor and tragedy in everything at once. She wore black jeans and a white T-shirt beneath a black blazer. She looked cool and tough and McCaleb knew from experience that she was. She had a habit of hooking her hair behind her ear frequently as she spoke. He found that endearing for some unknown reason. He had always thought that if he had not connected with Graciela he might have tried to know Jaye Winston better. He also sensed that Winston intuitively knew that.

'Makes me feel guilty about why I came,' she said. 'Sort of.'

McCaleb nodded at the binder and the tape.

'You came on business. You could have just called, Jaye. Saved some time, probably.'

'No, you didn't send out any change-of-address or phone cards. Like maybe you didn't want people to know where you ended up.'

She hooked her hair behind her left ear and smiled again.

'Not really,' he said. 'I just didn't think people would want to know where I was. So how did you find me?'

'Asked around over at the marina on the mainland.'

'Overtown. They call it overtown here.'

'Overtown, then. They told me in the harbor master's office that you still kept a slip there but you moved the boat over here. I came over and took a water taxi around the harbor until I found it. Your friend was there. He told me how to get up here.'

'Buddy.'

McCaleb looked down into the harbor and picked out *The Following Sea.* It was about a half mile or so away. He could see Buddy Lockridge bent over in the stern. After a few moments he could tell that Buddy was washing off the reels with the hose from the freshwater tank.

'So what's this about, Jaye?' McCaleb said without looking at Winston. 'Must be important for you to go through all of that on your day off. I assume you're off on Sundays.'

'Most of them.'

She pushed the tape aside and opened the binder. Now McCaleb looked over. Although it was upside down to him, he could tell the top page was a standard homicide occurrence report, usually the first page in every murder book he had ever read. It was the starting point. His eyes went to the address box. Even upside down he could make out that it was a West Hollywood case.

'I've got a case here I was hoping you'd take a look at. In your spare time, I mean. I think it might be your sort of thing. I was hoping you'd give me a read, maybe point me someplace I haven't been yet.'

He had known as soon as he saw the binder in her hands that this was what she was going to ask him. But now that it had been asked he felt a confusing rush of sensations. He felt a thrill at the possibility of having a part of his old life again. He also felt guilt over the idea of bringing death into a home so full of new life and happiness. He glanced toward the open slider to see if Graciela was looking out at them. She wasn't.

'My sort of thing?' he said. 'If it's a serial, you shouldn't waste time. Go to the bureau, call Maggie Griffin. She'll—'

'I did all of that, Terry. I still need you.'

'How old is this thing?'

'Two weeks.'

Her eyes looked up from the binder to his.

'New Year's Day?'

She nodded.

'First murder of the year,' she said. 'For L.A. County, at least. Some people think the true millennium didn't start until this year.'

'You think this is a millennium nut?'

'Whoever did this was a nut of some order. I think. That's why I'm here.'

'What did the bureau say? Did you take this to Maggie?'

'You haven't kept up, Terry. Maggie was sent back to Quantico. Things slowed down in the last few years out here and Behavioral Sciences pulled her back. No outpost in L.A. anymore. So, yes, I talked to her. But over the phone at Quantico. She ran it through VICAP and got zilched.'

McCaleb knew she meant the Violent Criminal Apprehension Program computer.

'What about a profile?' he asked.

'I'm on a waiting list. Do you know that across the country there were thirty-four millennium-inspired murders on New Year's Eve and New Year's Day? So they have their hands full at the moment and the bigger departments like us, we're at the end of the line because the bureau figures the smaller departments with less experience and expertise and manpower need their help more.'

She waited a moment while letting McCaleb consider all of this. He understood the bureau's philosophy. It was a form of triage.

'I don't mind waiting a month or so until Maggie or somebody else over there can work something up for me, but my gut on this one tells me time is a consideration, Terry. If it is a serial, a month may be too long to wait. That's why I thought of coming to you. I am banging my head on the wall on this one and you might be our last best hope of coming up with something to move on now. I still remember the Cemetery Man and the Code Killer. I know what you can do with a murder book and some crime scene tape.'

The last few lines were gratuitous and her only false move so far, McCaleb thought. Otherwise he believed she was sincere in the expression of her belief that the killer she was looking for might strike again.

'It's been a long time for me, Jaye,' McCaleb began. 'Other than that thing with Graciela's sister, I haven't been involved in—'

'Come on, Terry, don't bullshit me, okay? You can sit here with a baby in your lap every day of the week and it still won't erase what you were and what you did. I know you. We haven't seen each other or talked in a long time but I know you. And I know that not a day goes by that you don't think about cases. Not a day.'

She paused and stared at him.

'When they took out your heart, they didn't take out what makes you tick, know what I mean?'

McCaleb looked away from her and back down at his boat. Buddy was now sitting in the main fighting chair, his feet up on the transom. McCaleb assumed he had a beer in his hand but it was too far to see that.

'If you're so good at reading people, what do you need me for?'

'I may be good but you're the best I ever knew. Hell, even if they weren't backed up till Easter in Quantico, I'd take you over any of those profilers. I mean that. You were—'

'Okay, Jaye, we don't need a sales pitch, okay? My ego is doing okay without all the—'

'Then what do you need?'

He looked back at her.

'Just some time. I need to think about this.'

'I'm here because my gut says I don't have much time.'

McCaleb got up and walked to the railing. His gaze was out to the sea. A *Catalina Express* ferry was coming in. He knew it would be almost empty. The winter months brought few visitors.

'The boat's coming in,' he said. 'It's the winter schedule, Jaye. You better catch it going back or you'll be here all night.'

'I'll have dispatch send a chopper for me if I have to. Terry, all I need from you is one day at the most. One night, even. Tonight. You sit down, read the book, look at the tape and then call me in the morning, tell me what you see. Maybe it's nothing or at least nothing that's new. But maybe you'll see something we've missed or you'll get an idea we haven't come up with yet. That's all I'm asking. I don't think it's a lot.'

McCaleb looked away from the incoming boat and turned so his back leaned against the rail.

'It doesn't seem like a lot to you because you're in the life. I'm not. I'm out of it, Jaye. Even going back into it for a day is going to change things. I moved out here to start over and to forget all the stuff I was good at. To get good at being something else. At being a father and a husband, for starters.'

Winston got up and walked to the railing. She stood next to him but looked out at the view while he remained facing his home. She spoke in a low voice. If Graciela was listening from somewhere inside, she could not hear this.

'Remember with Graciela's sister what you told me? You told me you got a second shot at life and that there had to be a reason for it. Now you've built this life with her sister and her son and now even your own child. That's wonderful, Terry, I really think so. But that can't be the reason you were looking for. You might think it is but it's not. Deep down you know it. You were good at catching these people. Next to that, what is catching fish?'

McCaleb nodded slightly and was uncomfortable with himself for doing it so readily.

'Leave the stuff,' he said. 'I'll call you when I can.'

On the way to the door Winston looked about for Graciela but didn't see her.

'She's probably in with the baby,' McCaleb said.

'Well, tell her I said good-bye.'

'I will.'

There was an awkward silence the rest of the way to the door. Finally, as McCaleb opened it, Winston spoke.

'So what's it like, Terry? Being a father.'

'It's the best of times, it's the worst of times.'

His stock answer. He then thought a moment and added something he had thought about but never said, not even to Graciela.

'It's like having a gun to your head all the time.'

Winston looked confused and maybe even a little concerned.

'How so?'

'Because I know if anything ever happens to her, anything, then my life is over.'

She nodded.

'I think I can understand that.'

She went through the door. She looked rather silly as she left. A seasoned homicide detective riding away in a golf cart.

2

Sunday dinner with Graciela and Raymond was a quiet affair. They ate white sea bass McCaleb had caught with the charter that morning on the back side of the island near the isthmus. His charters always wanted to keep the fish they caught but then often changed their minds when they got back to the harbor. It was something about the killing instinct in men, McCaleb believed. It wasn't enough just to catch their quarry. They must kill it as well. It meant fish was often served at dinner at the house on La Mesa.

McCaleb had grilled the fish along with corn still in the husks on the porch barbecue. Graciela had made a salad and biscuits. They both had a glass of white wine in front of them. Raymond had milk. The meal was good but the silence wasn't. McCaleb looked over at Raymond and realized the boy had picked up on the vibe passed between the adults and was going along with the tide. McCaleb remembered how he had done the same thing when he was a boy and his parents were throwing silence at each other. Raymond was the son of Graciela's sister, Gloria. His father had never been part of the picture. When Glory died – was murdered – three years before, Raymond had come to live with Graciela. McCaleb met them both when he investigated the case.

'How was softball today?' McCaleb finally asked.

'It was okay, I guess.'

'Get any hits?'

'No.'

'You will. Don't worry. Just keep trying. Keep swinging.'

McCaleb nodded. The boy had wanted to go out on the charter that morning but had not been allowed. The charter was for six men from overtown. With McCaleb and Buddy, that made eight on *The Following Sea* and that was the limit the boat could carry under the rules of safety. McCaleb never broke those rules.

'Well, listen, our next charter isn't until Saturday. Right now it's only four people. In winter season I doubt we'll pick up anybody else. If it stays that way, you can come.'

The boy's dark features seemed to lighten and he nodded vigorously as he worked his fork into the pure white meat of the fish on his plate. The fork looked big in his hand and McCaleb felt a momentary sadness for the boy. He was exceedingly small for a boy of ten. This bothered Raymond a great deal and he often asked McCaleb when he would grow. McCaleb always told him that it would happen soon, though privately he thought the boy would always be small. He knew that his mother had been of average size but Graciela had told McCaleb that Raymond's father had been a very small man – in size and integrity. He had disappeared before Raymond was born.

Always picked last for the team, too small to be competitive with other boys his age, Raymond had gravitated toward pastimes other than team sports. Fishing was his passion and on off days McCaleb usually took him out into the bay to fish for halibut. When he had a charter, the boy always begged to go and when there was room he was allowed to come along as second mate. It was always McCaleb's great pleasure to put a five-dollar bill into an envelope, seal it and hand it to the boy at the end of the day.

'We'll need you in the tower,' McCaleb said. 'This party wants to go down south for marlin. It'll be a long day.'

'Cool!'

McCaleb smiled. Raymond loved being the lookout in the tower, watching for black marlin sleeping or rolling on the surface. And with a pair of binoculars, he was becoming adept at it. McCaleb looked over at Graciela to share the moment but she was looking down at her plate. There was no smile on her face.

In a few more minutes Raymond had finished eating and asked to be excused so he could play on the computer in his room. Graciela told him to keep the sound down so as not to wake the baby. The boy took his plate into the kitchen and then Graciela and McCaleb were alone.

He understood why she was silent. She knew she could not voice her objection to his getting involved in an investigation because her own request that he investigate her sister's death was what had brought them together three years before. Her emotions were caught in this irony.

'Graciela,' McCaleb began. 'I know you don't want me to do this but—'

'I didn't say that.'

'You didn't have to. I know you and I can tell by the look that's been on your face ever since Jaye was here that—'

'I just don't want everything to change, that's all.'

'I understand that. I don't want anything to change either. And it won't. All I'm going to do is look at the file and the tape and tell her what I think.'

'It won't be just that. *I* know *you*. I've seen you do this. You'll get hooked. It's what you are good at.'

'I won't get hooked. I'll just do what she asked and that's it. I'm not even going to do it here. I'm going to take what she gave me and go over to the boat. So it won't even be in the house. Okay? I don't want it in the house.'

He knew he was going to do it with or without her approval but he wanted it from her just the same. Their relationship was still so new that he seemed to always be seeking her approval. He had thought about this and wondered if it was something to do with his second chance. He had fought through a lot of guilt in the past three years but it still came up like a roadblock every few miles. Somehow he felt as though if he could just win this one woman's approval for his existence, then it would all be okay. His cardiologist had called it survivor's guilt. He had lived because someone else had died and must now attain some sense of redemption for it. But McCaleb thought the explanation was not as simple as that.

Graciela frowned but it did not detract from his view of her as beautiful. She had copper skin and dark brown hair that framed a face with eyes so darkly brown that there was almost no demarcation between iris and pupil. Her beauty was another reason he sought her approval of all things. There was something purifying about the light of her smile when it was cast on him.

'Terry, I listened to you two on the porch. After the baby got quiet. I heard what she said about what makes you tick and how a day doesn't go by that you don't think about it, what you used to do. Just tell me this, was she right?'

McCaleb was silent a moment. He looked down at his empty plate and then off across the harbor to the lights in the houses going up the opposite hillside to the inn at the top of Mount Ada. He slowly nodded and then looked back at her.

'Yes, she was right.'

'Then all of this, what we are doing here, the baby, it's all a lie?'

'No. Of course not. This is everything to me and I would protect it with everything I've got. But the answer is yes, I think about what I was and what I did. When I was with the bureau I saved lives, Graciela, plain and simple. And I took evil out of this world. Made it a little less dark out there.'

He raised his hand and gestured toward the harbor.

'Now I have a wonderful life with you and Cielo and Raymond. And I . . . I catch fish for rich people with nothing better to do with their money.'

'So you want both.'

'I don't know what I want. But I know that when she was here I was saying things to her because I knew you were listening. I was saying what I knew you wanted to hear but I knew in my heart it wasn't what I wanted. What I wanted to do was open that book right then and go to work. She was right about me, Gracie. She hadn't seen me in three years but she had me pegged.'

Graciela stood up and came around the table to him. She sat on his lap.

'I'm just scared for you, that's all,' she said.

She pulled him close.

McCaleb took two tall glasses from the cabinet and put them on the counter. He filled the first with bottled water and the second with orange juice. He then began ingesting the twenty-seven pills he had lined up on the counter, intermittently taking swallows of water and orange juice to help them go down. Eating the pills – twice a day – was his ritual and he hated it. Not because of the taste – he was long past that after three years. But because the ritual was a reminder of how dependent he was on exterior concerns for his life. The pills were a leash. He could not live long without them. Much of his world now was built around ensuring that he would always have them. He planned around them. He hoarded them. Sometimes he even dreamed about taking pills.

When he was done, McCaleb went into the living room, where Graciela was reading a magazine. She didn't look up at him when he stepped into the room, another sign that she was unhappy with what was suddenly happening in her home. He stood there waiting for a moment and when things didn't change he went down the hallway into the baby's room.

Cielo was still asleep in her crib. The overhead light was on a dimmer switch and he raised the illumination just enough so that he could see her clearly. McCaleb went to the crib and leaned down so he could listen to her breathe and see her and smell her baby scent. Cielo had her mother's coloring – dark skin and hair – except for her eyes, which were ocean blue. Her tiny hands were balled in fists as if she were showing her readiness to fight for life. McCaleb fell most in love with her when he watched her sleep. He thought about all the preparation they had gone through, the books and classes and advice from Graciela's friends at the hospital who were pediatric nurses. All of it so that they would be ready to care for a fragile life so dependent on them. Nothing had been said or read to prepare him for the opposite: the knowledge that came the first moment he held her, that his own life was now dependent on her.

He reached down to her, the spread of his hand covering her back. She didn't stir. He could feel her tiny heart beating. It seemed quick and desperate, like a whispered prayer. Sometimes he pulled the rocking chair over next to the crib and watched over her until late into the night. This night was different. He had to go. He had work to do. Blood work. He wasn't sure if he was there to simply say good-bye for the night or to somehow gain inspiration or approval from her as well. In his mind it didn't quite make sense. He just knew that he had to watch her and touch her before he went to his work.

McCaleb walked out on the pier and then down the steps to the skiff dock. He found his Zodiac among the other small boats and climbed aboard, careful to put the videotape and the murder book in the shelter of the inflatable's bow so they wouldn't get wet. He pulled the engine cord twice before it started and then headed off down the middle lane of the harbor.

There were no docks in Avalon Harbor. The boats were tied to mooring buoys set in lines that followed the concave shape of the natural harbor. Because it was winter there were few boats in the harbor, but McCaleb didn't cut between the buoys. He followed the fairways, as if driving a car on the streets of a neighborhood. You didn't cut across lawns, you stayed on the roadway.

It was cold on the water and McCaleb zipped up his windbreaker. As he approached *The Following Sea* he could see the glow of the television behind the curtains of the salon. This meant Buddy Lockridge had not finished up in time to catch the last ferry and was staying over.

McCaleb and Lockridge worked the charter business together. While the boat's ownership was in Graciela's name, the marine charter license and all other documentation relating to the business were in Lockridge's name. The two had met more than three years earlier when McCaleb had docked *The Following Sea* at Cabrillo Marina in the Los Angeles Harbor and was living aboard it while restoring it. Buddy was a neighbor, living on a sailboat nearby. They had struck up a friendship that ultimately became a partnership.

During the busy spring and summer season Lockridge stayed most nights on *The Following Sea.* But during the slow times he usually caught a ferry back overtown to his own boat at Cabrillo. He seemed to have greater success finding female companions in the overtown bars than in the handful of places on the island. McCaleb assumed he would be heading back in the morning since they did not have a charter for another five days.

McCaleb bumped the Zodiac into the fantail of *The Following Sea.* He cut the engine and got out with the tape and the binder. He tied the Zodiac off on a stern cleat and headed for the salon door. Buddy was there waiting, having heard the Zodiac or felt its bump on the fantail. He slid the door open, holding a paperback novel down at his side. McCaleb glanced at the television but couldn't tell what it was he had on.

'What's up, Terror?' Lockridge asked.

'Nothing. I just need to do a little work. I'm going to be using the forward bunk, okay?'

He stepped into the salon. It was warm. Lockridge had the space heater fired up.

'Sure, fine. Anything I can do to help?'

'Nah, this isn't about the business.'

'It about that lady who came by? The sheriff's lady?'

McCaleb had forgotten that Winston had come to the boat first and gotten directions from Buddy.

'Yeah.'

'You working a case for her?'

'No,' McCaleb said quickly, hoping to limit Lockridge's interest and involvement. 'I just need to look at some stuff and give her a call back.'

'Very cool, dude.'

'Not really. It's just a favor. What are you watching?'

'Oh, nothing. Just a show about this task force that goes after computer hackers. Why, you seen it?'

'No, but I was wondering if I could borrow the TV for a little while.'

McCaleb held up the videotape. Lockridge's eyes lit up.

'Be my guest. Pop that baby in there.'

'Um, not up here, Buddy. This is – Detective Winston asked me to do this in confidence. I'll bring the TV back up as soon as I'm done.'

Lockridge's face registered his disappointment but McCaleb wasn't worried about it. He went over to the counter that separated the galley from the salon and put down the binder and tape. He unplugged the television and removed it from the locking frame that held it in place so it wouldn't fall when the boat encountered high seas. The television had a built-in videocassette player and was heavy. McCaleb lugged it down the narrow stairway and took it to the forward stateroom, which had been partially converted into an office. Two sides of the room had been lined with twin bunk beds. The bottom berth on the left had been changed into a desk and the two top bunks were used by McCaleb to store his old bureau case files – Graciela didn't want them in the house where Raymond might stumble upon them. The only problem was that McCaleb was sure that on occasion Buddy had gone through the boxes and looked at the files. And it bothered him. It was an invasion of some kind. McCaleb had thought about keeping the forward stateroom locked but knew that could be a deadly mistake. The only ceiling hatch on the lower deck was in the forward room and access to it ought not be blocked in case there was ever a need for an emergency evacuation through the bow.

He put the television down on the desk and plugged it in. He turned to go back up to the salon to retrieve the binder and tape when he saw Buddy coming down the stairs, holding the tape and leafing through the binder.

'Hey, Buddy—'

'Looks like a weird one, man.'

McCaleb reached out and closed the binder, then took it and the tape from his fishing partner's hands.

'Just taking a peek.'

'I told you, it's confidential.'

'Yeah, but we work good together. Just like before.'

It was true that by happenstance Lockridge had been a great help when McCaleb had investigated the death of Graciela's sister. But that had been an active street investigation. This was just going to be a review. He didn't need anybody looking over his shoulder.

'This is different, Buddy. This is a one-night stand. I'm just going to take a look at this stuff and then that will be it. Now let me get to work so I'm not here all night.'

Lockridge didn't say anything and McCaleb didn't wait. He closed the door to the forward bunk and then turned to the desk. As he looked down at the murder book in his hands he felt a sharp thrill as well as the familiar rising of dread and guilt.

McCaleb knew it was time to go back to the darkness. To explore it and know it. To find his way through it. He nodded, though he was alone now. It was in acknowledgment that he had waited a long time for this moment.

3

The video was clear and steady, the lighting was good. The technical aspects of crime scene videotaping had vastly improved since McCaleb's days with the bureau. The content had not changed. The tape McCaleb watched showed the starkly lit tableau of murder. McCaleb finally froze the image and studied it. The cabin was silent, the gentle lapping sound of the sea against the boat's hull the only intrusion from outside.

At center focus was the nude body of what appeared to be a man who had been trussed with baling wire, his arms and legs held tightly behind his torso to such an extreme that the body appeared to be in a reverse fetal position. The body was face down on an old and dirty rug. The focus was too tight on the body to determine in what sort of location it had been found. McCaleb judged that the victim was a man solely on the basis of body mass and musculature. For the head of the victim was not visible. A gray plastic mop bucket had been placed entirely over the victim's head. McCaleb could see that a length of the baling wire was stretched taut from the victim's ankles, up his back and between his arms, and beneath the lip of the bucket where it wrapped around his neck. It appeared on first measure to be a ligature strangulation in which the leverage of the legs and feet pulled the wire tight around the victim's neck, causing asphyxia. In effect, the victim had been bound in such a way that he ultimately killed himself when he could no longer hold his legs folded backward in such an extreme position.

McCaleb continued studying the scene. A small amount of blood had poured onto the carpet from the bucket, indicating that some kind of head wound would be found when the vessel was removed.

McCaleb leaned back in his old desk chair and thought about his initial impressions. He had not yet opened the binder, choosing instead to watch the crime scene videotape first and to study the scene as close as possible to the way the investigators had originally seen it. Already he was fascinated by what he was looking at. He felt the implication of ritual in the scene on the television screen. He also felt the trilling of adrenaline in his blood again. He pressed the button on the remote and the video continued.

The focus pulled back as Jaye Winston entered the frame of the video.

McCaleb could see more of the room now and noted that it appeared to be in a small, sparsely furnished house or apartment.

Coincidentally, Winston was wearing the same outfit she had worn when she had come to the house with the murder book and videotape. She had on rubber gloves that she had pulled up over the cuffs of her blazer. Her detective's shield hung on a black shoelace which had been tied around her neck. She took a position on the left side of the dead man while her partner, a detective McCaleb did not recognize, moved to the right side. For the first time there was talking on the video.

'The victim has already been examined by a deputy coroner and released for crime scene investigation,' Winston said. 'The victim has been photographed in situ. We're now going to remove the bucket to make further examination.'

McCaleb knew that she was carefully choosing her words and demeanor with the future in mind, a future that would include a trial for an accused killer in which the crime scene tape would be viewed by a jury. She had to appear professional and objective, completely emotionally removed from what she was encountering. Anything deviating from this could be cause for a defense attorney to seek removal of the tape from evidence.

Winston reached up and hooked her hair behind her ears and then placed both hands on the victim's shoulders. With her partner's help she turned the body on its side, the dead man's back to the camera.

The camera then came in over the victim's shoulder and closed in as Winston gently pulled the bucket handle from under the man's chin and proceeded to carefully lift it off the head.

'Okay,' she said.

She showed the interior of the bucket to the camera – blood had coagulated inside it – and then placed it in an open cardboard box used for evidence storage. She then turned back and gazed down at the victim.

Gray duct tape had been wrapped around the dead man's head to form a tight gag across the mouth. The eyes were open and distended – bugged. The cornea of each eye was rouged with hemorrhage. So was the skin around the eyes.

'CP,' the partner said, pointing to the eyes.

'Kurt,' Winston said. 'We're on sound.'

'Sorry.'

She was telling her partner to keep all observations to himself. Again, she was safeguarding the future. McCaleb knew that what her partner was pointing out was the hemorrhaging, or conjunctive petechiae, which always came with ligature strangulation. However, the observation was one that should be made to a jury by a medical examiner, not a homicide detective.

Blood matted the dead man's medium-length hair and had pooled inside the bucket against the left side of his face. Winston began manipulating the head and combing her fingers through the hair in search of the origin of the blood. She finally found the wound on the crown of the head. She pulled the hair back as much as possible to view it.

'Barney, come in close on this if you can,' she said.

The camera moved in. McCaleb saw a small, round puncture wound that did not appear to penetrate the skull. He knew that the amount of blood evidenced was not always in concert with the gravity of the wound. Even inconsequential wounds to the scalp could produce a lot of blood. He would get a formal and complete description of the wound in the autopsy report.

'Barn, get this,' Winston said, her voice up a notch from the previous monotone. 'We've got writing or something on the tape, on the gag.'

She had noticed it while manipulating the head. The camera moved in. McCaleb could make out lightly marked letters on the tape where it crossed the dead man's mouth. The letters appeared to be written in ink but the message was obliterated by blood. He could make out what appeared to be one word of the message.

'Cave,' he read out loud. 'Cave?'

He then thought maybe it was only a partial word but he couldn't think of any larger word – other than *cavern* – that contained those letters in that order.

McCaleb froze the picture and just looked. He was enthralled. What he was seeing was pulling him backward in time to his days as a profiler, when almost every case he was assigned left him with the same question: *What dark, tortured mind did this come from?*

Words from a killer were always significant and put a case on a higher plane. It most often meant that the killing was a statement, a message transmitted from killer to victim and then from the investigators to the world as well.

McCaleb stood up and reached to the upper bunk. He pulled down one of the old file boxes and let it drop heavily to the floor. Quickly lifting the lid, he began combing through the files for a notebook with some unused pages in it. It had been his ritual with the bureau to start each case he was assigned with a fresh spiral notebook. He finally came across a file with only a BAR form and a notebook in it. With so little paperwork in the file he knew it was a short case and that the notebook should have plenty of blank pages.

McCaleb leafed through the notebook and found it largely unused. He then took out the Bureau Assistance Request form and quickly read the top sheet to see what case it was. He immediately remembered it because he had handled it with one phone call. The request had come from a detective in the small town of White Elk, Minnesota, almost ten years before, when McCaleb still worked out of Quantico. The detective's report said two men had gotten into a drunken brawl in the house they shared, challenged each other to a duel and proceeded to kill each other with simultaneous shots from ten yards apart in the back yard. The detective needed no help with the double homicide case because it was cut and dried. But he was puzzled by something else. In the course of searching the victims' house, investigators had come across something strange in the basement freezer. Pushed into a corner of the freezer cabinet were plastic bags containing dozens and dozens of used tampons. They were of various makes and brands, and preliminary tests on a sampling of the tampons had identified the menstrual blood on them as having come from several different women.

The case detective didn't know what he had but feared the worst. What he wanted from the FBI's Behavioral Sciences Unit was an idea about what these bloody tampons could mean and how to proceed. More specifically, he wanted to know if the tampons could possibly be souvenirs kept by a serial killer or killers who had gone undiscovered until they happened to kill each other.

McCaleb smiled as he remembered the case. He had come across tampons in a freezer before. He called the detective and asked him three questions. What did the two men do for a living? In addition to the firearms used during the duel, were there any long weapons or a hunting license found in the apartment? And, lastly, when did bear hunting season begin in the woods of northern Minnesota?

The detective's answers quickly solved the tampon mystery. Both men worked at the airport in Minneapolis for a subcontractor that provided clean-out crews who prepared commercial airliners for flights. Several hunting rifles were found in the house but no hunting license. And, lastly, bear season was three weeks away.

McCaleb told the detective that it appeared that the men were not serial killers but had probably been collecting the contents from the tampon disposal receptacles in lavatories of the planes they cleaned. They were taking the tampons home and freezing them. When hunting season began they would most likely thaw the tampons and use them to bait bear, which can pick up the scent of blood at a great distance. Most hunters use garbage as bait but nothing is better than blood.

McCaleb remembered that the detective had actually seemed disappointed that he had no serial killer or killers at hand. He had either been embarrassed that an FBI agent sitting at a desk in Quantico had so quickly solved his mystery or he was simply annoyed that there would be no national media ride from his case. He abruptly hung up and McCaleb never heard from him again.

McCaleb tore the few pages of notes from the case out of the notebook, put them in the file with the BAR form and returned the file to its spot. He then put the lid on the box and hoisted it back up onto the shelf that had been the top bunk. He shoved the box back into place and it banged hard on the bulkhead.

Sitting back down, McCaleb glanced at the frozen image on the television screen and then considered the blank page in the notebook. Finally, he took the pen out of his shirt pocket and was about to begin writing when the door to the room suddenly opened and Buddy Lockridge stood there.

'You okay?'

'What?'

'I heard all this banging. The whole boat moved.'

'I'm fine, Buddy, I just—'

'Oh, shit, what the hell is that?'

He was staring at the TV screen. McCaleb immediately raised the remote and killed the picture.

'Buddy, look, I told you this is confidential and I can't—'

'Okay, okay, I know. I was just checking to make sure you didn't keel over or something.'

'Okay, thanks, but I'm fine.'

'I'll be up for a little while if you need something.'

'I won't, but thanks.'

'You know, you're using a lot of juice. You're going to have to run the generator tomorrow after I split.'

'No problem. I'll do it. I'll see you later, Buddy.'

Buddy pointed at the now empty television screen.

'That's a weird one.'

'Good-bye, Buddy,' McCaleb said impatiently.

He got up and closed the door while Lockridge was still standing there. This time he locked it. He returned to the seat and the notebook. He started writing and in a few moments he had constructed a list.

SCENE
1. Ligature
2. Nude
3. Head Wound
4. Tape/Gag – 'Cave'?
5. Bucket?

He studied the list for a few moments, waiting for an idea, but nothing came through. It was too early. Instinctively, he knew the wording on the tape was a key that he wouldn't be able to turn until he had the complete message. He fought the urge to open the murder book and get to it. Instead, he turned the television back on and began running the tape from the spot he had left off. The camera was in and tight on the dead man's mouth and the tape stretched tightly across it.

'We'll leave this for the coroner,' Winston said. 'You got what you can of this, Barn?'

'I got it,' said the unseen videographer.

'Okay, let's pull back and look at these bindings.'

The camera traced the baling wire from the neck to the feet. The wire looped around the neck and passed through a slip knot. It then went down the spine to where it had been wrapped several times around the ankles, which had been pulled so far back that the victim's heels now rested on his buttocks.

The wrists were bound with a separate length of wire that had been wrapped six times around and then pulled into a knot. The bindings had caused deep furrow marks in the skin of the wrists and ankles, indicating that the victim had struggled for a period before finally succumbing.

When the videography of the body was completed, Winston told the unseen man with the camera to make a video inventory of every room in the apartment.

The camera panned away from the body and took in the rest of the living-room/dining-room space. The home seemed to have been furnished out of a secondhand store. There was no uniformity, none of the pieces of furniture matched. The few framed pictures on the walls looked as though they could have come out of a room at a Howard Johnson's ten years before – all orange and aqua pastels. At the far end of the room was a tall china cabinet with no china in it. There were some books on a few of the shelves but most were barren. On top of the cabinet was something McCaleb found curious. It was a two-foot-high owl that looked hand painted. McCaleb had seen many of these before, especially in Avalon Harbor and Cabrillo Marina. Most often the owls were made of hollow plastic and placed at the tops of masts or on the bridges of power boats in a usually unsuccessful attempt to scare gulls and other birds away from the boats. The theory was that the owl would be seen by the other birds as a predator and they would stay clear, thereby leaving the boats unfouled by their droppings.

McCaleb had also seen the owls used on the exteriors of public buildings where pigeons were a nuisance. But what interested him about the plastic owl here was that he had never seen or heard of one being used inside a private home as ornamentation or otherwise. He knew that people collected all manner of things, including owls, but he had so far seen none in the apartment other than the one positioned at center on the cabinet. He quickly opened the binder and found the victim identification report. It listed the victim's occupation as house painter. McCaleb closed the binder and considered for a moment that perhaps the victim had taken the owl from a job or removed it from a structure while prepping it to be painted.

He backed the tape up and watched again as the videographer panned from the body to the cabinet atop which the owl was perched. It appeared to McCaleb that the videographer had made a 180-degree turn, meaning the owl would have been directly facing the victim, looking down upon the scene of the murder.

While there were other possibilities, McCaleb's instinct told him the plastic owl was somehow part of the crime scene. He took up the notebook and made the owl the sixth entry on his list.

The rest of the crime scene videotape fostered little interest in McCaleb. It documented the remaining rooms of the victim's apartment – the bedroom, bathroom and kitchen. He saw no more owls and took no more notes. When he got to the end of the tape he rewound it and watched it all the way through once more. Nothing new caught his attention. He ejected the tape and slid it back into its cardboard slipcase. He then carried the television back up to the salon, where he locked it into its frame on the counter.

Buddy was sprawled on the couch reading his paperback. He didn't say anything and McCaleb could tell he was hurt that McCaleb had closed and locked the door to the office on him. He thought about apologizing but decided to let it go. Buddy was too nosy about McCaleb, past and present. Maybe this rejection would let him know that.

'What are you reading?' he asked instead.

'A book,' Lockridge answered without looking up.

McCaleb smiled to himself. Now he was sure that he had gotten to Buddy.

'Well, there's the TV if you want to watch the news or something.'

'The news is over.'

McCaleb looked at his watch. It was midnight. He had not realized how much time had gone by. This had often been the case with him – while at the bureau it was routine for him to work through lunch or late into the night without realizing it when he became fully engaged in a case.

He left Buddy to sulk and went back down to the office. He closed the door again, loudly, and locked it.

4

After turning to a fresh page in his notebook, McCaleb opened the murder book. He snapped open the rings and pulled the documents out and stacked them neatly on the desk. It was a little quirk but he never liked reviewing cases by turning pages in a book. He liked to hold the individual reports in his hands. He liked squaring off the corners of the whole stack. He put the binder aside and began carefully reading through the investigative summaries in chronological order. Soon he was fully immersed in the investigation.

The homicide report had come in anonymously to the front desk of the West Hollywood substation of the Los Angeles County Sheriff's Department at noon on Monday, January 1. The male caller said there was a man dead in apartment 2B in the Grand Royale Apartments on Sweetzer near Melrose. The caller hung up without giving his name or any other message. Because the call came in on one of the non-emergency lines at the front desk it was not recorded, and there was no caller ID function on the phone.

A pair of patrol deputies were dispatched to the apartment and found the front door slightly ajar. After receiving no answer to their knocks and calls, the deputies entered the apartment and quickly determined that the anonymous caller had given correct information. A man was dead inside. The deputies backed out of the apartment and the homicide squad was called. The case was assigned to partners Jaye Winston and Kurt Mintz, with Winston as lead detective.

The victim was identified in the reports as Edward Gunn, a forty-four-year-old itinerant house painter. He had lived alone in the Sweetzer Avenue apartment for nine years.

A computer search for criminal records or known criminal activity determined that Gunn had a history of convictions for small-time crimes ranging from soliciting for prostitution and loitering to repeated arrests for public intoxication and drunk driving. He had been arrested twice for drunk driving in the three months prior to his death, including the night of December 30. He posted bail on the 31st and was released. Less than twenty-four hours later he was dead. The records also showed an arrest for a serious crime without subsequent conviction. Six years earlier Gunn had been taken into custody by the Los Angeles Police Department and questioned in a homicide. He was later released and no charges were ever filed.

According to the investigative reports Winston and her partner had put into the murder book, there was no apparent robbery of Gunn or his apartment, leaving the motive for his slaying unknown. Other residents in the eight-unit apartment building said that they had heard no disturbances in Gunn's apartment on New Year's Eve. Any sounds that might have emanated from the apartment during the murder were likely camouflaged by the sounds of a party being held by a tenant in the apartment directly below Gunn's. The party had lasted well into the morning of January 1. Gunn, according to several partygoers who were interviewed, had not attended the party or been invited.

A canvass of the neighborhood, which was primarily lined with small apartment buildings similar to the Grand Royale, found no witnesses who remembered seeing Gunn in the days leading up to his death.

All indications were that the murderer had come to Gunn. The lack of damage to doors and windows of the apartment indicated that there had been no break-in and that Gunn might very well have known his killer. To that end, Winston and Mintz interviewed all known coworkers and associates, as well as every tenant and every person who had attended the party at the complex, in an effort to draw out a suspect. They got nothing for their effort.

They also checked all of the victim's financial records for a clue to a possible monetary motivation and found nothing. Gunn had no steady employment. He mostly loitered around a paint and design store on Beverly Boulevard and offered his services to customers on a day-work basis. He lived a hand-to-mouth existence, making just enough to pay for and maintain his apartment and a small pickup truck in which he carried his painting equipment.

Gunn had one living relative, a sister who lived in Long Beach. At the time of his death, he had not seen her in more than a year, though he happened to call her the night before his death from the holding tank of the LAPD's Hollywood Division station. He was being held there following his DUI arrest. The sister reported that she'd told her brother she could no longer keep helping him and bailing him out. She'd hung up. And she could not offer the investigators any useful information in regard to his murder.

The incident in which Gunn had been arrested six years before was fully reviewed. Gunn had killed a prostitute in a Sunset Boulevard motel room. He had stabbed her with her own knife when she attempted to stab and rob him, according to his statement in the report forwarded by the LAPD's Hollywood Division. There were minor inconsistencies between Gunn's original statement to responding patrol officers and the physical evidence but not enough for the district attorney's office to seek charges against him. Ultimately, the case was reluctantly written off as self-defense and dropped.

McCaleb noticed that the lead investigator on the case had been Detective Harry Bosch. Years earlier McCaleb had worked with Bosch on a case, an investigation he still often thought about. Bosch had been abrasive and secretive at times, but still a good cop with excellent investigative skills, intuition and instincts. They had actually bonded in some way over the emotional turmoil the case had caused them both. McCaleb wrote Bosch's name down in the notebook as a reminder to call the detective to see if he had any thoughts on the Gunn case.

He went back to reading the summaries. With Gunn's record of prior engagement with a prostitute in mind, Winston's and Mintz's next step was to comb through the murder victim's phone records as well as check and credit card purchases for indications that he might have continued to use prostitutes. There was nothing. They cruised Sunset Boulevard with an LAPD vice crew for three nights, stopping and interviewing street prostitutes. But none admitted knowing the man in the photos the detectives had borrowed from Gunn's sister.

The detectives scanned the sex want ads in the local alternative papers for an advertisement Gunn might have placed. One more time their efforts hit a wall.

Finally, the detectives took the long shot of tracking the family and associates of the dead prostitute of six years before. Although Gunn had never been charged with the killing, there was still a chance someone believed he had not acted in self-defense – someone who might have sought retribution.

But this, too, was a dead end. The woman's family was from Philadelphia. They had lost contact years before. No family member had even come out to claim the body before it was cremated at county taxpayers' expense. There was no reason for them to seek vengeance for a killing six years old when they had not cared much about the killing in the first place.

The case had hit one investigative dead end after another. A case not solved in the first forty-eight hours had a less than 50 percent chance of being cleared. A case unsolved after two weeks was like an unclaimed body in the morgue – it was going to sit there in the cold and the dark for a long, long time.

And that was why Winston had finally come to McCaleb. He was the last resort on a hopeless case.

Finished with the summaries, McCaleb decided to take a break. He checked his watch and saw it was now almost two. He opened the cabin door and went up to the salon. The lights were off. Buddy had apparently gone to bed in the master cabin without making any noise. McCaleb opened the cold box and looked in. There was a six-pack of beer left over from the charter but he didn't want that. There was a carton of orange juice and some bottled water. He took the water and went out through the salon door to the cockpit. It was always cool on the water but this night seemed crisper than usual. He folded his arms across his chest and looked across the harbor and up the hill to the house where he knew his family slept. A single light shone from the back deck.

A momentary pang of guilt passed through him. He knew that despite his deep love for the woman and two children behind that light, he would rather be on the boat with the murder book than up there in the sleeping house. He tried to push away these thoughts and the questions they raised but could not completely blind himself to the essential conclusion that there was something wrong with him, something missing. It was something that prevented him from fully embracing that which most men seemed to long for.

He went back inside the boat. He knew that immersing himself in the case reports would shut out the guilt.

The autopsy report contained no surprises. The cause of death was as McCaleb had guessed from the video: cerebral hypoxia due to compression of the carotid arteries by ligature strangulation. The time of death was estimated to have been between midnight and 3 A.M. on January 1.

The deputy medical examiner who conducted the autopsy noted that interior damage to the neck was minimal. Neither the hyoid bone nor the thyroid cartilage was broken. This aspect, coupled with multiple ligature furrows on the skin, led the examiner to conclude that Gunn suffocated slowly while desperately struggling to keep his feet behind his torso so that the wire noose was not pulled tight around his neck. The autopsy summation suggested that the victim could have struggled in this position for as long as two hours.

McCaleb thought about this and wondered if the killer had been there in the apartment the whole time, watching the dying man struggle. Or had he set the ligature and left before his victim was dead, possibly to set some kind of alibi scheme into motion – perhaps appearing at a New Year's Eve party so that there would be multiple witnesses able to account for him at the time of the victim's death.

He then remembered the bucket and decided that the killer had stayed. The covering of the victim's face was a frequent occurrence in sexually motivated and rage killings, the attacker covering his victim's face as a means of dehumanizing the victim and avoiding eye contact. McCaleb had worked dozens of cases where he had noted this phenomenon, women who had been raped and murdered with nightgowns or pillowcases covering their faces, children with their heads wrapped in towels. He could write a list of examples that would fill the entire notebook. Instead he wrote one line on the page under Bosch's name.

UNSUB was there the whole time. He watched.

The unknown subject, McCaleb thought. So we meet again.

Before moving on, McCaleb looked through the autopsy report for two other pieces of information. First was the head wound. He found a description of the wound in the examiner's comments. The perimortem laceration was circular and superficial. Its damage was minimal and it was possibly a defensive wound.

McCaleb dismissed the possibility of it being a defensive wound. The only blood on the rug at the crime scene was that spilled from the bucket after it was placed over the victim's head. Plus, the flow of blood from the wound at the point of the crown was forward and over the victim's face. This indicated the head was bowed forward. McCaleb took all of this to mean that Gunn was already bound and on the floor when the blow had been struck to his head and then the bucket placed over it. His instinct told him this might have been a blow delivered with the intention of hurrying the victim's demise; an impact to the head that would weaken the victim and shorten his struggle against the ligature.

He wrote these thoughts down in the notebook and then went back into the autopsy report. He located the findings on the examination of the anus and penis. Swabs indicated no sexual activity had occurred in the time prior to death. McCaleb wrote down *No Sex* in the notebook. Beneath this he wrote the word *Rage* and circled it.

McCaleb realized that many, if not all, of the suspicions and conclusions he was coming up with had probably already been reached by Jaye Winston. But this had always been his routine in analyzing murder scenes. He made his own judgments first, then looked to see how they stacked up next to the primary investigator's conclusions afterward.

After the autopsy he went to the evidence analysis reports. He first looked at the recovered evidence list and noticed that the plastic owl he had seen on the videotape had not been bagged and tagged. He felt sure that it should have been and made a note of it. Also missing from the list was any mention of a weapon recovery. It appeared that whatever had been used to open up the wound on Gunn's scalp had been taken away from the scene by the killer. McCaleb made a note of this as well because it was another piece of information supportive of a profile of the killer as organized, thorough and cautious.

The report on the analysis of the tape used to gag the victim was folded into a separate envelope that McCaleb found in one of the binder's pockets. In addition to a computer printout and an addendum there were several photographs that showed the full length of the tape after it had been cut and peeled away from the victim's face and head. The first set of photos documented the tape front and back as it was found, with a significant amount of coagulated blood obscuring the message written on it. The next set of photos showed the tape front and back after the blood had been removed with a solution of soapy water. McCaleb stared at the message for a long moment even though he knew he would never be able to decipher it on his own.

Cave Cave Dus Videt

He finally put the photos aside and picked up the accompanying reports. The tape was found to be clear of fingerprints but several hairs and microscopic fibers were collected from the underside adhesive. The hair was determined to have belonged to the victim. The fibers were held pending further orders for analysis. McCaleb knew this meant there was a time and cost constraint. The fibers would not be analyzed until the investigation reached a point where there were fibers from a suspect's possessions that also could be analyzed and compared. Otherwise, the costly and time-consuming analysis of the collected fibers would be for nothing. McCaleb had seen this sort of investigative prioritizing before. It was a routine in local law enforcement not to take expensive steps until necessary. But he was a bit surprised that it had not been deemed necessary in this case. He concluded that Gunn's background as a one-time murder suspect might have dropped him into a lower class of victim, one for which the extra step is not taken. Maybe, McCaleb thought, this was why Jaye Winston had come to him. She hadn't said anything about paying him for his time – not that he could accept a monetary payment anyway.

He moved on to an addendum report that had been filed by Winston. She had taken a photograph of the tape and the message to a linguistics professor at UCLA who had identified the words as Latin. She was then referred to a retired Catholic priest who lived in the rectory at St. Catherine's in Hollywood and had taught Latin at the church's school for two decades until it was dropped from the curriculum in the early seventies. He easily translated the message for Winston.

As McCaleb read the translation he felt the feathery run of adrenaline rise up his spine to his neck. His skin tightened and he felt a sensation that came close to lightheadedness.

Cave Cave Dus Videt
Cave Cave D(omin)us Videt
Beware Beware God Sees

'Holy shit,' McCaleb said quietly to himself.

It was not said as an exclamation. Rather, it was the phrase he and fellow bureau profilers had used to informally classify cases in which religious overtures were part of the evidence. When God was discovered to be part of the probable motivation for a crime, it became a 'holy shit' case when spoken of in casual conversation. It also changed things significantly, for God's work was never done. When a killer was out there using His name as part of the imprint of a crime, it often meant there would be more crimes. It was said in the bureau profiling offices that God's killers never stopped of their own volition. They had to be stopped. McCaleb now understood Jaye Winston's apprehension about letting this case gather dust. If Edward Gunn was the first known victim, then somebody else was likely in the sights of the killer right now.

McCaleb scribbled down a translation of the killer's message and some other thoughts. He wrote *Victim Acquisition* and underlined it twice.

He looked back at Winston's report and noticed that at the bottom of the page containing the translation there was a paragraph marked with an asterisk.

> *Father Ryan stated that the word 'Dus' as seen on the duct tape was a short form of 'Deus' or 'Dominus' primarily found in medieval Bibles as well as church carvings and other artwork.

McCaleb leaned back in his chair and drank from the water bottle. He found this final paragraph the most interesting of the whole package. The information it contained could be a means by which the killer might be isolated in a small group and then found. Initially the pool of potential suspects was huge – it would essentially include anyone who had had access to Edward Gunn on New Year's Eve. But the information from Father Ryan narrowed it significantly to those who had knowledge of medieval Latin, or someone who had gotten the word *Dus* and possibly the whole message from something he had seen.

Perhaps something in a church.

5

McCaleb was too jazzed by what he had read and seen to think about sleep. It was four-thirty and he knew he would complete this night awake and in the office. It was probably too early in Quantico, Virginia, for anyone to be in the Behavioral Sciences Unit but he decided to make the call anyway. He went up to the salon, got the cell phone out of the charger and punched in the number from memory. When the general operator answered he asked to be transferred to Special Agent Brasilia Doran's desk. There were a lot of people he could have asked for but he had decided on Doran because they had worked well together – and often from long distances – when he had been in the bureau. Doran also specialized in icon identification and symbology.

The call was picked up by a machine and while listening to Doran's outgoing message McCaleb quickly tried to decide whether to leave a message or just call back. Initially, he thought it would be better to hang up and try to catch Doran live later because a personal call is much more difficult to deflect than a taped message. But then he decided to put faith in their former camaraderie, even if he had been out of the bureau for nearly five years.

'Brass, it's Terry McCaleb. Long time no see. Uh, listen, I'm calling because I need a favor. Could you call me back as soon as you get a moment? I'd really appreciate it.'

He gave the number for his cell phone, thanked her and hung up. He could take the phone with him back to the house and wait for the call there but that would mean that Graciela might overhear the conversation with Doran and he didn't want that. He went back down to the forward bunk and started through the murder book documents again. He checked every page again for something that stood out in its inclusion or exclusion. He took a few more notes and made a list of things he still needed to do and know before drawing up a profile. But primarily he was just waiting for Doran. She finally returned his call at five-thirty.

'Long time is right,' she said by way of greeting.

'Too long. How y'doin', Brass?'

'Can't complain because nobody listens.'

'I heard you guys are looking for the Drano over there.'

'You're right about that. We are clogged and flogged. You know last year we sent half the staff to Kosovo to help in the war crimes investigations. On six-week rotations. That just killed us. We are still so far behind it's getting critical.'

McCaleb wondered if she was giving him the woe-is-me pitch so he might not ask the favor he had mentioned on the message. He decided to go ahead with it anyway.

'Well, then you aren't going to like hearing from me,' he said.

'Oh boy, I'm shaking in my boots. What do you need, Terry?'

'I'm doing a favor for a friend out here. Sheriff's homicide squad. Taking a look at a homicide and—'

'Did he already run it through here?'

'It's a she. And, yeah, she ran it on the VICAP box and got blanked. That's all. She got the word on how backed up you guys are on profiling and came to me instead. I sort of owe her one so I said I'd take a look.'

'And now you want to cut in line, right?'

McCaleb smiled and hoped she was smiling as well on the other end of the line.

'Sort of. But I think it's a quickie. It's just one thing I want.'

'Then out with it. What?'

'I need an iconography baseline. I'm following a hunch on something.'

'Okay. Doesn't sound too involving. What's the symbol?'

'An owl.'

'An owl? Just an owl?'

'More specifically, a plastic owl. But an owl just the same. I want to know if it's turned up before and what it means.'

'Well, I remember the owl on the bag of potato chips. What's that brand?'

'Wise. I remember. It's an East Coast brand.'

'Well, there you go. The owl is smart. He is wise.'

'Brass, I was hoping for something a little more—'

'I know, I know. Tell you what, I'll see what I can find. The thing to remember is, symbols change. What means one thing at one time might mean something completely different at another time. You just looking for contemporary uses and examples?'

McCaleb thought for a moment about the message on the duct tape.

'Can you throw in the medieval time period?'

'Sounds like you got a weird one – but ain't they all. Let me guess, a holy shit case?'

'Could be. How'd you know that?'

'Oh, all that medieval Inquisition and church stuff. Seen it before. I've got your number. I'll try to get back today.'

McCaleb thought about asking her to run an analysis of the message from the duct tape but decided not to pile it on. Besides, the message must have been included on the computer run Jaye Winston completed. He thanked her and was about to disconnect when she asked about his health and he told her he was fine.

'You still living on that boat I heard about?'

'Nope. I'm living on an island now. But I still have the boat. I've got a wife and new baby daughter, too.'

'Wow! Is this the Terry "TV Dinner" McCaleb I used to know?'

'Same one, I guess.'

'Well, it sounds like you got your stuff together.'

'I think I finally do.'

'Then be careful with it. What are you doing chasing a case again?'

McCaleb hesitated in his reply.

'I'm not sure.'

'Don't bullshit me. We both know why you're doing it. Tell you what, let me see what I can find out and I'll call you back.'

'Thanks, Brass. I'll be waiting.'

McCaleb went into the master cabin and shook Buddy Lockridge awake. His friend startled and began swinging his arms wildly.

'It's me, it's me!'

Before he calmed down, Buddy clapped McCaleb on the side of the head with a book he had fallen asleep holding.

'What are you doing?' Buddy exclaimed.

'I'm trying to wake you, man.'

'What for? What time is it?'

'It's almost six. I want to take the boat across.'

'Now?'

'Yeah, now. So get up and help me. I'll get the lines.'

'Man, now? We're going to hit the layer. Why don't you wait until it burns off?'

'Because I don't have the time.'

Buddy reached up and turned on the reading lamp that was attached to the cabin wall just above the headboard. McCaleb noticed the book he was reading was called *The Wire in the Blood.*

'Something sure put a wire in your blood, man,' he said as he rubbed his ear where the book had hit him.

'Sorry about that. Why you in such a hurry to cross, anyway? It's that case, isn't it?'

'I'll be on top. Let's get it going.'

McCaleb headed out of the cabin. Buddy called after him as he expected he would.

'You going to need a driver?'

'No, Buddy. You know I've been driving a couple years now.'

'Yeah, but you might need help with the case, man.'

'I'll be all right. Hurry up, Bud, I want to get over there.'

McCaleb took the key off the hook next to the salon door and went out and climbed up into the bridge. The air was still chilled and tendrils of dawn light were working their way through the morning mist. He flicked on the Raytheon radar and started the engines. They turned over immediately – Buddy had taken the boat over to Marina del Rey the week before to have them overhauled.

McCaleb left them idling while he climbed back down and went to the fantail. He untied the stern line and then the Zodiac and led it around to the bow. He tied the Zodiac to the line from the mooring buoy after releasing it from the forward cleat. The boat was free now. He turned in the bow pulpit and looked up at the bridge just as Buddy, his hair a wiry nest from sleep, slid into the pilot seat. McCaleb signaled that the boat was loose. Buddy pushed the throttles forward and *The Following Sea* began to move. McCaleb picked the eight-foot gaff pole up off the deck and used it to keep the buoy off the bow as the boat made the turn into the fairway and slowly headed toward the mouth of the harbor.

McCaleb stayed in the pulpit, leaning back against the railing and watching the island slip away behind the boat. He looked up once again toward his house and saw only the one light still on. It was too early for his family to be awake. He thought about the mistake he had knowingly just made. He should have gone up to the house and told Graciela what he was doing, tried to explain it. But he knew it would lose him a lot of time and that he would never be able to explain it to her satisfaction. He decided to just go. He would call his wife after the crossing and he would deal with the consequences of his decision later.

The cool air of the shark-gray dawn had tightened the skin on his arms and neck. He turned in the bow pulpit and looked forward and across the bay to where he knew overtown lay hidden beneath the marine layer. Not being able to see what he knew to be there gave him an ominous feeling and he looked down. The water the bow cut through was flat and as blue-black as a marlin's skin. McCaleb knew he needed to get up into the bridge to help Buddy. One of them would drive while the other kept an eye on the radar screen to chart a safe course to Los Angeles Harbor. Too bad, he thought, that there would be no radar for him to use once he was on land again and trying to chart his way through the case that now gripped him. A mist of a different kind awaited him there. And these thoughts of trying to see his way through turned his mind to the thing about the case that had hooked him so deeply.

Beware Beware God Sees

The words turned in his head like a newfound mantra. There was someone in the cloaking mist ahead who had written those words.

Someone who had acted on them in an extreme capacity at least once and who would likely act on them again. McCaleb was going to find that person. And in doing so, he wondered, whose words would he be acting on? Was there a true God sending him on this journey?

He felt a touch on his shoulder and startled and turned, nearly dropping the gaff pole overboard. It was Buddy.

'Jesus, man, don't do that!'

'You all right?'

'I was till you scared the hell out of me. What are you doing? You should be driving.'

McCaleb glanced over his shoulder to make sure they were clear of the harbor markers and into the open bay.

'I don't know,' Buddy said. 'You looked like Ahab standing out here with that gaff. I thought something was wrong. What are you doing?'

'I was thinking. Do you mind? Don't sneak up on me like that, man.'

'Well, I guess that makes us even then.'

'Just go drive the boat, Buddy. I'll be up in a minute. And check the generator – might as well juice the batteries.'

As Buddy moved away McCaleb felt his heart even out again. He stepped off the pulpit and snapped the gaff back into its clamps on the deck. As he was bent over he felt the boat rise and fall as it went over a three- or four-foot roller. He straightened up and looked around for the origin of the wake. But he saw nothing. It had been a phantom moving across the flat surface of the bay.

6

Harry Bosch raised his briefcase like a shield and used it to push his way through the crowd of reporters and cameras gathered outside the doors of the courtroom.

'Let me through, please, let me through.'

Most of them didn't move until he used the briefcase to lever them out of the way. They were desperately crowding in and reaching tape recorders and cameras toward the center of the human knot where the defense lawyer was holding court.

Bosch finally made it to the door, where a sheriff's deputy was pressed against the handle. He recognized Bosch and stepped sideways so he could open the door.

'You know,' Bosch said to the deputy, 'this is going to happen every day. This guy has more to say outside court than inside. You might want to think about setting up some rules so people can get in and out.'

As Bosch went through the door, he heard the deputy tell him to talk to the judge about it.

Bosch walked down the center aisle and then through the gate to the prosecution table. He was the first to arrive. He pulled the third chair out and sat down. He opened his briefcase on the table, took out the heavy blue binder and put it to the side. He then closed and snapped the briefcase locks and put it down on the floor next to his chair.

Bosch was ready. He leaned forward and folded his arms on top of the binder. The courtroom was still, almost empty except for the judge's clerk and a court reporter who were getting ready for the day. Bosch liked these times. The quiet before the storm. And he knew without a doubt that a storm was surely coming. He nodded to himself. He was ready, ready to dance with the devil once more. He realized that his mission in life was all about moments like these. Moments that should be savored and remembered but that always caused a tight fisting of his guts.

There was a loud metallic clacking sound and the door to the side holding cell opened. Two deputies led a man through the door. He was young and still tanned somehow despite almost three months in lockup. He wore a suit that would easily take the weekly paychecks of the men on either side of him. His hands were cuffed at his sides to a waist chain which looked incongruous with the perfect blue suit. In one hand he clasped an artist's sketch pad. The other held a black felt-tip pen, the only kind of writing instrument allowed in lockdown.

The man was led to the defense table and positioned in front of the middle seat. He smiled and looked forward as the cuffs and the chain were removed. A deputy put a hand on the man's shoulder and pushed him down into the seat. The deputies then moved back and took positions in chairs to the man's rear.

The man immediately leaned forward and opened the sketch pad and went to work with his pen. Bosch watched. He could hear the point of the pen scratching furiously on the paper.

'They don't allow me a charcoal, Bosch. Do you believe that? What threat could a piece of charcoal possibly be?'

He hadn't looked at Bosch as he said it. Bosch didn't reply.

'It's the little things like that that bother me the most,' the man said.

'Better get used to it,' Bosch said.

The man laughed but still did not look at Bosch.

'You know, somehow I knew that was exactly what you were going to say.'

Bosch was quiet.

'You see, you are so predictable Bosch. All of you are.'

The rear courtroom door opened and Bosch turned his eyes away from the defendant. The attorneys were coming in now. They were about to start.

7

By the time McCaleb got to the Farmers' Market he was thirty minutes late for the meeting with Jaye Winston. He and Buddy had made the crossing in an hour and a half and McCaleb had called the sheriff's detective after they tied up at Cabrillo Marina. They arranged to meet but then he found the battery in the Cherokee dead because the car hadn't been used in two weeks. He had to get Buddy to give him a jump from his old Taurus and that had taken up the time.

He walked into Dupar's, the corner restaurant in the market, but didn't see Winston at any of the tables or the counter. He hoped she hadn't come and gone. He chose an unoccupied booth that afforded the most privacy and sat down. He didn't need to look at a menu. They had chosen the Farmer's Market to meet because it was near Edward Gunn's apartment and because McCaleb wanted to eat breakfast at Dupar's. He had told Winston that more than anything else about Los Angeles, he missed the pancakes at Dupar's. Often when he and Graciela and the children made their once-a-month trip overtown to buy clothing and supplies not available on Catalina, they ate a meal at Dupar's. It didn't matter whether it was breakfast, lunch or dinner, McCaleb always ordered pancakes. Raymond did, too. But he was boysenberry while McCaleb was traditional maple.

McCaleb told the waitress he was waiting for another party but ordered a large orange juice and a glass of water. After she brought the two glasses he opened his leather bag and took out the plastic pill box. He kept a week's supply of his pills on the boat and another couple days' worth in the glove box of the Cherokee. He'd prepared the box after docking. Alternating gulps of orange juice and water, he downed the twenty-seven pills that made up his morning dosage. He knew their names by their shapes and colors and tastes; Prilosec, Imuran, digoxin. As he methodically went through the lineup he noticed a woman in a nearby booth watching, her eyebrows arched in wonder.

He would never get rid of the pills. They were as certain for him as the proverbial death and taxes. Over the years some would be changed, some subtracted and new ones added, but he knew he would be swallowing pills and washing away their awful tastes with orange juice for the rest of his life.

'I see you ordered without me.'

He looked up from the last three cyclosporine pills he was about to take as Jaye Winston slid into the opposite side of the booth.

'Sorry, I'm so late. Traffic on the ten was a complete bitch.'

'It's all right. I was late, too. Dead battery.'

'How many of those you take now?'

'Fifty-four a day.'

'Unbelievable.'

'I had to turn a hallway closet into a medicine cabinet. The whole thing.'

'Well, at least you're still here.'

She smiled and McCaleb nodded. The waitress came to the table with a menu for Winston but she said they had better order.

'I'll have what he's having.'

McCaleb ordered a large stack with melted butter. He told the waitress they would share one order of well-done bacon.

'Coffee?' asked the waitress. She looked as though this might have been the one-millionth pancake order she had taken.

'Yes, please,' said Winston. 'Black.'

McCaleb said he was fine with the orange juice.

When they were alone McCaleb looked across the table at Winston.

'So, you get ahold of the manager?'

'He's going to meet us at ten-thirty. The place is still vacant but it has been cleaned. After we released it, the vic's sister came up and went through his things, took what she wanted.'

'Yeah, I was afraid of something like that.'

'The manager didn't think it was very much – the guy didn't have much.'

'What about the owl?'

'He didn't remember the owl. Frankly, I didn't either until you mentioned it this morning.'

'It's just a hunch. I'd like to take a look at it.'

'Well, we'll see if it's there. What else do you want to do? I hope you didn't come all the way across just to look at the guy's apartment.'

'I was thinking about checking out the sister. And maybe Harry Bosch, too.'

Winston was silent but he could tell by her demeanor she was waiting for an explanation.

'In order to profile an unknown subject, it's important to know the victim. His routines, personality, everything. You know the drill. The sister and, to a lesser extent, Bosch can help with that.'

'I only asked you to look at the book and the tape, Terry. You're going to make me start feeling guilty here.'

McCaleb paused while the waitress brought Winston's coffee and put down two small glass pitchers containing boysenberry and maple syrup. After she went away he spoke.

'You knew I'd get hooked, Jaye. "Beware, beware, God sees?" I mean, come on. You're going to tell me you thought I'd look it all over and phone in the report? Besides, I'm not complaining. I'm here because I want to be. If you feel guilty, you can buy the pancakes.'

'What did your wife say about it?'

'Nothing. She knows it's something I have to do. I called her from the dock after I crossed. It was too late for her to really say anything by then anyway. She just told me to pick up a bag of green corn tamales at El Cholo before I headed back. They sell 'em frozen.'

The pancakes came. They stopped talking and McCaleb politely waited for Winston to choose a syrup first but she was using a fork to move her pancakes around on her plate and he finally couldn't wait. He doused his stack with maple syrup and started eating. The waitress came back by and put a check down. Winston quickly grabbed it.

'The sheriff will pay for this.'

'Tell him thanks.'

'You know, I don't know what you expect from Harry Bosch. He told me he'd only had a handful of contacts with Gunn in the six years since the prostitute case.'

'When were those, when he got popped?'

Winston nodded as she poured boysenberry syrup on her pancakes.

'That means he would have seen him the night before he was killed. I didn't see anything about it in the book.'

'I haven't written it up. There's not much to it. The watch sergeant called him and told him Gunn was in the drunk tank on a DUI.'

McCaleb nodded.

'And?'

'And he came in to look at the guy. That was it. He said they didn't even talk because Gunn was too blitzed.'

'Well . . . I still want to talk to Harry. I worked a case with him once. He's a good cop. Intuitive and observant. He might know something I could use.'

'That is, if you can get to talk to him.'

'What do you mean?'

'You don't know? He's riding the prosecution table on the David Storey murder case. Up in Van Nuys. Don't you watch the news?'

'Ah, damn, I forgot about that. I remember reading his name in the newspapers after they took Storey down. That was, what, in October? They're already in trial?'

'They sure are. No delays and they didn't need a prelim because they went through the grand jury. They started jury selection right after the first. Last I heard, they had the panel so openers will probably be this week, maybe even today.'

'Shit.'

'Yeah, good luck getting to Bosch. I'm sure this is just what he'll want to hear about.'

'Are you saying you don't want me to talk to him?'

Winston shrugged her shoulders.

'No, I'm not saying that at all. Do whatever you want to do. I just didn't think you'd be doing so much legwork on this. I can talk to my captain about maybe getting a consulting fee for you but—'

'Don't worry about it. The sheriff's buying breakfast. That's enough.'

'Doesn't seem like it.'

He didn't tell her that he'd work the case for free, just to be back in the life for a few days. And he didn't tell her that he couldn't take any money from her anyway. If he made any 'official' income he would lose his eligibility for the state medical assistance that paid for the fifty-four pills he swallowed every day. The pills were so expensive that if he had to pay for them himself he'd be bankrupt inside six months, unless he happened to be drawing a six-figure salary. It was the ugly secret behind the medical miracle that had saved him. He got a second chance at life, just as long as he didn't use it to try to earn a living. It was the reason the charter business was in Buddy Lockridge's name. Officially, McCaleb was an unpaid deckhand. Buddy simply rented the boat for charter from Graciela, the rent being 60 percent of all charter fees after expenses.

'How are your pancakes?' he asked Winston.

'The best.'

'Damn right.'

8

The Grand Royale was a two-story eyesore, a deteriorating stucco box whose attempt at style began and ended with the modish design of the letters of its name tacked over the entranceway. The streets of West Hollywood and elsewhere in the flats were lined with such banal designs, the high-density apartments that crowded out smaller bungalow courts in the fifties and sixties. They replaced true style with phony ornamental flourishes and names that reflected exactly what they were not.

McCaleb and Winston entered the second-floor apartment that had belonged to Edward Gunn with the building manager, a man named Rohrshak – 'Like the test, only spelled different.'

If he hadn't known where to look, McCaleb would have missed what was left of the bloodstain on the carpet where Gunn had died. The carpet had not been replaced. Instead it had been shampooed, leaving only a small, light brown trace stain that would probably be mistaken by the next renter as the remnant of a soda or coffee spill.

The place had been cleaned and readied for renting. But the furnishings were the same. McCaleb recognized them from the crime scene video.

He looked across the room at the china cabinet but it was empty. There was no plastic owl perched atop it. He looked at Winston.

'It's gone.'

Winston turned to the manager.

'Mr. Rohrshak. The owl that was on top of that cabinet. We think it was important. Are you sure you don't know what happened to it?'

Rohrshak spread his arms wide and then dropped them to his side.

'No, I don't know. You asked before and I thought, "I don't remember any owl." But if you say so ...'

He shrugged his shoulders and jutted his chin, then nodded as if reluctantly agreeing that there had been an owl on the china cabinet.

McCaleb read his body language and words as the classic mannerisms of a liar. Deny the existence of the object you have stolen and you eliminate the theft. He assumed Winston had picked up on it as well.

'Jaye, you have a phone? Can you call the sister to double-check?'

'I've been holding out until the county buys me one.'

McCaleb had wanted to keep his phone free in case Brass Doran called back but put his leather bag down on an overstuffed couch and dug out his phone and handed it to her.

She had to get the sister's number out of a notebook in her briefcase. While she made the call McCaleb walked slowly around the apartment, taking it all in and trying to get a vibe from the place. In the dining area he stopped in front of the round wooden table with four straight-back chairs placed around it. The crime scene analysis report said that three of the chairs had numerous smears, partials and complete latent fingerprints on them – all of them belonging to the victim, Edward Gunn. The fourth chair, the one found on the north side of the table, was completely devoid of fingerprint evidence in any condition. The chair had been wiped down. Most likely, the killer had done this after handling the chair for some reason.

McCaleb checked his directions and went to the chair on the north side of the table. Careful not to touch the back of it, he hooked his hand under the seat and pulled it away from the table and over to the china cabinet. He positioned it at center and then stepped up onto the seat. He raised his arms as if placing something on top of the cabinet. The chair wobbled on its uneven legs and McCaleb instinctively reached one hand to the top edge of the china cabinet to steady himself. Before he grabbed on he realized something and stopped himself. He braced his forearm across the frame of one of the cabinet's glass doors instead.

'Steady there, Terry.'

He looked down. Winston was standing next to him. His phone was folded closed in her hand.

'I am. So does she have the bird?'

'No, she didn't know what I was talking about.'

McCaleb raised himself on his toes and looked over the top edge of the cabinet.

'She tell you what she did take?'

'Just some clothes and some old photos of them when they were kids. She didn't want anything else.'

McCaleb nodded. He was still looking up and down the top of the cabinet. There was a thick layer of dust on top.

'You say anything about me coming down to talk to her?'

'I forgot. I can call her back.'

'You have a flashlight, Jaye?'

She dug through her purse and then handed up a small penlight. McCaleb flicked it on and held it at a low angle to the top of the cabinet. The light made the surface dust more distinct and now he could clearly see an octagonal-shaped impression that had been left by something that had been put on top of the cabinet and the dust. The base of the owl.

He next moved the light along the edges of the top board, then turned it off and got down off the chair. He handed Jaye the penlight.

'Thanks. You might want to think about getting a print team back out here.'

'How come? The owl's not up there, is it?'

McCaleb glanced at Rohrshak for a moment.

'Nope, it's gone. But whoever put it up there used that chair. When it wobbled they grabbed a hold.'

He took a pen out of his pocket and reached up and tapped the front edge of the cabinet in the area where he had seen finger impressions in the dust.

'It's pretty dusty but there might be prints.'

'What if it was whoever took the owl?'

McCaleb looked pointedly at Rohrshak when he answered.

'Same thing. There might be prints.'

Rohrshak looked away.

'Can I use this again?'

Winston held up his phone.

'Go ahead.'

As Winston called for a print team, McCaleb dragged the chair into the middle of the living room, positioning it a few feet from the bloodstain. He then sat down on it and took in the room. In this position the owl would have looked down on the killer as well as the victim. Some instinct told McCaleb that this was the configuration the killer had wanted. He looked down at the bloodstain and imagined he was looking down at Edward Gunn struggling for his life and slowly losing the battle. The bucket, he thought. Everything fit but the bucket. The killer had set the stage but then couldn't watch the play. He needed the bucket so that he wouldn't see his victim's face. It bothered McCaleb that it didn't fit.

Winston came over and handed him the phone.

'There's a crew just finishing a break-in on Kings. They'll be here in fifteen minutes.'

'That's lucky.'

'Very. What are you doing?'

'Just thinking. I think he sat here and watched but then couldn't take it. He struck the victim on the head, to maybe hurry it up. Then he got the bucket and put it on so he wouldn't have to watch.'

Winston nodded.

'Where'd the bucket come from? There was nothing in the—'

'We think it came from under the sink in the kitchen. There's a ring, a water ring on the shelf that fits the base of the bucket. It's on a supplemental Kurt typed up. He must've forgotten to put it in the book.'

McCaleb nodded and stood up.

'You're going to wait for the print crew, right?'

‘Yes, it shouldn’t be long.’

‘I’m going to take a walk.’

He headed for the open door.

‘I will go with you,’ Rohrshak said.

McCaleb turned.

‘No, Mr. Rohrshak, you need to stay here with Detective Winston. We need an independent witness to monitor what we do in the apartment.’

He glanced over Rohrshak’s shoulder at Winston. She winked, telling him she understood the phony story and what he was doing.

‘Yes, Mr. Rohrshak. Please stay here, if you don’t mind.’

Rohrshak shrugged his shoulders again and raised his hands.

McCaleb went down the stairs to the enclosed courtyard in the center of the apartment building. He turned in a complete circle and his eyes traveled up to the line of the flat roof. He didn’t see the owl anywhere and turned and walked out through the entrance hall to the street.

Across Sweetzer was the Braxton Arms, a three-story, L-shaped apartment building with exterior walkways and stairwells. McCaleb crossed and found a six-foot security gate and fence at the entrance. It was more for show than as a deterrent. He took off his windbreaker, folded it and pushed it between two of the gate’s bars. He then brought his foot up onto the gate’s handle, tested it with his weight, then hoisted himself up to the top of the gate. He dropped down on the other side and looked around to see if anyone was watching him. He was clear. He grabbed his windbreaker and headed for the stairwell.

He walked up to the third level and followed the walkway to the front of the building. His breathing was loud and labored from climbing the gate and then the stairs. When he got to the front he put his hands on the safety railing and leaned forward until he had caught his breath. He then looked across Sweetzer to the flat roof of the apartment building where Edward Gunn had lived. Again, the plastic owl wasn’t there.

McCaleb leaned his forearms down on the railing and continued to labor for breath. He listened to the cadence of his heart as it finally settled. He could feel sweat popping on his scalp. He knew it wasn’t his heart that was weak. It was his body, weakened by all the drugs he took to keep his heart strong. It frustrated him. He knew that he would never be strong, that he would spend the rest of his life listening to his heart the way a night burglar listens to creaks in the floor.

He looked down when he heard a vehicle and saw a white van with the sheriff’s seal on the driver’s door pull to a stop in front of the apartment building across the street. The print crew had arrived.

McCaleb glanced at the roof across the street once more and then turned to head back down, defeated. He suddenly stopped. There was the owl. It was perched atop a compressor for a central air-conditioning system on the roof of the L-extension of the building he was in.

He quickly went to the stairs and climbed up to the roof landing. He had to work his way around some furniture that was stacked and stored on the landing but found the door unlocked and hurried across the flat, gravel-strewn roof to the air conditioner.

McCaleb first studied the owl before touching it. It matched his memory of the owl on the crime scene tape. Its base was an octagonal stump. He knew it was the missing owl. He removed the wire that had been wrapped around the base and attached to the intake grill of the air conditioner. He noticed that the grill and metal covering of the unit were covered with old bird droppings. He surmised that the droppings were a maintenance problem and Rohrshak, who apparently managed this building as well as the one across the street, had taken the owl from Gunn's apartment to use to keep the birds away.

McCaleb took the wire and looped it around the owl's neck so that he could carry it without touching it, though he doubted there would be any usable fingerprint or fiber evidence remaining on it. He lifted it off the air conditioner and headed back to the stairs.

When McCaleb stepped back into Edward Gunn's apartment he saw two crime scene techs getting equipment out of a toolbox. A stepladder was standing in front of the china cabinet.

'You might want to start with this,' he said.

He watched Rohrshak's eyes widen as he entered the room and placed the plastic owl on the table.

'You manage the place across the street, don't you, Mr. Rohrshak?'

'Uh . . .'

'It's okay. It's easy enough to find out.'

'Yes, he does,' Winston said, bending down to look at the owl. 'He was over there when we needed him on the day of the murder. He lives there.'

'Any idea how this ended up on the roof?' McCaleb asked.

Rohrshak still didn't answer.

'Guess it just flew over, right?'

Rohrshak couldn't take his eyes off the owl.

'Tell you what, you can go now, Mr. Rohrshak. But stay around your place. If we get a print off the bird or the cabinet, we're going to need to take a set of yours for comparison.'

Now Rohrshak looked at McCaleb and his eyes grew even wider.

'Go on, Mr. Rohrshak.'

The building manager turned and slowly headed out of the apartment.

'And shut the door, please,' McCaleb called after him.

After he was gone and the door was shut Winston almost burst into laughter.

'Terry, you're being so hard on him. He didn't really do anything wrong, you know. We cleared the place, he let the sister take what she wanted and then what was he supposed to do, try to rent the place with this stupid owl up there?'

McCaleb shook his head.

'He lied to us. That was wrong. I almost blew a gasket climbing that building across the street. He could have just told us it was up there.'

'Well, he's properly scared now. I think he learned his lesson.'

'Whatever.'

He stepped back so one of the techs could go to work on the owl while the other climbed the ladder to work on the top of the cabinet.

McCaleb studied the bird as the tech brushed on black fingerprint powder. It appeared that the owl was hand painted. It was dark brown and black on its wings, head and back. Its chest was a lighter brown with some yellow highlighting. Its eyes were a shiny black.

'Has this been outside?' the tech asked.

'Unfortunately,' McCaleb answered, remembering the rains that had swept off the mainland and out to Catalina the week before.

'Well, I'm not getting anything.'

'Figures.'

McCaleb looked at Winston, his eyes portraying renewed anger with Rohrshak.

'Nothing up here, either,' the other tech said. 'Too much dust.'

9

The trial of David Storey was being held in the Van Nuys courthouse. The crime the case centered on was not remotely connected to Van Nuys or even the San Fernando Valley, but the courthouse had been chosen by schedulers in the district attorney's office because Department N was available and it was the single largest courtroom in the county – constructed out of two courtrooms several years earlier to comfortably hold the two juries as well as the attendant media crush of the Menendez brothers murder case. The Menendezes' slaying of their parents had been one of several Los Angeles court cases in the previous decade to capture the media's and, therefore, the public's attention. When it was over, the DA's office did not bother deconstructing the huge courtroom. Somebody there had the foresight to realize that in L.A. there would always be a case that could fill Department N.

And at the moment it was the David Storey case.

The thirty-eight-year-old film director, known for films that pushed the limits of violence and sexuality within an R rating, was charged with the murder of a young actress he had taken home from the premiere of his most recent film. The twenty-three-year-old woman's body was found the next morning in the small Nichols Canyon bungalow she shared with another would-be actress. The victim had been strangled, her nude body arranged in her bed in a pose investigators believed to be part of a careful plan by her killer to avoid discovery.

The case's elements – power, celebrity, sex and money – and the added Hollywood connection served to bring the case maximum media attention. David Storey worked on the wrong side of the camera to be a fully realized celebrity himself, but his name was known and he wielded the awesome power of a man who had delivered seven box office hits in as many years. The media were drawn to the Storey trial in the way young people are drawn by the dream of Hollywood. The advance coverage clearly delineated the case as a parable on unchecked Hollywood avarice and excess.

The case also had a degree of secrecy not usually seen in criminal trials. The prosecutors assigned to the case took their evidence to a grand jury in order to seek charges against Storey. The move allowed them to bypass a preliminary hearing, where most of the evidence accumulated against a defendant is usually made public. Without that fount of case information, the media were left to mine their sources in both the prosecution and defense camps. Still, little about the case was leaked to the media other than generalities. The evidence the prosecution would use to tie Storey to the murder remained cloaked, and all the more cause for the media frenzy around the trial.

It was just that frenzy that had convinced the district attorney to move the trial to the large Department N courtroom in Van Nuys. The second jury box would be used to accommodate more media members in the courtroom, while the unused deliberation room would be converted into a media room where the video feed could be watched by the second- and third-tier journalists. The move, which would give all media – from the *National Enquirer* to the *New York Times* – full access to the trial and its players, guaranteed the proceedings would become the first full-blooded media circus of the new century.

In the center ring of this circus, sitting at the prosecution table, was Detective Harry Bosch, the lead investigator of the case. All the pretrial media analysis came down to one conclusion: the charges against David Storey would rise and fall with Bosch. All evidence in support of the murder charge was said to be circumstantial; the foundation of the case would come from Bosch. The one solid piece of evidence that had been leaked to the media was that Bosch would testify that in a private moment, with no other witnesses or devices at hand to record the statement, Storey had smugly admitted to him that he had committed the crime and boasted that he would surely get away with it.

McCaleb knew all of this as he walked into the Van Nuys courthouse shortly before noon. He stood in line to go through the metal detector and felt a reminder of all that had changed in his life. When he had been a bureau agent all he needed to do was hold his badge up and walk around the line. Now he was just a citizen. He had to wait.

The fourth-floor hallway was crowded with people milling about. McCaleb noticed that many clutched stacks of eight-by-ten black-and-white glossies of the movie stars they hoped would be attending the trial – either as witnesses or as spectators in support of the defendant. He walked to the double-door entrance to Department N but one of the two sheriff's deputies posted there told him the courtroom was at full capacity. The deputy pointed to a long line of people standing behind a rope. He said it was the line for people waiting to go in. Every time one person left the courtroom another could go in. McCaleb nodded and stepped away from the doors.

He saw that further down the hallway was an open door with people milling about it. He recognized one man as a reporter on a local television news program. He guessed it was the media room and headed that way.

When he got to the open door he could look in and see two large televisions mounted high up in either corner above the room where there were several people crowded around a large jury table. Reporters. They were typing on laptop computers, taking notes on pads, eating sandwiches from to-go bags. The center of the table was crowded with plastic coffee and soda cups.

He looked up at one of the televisions and saw that court was still in session though it was now past noon. The camera focused on a wide angle and he recognized Harry Bosch sitting with a man and a woman at the prosecution table. It did not look as though he was paying attention to the proceedings. A man McCaleb recognized stood at the lectern between the prosecution and defense tables. He was J. Reason Fowkkes, the lead defense attorney. At the table to his left sat the defendant, David Storey.

McCaleb could not hear the audio feed but he knew that Fowkkes was not delivering his opening statement. He was looking up at the judge, not in the direction of the jury box. Most likely last-minute motions were being argued by the attorneys before openers began. The twin television screens switched to a new camera, this angle directly on the judge, who began speaking, apparently delivering his rulings. McCaleb noted the name plate in front of the judge's bench. It said Superior Court Judge John A. Houghton.

'Agent McCaleb?'

McCaleb turned from the television to see a man he recognized but couldn't immediately place standing next to him.

'Just McCaleb. Terry McCaleb.'

The man perceived his difficulty and held out his hand.

'Jack McEvoy. I interviewed you once. It was pretty brief. It was about the Poet investigation.'

'Oh, right, I remember now. That was a while back.'

McCaleb shook his hand. He did remember McEvoy. He had become entwined in the Poet case and then wrote a book about it. McCaleb had had a very peripheral part in the case – when the investigation had shifted to Los Angeles. He never read McEvoy's book but was sure he had not added anything to it and likely wasn't mentioned in it.

'I thought you were from Colorado,' he said, recalling that McEvoy had worked for one of the papers in Denver. 'They sent you out to cover this?'

McEvoy nodded.

'Good memory. I was from there but I live out here now. I work freelance.'

McCaleb nodded, wondering what else there was to say.

'Who are you covering this for?'

'I've been writing a weekly dispatch on it for the *New Times.* Do you read it?'

McCaleb nodded. He was familiar with the *New Times.* It was a weekly tabloid with an anti-authority, muckraking stance. It appeared to subsist mostly on entertainment ads, ranging from movies to the escort services that filled its back pages. It was free and Buddy always seemed to leave issues lying around the boat. McCaleb looked at it from time to time but hadn't noticed McEvoy's name before.

'I'm also doing a general wrap for *Vanity Fair,*' McEvoy said. 'You know, a more discursive, dark-side-of-Hollywood piece. I'm thinking about another book, too. What brings you here? Are you . . . involved with this in some . . .'

'Me, no. I was in the area and I have a friend involved. I was hoping I might be able to get a chance to say hello to him.'

As he told the lie McCaleb looked away from the writer and back through the door to the televisions. The full courtroom camera angle was now being shown. It looked like Bosch was gathering things into a briefcase.

'Harry Bosch?'

McCaleb looked back at him.

'Yeah, Harry. We worked a case together before and . . . uh, what's going on in there now, anyway?'

'Final motions before they start. They started with a closed session and they're just doing some housekeeping. Not worth being in there. Everybody thinks the judge will probably finish before lunch and then give the lawyers the rest of the day to work on openers. They start tomorrow at ten. You think things are crowded here now? Wait till tomorrow.'

McCaleb nodded.

'Oh, well, okay then. Uh, nice seeing you again, Jack. Good luck with the story. And the book, if it comes to that.'

'You know, I would have liked to write your story. You know, with the heart and everything.'

McCaleb nodded.

'Well, I owed Keisha Russell one and she did a good job with it.'

McCaleb noticed people start to push their way out of the media room. Behind them he could see on the television screens that the judge had left the bench. Court was out of session.

'I better go down the hall and see if I can catch Harry. Good to see you again, Jack.'

McCaleb offered his hand and McEvoy shook it. He then followed the other reporters down to the courtroom doors.

The main doors to Department N were opened by the two deputies and out flowed the crowd of lucky citizens who had gotten seats during the session, which had most likely been mind-numbingly boring. Those who had not made it inside pushed up close for a glimpse of a celebrity but they were disappointed. The celebrities wouldn't start showing until the next day. Opening statements were like the opening credits of a film. That's where they would want to be seen.

At the tail end of the crowd came the lawyers and staff. Storey had been returned to lockup but his attorney strode right to the semicircle of reporters and began giving his view of what had transpired inside. A tall man with jet-black hair, a deep tan and ever-shifting green eyes took a position directly behind the lawyer to cover his back. He was striking and McCaleb thought he recognized him but he couldn't think from where. He looked like one of the actors Storey normally put in his films.

The prosecutors came out and soon had their own knot of reporters to deal with. Their answers were shorter than the defense lawyer's. They often declined to comment when asked questions about the evidence they would present.

McCaleb watched for Bosch and finally saw him slip out last. Bosch skirted the crowd by staying close to the wall and headed toward the elevators. One reporter moved in on him but he held up his hand and waved her away. She stopped and moved back like a loose molecule to the pack standing around J. Reason Fowkkes.

McCaleb followed Bosch down the hall and caught him when he stopped to wait for an elevator.

'Hey, Harry Bosch.'

Bosch turned, already putting on his no-comment face, when he saw it was McCaleb.

'Hey . . . McCaleb.'

He smiled. The men shook hands.

'Looks like the world's worst eight-by-ten case,' McCaleb said.

'You're telling me. What are you doing here? Don't tell me you're writing a book on this thing.'

'What?'

'All these ex-bureau guys writing books nowadays.'

'Nah, that's not me. Actually, though, I was hoping I could maybe buy you lunch. There's something I wanted to talk to you about.'

Bosch looked at his watch and was deciding something.

'Edward Gunn.'

Bosch looked up at him.

'Jaye Winston?'

McCaleb nodded.

'She asked me to take a look.'

The elevator came and they stepped onto it with a crowd of people who had been in the courtroom. They all seemed to be looking at Bosch while trying not to show it. McCaleb decided not to continue until they were off.

On the first floor they headed toward the exit.

'I told her I'd profile it. A quick one. To do it I need to get a handle on Gunn. I thought maybe you could tell me about that old case and about what kind of guy he was.'

'He was a scumbag. Look, I have about forty-five minutes max. I need to get on the road. I'm running down wits today, making sure everybody's ready to go after openers.'

'I'll take the forty-five if you can spare it. Any place to eat around here?'

'Forget the cafeteria here – it's awful. There's a Cupid's up on Victory.'

'You cops always eat at the best.'

'It's why we do what we do.'

10

They ate their hot dogs at an outdoor table without an umbrella. Though it was a mildly warm winter day, McCaleb found himself sweating. On any given day the Valley could be counted on to be fifteen to twenty degrees warmer than Catalina and he wasn't used to the change. His internal heating and cooling systems had never been normal since the transplant and he was prone to quick chills and sweats.

He began with some small talk about Bosch's current case.

'You ready to become Hollywood Harry with this case?'

'Yeah, no thanks,' Bosch said between bites of what was billed as a Chicago dog. 'I think I'd rather be on midnight shift in the Seventy-seventh.'

'Well, you think you got it together? You got him?'

'Never know. The DA's office hasn't won a big one since disco. I don't know how it will go. The lawyers all say it depends on the jury. I always thought it was the quality of the evidence but I'm just a dumb detective. John Reason brought in O. J.'s jury consultant and they're acting pretty happy with the twelve in the box. Shit, John Reason. See, I'm even calling the guy by the name the reporters use. It shows how good he is at controlling things, sculpting things.'

He shook his head and took another bite of his lunch.

'Who is the big guy I saw him with?' McCaleb asked. 'The guy standing behind him like Lurch.'

'Rudy Valentino, his investigator.'

'That's his name?'

'No, it's Rudy Tafero. He's former LAPD. He worked Hollywood detectives until a few years back. People in the bureau called him Valentino 'cause of his looks. He got off on it. Anyway, he went private. Has a bail bonds license. Don't ask me how but he started getting security contracts with a lot of Hollywood people. He showed up on this one right after we popped Storey. In fact, Rudy brought Storey to Fowkkes. Probably got a nice finder's fee for that.'

'And how about the judge? How's he going to be?'

Bosch nodded as if he had found something good in the conversation.

'Shootin' Houghton. He's no Second Chance Lance. He's no bullshit. He'll slap Fowkkes down if he needs to. At least we have that going for us.'

'Shootin' Houghton?'

'Under that black robe he's usually strapped – or at least most people think so. About five years ago he had a Mexican Mafia case, and when the jury came in guilty a bunch of the defendants' buddies and family in the audience got mad and nearly started a riot in the courtroom. Houghton pulled his Glock and put a round into the ceiling. It quieted things down pretty quick. Ever since he's been reelected by the highest percentage of any incumbent judge in the county. Go in his courtroom and check the ceiling. The bullet hole's still there. He won't let anybody fix it.'

Bosch took another bite and looked at his watch. He changed the subject, talking with his mouth full.

'Nothing personal but I take it they've hit the wall on Gunn if they're going to outside help already.'

McCaleb nodded.

'Something like that.'

He looked down at the chili dog in front of him and wished he had a knife and fork.

'What's wrong? We didn't have to come here.'

'Nothing. I was just thinking. Between pancakes at Dupar's this morning and this, I might need another heart by dinner.'

'You want to stop your heart, next time you go to Dupar's top it off with a stop at Bob's Donuts. Right there in the Farmers' Market. Raised glaze. A couple of those and you'll feel your arteries harden and snap like icicles hanging off a house. They never came up with suspect one, right?'

'Right. Nothing.'

'So what makes you so interested?'

'Same as Jaye. Something about this one. We think whoever it was might be just starting.'

Bosch just nodded. His mouth was full.

McCaleb appraised him. His hair was shorter than McCaleb had remembered it. More gray but that was to be expected. He still had the mustache and the eyes. They reminded him of Graciela's, so dark there was almost no delineation between iris and pupil. But Bosch's eyes were weary and slightly hooded by wrinkles at the corners. Still, they were always moving, observing. He sat leaning slightly forward, as if ready to move. McCaleb remembered that there had always been a spring-loaded feel to Bosch. He felt as though at any moment or for any reason Bosch could put the needle into the red zone.

Bosch reached inside his suit coat and took out a pair of sunglasses and put them on. McCaleb wondered if that had been in response to realizing that McCaleb had been studying him. He bent down, raised up his chili dog and finally took a bite. It tasted delicious and deadly at the same time.

He put the dripping mess back on the paper plate and wiped his hand on a napkin.

'So tell me about Gunn. You said he was a scumbag. What else?'

'What else? That's about it. He was a predator. Used women, bought women. He murdered that girl in that motel room, no doubt in my mind.'

'But the DA kicked the case.'

'Yeah. Gunn claimed self-defense. He said some things that didn't add up but not enough to add up to charges. He claimed self-defense and there wasn't going to be enough to go against that in a trial. So they no-billed it, end of story, on to the next case.'

'Did he ever know you didn't believe him?'

'Oh, sure. He knew.'

'Did you try to sweat him at all?'

Bosch gave him a look that McCaleb could read through the sunglasses. The last question went to Bosch's credibility as an investigator.

'I mean,' McCaleb said quickly, 'what happened when you tried to sweat him?'

'Actually, the truth is we never really got the chance. There was a problem. See, we did set it up. We brought him in and put him in one of the rooms. My partner and I were planning to leave him there a while, let him percolate a little and think about things. We were going to do all the paper, put it in the book and then take a run at him, try to break his story. We never got the chance. I mean, to do it right.'

'What happened?'

'Me and Edgar – that's my partner, Jerry Edgar – we went down the hall to get a cup of coffee and talk about how we were going to play it. While we were down there the squad lieutenant sees Gunn sitting in the interview room and doesn't know what the fuck he's doing there. He takes it upon himself to go in and make sure the guy's been properly advised of his rights.'

McCaleb could see the anger working its way into Bosch's face, even six years after the fact.

'You see, Gunn had come in as a witness and ostensibly as the victim of a crime. He said she came at him with the knife and he turned it on her. So we didn't need to advise him. The plan was to go in there, shake his story down and get him to make a mistake. Once we had that, then we were going to advise him. But this dipshit lieutenant didn't know any of this and he just went in and advised the guy. After that, we were dead. He knew we were coming after him. He asked for a lawyer as soon as we walked into the room.'

Bosch shook his head and looked out onto the street. McCaleb followed his eyes. Across Victory Boulevard was a used-car lot with red, white and blue pennants flapping in the wind. To McCaleb, Van Nuys was always synonymous with car lots. They were all over, new and used.

'So what did you say to the lieutenant?' he asked.

'Say? I didn't say anything. I just shoved him through the window of his office. I got a suspension out of it – involuntary stress leave. Jerry Edgar eventually took the case in to the DA and they sat on it a while and then finally kicked it.'

Bosch nodded. His eyes rested on his empty paper plate.

'I sort of blew it,' he said. 'Yeah, I blew it.'

McCaleb waited a moment before speaking. A gust of wind blew Bosch's plate off the table and the detective watched it skitter across the picnic area. He made no move to chase it down.

'You still working for that lieutenant?'

'Nope. He's no longer with us. Not too long after that he went out one night and didn't come home. They found him in his car up in the tunnel in Griffith Park near the Observatory.'

'What, he killed himself?'

'No. Somebody did it for him. It's still open. Technically.'

Bosch looked back at him. McCaleb dropped his eyes and noticed that Bosch's tie tack was a tiny pair of silver handcuffs.

'What else can I tell you?' Bosch said. 'None of this had anything to do with Gunn. He was just a fly in the ointment – the ointment being the bullshit they call the justice system.'

'Doesn't sound like you had time to do much background on him.'

'None, actually. All that I told you took place in the span of eight or nine hours. Afterward, with what happened, I was off the case and the guy walked out the door.'

'But you didn't give up. Jaye told me you visited him in the drunk tank the night before he got himself killed.'

'Yeah, he got popped on a duice while cruising whores on Sunset. He was in the tank and I got a call. I went in to take a look, maybe jerk his chain a little, see if he was ready to talk. But the guy was piss drunk, just lying there on the floor in the puke. So that was it. You could say that we didn't communicate.'

Bosch looked at McCaleb's unfinished chili dog and then his watch.

'Sorry, but that's all I got. You going to eat that or can we go?'

'Couple more bites, couple more questions. Don't you want to have a smoke?'

'I quit a couple years ago. I only smoke on special occasions.'

'Don't tell me, it was the Marlboro-man-gone-impotent sign on Sunset.'

'No, my wife wanted us both to quit. We did.'

'Your wife? Harry, you're full of surprises.'

'Don't get excited. She's come and gone. But at least I don't smoke anymore. I don't know about her.'

McCaleb just nodded, feeling he had stepped too far into the other man's personal world. He got back to the case.

'So any theories on who killed him?'

McCaleb took another bite while Bosch answered.

'My guess is he probably met up with somebody just like himself. Somebody who crossed a line somewhere. Don't get me wrong, I hope you and Jaye get the guy. But so far, whoever he or she is hasn't done anything I'm too upset about. Know what I mean?'

'It's funny you mentioned a "she." You think it could have been a woman?'

'I don't know enough about it. But like I said, he preyed on women. Maybe one of them put a stop to it.'

McCaleb just nodded. He couldn't think of anything else to ask. Bosch had been a long shot anyway. Maybe he'd known it would come to this and he just wanted to reconnect with Bosch for other reasons. He spoke with his eyes down on his paper plate.

'You still think about the girl on the hill, Harry?'

He didn't want to say out loud the name Bosch had given her.

Bosch nodded.

'From time to time I do. It sticks with me. They all do, I guess.'

McCaleb nodded.

'Yeah. So nothing . . . nobody ever made a claim on her?'

'Nope. And I tried with Seguin one last time, went up to see him at Q last year, about a week before he got the juice. Tried one more time to find out from him but he just smiled at me. It was like he knew it was the last thing he could hold over me or something. He enjoyed it, I could tell. So I got up to leave and I told him to enjoy himself in hell and know what he said to me? He said, "I hear it's a dry heat."

Bosch shook his head.

'Fucker. I drove up and back on my day off. Twelve hours in the car and the air conditioner didn't work.'

He looked directly at McCaleb and even through the shades McCaleb again felt the bond he had known so long ago with this man.

Before he could say anything he heard his phone begin to chirp from the pocket of his windbreaker, which was folded on the bench next to him. He struggled with the jacket to find the pocket and got to the phone before the caller hung up. It was Brass Doran.

'I have some stuff for you. Not a lot, but maybe a start.'

'You someplace I can call you back in a few minutes?'

'Actually, I'm in the central conference room. We're about to brainstorm a case and I'm the leader. It could be a couple hours before I'm free. You could call me at home tonight if you—'

'No, hold on.'

He held the phone down and looked at Bosch.

'I better take this. I'll talk to you later if anything comes up, okay?'

'Sure.'

Bosch started getting up. He was going to carry his Coke with him.

'Thanks,' McCaleb said, extending his hand. 'Good luck with the trial.'

Bosch shook his hand.

'Thanks. We'll probably need it.'

McCaleb watched him walk out of the picnic area and to the sidewalk leading back to the courthouse. He brought the phone back up then.

'Brass?'

'Here. Okay, you were talking about owls in general, right? You don't know the specific kind or breed, right?'

'Right. It's just a generic owl, I think.'

'What color is it?'

'Uh, it's brown mostly. Like on the back and the wings.'

As he spoke he took a couple of folded pages of notebook paper and a pen out of his pockets. He shoved his half-eaten chili dog out of the way and got ready to take notes.

'Okay, modern iconography is what you'd expect. The owl is the symbol of wisdom and truth, denotes knowledge, the view of the greater picture as opposed to the small detail. The owl sees in the night. In other words, seeing through the darkness is seeing the truth. It is learning the truth, therefore, knowledge. And from knowledge comes wisdom. Okay?'

McCaleb didn't need to take notes. What Doran had said was obvious. But just to keep his head in it he wrote down a line.

Seeing in the dark = Wisdom

He then underlined the last word.

'Okay, fine. What else?'

'That's basically what I have as far as contemporary application. But when I go backward it gets pretty interesting. Our friend the owl has totally rejuvenated his reputation. He used to be a bad guy.'

'Tell me, Brass.'

'Get your pencil out. The owl is seen repeatedly in art and religious iconography from early medieval through late Renaissance periods. It is found often depicted in religious allegorical displays – paintings, church panels and stations of the cross. The owl was—'

'Okay, Brass, but what did it mean?'

'I'm getting to that. Its meaning could be different from depiction to depiction and according to species depicted. But essentially its depiction was the symbol of evil.'

McCaleb wrote the word down.

'Evil. Okay.'

'I thought you'd be more excited.'

'You can't see me. I'm standing on my hands here. What else you have?'

'Let me run down the list of hits. These are taken from the extracts, the critical literature of the art of the period. References to depictions of owls come up as the symbol of – and I quote – doom, the enemy of innocence, the Devil himself, heresy, folly, death and misfortune, the bird of darkness, and finally, the torment of the human soul in its inevitable journey to eternal damnation. Nice, huh? I like that last one. I guess they didn't sell too many bags of potato chips with owls on them back in the fourteen hundreds.'

McCaleb didn't answer. He was busy scribbling down the descriptions she had read to him.

'Read that last one again.'

She did and he wrote it down verbatim.

'Now, there is more,' Doran said. 'There is also some interpretation of the owl as being the symbol of wrath as well as the punishment of evil. So it obviously was something that meant different things at different times *and* to different people.'

'The punishment of evil,' McCaleb said as he wrote it down.

He looked at the list he had written.

'Anything else?'

'Isn't that enough?'

'Probably. Was there anything about books showing some of this stuff or the names of artists or writers who used the so-called "bird of darkness" in their work?'

McCaleb heard some pages turning over the phone and Doran was silent for a few moments.

'I don't have a lot here. No books but I can give you the name of some of the artists mentioned and you could probably get something over the Internet or maybe the library at UCLA.'

'All right.'

'I have to do this quickly. We're about to go here.'

'Give it to me.'

'All right, I have an artist named Bruegel who painted a huge face as the gateway to hell. A brown owl was nesting in the nostril of the face.'

She started laughing.

'Don't ask me,' she said. 'I'm just giving you what I found.'

'Fine,' McCaleb said, writing the description down. 'Go on.'

'Okay, two others noted for using the owl as the symbol of evil were Van Oostanen and Dürer. I don't have specific paintings.'

He heard more pages turning. He asked for spellings of the artists' names and wrote them down.

'Okay, here it is. This last guy's work is supposedly replete with owls all over the place. I can't pronounce his first name. It's spelled H-I-E-R-O-N-Y-M-U-S. He was Netherlandish, part of the Northern Renaissance. I guess owls were big up there.'

McCaleb looked at the paper in front of him. The name she had just spelled seemed familiar to him.

'You forgot his last name. What's his last name?'

'Oh, sorry. It's Bosch. Like the spark plugs.'

McCaleb sat frozen. He didn't move, he didn't breathe. He stared at the name on the page, unable to write the last part that Doran had just given him. Finally, he turned his head and looked out of the picnic area to the spot on the sidewalk where he had last seen Harry Bosch walking away.

'Terry, you there?'

He came out of it.

'Yeah.'

'That's really all I have. And I have to go. We're starting here.'

'Anything else on Bosch?'

'Not really. And I'm out of time.'

'Okay, Brass. Listen, thanks a lot. I owe you one for this.'

'And I'll collect one day. Let me know how it all comes out, okay?'

'You got it.'

'And send me a photo of that little girl.'

'I will.'

She hung up and McCaleb slowly closed his phone. He wrote a note at the bottom of the page reminding him to send Brass a photo of his daughter. It was just an exercise in avoiding the name of the painter he had written down.

'Shit,' he whispered.

He sat with his thoughts for a long time. The coincidence of receiving the eerie information just minutes after eating with Harry Bosch was unsettling. He studied his notes for a few more moments but knew they did not contain the immediate information he needed. He finally reopened the phone and called 213 information. A minute later he called the personnel office of the Los Angeles Police Department. A woman answered after nine rings.

'Yes, I'm calling on behalf of the L.A. County Sheriff's Department and I need to contact a particular LAPD officer. Only I don't know where he works. I only have his name.'

He hoped the woman wouldn't ask what he meant by *on behalf of.* There was what seemed to be a long silence and then he heard the sound of typing on a keyboard.

'Last name?'

'Uh, it's Bosch.'

He spelled it and then looked down at his notes, ready to spell the first name.

'And the first na – never mind, there's only one. Higher – ronny – mus. Is that it? I can't pronounce it, I don't think.'

'Hieronymus. Yes, that's it.'

He spelled the name and asked if it was a match. It was.

'Well, he's a detective third grade and he works in Hollywood Division. Do you need that number?'

McCaleb didn't answer.

'Sir, do you need—'

'No, I have it. Thank you very much.'

He closed the phone, looked at his watch, and then reopened the phone. He called Jaye Winston's direct number and she picked up right away. He asked if she had gotten anything back from the lab on the examination of the plastic owl.

'Not yet. It's only been a couple hours and one of them was lunch. I'm going to give it until tomorrow before I start knocking on their door.'

'Do you have time to make a few calls and do me a favor?'

'What calls?'

He told her about the icon search Brass Doran had conducted but left out any mention of Hieronymus Bosch. He said that he wanted to talk with an expert on Northern Renaissance painting but thought the arrangements could be made more quickly and cooperation would be more forthcoming if the request came from an official homicide detective.

'I'll do it,' Winston said. 'Where should I start?'

'I'd try the Getty. I'm in Van Nuys now. If somebody will see me I could be there in a half hour.'

'I'll see what I can do. You talk to Harry Bosch?'

'Yeah.'

'Anything new?'

'Not really.'

'I didn't think so. Hang tight. I'll call you back.'

McCaleb dumped what was left of his lunch into one of the trash barrels and headed back toward the courthouse, where he had left the Cherokee parked on a side street by the state parole offices. As he walked he thought about how he had lied by omission to Winston. He knew he should have told her about the Bosch connection or coincidence, whichever it was. He tried to understand what it was that made him hold it back. He found no answer.

His phone chirped just as he got to the Cherokee. It was Winston.

'You have an appointment at the Getty at two. Ask for Leigh Alasdair Scott. He's an associate curator of paintings.'

McCaleb got out his notes and wrote the name down, using the front hood of the Cherokee, after asking Winston to spell it.

'That was quick, Jaye. Thanks.'

'We aim to please. I spoke directly to Scott and he said if he couldn't help you he would find someone who could.'

'You mention the owl?'

'No, it's your interview.'

'Right.'

McCaleb knew he had another chance to tell her about Hieronymus Bosch. But again he let it pass.

'I'll call you later, okay?'

'See ya.'

He closed the phone and unlocked the car. He looked over the roof at the parole offices and saw a large white banner with blue lettering hanging across the facade above the building's entrance.

WELCOME BACK THELMA!

He got into the car wondering whether the Thelma being welcomed back was a convict or an employee. He drove off in the direction of Victory Boulevard. He'd take it to the 405 and then head south.

11

As the freeway rose to cross the Santa Monica Mountains in the Sepulveda Pass, McCaleb saw the Getty rise in front of him on the hilltop. The structure of the museum itself was as impressive as any of the great artworks housed within. It looked like a castle sitting atop a medieval hill. He saw one of the double trams slowly working its way up the side of the hill, delivering another group to the altar of history and art.

By the time he parked at the bottom of the hill and caught his own tram ride up, McCaleb was fifteen minutes late for his appointment with Leigh Alasdair Scott. After getting directions from a museum guard, McCaleb hurried across the travertine stone plaza to a security entrance. Having checked in at the counter he waited on a bench until Scott came for him.

Scott was in his early fifties and spoke with an accent McCaleb placed as originating in either Australia or New Zealand. He was friendly and happy to oblige the L.A. County sheriff's office.

'We have had occasion to offer our help and expertise to detectives in the past. Usually in regard to authenticating artwork or offering historical background to specific pieces,' he said as they walked down a long hallway to his office. 'Detective Winston indicated this would be different. You need some general information on the Northern Renaissance?'

He opened a door and ushered McCaleb into a suite of offices. They stepped into the first office past the security counter. It was a small office with a view through a large window across the Sepulveda Pass to the hillside homes of Bel-Air. The office felt crowded because of the bookshelves lining two walls and the cluttered worktable. There was just room for two chairs. Scott pointed McCaleb to one while he took the other.

'Actually, things have changed a bit since Detective Winston spoke to you,' McCaleb said. 'I can be more specific about what I need now. I've been able to narrow down my questions to a specific painter of that period. If you can tell me about him and maybe show me some of his work, that would be a big help.'

'And what is his name?'

'I'll show it to you.'

McCaleb took out his folded notes and showed him. Scott read the name aloud with obvious familiarity. He pronounced the first name Her-ron-i-mus.

'I thought that was how you said it.'

'Rhymes with anonymous. His work is actually quite well known. You are not familiar with it?'

'No. I never did much studying of art. Does the museum have any of his paintings?'

'None of his works are in the Getty collection but there is a descendant piece in the conservation studio. It is undergoing heavy restoration. Most of his verified works are in Europe, the most significant representations in the Prado. Others scattered about. I am not the one you should be talking to, however.'

McCaleb raised his eyebrows in way of a question.

'Since you have narrowed your query to Bosch specifically, there is someone here you would be better advised to talk to. She is a curatorial assistant. She also happens to be working on a catalogue raisonné on Bosch – a rather long-term project for her. A labor of love, perhaps.'

'Is she here? Can I speak to her?'

Scott reached for his phone and pushed the speaker button. He then consulted an extensions list taped to the table next to it and punched in three digits. A woman answered after three rings.

'Lola Walter, can I help you?'

'Lola, it's Mr. Scott. Is Penelope available?'

'She's working on *Hell* this morning.'

'Oh, I see. We'll go to her there.'

Scott hit the speaker button, disconnecting the call, and headed toward the door.

'You're in luck,' he said.

'Hell?' McCaleb asked.

'It's the descendant painting. If you'll come with me please.'

Scott led the way to an elevator and they went down one floor. Along the way Scott explained that the museum had one of the finest conservation studios in the world. Consequently, works of art from other museums and private collections were often shipped to the Getty for repair and restoration. At the moment a painting believed to have come from a student of Bosch's or a painter from his studio was being restored for a private collector. The painting was called *Hell*.

The conservation studio was a huge room partitioned into two main sections. One section was a workshop where frames were restored. The other section was dedicated to the restoration of paintings and was broken into a series of work bays that ran along a glass wall with the same views Scott had in his office.

McCaleb was led to the second bay, where there was a woman standing behind a man seated before a painting attached to a large easel. The man wore an apron over a dress shirt and tie and a pair of what looked like jeweler's magnifying glasses. He was leaning toward the painting and using a paintbrush with a tiny brush head to apply what looked like silver paint to the surface.

Neither the man nor the woman looked at McCaleb and Scott. Scott held his hands up in a *Hold here* gesture while the seated man completed his paint stroke. McCaleb looked at the painting. It was about four feet high and six feet wide. It was a dark landscape depicting a village being burned to the ground in the night while its inhabitants were being tortured and executed by a variety of otherworldly creatures. The upper panels of the painting, primarily depicting the swirling night sky, were spotted with small patches of damage and missing paint. McCaleb's eyes caught on one segment of the painting below this which depicted a nude and blindfolded man being forced up a ladder to a gallows by a group of birdlike creatures with spears.

The man with the brush completed his work and placed the brush on the glass top of the worktable to his left. He then leaned back toward the painting to study his work. Scott cleared his throat. Only the woman turned around.

'Penelope Fitzgerald, this is Detective McCaleb. He is involved in an investigation and needs to ask about Hieronymus Bosch.'

He gestured toward the painting.

'I told him you would be the most appropriate member of staff to speak with.'

McCaleb watched her eyes register surprise and concern, a normal response to a sudden introduction to the police. The seated man did not even turn around. This was not a normal response. Instead he picked up his brush and went back to work on the painting. McCaleb held his hand out to the woman.

'Actually, I'm not officially a detective. I've been asked by the sheriff's department to help out with an investigation.'

They shook hands.

'I don't understand,' she said. 'Has a Bosch painting been stolen?'

'No, nothing like that. This is a Bosch?'

He gestured toward the painting.

'Not quite. It may be a copy of one of his pieces. If so, then the original is lost and this is all we have. The style and design are his. But it's generally agreed to be the work of a student from his workshop. It was probably painted after Bosch was dead.'

As she spoke her eyes never left the painting. They were sharp and friendly eyes that easily betrayed her passion for Bosch. He guessed that she was about sixty and had probably dedicated her life to the study and love of art. She had surprised him. Scott's brief description of her as an assistant working on a catalog of Bosch's work had made McCaleb think she would be a young art student. He silently chastised himself for making the assumption.

The seated man put his brush down again and picked up a clean white cloth off the worktable to wipe his hands. He swiveled in his chair and looked up when he noticed McCaleb and Scott. It was then that McCaleb knew he had made a second error of assumption. The man had not been ignoring them. He just hadn't heard them.

The man flipped the magnifiers up to the top of his head while reaching beneath the apron to his chest and adjusted a hearing aid control.

'I am sorry,' he said. 'I didn't know we had visitors.'

He spoke with a hard German accent.

'Dr. Derek Vosskuhler, this is Mr. McCaleb,' Scott said. 'He's an investigator and he needs to steal Mrs. Fitzgerald away from you for a short while.'

'I understand. This is fine.'

'Dr. Vosskuhler is one of our restoration experts,' Scott volunteered.

Vosskuhler nodded and looked up at McCaleb and studied him in the way he might study a painting. He made no move to extend his hand.

'An investigation? In regard to Hieronymus Bosch, is it?'

'In a peripheral way. I just want to learn what I can about him. I'm told Mrs. Fitzgerald is the expert.'

McCaleb smiled.

'No one is an expert on Bosch,' Vosskuhler said without a smile. 'Tortured soul, tormented genius . . . how will we ever know what is truly in a man's heart?'

McCaleb just nodded. Vosskuhler turned and appraised the painting.

'What do you see, Mr. McCaleb?'

McCaleb looked at the painting and didn't answer for a long moment.

'A lot of pain.'

Vosskuhler nodded approvingly. Then he stood and looked closely at the painting, flipping the glasses down and leaning close to the upper quarter panel, his lenses just inches from the night sky above the burning village.

'Bosch knew all of the demons,' he said without turning from the painting. 'The darkness . . .'

A long moment went by.

'A darkness more than night.'

There was another long moment of silence until Scott abruptly punctuated it by saying he needed to get back to his office. He left then, and after another moment Vosskuhler finally turned from the painting. He didn't bother flipping up the glasses when he looked at McCaleb. He slowly reached into his apron and switched off sound to his ears.

'I, too, must go back to work. Good luck with your investigation, Mr. McCaleb.'

McCaleb nodded as Vosskuhler sat back in his swivel chair and picked up his tiny brush again.

'We can go to my office,' Fitzgerald said. 'I have all the plate books from our library there. I can show you Bosch's work.'

'That would be fine. Thank you.'

She headed toward the door. McCaleb delayed a moment and took one last look at the painting. His eyes were drawn to the upper panels, toward the swirling darkness above the flames.

Penelope Fitzgerald's office was a six-by-six pod in a room shared by several curatorial assistants. She pulled a chair into the tight space from a nearby pod where no one was working and told McCaleb to sit down. Her desk was L-shaped, with a laptop computer set up on the left side and a cluttered work space on the right. There were several books stacked on the desk. McCaleb noticed that behind one stack was a color print of a painting very much in the same style as the painting Vosskuhler was working on. He pushed the books a half foot to the side and bent down to look at the print. It was in three panels, the largest being the centerpiece. Again it was a ramble. Dozens and dozens of figures spread across the panels. Scenes of debauchery and torture.

'Do you recognize it?' Fitzgerald said.

'I don't think so. But it's Bosch, right?'

'His signature piece. The triptych called *The Garden of Earthly Delights.* It's in the Prado in Madrid. I once stood in front of it for four hours. It wasn't enough time to take it all in. Would you like some coffee or some water or anything, Mr. McCaleb?'

'No, I'm fine. Thank you. You can call me Terry if you want.'

'And you can call me Nep.'

McCaleb put a quizzical look on his face.

'Childhood nickname.'

He nodded.

'Now,' she said. 'In these books I can show you every piece of Bosch's identified work. Is it an important investigation?'

McCaleb nodded.

'I think so. It's a homicide.'

'And you are some kind of consultant?'

'I used to work for the FBI here in L.A. The sheriff's detective assigned to the case asked me to look at it and see what I think. It led me here. To Bosch. I am sorry but I can't get into the details of the case and I know that will probably be frustrating to you. I want to ask questions but I can't really answer any from you.'

'Darn.' She smiled. 'It sounds really interesting.'

'Tell you what, if there is ever a point I can tell you about it, I will.'

'Fair enough.'

McCaleb nodded.

'From what Dr. Vosskuhler said, I take it that there isn't a lot known about the man behind the paintings.'

Fitzgerald nodded.

'Hieronymus Bosch is certainly considered an enigma and he probably always will be.'

McCaleb unfolded his notepaper on the table in front of him and started taking notes as she spoke.

'He had one of the most unconventional imaginations of his time. Or any time for that matter. His work is quite extraordinary and still subject these five centuries later to restudy and reinterpretation. However, I think you will find that the majority of the critical analysis to date holds that he was a doomsayer. His work is informed with the portents of doom and hellfire, of warnings of the wages of sin. To put it more succinctly, his paintings primarily carried variations on the same theme: that the folly of humankind leads us all to hell as our ultimate destiny.'

McCaleb was writing quickly, trying to keep up. He wished he had brought a tape recorder.

'Nice guy, huh?' Fitzgerald said.

'Sounds like it.' He nodded to the print of the triptych. 'Must've been fun on a Saturday night.'

She smiled.

'Exactly what I thought when I was in the Prado.'

'Any redeeming qualities? He took in orphans, was nice to dogs, changed flat tires for old ladies, anything?'

'You have to remember his time and place to fully understand what he was doing with his art. While his work is punctuated with violent scenes and depictions of torture and anguish, this was a time when those sorts of things were not unusual. He lived in a violent time; his work clearly reflects that. The paintings also reflect the medieval belief in the existence of demons everywhere. Evil lurks in all of the paintings.'

'The owl?'

She stared blankly at him for a moment.

'Yes, the owl is one symbol he used. I thought you said you were unfamiliar with his work.'

'I *am* unfamiliar with it. It was an owl that brought me here. But I shouldn't go into that and I shouldn't have interrupted you. Please go on.'

'I was just going to add that it is telling when you consider that Bosch was a contemporary of Leonardo, Michelangelo and Raphael. Yet if you were to look at their works side by side you would have to believe Bosch – with all the medieval symbols and doom – was a century behind.'

'But he wasn't.'

She shook her head as though she felt sorry for Bosch.

'He and Leonardo da Vinci were born within a year or two of each other. By the end of the fifteenth century, da Vinci was creating pieces that were full of hope and celebration of human values and spirituality while Bosch was all gloom and doom.'

'That makes you feel sad, doesn't it?'

She put her hands on the top book in the stack but didn't open it. It was simply labeled BOSCH on the spine and there was no illustration on the black leather binding.

'I can't help but think about what could have been if Bosch had worked side by side with da Vinci or Michelangelo, what could have happened if he had used his skill and imagination in celebration rather than damnation of the world.'

She looked down at the book and then back up at him.

'But that is the beauty of art and why we study and celebrate it. Each painting is a window to the artist's soul and imagination. No matter how dark and disturbing, his vision is what sets him apart and makes his paintings unique. What happens to me with Bosch is that the paintings serve to carry me into the artist's soul and I sense the torment.'

He nodded and she looked down and opened the book.

The world of Hieronymus Bosch was as striking to McCaleb as it was disturbing. The landscapes of misery that unfolded in the pages Penelope Fitzgerald turned were not unlike some of the most horrible crime scenes he had witnessed, but in these painted scenes the players were still alive and in pain. The gnashing of teeth and the ripping of flesh were active and real. His canvases were crowded with the damned, humans being tormented for their sins by visible demons and creatures given image by the hand of a horrible imagination.

At first he studied the color reproductions of the paintings in silence, taking it all in the way he would first observe a crime scene photograph. But then a page was turned and he looked at a painting that depicted three people gathered around a sitting man. One of those standing used what looked like a primitive scalpel to probe a wound on the crown of the sitting man's head. The image was depicted in a circle. There were words painted above and below the circle.

'What is this one?' he asked.

'It's called *The Stone Operation,*' Fitzgerald said. 'It was a common belief at the time that stupidity and deceit could be cured by the removal of a stone from the head of the one suffering the malady.'

McCaleb leaned over her shoulder and looked closely at the painting, specifically at the location of the surgery wound. It was in a location comparable to the wound on Edward Gunn's head.

'Okay, you can go on.'

Owls were everywhere. Fitzgerald did not have to point them out most of the time, their positions were that obvious. She did explain some of the attendant imagery. Most often in the paintings when the owl was depicted in a tree, the branch upon which the symbol of evil perched was leafless and gray – dead.

She turned the page to a three-panel painting.

'This is called *The Last Judgment,* with the left panel subtitled *The Fall of Mankind* and the right panel simply and obviously called *Hell.*'

'He liked painting hell.'

But Nep Fitzgerald didn't smile. Her eyes studied the book.

The left panel of the painting was a Garden of Eden scene with Adam and Eve at center taking the fruit from the serpent in the apple tree. On a dead branch of a nearby tree an owl watched the transaction. On the opposite panel Hell was depicted as a dark place where birdlike creatures disemboweled the damned, cut their bodies up and placed them in frying pans to be slid into fiery ovens.

'All of this came from this guy's head,' McCaleb said. 'I don't . . .'

He didn't finish because he was unsure what he was trying to say.

'A tormented soul,' Fitzgerald said and turned the page.

The next painting was another circular image with seven separate scenes depicted along the outer rim and a portrait of God at center. In a circle of gold surrounding the portrait of God and separating him from the other scenes were four Latin words McCaleb immediately recognized.

'Beware, beware, God sees.'

Fitzgerald looked up at him.

'You obviously have seen this before. Or you just happen to know fifteenth-century Latin. This must be one strange case you are working on.'

'It's getting that way. But I only know the words, not the painting. What is it?'

'It's actually a tabletop, probably created for a church rectory or a holy person's house. It's the eye of God. He is at center and what he sees as he looks down are these images, the seven deadly sins.'

McCaleb nodded. By looking at the distinct scenes he could pick out some of the more obvious of the sins; gluttony, lust and pride.

'And now his masterpiece,' his tour guide said as she turned the page.

She came to the same triptych she had pinned to the wall of the pod. *The Garden of Earthly Delights.* McCaleb studied it closely now. The left panel was a bucolic scene of Adam and Eve being placed in the garden by the creator. An apple tree stood nearby. The center panel, the largest, showed dozens of nudes coupling and dancing in uninhibited lust, riding horses and beautiful birds and wholly imagined creatures from the lake in the foreground. And then the last panel, the dark one, was the payoff. Hell, a place of torment and anguish administered by monster birds and other ugly creatures. The painting was so detailed and enthralling that McCaleb understood how someone might stand before it – the original – for four hours and still not see everything.

'I am sure you are grasping the ideas of Bosch's often repeated themes by now,' Fitzgerald said. 'But this is considered the most coherent of his works as well as the most beautifully imagined and realized.'

McCaleb nodded and pointed to the three panels as he spoke.

'You have Adam and Eve here, the good life until they eat that apple. Then in the center you have what happens after the fall from grace: life without rules. Freedom of choice leads to lust and sin. And where does all of this go? Hell.'

'Very good. And if I could just point out a few specifics that might interest you.'

'Please.'

She started with the first panel.

'The earthly paradise. You are correct in that it depicts Adam and Eve before the Fall. This pool and fountain at center represent the promise of eternal life. You already noted the fruit tree at left center.'

Her finger moved across the plate to the fountain structure, a tower of what looked like flower petals that somehow delivered water in four distinct trickles to the pool below. Then he saw it. Her finger stopped below a small dark entrance at the center of the fountain structure. The face of an owl peered from the darkness.

'You mentioned the owl before. Its image is here. You see all is not right in this paradise. Evil lurks and, as we know, will ultimately win the day. According to Bosch. Then, going to the next panel we see the imagery again and again.'

She pointed out two distinct representations of owls and two other depictions of owl-like creatures. McCaleb's eyes held on one of the images. It showed a large brown owl with shiny black eyes being embraced by a nude man. The owl's coloring and eyes matched that of the plastic bird found in Edward Gunn's apartment.

'Do you see something, Terry?'

He pointed to the owl.

'This one. I can't really go into it with you but this one, it matches up with the reason I am here.'

'A lot of symbols are at work in this panel. That is one of the obvious ones. After the Fall, man's freedom of choice leads him to debauchery, gluttony, folly and avarice, the worst sin of all in Bosch's world being lust. Man wraps his arms around the owl; he embraces evil.'

McCaleb nodded.

'And then he pays for it.'

'Then he pays for it. As you notice in the last panel, this is a depiction of hell without fire. Rather, it is a place of myriad torments and endless pain. Of darkness.'

McCaleb stared silently for a long time, his eyes moving across the landscape of the painting. He remembered what Dr. Vosskuhler had said.

A darkness more than night.

12

Bosch cupped his hands and held them against the window next to the front door of the apartment. He was looking into the kitchen. The counters were spotless. No mess, no coffee maker, not even a toaster. He started to get a bad feeling. He stepped over to the door and knocked once more. He then paced back and forth waiting. Looking down he saw an outline on the pavement of where a welcome mat had once been.

'Damn,' he said.

He reached into his pocket and took out a small leather pouch. He unzipped it and removed two small steel picks he had made from hacksaw blades. Glancing around he saw no one. He was in a shielded alcove of a large apartment complex in Westwood. Most residents were probably still at work. He stepped up to the door and went to work with the picks on the deadbolt. Ninety seconds later he had the door open and he went inside.

He knew the apartment was vacant as soon as he stepped in but he covered every room anyway. All of them were empty. Hoping for an empty prescription bottle he even checked the bathroom medicine cabinet. There was a used razor made of pink plastic on a shelf, nothing else.

He walked back into the living room and took out his cell phone. He had just put Janis Langwiser's cell phone on the speed dial the day before. She was co-prosecutor on the case and they had worked on Bosch's testimony throughout the weekend. His call found her still in the trial team's temporary office in the Van Nuys courthouse.

'Listen, I don't want to rain on the parade but Annabelle Crowe is gone.'

'What do you mean, gone?'

'I mean gone, baby, gone. I'm standing in what was her apartment. It's empty.'

'Shit! We really need her, Harry. When did she move out?'

'I don't know. I just discovered she was gone.'

'Did you talk to the apartment manager?'

'Not yet. But he's not going to know much more than how long ago she split. If she's running from the trial she wouldn't be leaving any forwarding addresses with the management.'

'Well, when did you talk to her last?'

'Thursday. I called her here. But that line is disconnected today. No forwarding number.'

'Shit!'

'I know. You said that.'

'She got the subpoena, right?'

'Yeah, she got it Thursday. That's why I called. To make sure.'

'Okay, then maybe she'll be here tomorrow.'

Bosch looked around the empty apartment.

'I wouldn't count on it.'

He looked at his watch. It was after five. Because he had been so sure about Annabelle Crowe, she had been the last witness he was going to check on. There had been no hint that she was going to split. Now he knew he would be spending the night trying to run her down.

'What can you do?' Langwiser asked.

'I've got some information on her I can run down. She's got to be in town. She's an actress, where else is she going to go?'

'New York?'

'That's where real actors go. She's a face. She'll stay here.'

'Find her, Harry. We'll need her by next week.'

'I'll try.'

There was a moment of silence while they both considered things.

'You think Storey got to her?' Langwiser finally asked.

'I'm wondering. He could've gotten to her with what she needs – a job, a part, a paycheck. When I find her I'll be asking that.'

'Okay, Harry. Good luck. If you get her tonight, let me know. Otherwise, I'll see you in the morning.'

'Right.'

Bosch closed the phone and put it down on the kitchen counter. From his jacket pocket he took out a thin stack of three-by-five cards. Each card had the name of one of the witnesses he was responsible for vetting and preparing for trial. Home and work addresses as well as phone numbers and pager numbers were noted on the cards. He checked the card assigned to Annabelle Crowe and then punched her pager number into his phone. A recorded message said the pager was no longer in service.

He clapped the phone closed and looked at the card again. The name and number of Annabelle Crowe's agent were listed at the bottom. He decided that the agent might be the one tie she wouldn't sever.

He put the phone and cards back into his pockets. This was one inquiry he was going to make in person.

13

McCaleb made the crossing by himself, *The Following Sea* arriving at Avalon Harbor just as darkness did. Buddy Lockridge had stayed behind at Cabrillo Marina because no new charters had come up and he wouldn't be needed until Saturday. As he arrived at the island McCaleb radioed the harbor master's boat on channel 16 and got help mooring the boat.

The added weight of the two heavy books he had found in the used-books section at Dutton's bookstore in Brentwood plus the smaller cooler filled with frozen tamales made the walk up the hill to his house exhausting. He had to stop twice on the side of the road to rest. Each time he sat down on the cooler and took one of the books out of his leather bag so that he could once more study the dark work of Hieronymus Bosch – even in the shadows of evening.

Since his visit to the Getty, the images in the Bosch paintings were never far from his thoughts. Nep Fitzgerald had said something at the end of the meeting in her office. Just before closing the book on the plates reproducing *The Garden of Earthly Delights* she looked at him with a small smile, as if she had something to say but was hesitant.

'What?' he said.

'Nothing really, just an observation.'

'Go ahead and make it. I'd like to hear it.'

'I was just going to mention that a lot of the critics and scholars who view Bosch's work see corollaries to contemporary times. That's the mark of a great artist – if his work stands the test of time. If it has the power to connect to people and . . . and maybe influence them.'

McCaleb nodded. He knew she wanted him to tell her what he was working on.

'I understand what you are saying. I'm sorry but at the moment I can't tell you about this. Maybe someday I will, or someday you will just know what it was. But thank you. You have helped a lot, I think. I don't know for sure yet.'

Sitting on the cooler now, McCaleb remembered the conversation. Corollaries to contemporary times, he thought. And crimes. He opened the larger of the two books he had bought and opened it to a color illustration of Bosch's masterpiece. He studied the owl with black eyes and all of his instincts told him he was on to something significant. Something very dark and dangerous.

When he got home Graciela took the cooler from him and opened it on the kitchen counter. She took three of the green corn tamales out and put them on a plate for defrosting in the microwave.

'I'm making chili relenos, too,' she said. 'It's a good thing you called from the boat or we would've gone ahead and eaten without you.'

McCaleb let her vent. He knew she was angry about what he was doing. He walked over to the table where Cielo was propped in a bouncing chair. She was staring up at the ceiling fan and moving her hands in front of her, getting used to them. McCaleb bent down and kissed both of them and then her forehead.

'Where's Raymond?'

'In his room. On the computer. Why did you only get ten?'

He looked over at her as he slid into a chair next to Cielo. She was putting the other tamales into a plastic Tupperware container for freezing.

'I took the cooler in and told them to fill it. That's how many fit, I guess.'

She shook her head, annoyed with him.

'We'll have one extra.'

'Then throw it out or invite one of Raymond's friends over for dinner next time. Who cares, Graciela? It's a tamale.'

Graciela turned and looked at him with dark, upset eyes that immediately softened.

'You're sweaty.'

'I just walked up the hill. The shuttle was closed for the night.'

She opened an overhead cabinet and took out a plastic box holding a thermometer. There was a thermometer in every room in the house. She took this one out and shook it and came over to him.

'Open.'

'Let's use the electronic.'

'No, I don't trust them.'

She put the end of the thermometer under his tongue and then used her hand to gently bring his jaw up and close his mouth. Very professional. She had been an emergency room nurse when he met her and was now the school nurse and an office clerk at Catalina Elementary. She had just gone back to work after the Christmas holiday. McCaleb sensed that she wanted to be a full-time mother, but they couldn't afford it so he never brought it up directly. He hoped that in a couple of years the charter service would be more established and they would have the choice then. Sometimes he wished they had kept a share of the money for the book-and-movie deal but he also knew that their decision to honor Graciela's sister by not making money from what happened had been the only choice. They had given half the money to the Make a Wish Foundation and put the other half in a trust fund for Raymond. It would pay for college if he wanted that.

Graciela held his wrist and checked his pulse while he sat silently watching her.

'You're high,' she said, dropping his wrist. 'Open.'

He opened his mouth and she took out the thermometer and read it. She went to the sink and washed it, then returned it to its case and the cabinet. She didn't say anything and McCaleb knew that meant his temperature was normal.

'You wish I had a fever, don't you?'

'Are you crazy?'

'Yes, you do. That way you could tell me to stop this.'

'What do you mean, tell you to stop it? Last night you said it was just going to be last night. Then this morning you said it was just going to be today. What are you telling me now, Terry?'

He looked over at Cielo and held out a finger for her to grasp.

'It's not over.' He now looked back at Graciela. 'Some things came up today.'

'Some *things?* Whatever they are, give them to Detective Winston. It's her job. It's not your job to be doing this.'

'I can't. Not yet. Not until I am sure.'

Graciela turned and walked back to the counter. She put the plate with the tamales on it into the microwave and set it for defrost.

'Will you take her in and change her? It's been a while. And she'll need a bottle while I make dinner.'

McCaleb carefully raised his daughter out of the bouncing seat and put her on his shoulder. She made some fussing noises and he gently patted her back to calm her. He walked over to Graciela's back, put his arm around the front of her and pulled her backward into him. He kissed the top of her head and held his face in her hair.

'It will all be over soon and we'll be back to normal.'

'I hope so.'

She touched his arm, which crossed her body beneath her breasts. The touch of her fingertips was the approval he sought. It told him this was a rough spot but they were okay. He held her tighter, kissed the back of her neck and then let her go.

Cielo watched the slowly moving mobile that hung over the changing table as he put a new diaper on her tiny body. Cardboard stars and half moons hung from threads. Raymond had made it with Graciela as a Christmas present. An air current from somewhere in the house gently turned it and Cielo's dark blue eyes focused on it. McCaleb bent down and kissed her forehead.

After wrapping her in two baby blankets he took her out to the porch and gave her the bottle while gently moving in the rocking chair. Looking down at the harbor he noticed he had left on the instrument lights on *The Following Sea*'s bridge. He knew he could call the harbor master on the pier and whoever was working nights could just motor over and turn them off. But he knew he'd be going back to the boat after dinner. He would get the lights then.

He looked down at Cielo. Her eyes were closed but he knew she was awake. She was working the bottle forcefully. Graciela had stopped full-time breastfeeding when she had gone back to work. Bottle feedings were new and he found them to be perhaps the single most pleasurable moments of being a new father. He often whispered to his daughter during these times. Promises mostly. Promises that he would always love her and be with her. He told her never to be afraid or feel alone. Sometimes when she would suddenly open her eyes and look at him, he sensed that she was communicating the same things back to him. And he felt a kind of love he had never known before.

'Terry.'

He looked up at Graciela's whisper.

'Dinner's ready.'

He checked the bottle and saw it was almost empty.

'I'll be there in a minute,' he whispered.

After Graciela left them he looked down at his daughter. The whispering had made her open her eyes. She stared up at him. He kissed her on the forehead and then just held her gaze.

'I have to do this, baby,' he whispered.

The boat was cold inside. McCaleb turned on the salon lights and then positioned the space heater in the center of the room and turned it on low. He wanted to warm up but not too much, for then he might get sleepy. He was still tired from the exertions of the day.

He was down in the front cabin going through his old files when he heard the cell phone start to chirp from his leather bag up in the salon. He closed the file he was studying and took it with him as he bounded up the stairs to the salon and grabbed the phone out of his bag. It was Jaye Winston.

'So how'd it go at the Getty? I thought you were going to call me back.'

'Oh, well it ran late and I wanted to get back to the boat and get across before dark. I forgot to call.'

'You're back on the island?'

She sounded disappointed.

'Yeah, I told Graciela this morning I'd be back. But don't worry, I'm still working on a few things.'

'What happened at the Getty?'

'Nothing much,' he lied. 'I talked to a couple people and looked at some paintings.'

'You see any owls that match ours?'

She laughed as she asked the question.

'A couple close ones. I got some books I want to look through tonight. I was going to call you, see if maybe we could get together tomorrow.'

'When? I've got a meeting in the morning at ten and another at eleven.'

'I was thinking the afternoon anyway. There's something I have to do in the morning myself.'

He didn't want to tell her that he wanted to watch the opening statements in the Storey trial. He knew they'd be carried live on *Court TV*, which he got up at the house with the satellite dish.

'Well, I could probably get a chopper to take me out there but I'll have to check with aero first.'

'No, I'll be coming back over.'

'You will? Great! You want to come here?'

'No, I was thinking about something more quiet and private.'

'How come?'

'I'll tell you tomorrow.'

'Getting mysterious on me. This isn't a scam to get the sheriff's to pay for pancakes again, is it?'

They both laughed.

'No scam. Any chance you could come out to Cabrillo and meet me at my boat?'

'I'll be there. What time?'

He made the appointment for three o'clock thinking that would give him plenty of time to prepare a profile and figure out how he would tell her what he had to say. It would also give him enough time to be ready for what he hoped she would allow him to do that night.

'Anything on the owl?' he asked once they had the meeting arranged.

'Very little, none of it good. Inside there are manufacturing markings. The plastic mold was made in China. The company ships them to two distributors over here, one in Ohio and one in Tennessee. From there they probably go all over. It's a long shot and a lot of work.'

'So you're going to drop it.'

'No, I didn't say that. It's just not a priority. It's on my partner's plate. He's got calls out. We'll see what he gets from the distributors, evaluate and decide where to go from there.'

McCaleb nodded. Prioritizing investigative leads and even investigations themselves was a necessary evil. But it still bothered him. He was sure the owl was a key and knowing everything about it would be useful.

'Okay, so we're all set?' she asked.

'About tomorrow? Yeah, we're set.'

'We'll see you at three.'

'We?'

'Kurt and I. My partner. You haven't met him yet.'

'Uh, look, tomorrow could it just be me and you? Nothing against your partner but I'd just like to talk to you tomorrow, Jaye.'

There was a moment of silence before she responded.

'Terry, what's going on with you?'

'I just want to talk to you about this. You brought me in, I want to give what I have to you. If you want to bring your partner in on it after, that's fine.'

There was another pause.

'I'm getting a bad vibe from all of this, Terry.'

'I'm sorry, but that's the way I want it. I guess you have to take it or leave it.'

His ultimatum made her go silent even longer this time. He waited for her.

'All right, man,' she finally said. 'It's your show. I'll take it.'

'Thanks, Jaye. I'll see you then.'

They hung up. He looked at the old case file he had pulled and still held in his hand. He put the phone down on the coffee table and leaned back on the couch and opened the file.

14

At first they called it the Little Girl Lost case because the victim had no name. The victim was thought to be about fourteen or fifteen years old; a Latina – probably Mexican – whose body was found in the bushes and among the debris below one of the overlooks off Mulholland Drive. The case belonged to Bosch and his partner at the time, Frankie Sheehan. This was before Bosch worked homicide out of Hollywood Division. He and Sheehan were a Robbery–Homicide team and it had been Bosch who contacted McCaleb at the bureau. McCaleb was newly returned to Los Angeles from Quantico. He was setting up an outpost for the Behavioral Sciences Unit and Violent Criminal Apprehension Program. The Little Girl Lost case was one of the first submitted to him.

Bosch came to him, bringing the file and the crime scene photos to his tiny office on the thirteenth floor of the federal building in Westwood. He came without Sheehan because the partners had disagreed on whether to bring the bureau in on the case. Cross-agency jealousies at work. But Bosch didn't care about all of that. He cared about the case. He had haunted eyes. The case was clearly working on him as much as he worked on it.

The body had been found nude and violated in many ways. The girl had been manually strangled by her killer's gloved hands. No clothes or purse were found on the hillside. Fingerprints matched no computerized records. The girl matched no description on an active missing persons case anywhere in Los Angeles County or on national crime computer systems. An artist's rendering of the victim's face put on the TV news and in the papers brought no calls from a loved one. Sketches faxed to five hundred police agencies across the Southwest and to the State Judicial Police in Mexico drew no response. The victim remained unclaimed and unidentified, her body reposing in the refrigerator at the coroner's office while Bosch and his partner worked the case.

There was no physical evidence found with the body. Aside from being left without her clothes or any identifying property, the victim had apparently been washed with an industrial-strength cleaner before being dumped late at night off Mulholland.

There was only one clue with the body. An impression in the skin of the left hip. Postmortem lividity indicated the blood in the body had settled on the left half, meaning the body had been lying on its left side in the time between the stilling of the heart and the dropping of the body down the hillside where it came to rest face down on a pile of empty beer cans and tequila bottles. The evidence indicated that during the time that the blood settled, the body had been lying on top of the object that left the impression on the hip.

The impression consisted of the number 1, the letter J and part of a third letter that could have been the upper left stem of an H, a K or an L. It was a partial reading of a license plate.

Bosch formed the theory that whoever had killed the girl with no name had hidden the body in the trunk of a car until it was time to dump it. After carefully cleaning the body the killer had put it into the trunk of his car, mistakenly putting it down on part of a license plate that had been taken off the car and also placed in the trunk. Bosch's theory was that the license plate had been removed and possibly replaced with a stolen plate as one more safety measure that would help the killer avoid detection if his car happened to be spotted by a suspicious passerby at the Mulholland overlook.

Though the skin impression gave no indication of what state issued the license plate, Bosch went with the percentages. From the state Department of Motor Vehicles he obtained a list of every car registered in Los Angeles County that carried a plate beginning 1JH, 1JK and 1JL. The list contained over three thousand names of car owners. He and his partner cut 40 percent of it by discounting the female owners. The remaining names were slowly fed into the National Crime Index computer and the detectives came up with a list of forty-six men with criminal records ranging from minor to the extreme.

It was at this point that Bosch came to McCaleb. He wanted a profile of the killer. He wanted to know if he and Sheehan were on the right track in suspecting that the killer had a criminal history, and he wanted to know how to approach and evaluate the forty-six men on the list.

McCaleb considered the case for nearly a week. He looked at each of the crime scene photos twice a day – first thing in the morning and last thing before going to sleep – and studied the reports often. He finally told Bosch that he believed they were on the right course. Using data accumulated from hundreds of similar crimes and analyzed in the bureau's VICAP program, he was able to provide a profile of a man in his late twenties with a history of having committed crimes of an escalating nature and likely including offenses of a sexual nature. The crime scene suggested the work of an exhibitionist – a killer who wanted his crime to be public and to instill horror and fear in the general population. Therefore, the location of the body dump site would have been chosen for these reasons as opposed to reasons of convenience.

In comparing the profile to the list of forty-six names, Bosch narrowed the possibilities to two suspects: a Woodland Hills office building custodian who had a record of arson and public indecency and a stage builder who worked for a studio in Burbank and had been arrested for the attempted rape of a neighbor when he was a teenager. Both men were in their late twenties.

Bosch and Sheehan leaned toward the custodian because of his access to industrial cleaners, like the one that had been used to wash the victim's body. However, McCaleb liked the stage builder as a suspect because the attempted rape of the neighbor in his youth indicated an impulsive action that was more in tune with the profile of the current crime's perpetrator.

Bosch and Sheehan decided to informally interview both men and invited McCaleb along. The FBI agent stressed that the men should be interviewed in their own homes so that he would have the opportunity to study them in their own environment as well as look for clues in their belongings.

The stage builder was first. His name was Victor Seguin. He seemed shell-shocked by seeing the three men at his door and the explanation Bosch gave for their visit. Nevertheless he invited them in. As Bosch and Sheehan calmly asked questions McCaleb sat on a couch and studied the clean and neat furnishings of the apartment. Within five minutes he knew they had the right man and nodded to Bosch – their prearranged signal.

Victor Seguin was informed of his rights and arrested. He was placed in the detectives' car and his small home under the landing zone of Burbank Airport was sealed until a search warrant could be obtained. Two hours later, when they reentered with the search warrant, they found a sixteen-year-old girl bound and gagged but alive in a soundproof coffin-like crawl space constructed by the stage builder beneath a trap door hidden under his bed.

Only after the excitement and adrenaline high of having broken a case and saved a life began to subside did Bosch finally ask McCaleb how he knew they had their man. McCaleb walked the detective over to the living-room bookcase, where he pointed out a well-worn copy of a book called *The Collector,* a novel about a man who abducts several women.

Seguin was charged with the unidentified girl's murder and the kidnapping and rape of the young woman the investigators rescued. He denied any guilt in the murder and pressed for a deal by which he would plead guilty to the kidnapping and rape of the survivor only. The DA's office declined any deal and proceeded to trial with what they had – the survivor's gut-wrenching testimony and the license plate impression on the dead girl's hip.

The jury convicted on all counts after less than four hours' deliberation. The DA's office then floated a possible deal to Seguin: a promise not to go for the death penalty during the second phase of the trial if the killer agreed to tell investigators who his first victim was and from where he had abducted her. To take the deal Seguin would have to drop his pose of innocence. He passed. The DA went for the death penalty and got it. Bosch never learned who the dead girl was and McCaleb knew it haunted him that no one apparently cared enough to come forward.

It haunted McCaleb, too. On the day he came to the penalty phase of the trial to testify, he had lunch with Bosch and noticed that a name had been written on the tabs of his files on the case.

'What's that?' McCaleb asked excitedly. 'You ID'd her?'

Bosch looked down and saw the name on the tabs and turned the files over.

'No, no ID yet.'

'Well, what's that?'

'Just a name. I sort of gave her a name, I guess.'

Bosch looked embarrassed. McCaleb reached over and turned the files back over to read the name.

'Cielo Azul?'

'Yeah, she was Spanish, I gave her a Spanish name.'

'It means blue sky, right?'

'Yeah, blue sky. I, uh . . .'

McCaleb waited. Nothing.

'What?'

'Well . . . I'm not that religious, you know what I mean?'

'Yes.'

'But I sort of figured if nobody down here wanted to claim her, then hopefully . . . maybe there's somebody up there that will.'

Bosch shrugged his shoulders and looked away. McCaleb could see his face turning red in the upper cheeks.

'It's hard to find God's hand in what we do. What we see.'

Bosch just nodded and they didn't speak about the name again.

McCaleb lifted the last page of the file marked Cielo Azul and looked at the inside rear flap of the manila folder. It had become his habit over time at the bureau to jot notes on the back flap, where they would not readily be seen because of the attached file pages. These were notes he made about the investigators who submitted the cases for profiling. McCaleb had come to realize that insights about the investigator were sometimes as important as the information in the case file. For it was through the investigator's eyes that McCaleb first viewed many aspects of the crime.

His case with Bosch had come up more than ten years earlier, before he began his more extensive profiling of the investigators as well as the cases. On this file he had written Bosch's name and just four words beneath it.

Thorough – Smart – M. M. – A. A.

He looked at the last two notations now. It had been part of his routine to use abbreviations and shorthand when making notes that needed to be kept confidential. The last two notations were his reading on what motivated Bosch. He had come to believe that homicide detectives, a breed of cop unto themselves, called upon deep inner emotions and motivations to accept and carry out the always difficult task of their job. They were usually of two kinds, those who saw their jobs as a skill or a craft, and those who saw it as a mission in life. Ten years ago he had put Bosch into the latter class. He was a man on a mission.

This motivation in detectives could then be broken down even further as to what gave them this sense of purpose or mission. To some the job was seen as almost a game; they had some inner deficit that caused them to need to prove they were better, smarter and more cunning than their quarry. Their lives were a constant cycle of validating themselves by, in effect, invalidating the killers they sought by putting them behind bars. Others, while carrying a degree of that same inner deficit, also saw themselves with the additional dimension of being speakers for the dead. There was a sacred bond cast between victim and cop that formed at the crime scene and could not be severed. It was what ultimately pushed them into the chase and enabled them to overcome all obstacles in their path. McCaleb classified these cops as avenging angels. It had been his experience that these cop/angels were the best investigators he ever worked with. He also came to believe that they traveled closest to that unseen edge beneath which lies the abyss.

Ten years before, he had classified Harry Bosch as an avenging angel. He now had to consider whether the detective had stepped too close to that edge. He had to consider that Bosch might have gone over.

He closed the file and pulled the two art books out of his bag. Both were simply titled *Bosch.* The larger one, with full-color reproductions of the paintings, was by R. H. Marijnissen and P. Ruyffelaere. The second book, which appeared to carry more analysis of the paintings than the other, was written by Erik Larsen.

McCaleb started with the smaller book and began scanning through the pages of analysis. He quickly learned that, as Penelope Fitzgerald had said, there were many different and even competing views of Hieronymus Bosch. The Larsen book cited scholars who called Bosch a humanist and even one who believed him to be part of a heretical group that believed the earth was a literal hell ruled over by Satan. There were disputes among the scholars about the intended meanings of some of the paintings, about whether some paintings could actually be attributed to Bosch, about whether the painter had ever traveled to Italy and viewed the work of his Renaissance contemporaries.

Finally, McCaleb closed the book when he realized that, at least for his purposes, the words about Hieronymus Bosch might not be important. If the painter's work was subject to multiple interpretations, then the only interpretation that mattered would be that of the person who killed Edward Gunn. What mattered was what that person saw and took from the paintings of Hieronymus Bosch.

He opened the larger book and began to slowly study the reproductions. His viewing of reproduction plates of the paintings at the Getty had been hurried and encumbered by his not being alone.

He put his notebook on the arm of the couch with the plan to keep a tabulation of the number of owls he saw in the paintings as well as descriptions of each bird. He quickly realized that the paintings were so minutely detailed in the smaller-scale reproductions that he might be missing things of significance. He went down to the forward cabin to find the magnifying glass he had always kept in his desk at the bureau for use while examining crime scene photos.

As he was bent over a box full of office supplies he had cleared out of his desk five years before, McCaleb felt a slight bump against the boat and straightened up. He had tied the Zodiac up on the fantail, so it could not have been his own skiff. He was considering this when he felt the unmistakable up-and-down movement of the boat indicating that some-one had just stepped aboard. His mind focused on the salon door. He was sure he had left it unlocked.

He looked down into the box he had just been sorting through and grabbed the letter opener.

As he came up the steps into the galley McCaleb surveyed the salon and saw no one and nothing amiss. It was difficult seeing past the interior reflection on the sliding door but outside in the cockpit, silhouetted by the streetlights on Crescent Street, there was a man. He stood with his back to the salon as if admiring the lights of the town going up the hill.

McCaleb moved quickly to the slider and pulled it open. He held the letter opener at his side but with the point of the blade up. The man standing in the cockpit turned around.

McCaleb lowered his weapon as the man stared at it with wide eyes.

'Mr. McCaleb, I—'

'It's all right, Charlie, I just didn't know who it was.'

Charlie was the night man in the harbor office. McCaleb didn't know his last name. But he knew that he often visited Buddy Lockridge on nights Buddy stayed over. McCaleb guessed that Buddy was a soft touch for a quick beer every now and then on the long nights. That was probably why Charlie had rowed his skiff over from the pier.

'I saw the lights and thought maybe Buddy was here,' he said. 'I was just paying a visit.'

'No, Buddy's overtown tonight. He probably won't be back till Friday.'

'Okay, then. I'll just be going. Everything all right with you? The missus isn't making you sleep on the boat, is she?'

'No, Charlie, everything's fine. Just doing a little work.'

He held up the letter opener as if that explained what he was doing.

'All right then, I'll be heading back.'

'Good night, Charlie. Thanks for checking on me.'

He went back inside and down to the office. He found the magnifying glass, with a light attachment, at the bottom of the box of office supplies.

For the next two hours he went through the paintings. The eerie landscapes of phantasmic demons surrounding human prey enthralled him once again. As he studied each work he marked particular findings such as the owls with yellow Post-its so that he could easily return to them.

McCaleb amassed a list of sixteen direct depictions of owls in the paintings and another dozen portrayals of owl-like creatures or structures. The owls were darkly painted and lurking in all the paintings like sentinels of judgment and doom. He looked at them and couldn't help but think of the analogy of the owl as detective. Both creatures of the night, both watchers and hunters – firsthand observers of the evil and pain humans and animals inflict upon each other.

The single most significant finding McCaleb made during his study of the paintings was not an owl. Rather, it was the human form. He made the discovery as he used the lighted glass to examine the center panel of a painting called *The Last Judgment.* Outside the depiction of hell's oven, where sinners were thrown, there were several bound victims waiting to be dismembered and burned. Among this grouping McCaleb found the image of a nude man bound with his arms and legs behind him. The sinner's extremities had been stretched into a painful reverse fetal position. The image closely reflected what he had seen at center focus in the crime scene videotape and photos of Edward Gunn.

McCaleb marked the finding with a Post-it and closed the book. When the cell phone on the couch next to him chirped just then, he bolted upright with a start. He checked his watch before answering and saw it was exactly midnight.

The caller was Graciela.

'I thought you were coming back tonight.'

'I am. I just finished and I'm on my way.'

'You took the cart down, right?'

'Yeah. So I'll be fine.'

'Okay, see you soon.'

'Yes, you will.'

McCaleb decided to leave everything on the boat, thinking that he needed to clear his mind before the next day. Carrying the files and the heavy books would only remind him of the heavy thoughts he carried within. He locked the boat and took the Zodiac to the skiff dock. At the end of the pier he climbed into the golf cart. He rode through the deserted business district and up the hill toward home. Despite his efforts to deflect them, his thoughts were of the abyss. A place where creatures with sharp beaks and claws and knives tormented the fallen in perpetuity. He knew one thing for sure at this point. The painter Bosch would have made a good profiler. He knew his stuff. He had a handle on the nightmares that rattle around inside most people's minds. As well as those that sometimes get out.

15

Opening statements in the trial of David Storey were delayed while the attorneys argued over final motions behind closed doors with the judge. Bosch sat at the prosecution table and waited. He tried to clear his mind of all extraneous diversions, including his fruitless search for Annabelle Crowe the night before.

Finally, at ten forty-five, the attorneys came into the courtroom and moved to their respective tables. Then the defendant – today wearing a suit that looked like it would cover three deputies' paychecks – was led into court from the holding cell and, at last, Judge Houghton took the bench.

It was time to begin and Bosch felt the tension in the courtroom ratchet up a considerable notch. Los Angeles had raised – or perhaps lowered – the criminal trial to the level of worldwide entertainment, but it was never seen that way by the players in the courtroom. They were playing for keeps and in this trial perhaps more than most there was a palpable sense of the enmity between the two opposing camps.

The judge instructed the deputy sheriff who acted as his bailiff to bring in the jury. Bosch stood with the others and turned and watched the jurors file in silently and take their seats. He thought he could see excitement in some of their faces. They had been waiting through two weeks of jury selection and motions for things to start. Bosch's eyes rose above them to the two cameras mounted on the wall over the jury box. They gave a full view of the courtroom, except for the jury box.

After everyone was seated Houghton cleared his throat and leaned forward to the bench microphone while looking at the jurors.

'Ladies and gentlemen, how are you this morning?'

There was a murmured response and Houghton nodded.

'I apologize for the delay. Please remember that the justice system is in essence run by lawyers. As such it runs slowwwwwwly.'

There was polite laughter in the courtroom. Bosch noticed that the attorneys – prosecution and defense – dutifully joined in, a couple of them overdoing it. It had been his experience that while in open court a judge could not possibly tell a joke that the lawyers did not laugh at.

Bosch glanced to his left, past the defense table, and saw the other jury box was packed with members of the media. He recognized many of the reporters from television newscasts and press conferences in the past.

He scanned the rest of the courtroom and saw the public observation benches were densely packed with citizens, except for the row directly behind the defense table. There sat several people with ample room on either side who looked as if they'd spent the morning in a makeup trailer. Bosch assumed they were celebrities of some sort, but it wasn't a realm he was familiar with and he could not identify any of them. He thought about leaning over to Janis Langwiser and asking but then thought better of it.

'We needed to clean up some last-minute details in my chambers,' the judge continued to the jury. 'But now we're ready to start. We'll begin with opening statements and I need to caution you that these are not statements of fact but rather statements about what each side *thinks* the facts are and what they will endeavor to prove during the course of the trial. These statements are not to be considered by you to contain evidence. All of that comes later on. So listen closely but keep an open mind because a lot is still coming down the pipe. Now we're going to start off with the prosecution and, as always, give the defendant the last word. Mr. Kretzler, you may begin.'

The lead prosecutor stood and moved to the lectern positioned between the two lawyers' tables. He nodded to the jury and identified himself as Roger Kretzler, deputy district attorney assigned to the special crimes section. He was a tall and gaunt prosecutor with a reddish beard beneath short dark hair and rimless glasses. He was at least forty-five years old. Bosch thought of him as not particularly likable but nevertheless very capable at his job. And the fact that he was still in the trenches prosecuting cases when others his age had left for the higher-paying corporate or criminal defense worlds made him all the more admirable. Bosch suspected he had no home life. On nights before the trial when a question about the investigation had come up and Bosch would be paged, the call-back number was always Kretzler's office line – no matter how late it was.

Kretzler identified his co-prosecutor as Janis Langwiser, also of the special crimes unit, and the lead investigator as LAPD detective third grade Harry Bosch.

'I am going to make this short and sweet so all the sooner we will be able to get to the facts, as Judge Houghton has correctly pointed out. Ladies and gentlemen, the case you will hear in this courtroom certainly has the trappings of celebrity. It has event status written all over it. Yes, the defendant, David N. Storey, is a man of power and position in this community, in this celebrity-driven age we live in. But if you strip away the trappings of power and glitter from the facts – as I promise we will do over the next few days – what you have here is something as basic as it is all too common in our society. A simple case of murder.'

Kretzler paused for effect. Bosch checked the jury. All eyes were fastened on the prosecutor.

'The man you see seated at the defense table, David N. Storey, went out with a twenty-three-year-old woman named Jody Krementz on the evening of last October twelfth. And after an evening that included the premiere of his latest film and a reception, he took her to his home in the Hollywood Hills where they engaged in consensual sexual intercourse. I don't believe you will find argument from the defense table about any of this. We are not here about that. But what happened during or after the sex is what brings us here today. On the morning of October thirteenth the body of Jody Krementz was found strangled and in her own bed in the small home she shared with another actress.'

Kretzler flipped up a page of the legal pad on the lectern in front of him even though it seemed clear to Bosch and probably everyone else that his statement was memorized and rehearsed.

'In the course of this trial the State of California will prove beyond a reasonable doubt that it was David Storey who took Jody Krementz's life in a moment of brutal sexual rage. He then moved or caused to be moved the body from his home to the victim's home. He arranged the body in such a way that the death might appear accidental. And following this, he used his power and position in an effort to thwart the investigation of the crime by the Los Angeles Police Department. Mr. Storey, who you will learn has a history of abusive behavior toward women, was so sure that he would walk away untouched from his crime that in a moment of—'

Kretzler chose this moment to turn from the lectern and look down upon the seated defendant with a disdainful look. Storey stared straight ahead unflinchingly and the prosecutor finally turned back to the jury.

'—shall we say candor, he actually boasted to the lead investigator on the case, Detective Bosch, that he would do just that, walk away from his crime.'

Kretzler cleared his throat, a sign he was ready to bring it all home.

'We are here, ladies and gentlemen of the jury, to find justice for Jody Krementz. To make it our business that her murderer not walk away from his crime. The State of California asks, and I personally ask, that you listen carefully during the trial and weigh the evidence fairly. If you do that, we can be sure that justice will be served. For Jody Krementz. For all of us.'

He picked up the pad from the lectern and turned to move back to his seat. But then he stopped, as if a second thought had just occurred to him. Bosch saw it as a well-practiced move. He thought the jury would see it that way as well.

'I was just thinking that we all know it has been part of our recent history here in Los Angeles to see our police department put on trial in these high-profile cases. If you don't like the message, then by all means shoot the messenger. It is a favorite from the defense bar's bag of tricks. I want you all to promise yourselves that you will remain vigilant and keep your eyes on the prize, that prize being truth and justice. Don't be fooled. Don't be misdirected. Trust yourself on the truth and you'll find the way.'

He stepped over to his seat and sat down. Bosch noticed Langwiser reaching over and gripping Kretzler's forearm in a congratulatory gesture. It, too, was part of the well-practiced play.

The judge told the jurors that in light of the brevity of the prosecution's address the trial would proceed to the defense statement without a break. But the break came soon enough anyway when Fowkkes stood and moved to the lectern and proceeded to spend even less time than Kretzler addressing the jury.

'You know, ladies and gentlemen, all this talk about shoot the messenger, don't shoot the messenger, well let me tell you something about that. Those fine words you got from Mr. Kretzler there at the end, well let me tell you every prosecutor in this building says those at the start of every trial in this place. I mean they must have 'em printed up on cards they carry in their wallets, it seems to me.'

Kretzler stood and objected to what he called such 'wild exaggeration' and Houghton admonished Fowkkes but then advised the prosecutor that he might make better use of his objections. Fowkkes moved on quickly.

'If I was outta line, I'm sorry. I know it's a touchy thing with prosecutors and police. But all I'm saying, folks, is that where there's smoke there's usually fire. And in the course of this trial we are going to try to find our way through the smoke. We may or may not come upon a fire but one thing I do know for sure we will come upon is the conclusion that this man—'

He turned and pointed strongly at his client.

'—this man, David N. Storey, is without a shadow of a doubt not guilty of the crime he is charged with. Yes, he is a man of power and position but, remember, it is not a crime to be so. Yes, he knows a few celebrities but, last time I checked *People* magazine, this too was not yet a crime. Now I think you may find elements of Mr. Storey's personal life and appetites to be offensive to you. I know I do. But remember that these do not constitute crimes that he is charged with in these proceedings. The crime here is *murder*. Nothing less and nothing more. It is a crime of which David Storey is *NOT* guilty. And no matter what Mr. Kretzler and Ms. Langwiser and Detective Bosch and their witnesses tell you, there is absolutely no evidence of guilt in this case.'

After Fowkkes bowed to the jury and sat down, Judge Houghton announced the trial would break for an early lunch before testimony began in the afternoon.

Bosch watched the jury file out through the door next to the box. A few of them looked back over their shoulders at the courtroom. The juror who was last in line, a black woman of about fifty, looked directly back at Bosch. He lowered his eyes and then immediately wished he hadn't. When he looked back up she was gone.

16

McCaleb turned off the television when the trial broke for lunch. He didn't want to hear all the analysis of the talking heads. He thought the best point had been scored by the defense. Fowkkes had made a smooth move telling the jury that he, too, found his client's personal life and habits offensive. He was telling them that if he could stand it, so could they. He was reminding them that the case was about taking a life, not about how one lived a life.

He went back to preparing for his afternoon meeting with Jaye Winston. He'd gone back to the boat after breakfast and gathered up his files and books. Now, with a pair of scissors and some tape, he was putting together a presentation he hoped would not only impress Winston but convince her of something McCaleb was having a difficult time believing himself. In a way, putting together the presentation was a dress rehearsal for putting on a case. In that respect, McCaleb found the time he labored over what he would show and say to Winston very useful. It allowed him to see logic holes and prepare answers for the questions he knew Winston would ask.

While he considered exactly what he would say to Winston, she called on his cell phone.

'We might have a break on the owl. Maybe, maybe not.'

'What is it?'

'The distributor in Middleton, Ohio, thinks he knows where it came from. A place right here in Carson called Bird Barrier.'

'Why does he think that?'

'Because Kurt faxed photos of our bird, and the man he was dealing with in Ohio noticed that the bottom of the mold was open.'

'Okay. What's it mean?'

'Well, apparently these are shipped with the base enclosed so it can be filled with sand to make the bird stand up in wind and rain and whatever.'

'I understand.'

'Well, they have one subdistributor who orders the owls with the bottom of the base punched out. Bird Barrier. They take them with the open base because they fit the owls on top of some kind of gizmo that shrieks.'

'What do you mean, shrieks?'

'You know, like a real owl. I guess it helps really scare birds away. You know what Bird Barrier's slogan is? "Number one when it comes to birds going number two." Cute, huh? That's how they answer the phone there.'

McCaleb's mind was churning too quickly to register humor. He didn't laugh.

'This place is in Carson?'

'Right, not far from your marina. I've got to go to a meeting now but I was going to drop by before coming to see you. You want to meet there instead? Can you make it over in time?'

'That would be good. I'll be there.'

She gave him the address, which was about fifteen minutes from Cabrillo Marina, and they agreed to meet there at two. She said that the company's president, a man named Cameron Riddell, had agreed to see them.

'Are you bringing the owl with you?' McCaleb asked.

'Guess what, Terry? I've been a detective going on twelve years now. *And* I've had a brain even longer.'

'Sorry.'

'See you at two.'

After clicking off the phone, McCaleb took a leftover tamale out of the freezer, cooked it in the microwave and then wrapped it in foil and put it in his leather bag for eating while crossing the bay. He checked on his daughter, who was in the family room sleeping in the arms of their part-time nanny, Mrs. Perez. He touched the baby's cheek and left.

Bird Barrier was located in a commercial and upscale warehouse district that hugged the eastern side of the 405 Freeway just below the airfield where the Goodyear blimp was tethered. The blimp was in its place and McCaleb could see the leashes that held it straining against the afternoon wind coming in from the sea. When he pulled into the Bird Barrier lot he noticed an LTD with commercial hubs that he knew had to be Jaye Winston's car. He was right. She was sitting in a small waiting room when he came in through a glass door. On the floor next to her chair were a briefcase and a cardboard box sealed at the top with red tape marked EVIDENCE. She immediately got up and went to a reception window through which McCaleb could see a seated young man wearing a telephone headset.

'Can you tell Mr. Riddell we're both here?'

The young man, who was apparently on a call, nodded to her.

A few minutes later they were ushered into Cameron Riddell's office. McCaleb carried the box. Winston made the introductions, calling McCaleb her colleague. It was the truth but it also concealed his badgeless status.

Riddell was a pleasant-looking man in his mid-thirties who seemed anxious to help in the investigation. Winston put on a pair of latex gloves from her briefcase, then ran a key along the red tape on the box and opened it. She removed the owl and placed it on Riddell's desk.

'What can you tell us about this, Mr. Riddell?'

Riddell remained standing behind his desk and leaned across to look at the owl.

'I can't touch it?'

'Tell you what, why don't you put these on.'

Winston opened her briefcase and handed another pair of gloves from the cardboard dispenser to Riddell. McCaleb just watched, having decided that he would not jump in unless Winston asked him to or she made an obvious omission during the interview. Riddell struggled with the gloves, slowly pulling them on.

'Sorry,' Winston said. 'They're medium. You look like a large.'

Once he had the gloves on, Riddell picked the owl up with both hands and studied the underside of the base. He looked up into the hollow plastic mold and then held the bird directly in front of him, seemingly studying the painted eyes. He then placed it on the corner of the desk and went back around to his seat. He sat down and pressed a button on an intercom.

'Monique, it's Cameron. Can you go to the back and get one of the screeching owls off the line and bring it in to me? I need it now, too.'

'On my way.'

Riddell took off the gloves and flexed his fingers. He then looked at Winston, having sensed that she was the important one. He gestured to the owl.

'Yes, it's one of ours but it's been . . . I don't know what the word you would use would be. It's been changed, modified. We don't sell them like this.'

'How so?'

'Well, Monique's getting us one so you can see, but essentially this one has been repainted a little bit and the screeching mechanism has been removed. Also, we have a proprietary label we attach here at the base and that's gone.'

He pointed to the rear of the base.

'Let's start with the painting,' Winston said. 'What was done?'

Before Riddell answered, there was a single knock on the door and a woman came in carrying another owl which was wrapped in plastic. Riddell told her to put it down on the desk and remove the plastic. McCaleb noticed that she made a face when she saw the painted black eyes of the owl Winston had brought. Riddell thanked her and she left the office.

McCaleb studied the side-by-side owls. The evidence owl had been painted darker. The Bird Barrier owl had five colors on its feathers, including white and light blue, as well as plastic eyes with pupils rimmed in a reflective amber color. Also, the new owl was sitting atop a black plastic base.

'As you can see, the owl you brought has been repainted,' Riddell said. 'Especially the eyes. When you paint over them like that, you lose a lot of the effect. These are called foil-reflect eyes. The layer of foil in the plastic catches light and gives the eyes the appearance of movement.'

'So the birds think it is real.'

'Exactly. You lose that when you paint them like this.'

'We don't think the person that painted this was worried about birds. What else is different?'

Riddell shook his head.

'Just that the plumage has been darkened quite a bit. You can see that.'

'Yes. Now you said the mechanism has been removed. What mechanism?'

'We get these from Ohio and then we paint them and attach one of two mechanisms. What you see here is our standard model.'

Riddell picked the owl up and showed them the underside. The black plastic base swiveled as he turned it. It made a loud screeching sound.

'Hear the screech?'

'Yes, that's enough, Mr. Riddell.'

'Sorry. But you see, the owl sits on this base and reacts to the wind. As it turns, it emits the screech and sounds like a predator. Works well, as long as the wind is blowing. We also have a deluxe model with an electronic insert in the base. It contains a speaker that emits recorded sounds of predator birds like the hawk. No reliance on wind.'

'Can you get one without either one of the inserts?'

'Yes, you can purchase a replacement that fits over one of our proprietary bases. In case the owl is damaged or lost. With exposure, particularly in marine settings, the paint lasts two to three years and after that the owl might lose some of its effectiveness. You have to repaint or simply get a new owl. The reality is, the mold is the least expensive part of the ensemble.'

Winston looked over at McCaleb. He had nothing to add or ask in the line of questioning she was pursuing. He simply nodded at her and she turned back to Riddell.

'Okay, then, I think we want to see if there is a method of tracing this owl from this point to its eventual owner.'

Riddell looked at the owl for a long moment as if it might be able to answer the question itself.

'Well, that could be difficult. It's a commodity item. We sell several thousand a year. We ship to retail outlets as well as sell through mail-order catalogs and an internet website.'

He snapped his fingers.

'There is one thing that will cut it down some, though.'

'What's that?'

'They changed the mold last year. In China. They did some research and decided the horned owl was considered a higher threat to other birds than the round head. They changed to the horns.'

'I'm not quite following you, Mr. Riddell.'

He held up a finger as if to tell her to wait a moment. He then opened a desk drawer and dug through some paperwork. He came out with a catalog and quickly started turning pages. McCaleb saw that Bird Barrier's primary business was not plastic owls, but large-scale bird deterrent systems that encompassed netting and wire coils and spikes. Riddell found the page showing the plastic owls and turned the catalog so that Winston and McCaleb could view it.

'This is last year's catalog,' he said. 'You see the owl has the round head. The manufacturer changed last June, about seven months ago. Now we have these guys.'

He pointed to the two owls on the table.

'The feathering turns up into the two points, or ears, on the top of the head. The sales rep said these are called horns and that these types of owls are sometimes called devil owls.'

Winston glanced at McCaleb, who raised his eyebrows momentarily.

'So you're saying this owl we have was ordered or bought since June,' she said to Riddell.

'More like since August or maybe September. They changed in June but we probably didn't start receiving the new mold until late July. We also would have sold off our existing supplies of the round head first.'

Winston then questioned Riddell about sales records and determined that information from mail-order and website purchases was kept complete and current on the company's computer files. But point-of-purchase sales from shipments to major hardware and home and marine products retailers would obviously not be recorded. He turned to the computer on his desk and typed in a few commands. He then pointed to the screen, though McCaleb and Winston were not at angles where they could see it.

'All right, I asked for sales of those part numbers since August one,' he said.

'Part numbers?'

'Yes, for the standard and deluxe models and then the replacement molds. We show we self-shipped four hundred and fourteen total. We also shipped six hundred even to retailers.'

'And what you're telling us is that we can only trace, through you at least, the four hundred fourteen.'

'Correct.'

'You have the names of buyers and the addresses the owls were shipped to there?'

'Yes, we do.'

'And are you willing to share this information with us without need of a court order?'

Riddell frowned as if the question was absurd.

'You said you're working on a murder, right?'

'Right.'

'We don't require a court order. If we can help, we want to help.'

'That's very refreshing, Mr. Riddell.'

They sat in Winston's car and reviewed the computer printouts Riddell had given them. The evidence box containing the owl was between them on the seat. There were three printouts, divided by orders for the deluxe, standard or replacement owls. McCaleb asked to see the replacement list because his instincts told him the owl in Edward Gunn's apartment had been bought for the express purpose of playing a part in the murder scene and therefore no attachment mechanisms were needed. Additionally, the replacement owl was the least expensive.

'We better find something here,' Winston said as her eyes scanned the list of purchasers of the standard owl model. 'Because chasing down buyers through the Home Depots and other retailers is going to mean court orders and lawyers and – hey, the Getty's on here. They ordered four.'

McCaleb looked over at her and thought about that. Finally, he shrugged his shoulders and went back to his list. Winston moved on as well, continuing her listing of the difficulties they would face if they had to go to the retail outlets where the horned owl was sold. McCaleb tuned her out when he got to the third-to-last name on his list. He traced his finger from a name he recognized along a line on the printout detailing the address the owl was shipped to, method of payment, origin of purchase order and the name of the person receiving it if different from purchaser. His breath must have caught, because Winston picked up on his vibe.

'What?'

'I got something here.'

He held the printout across the seat to her and pointed to the line.

'This buyer. Jerome Van Aiken. He had one shipped the day before Christmas to Gunn's address and apartment number. The order was paid for by a money order.'

She took the printout from him and started reading the information.

'Shipped to the Sweetzer address but to a Lubbert Das care of Edward Gunn. Lubbert Das. Nobody named Lubbert Das came up in the investigation. I don't remember that name on the residents list of that building, either. I'll call Rohrshak to see if Gunn ever had a roommate with that name.'

'Don't bother. Lubbert Das never lived there.'

She looked up from the pages and over at him.

'You know who Lubbert Das is?'

'Sort of.'

Her brow creased deeply.

'Sort of? *Sort of?* What about Jerome Van Aiken?'

He nodded. Winston dropped the pages on the box between them. She looked at him with an expression that imparted both curiosity and annoyance.

'Well, Terry, I think it's about time you started telling me what you know.'

McCaleb nodded again and put his hand on the door handle.

'Why don't we go over to my boat? We can talk there.'

'Why don't we talk right here, right fucking now?'

McCaleb tried a small smile on her.

'Because it's what you'd call an audiovisual demon-stration.'

He opened the door and got out, then looked back in at her.

'I'll see you over there, okay?'

She shook her head.

'You better have one hell of a profile worked out for me.'

Then he shook his head.

'I don't have a profile ready for you yet, Jaye.'

'Then what *do* you have?'

'A suspect.'

He closed the door then and he could hear her muffled curses as he walked to his car. As he crossed the parking lot a shadow fell over him and everything else. He looked up to see the Goodyear blimp cross overhead, totally eclipsing the sun.

17

They reconvened fifteen minutes later on *The Following Sea.* McCaleb got out some Cokes and told Winston to sit on the stuffed chair at the end of the coffee table in the salon. In the parking lot he had told her to bring the plastic owl with her to the boat. He now used two paper towels to remove it from its box and place it on the table in front of her. Winston watched him, her lips tight with annoyance. McCaleb told her he understood her anger at being manipulated on her own case but added that she would be back in control of things as soon as he presented his findings.

'All I can say, Terry, is that this better be fucking good.'

He remembered that he had once noted on the inside file flap on the first case he ever worked with her that she was prone to using profanity when under stress. He had also noted that she was smart and intuitive. He hoped now that those characteristics had not changed.

He stepped over to the counter where he had his presentation file waiting. He opened it and took the top sheet over to the coffee table. He pushed the Bird Barrier printout aside and put the sheet down at the base of the plastic owl.

'What do you think? This our bird?'

Winston leaned forward to study the color image he had put down. It was an enlarged detail from the Bosch painting *The Garden of Earthly Delights* showing the nude man embracing the dark owl with shining black eyes. He had cut it and other details from the Marijnissen book. He watched as Winston's eyes moved back and forth between the plastic owl and the detail from the painting.

'I'd say it's a match,' she finally said. 'Where'd you get this, the Getty? You should have told me about this yesterday, Terry. What the fuck is going on?'

McCaleb raised his hands in a calming gesture.

'I'll explain everything. Just let me show you this stuff the way I want to. Then I'll answer any question you ask.'

She waved a hand, indicating he could go on. He went over to the counter and got the second sheet and brought it over. He put it down in front of her.

'Same painter, different painting.'

She looked. It was a detail from *The Last Judgment* depicting the sinner bound in the reverse fetal position, waiting to be delivered to hell.

'Don't do this to me. Who painted these?'

'I'll tell you in a minute.'

He went back to the counter and the file.

'Is this guy still alive?' she called after him.

He walked the third sheet over and put it down on the table next to the other two.

'He's been dead about five hundred years.'

'Jesus.'

She picked up the third sheet and looked closely at it. It was the full copy of the *Seven Deadly Sins* tabletop.

'That's supposed to be God's eye seeing all the sins of the world,' McCaleb explained. 'You recognize the words in the center, running around the iris?'

'Beware, beware . . .' she whispered the translation. 'Oh, God, we've got a real nut here. Who is this?'

'One more. This one really falls into place now.'

He went back to the file for the fourth time and came back with another reproduction of a painting from the Bosch book. He handed it to her.

'It's called *The Stone Operation.* In medieval times it was believed by some that an operation to remove a stone from the brain was a cure for stupidity and deceit. Note the location of the incision.'

'I noted, I noted. Just like our guy. What's all of this around here?'

She traced the exterior of the circular painting with a finger. In the outer black margin were words that were once ornately painted in gold but which had deteriorated over time and were almost indecipherable.

'The translation is "Master, cut out the stone. My name is Lubbert Das." The critical literature on the painter who created this piece notes that in his time the name Lubbert was a derisive name applied to those who were perverted or stupid.'

Winston put the sheet down on top of the others and raised her hands, palms out.

'All right, Terry, enough. Who was the painter and who is this suspect you say you've come up with?'

McCaleb nodded. It was time.

'The painter's name was Jerome Van Aiken. He was Netherlandish, considered to be one of the greats of the Northern Renaissance. But his paintings were dark, full of monsters and phantasmic demons. Owls, too. Lots of owls. The literature suggests the owls found in his paintings symbolized everything from evil to doom to the fall of mankind.'

He sorted through the sheets on the coffee table and held up the detail of the man embracing the owl.

'This kind of says it all about him. Man's embracing of evil – the devil owl, to use Mr. Riddell's description – leads to the inevitable destiny of hell. Here's the whole painting.'

He went back to the file and brought to her the full copy of *The Garden of Earthly Delights.* He watched her eyes as she studied the images. He saw repulsion as well as fascination. He pointed out the four owls he had found in the painting, including the detail he had already shown her.

She suddenly pulled the sheet aside and looked at him.

'Wait a minute. I know I've seen this before. In a book or maybe an art class I took at CSUN. But I never heard of this Van Aiken, I don't think. He painted this?'

McCaleb nodded.

'*The Garden of Earthly Delights.* Van Aiken painted it but you've never heard of him because he wasn't known by his real name. He used the Latin version of Jerome and took the name of his hometown for a last name. He was known as Hieronymus Bosch.'

She just looked at him for a long moment as it all clicked together, the images he had shown her, the names on the printout, her knowledge of the Edward Gunn case.

'Bosch,' she said, almost as an expulsion of breath. 'Is Hieronymus . . .?'

She didn't finish. McCaleb nodded.

'Yeah, that's Harry's real name.'

They were both pacing in the salon now, heads down but careful not to collide. Talking in sprints, a bad but fast-moving jazz in their blood.

'This is too far out there, McCaleb. Do you know what you are saying?'

'I know exactly what I'm saying. And don't think that I didn't think long and hard about it before I said it. I consider him to be a friend, Jaye. There was . . . I don't know, at one time I thought we were a lot alike. But look at this stuff, look at the connections, the parallels. It fits. It all fits.'

He stopped and looked at her. She kept pacing.

'He's a cop! A homicide cop, for God's sake.'

'What, are you going to tell me it's beyond the realm because he's a cop? This is Los Angeles – the modern Garden of Earthly Delights. With all the same temptations and demons. You don't even have to go beyond the city limits for examples of cops crossing the line – dealing drugs, robbing banks, even murder.'

'I know, I know. It's just that . . .'

She didn't finish.

'At minimum it fits well enough that you know we have to take a good hard look.'

She stopped and looked back at him.

'We? Forget it, Terry. I asked you to take a look at the book, not run down the leads. You're out after this.'

'Look, if I didn't run some of this down you'd have nothing. This owl would still be sitting on top of that guy Rohrshak's other building.'

'I'll give you that. And thank you very much. But you're a civilian. You're out.'

'I'm not walking away, Jaye. If I'm the one who puts Bosch under the glass, then I'm not walking away from it.'

Winston sat down heavily in the chair.

'All right, can we talk about that when and if we come to it? I'm still not sold on this.'

'Good. I'm not either.'

'Well, you sure made a nice show of giving me the pictures and building your case.'

'All I am saying is that Harry Bosch is connected to this. And that cuts two ways. One, he did it. Two, he's been set up. He's been a cop a long time.'

'Twenty-five, thirty years. The list of people he's put in the penitentiary has got to be a yard long. And the ones who have been in and out is probably half the list. It'll take a fucking year to run all of them down.'

McCaleb nodded.

'And don't think he didn't know that.'

She looked up sharply at him. He started pacing again, his head down. After too long a silence he glanced up and saw her staring at him.

'What?'

'You really like Bosch for this, don't you? You know something else.'

'No, I don't. I am trying to stay open. All avenues of possibility need to be pursued.'

'Bullshit, you're driving down one avenue.'

McCaleb didn't answer. He felt enough guilt about it without Winston having to apply more.

'Okay,' she said. 'Then why don't you spell it out for me? And don't worry, I'm not going to hold it against you when you end up wrong.'

He stopped and looked at her.

'Come on, spell it out for me.'

McCaleb shook his head.

'I'm not all the way there yet. All I know is that what we have here is way, *way* beyond the realm of coincidence. So there has to be an explanation.'

'So tell me the explanation involving Bosch. I know you. You've been thinking about it.'

'All right, but remember, it's all theory at this point.'

'I'll remember. Go.'

'First of all, you start with *Detective* Hieronymus Bosch believing – no, make that *knowing* – that this guy, Edward Gunn, walked on a homicide. Okay, then you have Gunn turn up strangled and looking like a figure out of a picture by the *painter* Hieronymus Bosch. You throw in one plastic owl and at least a half dozen other connection points between the two Boschs, let alone the name, and there it is.'

'What's there? Those connections don't mean it was Bosch who did it. You said it yourself, someone could have set this up for us to find and put on Bosch.'

'I don't know what it is. Gut instinct, I guess. There's something about Bosch – something off the page.'

He remembered how Vosskuhler had described the paintings.

'A darkness more than night.'

'What's that supposed to mean?'

McCaleb waved off the question. He reached over and picked up the detail of the owl embraced by the man. He held it up in front of her face.

'Look at the darkness there. In the eyes. There's something about Harry that is the same.'

'Now you're getting downright spooky, Terry. What are you saying, in a previous life Harry Bosch was a painting? I mean, listen to what you are saying here.'

He put the sheet back down and stepped away from her, shaking his head.

'I don't know *how* to say it,' he said. 'There's just something there. A connection of some kind between them that is more than the name.'

He made a motion of waving away the thought.

'All right, then let's move on,' Winston said. 'Why now, Terry? If it is Bosch, why now? And why Gunn? He walked away from him six years ago.'

'It's interesting that you say walked away from *him* and not justice.'

'I didn't mean anything by it. You just like to take—'

'Why now? Who knows? But there was that re-encounter the night before in the drunk tank and before that there was the time in October and it goes further back. Whenever this guy ended up in the can Bosch was there.'

'But on that last night Gunn was too drunk to talk.'

'Says who?'

She nodded. They only had Bosch's account of the drunk-tank encounter.

'All right, fine. But why Gunn? I mean, I don't want to put a qualitative judgment on a murderer or his victims but, come on, the guy stabbed a prostitute in a Hollywood hot sheet hotel. We all know that some count more than others and this one couldn't have counted for much. If you read the book, you saw – her own family didn't even care about her.'

'Then there's something missing, something else that we don't know. Because Harry cared. I don't think he's the kind who ever counts one case, one person more important than another, anyway. But there's something about Gunn we don't know yet. There has to be – six years ago it was enough for Harry to shove his lieutenant through a window and take a suspension for it. It was enough for him to visit Gunn every time he got hooked up and put in a cell.'

McCaleb nodded to himself.

'We need to find the trigger. The stressor. The thing that forced the action now as opposed to a year ago, two years ago, whenever.'

Winston abruptly stood up.

'Would you stop saying "we"? And, you know, there is something you are conveniently missing here. Why would this man, this veteran cop and homicide detective, kill this guy and leave all of these clues leading back to himself? It makes no sense – not with Harry Bosch. He'd be too smart for that.'

'Only from this side of it. These things may only seem obvious now that we have discovered them. And you are forgetting the act of murder itself is evidence of aberrant thinking, of a dissembling personality. If Harry Bosch has veered off the path and crashed into the ditch – into the abyss – then we can't assume anything about his thinking or planning of a murder. His leaving of these markers could be symptomatic.'

She waved off his explanation.

'That's the Quantico dance there. Too much mumbo jumbo.'

Winston picked the copy of *The Garden of Earthly Delights* off the table and studied it.

'I talked to Harry about this case two weeks ago,' she said. 'You talked to him yesterday. He wasn't exactly climbing the walls and foaming at the mouth. And look at this trial he's riding now. He's cool, calm and has his shit together. Know what some of the guys in the office call him, the ones who know him? The Marlboro Man.'

'Yeah, well, he stopped smoking. And maybe this Storey case was the stressor. A lot of pressure. It's gotta come out someplace.'

McCaleb could tell she wasn't listening. Her eyes had caught on something in the painting. She dropped the sheet and picked up the detail of the dark owl embraced by the nude man.

'Let me ask you something,' she said. 'If our guy sent the owl directly from that warehouse to our victim, then how the fuck did it get this nice custom paint job?'

McCaleb nodded.

'Good question. He must've painted it right there in the apartment. Maybe while watching Gunn try to stay alive.'

'There was no paint like this found in the apartment. And we checked the building's dumpster, too. I saw no paint.'

'He took it with him, got rid of it somewhere else.'

'Or maybe plans to use it again on the next one.'

She paused and thought for a long moment. McCaleb waited.

'So what do we do?' she finally asked.

'So it's "we" now?'

'For now. I changed my mind. I can't take this inside. Too dangerous. If it's wrong I could kiss everything good-bye.'

McCaleb nodded.

'Do you and your partner have other cases?'

'We've got three open files, including this one.'

'Well, put him on one of the others while you work this one – with me. We work on Bosch until we have something solid – one way or the other – that you can take in and make official.'

'And what do I do, call up Harry Bosch and tell him I need to talk to him because he's a suspect in a murder?'

'I'll take Bosch first. It will be less obvious if I make the first run. Let me get a feel for him and, who knows, maybe my current instincts will be wrong. Or maybe I'll find the trigger.'

'That's easier said than done. We move too close and he'll know. I don't want this blowing up in our faces – my face, in particular.'

'That's where I can be an advantage.'

'Yeah? How so?'

'I'm not a cop. I'll be able to get closer to him. I need to get inside his house, see how he lives. Meantime, you—'

'Wait a minute. You're not talking about breaking into his house. I can't be a party to that.'

'No, nothing illegal.'

'Then how are you going to get in?'

'Knock on the door.'

'Good luck. What were you going to say? Meantime, I do what?'

'You work the outside line, the obvious stuff. Trace down the money order for the owl. Find out more about Gunn and the murder six years ago. Find out about the incident between Harry and his old lieutenant – and find out about the lieutenant. Harry said the guy went out one night and ended up dead in a tunnel.'

'Damn, I remember that. That was related to Gunn?'

'I don't know. But Bosch made some kind of elliptical reference to it yesterday.'

'I can pull stuff on it and I can ask questions about the other stuff. But any one of these moves could get back to Bosch.'

McCaleb nodded. He thought it was a risk that had to be taken.

'You know anybody who knows him?' he said.

She shook her head in annoyance.

'Look, don't you remember? Cops are paranoid people. The minute I ask one question about Harry Bosch, people are going to know what we are doing.'

'Not necessarily. Use the Storey case. It's high profile. Maybe you've been watching the guy on TV and he doesn't look so good. "Is he all right? What's going on with him?" Like that. Make it like you're gossiping.'

She didn't look mollified. She stepped over to the sliding door and looked out across the marina. She leaned her forehead against the glass.

'I know his former partner,' she said. 'There's an informal group of women who get together once a month. We all work homicide from all the local departments. About a dozen of us. Harry's old partner Kiz Rider just got moved from Hollywood to Robbery–Homicide. The big time. But I think they were close. He was kind of a mentor. I might be able to hit on her. If I use a little finesse.'

McCaleb nodded and thought of something.

'Harry told me he was divorced. I don't know how long ago but you could ask Rider about him like, you know, you're interested and what's he like, that sort of thing. You ask like that and she might give you the real lowdown.'

Winston looked away from the slider and back at McCaleb.

'Yeah, that will make us good friends when she finds out it was all bullshit and I was setting up on her ex-partner – her mentor.'

'If she's a good cop she'll understand. You had to clear him or bag him and either way you wanted to do it as quietly as possible.'

Winston looked back out the door.

'I'm going to need deniability on this.'

'Meaning?'

'Meaning if we do this and you go in there and it all blows up, I need to be able to walk away.'

McCaleb nodded. He wished she hadn't said it but he could see her need to protect herself.

'I'm just telling you up front, Terry. If it all goes to hell it's going to look like you overstepped, that I asked you to take a look at the book and you went off on your own. I'm sorry but I have to protect myself here.'

'I understand, Jaye. I can live with it. I'll take my chances.'

18

Winston was silent for a long time while she stared out the salon's door. McCaleb sensed that she was building up to something and just waited.

'I'll tell you a story about Harry Bosch,' she finally said. 'The first time I ever met him was about four years ago. It was a joint case. Two kidnap–murders. The one in Hollywood was his, the one in West Hollywood was mine. Young women, girls really. Physical evidence tied the cases together. We were basically working them separately but would meet for lunch every Wednesday to compare notes.'

'Did you profile it?'

'Yeah. This was when Maggie Griffin was still out here at the bureau. She worked something up for us. The usual. Anyway, things heated up when a third one disappeared. A seventeen-year-old this time. The evidence from the first two indicated the doer was keeping them alive four or five days before he got tired of them and killed them. So we had a big clock on us. We got reinforcements and we were running down common denominators.'

McCaleb nodded. It sounded as though they were going by the book on tracking a serial.

'A long shot came up,' she said. 'All three of the victims used the same dry cleaner on Santa Monica near La Cienega. The latest – the girl – had a summer job at Universal and took her uniforms in for dry cleaning. Anyway, before we even went in there to the management we went into the employee parking lot and took down tags to run, just in case we got something before we had to go in and announce ourselves. And we got a hit. The manager himself. He'd gotten popped about ten years before on a public indecency. We pulled the jacket and it was a garden-variety flasher case. He pulled up in a car next to a bus stop and opened the door so the woman on the bench could get a look at his johnson. Turned out she was an undercover – they knew a wagger was working the neighborhood and put out decoys. Anyway, he got probation and counseling. He lied about it on his application at the job and over the years worked his way up to manager of the shop.'

'Higher job, higher stress, higher level of offense.'

'That's what we thought. But we didn't have any evidence. So Bosch had an idea. He said all of us – me, him and our partners – would go see this guy, his name was Hagen, at his home. He said an FBI agent once told him to always brace a suspect at home if you get the chance because sometimes you get more from the surroundings than you get from their mouths.'

McCaleb suppressed a smile. It had been a lesson Bosch learned on the Cielo Azul case.

'So we followed Hagen home. He lived over in Los Feliz in a big old rundown house off Franklin. This was the fourth day of the third woman's disappearance, so we knew we were running out of time. We knocked on his door and the plan was to act like we didn't know about his record and that we were just there to enlist his help in checking out employees in the shop. You know, to see how he reacted or if he made a slip.'

'Right.'

'Well, we were in there in this guy's living room and I was doing most of the talking because Bosch wanted to see how the guy took it. You know, a woman in control. And we weren't there but five minutes when Bosch suddenly stood up and said, "It's him. She's here somewhere." And when he said that, Hagen up and bolted for the door. He didn't get far.'

'Was it a bluff or part of the plan?'

'Neither. Bosch just knew. On this little table next to the couch was one of those baby monitor things, you know? Bosch saw that and he just knew. It was the wrong end. It was the transmitter part. It meant the receiver was somewhere else. If you have a kid it's the other way around. You listen in the living room for noise from the baby room. But this was backwards. The profile from Griffin said this guy was a controller, that he likely used verbal coercion on his victim. Bosch saw that transmitter and something just clicked; this guy had her somewhere and got off on talking to her.'

'He was right?'

'Dead on. We found her in the garage in an unplugged freezer with three air holes drilled in it. It was like a coffin. The receiver part of the monitor was in there with her. She later told us that Hagen talked to her incessantly whenever he was in the house. He sang to her, too. Top forties. He'd change the words and sing about raping and killing her.'

McCaleb nodded. He wished he had been there on the case, for he knew what Bosch had felt, that sudden moment of coalescing, when the atoms smash together. When you just knew. A moment as thrilling as it was dreadful. The moment every homicide detective privately lives for.

'The reason I tell this story is because of what Bosch did and said after. Once we had Hagen in the back seat of one of the cars and started searching the house, Bosch stayed in the living room with that baby monitor. He turned it on and he spoke to her. He never stopped until we found her. He said, "Jennifer, we're here. It's all right, Jennifer, we're coming. You're safe and we're coming for you. Nobody's going to hurt you." He never stopped talking to her, soothing her like that.'

She stopped for a long moment and McCaleb saw her eyes were on the memory.

'After we found her we all felt so good. It was the best high I've ever had on this job. I went to Bosch and said, "You must have kids. You spoke to her like she was one of your own." And he just shook his head and said no. He said, "I just know what it's like to be alone and in the dark." Then he sort of walked away.'

She looked from the door back at McCaleb.

'Your talking about darkness reminded me of that.'

He nodded.

'What do we do if we come to a point that we know flat out that it was him?' she asked, her face turned back to the glass.

McCaleb answered quickly so that he wouldn't have to think about the question.

'I don't know,' he said.

After Winston had put the plastic owl back in the evidence box, gathered all of the pages he had shown her and left, McCaleb stood at the sliding door and watched her make her way up the ramp to the gate. He checked his watch and saw there was a lot of time before he needed to get ready for the night. He decided he would watch some of the trial on *Court TV.*

He looked back out the door and saw Winston putting the evidence box into the trunk of her car. Behind him somebody cleared his throat. McCaleb abruptly turned and there was Buddy Lockridge in the stairwell looking up at him from the lower deck. He had a pile of clothes clasped in his arms.

'Buddy, what the hell are you doing?'

'Man, that's one weird case you're working on.'

'I said *what* the hell are you doing?'

'I was going to do laundry and I came over here 'cause half my stuff was down in the cabin. Then you two showed up and when you started talking I knew I couldn't come up.'

He held the pile of clothes in his arms up as proof of his story.

'So I just sat down there on the bed and waited.'

'And listened to everything we said.'

'It's a crazy case, man. What are you going to do? I've seen that Bosch guy on *Court TV.* He kind of looks like he's wound a little too tight.'

'I know what I'm not going to do. I'm not going to talk about this with you.'

He pointed to the glass door.

'Leave, Buddy, and don't tell a word of this to anybody. You understand me?'

'Sure, I understand. I was just—'

'Leaving.'

'Sorry, man.'

'So am I.'

McCaleb opened the slider and Lockridge walked out like a dog with his tail between his legs. McCaleb had to hold himself back from kicking him in the rear. Instead he angrily slid the door closed and it banged loudly in its frame. He stood there looking out through the glass until he saw Lockridge make it all the way up the ramp and over to the facilities building where there was a coin laundry.

His eavesdropping had compromised the investigation. McCaleb knew he should page Winston immediately and tell her, see how she wanted to handle it. But he let it go. The truth was, he didn't want to make any move that might take him out of the investigation.

19

After putting his hand on the Bible and promising the whole truth, Harry Bosch took a seat in the witness chair and glanced up at the camera mounted on the wall above the jury box. The eye of the world was upon him, he knew. The trial was being broadcast live on *Court TV* and locally on Channel 9. He tried to give no appearance of nervousness. But the fact was that more than the jurors would be studying him and judging his performance and personality. It was the first time in many years of testifying in criminal trials that he did not feel totally at ease. Being on the side of the truth was not a comfort when he knew the truth had to run a treacherous obstacle course set before it by a wealthy, connected defendant and his wealthy, connected attorney.

He put the blue binder – the murder book – down on the front ledge of the witness box and pulled the microphone toward him, creating a high-pitched squeal that hurt every set of ears in the courtroom.

'Detective Bosch, please don't touch the microphone,' Judge Houghton intoned.

'Sorry, Your Honor.'

A deputy sheriff who acted as the judge's bailiff came over to the witness box, turned the microphone off and adjusted its location. When Bosch nodded at its new position, the bailiff turned it back on. The judge's clerk then asked Bosch to state his full, formal name and spell it for the record.

'Very well,' the judge said after Bosch finished. 'Ms. Langwiser?'

Deputy District Attorney Janis Langwiser got up from the prosecution table and went to the attorney's lectern. She carried a yellow legal tablet with her questions on it. She was second seat at the prosecution table but had worked with the investigators since the start of the case. It had been decided that she would handle Bosch's testimony.

Langwiser was a young up-and-coming lawyer in the DA's office. In the span of a few short years she had risen from a position of filing cases for more experienced lawyers in the office to handle to taking them all the way to court herself. Bosch had worked with her before on a politically sensitive and treacherous case known as the Angels Flight murders. The experience resulted in his recommendation of her as second chair to Kretzler. Since working with her again, Bosch had found his earlier impressions were well founded. She had complete command and recall of the facts of the case. While most other lawyers would have to sift through evidence reports to locate a piece of information, she would have the information and its location in the reports memorized. But her skill was not confined to the minutiae of the case. She never took her eye off the big picture – the fact that all their efforts were focused on putting David Storey away for good.

'Good afternoon, Detective Bosch,' she began. 'Could you please tell the jury a bit about your career as a police officer.'

Bosch cleared his throat.

'Yes. I've been with the Los Angeles Police Department twenty-eight years. I have spent more than half of that time investigating homicides. I am a detective three assigned to the homicide squad of the Hollywood Division.'

'What does "detective three" mean?'

'It means detective third grade. It is the highest detective rank, equivalent to sergeant, but there are no detective sergeants in the LAPD. From detective three the next rank up would be detective lieutenant.'

'How many homicides would you say you have investigated in your career?'

'I don't keep track. I would say at least a few hundred in fifteen years.'

'A few *hundred*.'

Langwiser looked over at the jury when she stressed the last word.

'Give or take a few.'

'And as a detective three you are currently a supervisor on the homicide squad?'

'I have some supervisory duties. I am also the lead officer on a three-person team that handles homicide investigations.'

'As such you were in charge of the team that was called to the scene of a homicide on October thirteenth of last year, correct?'

'That is correct.'

Bosch glanced over at the defense table. David Storey had his head down and was using his felt-tip pen to draw on the sketch pad. He'd been doing it since jury selection began. Bosch's eyes traveled to the defendant's attorney and locked on those of J. Reason Fowkkes. Bosch held the stare until Langwiser asked her next question.

'This was the murder of Donatella Speers?'

Bosch looked back over at Langwiser.

'Correct. That was the name she used.'

'It was not her real name?'

'It was her stage name, I guess you would call it. She was an actress. She changed her name. Her real name was Jody Krementz.'

The judge interrupted and asked Bosch to spell the names for the court reporter, then Langwiser continued.

'Tell us the circumstances of the call out. Walk us through it, Detective Bosch. Where were you, what were you doing, how did this become your case?'

Bosch cleared his throat and had reached to the microphone to pull it closer when he remembered what happened the last time. He left the microphone where it was and leaned forward to it.

'My two partners and I were eating lunch at a restaurant called Musso and Frank's on Hollywood Boulevard. It was Friday and we usually eat there if we have the time. At eleven forty-eight my pager went off. I recognized the number as belonging to my supervisor, Lieutenant Grace Billets. While I was calling her, the pagers of my partners, Jerry Edgar and Kizmin Rider, also went off. At that point we knew we had probably drawn a case. I got ahold of Lieutenant Billets and she directed my team to one-thousand-one Nichols Canyon Road, where patrol officers had earlier responded along with paramedics to an emergency call at that location. They reported a young woman was found dead in her bed under suspicious circumstances.'

'You then went to the address?'

'No. I had driven all three of us to Musso's. So I drove back to the Hollywood station, which is a few blocks away, and dropped off my partners so they could get their own vehicles. Then all three of us proceeded separately to the address. You never know where you might have to go from a crime scene. It's good procedure for each detective to have his or her own car.'

'At this time did you know who the victim was or what the suspicious circumstances of her death were?'

'No, I did not.'

'What did you find when you got there?'

'It was a small two-bedroom house overlooking the canyon. Two patrol cars were on the scene. The paramedics had already left once it was determined the victim was dead. Inside the house were two patrol officers and a patrol sergeant. In the living room there was a woman seated on the couch. She was crying. She was introduced to me as Jane Gilley. She shared the house with Ms. Krementz.'

Bosch stopped there and waited for a question. Langwiser was bent over the prosecution table whispering to her co-prosecutor, Roger Kretzler.

'Ms. Langwiser, does that conclude your questioning of Detective Bosch?' Judge Houghton asked.

Langwiser jerked upright, not having noticed that Bosch had stopped.

'No, Your Honor.'

She moved back to the lectern.

'Go on, Detective Bosch, tell us what happened after you entered the house.'

'I spoke to Sergeant Kim and he informed me that there was a young woman who was deceased in her bed in the bedroom to the right rear of the house. He introduced the woman on the couch and he said that his people had backed out of the bedroom without disturbing anything once the paramedics determined that the victim was dead. I then went down the short hallway to the bedroom and entered.'

'What did you find in there?'

'I saw the victim in the bed. She was a white female of slim build and blond hair. Her identification would later be confirmed as Jody Krementz, age twenty-three.'

Langwiser asked permission to show a set of photographs to Bosch. Houghton allowed it and Bosch identified the police evidence photos as being that of the victim in situ – as the body had been seen at first by police. The body was face up. The bedclothes were pulled to the side to reveal the body to be nude with the legs spread about two feet apart at the knees. The large breasts held their full shape despite the body being in a horizontal position, an indication of breast implants. The left arm was extended over the stomach. The palm of the left hand covered the pubic region. Two fingers of the left hand penetrated the vagina.

The victim's eyes were closed and her head rested on a pillow but at a sharp angle to her neck. Wrapped tightly around her neck was a yellow scarf with one end looped up and over the top crossbar of the bed's headboard. The end of the scarf came off the crossbar and extended to the victim's right hand on the pillow above her head. The end of the silk scarf was wrapped several times around the hand.

The photographs were in color. A purplish-red bruise could be seen on the victim's neck where the scarf had tightened against the skin. There was a rouge-like discoloration in and around the eye sockets. There was also a bluish discoloration running down the complete left side of the body, including the left arm and leg.

After Bosch identified the photographs as being of Jody Krementz in situ, Langwiser asked that they be shown to the jury. J. Reason Fowkkes objected, stating that the photos would be highly inflammatory and prejudicial for jurors to see. The judge overruled the objection but told Langwiser to choose just one photo which would be representative of the lot. Langwiser chose the photo taken closest to the victim and it was handed to a man who sat in the first seat of the jury. While the photo was slowly passed from juror to juror and then to the alternates, Bosch watched their faces tighten with shock and horror. He pushed back on his seat and drank from a paper cup of water. After he drained it he caught the eye of the sheriff's deputy and signaled for a refill. He then pulled himself back close to the microphone.

After the photo made its way through the jury, it was delivered to the clerk. It would be returned to the jurors, along with all other exhibits presented during the trial, during deliberation of a verdict.

Bosch watched Langwiser return to the lectern to continue the questioning. He knew she was nervous. They'd had lunch together in the basement cafeteria of the other court building and she had voiced her concerns. Though she was second seat to Kretzler, it was a big trial with potential career enhancing or destroying aspects for both of them.

She checked her legal pad before going on.

'Detective Bosch, did there come a time after you had inspected the body that you declared the death to be subject to a homicide investigation?'

'Right away – before my partners even got there.'

'Why is that? Did it not appear to be an accidental death?'

'No, it—'

'Ms. Langwiser,' Judge Houghton interrupted. 'One question at a time, please.'

'Sorry, Your Honor. Detective, did it not appear to you that the woman may have accidentally killed herself?'

'No, it did not. It appeared to me that someone attempted to make it look that way.'

Langwiser looked down at her pad for a long moment before going on. Bosch was pretty sure the pause was planned, now that the photograph and his testimony had secured the full attention of the jury.

'Detective, are you familiar with the term autoerotic asphyxia?'

'Yes, I am.'

'Could you please explain it to the jury?'

Fowkkes stood up and objected.

'Y'Honor, Detective Bosch may be a lot of things but there has been no proffer made to the court that he is an expert in human sexuality.'

There was a murmur of quiet laughter in the courtroom. Bosch saw a couple of the jurors suppress smiles. Houghton hit his gavel once and looked at Langwiser.

'What about that, Ms. Langwiser?'

'Your Honor, I can make a proffer.'

'Proceed.'

'Detective Bosch, you said you have worked hundreds of homicides. Have you investigated deaths that turned out not to be caused by homicide?'

'Yes, probably hundreds of those as well. Accidental deaths, suicides, even deaths by natural causes. It is routine for a homicide detective to be called out to a death scene by patrol officers to help in making a determination as to whether a death should be investigated as a homicide. This is what happened in this case. The patrol officers and their sergeant weren't sure what they had. They called it in as suspicious and my team got the call out.'

'Have you ever been called out or investigated a death that was ruled, either by you or the medical examiner's office, an accidental death by autoerotic asphyxia?'

'Yes.'

Fowkkes stood up again.

'Same objection, Y'Honor. This is leading to an area where Detective Bosch is not an expert.'

'Your Honor,' Langwiser said. 'It has clearly been established that Detective Bosch is an expert in the investigation of death – that would include all kinds. He has seen this before. He can testify to it.'

There was a note of exasperation in her voice. Bosch thought it was intended for the jury, not Houghton. It was a subliminal way of communicating to the twelve that she wanted to get at the truth, while others wanted to block the way.

'I tend to agree, Mr. Fowkkes,' Houghton said after a slight pause. 'Objections to this line of questioning are overruled. Proceed, Ms. Langwiser.'

'Thank you, Your Honor. So then, Detective Bosch, you are familiar with cases of autoerotic asphyxia?'

'Yes, I have worked on three or four. I have also studied the literature on the subject. It is referenced in books on homicide investigation techniques. I have also read summaries of in-depth studies conducted by the FBI and others.'

'Was this before this case occurred?'

'Yes, before.'

'What is autoerotic asphyxia? How does it occur?'

'Ms. Langwiser,' the judge began.

'Sorry, Your Honor. Restating. What is autoerotic asphyxia, Detective Bosch?'

Bosch took a drink of water, using the time to draw his thoughts together. They had gone over these questions during lunch.

'It is an accidental death. It occurs when the victim attempts to increase sexual sensations during masturbation by cutting off or disrupting the flow of arterial blood to the brain. This is usually done with a form of ligature around the neck. The tightening of the ligature results in hypoxia – the diminishing of oxygenation of the brain. It is believed by people who . . . uh, practice this that hypoxia – the light-headedness that ensues – heightens masturbatory sensations. However, it can lead to accidental death if the victim goes too far, to the point where he damages the carotid arteries and/or passes out with the ligature still tightly in place and asphyxiates.'

'You said "he," Detective. But in this case the victim is a woman.'

'This case does not involve autoerotic asphyxia. The cases I have seen and investigated involving this form of death all involved male victims.'

'Are you saying that in this case the death was made to look like autoerotic asphyxia?'

'Yes, that was my immediate conclusion. It remains so today.'

Langwiser nodded and paused. Bosch sipped some water. As he brought the cup up to his mouth he glanced at the jury. Everyone in the box seemed to be paying close attention.

'Walk us through it, Detective. What led you to that conclusion?'

'Can I refer to my reports?'

'Please.'

Bosch opened the binder in front of him. The first four pages were the OIR – the original incident report. He turned to the fourth page, which included the lead officer's summary. The report had actually been typed out by Kiz Rider, though Bosch was the LO on the case. He quickly scanned the summary to refresh his mind, then looked up at the jury.

'Several things contradicted the death being an accident caused by autoerotic asphyxia. First off, I was immediately concerned because statistically it is rare that this occurs with female victims. It is not one hundred percent males but it is close. This knowledge made me pay very close attention to the body and the crime scene.'

'Would it be fair to say you were immediately skeptical of the crime scene?'

'Yes, that would be fair.'

'Okay, go on. What else concerned you?'

'The ligature. In almost all cases involving this that I have been aware of firsthand or through the literature on the subject, the victim uses some sort of padding around the neck to prevent bruising or breaking of the skin. Most often a piece of heavy clothing like a sweater or a towel is wrapped around the neck. The ligature is then wrapped around this padding. It prevents the ligature from making a contusion line running around the neck. In this case there was no padding.'

'And what did that mean to you?'

'Well, it didn't make sense if you looked at it from the victim's viewpoint. I mean, if you were to assume that she had engaged in this activity, then the scene didn't make sense. It would mean that she didn't use any kind of padding because she didn't mind having the bruises on her neck. This to me was a contradiction between what we had there at the scene and common sense. Add in that she was an actress – which I knew right away because she had a stack of head shots on the bureau – and the contradiction was even greater. She relied on her physical presence and attributes while seeking acting work. That she would knowingly engage in an activity, sexual or otherwise, that would leave visible bruises on her neck – I just didn't buy it. That and other things led me to conclude the scene was a setup.'

Bosch looked over at the defense table. Storey still had his head down and was working on the sketch pad as though he were sitting on a bench in a park somewhere. Bosch noticed Fowkkes was writing on a legal tablet. Harry wondered if he had said something in his last answer that could somehow be turned against him. He knew Fowkkes was an expert in taking phrases of testimony and giving them new meaning when taken out of context.

'What other things added to this conclusion?' Langwiser asked him.

Bosch looked at the OIR summary page again.

'The biggest single thing was the indication from postmortem lividity that the body had been moved.'

'In layman's terms, Detective, what does postmortem lividity mean?'

'When the heart ceases to pump blood through the body, the blood then settles in the lower half of the body, depending on the position of the body. Over time it creates a bruising effect on the skin. If the body is moved, the bruising remains in the original position because the blood has coagulated. Over time the bruising becomes more apparent.'

'What happened in this case?'

'In this case there was clear indication that the blood had settled in the left side of the body, meaning the victim's body had been lying on the left side at or shortly after the time of death.'

'However, that was not the way the body was found, correct?'

'That is correct. The body was found in the supine position – lying on the back.'

'What did you conclude from this?'

'That the body had been moved after death. That the woman had been positioned on her back as part of the setup to make her death look like an autoerotic asphyxiation.'

'What did you think was the cause of death?'

'At that point I wasn't sure. I just didn't think it was as presented. The bruising on the neck beneath the ligature led me to believe we were looking at a strangulation – just not at her own hands.'

'At what point did your partners arrive on the scene?'

'While I was making the initial observations of the body and crime scene.'

'Did they come to the same conclusions as you?'

Fowkkes objected, saying the question called for an answer that would be hearsay. The judge sustained the objection. Bosch knew it was a minor point. If Langwiser wanted the conclusions of Edgar and Rider on the record, she could just call them to testify.

'Did you attend the autopsy of Jody Krementz's body?'

'Yes, I did.' He flipped through the binder until he found the autopsy protocol. 'On October seventeenth. It was conducted by Dr. Teresa Corazón, chief of the medical examiner's office.'

'Was a cause of death determined by Dr. Corazón during autopsy?'

'Yes, the cause of death was asphyxiation. She was strangled.'

'By ligature?'

'Yes.'

'Now doesn't this contradict your theory that the death was not caused by autoerotic asphyxiation?'

'No, it confirmed it. The pose of autoerotic asphyxiation was used to cover the strangulation murder of the victim. The interior damage to both carotid arteries, to the muscular tissue of the neck and the hyoid bone, which was crushed, led Dr. Corazón to confirm that death was at the hand of another. The damage was too great to be knowingly self-inflicted.'

Bosch realized he was holding a hand to his neck as he described the injuries. He dropped it back down to his lap.

'Did the medical examiner find any independent evidence of homicide?'

He nodded.

'Yes, examination of the victim's mouth determined that there was a deep laceration caused by biting on the tongue. Such injury is common in cases of strangulation.'

Langwiser flipped a page over on her tablet.

'Okay, Detective Bosch, let's go back to the crime scene. Did you or your partners interview Jane Gilley?'

'Yes, I did. Along with Detective Rider.'

'From that interview were you able to ascertain where the victim had been in the twenty-four hours prior to the discovery of her death?'

'Yes, we first determined that she had met the defendant several days earlier at a coffee shop. He invited her to attend a premiere of a movie as his date on the night of October twelfth at the Chinese Theater in Hollywood. He picked her up between seven and seven-thirty that night. Ms. Gilley watched from a window in the house and identified the defendant.'

'Did Ms. Gilley know when Ms. Krementz returned that night?'

'No. Ms. Gilley left the house shortly after Ms. Krementz went on her date and spent the night elsewhere. Consequently, she did not know when her roommate returned home. It was when Ms. Gilley returned to the house at eleven A.M. on October thirteenth that she discovered Ms. Krementz's body.'

'What was the name of the movie which was premiered the night before?'

'It was called *Dead Point.*'

'And who directed it?'

'David Storey.'

Langwiser waited through a long pause before looking at her watch and then up at the judge.

'Your Honor,' she said, 'I am going to move into a new line of questioning now with Detective Bosch. If appropriate, this might be the best time to break for the day.'

Houghton pulled back the baggy black sleeve of his robe and looked at his watch. Bosch looked at his. It was a quarter to four.

'Okay, Ms. Langwiser, we'll adjourn until nine o'clock tomorrow morning.'

Houghton told Bosch he could step down from the witness stand. He then admonished the jurors not to read newspaper accounts or watch TV reports on the trial. Everyone stood as the jurors filed out. Bosch, who was now standing next to Langwiser at the prosecution table, glanced over at the defense side. David Storey was looking at him. His face betrayed no emotion at all. But Bosch thought he saw something in his pale blue eyes. He wasn't sure but he thought it was mirth.

Bosch was the first to look away.

20

After the courtroom emptied, Bosch conferred with Langwiser and Kretzler about their missing witness.

'Anything yet?' Kretzler asked. 'Depending on how long John Reason keeps you up there, we're going to need her tomorrow afternoon or the next morning.'

'Nothing yet,' Bosch said. 'But I've got something in the works. In fact, I better get going.'

'I don't like this,' Kretzler said. 'This could blow up. If she's not coming in, there's a reason. I've never been a hundred percent on her story.'

'Storey could have gotten to her,' Bosch offered.

'We need her,' Langwiser said. 'It shows pattern. You have to find her.'

'I'm on it.'

He got up from the table to leave.

'Good luck, Harry,' Langwiser said. 'And, by the way, so far I think you're doing very well up there.'

Bosch nodded.

'The calm before the storm.'

On his way down the hall to the elevators Bosch was approached by one of the reporters. He didn't know his name but he recognized him from the press seats in the courtroom.

'Detective Bosch?'

Bosch kept walking.

'Look, I've told everybody, I'm not commenting until the trial is over. I'm sorry. You'll have to get—'

'No, that's okay. I just wanted to see if you hooked up with Terry McCaleb.'

Bosch stopped and looked at the reporter.

'What do you mean?'

'Yesterday. He was looking for you here.'

'Oh, yeah, I saw him. You know Terry?'

'Yeah, I wrote a book a few years ago about the bureau. I met him then. Before he got the transplant.'

Bosch nodded and was about to move on when the reporter put out his hand.

'Jack McEvoy.'

Bosch reluctantly shook his hand. He recognized the name. Five years earlier the bureau had tracked a serial cop killer to L.A., where it was believed he was about to strike his next victim – a Hollywood homicide detective named Ed Thomas. The bureau had used information from McEvoy, a reporter for the *Rocky Mountain News* in Denver, to track the so-called Poet and Thomas's life was never threatened. He was retired from the force now and running a bookshop down in Orange County.

'Hey, I remember you,' Bosch said. 'Ed Thomas is a friend of mine.'

Both men appraised each other.

'You're covering this thing?' Bosch asked, an obvious question.

'Yeah. For the *New Times* and *Vanity Fair*. I'm thinking about a book, too. So when it's all over, maybe we can talk.'

'Yeah, maybe.'

'Unless you're doing something with Terry on it.'

'With Terry? No, that was something else yesterday. No book.'

'Okay, then keep me in mind.'

McEvoy dug into his pocket for his wallet and then removed a business card.

'I mostly work out of my home in Laurel Canyon. Feel free to give me a call if you want.'

Bosch held the card up.

'Okay. I gotta go. See you around, I guess.'

'Yeah.'

Bosch walked over and pushed the button for an elevator. He looked at the card again while he waited and thought about Ed Thomas. He then put the card into the pocket of his suit jacket.

Before the elevator came he looked down the hallway and saw McEvoy was still in the hallway, now talking to Rudy Tafero, the defense's investigator. Tafero was a big man and he was leaning forward, close to McEvoy, as if it was some sort of conspiratorial rendezvous. McEvoy was writing in a notebook.

The elevator opened and Bosch stepped on. He watched them until the doors closed.

Bosch took Laurel Canyon Boulevard over the hill and dropped down into Hollywood ahead of the evening traffic. At Sunset he took a right and pulled to the curb a few blocks into West Hollywood. He fed the meter and went into the small, drab white office building across Sunset from a strip bar. The two-story courtyard building catered to small production companies. They were small offices with small overheads. The companies lived from movie to movie. In between there was no need for opulent offices and space.

Bosch checked his watch and saw that he was right on time. It was quarter to five and the audition was set for five. He took the stairs up to the second floor and went through a door with a sign saying NUFF SAID PRODUCTIONS. It was a three-room suite, one of the biggest in the building. Bosch had been there before and knew the layout: a waiting room with a secretary's desk, the office of Bosch's friend, Albert 'Nuff' Said, and then a conference room. A woman behind the secretary's desk looked up at Bosch as he stepped in.

'I'm here to see Mr. Said. My name's Harry Bosch.'

She nodded and picked up the phone and punched a number. Bosch could hear it beep in the other room and recognized Said's voice answering.

'It's Harry Bosch,' the secretary said.

Bosch heard Said order her to send him in. He headed that way before she was off the phone.

'Go on in,' she said to his back.

Bosch stepped into an office that was furnished simply with a desk, two chairs, a black leather couch and a television/video console. The walls were crowded with framed one-sheet posters advertising Said's movies and other mementos, such as the back panels of the producers' chairs with the names of the movies printed on them. Bosch had known Said at least fifteen years, ever since the older man had hired him as a technical adviser on a movie thinly based on one of Bosch's cases. They had kept in touch sporadically over the ensuing decade, Said usually calling Bosch when he had a technical question about a police procedure he was using in a movie. Most of Said's productions were never seen on the silver screen. They were television and cable movies.

Albert Said stood up behind the desk and Bosch extended his hand.

'Hey, Nuff, howzit going?'

'Going fine, my friend.'

He pointed to the television.

'I watched your fine performance on *Court TV* today. Bravo.'

He politely clapped his hands. Bosch waved the demonstration off and looked at his watch again.

'Thanks. So are we all set here?'

'I believe so. Marjorie will have her wait for me in the conference room. You can take it from there.'

'I appreciate this, Nuff. Let me know what I can do to square it.'

'You can be in my next movie. You have a real presence, my friend. I watched the whole thing today. I taped it if you would like to see for yourself.'

'No, I don't think so. I don't think we'll have the time anyway. What have you got going these days?'

'Oh, you know, waiting for the light to turn green. I have a project I think is about to go with overseas financing. It is about this cop who gets sent to prison and the trauma of being stripped of his badge and his respect and everything gives him amnesia. And so there he is in prison and he can't remember which guys he put there and which ones he didn't. He's in a constant fight to survive. The one convict who befriends him turns out to be a serial killer he sent there in the first place. It's a thriller, Harry. What do you think? Steven Segal is reading the script.'

Said's bushy black eyebrows were arched into sharp points on his forehead. He was clearly excited by the premise of the movie.

'I don't know, Nuff,' Bosch said. 'I think it's been done before.'

'Everything's been done before. But what do you think?'

Bosch was saved by the bell. In the silence after Said's question they both could hear the secretary talking to someone in the next room. Then the speakerphone on Said's desk beeped and the secretary said, 'Ms. Crowe is here. She will be waiting in the conference room.'

Bosch nodded at Said.

'Thanks, Nuff,' he whispered. 'I'll take it from here.'

'Are you sure?'

'I'll let you know if I need any help.'

He turned to the office door but then went back to the desk and put out his hand.

'I may have to split kind of fast. So I'll say good-bye. Good luck with that project. Sounds like another winner.'

They shook hands.

'Yes, we shall see,' Said said.

Bosch left the office and crossed a small hallway and entered the conference room. There was a square, glass-topped table at center with a chair on each side. Annabelle Crowe sat in the chair on the side opposite the door. She was studying a black-and-white photograph of herself as Bosch entered. She looked up with a bright smile and perfect teeth. The smile held for a little longer than a second and then crashed off her face like a Malibu mudslide.

'What – what are you doing here?'

'Hello, Annabelle, how've you been?'

'This is an audition – you can't just—'

'You're right, this is an audition. I am auditioning you for the role of witness in a murder trial.'

The woman stood up. Her head shot and a résumé slipped off the table to the floor.

'You can't just – what is going on here?'

'You know what is going on. You moved and left no forwarding. Your parents wouldn't help. Your agent wouldn't help me. The only way I could get to you was to set up an audition. Now sit down and we're going to talk about where you've been and why you're ducking the trial.'

'So there is no part?'

Bosch almost laughed. She still didn't get it.

'No, no part.'

'And they're not remaking *Chinatown?*'

This time he did laugh but quickly covered.

'One of these days they'll get around to it. But you're too young for the part and I'm no Jake Gittes. Sit down, please.'

Bosch started to pull out the chair opposite hers. But she refused to sit down. She looked very put out. She was a beautiful young woman with a face that often got her what she wanted. But not this time.

'I said sit down,' Bosch said sternly. 'You have to understand something here, Miss Crowe. You broke the law when you did not respond to a court-issued subpoena to appear today. That means if I want, I can just place you under arrest and we can talk about this in lockup. Or the alternative is that we sit down here because they're letting us use the nice room and talk about this in a civilized manner. Your choice, Annabelle.'

She dropped back into her chair. Her mouth was a thin, tight line. The lipstick she had carefully painted on for a casting session was already starting to crack and wear. Bosch studied her for a long moment before beginning.

'Who got to you, Annabelle?'

She looked at him sharply.

'Look,' she said, 'I was scared, okay? I still am. David Storey is a powerful man. He has some scary people behind him.'

Bosch leaned across the table.

'Are you saying you were threatened by him? By them?'

'No, I am not saying that. They didn't need to threaten me. I know the picture.'

Bosch leaned back away from her and quietly studied her. Her eyes moved everywhere around the room but to him. The traffic noise from out on Sunset filtered through the room's one closed window. Somewhere in the building a toilet was flushed. Finally, she looked at Bosch.

'What? What do you want?'

'I want you to testify. I want you to make a stand against this guy. For what he tried to do to you. For Jody Krementz. And Alicia Lopez.'

'Who is Alicia Lopez?'

'Another one we found. She wasn't lucky like you.'

Bosch could read the turmoil on her face. She clearly viewed testifying as some sort of danger.

'If I testify I'll never work again. And maybe worse.'

'Who told you that?'

She didn't answer.

'Come on, who? Did that come from them, your agent, who?'

She hesitated and then shook her head as if she couldn't believe she was talking to him.

'I was working out at Crunch and I was on a Stairmaster and this guy got on the machine next to me. He was reading the newspaper. It was folded to the story he was reading. And I was minding my own business when suddenly he just started talking. He never looked at me. He just talked while he was looking down at the newspaper. He said the story he was reading was about the David Storey trial and how he'd hate to be a witness who went against him. He said that person would never work in this town again.'

She stopped but Bosch waited. He studied her. Her anguish in recounting the story seemed genuine. She was on the verge of tears.

'And I . . . I got so panicked with him right there next to me I just got off the machine and ran into the locker room. I stayed in there for an hour and even then I was scared that he might still be out there waiting for me. Watching me.'

She started crying. Bosch got up and left the room and looked into the bathroom in the hallway. There was a box of tissues. He took it back with him to the conference room and handed it to Annabelle Crowe. He sat back down.

'Where is Crunch?'

'Just down the street from here. Sunset and Crescent Heights.'

Bosch nodded. He knew where it was now. The same shopping and entertainment complex where Jody Krementz had met David Storey in a coffee shop. He wondered if there was a connection. Maybe Storey belonged to Crunch. Maybe he got a workout pal to threaten Annabelle Crowe.

'Did you get a look at the guy?'

'Yes, but it doesn't matter. I don't know who he was. I never saw him before or since.'

Bosch thought about Rudy Tafero.

'Do you know who the defense team's investigator is? A guy named Rudy Tafero? He's tall, black hair and a nice tan. Good-looking guy?'

'I don't know who that is but he's not the man who was there that day. This man was short and bald. He had glasses.'

The description didn't register with Bosch. He decided to let it go for the time being. He'd have to let Langwiser and Kretzler know about the threat. They might want to take it to Judge Houghton. They might want to have Bosch go to Crunch and start asking questions, see if he could confirm anything.

'So what are you going to do?' she asked. 'Are you going to make me testify?'

'It's not up to me. The prosecutors will decide after I tell them your story.'

'Do you believe it?'

Bosch hesitated and then nodded.

'You still have to show up. You're under subpoena. Be there between twelve and one tomorrow and they'll let you know what they want to do.'

Bosch knew that they would make her testify. They wouldn't care if the threat was real or not. They had the case to worry about. Annabelle Crowe would be sacrificed to get David Storey. A small fish to get a big fish, the name of the game.

Bosch made her empty her purse. He looked through her things and found an address and phone number written down. It was a temp apartment in Burbank. She admitted that she had put her belongings in storage and was living in the temp, waiting for the trial to be over.

'I'm going to give you a break, Annabelle, and not hold you in lockup overnight. But I found you this time and I can find you again. You don't show up tomorrow and I'll come looking for you. And you'll go right to lockup at Sybil Brand, you understand that?'

She nodded her head.

'You going to be there?'

She nodded again.

'I should've never come to you people.'

Bosch nodded. She was right.

'It's too late for that,' he said. 'You did the right thing. Now you have to live with it. That's the funny thing about the courts. You decide to be brave and stick your neck out and they don't let you back down from it.'

21

Art Pepper was on the stereo and Bosch was on the telephone with Janis Langwiser when there was a knock on his screen door. He stepped into the hallway from the kitchen and saw a figure looking in through the mesh. Annoyed by the intrusion of a solicitor, he walked to the door and was about to simply close it without a word when he recognized the visitor as Terry McCaleb. Still on the phone and listening to Langwiser fume about possible witness tampering, he flicked on the outside light, opened the screen door and signaled McCaleb in.

McCaleb made a signal that he would be quiet until Bosch was off the call. Bosch watched him walk through the living room and step out onto the rear deck to look down at the lights of the Cahuenga Pass. He tried to concentrate on what Langwiser was saying but he was curious as to why McCaleb would drive all the way up into the hills to see him.

'Harry, are you listening?'

'Yeah. What was that last part?'

'I said do you think Shootin' Houghton will delay the trial if we open up an investigation.'

Bosch didn't have to think long to answer that.

'No way. The show must go on.'

'Yeah, that's what I figure. I'm going to call Roger and see what he wants to do. Anyway, it's the least of our worries. As soon as you mention Alicia Lopez on the stand there's going to be a brutal fight.'

'I thought we already won that. Houghton ruled—'

'It doesn't mean Fowkkes won't try a new attack. We're not clear yet.'

There was a pause. There had not been much confidence in her voice.

'I guess I'll see you tomorrow, Harry.'

'All right, Janis, I'll see you.'

Bosch clicked the phone off and put it back in its cradle in the kitchen. When he stepped back out McCaleb was standing in the living room, looking at the shelves over the stereo, at a framed photograph of Bosch's wife in particular.

'Terry, what's up?'

'Hey, Harry, sorry to drop in unannounced like this. I didn't have your home number to call first.'

'How'd you find the place? You want a beer or something?'

Bosch pointed to his chest.

'Can you have a beer?'

'I can now. Just got clearance, in fact. I can drink again. In moderation. A beer sounds good.'

Bosch went into the kitchen. McCaleb continued talking from the living room.

'I've been here before. You don't remember?'

Bosch came out with two open bottles of Anchor Steam. He handed one to McCaleb.

'You need a glass? When were you here?'

McCaleb took the bottle.

'Cielo Azul.'

He took a long pull from the bottle, answering Bosch's question about the glass.

Cielo Azul, Bosch thought and then he remembered. They had gotten drunk on the back porch once, both of them dulling the edges of a case that was too terrible to think deeply about with a sober mind. He remembered being embarrassed about it the next day, about how he had lost control and kept rhetorically asking in an alcohol-slowed voice, 'Where is God's hand, where is God's hand?'

'Oh, yeah,' Bosch said. 'One of my finer existential moments.'

'Yeah. Except the place is different now. The old one slide down the hill in the quake?'

'Just about. Red-tagged, the whole bit. Started over from the ground up.'

'Yeah, I didn't recognize it. I drove up here looking for the old place. But then I saw the Shamu and figured there couldn't be another cop in the neighborhood.'

Bosch thought about the black-and-white parked in the carport. He hadn't bothered to take it to the station to exchange for his personal car. It would save him time in the morning by allowing him to drive straight to court. The car was a slickback – a black-and-white without the emergency lights on top. Detectives from the divisions used them as part of a program designed to make it look as if there were more cops on the street than there really were.

McCaleb reached over and clicked Bosch's bottle with his own.

'To Cielo Azul,' he said.

'Yeah,' Bosch said.

He drank from the bottle. It was ice cold and good. His first beer since the start of the trial. He decided he would keep it to one, even if McCaleb pressed on.

'This your ex?' McCaleb asked, pointing to the photo on the shelves.

'My wife. Not my ex, yet – at least as far as I know. But I guess it's heading that way.'

Bosch stared at the photo of Eleanor Wish. It was the only picture of her he had.

'That's too bad, man.'

'Yeah. So what's up, Terry? I've got some stuff I have to go over for—'

'I know, the trial. I'm sorry to intrude, man. I know that's gotta be all-consuming. I just had a couple things on the Gunn case I wanted to clear up. But also I wanted to tell you something. I mean, show you, too.'

He pulled his wallet out of his back pocket, opened it and took out a photo. He handed it to Bosch. The photo had taken on the contour line of the wallet. It showed a dark-haired baby in the arms of a dark-haired woman.

'That's my daughter, Harry. And my wife.'

Bosch nodded and studied the photo. Both mother and child had dark hair and skin and were quite beautiful. He knew they were probably even more so to McCaleb.

'Beautiful,' he said. 'The baby looks brand new. So tiny.'

'She's about four months now. That picture's a month old, though. Anyway, I forgot to tell you yesterday at lunch. We named her Cielo Azul.'

Bosch's eyes came up from the photo to McCaleb's. They held for a moment and then he nodded.

'Nice.'

'Yeah, I told Graciela I wanted to do it and I told her why. She thought it was a good idea.'

Bosch handed the photo back.

'I hope someday the kid does, too.'

'Me, too. We call her CiCi most of the time. Anyway, remember that night up here, how you kept asking that question about the hand of God and how you couldn't find it in anything anymore? That happened to me, too. I lost it. This kind of job . . . it's hard not to. Then . . .'

He held up the photo.

'Here it is right here. I found it again. The hand of God. I see it in her eyes.'

Bosch looked at him for a long moment and then nodded.

'Good for you, Terry.'

'I mean, I'm not trying to come off like . . . I mean I'm not trying to convert you or anything. I'm just saying I found that thing that was missing. And I don't know if you're still looking for it . . . I just wanted to say, you know, that it is out there. Don't give up.'

Bosch glanced away from McCaleb and out the glass doors to the darkness.

'For some people I'm sure it is.'

He drained his bottle and went into the kitchen to break his promise to himself to have only one. He called back to McCaleb to see if he was ready for a second but his visitor passed. As he bent into the open refrigerator he paused and closed his eyes as the cool air caressed his face. He thought about what McCaleb had just told him.

'You don't think you are one of them?'

Bosch jerked up at the sound of McCaleb's voice. He was standing in the kitchen's doorway.

'What?'

'You said it was out there for some people. You don't think you are one of them?'

Bosch took a beer out of the refrigerator and slid it into the bottle opener mounted on the wall. He snapped the bottle open and drank deeply from it before answering.

'What is this, Terry, twenty questions? You thinking of becoming a priest or something?'

McCaleb smiled and shook his head.

'Sorry, Harry. A new father, you know? I guess I want to tell the world, that's all.'

'That's nice. You want to talk about Gunn now?'

'Sure.'

'Let's go out and look at the night.'

They walked out to the back deck and both looked at the view. The 101 was its usual ribbon of light, a glowing vein cutting through the mountains. The sky was clear, the smog having been washed out by rain the week before. Bosch could see the lights on the floor of the Valley seemingly extending into infinity. Closer to the house there was only darkness held in the brush on the hillside below. He could smell the eucalyptus from below; it was always strongest after the rain.

McCaleb was the first to speak.

'You've got a nice place here, Harry. A nice spot. You must hate having to ride down into the plague every morning.'

Bosch looked over at him.

'Not as long as I get a shot at the carriers every now and then. People like David Storey. I don't mind that.'

'And what about the ones who walk away? Like Gunn.'

'Nobody walks away, Terry. If I believed that they did, then I couldn't do this. Sure we might not get every one of them, but I believe in the circle. The big wheel. What goes around comes around. Eventually. I might not see the hand of God too often like you do but I believe in that.'

Bosch put his bottle down on the railing. It was empty and he wanted another but knew he had to put on the brakes. He'd need every brain cell he could muster in court the next day. He thought about a cigarette and knew there was a fresh pack in a kitchen cabinet. But he decided to hold off on that, too.

'Then I guess what happened with Gunn must be a confirmation of your faith in the big wheel theory.'

Bosch didn't say anything for a long time. He just stared out across the valley of light.

'Yeah,' he finally said. 'I guess it does.'

He broke his stare away and turned his back on the view. He leaned against the railing and looked at McCaleb again.

'So what about Gunn? I thought I told you everything there was to tell yesterday. You've got the file, right?'

McCaleb nodded.

'You probably did and I do have the file. But I was just wondering if anything else came up. You know, if maybe our conversation jump-started your thinking on it.'

Bosch sort of laughed and picked up the bottle before remembering it was empty.

'Terry, come on, man, I'm in the middle of a trial. I'm on the stand, I've been chasing down an AWOL wit. I mean I stopped thinking about your investigation the minute I got up from the table at Cupid's. What exactly do you want from me?'

'Nothing, Harry. I don't want anything from you that you don't have. I just thought it might be worth a shot, is all. I'm working on this thing and scratching around for anything. I thought maybe . . . don't worry about it.'

'You're a weird guy, McCaleb. I'm remembering that now. The way you used to stare at crime scene photos. You want another beer?'

'Yeah, why not?'

Bosch pushed off the railing and reached over for his bottle and then McCaleb's. It was still at least a third full. He put it back down.

'Well, finish that.'

He went into the house and got two more beers out of the refrigerator. This time McCaleb was standing in the living room when he came back from the kitchen. He handed Bosch his empty bottle and Bosch wondered for a moment if he had finished it or poured the beer over the side of the deck. He took the empty into the kitchen and when he came back McCaleb was standing at the stereo studying a CD case.

'This what's playing?' he asked. 'Art Pepper meets the Rhythm Section?'

Bosch stepped over.

'Yeah. Art Pepper and Miles's side men. Red Garland on piano, Paul Chambers on bass, Philly Joe Jones on drums. Recorded here in L.A., January 19, 1957. One day. The cork in the neck of Pepper's sax was supposedly cracked but it didn't matter. He had one shot with these guys. He made the most of it. One day, one shot, one classic. That's the way to do it.'

'These guys were in Miles Davis's band?'

'At the time.'

McCaleb nodded. Bosch leaned close to look at the CD cover in McCaleb's hands.

'Yeah, Art Pepper,' he said. 'When I was growing up I never knew who my father was. My mother, she used to have a lot of this guy's records. She hung out at some of the jazz clubs where he'd play. Handsome devil, Art was. For a hype. Just look at that picture. Too cool to fool. I made up this whole story about how he was my old man and he wasn't around 'cause he was always on the road and making records. Almost got to the point I believed it. Later on – I mean years later – I read a book about him. It said he was junk sick when they took that picture. He puked as soon as it was over and went back to bed.'

McCaleb studied the photograph on the CD. A handsome man leaning against a tree, his sax cradled in his right arm.

'Well, he could play,' McCaleb said.

'Yeah, he could,' Bosch agreed. 'Genius with a needle in his arm.'

Bosch stepped over and turned the volume up slightly. The song was 'Straight Life,' Pepper's signature composition.

'Do you believe that?' McCaleb asked.

'What, that he was a genius? Yeah, he was with the sax.'

'No, I mean do you think that every genius – musician, artist, even a detective – has a fatal flaw like that? The needle in the arm.'

'I think everybody's got a fatal flaw, whether they're a genius or not.'

Bosch turned it up louder. McCaleb put his beer down on top of one of the floor speakers. Bosch picked it up and handed it back. He used his palm to wipe the wet ring off the wood surface. McCaleb turned the music down.

'Come on, Harry, give me something.'

'What are you talking about?'

'I made the journey up here. Give me something on Gunn. I know you don't care about him – the wheel turned and he didn't walk away. But I don't like the way this one looked. This guy – whoever he is – is still out there. And he's going to do this again. I can tell.'

Bosch shrugged his shoulders like he still didn't care.

'All right, here's something. It's thin but it might be worth a try. When he was in the tank the night before he got put down and I checked in on him, I also talked with the Metro guys who brought him in on the duice. They said they asked him where he'd been drinking and he said he'd come out of a place called Nat's. It's on the Boulevard about a block from Musso's and on the south side.'

'Okay, I can find it,' McCaleb said, a what-about-it tone in his voice. 'What's the connection?'

'Well, see, Nat's was the same place he'd been drinking that night six years ago that I first made his acquaintance. It's where he picked up that woman, the one he killed.'

'So he was a regular.'
'Looks it.'
'Thanks, Harry. I'll check it out. How come you didn't tell this to Jaye Winston?'
Bosch shrugged his shoulders.
'I guess I didn't think about it and she didn't ask.'
McCaleb almost put his beer down on the speaker again but instead handed it to Bosch.
'I might go check down there tonight.'
'Don't forget.'
'Forget what?'
'You hook the guy who did it, you shake his hand for me.'
McCaleb didn't respond. He looked around the place as if he had just walked in.
'Can I use the bathroom?'
'Down the hall on the left.'
McCaleb headed that way while Bosch took the bottles into the kitchen and put them in the recycle bin with the others. He opened the refrigerator and saw he was down to one soldier left in the six-pack he'd bought on the way home from tricking Annabelle Crowe. He closed the refrigerator when McCaleb stepped into the room.
'That's a crazy fucking picture you got hanging in the hallway,' he said.
'What? Oh, yeah. I like that picture.'
'What's it supposed to mean?'
'I don't know. I guess it means the big wheel keeps turning. Nobody walks away.'
McCaleb nodded.
'I suppose.'
'You heading down there to Nat's?'
'Thinking about it. You want to go?'
Bosch considered it even though he knew it would be foolish. He had to review half of the murder book in preparation for his continuing testimony the next morning.
'Nah, I better do some work here. Get ready for tomorrow.'
'Okay. How'd it go today, anyway?'
'So far so good. But we're playing softball right now – direct. Tomorrow the ball goes to John Reason and he throws it back inside and fast.'
'I'll watch the news.'
McCaleb stepped over and stuck his hand out. Bosch shook it.
'Be careful out there.'
'You, too, Harry. Thanks for the beers.'
'No problem.'
He walked McCaleb to the door and then watched him get into a black

Cherokee parked on the street. It started up immediately and pulled away, leaving Bosch standing in the lighted doorway.

Bosch locked up and turned off the living-room lights. He left the stereo on. It would automatically turn off at the end of Art Pepper's classic moment in time. It was early but Bosch was tired from the pressures of the day and the alcohol moving in his blood. He decided he would sleep now and wake up early to prepare for his testimony. He went into the kitchen and got the last bottle of beer out of the refrigerator.

On the way down the hall to his bedroom he stopped and looked at the framed picture McCaleb had referred to. It was a print of the Hieronymus Bosch painting called *The Garden of Earthly Delights.* He'd had it for a long time, since he was a kid. The surface of the print was warped and scratched. It was in bad shape. It had been Eleanor who moved it from the living room to the hallway. She didn't like it being in the place where they sat every night. Bosch never understood whether that was because of what was in the painting or because the print was old and deteriorated.

As he looked at the landscape of human debauchery and torment depicted in the painting, Bosch thought about maybe moving it back to its spot in the living room.

In Bosch's dream he was moving through dark water, unable to see his hands in front of his own face. There was a ringing sound and he pushed upward through the darkness.

He came awake. The light was on but all was silent. The stereo was off. He started to look at his watch when the phone rang again and he quickly grabbed it off the bedside table.

'Yeah.'

'Hey, Harry, it's Kiz.'

His old partner.

'Kiz, what's up?'

'You okay? You sound . . . out of it.'

'I'm fine. I was just . . . I was asleep.'

He looked at his watch. It was just after ten.

'Sorry, Harry, I thought you'd be burning the oil, getting ready for tomorrow.'

'I'm going to get up early and do it.'

'Well, you did good today. We had the box on in the squad. Everybody was pulling for you.'

'I'll bet. How is it going down there?'

'It's going. In a way I'm starting over. I've got to prove myself to them.'

'Don't worry about it. You'll be passing those guys like they're standing still. Just like you did with me.'

'Harry . . . you're the best. I learned more from you than you'll ever know.'

Bosch hesitated. He was genuinely touched by what she had said.

'That's nice of you to say, Kiz. You should call me more often.'

She laughed.

'Well, that's not why I'm calling. I told a friend I'd do this. It reminds me of high school but here goes. There's somebody that is interested in you. I said I'd check to see if you were back out in the field, if you know what I mean?'

Bosch didn't even have to think before answering.

'Nah, Kiz, I'm not. I . . . I'm not giving up on Eleanor yet. I'm still hoping she'll call or show up and maybe we can work it out. You know how it is.'

'I do. And that's cool, Harry. I just said I'd ask. But if you change your mind, she's a neat lady.'

'I know her?'

'Yeah, you know her. Jaye Winston, over at the sheriff's. We're in a women's group together. Dicks without Dicks. We got to talking about you tonight.'

Bosch didn't say anything. A strange constricting feeling filled his gut. He didn't believe in coincidences.

'Harry, you there?'

'Yeah, I'm here. I was just thinking about something.'

'Well, I'll let you go. And listen, Jaye asked me not to give you her name. You know, she just wanted to ask about you and put an anonymous feeler out. So next time you both run across each other on the job it wouldn't be embarrassing. So you didn't get it from me, right?'

'Right. She asked you questions about me?'

'A few. Nothing big. I hope you don't mind. I told her she made a good choice. I said if I wasn't, you know, the way I was, I'd be interested too.'

'Thanks, Kiz,' Bosch said but his mind was flying.

'Well, look, I'm gonna go. I'll see you. Knock 'em dead tomorrow, okay?'

'I'll try.'

She hung up and Bosch slowly put the phone back in its cradle. The tightening in his gut got more intense. He started thinking about McCaleb's visit and what he had asked and what Harry had said. Now Winston was asking questions about him.

He did not believe it was a coincidence. It was clear to Bosch that they had a bead on him. They were looking at him for the Edward Gunn killing. And he knew he had probably given McCaleb the right amount of psychological insight to believe he was on the right course.

Bosch drained the bottle of beer that was on the nightstand. The last swallow was room temperature and sour. He knew there were no more bottles in the refrigerator. He got up to get a cigarette instead.

22

Nat's was a railroad car-sized bar that was like a lot of Hollywood haunts – favored during daylight hours by hard-core drinkers, during early evening hours by casual hookers and their clientele, and late at night by the black leather and tattoo crowd. It was the kind of place where a person would stand out as a target if he tried to pay for drinks with a gold credit card.

McCaleb had stopped at Musso's for dinner – his body clock demanding nourishment before a complete shutdown occurred – and didn't get to Nat's until after ten. While eating his chicken pot pie he had wondered whether going to the bar to ask questions about Gunn was even worth the time. The tip had come from the suspect. Would the suspect knowingly point the investigator in the right direction? It seemed not, but McCaleb factored in Bosch's drinking and his being unaware of McCaleb's true mission during the visit to the house on the hill. The tip might very well be valid and he decided no part of the investigation should be overlooked.

As he walked in it took him a few seconds to adjust to the dim, reddish lighting. When the room became clear he saw it was half empty. It was the time between the early evening crowd and the late night group. Two women – one black, one white – sitting at one end of the bar that ran along the left side of the room sized him up and McCaleb could see *cop* register in their eyes at the same moment *hookers* registered in his. It secretly pleased him that he still had the look. He walked by them and further into the lounge. The booths lining the right side of the room were mostly full. No one in these bothered to give him a glance.

He stepped up to the bar between two empty stools and signaled one of the bartenders.

An old Bob Seger song, 'Night Moves,' was blaring from a jukebox in the back. The bartender leaned over the bar so she could get McCaleb's order. She was wearing a buttoned black vest with no shirt underneath. She had long straight black hair and a thin gold hoop pierced her left eyebrow.

'What can I get you?'

'Some information.'

McCaleb slid a driver's-license picture of Edward Gunn across the counter. It was a three-by-five blowup that had been in the files Winston gave him. The bartender looked at it for a moment and then back up at McCaleb.

'What about him? He's dead.'

'How do you know that?'

She shrugged her shoulders.

'I don't know. Word just got around, I guess. You a cop?'

McCaleb nodded, lowered his voice so the music would cover it and said, 'Something like that.'

The bartender leaned further over the bartop so she could hear him. This position opened the top of her vest, exposing most of her small but round breasts. There was a tattoo of a heart wrapped in barbed wire on the left side. It looked like a bruise on a pear, not very appetizing. McCaleb looked away.

'Edward Gunn,' he said. 'He was a regular, right?'

'He came in a lot.'

McCaleb nodded. Her acknowledgment confirmed Bosch's tip.

'You work New Year's Eve?'

She nodded.

'You know if he came in that night?'

She shook her head.

'I can't remember. A lot of people were in here New Year's Eve. We had a party. I don't know if he was here or not. It wouldn't surprise me, though. People came and went.'

McCaleb nodded toward the other bartender. A Latino who also wore a black vest with no shirt beneath.

'What about him? Think he'd remember?'

'No, 'cause he only started last week. I'm breaking him in.'

A thin smile played on her face. McCaleb ignored it. 'Twisting the Night Away' began playing. The Rod Stewart version.

'How well did you know Gunn?'

She let out a short burst of laughter.

'Honey, this is the kind of place where people don't exactly like to let on who they are or what they are. How well did I know him? I knew him, okay? Like I said, he came in. But I didn't even know his name until he was dead and people started talking about him. Somebody said Eddie Gunn got himself killed and I said, "Who the fuck is Eddie Gunn?" They had to describe him. The whiskey rocks who always had the paint in his hair. Then I knew who Eddie Gunn was.'

McCaleb nodded. He reached inside his coat pocket and brought out a folded piece of newspaper. He slid it across the bartop. She leaned down to look, showing another view of her breasts. McCaleb thought it was intentional.

'This is that cop, the one from the trial, right?'

McCaleb didn't answer the question. The newspaper had been folded to a photo of Harry Bosch that had run that morning in the *Los Angeles Times* as an advance on the testimony expected to begin in the Storey trial. It was a candid shot of Bosch standing outside the courtroom door. He probably didn't even know it had been taken.

'You seen him in here?'

'Yeah, he comes in. Why are you asking about him?'

McCaleb felt a charge go up the back of his neck.

'When does he come in?'

'I don't know, from time to time. I wouldn't call him a regular. But he'd come in. And he wouldn't stay long. A one-timer – one drink and out. He's . . .'

She pointed a finger up and cocked her head to the side as she rifled through her interior files. She then slashed her finger down as if making a notch.

'Got it. Bottled beer. Asks for Anchor Steam every time because he always forgets we don't carry it – too expensive, we'd never sell it. He then settles for the old thirty-three.'

McCaleb was about to ask what that was when she answered his unspoken question.

'Rolling Rock.'

He nodded.

'Was he in here New Year's Eve?'

She shook her head.

'Same answer. I don't remember. Too many people, too many drinks, too many days since then.'

McCaleb nodded and pulled the newspaper back across the bar and put it in his pocket.

'He in some kind of trouble, that cop?'

McCaleb shook his head. One of the women at the end of the bar tapped the corner of her empty glass on the bartop and called to the bartender.

'Hey, Miranda, you got payin' customers over here.'

The bartender looked around for her partner. He was gone, apparently in the back room or the bathroom.

'Gotta go to work,' she said.

McCaleb watched her go to the end of the bar and make two fresh vodka rocks for the hookers. During a lull in the music, he overheard one of them tell her to stop talking to the cop so he would leave. As Miranda headed back toward McCaleb's position one of the hookers called after her.

'And stop giving him the freebie or he'll never leave.'

McCaleb acted like he didn't hear it. Miranda exhaled like she was tired when she got to him.

'I don't know where Javier went. I can't be standing here talking to you all night.'

'Let me ask you one last thing,' he said. 'You ever remember the cop being in here with Eddie Gunn at the same time – either together or apart?'

She thought a moment and leaned forward.

'Maybe, it could've happened. But I don't remember.'

McCaleb nodded. He was pretty sure that was the best he could get out of her. He wondered if he should leave some money on the bar. He'd never been good at that sort of thing when he was an agent. He never knew when it would be appropriate and when it would be insulting.

'Can I ask you something now?' Miranda asked.

'What?'

'You like what you see?'

He felt his face immediately begin to color with embarrassment.

'I mean, you were looking enough. I just thought I'd ask.'

She glanced over at the hookers and shared a smile. They were all enjoying McCaleb's embarrassment.

'They're real nice,' he said as he stepped away from the bar, leaving a twenty-dollar bill for her. 'I'm sure they keep people coming back. Probably kept Eddie Gunn comin' in.'

He headed toward the door and she called after him, her words hitting him in the back all the way to the door.

'Then maybe you oughta come back and try 'em out some time, *Officer!*'

As he went through the door he heard the hookers whoop and slap hands in a high five.

McCaleb sat in the Cherokee in front of Nat's and tried to shake off the embarrassment. He concentrated on the information he had gotten from the bartender. Gunn was a regular and might or might not have been in there on the last night of his life. Secondly, she was familiar with Bosch as a customer. He, too, might or might not have been in there on the last night of Gunn's life. The fact that this information had indirectly come from Bosch was puzzling. Again, he wondered why Bosch – if he was Gunn's killer – had given him a valid clue to follow. Was it arrogance, a belief that he would never be considered a suspect and therefore not be brought up during the questioning at the bar? Or could there be a deeper psychological motivation? McCaleb knew that many criminals make mistakes that ensure their apprehension because subconsciously they do not want to get away with their crimes. The big wheel theory, McCaleb thought. Maybe Bosch was subconsciously making sure the wheel turned for him as well.

He opened his cell phone and checked the signal. It was good. He called Jaye Winston's home number. He checked his watch while the phone was ringing and thought that it was not too late to call. After five rings she finally picked up.

'It's me. I've got some stuff.'

'So do I. But I'm still on the phone. Can I call you when I'm done?'

'Yeah, I'll be here.'

He clicked off and sat in the car waiting and thinking about things. He watched through the windshield as the white hooker from the bar stepped through the door with a man in a baseball cap in tow. They both lit cigarettes and headed down the sidewalk toward a motel called the Skylark.

His phone chirped. It was Winston.

'It's coming together, Terry. I'm a believer.'

'What did you get?'

'You first. You said you got some stuff.'

'No, you. What I got is minor. It sounds like you hooked something big.'

'Okay, listen to this. Harry Bosch's mother was a prostitute. In Hollywood. She got murdered when he was a little kid. And whoever did it got away with it. How is that for psychological underpinnings, Mr. Profiler?'

McCaleb didn't answer. The new information was stunning and provided many of the missing pieces in the working theory. He watched the hooker and her customer at the window of the motel office. The man passed cash through and received a key. They went in through a glass door.

'Gunn kills a prostitute and walks away,' Winston said when he didn't respond. 'Just like what happened with his mother.'

'How'd you find this out?' McCaleb finally asked.

'I made that call we talked about. To my friend, Kiz. I acted like I was interested in Bosch and asked her if she knew if he was, you know, over his divorce yet. She told me what she knew about him. The stuff about his mother apparently came out a few years ago in a civil trial when Bosch got sued for a wrongful death – the Dollmaker, you remember that one?'

'Yeah, the LAPD refused to call us in on that one. That was also a guy who killed prostitutes. Bosch killed him. He was unarmed.'

'There's a psychology going on here. A goddamn pattern.'

'What happened to Bosch after his mother was killed?'

'Kiz didn't really know. She called him an institutional man. It happened when he was ten or eleven. After that he grew up in youth halls and foster homes. He went into the service and then the department. The point is, this is the thing we were missing. The thing that turned a no-count case into something Bosch wouldn't let go.'

McCaleb nodded to himself.

'And there's more,' Winston said. 'I went through all the accumulated files – extraneous things I didn't put in the murder book. I looked at the autopsy on the woman Gunn killed six years ago. Her name was Frances Weldon, by the way. There was one thing in there that seems significant in light of what we now know about Bosch. Examination of the uterus and hips showed that at some point she'd had a child.'

McCaleb shook his head.

'Bosch wouldn't have known that. He pushed his lieutenant through a window and was on suspension by the time there was an autopsy.'

'True. But he could and probably did look at the case files after he came back. He would have known that Gunn did to some other kid what was done to him. You see, it is all fitting. Eight hours ago I thought you were grasping at straws. Now it looks to me like you're dead on.'

It didn't feel all that good to be dead on. But he understood Winston's excitement. When cases fell together the excitement could sometimes obscure the reality of the crime.

'What happened to her kid?' he asked.

'No idea. She probably gave the child up after the birth. That doesn't matter. What matters is what it meant to Bosch.'

She was right. But McCaleb didn't like the loose end.

'Going back to your call to Bosch's old partner. Is she going to call him and tell him you asked about him?'

'She already did.'

'This is tonight?'

'Yeah, this all just went down. That was that call, her getting back to me. He passed. He told her he was still holding out hope for his wife coming back.'

'Did she tell him it was you who was interested?'

'She wasn't supposed to.'

'But she probably did. This might mean he knows we're looking at him.'

'That's impossible. How?'

'I was just up there tonight. I was in his house. Then the same night he gets this call about you. A guy like Harry Bosch, he doesn't believe in coincidences, Jaye.'

'Well, when you were up there, how did you handle it?' Winston finally asked.

'Like we said. I wanted more info on Gunn but sidetracked into talking about Bosch. That's why I was calling you. I got some interesting stuff. Nothing that compares to what you got but stuff that also fits. But if he got this call about you right after I was there . . . I don't know.'

'Tell me about your stuff.'

'All little stuff. He's got the photo of the estranged wife prominently displayed in the living room. I was there less than an hour and the guy downed three beers. So there's the alcohol syndrome. Symptomatic of interior pressures. He also spoke of something he called "the big wheel." It's part of his belief system. He doesn't see the hand of God in things. He sees the big wheel. What goes around comes around. He said guys like Gunn don't really get away. Something always catches up to them. The wheel. I used some specific phrases to see if I could draw a reaction or disagreement. I called the world outside his door the plague. He didn't disagree. He said he could deal with the plague as long as he got his shots at the carriers. It's all very subtle, Jaye, but it's all there. He's got a Bosch print on the wall in the hallway. *The Garden of Earthly Delights.* It's got our owl in it.'

'So, he's named after the guy. If my name was Picasso I'd have a Picasso print on the wall.'

'I acted like I'd never seen it before and asked him what it meant. All he said was that it was the big wheel turning. That's what it meant to him.'

'Little pieces that fit.'

'There's still work to be done.'

'Well, are you still on it? Or are you going back?'

'For the time being I'm on it. I'll be staying over tonight. But I have a charter Saturday. I have to go back for that.'

She didn't say anything.

'You got anything else?' he finally asked.

'Yeah, I almost forgot.'

'What?'

'The owl from Bird Barrier. It was paid for with a money order from the Postal Service. I got the number from Cameron Riddell and ran a trace on it. It was bought December twenty-second at the post office on Wilcox in Hollywood. It's about four blocks from the police station where Bosch works.'

He shook his head.

'The laws of physics.'

'What do you mean?'

'For every action there is an equal and opposite reaction. When you look into the abyss the abyss looks into you. You know, all the clichés. They're clichés because they're true. You don't go into the darkness without it going into you and taking its piece. Bosch may have gone in too many times. He's lost his way.'

They were silent for a little while after that and then made plans to meet the following day. As he hung up he saw the hooker leaving the Skylark by herself and heading back up toward Nat's. She was wearing a denim jacket which she pulled tight around her against the cool night air. She adjusted her wig as she walked toward the bar where she would seek another customer.

Watching her and thinking about Bosch, McCaleb was reminded of all he had and how lucky in life he had been. He was reminded that luck could be a fleeting thing. It had to be earned and then guarded with everything you had. He knew he was not doing that now. He was leaving things unguarded while he went into the dark.

23

Trial resumed twenty-five minutes after the scheduled nine o'clock start because of the prosecution's unsuccessful bid to seek both sanctions against the defense for witness intimidation and a delay while the statements of Annabelle Crowe were fully investigated. Sitting behind his cherrywood desk in chambers, Judge Houghton encouraged the investigation but said the trial would not be delayed to accommodate it and no sanctions or other penalties would be issued unless evidence corroborating the witness's statements could be found. He warned the prosecutors and Bosch, who had taken part in the closed-door meeting by recounting his interview with Crowe, not to leak word of the witness's accusations to the media.

Five minutes later they were convened in the courtroom and the jurors were brought to their two rows of seats. Bosch returned to the witness stand and was reminded by the judge that he was still under oath. Janis Langwiser went back to the lectern with her legal pad.

'Now, Detective Bosch, we left off yesterday with your conclusion in regard to the death of Jody Krementz being determined to be a homicide. Is that correct?'

'Yes.'

'And that conclusion was based not only on your investigation but on the investigation and autopsy conducted by the coroner's office as well, correct?'

'Correct.'

'Could you please tell the jurors how the investigation proceeded once you had established the death as a homicide?'

Bosch turned in his seat so that he was looking directly at the jury box as he spoke. The movement was jarring. He had a pounding ache on the left side of his head that was so intense he wondered if people could actually see his temple throbbing.

'Well, my two partners – Jerry Edgar and Kizmin Rider – and I began to sit through – I mean, sift through the physical evidence we had accumulated. We also began conducting extensive interviews with those who knew the victim and were known to have been with her in the last twenty-four hours of her life.'

'You mentioned physical evidence. Please explain to the jury what physical evidence you had accumulated.'

'Actually, there was not a whole lot gathered. There were fingerprints throughout the house that we needed to run down. And there also was a quantity of fiber and hair evidence gathered from on and about the victim's body.'

J. Reason Fowkkes quickly objected before Bosch could continue his answer.

'Objection to the phrase "on or about" as being vague and misleading.'

'Your Honor,' Langwiser countered, 'I think if Mr. Fowkkes gave Detective Bosch a chance to finish the answer to the question there would be nothing vague or misleading. But interrupting a witness in mid-answer to say the answer is vague or misleading is not appropriate.'

'Overruled,' Judge Houghton said, before Fowkkes could get in a rejoinder. 'Let the witness complete his answer and then we'll see how vague it is. Go ahead, Detective Bosch.'

Bosch cleared his throat.

'I was going to say that several samples of pubic hair not—'

'What is "several," Your Honor,' Fowkkes said. 'My ongoing objection is to the lack of precision this witness is offering the jury.'

Bosch looked at Langwiser and saw how mad she was getting.

'Judge,' she said, 'could we please have direction from the court as to when objections can be raised? Defense counsel is seeking to constantly interrupt the witness because he knows we are moving into an area that is particularly devastating to his—'

'Ms. Langwiser, this isn't the time for closing arguments,' the judge said, cutting her off. 'Mr. Fowkkes, unless you are seeing a dire miscarriage of justice, I want objections stated either before a witness speaks or after he has completed at least a sentence.'

'Your Honor, the consequences *are* dire here. The state is trying to take away my client's life, simply because his moral views are—'

'Mr. Fowkkes!' the judge boomed. 'That goes for you, too, on the closing arguments. Let's continue the testimony, shall we?'

He turned to Bosch.

'Detective, continue – and try to be a little more precise in your answers.'

Bosch looked at Langwiser and saw her close her eyes momentarily. The judge's offhand direction to Bosch had been what Fowkkes was going for. A hint to the jurors that there might be vagueness, maybe even obfuscation in the prosecution's case. Fowkkes had successfully goaded the judge into appearing to agree with his objections.

Bosch glanced over at Fowkkes and saw him sitting with arms folded and a satisfied, if not smug, look on his face. Bosch looked back down at the murder book in front of him.

'Can I refer to my notes?' he asked.

He was told he could. He opened the binder and turned to the evidence reports. Looking at the medical examiner's evidence collection report, he began again.

'Prior to autopsy an evidence-collecting brush was passed through the victim's pubic hair. The comb collected eight samples of pubic hair that subsequent laboratory testing showed to have come from someone other than the victim.'

He looked up at Langwiser.

'Were those pubic hairs from eight different people?'

'No, the lab tests identified them as coming from the same unknown person.'

'And what did this indicate to you?'

'That the victim likely had sexual relations with someone between the time of her last bathing and her death.'

Langwiser looked down at her notes.

'Was there any other hair evidence collected on the victim or at the scene of the crime, Detective?'

Bosch turned a page in the murder book.

'Yes, a single strand of hair measuring two and one half inches long was found entangled on the clasp of a gold necklace the victim wore around her neck. The clasp was located at the back of the victim's neck. This, too, was identified during lab analysis as coming from someone other than the victim.'

'Going back for a moment to the pubic hair. Were there any other indications or evidence collected from the body or the crime scene indicating the victim had engaged in sexual relations in the time between bathing and her death?'

'No, there wasn't. No semen was collected from the vagina.'

'Is there a conflict between that and the finding of the pubic hair?'

'No conflict. It was simply an indication that a condom could have been used during the sex act.'

'Okay, moving on, Detective. Fingerprints. You mentioned fingerprints were found in the house. Please tell us about that area of the investigation.'

Bosch turned to the fingerprint report in the binder.

'There were a total of sixty-eight exemplars of fingerprints gathered inside the house where the victim was found. The victim and her roommate accounted for fifty-two of these. It was determined that the remaining sixteen were left by a total of seven people.'

'And who were these people?'

Bosch read the list of names from the binder. Through questioning from Langwiser he explained who each person was and how the detectives traced down when and why they had been in the house. They were friends of the roommates as well as family members, a former boyfriend and a prior date.

The prosecution team knew that the defense would attempt to go to town on the prints, using them as red herrings to bait the jury away from the facts of the case. So the testimony moved slowly as Bosch tediously explained the location and origin of each fingerprint found and identified in the house. He ended with testimony about a full set of fingerprints found on the headboard of the bed in which the victim was found. He and Langwiser knew that these were the prints that Fowkkes would get the most yardage out of, so Langwiser attempted to minimize the potential damage by having it revealed during her examination of the witness.

'How far from the victim's body were these prints located?'

Bosch looked at the report in the binder.

'Two point three feet.'

'Exactly where on the headboard?'

'On the outside facing, between the headboard and the wall.'

'Was there a lot of space there?'

'About two inches.'

'How would someone get their fingerprints there?'

Fowkkes objected, saying it was outside Bosch's realm of expertise to determine how a set of fingerprints got anywhere, but the judge allowed the question.

'Only two ways I can think of,' Bosch answered. 'They got there when the bed was not pushed quite up to the wall. Or the person who left the prints had reached their fingers through the opening in the slats of the headboard and left them while holding onto that particular cross board.'

Langwiser introduced a photo taken by a fingerprint technician as an exhibit and it was shown to the jury.

'To accomplish the latter explanation you offered, the person would have to be lying in the bed, would they not?'

'It would seem that way.'

'Face down?'

'Yes.'

Fowkkes stood to object but the judge sustained it before the lawyer uttered a word.

'You are going too far afield with suppositions, Ms. Langwiser. Move on.'

'Yes, Your Honor.'

She referred to her pad for a moment.

'This print on the victim's bed, didn't that make you think the person who left it should be considered a prime suspect?'

'Not initially. It is impossible to tell how long a print has been at a specific location. Plus we had the additional factor that we knew the victim had not been killed in her bed, but rather taken to the bed after being killed elsewhere. It appeared to us that the location of the print was not a place that would have been touched by the killer when he put the body in the bed.'

'Who did these prints belong to?'

'A man named Allan Wiess, who had dated Ms. Krementz on three prior occasions, the most recent date being three weeks before her death.'

'Did you interview Allan Wiess?'

'Yes, I did. Along with Detective Edgar.'

'Did he acknowledge ever being in the victim's bed?'

'Yes, he did. He said he slept with her on that last occasion that he saw her, three weeks prior to her death.'

'Did he say he touched the bed board in the location you have shown us where the fingerprints were located?'

'He said he could have done it but he did not specifically remember doing it.'

'Did you investigate Allan Weiss's activities on the night of Jody Krementz's death?'

'Yes, we did. He had a solid alibi.'

'And what was that?'

'He told us he was in Hawaii at a real estate seminar. We checked airline and hotel records as well as with the seminar's producers. We confirmed he was there.'

Langwiser looked at Judge Houghton and said that it would be a good time to take the morning break. The judge said it was a little early but granted the request and ordered the jurors back in fifteen minutes.

Bosch knew she wanted the break now because she was about to move into questions about David Storey and wanted them clearly separated from all the other testimony. As he stepped off the witness stand and went back to the prosecution table, Langwiser was flipping through some files. She spoke to him without looking up.

'What's wrong, Harry?'

'What do you mean?'

'You're not crisp. Not like yesterday. Are you nervous about something?'

'No. Are you?'

'Yeah, the whole thing. We've got a lot riding on this.'

'I'll be crisper.'

'I'm serious, Harry.'

'So am I, Janis.'

He then walked away from the prosecution table and out through the courtroom.

He decided he would get a cup of coffee at the second-floor cafeteria. But first he stepped into the restroom next to the elevators and went to one of the sinks to splash cold water on his face. He bent fully over the sink, careful not to get water on his suit. He heard a toilet flush and when he straightened up and looked in the mirror he saw Rudy Tafero pass behind him and go to the sink furthest away. Bosch bent down again and brought more water up and held it. Its chill felt good against his eyes and eased his headache.

'What's it like, Rudy?' he asked without looking at the other man.

'What's what like, Harry?'

'You know, doing the devil's bidding. You get any sleep at night?'

Bosch walked over to the paper towel dispenser and tore off several sheets to dry his hands and face. Tafero came over and tore off a towel and began drying his hands.

'It's funny,' Tafero said. 'The only time in my life I had trouble sleeping was when I was a cop. I wonder why that was.'

He balled the towel in his hands and threw it into the wastebasket. He smiled at Bosch and then walked out. Bosch watched him go, still rubbing his hands on the towels.

24

Bosch could feel the coffee working in his blood. The second wind was coming. The headache was easing. He was ready. This would be how they planned it, how they had choreographed it. He leaned forward to the microphone and waited for the question.

'Detective Bosch,' Langwiser said from the lectern, 'did there come a time when the name David Storey came up in your investigation?'

'Yes, almost immediately. We received information from Jane Gilley, who was Jody Krementz's roommate, that on the last night of Jody's life she had a date with David Storey.'

'Did there come a time when you questioned Mr. Storey about that last night?'

'Yes. Briefly.'

'Why briefly, Detective Bosch? This *was* a homicide.'

'That was Mr. Storey's choosing. We attempted several times to interview him on that Friday that the body was discovered and the next day as well. He was difficult to locate. Finally, through his attorney, he agreed to be interviewed the next day, which was Sunday, on the condition that we come to him and conduct the interview in his office at Archway Studios. We reluctantly agreed to do it that way but did so in the spirit of cooperation and because we needed to talk to this man. At that point we were two days into the case and had not been able to talk to the last person known to have seen the victim alive. When we arrived at the office, Mr. Storey's personal attorney, Jason Fleer, was there. We began interviewing Mr. Storey but in less than five minutes his attorney terminated the interview.'

'Was this conversation tape-recorded?'

'Yes, it was.'

Langwiser made the motion to play the recording and it was approved by Judge Houghton over Fowkkes's objection. Fowkkes had asked the judge to simply allow jurors to read his already prepared transcripts of the short interview. But Langwiser objected to that, saying that she had not had time to check the transcripts for accuracy and that it was important for the jurors to hear David Storey's tone and demeanor. With the wisdom of

Solomon the judge ruled that the tape would be heard and that the transcripts would be handed out anyway as an aid to the jurors. He encouraged Bosch and the prosecution team to read along as well so they could check the transcript for accuracy.

BOSCH: My name is Detective Hieronymus Bosch of the Los Angeles Police Department. I am accompanied by my partners, Detectives Jerry Edgar and Kizmin Rider. The date is October 15, 2000. We are interviewing David Storey in his offices at Archway Studios in regard to case number zero-zero-eight-nine-seven. Mr. Storey is accompanied by his attorney, Jason Fleer. Mr. Storey, Mr. Fleer? Any questions before we begin?

FLEER: No questions.

BOSCH: Oh, and, obviously, we are recording this statement. Mr. Storey, did you know a woman named Jody Krementz? Also known as Donatella Speers.

STOREY: You know the answer to that.

FLEER: David . . .

STOREY: Yes, I knew her. I was with her last Thursday night. It does not mean I killed her.

FLEER: David, please. Answer only the questions they ask you.

STOREY: Whatever.

BOSCH: Can I continue?

FLEER: By all means. Please.

STOREY: Yes, by all means. Please.

BOSCH: You mentioned that you were with her on Thursday evening. This was a date?

STOREY: Why ask things you already know the answer to? Yes, it was a date, if you want to call it that.

BOSCH: What do you want to call it?

STOREY: Doesn't matter.

(pause)

BOSCH: Could you give us a framework of time that you were with her?

STOREY: Picked her up at seven-thirty, dropped her off about midnight.

BOSCH: Did you enter her home when you came to pick her up?

STOREY: Matter of fact, I didn't. I was running very late and called on my cell phone to tell her to come outside because I didn't have time to come in. I think she wanted me to meet her roommate – another actress, no doubt – but I didn't have the time.

BOSCH: So when you pulled up she was waiting outside.

STOREY: That's what I said.

BOSCH: Seven-thirty until midnight. That is four and a half hours.

STOREY: You are good at math. I like that in a detective.

FLEER: David, let's try to get this done.

STOREY: I am.

BOSCH: Could you tell us what you did during the time period you were with Jody Krementz?

STOREY: We covered the three Fs. Film, food and a fuck.

BOSCH: Excuse me?

STOREY: We went to the premiere of my movie, then we went to the reception and had something to eat, then I took her to my place and we had sex. Consensual sex, Detective. Believe it or not, people do it on dates all the time. And not just Hollywood people. It happens across this great country of ours. It's what makes it great.

BOSCH: I understand. Did you take her home when you were finished?

STOREY: Always the gentleman, I did.

BOSCH: Did you enter her house at this time?

STOREY: No. I was in my fucking bathrobe. I just drove up, she got out and went inside. I then drove back home. Whatever happened after that I don't know. I am not involved in this in any way, shape or form. You people are—

FLEER: David, please.

STOREY: – completely full of shit if for one fucking moment you think—

FLEER: David, stop!

(pause)

Detective Bosch, I think we need to stop this.

BOSCH: We're in the middle of an interview here and—

FLEER: David, where are you going?

STOREY: Fuck these people. I'm going out for a smoke.

BOSCH: Mr. Storey has just left the office.

FLEER: I think at this point he is exercising his rights under the Fifth Amendment. This interview is over.

The tape went blank and Langwiser turned it off. Bosch looked at the jury. Several of them were looking at Storey. His arrogance had come through loud and clear on the tape. This was important because they would soon be asking the jury to believe that Storey had privately boasted to Bosch about the murder and how he would get away with it. Only an arrogant man would do that. The prosecution needed to prove Storey was not only a murderer, but an arrogant one at that.

'Okay, then,' Langwiser said. 'Did Mr. Storey return to continue the interview?'

'No, he did not,' Bosch answered. 'And we were asked to leave.'

'Did Mr. Storey's denial of any involvement in the murder of Jody Krementz end your interest in him?'

'No, it did not. We had an obligation to investigate the case fully and that included either ruling him in or ruling him out as a suspect.'

'Was his behavior during the short interview cause for suspicion?'

'You mean his arrogance? No, he—'

Fowkkes jumped up with an objection.

'Your Honor, one man's arrogance is another man's confidence in his innocence. There is no—'

'You are right, Mr. Fowkkes,' Houghton said.

He sustained the objection, struck Bosch's answer and turned to the jurors to tell them to ignore the remark.

'His behavior during the interview was not cause for suspicion,' Bosch began again. 'His being the last known person to be with the victim was cause for our immediate attention and focus. His lack of cooperation was suspicious but at this point we were keeping an open mind about everything. My partners and I have a combined total of more than twenty-five years' experience investigating homicides. We know that things are not always what they seem.'

'Where did the investigation go next?'

'We continued all avenues of investigation. One of those avenues was obviously Mr. Storey. Based on his statement that he and the victim had gone to his home on their date, my partners filed a search warrant application in Municipal Court and received approval to search David Storey's home.'

Langwiser brought the search warrant forward to the judge and it was received into evidence. She took it back with her to the lectern. Bosch then testified that the search of the home on Mulholland Drive was conducted at 6 A.M. two days after the initial interview with Storey.

'The search warrant authorized you to seize any evidence of Jody Krementz's murder, any evidence of her belongings and any evidence of her presence in that location, is that correct?'

'Correct.'

'Who conducted the search?'

'Myself, my partners and a two-man forensics team. We also had a photographer, for video and stills. A total of six.'

'How long did the search last?'

'Approximately seven hours.'

'Was the defendant present during the search?'

'For most of it. He had to leave at one point for a meeting with a movie actor he said he couldn't postpone. He was gone approximately two hours. During that time his personal attorney, Mr. Fleer, remained in the house and monitored the search. We were never left alone in the house, if that is what you are asking.'

Langwiser flipped through the pages of the search warrant, coming to the end of it.

'Now, Detective, when you seize any items during a court-approved search, you are required by law to keep an inventory on the search warrant receipt, correct?'

'Yes.'

'This receipt is then filed with the court, correct?'

'Yes.'

'Can you tell us then, why is this receipt blank?'

'We did not take any items from the house during the search.'

'You found nothing that indicated that Jody Krementz had been inside Mr. Storey's house, as he had told you she had been?'

'Nothing.'

'This search took place how many days after the evening Mr. Storey told you he had taken Ms. Krementz to his house and engaged in sexual relations with her?'

'Five days from the night of the murder, two days from our interview with Mr. Storey.'

'You found nothing in support of Mr. Storey's statement.'

'Nothing. The place was clean.'

Bosch knew she was trying to turn a negative into a positive, somehow trying to imply that the unsuccessful search was an indication of Storey's guilt.

'Would you call this an unsuccessful search?'

'No. Success doesn't enter into it. We were looking for evidence that would corroborate his statement as well as any evidence of possible foul play relating to Ms. Krementz. We found nothing in the house indicative of this. But sometimes it is not what you find, it's what you don't.'

'Can you explain that to the jury?'

'Well, it is true we didn't take any evidence from the house. But we found something missing that would later become important to us.'

'And what was that?'

'A book. A missing book.'

'How did you know it was missing if it wasn't there?'

'In the living room of the house there was a large built-in bookcase. Each shelf was full of books. On one shelf there was a space – a slot – where a book had been but was now gone. We could not find what book that might be. There were no books sitting out loose in the house. At the time it was just a small thing. Someone had obviously taken a book from the shelf and not replaced it. It was just kind of curious to us that we could not figure out where or what it was.'

Langwiser offered two still photographs of the bookcase taken during the search as exhibits. Houghton accepted them over a routine objection from Fowkkes. The photos showed the bookcase in its entirety and a close-up of the second shelf with the open space between a book called *The Fifth Horizon* and a biography of the film director John Ford called *Print the Legend.*

'Now, Detective,' Langwiser said, 'you said that at the time you did not know if this missing book had any importance or bearing on the case, correct?'

'That is right.'

'Did you eventually determine what book had been taken from the shelf?'

'Yes, we did.'

Langwiser paused. Bosch knew what she was going to do. The dance had been choreographed. He thought of her as a good storyteller. She knew how to string it along, keep people hooked in, take them to the edge of the cliff and then pull them back.

'Well, let's take things in order,' she said. 'We'll come back to the book. Now did you have occasion to talk to Mr. Storey on the day of the search?'

'He mostly kept to himself and was on the phone most of the time. But we spoke when we first knocked on the door and announced the search. And then at the end of the day when I told him we were leaving and that we were not taking anything with us.'

'Did you wake him up when you came at six in the morning?'

'Yes, we did.'

'Was he alone in the house?'

'Yes.'

'Did he invite you in?'

'Not at first. He objected to the search. I told him—'

'Excuse me, Detective, we might make this easier if we show it. You said there was a videographer with you. Was he running the camera when you knocked at six in the morning?'

'Yes, he was.'

Langwiser then made the appropriate motions to introduce the search video. It was accepted under objection from the defense. A large television was rolled into the courtroom and placed at center in front of the jury box. Bosch was asked to identify the tape. The lights in the courtroom were dimmed and it was played.

The tape began with a focus on Bosch and the others outside the red front door of a house. He identified himself and the address and the case number. He spoke quietly. He then turned and knocked sharply on the door. He announced it was the police and knocked sharply again. They waited. Bosch knocked on the door every fifteen seconds until it was finally opened about two minutes after the first pounding. David Storey looked out through the opening, his hair disheveled, his eyes showing exhaustion.

'What?' he asked.

'We have a search warrant here, Mr. Storey,' Bosch said. 'It allows us to conduct a search of these premises.'

'You have to be fucking kidding.'

'No, we're not, sir. Could you step back and let us in? The sooner we're in the sooner we're out.'

'I'm calling my lawyer.'

Storey closed and locked the door. Bosch immediately stepped up and put his face close to the jamb. He called out loudly.

'Mr. Storey, you have ten minutes. If this door is not opened by six-fifteen then we're going to take it down. We have a court-ordered search warrant and we will execute it.'

He turned back to the camera and made the cut signal across his throat.

The video jumped to another focus on the door. The time readout in the bottom corner now showed it was 6:13 A.M. The door opened and Storey stepped back and signaled the search team in. His hair looked as though it had been combed with his hands. He was wearing black jeans and a black T-shirt. He was in bare feet.

'Do what you have to do and get out. My lawyer's coming and he's going to watch you people. You break one fucking thing in this house and I'm going to sue the shit out of you. This is a David Serrurier house. You so much as put a scratch on one of the walls and it'll be your jobs. All of you.'

'We'll be careful, Mr. Storey,' Bosch said as he walked in.

The cameraman was the last to enter the house. Storey looked into the lens as if seeing it for the first time.

'And get that shit off of me.'

He made a motion and the camera angle shot upward to the ceiling. It remained there while the voices of the videographer and Storey continued off camera.

'Hey! Don't touch the camera!'

'Then get it out of my face!'

'Okay. Fine. Just don't touch the camera.'

The screen went blank and the lights of the courtroom came back up. Langwiser continued the questioning.

'Detective Bosch, did you or members of the search team have further ... conversation with Mr. Storey after that?'

'Not during the search. Once his lawyer got there Mr. Storey stayed in his office. When we searched his office he moved into the bedroom. When he was leaving for his appointment I questioned him briefly about that and he left. That was about it as far as it went during the search and while we were inside the house.'

'What about at the end of the day – seven hours later – when the search was completed, did you speak to the defendant again?'

'Yes, I spoke to him briefly at the front door. We were packed up and ready to leave. The lawyer had left. I was in my car with my partners. We were backing out when I realized I had forgotten about giving Mr. Storey a copy of the search warrant. It's required by law. So I went back to his door and knocked on it.'

'Did Mr. Storey answer the door himself?'

'Yes, he answered after about four hard knocks. I gave him the receipt and told him it was required.'

'Did he say anything to you?'

Fowkkes stood up and objected for the record but the issue had already been disposed of in pretrial motions and rulings. The judge noted the objection for the record and overruled it for the record. Langwiser asked the question again.

'Can I refer to my notes?'

'Please.'

Bosch turned to the notes he had taken in the car right after the conversation.

'First, he said, "You didn't find a goddamn thing, did you?" And I told him he was right, that we weren't taking anything with us. He then said, "Because there was nothing to take." I nodded and was turning to leave when he spoke again. He said, "Hey, Bosch." I turned back and he leaned toward me and said, "You'll never find what you are looking for." I said, "Oh really, what is it that I am looking for?" He didn't respond. He just looked at me and smiled.'

After a pause, Langwiser asked, 'Was that the end of it?'

'No. I sensed at that point that I might be able to bait him into saying more. I said to him, "You did it, didn't you?" He continued to smile and then he slowly nodded. And he said, "And I'll get away with it." He said, "I'm a —"

'Bullshit! You're a fucking liar!'

It was Storey. He had stood up and was pointing at Bosch. Fowkkes had his hand on him and was trying to pull him back into his place. A deputy sheriff, who had been positioned at a desk to the rear of the defense table was up and moving toward Storey from behind.

'The defendant will sit DOWN!' the judge boomed from the bench at the same moment he brought the gavel down.

'He's fucking lying!'

'Deputy, sit him down!'

The deputy moved in, put both hands on Storey's shoulders from behind and roughly pulled him back down into his seat. The judge pointed another deputy toward the jury.

'Remove the jury.'

While the jurors were quickly hustled into the deliberation room, Storey continued to struggle with the deputy and Fowkkes. As soon as the jurors were gone he seemed to relax his efforts and then calmed. Bosch looked over at the reporters, trying to see if any of them had noted how Storey's demonstration ended as soon as the jurors were out of sight.

'Mr. Storey!' the judge yelled from a standing position. 'That behavior and language is not acceptable in this courtroom. Mr. Fowkkes, if you can't control your client, my people will. One more outburst and I will have him gagged and chained to that chair. Am I clear on this?'

'Absolutely, Your Honor. I apolo—'

'That is a zero tolerance rule. Any outburst from here on out and he'll be shackled. I don't care who he is or who his friends are.'

'Yes, Your Honor. We understand.'

'I am taking five minutes and then we'll start again.'

The judge abruptly left the bench, his feet resounding loudly as he quickly took the three steps down. He disappeared through a door to the rear hallway that led to his chambers.

Bosch looked over at Langwiser and her eyes betrayed her delight at what had just happened. To Bosch it was a trade-off. On one hand the jurors saw the defendant acting angry and out of control – possibly exhibiting the same rage that had led to murder. But on the other hand, he was registering his objection to what was happening to him in the courtroom. And that could register an empathic response from the jurors. Storey had to reach only one of them in order to walk.

Before the trial Langwiser had predicted that they would draw Storey into an outburst. Bosch had thought she was wrong. He thought Storey was too cool and calculating. Unless, of course, the outburst was a calculated move. Storey was a man who directed dramatic scenes and characters for a living. Bosch knew he should have seen that a time might come when he would be unwittingly used as a supporting actor in one of those scenes.

25

The judge returned to the bench two minutes after leaving and Bosch wondered if he had retreated to his chambers to put a holster on under the robes. As soon as he sat down Houghton looked at the defense table. Storey was sitting with his face somberly pointed down at the sketch pad in front of him.

'Are we ready?' the judge asked.

All parties murmured they were ready. The judge called for the jury and they were brought in, most of them looking directly at Storey as they entered.

'Okay, folks, we're going to try this again,' Judge Houghton said. 'The exclamations you heard a few minutes ago from the defendant are to be ignored. They are not evidence, they are not anything. If Mr. Storey wants to personally deny the charges or anything else said about him in testimony, he'll get that chance.'

Bosch watched Langwiser's eyes dance. The judge's comments were his way of slapping back at the defense. He was setting up the expectation that Storey would testify during the defense phase. If he didn't, then it could be a letdown for the jurors.

The judge turned it back over to Langwiser, who continued her questioning of Bosch.

'Before we were interrupted, you were testifying about your conversation with the defendant at the door to his house.'

'Yes.'

'You quoted the defendant as saying, "And I'll get away with it," is that correct?'

'Correct.'

'And you took this comment to be referring to the death of Jody Krementz, correct?'

'That's what we were talking about, yes.'

'Did he say anything else after that?'

'Yes.'

Bosch paused, wondering if Storey would make another outburst. He didn't.

'He said, "I am a god in this town, Detective Bosch. You don't fuck with the gods." '

Nearly ten seconds of silence went by before Langwiser was prompted by the judge to move on.

'What did you do after the defendant made this statement to you?'

'Well, I was kind of taken aback. I was surprised that he would say this to me.'

'You were not recording the conversation, is that correct?'

'That is correct. It was just a conversation at the door after I knocked.'

'So what happened next?'

'I went to the car and immediately wrote out these notes of the conversation so I would have it verbatim from when it was freshest in my mind. I told my partners what had just transpired and we decided to call the district attorney's office for advice as to whether this admission to me would give us probable cause to arrest Mr. Storey. Um, what happened was that none of us could get a signal on our cell phones because we were up there in the hills. We left the house and drove to the fire station on Mulholland just east of Laurel Canyon Boulevard. We asked to use a phone there and I made the call to the DA.'

'And who did you speak with?'

'You. I recounted the case, what had transpired during the search and what Mr. Storey said at the door. It was decided to continue the investigation at that point and not make the arrest.'

'Did you agree with that decision?'

'Not at the time. I wanted to arrest him.'

'Did Mr. Storey's admission change the investigation?'

'It pretty much closed the focus. The man had admitted the crime to me. We began looking only at him.'

'Did you ever consider that perhaps the admission was an empty boast, that at the same time you were in essence baiting the defendant, he was baiting you?'

'Yes, I considered it. But ultimately I believed he made the statements because they were true and because he believed he was in an invincible position at that point.'

There was a sharp ripping sound as Storey tore the top page off his sketch pad. He crumpled the paper and bounced it across the table. It hit a computer screen and bounced off the table to the floor.

'Thank you, Detective,' Langwiser said. 'Now, you said the decision was to continue the investigation. Can you tell the jury what that entailed?'

Bosch described how he and his partners had interviewed dozens of witnesses who had seen the defendant and the victim at the film premiere or at the reception that followed in a circus tent erected in a nearby parking lot. They also interviewed dozens more people who knew Storey or had worked with him. Bosch acknowledged that none of these interviews had produced information important to the investigation.

'You mentioned earlier that during the search of the defendant's home you became curious about a missing book, correct?'

'Yes.'

Fowkkes objected.

'There has been no evidence whatsoever about a missing book. There was a space on the shelf. It does not mean there was ever a book in that place.'

Langwiser promised she would tie it all up promptly and the judge overruled.

'Did there come a time when you determined what book had been in that space on the shelf in the defendant's home?'

'Yes, in the course of our gathering of background information on Mr. Storey, my partner, Kizmin Rider, who was aware of his work and professional reputation, remembered that she had read a story about him in a magazine called *Architectural Digest.* She was able to do an Internet search and determine that the issue she remembered was from February of last year. She then ordered a copy of the magazine from the publisher. What she had remembered was that there were photos in the article of Mr. Storey in his house. She remembered his bookshelves because she is an avid reader and was curious about what books this movie director would have on his shelves.'

Langwiser made a motion to introduce the magazine as her next exhibit. It was received by the judge and Langwiser gave it to Bosch on the witness stand.

'Is that the magazine your partner received?'

'Yes.'

'Could you turn to the story on the defendant and describe the photograph on the opening page of the story?'

Bosch flipped to a marker in the magazine.

'It is a photograph of David Storey sitting on the couch in the living room of his house. To his left are the bookshelves.'

'Can you read the titles of the books on the spines of the books?'

'Some of them. They are not all clear.'

'When you received this magazine from the publisher, what did you do with it?'

'We saw that not all of the books were clear. We contacted the publisher again and attempted to borrow the negative of this photo. We dealt with the editor in chief, who would not allow the negatives out of the office. He cited media law and free-press restraints.'

'So what happened next?'

'The editor said he would even fight a court order. An attorney from the city attorney's office was called in and began negotiating with the magazine's lawyer. The result was that I flew to New York City and was allowed access to the negative in the photo lab in the *Architectural Digest* offices.'

'For the record, what date were you there?'

'I took a redeye on October twenty-ninth. I was at the magazine's office the following morning. It was a Monday, October thirtieth.'

'And what did you do there?'

'I had the magazine's photo lab manager make blowups of the shot containing the bookshelves.'

Langwiser introduced two large blowup photographs on hard backing as her next exhibits. After they were approved over unsustained objection she put them on easels set in front of the jury. One showed the bookcase in full while the other was a blowup of one shelf. The image was grainy but the titles on the spines of the books could be read.

'Detective, did you compare these photos with those taken during the search of the defendant's house?'

'Yes, we did.'

Langwiser asked permission to set up a third and fourth easel and to put blowup photos taken during the search of the full bookcase and the shelf with the space for a missing book. The judge approved. She then asked Bosch to step down from the witness stand and use a pointer to explain what he found during his comparison study. It was obvious to anyone looking at the photos what he found but Langwiser was painstakingly going through the motions so that no juror could be confused.

Bosch put the pointer on the photo showing the open space in the shelved books. He then brought it over and put the tip on a book that was in the same spot.

'When we searched the house on October seventeenth there was no book here between *The Fifth Horizon* and *Print the Legend.* Here in this photo, taken ten months before, there is a book between *The Fifth Horizon* and *Print the Legend.*'

'And what is the title of that book?'

'*Victims of the Night.*'

'Okay, and did you look at photos you had from the search of the full bookcase in order to see if this book, *Victims of the Night,* had been shelved elsewhere?'

Bosch pointed to the October 17 blowup of the entire bookcase.

'We did. It's not there.'

'Did you find this book anywhere in the house?'

'No, we did not.'

'Thank you, Detective. You can return to the witness stand now.'

Langwiser introduced a copy of *Victims of the Night* as an exhibit and handed it to Bosch.

'Can you tell the jury what that is, Detective?'

'It is a copy of *Victims of the Night.*'

'Is that the book that was on the defendant's shelf when his photograph was taken for *Architectural Digest* in January of last year?'

'No, it's not. It's a copy of the same book. I bought it.'

'Where?'

'A place called Mystery Bookstore in Westwood.'

'Why did you buy it there?'

'I called around. It was the only place I could find that had it in stock.'

'Why was it so hard to find?'

'The man at Mystery Bookstore told me it was a small printing by a small publisher.'

'Did you read this book?'

'Parts of it. It is mostly photographs of unusual crime scenes and accident scenes, that sort of thing.'

'Is there anything in there that struck you as unusual or perhaps relating to the killing of Jody Krementz?'

'Yes, there is a photograph of a death scene on page seventy-three that immediately drew my attention.'

'Describe it, please.'

Bosch opened the book to a marker. He spoke as he looked at the full-page photograph on the right side of the book.

'It shows a woman in a bed. She's dead. A scarf is tied around her neck and looped over one of the bars of the headboard. She is nude from the waist down. Her left hand is between her legs and two of her fingers have penetrated the vagina.'

'Can you read the caption beneath the photo, please?'

'It says, "Autoerotic Death: This woman was found in her bed in New Orleans, a victim of autoerotic asphyxia. It is estimated that around the world more than five hundred people die from this accidental misadventure each year." '

Langwiser asked and received permission to place two more blowup photos on the easels as exhibits. She placed them right over two of the bookshelf photos. Side by side the photos were of Jody Krementz's body in her bed and of the page from *Victims of the Night.*

'Detective, did you make a comparison between the photo of the victim in this case, Jody Krementz, and the photo from the book?'

'Yes, I did. I found them to be very similar.'

'Did it appear to you that the body of Ms. Krementz could have been staged, using the photo from the book as a model or baseline?'

'Yes, it did.'

'Did you ever have occasion to ask the defendant what happened to his copy of the book *Victims of the Night*?'

'No, since the day of the search of his home, Mr. Storey and his attorneys have refused repeated requests for an interview.'

Langwiser nodded and looked at the judge.

'Your Honor, may I take these exhibits down and offer them to the court clerk?'

'Please do,' the judge responded.

Langwiser made a show of taking the photos of the two dead women down first by folding them in toward each other like two sides of a mirror closing. It was a little thing but Bosch saw the jurors watching.

'Okay, Detective Bosch,' Langwiser said when the easels were cleared. 'Did you make any inquiries or do any further investigation into autoerotic deaths?'

'Yes. I knew that if this case ever moved to a trial that the classification of the death as a homicide staged to look like this sort of accident might be challenged. I was also curious about what that caption in the book said. Frankly, I was surprised by the figure of five hundred deaths a year. I did some checking with the FBI and found that the figure was actually accurate, if not low.'

'And did that cause you to do any further research?'

'Yes, on a more local level.'

With Langwiser prompting, Bosch testified that he checked through records at the medical examiner's office for deaths due to autoerotic asphyxia. His search went back five years.

'And what did you find?'

'In those five years, sixteen deaths in Los Angeles County classified as accidental death by misadventure had been attributed specifically to autoerotic asphyxia.'

'And how many of these cases involved female victims?'

'Only one case involved a female.'

'Did you examine this case?'

Fowkkes was up with an objection and this time asked for a sidebar conference. The judge allowed it and the attorneys gathered at the side of the bench. Bosch could not hear the whispered conversation but knew that Fowkkes was most likely trying to stop the direction of the testimony. Langwiser and Kretzler had anticipated he would move once more to block any mention of Alicia Lopez in front of the jurors. It would likely be the pivotal decision in the trial – for both sides.

After five minutes of whispered argument, the judge sent the lawyers back to their places and told the jurors that the issue before the court would take longer than anticipated. He adjourned for another fifteen-minute break. Bosch returned to the prosecution table.

'Something new?' Bosch asked Langwiser.

'No, the same old argument. For some reason the judge wants to hear it again. Wish us luck.'

The lawyers and the judge retreated to chambers to argue the point. Bosch was left at the table. He used his cell phone to check messages at his home and office. There was one message at work. It was from Terry McCaleb. He thanked Bosch for the tip from the night before. He said he got some good information at Nat's and that he'd be in touch. Bosch erased it and closed the phone, wondering what it was that McCaleb had picked up.

When the lawyers returned through the rear door of the courtroom, Bosch read the judge's decision in their faces. Fowkkes looked dour, with his eyes downcast. Kretzler and Langwiser came back smiling.

After the jurors were brought back and the trial resumed, Langwiser went directly in for the hit. She asked the court reporter to read back the last question before the objection.

'Did you examine this case?' the reporter read.

'Let's strike that,' Langwiser said. 'Let's not confuse the issue. Detective, the one female case of the sixteen you found in the medical examiner's records, what was the name of the deceased in that case?'

'Alicia Lopez.'

'Can you tell us a little bit about her?'

'She was twenty-four and lived in Culver City. She worked as an administrative assistant to the vice-president of production at Sony Pictures, also in Culver City. She was found dead in her bed on the twentieth of May, nineteen ninety-eight.'

'She lived alone?'

'Yes.'

'What were the circumstances of her death?'

'She was found in her bed by a coworker who became concerned when she had missed two days of work following the weekend without calling in. The coroner estimated she had been dead three to four days by the time she was found. Decomposition of the body was extensive.'

'Ms. Langwiser?' Judge Houghton interrupted. 'It was agreed that you would lay foundation connecting the cases quickly.'

'I'm right there, Your Honor. Thank you. Detective, did anything about this case alert you or draw your attention in any way?'

'Several things. I looked at photos taken at the death scene and though decomposition was extensive I was able to note that the victim in this case was in a posture closely paralleling that of the victim in the present case. I also noted that the ligature in the Lopez case was also used without a buffering, which was the same with the present case. I also knew from our backgrounding investigation of Mr. Storey that at the time of Ms. Lopez's death he was making a film for a company called Cold House Films, a company which was being financed in part by Sony Pictures.'

In the moment following his answer Bosch noticed that the courtroom had become unusually still and silent. No one was whispering in the gallery or clearing their throat. It was as if everyone – jurors, lawyers, spectators and media – all decided to hold their breath at once. Bosch glanced at the jurors and saw that almost all of them were looking at the defense table. Bosch looked there as well and saw Storey, his face still aimed downward, silently seething. Langwiser finally broke the silence.

'Detective, did you make further inquiries about the Lopez case?'

'Yes, I spoke to the detective who handled it for the Culver City Police Department. I also made inquiries about Ms. Lopez's job at Sony.'

'And what did you learn about her that would have bearing on the present case?'

'I learned that at the time of her death she was acting as a liaison between the studio and the field production of the film David Storey was directing.'

'Do you recall the name of that film?'

'The Fifth Horizon.'

'Where was it being filmed?'

'In Los Angeles. Mostly in Venice.'

'And as a liaison would Ms. Lopez have had any direct contact with Mr. Storey?'

'Yes. She spoke with him by phone or in person every day of the shoot.'

Again the silence seemed to be roaring. Langwiser milked it for as long as she could and then started driving home the nails.

'Let me see if I have all of this straight, Detective. Your testimony is that in the past five years there has been only one death of a female in Los Angeles County attributed to autoerotic asphyxia and that the present case involving the death of Jody Krementz was staged to appear as an autoerotic asphyxia?'

'Objection,' Fowkkes interjected. 'Asked and answered.'

'Overruled,' Houghton said without argument from Langwiser. 'The witness may answer.'

'Yes,' Bosch said. 'Correct.'

'And that both of these women knew the defendant, David Storey?'

'Correct.'

'And that both of these deaths show similarities to a photograph of an autoerotic death contained in a book known at one time to be in the defendant's collection at home?'

'Correct.'

Bosch looked over at Storey as he said it, hoping he would look up so that they could lock eyes one more time.

'What did the Culver City Police Department have to say about this, Detective Bosch?'

'Based upon my inquiries they have reopened the case. But they are hampered.'

'Why is that?'

'The case is old. Because it was originally ruled an accidental death, not all the records were kept in archives. Because decomposition was advanced at the time of the body's discovery it is hard to make definitive observations and conclusions. And the body cannot be exhumed because it was cremated.'

'It was? By whom?'

Fowkkes stood and objected but the judge said the argument had already been heard and overruled. Langwiser prompted Bosch before Fowkkes had even sat back down.

'By whom, Detective Bosch?'

'By her family. But it was paid for . . . the cremation, the service, everything was paid for by David Storey as a gift in Alicia Lopez's memory.'

Langwiser loudly flipped up a page on her legal tablet. She was on a roll and everybody knew it. It was what cops and prosecutors called being in the tube. It was a surfing reference. It meant they had ridden the case into the water tunnel where everything was going smoothly and perfectly and was surrounding them in glorious balance.

'Detective, subsequent to this part of the investigation, did there come a time when a woman named Annabelle Crowe came to see you?'

'Yes. A story had broken in the *Los Angeles Times* about the investigation and how David Storey was the focus. She read the story and came forward.'

'And who is she?'

'She's an actress. She lives in West Hollywood.'

'And what bearing did she have on this case?'

'She told me that she had dated David Storey at one time last year and he choked her while they were having sex.'

Fowkkes made another objection, this one without the force of his other protestations. But again he was overruled, as the testimony had been cleared by the judge in earlier motions.

'Where did Ms. Crowe say this incident took place?'

'In Mr. Storey's home on Mulholland Drive. I asked her to describe the place and she was able to do so accurately. She had been there.'

'Couldn't she have seen the issue of *Architectural Digest* that showed photos of the defendant's home?'

'She was able to describe in accurate detail areas of the master bedroom and bath that were not shown in the magazine.'

'What happened to her when the defendant choked her?'

'She told me she passed out. When she awoke Mr. Storey was not in the room. He was taking a shower. She grabbed her clothing and fled from the home.'

Langwiser underlined that with a long silence. She then flipped the pages of her pad down, glanced over at the defense table and then looked up at Judge Houghton.

'Your Honor, that is all I have for Detective Bosch at this time.'

26

McCaleb got to El Cochinito at quarter to twelve. He hadn't been inside the store-front restaurant in Silver Lake in five years but he remembered the place had only a dozen or so tables and they were usually taken quickly at lunchtime. And often those tables were taken by cops. Not because the name of the restaurant was a draw – the Little Pig – but because the food was of high quality and low cost. It had been McCaleb's experience that cops were highly skilled in finding such establishments among the many restaurants in any city. When he had traveled on assignment for the bureau, he would always ask the local street cops for recommendations on food. He had rarely been disappointed.

While he waited for Winston he carefully studied the menu and planned his meal. In the past year his palate had finally returned with a vengeance. For the first eighteen months of his life after surgery, his sense of taste had deserted him. He had not cared what he ate because it all tasted the same – bland. Even a heavy dousing of habañera sauce on everything from sandwiches to pasta only registered a minor blip on his tongue. But then, slowly, his taste started coming back and it became a second rebirth for him following the transplant itself. He now loved everything Graciela made. He even loved everything *he* made – and this despite his general ineptitude with anything other than the barbecue grill. He ate everything with a gusto he'd never had before, even before the transplant. A peanut butter and jelly sandwich in the middle of the night was something he privately savored as much as a trip overtown with Graciela to dine in style at Jozu on Melrose. Consequently, he had started filling out, gaining back the twenty-five pounds he'd lost while his own heart had withered and he'd waited for a new one. He was now back to his pre-illness weight of 180 and food intake, for the first time in four years, was something he had to watch. On his last cardio checkup, his doctor had taken notice and raised a warning. She told him that he had to slow down the intake of calories and fat.

But not at this lunch. He had been waiting a long time for a chance to come to this place. Years earlier he had spent a good bit of time in Florida on a serial case and the only good that had come out of it was his love of

Cuban food. When he later transferred to the Los Angeles field office it was hard to find a Cuban restaurant that compared with the places where he had eaten in Ybor City outside of Tampa. Once on an L.A. case he'd come across a patrol cop who he learned was of Cuban descent. McCaleb asked him where he went to eat when he wanted real home cooking. The cop's answer was El Cochinito. And McCaleb quickly became a regular.

McCaleb decided that studying the menu was a waste of time because he had known all along what he wanted. Lechon asada with black beans and rice, fried bananas and yucca on the side and don't bother telling the doctor. He just wished Winston would hurry up and get there so he could place his order.

He put the menu aside and thought about Harry Bosch. McCaleb had spent most of the morning on the boat, watching the trial on television. He thought Bosch's performance on the witness stand had been outstanding. The revelation that Storey had been linked to another death was shocking to McCaleb and apparently to the media horde as well. During the breaks the talking heads in the studio were beside themselves with excitement over the prospect of this new fodder. They cut at one point to the hallway outside the courtroom where J. Reason Fowkkes was being peppered with questions about these new developments. Fowkkes, for probably the only time in his life, was not commenting. The talking heads were left to speculate about this new information and to comment on the methodical yet thoroughly gripping procession of the prosecution's case.

Still, watching the trial only caused uneasiness within McCaleb. He had a difficult time coming to terms with the idea that the man he had watched so capably describing the aspects and moves of a difficult investigation was also the man he was investigating, the man his gut instincts told him had committed the same kind of crime he was now involved in prosecuting.

At noon, their agreed-upon meeting time, McCaleb looked up from his thoughts to see Jaye Winston come through the restaurant's front door. She was followed by two men. One was black and one was white and that was the best way to differentiate between them because they wore almost identical gray suits and maroon ties. Before they even got to his table McCaleb knew they were bureau men.

Winston had a look of washed-out resignation on her face.

'Terry,' she said before sitting down, 'I want you to meet a couple guys.'

She indicated the black agent first.

'This is Don Twilley and this is Marcus Friedman. They're with the bureau.'

All three of them pulled out chairs and sat down. Friedman sat next to McCaleb, Twilley directly across from him. Nobody shook hands.

'I've never had Cuban food before,' Twilley said as he pulled a menu from the napkin stand. 'Is it good here?'

McCaleb looked at him.

'No. That's why I like to eat here.'

Twilley's eyes came up from the menu and he smiled.

'I know, stupid question.' He looked down at the menu and then back up at McCaleb. 'You know I know about you, Terry. You're a fucking legend in the FO. Not 'cause of the heart, 'cause of the cases. I'm glad to finally meet you.'

McCaleb looked over at Winston with a look that said what the hell is going on?

'Terry, Marc and Don are from the civil rights section.'

'Yeah? That's great. Did you guys come all the way from the field office to meet the legend and try Cuban food, or is there something else?'

'Uh . . .' Twilley began.

'Terry, the shit's hit the fan,' Winston said. 'A reporter called my captain this morning to ask if we were investigating Harry Bosch as a suspect in the Gunn case.'

McCaleb leaned back in his seat, shocked by the news. He was about to respond when the waiter came to the table.

'Give us a couple minutes,' Twilley said gruffly to the man, waving him off with a dismissive gesture, which annoyed McCaleb.

Winston continued.

'Terry, before we go further with this, I have to know something. Did you leak this?'

McCaleb shook his head in disgust.

'Are you kidding me? You're asking *me* that?'

'Look, all I know is that it didn't come from me. And I didn't tell anyone, not Captain Hitchens and not even my own partner, let alone a reporter.'

'Well, it wasn't me. Thanks for asking.'

He glanced at Twilley and then back at Winston. He hated having this dispute with Jaye in front of them.

'What are these guys doing here?' he asked. Then looking at Twilley again, he added, 'What do you want?'

'They're taking over the case, Terry,' Winston answered. 'And you're out.'

McCaleb looked back at Winston. His mouth opened a little before he realized how he looked and closed it.

'What are you talking about? I'm out? I'm the only one in. I've been working this as—'

'I know, Terry. But things are different now. After the reporter called Hitchens I had to tell him what was happening, what we'd been doing. He threw a fit and after he was done throwing a fit he decided the best way to handle this was to go to the bureau with it.'

'The civil rights section, Terry,' Twilley said. 'Investigating cops is our bread and butter. We'll be able to—'

'Fuck you, Twilley. Don't try that bureau rap with me. I used to be in the club, remember? I know how it goes. You guys will come in, piggyback my trail and then waltz Bosch past the cameras on the way to the lockup.'

'Is that what this is about?' Friedman said. 'Getting the credit?'

'You don't have to worry about that, Terry,' Twilley said. 'We can put you in front of the cameras if that's what you want.'

'It's *not* what I want. And don't call me Terry. You don't even fuckin' know me.'

He looked down at the table, shaking his head.

'Fuck, I've been waiting to come back to this place for a long time and now I don't even feel like eating.'

'Terry . . .' Winston said, not offering anything else.

'What, you're going to tell me this is right?'

'No. It's not right or wrong. It's just the way it is. The investigation is official now. You're not official. You knew this could happen from the start.'

He reluctantly nodded. He brought his elbows up onto the table and put his face into his hands.

'Who was the reporter?'

When Winston didn't answer he dropped his hands and looked pointedly at her.

'Who?'

'A guy named Jack McEvoy. He works for the *New Times*, an alternative weekly that likes to stir up shit.'

'I know what it is.'

'You know McEvoy?' Twilley asked.

McCaleb's cell phone began to chirp. It was in the pocket of his jacket draped over his chair. It got caught in the pocket as he tried to get it out. He anxiously struggled with it because he assumed it would be Graciela. Other than Winston and Buddy Lockridge, he'd only given the number to Brass Doran in Quantico and he had finished his business with her.

He finally answered after the fifth chirp.

'Hey, Agent McCaleb, it's Jack McEvoy from the *New Times*. You got a couple minutes to talk?'

McCaleb looked across the table at Twilley, wondering if he could hear the voice on the phone.

'Actually, I don't. I'm in the middle of something here. How'd you get this number?'

'Information on Catalina. I called the number and your wife answered. She gave me your cell. That a problem?'

'No, no problem. But I can't talk now.'

'When can we talk? It's important. Something's come up that I really want to talk—'

'Just call me later. In an hour.'

McCaleb closed the phone and put it down on the table. He looked at it, half expecting McEvoy to call back right away. Reporters were like that.

'Terry, everything all right?'

He looked up at Winston.

'Yeah, fine. My charter tomorrow. He wanted to know about the weather.'

He looked at Twilley.

'What was your question again?'

'Do you know Jack McEvoy? The reporter who called Captain Hitchens.'

McCaleb paused, looking at Winston and then back at Twilley.

'Yeah, I know him. You know I know him.'

'That's right, the Poet case. You had a piece of that.'

'A small piece.'

'When was the last time you talked to McEvoy?'

'Well, that would've been, let's see . . . that would have been a couple days ago.'

Winston visibly stiffened. McCaleb looked over at her.

'Relax, would you, Jaye? I ran into McEvoy at the Storey trial. I went up there to talk to Bosch. McEvoy's covering it for *New Times* and he said hello – I hadn't talked to him in five years. And I did *not* tell him what I was doing or what I was working on. In fact, at the time I saw him Bosch wasn't even a suspect.'

'Well, did he see you with Bosch?'

'I'm sure he did. Everybody did. There's as much media up there as there was for O. J. Did he specifically mention me to your captain?'

'If he did, Hitchens didn't tell me.'

'All right, then, if it wasn't you and it wasn't me, where else did the leak come from?'

'That's what we are asking you,' Twilley said. 'Before we come into this case we want to know the lay of the land and who's talking to who.'

McCaleb didn't reply. He was getting claustrophobic. Between the conversation and Twilley being in his face, and the people standing around in the small restaurant waiting for tables, he was beginning to feel like he couldn't breathe.

'What about this bar you went to last night?' Friedman asked.

McCaleb leaned back and looked over at him.

'What about it?'

'Jaye told us what you told her. You specifically asked about Bosch *and* Gunn there, right?'

'Yeah, right. And what? You think the bartender then jumped on the phone and called the *New Times* and asked for Jack McEvoy? All because I showed her a picture of Bosch? Give me a fucking break.'

'Hey, it's a media-conscious town. People are plugged in. People sell stories, info, data all the time.'

McCaleb shook his head, refusing to buy into the possibility that the bartender in the vest had enough intelligence to put together what he was doing and to then make a call to a reporter.

Suddenly, he realized who did have the intelligence and information to do it. Buddy Lockridge. And if it had been him, it might as well have been McCaleb who leaked the story. He felt sweat start to warm his scalp as he thought about Lockridge hiding down on the lower deck while he had made his case against Bosch to Winston.

'Did you have anything to drink while you were in the bar? I hear you take a mess of pills every day. Mixing that with alcohol . . . you know, loose lips sink ships.'

Twilley had asked the question but McCaleb looked sharply at Winston. He was stung with a sense of betrayal by the whole scene and at how quickly things had shifted. But before he could say anything he saw the apology in her eyes and he knew she wished things had been handled differently. He finally looked back at Twilley.

'You think maybe I mixed a few too many drinks and pills, Twilley? That it? You think I started shooting my mouth off in the bar?'

'I don't think that. I'm just asking, okay? No reason to get defensive here. I'm just trying to figure out how this reporter knows what he thinks he knows.'

'Well, figure it out without me.'

McCaleb pushed back his chair to get up.

'Try the lechon asada,' he said. 'It's the best in the city.'

As he began to get up, Twilley reached across the table and grabbed his forearm.

'Come on, Terry, let's talk about this,' Twilley said.

'Terry, please,' Winston said.

McCaleb pulled his arm loose from Twilley's grip and stood up. He looked over at Winston.

'Good luck with these guys, Jaye. You'll probably need it.'

Then he looked down at Friedman and then Twilley.

'And fuck you guys very much.'

He made his way through the crowd of people waiting and out the front door. Nobody followed him.

He sat in the Cherokee parked on Sunset and watched the restaurant while letting the anger slowly leach out of his body. On one level McCaleb knew the moves Winston and her captain were making were the right moves. But on another he didn't like being moved out of his own case. A case was like a car. You could be driving it or riding in the front or back. Or you could be left on the side of the road as the car went by. McCaleb had just gone from having his hands on the wheel to thumbing it from the side of the road. And it hurt.

He began to think about Buddy Lockridge and how he would handle him. If he determined that it had been Buddy who had talked to McEvoy after eavesdropping on McCaleb's briefing of Winston on the boat, then he would cleanly sever all ties to him. Partner or not, he wouldn't be able to work with Buddy again.

He realized that Buddy had the number to his cell phone and could have been the one who gave it to McEvoy. He got the phone out and called his home. Graciela answered, Fridays being one of her half days at the school.

'Graciela, did you give my cell number to anybody lately?'

'Yes, a reporter who said he knew you and needed to speak with you right away. A Jack something. Why, is something wrong?'

'No, nothing's wrong. I was just checking.'

'Are you sure?'

McCaleb got a call-waiting beep. He looked at his watch. It was ten to one. McEvoy wasn't supposed to call back until after one.

'Yes, I'm sure,' he told Graciela. 'Look, I've got another call. I'll be home by dark tonight. I'll see you then.'

He switched to the other call. It was McEvoy, who explained that he was at the courthouse and had to get back into the trial at one or he'd lose his precious seat. He couldn't wait the full hour to call back.

'Can you talk now?' he asked.

'What do you want?'

'I need to talk to you.'

'You keep saying that. About what?'

'Harry Bosch. I'm working on a story about—'

'I don't know anything about the Storey case. Only what's on TV.'

'It's not that. It's about the Edward Gunn case.'

McCaleb didn't answer. He knew this was not good. Dancing with a reporter over something like this could only lead to trouble. McEvoy spoke into the silence.

'Is that what you wanted to see Harry Bosch about the other day when I saw you here? Are you working on the Gunn case?'

'Listen to me. I can honestly tell you that I am not working on the Edward Gunn case. Okay?'

Good, McCaleb thought. So far he hadn't lied.

'*Were* you working on the case? For the sheriff's department?'

'Can I ask you something? Who told you this? Who said I was working this case?'

'I can't answer that. I have to protect my sources. If you want to give me information I will protect your identity as well. But if I give up a source, I'm fucked in this business.'

'Well, I'll tell you what, Jack. I'm not talking to you unless you are talking to me, know what I mean? It's a two-way street. You want to tell me who is saying this shit about me and I'll talk to you. Otherwise, we've got nothing to say to each other.'

He waited. McEvoy said nothing.

'I thought so. Take it easy, Jack.'

He closed the phone. Whether McEvoy had mentioned his name or not to Captain Hitchens, it was clear that McEvoy was tapped in to a credible pipeline of information. And again McCaleb narrowed it down to one person besides himself and Jaye Winston.

'Goddamnit!' he said out loud in the car.

A few minutes after one he watched Jaye Winston come out of El Cochinito. McCaleb was hoping for the chance to corner her and talk to her alone, maybe tell her about Lockridge. But Twilley and Friedman followed her out and all three got into the same car. A bureau car.

McCaleb watched them pull out into traffic and drive off in the direction of downtown. He got out of the Cherokee and went back into the restaurant. He was starved. There were no tables available so he made an order to go. He'd eat in the Cherokee.

The old woman who took his order looked up at him with sad brown eyes. She said it had been a busy week and the kitchen had just run out of lechon asada.

27

John Reason surprised the spectators, the jurors and probably most of the media when he reserved his cross-examination of Bosch until the defense's case began, but it had been anticipated by the prosecution team. If the defense strategy was to shoot the messenger, that messenger was Bosch and the best place from which to take the shot was during the presentation of the defense's side. That way, Fowkkes's attack on Bosch could be part of an orchestrated attack on the entire case against David Storey.

Following a lunch break during which Bosch and the prosecutors were relentlessly pursued by the media with questions about Bosch's testimony, the prosecution began to move quickly with the momentum gained in the morning's session. Kretzler and Langwiser took turns examining a series of witnesses with short stays on the stand.

The first of these was Teresa Corazón, chief of the medical examiner's office. Under Kretzler's questioning, she testified to her findings during the autopsy and put Jody Krementz's time of death at some point between midnight and 2 A.M. on Friday, October 13. She also gave corroborating testimony on the rarity of autoerotic deaths involving female victims.

Once more Fowkkes reserved the right to question the witness during the defense phase of the trial. Corazón was dismissed after less than a half hour on the stand.

Now that his own testimony was completed – as far as the prosecution's case went – it was not vital for Bosch to be in the courtroom for every moment of the trial. While Langwiser called the next witness – a lab tech who would identify the hair samples gathered from the victim's body as belonging to Storey – Bosch walked Corazón to her car. They had been lovers many years before in what current culture would term a casual relationship. But while there may not have been any love involved, there had been nothing casual about it to Bosch. In his view it had been two people who looked at death every day pushing it away with the ultimate life-affirming act.

Corazón had broken it off after she was named to the top slot in the coroner's office. Their relationship since that point had been strictly professional, though Corazón's new position reduced her time in the autopsy suites and Bosch did not see her often. The Jody Krementz case was different. Corazón had instinctively known it might become a case that drew the bead of the media horde and had taken the autopsy herself. It had paid off. Her testimony would be seen across the nation and probably around the globe. She was attractive, smart, skilled and thorough. That half hour on the stand would be like a half-hour commercial for lucrative jobs as an independent examiner or commentator. Bosch knew one thing about her from his time with her: Teresa Corazón always had her eye on the next step.

She was parked in the garage next to the state parole office on the back side of the justice complex. They spoke of banalities – the weather, Harry's attempts to stop smoking – until Corazón brought the case up.

'It seems to be going well.'

'So far.'

'It'd be nice if we won one of these big ones for a change.'

'It would.'

'I watched you testify this morning. In my office I had the TV on. You did very well, Harry.'

He knew her tone. She was leading to something.

'But?'

'But you look tired. And you know they're going to come after you. This kind of case, if they destroy the cop they destroy the case.'

'O. J. one-oh-one.'

'Right. So are you ready for them?'

'I think so.'

'Good. Just rest up.'

'Easier said than done.'

As they approached the garage Bosch looked over at the parole office and saw a gathering of the staff out front for some kind of presentation. The group was standing below a banner hanging from the roof line that said WELCOME BACK THELMA. A man in a suit was presenting a plaque to a heavyset black woman who was leaning on a cane.

'Oh . . . that's that parole agent,' Corazón said. 'The one who got shot last year. By that hit man from Vegas?'

'Right, right,' Bosch said, remembering the story. 'She came back.'

He noticed that there were no television cameras recording the presentation. A woman got shot in the line of duty and then fought her way back to the job. It apparently wasn't worth wasting videotape over.

'Welcome back,' he said.

Corazón's car was on the second floor. It was a two-seat, shining black Mercedes.

'I see the outside work must be going pretty well,' Bosch said.

Corazón nodded.

'In my last contract I got four weeks' professional leave. I'm making the most of it. Trials, TV, that sort of thing. I did a case on that autopsy show on HBO, too. It airs next month.'

'Teresa, you're going to be world famous before we know it.'

She smiled and stepped close to him and straightened his tie.

'I know what you think about it, Harry. That's okay.'

'Doesn't matter what I think about it. Are you happy?'

She nodded.

'Very.'

'Then I'm happy for you. I better get back in there. I'll see you, Teresa.'

She suddenly rose on her toes and kissed him on the cheek. It had been a long time since he had gotten one of those.

'I hope you make it through, Harry.'

'Yeah, me too.'

Bosch stepped out of the elevator into the hallway and headed toward the Department N courtroom. He saw a line of people cordoned off by the courtroom door: people waiting for a spectator seat to possibly open. A few reporters were milling about the open door of the pressroom but everybody else was at stations, watching the trial.

'Detective Bosch?'

Bosch turned. Standing in a pay-phone alcove was Jack McEvoy, the reporter he had met the day before. He stopped.

'I saw you walk out and I hoped I'd catch you.'

'I have to get back in there.'

'I know. I just wanted to tell you that it is very important that I talk to you about something. The sooner the better.'

'What are you talking about? What's so important?'

'Well, it's about you.'

McEvoy stepped out of the alcove so that he was closer to Bosch and did not have to speak as loud.

'What about me?'

'Do you know you are under investigation by the sheriff's department?'

Bosch looked up the hall toward the courtroom door and then back at McEvoy. The reporter was slowly bringing a pad of paper and pen up in his hands. He was ready to take notes.

'Wait a minute.' Bosch put his hand on the notebook. 'What are you talking about? What investigation?'

'Edward Gunn, you remember him? He's dead and you're their suspect.'

Bosch just stared at him, his mouth coming slightly open.

'I wondered if you wanted to comment on this. You know, defend yourself. I'll be writing a story for next week's edition and wanted you to have the chance to tell your—'

'No, no comment. I have to get back.'

Bosch turned and walked a few paces toward the courtroom door but then stopped. He walked back to McEvoy, who was writing in the notebook.

'What are you writing? I didn't say anything.'

'I know. That's what I'm writing.'

McEvoy looked up from the notebook to him.

'You said next week,' Bosch said. 'When does it come out?'

'*New Times* is published every Thursday morning.'

'So until when do I have, if I decide to talk to you?'

'About Wednesday lunch. But that will be pressing it. I won't be able to do much then but drop in some quotes. The time to talk is now.'

'Who told you this? Who's your source?'

McEvoy shook his head.

'I can't discuss sources with you. What I want to talk about is this allegation. Did you kill Edward Gunn? Are you some kind of avenging angel? That's what they think.'

Bosch studied the reporter for a long moment before finally speaking.

'Don't quote me on this, but fuck you. You know what I mean? I don't know if this is a bullshit bluff or not, but let me give you some advice. You better make damn sure you've got it right before you put anything in that paper of yours. A good investigator always knows the motivation of his sources – it's called having a bullshit meter. Yours better be working real well.'

He turned and walked quickly to the courtroom door.

Langwiser had just finished with the hair specialist when Bosch came back into the courtroom. Once again Fowkkes stood up and reserved the right to recall the witness during the defense case.

While the witness came through the gate behind the attorneys' lectern, Bosch slipped past him and went to his seat at the prosecution table. He didn't look at or say anything to Langwiser or Kretzler. He folded his arms and looked down at the notepad he had left on the table. He realized he had adopted the same position and posture he had seen David Storey take at the defense table. The posture of a guilty man. Bosch quickly dropped his arms to his lap and looked up at the seal of the State of California which hung on the wall above the judge's bench.

Langwiser got up and called the next witness, a fingerprint technician. His testimony was quick and more corroboration of Bosch's testimony. It went unchallenged by Fowkkes. The technician was followed to the stand by the patrol officer who answered the first call from Krementz's roommate and then by his sergeant, who was the next to arrive.

Bosch barely listened to the testimony. There was nothing new in it and his mind was racing in another direction. He was thinking about McEvoy and the story he was working on. He knew he should inform Langwiser and Kretzler but wanted time to think about things. He decided to hold off until after the weekend.

The victim's roommate, Jane Gilley, was the first witness to appear who was not part of the law enforcement community. She was tearful and sincere in her testimony, confirming details of the investigation already revealed by Bosch but also adding more personal bits of information. She testified about how excited Jody Krementz had been at the prospect of dating a major Hollywood player and how both of them had spent the day before her date getting manicures, pedicures and hair stylings.

'She paid for me,' Gilley testified. 'That was so sweet.'

Her testimony put a very human face on what so far had been an almost antiseptic analysis by law enforcement professionals of a murder.

When Gilley's examination by Langwiser was concluded, Fowkkes finally broke with his pattern and announced he had a few questions for the witness. He stepped to the lectern without any notes. He clasped his hands behind his back and leaned slightly forward to the microphone.

'Now, Ms. Gilley, your roommate was an attractive young woman, wasn't she?'

'Yes, she was beautiful.'

'And was she popular? In other words, did she date a lot of fellows?'

Gilley nodded hesitantly.

'She went out.'

'A lot, a little, how often?'

'It would be hard to say. I wasn't her social secretary and I have my own boyfriend.'

'I see. Then let's take, say, the ten weeks prior to her death. How many of those ten weeks would you say went by without Jody going out on a date?'

Langwiser stood up and objected.

'Your Honor, this is ridiculous. It has nothing to do with the night of October twelfth going into the morning of the thirteenth.'

'Oh, but Your Honor, I think it does,' Fowkkes responded. 'And I think Ms. Langwiser knows it does. If you allow me a little bit of string here, I will be able to quickly tie it up.'

Houghton overruled the objection and told Fowkkes to ask the question again.

'In the ten weeks prior to her death, how many weeks went by without Jody Krementz having a date with a man?'

'I don't know. Maybe one. Maybe none.'

'Maybe none,' Fowkkes repeated. 'And, Ms. Gilley, how many of those weeks would you say your roommate had at least two dates?'

Langwiser objected again but was overruled again.

'I don't know the answer,' Gilley said. 'A lot of them.'

'A lot of them,' Fowkkes repeated.

Langwiser rose and asked the judge to direct Fowkkes not to repeat the witness's answer unless it was in the form of a question. The judge complied and Fowkkes went on as if he had not been corrected at all.

'Were these dates all with the same fellow?'

'No. Different guys mostly. A few repeats.'

'So she liked to play the field, is that correct?'

'I guess so.'

'Is that a yes or no, Ms. Gilley?'

'It's a yes.'

'Thank you. In the ten weeks prior to her death, weeks in which you said she most often had at least two dates, how many different men did she see?'

Gilley shook her head in exasperation.

'I have no idea. I didn't count them. Besides, what does this have to do—'

'Thank you, Ms. Gilley. I would appreciate it if you would just answer the questions I pose to you.'

He waited. She said nothing.

'Now, did Jody ever encounter difficulties when she stopped dating a man? When she moved on to the next?'

'I don't know what you mean.'

'I mean were all the men happy not to have a return engagement?'

'Sometimes they'd get mad if she didn't want to go out again. Nothing serious.'

'No threats of violence? She wasn't afraid of anyone?'

'Not that she told me about.'

'Did she tell you about every man she dated?'

'No.'

'Now, on these dates, did she often bring the men back to the home you two shared?'

'Sometimes.'

'Did they stay over?'

'Sometimes, I don't know.'

'You often weren't there, is that correct?'

'Yes, I often stayed at my boyfriend's.'

'Why is that?'

She gave a short laugh.

'Because I love him.'

'Well, did you ever stay together overnight at your home?'

'I don't remember him ever staying over.'

'Why is that?'

'I guess because he lives alone. It was more private.'

'Isn't it true, Ms. Gilley, that you stayed overnight several times a week at your boyfriend's home?'

'Sometimes. So what?'

'And that this was because you were unhappy with your roommate's constant procession of overnight guests.'

Langwiser stood up.

'Your Honor, that's not even a question. I object to its form and content. Jody Krementz's lifestyle is not on trial here. David Storey is on trial for her murder and it's not fair for the defense to be allowed to go after someone who—'

'Okay, Ms. Langwiser, that's enough,' Judge Houghton said. He looked over at Fowkkes. 'Mr. Fowkkes, that's about all the string I'm going to allow you to run with in that direction. Ms. Langwiser makes her point. I want you to move on with this witness.'

Fowkkes nodded. Bosch studied him. He was a perfect actor. In his demeanor he was able to convey the frustration of a man being pulled back from a hidden truth. He wondered if the jury would see it as an act.

'Very well, Your Honor,' Fowkkes said, putting the frustration into the inflection of his voice. 'I have no further questions for this witness at this time.'

The judge adjourned for the afternoon break of fifteen minutes. Bosch ushered Gilley through the reporters, down the elevator and out to her car. He told her she had done very well and handled Fowkkes's cross-examination perfectly. He then joined Kretzler and Langwiser in the second-floor DA's office where the prosecution team had a temporary office during the trial. There was a small coffeemaker in the room and it was half-filled with coffee brewed during the morning break. There wasn't enough time for a fresh brew so they all drank the stale coffee while Kretzler and Langwiser considered the progress of the day.

'I think the she's-a-whore defense is going to backfire on them big time,' Langwiser said. 'They have to have more than that.'

'He's just trying to show there were a lot of men,' Kretzler said. 'And it could have been any of them. The shotgun defense. You shoot a lot of pellets and one's bound to hit the target.'

'It's still not going to work.'

'I'll tell you one thing, with John Reason reserving on all of these wits, we're moving really quickly. He keeps this up, we're going to finish our case Tuesday or Wednesday.'

'Good. I can't wait to see what they've got.'

'I can,' Bosch interjected.

Langwiser looked at him.

'Oh, Harry. You've weathered these storms before.'

'Yeah, but I've got a bad feeling about this one.'

'Don't worry about it,' Kretzler said. 'We're going to kick their ass across the courtroom. We're in the tube, man, and we ain't coming out.'

They put their three Styrofoam cups together in a toast.

Bosch's current partner, Jerry Edgar, and former partner, Kizmin Rider, testified during the afternoon session. Both were asked by the prosecutors to recall the moments after the search of David Storey's home when Bosch got into the car and reported to them that Storey had just bragged of committing the crime. Their testimony was solidly in tandem with Bosch's own testimony and would act to buttress the case against defense assaults on Bosch's character. Bosch also knew that the prosecutors hoped to gain additional credence with the jury because both Edgar and Rider were black. Five members of the jury and the two alternates were black. In a time when the veracity of any white police officer in Los Angeles would fall under suspicion by black jurors, having Edgar and Rider join a line of solidarity with Bosch was a plus.

Rider testified first and Fowkkes passed on cross-examination. Edgar's testimony mirrored hers but he was asked additional questions because he had delivered the second search warrant issued in the case. This one was a court order seeking hair and blood samples from David Storey. It had been approved and signed by a judge while Bosch was in New York following the *Architectural Digest* lead and Rider was on a Hawaiian vacation planned before the murder. With a patrol officer in tow, Edgar had once again appeared at Storey's house at 6 A.M. with the warrant. He testified that Storey kept them waiting outside while he contacted his lawyer, who by now was the criminal defense attorney J. Reason Fowkkes.

Once Fowkkes was apprised of the situation he told Storey to cooperate and the suspect was taken to Parker Center in downtown where samples of his pubic hair, scalp hair and blood were collected by a lab nurse.

'Did you at any point during this traveling time and collection process question the defendant about the crime?' Kretzler asked.

'No, I did not,' Edgar responded. 'Before we left his residence he gave me his phone and I spoke to Mr. Fowkkes. He told me his client did not wish to be questioned or harassed, as he put it, in any way. So we basically drove in silence – at least on my part. And we didn't talk at Parker Center either. When we were finished, Mr. Fowkkes was there and he drove Mr. Storey home.'

'Did Mr. Storey make any unsolicited comments to you during the time he was with you?'

'Just one.'

'And where was that?'

'In the car while we were driving to Parker Center.'

'And what did he say?'

'He was looking out the window and just said, "You people are fucked if you think I'm going down for this."'

'And was this piece of conversation tape-recorded?'

'Yes, it was.'

'Why is that?'

'Because of his earlier admission to Detective Bosch, we thought there was a chance he might go ahead and make another statement like that. On the day I served the hair and blood warrant, I used a car borrowed from the narcotics unit. It's a car they use for making street buys. It is wired for sound.'

'Did you bring the tape from that day with you, Detective?'

'Yes.'

Kretzler introduced the tape as evidence. Fowkkes objected, saying that Edgar had already testified as to what was said and the audio wasn't necessary. Again the judge overruled and the tape was played. Kretzler started the tape well before the statement made by Storey so that the jurors would hear the hum of the car engine and traffic noise and know that Edgar did not violate the defendant's rights by questioning him in order to elicit the statement.

When the tape came to Storey's comment, the tone of arrogance and even hate for his investigators came through loud and clear.

Wanting that tone to be what carried the jurors into the weekend, Kretzler ended his questioning of Edgar.

Fowkkes, perhaps understanding the ploy, said he would have a brief cross-examination. He proceeded to ask Edgar a series of innocuous questions that added little to the record in favor of the defense or disfavor of the prosecution. At precisely 4:30 P.M. he ended the cross-examination and Judge Houghton promptly recessed for the weekend.

As the courtroom emptied into the hallway, Bosch looked around for McEvoy but didn't see him. Edgar and Rider, who had hung around after her testimony, came up to him.

'Harry, how 'bout we go get a drink?' Rider said.

'How 'bout we go get drunk?' Bosch replied.

28

They waited until ten-thirty Saturday morning for their charter clients to arrive but no one showed. McCaleb was sitting silently on the gunwale in the stern doing a slow burn over everything. The missing charter, his dismissal from the case, the most recent phone call from Jaye Winston, everything. Before he left the house Winston had called to apologize for how things had gone the day before. He feigned indifference and told her to forget about it. And he still didn't tell her about Buddy Lockridge overhearing them on the boat two days earlier. When Jaye said Twilley and Friedman had decided it would be best if he returned the copies of all the documents relating to the case, he told her to tell them they could come get them if they wanted them. He said he had a charter and had to go. They abruptly said good-byes and hung up.

Raymond was bent over the stern, fishing with a little spinner reel McCaleb had gotten him after they moved to the island. He was looking through the clear water at the moving shapes of the orange garibaldi fish twenty feet below. Buddy Lockridge was sitting in the fighting chair reading the Metro section of the *Los Angeles Times.* He seemed as relaxed as a summer wave. McCaleb had not yet confronted him with his suspicions that he was the leak. He had been waiting for the right moment.

'Hey, Terror, you see this story?' Lockridge said. 'About Bosch giving his testimony yesterday in Van Nuys court?'

'Nope.'

'Man, what they're hinting at here is that this director's a serial killer. Sounds like one of your old cases. And here the guy on the witness stand putting the finger on him is a—'

'Buddy, I told you, don't talk about that. Or did you forget what I said?'

'Okay, sorry. I was just saying, if this ain't irony I don't know what is, that's all.'

'Fine. Leave it at that.'

McCaleb checked his watch again. The clients should have been there at ten. He straightened up and went to the salon door.

'I'll make some calls,' he said. 'I don't want to be waiting around all day for these people.'

At the little chart table in the boat's salon he opened a drawer and took out the clipboard where they attached the charter reservations. There were only two pages on it. The current day's charter and a reservation for the following Saturday. The winter months were slow. He looked at the information on the top sheet. He was unfamiliar with it because Buddy had taken the reservation. The charter was for four men from Long Beach. They were supposed to come over Friday night and stay at the Zane Grey. A four-hour charter – ten to two on Saturday – and then they'd take a late ferry back to overtown. Buddy had taken the organizer's home number and the name of the hotel as well as a deposit of half the charter fee.

He looked at the list of hotels and phone numbers taped to the chart table and called the Zane Grey first. He quickly learned that no one with the charter organizer's name – the only one of the four names McCaleb had – was staying at the hotel. He then called the man's home number and got his wife. She said her husband wasn't home.

'Well, we're kind of waiting for him on a boat over here on Catalina. Do you know if he and his friends are on their way?'

There was a long silence.

'Ma'am, you there?'

'Uh, yes, yes. It's just that, they're not going fishing today. They told me they canceled that trip. They're out golfing right now. I can give you my husband's cell phone if you would like. You could talk—'

'That's not necessary, ma'am. Have a nice day.'

McCaleb closed his phone. He knew exactly what had happened. Neither he nor Buddy had checked the answering service that handled calls to the phone number they had placed on their charter ads in various phone books and fishing publications. He called the number now, punched in the code and, sure enough, there had been a message waiting since Wednesday. The party canceled the charter. They'd reschedule later.

'Yeah, sure,' McCaleb said.

He erased the message and closed the phone. He felt like throwing it through the glass slider at Buddy's head but he tried to calm himself. He walked into the little galley and got a quart carton of orange juice out of the cooler. He took it out with him to the stern.

'No charter today,' he said before taking a long drink from the carton.

'Why not?' Raymond asked, his disappointment obvious.

McCaleb wiped his mouth on the sleeve of his long-sleeve T-shirt.

'They canceled.'

Lockridge looked up from the newspaper and McCaleb hit him with a laser stare.

'Well, we keep the deposit, right?' Buddy asked. 'I took a two-hundred-dollar deposit on Visa.'

'No, we don't keep the deposit because they canceled on Wednesday.

We've both been too *busy* I guess to check the charter line like we're supposed to.'

'Ah, fuck! That's my fault.'

'Buddy, not in front of the boy. How many times do I have to tell you that?'

'Sorry. Sorry.'

McCaleb continued to stare at him. He had not wanted to talk about the leak to McEvoy until after the charter because he needed Buddy's help running a four-man fishing party. Now it didn't matter. Now was the time.

'Raymond,' he said while still staring at Lockridge. 'Do you still want to earn your money?'

'Yeah.'

'You mean "yes," don't you?'

'Yeah. I mean, yes. Yes.'

'Okay, then reel in, hook your line and start taking these rods in and put them in the rack. Can you do that?'

'Sure.'

The boy quickly reeled in his line, took off his bait and threw it into the water. He attached the hook to one of the rod's eyelets and then leaned it in the corner of the stern so he could take it home with him. He liked to practice his casting technique on the rear deck of the house, dropping a rubber practice weight onto the roofs and backyards below.

Raymond started taking the deep-sea rods out of the holders where Buddy had placed them in preparation for the charter. Two by two he took them into the salon and put them in the overhead racks. He had to stand on the couch to do it but it was an old couch in dire need of a new slipcover and McCaleb didn't care about it.

'Something wrong, Terror?' Buddy tried. 'It's just a charter, man. We knew it was going to be slow this month.'

'It's not the charter, Bud.'

'Then what? The case?'

McCaleb took a smaller gulp of juice and put the carton down on the gunwale.

'You mean the case I'm not on anymore?'

'I guess. I don't know. You're not on it anymore? When did that—'

'No, Buddy, I'm not on it. And there's something I want to talk to you about.'

He waited for Raymond to move another set of rods into the salon.

'You ever read the *New Times*, Buddy?'

'You mean that free weekly?'

'Yeah, that free weekly. The *New Times,* Buddy. Comes out every Thursday. There's always a stack in the laundry building at the marina. In fact, why am I asking this? I know you read the *New Times*.'

Lockridge's eyes suddenly fell to the deck. He looked crestfallen with guilt. He brought one hand up and rubbed his face. He kept it over his eyes when he spoke.

'Terry, I'm sorry. I never thought it would get back to you. What happened?'

'What's the matter, Uncle Buddy?'

It was Raymond in the door of the salon.

'Raymond, would you go inside and close that door for a few minutes?' McCaleb said. 'You can put on the TV. I need to talk to Buddy by myself.'

The boy hesitated, staring the whole time at Buddy covering his face.

'Raymond, please. And take this back to the cooler.'

The boy finally stepped out and took the orange juice carton. He went back in and slid the door closed. McCaleb looked back at Lockridge.

'How could you not think it would get back to me?'

'I don't know. I just thought nobody would know.'

'Well, you were wrong. And it has caused me a lot of trouble. But most of all it's a fucking betrayal, Buddy. I just can't believe you would do something like this.'

McCaleb glanced at the glass door to make sure the boy wasn't in earshot. There was no sign of Raymond. He must've gone down to one of the staterooms. McCaleb realized his breathing was way up. He was so angry he was hyperventilating. He had to end this and calm down.

'Does Graciela have to know about it?' Buddy asked in a pleading voice.

'I don't know. It doesn't matter what she knows. What matters is that we had this relationship and then you do something like this behind my back.'

Lockridge still hid his eyes behind his hand.

'I just didn't think it would mean that much to you, even if you found out. It was no big deal. I'm—'

'Don't try to mitigate it or tell me what kind of deal it is, okay? Don't even talk to me in that pleading, whiny voice. Just shut up.'

McCaleb walked to the stern, pressing his thighs against the padded combing. His back to Lockridge, he looked up the hillside above the commercial part of the little town. He could see his house. Graciela was on the deck holding the baby. She waved and then held Cielo's hand up in a baby wave. McCaleb waved back.

'What do you want me to do?' Buddy said from behind him. His voice was more controlled now. 'What do you want me to say? I won't do it again? Fine, I won't do it again.'

McCaleb didn't turn around. He continued looking up at his wife and his daughter.

'It doesn't matter what you won't do again. The damage is done. I have to think about this. We're partners as well as friends. Or we were, at least. All I want now is for you to just go. I'm going inside with Raymond. Take the skiff and go back to the pier. Take a ferry back tonight. I just don't want you around here, Buddy. Not now.'

'How will you guys get back to the pier?'

It was a desperate question with an obvious answer.

'I'll call the water taxi.'

'We've got a charter next Saturday. It's five people and—'

'I'll worry about Saturday when I come to it. I can cancel it if I have to or turn it over to Jim Hall's charter.'

'Terry, are you sure about this? All I did was—'

'I'm sure. Go on, Buddy. I don't want to talk anymore.'

McCaleb turned from the view and walked past Lockridge and to the salon door. He opened it and stepped in, then slid the door closed behind him. He didn't look back at Buddy. He went to the chart table and got an envelope out of the drawer. He slipped a five-dollar bill from his pocket into it, sealed it and wrote Raymond's name on it.

'Hey, Raymond where are you?' he called out.

For dinner they had grilled cheese sandwiches and chili. The chili was from the Busy Bee. McCaleb had picked it up on his way up from the boat with Raymond.

McCaleb sat across the table from his wife with Raymond to his left and the baby to his right in a jumper seat perched on the table. They were eating inside as an evening fog had enshrouded the island in a chilly grip. McCaleb remained morosely quiet through the meal, as he had been through much of the day. When they had come back early, Graciela decided to keep her distance. She took Raymond for a hike in the Wrigley Botanical Garden in Avalon Canyon. McCaleb was left with the baby, who fussed most of the day. He didn't mind, though. It took his mind off things.

Finally, at dinner, there was no avoiding each other. McCaleb had made the sandwiches so he was the last to sit down. He had barely begun eating when Graciela asked him what his trouble was.

'Nothing,' he said. 'I'm fine.'

'Raymond said you and Buddy had an argument.'

'Maybe Raymond should mind his own business.'

He looked at the boy as he said this and Raymond looked down at his food.

'That's not fair, Terry,' Graciela said.

She was right. McCaleb knew it. He reached over and tousled the boy's hair. It was so soft. He liked doing it. He hoped the gesture conveyed his apology.

'I'm off the case because Buddy leaked it to a reporter.'

'What?'

'We came up – I came up – with a suspect. A cop. Buddy overheard me telling Jaye Winston about my findings. He turned around and told a reporter. The reporter turned around and started making calls. Jaye and her captain think I was the leak.'

'That doesn't make sense. Why would Buddy do that?'

'I don't know. He didn't say. Actually, he did say. He said he didn't think I'd care or that it mattered. Words to that effect. That was today on the boat.'

He gestured toward Raymond, meaning this was the tense conversation he had caught part of and told Graciela about.

'Well, did you call Jaye and tell her it was him?'

'No, it doesn't matter. It came through me. I was dumb enough to let him on the boat. Can we talk about something else? I'm tired of thinking and talking about this.'

'Fine, Terry, what else do you want to talk about?'

He was silent. She was silent. After a long moment he started to laugh.

'I can't think of anything right now.'

Graciela finished eating a bite of her sandwich. McCaleb looked over at Cielo, who was looking at a blue-and-white ball that was suspended over her on a wire attached to the side of her bouncer seat. She was trying to reach for it with her tiny hands but couldn't quite make it. McCaleb could see her getting frustrated and he understood the feeling.

'Raymond, tell your father what you saw today in the gardens,' Graciela said.

She had recently begun referring to McCaleb as Raymond's father. They had adopted him but McCaleb didn't want to put any pressure on the boy to think of or refer to him as his father. Raymond usually called him Terry.

'We saw a Channel Islands fox,' he said now. 'It was hunting in the canyon.'

'I thought foxes hunted at night and slept during the day.'

'Well, somebody woke him up then because we saw him. He was big.'

Graciela nodded, confirming the sighting.

'Pretty cool,' McCaleb said. 'Too bad you didn't get a picture.'

They ate in silence for a few minutes. Graciela used her napkin to clean spittle off the baby's chin.

'Anyway,' McCaleb said, 'I'm sure you're happy that I'm off it and things will be normal around here again.'

Graciela looked at him.

'I want you to be safe. I want the whole family to be together and safe. That's what makes me happy, Terry.'

He nodded and finished his sandwich. She continued.

'I want you to be happy but if that means working these cases, then that is a conflict with your personal well-being as far as your health is concerned and the well-being of this family.'

'Well, you don't have to worry about it anymore. I don't think anybody will come calling on me again after this.'

He got up to clear the table. But before picking up plates he leaned over his daughter's chair and bent the wire so that the blue-and-white ball would be within her reach.

'It's not supposed to be like that,' Graciela said.

McCaleb looked at her.

'Yes, it is.'

29

McCaleb stayed up into the early morning hours with the baby. He and Graciela alternated nights on duty so that at least one of them got a decent night of sleep. Cielo seemed to have an almost hourly feed clock. Each time she awoke he would feed her and walk her through the dark house. He would gently pat her back until he heard her burp and then he would put her down again. In an hour the process would begin again.

After each cycle McCaleb would walk through the house and check the doors. It was a nervous habit, his routine. The house, by virtue of being up on the hillside, was fogged in tight. Looking through the rear windows, he couldn't even see the lights of the pier down below. He wondered if the fog stretched across the bay to the mainland. Harry Bosch's house was up high. He wondered if he was standing at his window looking into the misty nothingness as well.

In the morning Graciela took the baby and McCaleb, exhausted from the night and everything else, slept until eleven. When he came to he found the house to be quiet. In his T-shirt and boxer shorts he wandered down the hall and found the kitchen and family room empty. Graciela had left a note on the kitchen table saying she had taken the children to St. Catherine's for the ten o'clock service and then to the market afterward. The note said they'd be back by noon.

McCaleb went to the refrigerator and got out the gallon jug of orange juice. He poured a full glass and then took his keys off the counter and went back into the hallway to the locking cabinet. He opened it up and got out a plastic Ziploc bag containing a morning dose of the drug therapy that kept him alive. The first of every month he and Graciela carefully put together the doses and put them in plastic bags marked with dates and whether they were the A.M. or P.M. dosage. It made it easier than having to open dozens of pill bottles twice a day.

He took the bag back to the kitchen and began taking the pills two and three at a time with gulps of juice. As he followed this routine he looked through the kitchen window and down to the harbor below. The fog had moved out. It was still misty but clear enough for him to see *The Following Sea* and a skiff tied at its fantail.

He went to one of the kitchen drawers and pulled out the set of binoculars Graciela liked to use when she was watching him on the boat heading in or out of the harbor with a charter party. He went out onto the deck and to the railing. He focused the binoculars. There was no one in the cockpit or up on the bridge of the boat. His view could not penetrate the reflective film on the sliding door of the salon. He moved his focus to the skiff. It was weathered green with a one-and-a-half-horse outboard. He recognized it as being one of the rentals from the concession on the pier.

McCaleb went back inside and left the binoculars on the counter while he swiped the remaining pills into his hand. He took them and the orange juice back to the bedroom. He quickly ingested the pills while he got dressed. He knew Buddy Lockridge would not have rented a boat to get to *The Following Sea.* Buddy knew which Zodiac was McCaleb's and would simply have borrowed that.

Somebody else was on his boat.

It took him twenty minutes to walk down to the pier because Graciela had the golf cart. He went to the boat rental booth first to ask who had rented the boat but the window was closed and there was a sign with a clock face that said the operator would not be back until twelve-thirty. McCaleb checked his watch. It was ten after twelve. He couldn't wait. He went down the ramp to the skiff dock and stepped onto his Zodiac and started the engine.

As McCaleb moved down the fairway toward *The Following Sea* he studied the side windows of the salon but still could not see any movement or indication that someone was on the boat. He cut the engine on the Zodiac when he was twenty-five yards away and the inflatable skiff glided the rest of the way silently. He unzipped the pocket of his windbreaker and removed the Glock 17, his service weapon from his time with the bureau.

The Zodiac bumped lightly into the fantail next to the rental skiff. McCaleb first looked into the skiff but saw nothing other than a life vest and a flotation cushion, nothing that indicated who had rented the boat. He stepped onto the fantail and while crouched behind the stern wrapped the Zodiac's line around one of the rear cleats. He looked over the transom and saw only himself in the sliding door. He knew he would have to approach the door not knowing if there would be someone on the other side watching him come in.

He crouched down again and looked around. He wondered if he should retreat and come back with the harbor patrol boat. After a moment he decided against it. He glanced up the hill at his house and then raised himself and swung his body over the transom. With the gun carried low and hidden behind his hip he walked to the door and looked down at the lock. There was no damage or indication it had been tampered with. He pulled the handle and the door slid open. McCaleb was sure he had locked it the day before when leaving with Raymond.

He stepped inside. The salon was empty, no sign of intruder or burglary. He slid the door closed behind him and listened. The boat was silent. There was the sound of water lapping against the outside surfaces and that was it. His eyes moved toward the steps leading to the lower-deck staterooms and the head. He moved that way, raising the gun in front of him now.

On the second of the four steps down McCaleb hit a cracked board that sighed with his weight. He froze and listened for a response. There was only silence and the relentless sound of water against the sides of the boat. At the bottom of the stairs was a short hallway with three doors. Directly ahead was the forward stateroom, which had been converted into an office and file storage room. To the right was the master stateroom. To the left was the head.

The door to the master stateroom was closed and McCaleb could not remember if it had been that way when he had left the boat twenty-four hours earlier. The door to the head was wide open and hooked on the inside wall so it wouldn't swing and slam when the boat was moving. The office door was partially open and swaying slightly with the movement of the boat. There was a light on inside the room and McCaleb could tell it was the light over the desk, which was built into the lower berth of a set of bunk beds to the left of the door. McCaleb decided he would check the head first, followed by the office and then the master last. As he approached the head he realized that he smelled cigarette smoke.

The head was empty and too small to be used as a hiding place anyway. As he turned toward the office door and raised his weapon, a voice called out from within.

'Come on in, Terry.'

He recognized the voice. He cautiously stepped forward and used his free hand to push open the door. He kept the gun raised.

The door swung open and there was Harry Bosch sitting at the desk, his body in a relaxed posture, leaning back and looking toward the door. Both his hands were in sight. Both were empty except for the unlit cigarette between two fingers of his right hand. McCaleb slowly moved into the small room, still holding the gun up and aimed at Bosch.

'You going to shoot me? You want to be my accuser *and* my executioner?'

'This is breaking and entering.'

'Then I guess that makes us even.'

'What are you talking about?'

'That little dance at my place the other night, what do you call that? "Harry, I gotta couple more questions about the case." Only you never asked any real questions, did you? Instead, you take a look at my wife's picture and ask about that, and you ask about the picture in the hallway and you drink my beer and, oh, yeah, you tell me all about finding God in your baby daughter's blue eyes. So what do you call all of that, Terry?'

Bosch casually turned the chair and glanced over his shoulder at the desk. McCaleb looked past him and saw his own laptop computer was open and turned on. On the screen he could see that Bosch had called up the file containing the notes for the profile he was going to compose until everything changed the day before. He wished he had protected it with a password.

'It feels like breaking and entering to me,' Bosch said, his eyes on the screen. 'Maybe worse.'

In Bosch's new posture the leather bomber jacket he was wearing fell open and McCaleb could see the pistol holstered on his hip. He continued to hold his own weapon up and ready.

Bosch looked back at him.

'I didn't get a chance to look at all of this yet. Looks like a lot of notes and analysis. Probably all first-rate stuff, knowing you. But somehow, someway, you got it wrong, McCaleb. I'm not the guy.'

McCaleb slowly slid back into the lower berth of the opposite set of bunks. He held the gun with a little less precision now. He sensed there was no immediate danger from Bosch. If he had wanted to, he could have ambushed him as he'd come in.

'You shouldn't be here, Harry. You shouldn't be talking to me.'

'I know, anything I say can and will be used against me in a court of law. But who am I going to talk to? You put the bead on me. I want it off.'

'Well, you're too late. I'm off the case. And you don't want to know who's on it.'

Bosch just stared at him and waited.

'The bureau's civil rights division. You think Internal Affairs has been a pain in your ass? These people live and breathe for one thing, taking scalps. And an LAPD scalp is worth more than Boardwalk and Park Place put together.'

'How'd that happen, the reporter?'

McCaleb nodded.

'I guess that means he talked to you, too.'

Bosch nodded.

'Tried to. Yesterday.'

Bosch looked around himself, noticed the cigarette in his hand and put it in his mouth.

'You mind if I smoke?'

'You already have been.'

Bosch pulled a lighter out of his jacket pocket and lit the cigarette. He pulled the trash can out from beneath the desk and next to his seat to be used as an ashtray.

'Can't seem to quit these.'

'Addictive personality. A good and bad attribute in a detective.'

'Yeah, whatever.'

He took a hit off the cigarette.

'We've known each other for what is it, ten, twelve years?'

'More or less.'

'We worked cases and you don't work a case with somebody without taking some kind of measure. Know what I mean?'

McCaleb didn't answer. Bosch flicked the cigarette on the side of the trash can.

'And you know what bothers me, even more than the accusation itself? It's that it came from you. It's how and why you could think this. You know, what was the measure you took of me that allowed you to make this jump?'

McCaleb gestured with both hands as if to say the answer was obvious.

'People change. If there was anything I learned about people from my job, it's that any one of us is capable of anything, given the right circumstances, the right pressures, the right motives, the right moment.'

'That's all psycho-bullshit. It doesn't . . .'

Bosch's sentence trailed off and he didn't finish. He looked back at the computer and the papers spread across the desk. He pointed the cigarette at the laptop's screen.

'You talk about darkness . . . a darkness more than night.'

'What about it?'

'When I was overseas . . .' He dragged deeply on the cigarette and exhaled, tilting his head back and shooting the smoke toward the ceiling. '. . .I was put into the tunnels and let me tell you, you want darkness? That was darkness. Down in there. Sometimes you couldn't see your fucking hand three inches in front of your face. It was so dark it hurt your eyes from straining to see just anything. Anything at all.'

He took another long hit from the cigarette. McCaleb studied Bosch's eyes. They were staring blankly at the memory. Then suddenly he was back. He reached down and ground the half-finished cigarette into the inside edge of the can and dropped it in.

'This is my way of trying to quit. I smoke these shitty menthol things and never more than a half at a time. I'm down to about a pack a week.'

'It's not going to work.'

'I know.'

He looked up at McCaleb and smiled crookedly in a sort of apologetic way. Quickly his eyes changed and he moved back to his story.

'And then sometimes it wasn't that dark down there. In the tunnels. Somehow there was just enough light to make your way. And the thing is, I never knew where it came from. It was like it was trapped down there with the rest of us. My buddies and me, we called it lost light. It was lost but we found it.'

McCaleb waited but that was all Bosch said.

'What are you telling me, Harry?'

'That you missed something. I don't know what it is but you missed something.'

He held McCaleb with his dark eyes. He reached back to the desk and picked up the stack of copied documents from Jaye Winston. He tossed them across the small room onto McCaleb's lap. McCaleb made no move to catch them and they spilled to the floor in a jumble.

'Look again. You missed something and what you did see added up to me. Go back in and find the missing piece. It will change the addition.'

'I told you, man, I'm off it.'

'I'm putting you back on it.'

It was said with a tone of permanence, as if there was no choice for McCaleb.

'You've got till Wednesday. That writer's deadline. You have to stop his story with the truth. You don't, and you know what J. Reason Fowkkes will do with it.'

They sat in silence for a long moment looking at each other. McCaleb had met and talked with dozens of killers in his time as a profiler. Few of them readily admitted their crimes. So in that Bosch was no different. But the intensity with which he stared unblinkingly at him was something McCaleb had never seen before in any man, guilty or innocent.

'Storey's killed two women, and those are just the two we know about. He's the monster you spent your life chasing, McCaleb. And now . . . and now you're giving him the key that unlocks the door to the cage. He gets out, he'll do it again. You know his kind. You know he will.'

McCaleb could not compete with Bosch's eyes. He looked down at the gun in his hands.

'What made you think I would listen, that I would do this?' he asked.

'Like I said, you take somebody's measure. I got yours, McCaleb. You'll do this. Or the monster you set free will haunt you the rest of your life. If God is really in your daughter's eyes, how will you be able to look at her again?'

McCaleb unconsciously nodded and immediately wondered what he was doing.

'I remember you once told me something,' Bosch said. 'You said if God is in the details, so is the Devil. Meaning, the person you are looking for is usually right there in front of us, hiding in the details all the time. I always remember that. It still helps me.'

McCaleb nodded again. He looked down at the documents on the floor.

'Listen, Harry, you should know. I was convinced about this when I took it to Jaye. I'm not sure I can be turned the other way. If you want help, I'm probably the wrong one to go to.'

Bosch shook his head and smiled.

'That's exactly why you're the right one. If you can be convinced, the world can be convinced.'

'Yeah, where were you on New Year's Eve? Why don't we start with that.'

Bosch shrugged his shoulders.

'Home.'

'Alone?'

Bosch shrugged his shoulders again and didn't answer. He stood up to go. He put his hands in the pockets of his jacket. He went through the narrow door first and up the steps to the salon. McCaleb followed, now holding the gun at his side.

Bosch slid the door open with his shoulder. As he stepped out onto the cockpit he looked up at the cathedral of the hillside, then he looked at McCaleb.

'So all that talk at my place about finding God's hand, was that bullshit? Interview technique or something? A statement designed to get a response that could fit into a profile?'

McCaleb shook his head.

'No, no bullshit.'

'Good. I was hoping it wasn't.'

Bosch climbed over the transom to the fantail. He untied his rental boat and got in and sat down on the rear bench. Before starting the engine he looked once more at McCaleb and pointed to the back of the boat.

'*The Following Sea.* What's that mean?'

'My father named the boat. It was his originally. The following sea is the wave that comes up behind you, that hits you before you see it coming. I guess he named the boat as sort of a warning. You know, always watch your back.'

Bosch nodded.

'Overseas we used to tell each other, "Watch six."'

Now McCaleb nodded.

'Same thing.'

They were silent a moment. Bosch put his hand on the boat motor's pull handle but didn't start the engine.

'You know the history of this place, Terry? I'm talking about back before the missionaries came.'

'No, do you?'

'A little. I used to read a lot of history books. When I was a kid. Whatever they had in the library. I liked local history. L.A. mostly, and California. I just liked reading it. We took a field trip here from the youth hall once. So I read up on it.'

McCaleb nodded.

'The Indians that lived out here – the Gabrielinos – were sun worshippers,' Bosch said. 'The missionaries came and changed all of that – in fact, they were the ones who called them Gabrielinos. They called themselves something else but I don't remember what it was. But before all that happened they'd been here and they worshipped the sun. It was so important to life on the island I guess they figured it had to be a god.'

McCaleb watched Bosch's dark eyes scan across the harbor.

'And the mainland Indians thought of the ones out here as these fierce wizards who could control weather and waves through worship and sacrifices to their god. I mean, they had to be fierce and strong to be able to cross the bay so they could trade their pottery and sealskins on the mainland.'

McCaleb studied Bosch, trying to get a bead on the message he was sure the detective was trying to convey.

'What are you saying, Harry?'

Bosch shrugged his shoulders.

'I don't know. I guess I'm saying that people find God where they need Him to be. In the sun, in a new baby's eyes . . . in a new heart.'

He looked at McCaleb, his eyes as dark and as unreadable as the painted owl's.

'And some people,' McCaleb began, 'find their salvation in truth, in justice, in that which is righteous.'

Now Bosch nodded and offered his crooked smile again.

'That sounds good.'

He turned and started the engine with one pull. He then mock saluted McCaleb and pulled away, angling the rental boat back toward the pier. Not knowing the etiquette of the harbor, he cut across the fairway and between unused mooring buoys. He didn't look back. McCaleb watched him all the way. A man all alone on the water in an old wooden boat. And in that thought came a question. Was he thinking about Bosch or himself?

30

On the ferry ride back Bosch bought a Coke at the concession stand and hoped it would settle his stomach and prevent seasickness. He asked one of the stewards where the steadiest ride on the boat was and he was directed to one of the middle seats on the inside. He sat down and drank some of the Coke, then pulled the folded pages he had printed in McCaleb's office out of his jacket pocket.

He had printed two files before he had seen McCaleb approaching in the Zodiac. One was titled SCENE PROFILE and the other was called SUBJECT PROFILE. He had folded them into his jacket and disconnected the portable printer from the laptop before McCaleb entered the boat. He'd only had time to glance at them on the computer and now began a thorough reading.

He took the scene profile first. It was only one page. It was incomplete and appeared to be simply a listing of McCaleb's rough notes and impressions from the crime scene video.

Still, it gave an insight into how McCaleb worked. It showed how his observations of a scene turned into observations about a suspect.

SCENE
1. Ligature
2. Nude
3. Head wound
4. Tape/gag – 'Cave'?
5. Bucket?
6. Owl – watching over?

highly organized
detail oriented
statement – the SCENE is his statement
he was there – he watched (the owl?)
exposure = victim humiliation
  = victim hatred, contempt
bucket – remorse?

killer – PRIOR KNOWLEDGE of victim
personal knowledge – previous interaction
personal hatred
KILLER INSIDE THE WIRE
what is the statement?

Bosch reread the page and then thought about it. Though he did not have full knowledge of the crime scene from which McCaleb's notes were drawn, he was impressed by the leaps in logic McCaleb had made. He had carefully gone down the ladder to the point where he concluded that Gunn's killer was someone he knew, that it was someone who would be found inside the perimeter wire that circled Gunn's existence. It was an important distinction to make in any case. Investigative priorities were usually set up on the determination of whether the suspect being sought had intersected with the victim only at the point of the killing or before. McCaleb's read on the nuances of the scene were that the killer was someone known to Gunn, that there was a prelude to this final and fatal crossing of killer and victim.

The second page continued the listing of shorthand notes that Bosch assumed McCaleb planned to turn into a fleshed-out profile. As he read he realized that some of the word groupings were phrases McCaleb had taken from him.

SUSPECT
Bosch:
institutional – youth hall, Vietnam, LAPD
outsider – alienation
obsessive-compulsive
eyes – lost, loss
mission man – avenging angel
the big wheel always turning –
  nobody walks away
what goes around comes around

alcohol
divorce – wife? why?
alienation/obsession
mother
cases
justice system – 'bullshit'
carriers of the plague
guilt?

Harry = Hieronymus

owl = evil
evil = Gunn
death of evil = release stressors

paintings – demons – devils – evil
darkness and light – the edge
punishment
mother – justice – Gunn
God's hand – police – Bosch
punishment = God's work

A darkness more than night – Bosch

Bosch wasn't sure how to interpret the notes. His eyes were drawn to the last line and he repeatedly read it, unsure what it was that McCaleb was saying about him.

After a while he carefully folded the page closed and sat still for a long moment. It felt somehow surreal to be sitting there on the boat, having just tried to interpret someone else's notes and reasons as to why he should be considered a murder suspect. He felt himself getting queasy and realized he might be getting seasick. He gulped down the rest of the Coke and got up, putting the pages back into his jacket pocket.

Bosch headed toward the front of the boat and pushed through the heavy door to the bow. The cool air blasted him immediately. He could see the dim outline of the mainland in the distance. He kept his eyes on the horizon and breathed in deeply. In a few minutes he started feeling better.

31

McCaleb sat on the old couch in the salon thinking about his encounter with Bosch for a long time. It was the first time in all of his experiences as an investigator that a murder suspect had come to him to enlist his aid. He had to decide if it had been the act of a desperate or a sincere man. Or, possibly, something else. What if McCaleb had not noticed the rental skiff and come to the boat. Would Bosch have waited for him?

He went down to the front stateroom and looked at the documents spread on the floor. He wondered if Bosch had intentionally tossed them so that they would fall to the floor and become mixed up. Had he taken something?

He went to the desk and studied his laptop. It was not attached to the printer but he knew that didn't mean anything. He closed the file that was on the screen and opened the print manager window. He clicked the jobs file and saw that two files had been printed that day – the scene and suspect profiles. Bosch had taken them.

McCaleb imagined Bosch riding on the *Express* ferry back across, sitting by himself and reading what McCaleb had written about him. It made him feel uncomfortable. He didn't think any suspect he had ever profiled had read the report McCaleb had put together on him.

He shook it off and decided to occupy his mind with something else. He slid off the chair to his knees and began picking up the murder book reports, putting them into a neat pile first before worrying about putting them back in order.

Once he had the mess cleaned up he sat down at the desk, the reports in a squared-off pile in front of him. McCaleb took a blank page of typing paper out of a drawer and wrote on it with the thick black marker he used for labeling cardboard boxes containing his files.

YOU MISSED SOMETHING

He took a piece of tape off a dispenser on the desk and taped the page to the wall behind the desk. He looked at it for a long time. Everything Bosch had said to him came down to that one line. He now had to decide if it was true, if it was possible. Or if it was the last manipulation of a desperate man.

He heard his cell phone begin to chirp. It was in the pocket of his jacket, which he had left on the couch in the salon. He hustled up the stairs and grabbed the jacket. When he reached into the pocket his hand closed around his gun. He then tried the other pocket and got the phone. It was Graciela.

'We're home,' she said. 'I thought you'd be here. I thought maybe we could all go down to lunch at El Encanto.'

'Um . . .'

McCaleb didn't want to leave the office or his thoughts about Bosch. But the last week had strained things with Graciela. He needed to talk to her about that, about how he saw things changing.

'Tell you what,' he finally said. 'I'm just finishing some stuff here. Why don't you take the kids down and I'll meet you there.'

He looked at his watch. It was quarter of one.

'Is one-thirty too late?'

'Fine,' she said abruptly. 'What stuff?'

'Oh, just . . . I'm sort of wrapping up this thing for Jaye.'

'I thought you told me you were off it.'

'I am but I have all the reports and I wanted to write up my final . . . you know, just wrap it up.'

'Don't be late, Terry.'

She said it with a tone that implied that he would miss more than his lunch if he was.

'I won't. I'll see you there.'

He closed the phone and went back down to the office. He looked at his watch again. He had about a half hour before he'd have to get on the skiff and go back to the pier. The El Encanto was about a five-minute walk from there. It was one of the few restaurants that remained open on the island during the winter months.

He sat down and started putting the stack of investigative documents in order. It was not a difficult task. Each page had a date stamp on the upper right-hand corner. But McCaleb stopped almost as soon as he started. He looked up at the message he had taped on the wall. He decided that if he was going to look for something he had not noticed before, that he had missed, he should come at the information from another angle. He decided not to put the documents in their correct order. Instead, he would read them in the random order they were now in. Doing it this way he would avoid thinking about the flow of the investigation and how one step followed the other. He would simply have each report to consider as a single piece of the puzzle. It was a simple mind trick but he had used it before on cases with the bureau. Sometimes it shook something new out, something he had previously missed.

He checked his watch again and began with the first document on the pile. It was the autopsy protocol.

32

McCaleb walked briskly to the front steps of the El Encanto. He saw his golf cart parked at the curb. Mostly, the carts on the island looked the same, but he could identify his because of the baby seat with the pink-and-white cushioning. His family was still here.

He went up the steps and the hostess, recognizing him as a local, pointed to the table where his family was seated. He hurried over and pulled out a chair next to Graciela. They were close to being finished. He noticed that the waitress had already left the check on the table.

'Sorry I'm late.'

He took a chip out of the basket at the center of the table and dragged it through the salsa and guacamole bowls before shoving it into his mouth. Graciela looked at her watch and then pierced him with her deep brown eyes. He weathered it and got ready for the next one which he knew was surely coming.

'I can't stay.'

She loudly put her fork down on her plate. She was finished.

'Terry . . .'

'I know, I know. But something's come up. I have to go across tonight.'

'What could've possibly come up? You're off the case. It's Sunday. People are watching football, not running around trying to solve murders that they're not even asked to.'

She pointed to a television mounted in the upper corner of the room. Three talking heads with thick necks sat at a counter with a football field behind them. McCaleb knew that the day's games would determine the Super Bowl contenders. He couldn't care less, though he did suddenly remember he had promised Raymond that they would watch at least one of the games together.

'I have been asked, Graciela.'

'What are you talking about? You said they asked you *off* the case.'

He told her about discovering Bosch on the boat that morning and what he had asked McCaleb to do.

'And this is the guy you told Jaye probably did it?'

McCaleb nodded.

'How'd he know where you lived?'

'He didn't. He knew about the boat, not where we live. You don't have to worry about that.'

'I think I do. Terry, you are going too far with this and you are going completely blind to the dangers to yourself and your family. I think—'

'Really? I think—'

He stopped and reached into his pocket and pulled out two quarters. He turned to Raymond.

'Raymond, are you finished eating?'

'Yeah.'

'You mean yes?'

'Yes.'

'Okay, take these. Go play the video machine over there by the bar.'

The boy took the quarters.

'You're excused.'

Raymond hesitantly hopped down and then trotted into the next room where there were tabletop video games that they had played before. He chose a game McCaleb knew was Pac-Man and sat down. He was not out of McCaleb's sight.

McCaleb looked back at Graciela, who had her purse up on her lap and was taking money out and putting it down on the check.

'Graciela, forget about that. Look at me.'

She finished with the money and pushed her wallet back into the purse. She looked at him.

'We have to go. CiCi has to take her nap.'

The baby was in her bouncing chair on the table, one hand grasping the blue-and-white ball on the wire.

'She's fine. She can sleep right there. Just listen to me for a minute.'

He waited and she put a conceding look on her face.

'All right. Say what you have to say and then I have to leave.'

McCaleb turned and leaned close to Graciela so that his words would be heard only by her. He noticed the edge of one of her ears poking through her hair.

'We are heading toward a big problem here, aren't we?'

Graciela nodded and immediately the tears came down her cheeks. It was as if his saying the words out loud had knocked down the thin defensive mechanism she had constructed inside to protect herself and her marriage. McCaleb pulled the unused napkin out from beneath his silverware setting and handed it to her. He then put his hand on the back of her neck and pulled her toward him and kissed her on the cheek. Over the top of her head he saw Raymond watching them with a scared look on his face.

'We've talked about this, Graci,' he began. 'You have it in your head that we can't have our home and our family and everything else if this is what I do. The problem is in that word "if." That is the mistake here. Because there is no "if" here. It's not "if this is what I do." It *is* what I do. And I've gone too long thinking otherwise, trying to convince myself of something else.'

More tears came and she held the napkin to her face. She cried silently but McCaleb was sure people in the restaurant had noticed and were watching them instead of the television above them. He checked on Raymond and saw the boy was back to playing the video game.

'I know,' Graciela managed to say.

He was surprised by her acknowledgment. He took it as a good sign.

'So then what do we do? I'm not talking about just now and this case. I mean, for now and forever. What do we do? Graci, I am tired of trying to be what I'm not and of ignoring the thing inside that I know is what I am truly all about. It took this case to finally make me realize it and admit it to myself.'

She didn't say anything. He wasn't expecting her to.

'You know I love you and the kids. That's not the issue. I think I can have both and you think I can't. You've adopted this one-or-the-other attitude and I don't think it's right. Or fair.'

He knew his words were hurting her. He was drawing a line. One of them had to capitulate. He was saying it wasn't going to be him.

'Look, let's think about this. This isn't a good place to talk. What I am going to do is finish my work on this thing and then we'll sit down and talk about our future. Is that okay?'

She slowly nodded but didn't look at him.

'You do what you have to do,' she said in a tone McCaleb knew would make him feel guilty forever. 'I just hope you'll be careful.'

He pulled himself over and kissed her again.

'I've got too much here with you not to be.'

He got up and came around the table to the baby. He kissed her on top of the head and then unhitched the chair's safety belt and lifted her out.

'I'll take her down to the cart,' he said. 'Why don't you get Raymond?'

He carried the baby down to the cart and secured her in the safety seat. He put her bouncing chair in the rear storage compartment. Graciela came down with Raymond a few minutes later. Her eyes were swollen from the crying. McCaleb put his hand on Raymond's shoulder and walked him to the front passenger seat.

'Raymond, you're going to have to watch the second game without me. I have some work I have to do.'

'I can go with you. I can help you.'

'No, it's not a charter.'

'I know, but I can still help you.'

McCaleb knew Graciela was looking at him and he felt the guilt like the sun on his back.

'Thanks but maybe next time, Raymond. Put on your seat belt.'

Once the boy was safely in, McCaleb stepped back from the cart. He looked at Graciela, who was no longer looking at him.

'Okay,' he said. 'I'll be back as soon as I can. And I'll have the phone with me if you want to call.'

Graciela didn't acknowledge him. She pulled the cart away from the curb and headed up Marilla Avenue. He watched them until they were out of sight.

33

On the walk back to the pier his cell phone chirped. It was Jaye Winston returning his call. She was talking very quietly and said she was calling from her mother's house. McCaleb had difficulty hearing so he sat down on one of the benches along the casino walk. He leaned forward with his elbows on his knees, one hand holding the phone tightly to one ear, his other hand clasped over the other.

'We missed something,' he said. 'I missed something.'

'Terry, what are you talking about?'

'In the murder book. In Gunn's arrest record. He was—'

'Terry, what are you doing? You're off the case.'

'Says who, the FBI? I don't work for them anymore, Jaye.'

'Then says me. I don't want you getting any further—'

'I don't work for you, either, Jaye. Remember?'

There was a long silence on the phone.

'Terry, I don't know what you are doing but it's got to stop. You have no authority, no standing in this case anymore. If those guys Twilley and Friedman find out you're still snooping around on this, they can arrest you for interference. And you know they're just the type that will.'

'You want standing, I have standing.'

'What? I withdrew my authorization to you yesterday. You can't use me on this.'

McCaleb hesitated and then decided to tell her.

'I have standing. I guess you could say I'm working for the accused.'

Now Winston's silence was even longer. Finally she spoke, her words delivered very slowly.

'Are you telling me that you went to Bosch with this?'

'No. He came to me. He showed up on my boat this morning. I was right about the other night. The coincidence; me showing up at his place, then the call from his partner about you. He put it together. The reporter from the *New Times* called him, too. He knew what was going on without me having to tell him a thing. The point is, Jaye, none of that matters. What matters is that I think I jumped on Bosch too soon. I missed something and now I'm not so sure. There's a chance all of this could be a setup.'

'He's convinced you.'

'No, I convinced myself.'

There were voices in the background and Winston told McCaleb to hold on. He then heard voices muffled by a hand over the phone. It sounded like arguing. McCaleb stood up and continued walking toward the pier. Winston came back on in a few seconds.

'Sorry,' she said. 'This is not a good time. I'm in the middle of something right now.'

'Can we meet tomorrow morning?'

'What are you talking about?' Winston said, her voice almost shrill. 'You just told me you are working for the target of an investigation. I'm not going to meet with you. How the fuck would that look? Hold on—'

He heard her muffled voice apologizing for her language to someone. She then came back on the line.

'I really have to go.'

'Look, I don't care how it would look. I'm interested in the truth and I thought you would be, too. You don't want to meet me, fine, don't meet me. I've gotta go myself.'

'Terry, wait.'

He listened. She said nothing. He sensed that she was distracted by something there.

'What, Jaye?'

'What is this thing you said we missed?'

'It was in the arrest package from Gunn's last duice. I guess after Bosch told you he had spoken to him in lockup you pulled all the records. I just scanned through it the first time I looked at the book.'

'I pulled the records,' she said in a defensive tone. 'He spent the night of December thirtieth in the Hollywood tank. That's where Bosch saw him.'

'And he bonded out in the morning. Seven-thirty.'

'Yeah. Okay? I don't get it.'

'Look who bailed him out.'

'Terry, I'm at my parents'. I don't have—'

'Right, sorry. He was bailed out by Rudy Tafero.'

Silence. McCaleb was at the pier. He walked out toward the gangway that led down to the skiff dock and leaned on the railing. He cupped his free hand over his ear again.

'Okay, he was bailed out by Rudy Tafero,' Winston said. 'I assume he is a licensed bail bondsman. What does that mean?'

'You haven't been watching your TV. You're right, Tafero is a licensed bail bondsman – at least he put a license number on the bail sheet. But he's also a PI and security consultant. And – ready for this – he works for David Storey.'

Winston didn't say anything but McCaleb could hear her breathing into the phone.

'Terry, I think you better slow down. You are reading too much into this.'

'No coincidences, Jaye.'

'What coincidence? The man's a bail bondsman. It's what he does. He gets people out of jail. I'll bet you a box of doughnuts his office is right across the street from Hollywood station with all the others. He probably bails every third drunk and fourth prostitute out of the tank there.'

'You don't believe it's that simple and you know it.'

'Don't tell me what I believe.'

'This was when he was in the middle of preparing for Storey's trial. Why would Tafero come over and write a duice ticket himself?'

'Because maybe he's a one-man show and maybe, like I said, all he had to do was cross the street.'

'I don't buy it. And there's something else. On his booking slip it says Gunn got his one phone call at three A.M. December thirty-first. The number's on the slip – he called his sister in Long Beach.'

'Okay, what about it? We knew that.'

'I called her today and asked if she'd called a bondsman for him. She said no. She said she was tired of getting calls in the middle of the night and literally bailing him out all the time. She told him he was on his own this time.'

'So he went with Tafero. What about it?'

'How'd he get him? He already used his call.'

Winston had no answer for that. They were both silent for a while. McCaleb looked out across the harbor. The yellow taxi boat was moving slowly down one of the fairways, empty except for the man at the wheel. Men alone in their boats, McCaleb thought.

'What are you going to do?' Winston finally asked. 'Where are you going with this?'

'I'm coming back across tonight. Can you meet me in the morning?'

'Where? When?'

The tone of her voice revealed that she was put out by the prospect of a meeting.

'Seven-thirty, out front at the Hollywood station.'

There was a pause and then Winston said, 'Wait a minute, wait a minute. I can't do this. If Hitchens gets wind of it, that will be the end. He'll ship me out to Palmdale. I'll spend the rest of my career pulling bones out of the desert sand.'

McCaleb was ready for that protest.

'You said the bureau guys want the murder book back, right? You meet me, I'll have it with me. What's Hitchens going to say about that?'

There was silence as Winston considered this.

'Okay, that'll work. I'll be there.'

34

When Bosch got home that evening he found the message light on his phone machine was blinking. He pushed the button and listened to two messages, one from each of the prosecutors on the Storey case. He decided to call Langwiser back first. As he punched her number into the phone, he wondered what urgency had caused both members of the prosecution team to call him. He thought maybe they had been contacted by the FBI agents McCaleb had mentioned. Or possibly by the reporter.

'What's up?' he asked when Langwiser answered. 'With both of you guys calling me I know it must be big and bad.'

'Harry? How are you?'

'Hanging in. What do you two have cooking?'

'It's funny you should mention that. Roger's on his way over and I'm going to cook tonight. We're going to go over Annabelle Crowe's grand jury testimony one more time. You want to come by?'

He knew she lived up in Agua Dulce, an hour's drive north.

'Uh, you know what, I've been driving all day. Down to Long Beach and back. You think you really need me there?'

'Totally optional. Just didn't want you to feel left out. But that's not why we were calling.'

'What was the reason?'

He was in the kitchen, sliding a six-pack of Anchor Steam onto a shelf in the refrigerator. He pulled one bottle out of its sleeve and closed the door.

'Roger and I have been conferencing all weekend about this. We also talked to Alice Short about it.'

Alice Short was a chief deputy who was in charge of major trials. Their boss. It sounded as though they had been contacted about the Gunn case.

'What's the "it" you're talking about?' Bosch asked.

He slid the bottle into the opener and yanked down, popping the cap.

'Well, we think the case has really gone by the numbers. Really fallen together. In fact, it's bulletproof, Harry, and we think we should pull the trigger tomorrow.'

Bosch was quiet a moment while he tried to decipher all the weaponry coding.

'You're saying you're going to rest tomorrow?'

'We think so. We'll probably talk about it again tonight but we have Alice's blessing and Roger really thinks it's the right move. What we'd do is put on a bunch of cleanup wits in the morning and then bring Annabelle Crowe out after lunch. We'd end with her – a human story. She'll be our closer.'

Bosch was speechless. It might be the right move from a prosecutorial point of view. But that would put J. Reason Fowkkes in control of things as early as Tuesday.

'Harry, what do you think?'

He took a long pull on the bottle. The beer wasn't that cold. It had been in the car for a while.

'I think you only get one shot,' he said, continuing the weaponry imagery. 'You two better think long and hard about it tonight while you're making the pasta. You don't get a second chance to put on a case.'

'We know, Harry. And how'd you know I was making pasta?'

He could hear the smile in her voice.

'Lucky guess.'

'Well, don't worry, we'll think long and hard. We have been.'

She paused, allowing him a chance to respond but he was silent.

'In case we go this way, what's the status on Crowe?'

'She's waiting in the wings. Good to go.'

'Can you reach her tonight?'

'No problem. I'll tell her to be there by noon tomorrow.'

'Thanks, Harry. See you in the morning.'

They hung up. Bosch thought about things. He wondered if he should call McCaleb and tell him what was happening. He decided to wait. He walked out into the living room and turned on the stereo. The Art Pepper CD was still in the play slot. The music soon filled the room.

35

McCaleb was leaning against the Cherokee parked in front of the LAPD's Hollywood station when Winston pulled up in a BMW Z3 and parked. When she got out she saw McCaleb studying her car.

'I was running late. I didn't have time to pick up a company car.'

'I like your wheels. You know what they say about L.A., you are what you drive.'

'Don't start profiling me, Terry. It's too fucking early. Where's the book and the tape?'

He noted her profanity but kept his thoughts on that to himself. He pushed off the car and went around to the passenger side. He opened the door and took out the murder book and the crime scene tape. He handed them to her and she took them back to her car. McCaleb closed and locked the Cherokee, looking down through the window to the floor of the backseat where he had covered the Kinko's box with the morning newspaper. Before coming to the rendezvous he had gone to the twenty-four-hour shop on Sunset and photocopied the entire murder book. The tape was a problem; he didn't know where to get it dubbed on short notice. So he'd simply bought a videocassette at the Rite-Aid near the marina and slipped the blank tape into the case Winston had given him. It was his guess that she wouldn't check to make sure he had returned the correct tape.

When she came back from her car he pointed with his chin across the street.

'I guess I owe you a box of doughnuts.'

She looked. Across Wilcox from the station was a shabby two-story building with a handful of storefront bail bond operations with phone numbers advertised in each window in cheap neon, maybe to help prospective clients memorize them from the backseat of passing patrol cars. The middle business had a painted sign above the window: Valentino Bonds.

'Which one?' Winston asked.

'Valentino. As in Rudy Valentino Tafero. That's what they used to call him when he worked this side of the street.'

McCaleb appraised the small business again and shook his head.

'I still don't see how a neon bondsman and David Storey ever hooked up.'

'Hollywood is just street trash with money. So what are we doing here? I don't have a lot of time.'

'You bring your badge?'

She gave him a don't-fuck-with-me look and he explained what he wanted to do. They went up the steps and into the station. At the front desk Winston flashed her badge and asked for the A.M. watch sergeant. A man with Zucker on his name plate and sergeant's stripes on the sleeve of his uniform came out from the small office. Winston showed her badge again, introduced herself and then introduced McCaleb as her associate. Zucker knitted his healthy set of eyebrows together but didn't ask what associate meant.

'We're working a homicide case from New Year's Eve. The victim spent the night before in your tank. We—'

'Edward Gunn.'

'Right. You knew him?'

'He'd been in a few times. And of course I heard he won't be coming back.'

'We need to talk to whoever runs the tank on A.M. watch.'

'Well, that would be me, I guess. We don't have a specific duty. It's sort of catch as catch can around here. What do you want to know?'

McCaleb took a set of photocopies from the murder book out of his jacket pocket and spread them on the counter. He noticed Winston's look but ignored it.

'We're interested in how he made bail,' he said.

Zucker turned the pages around so he could read them. He put his finger on Rudy Tafero's signature.

'Says it right here. Rudy Tafero. He's got a place across the street. He came over and bailed him out.'

'Did someone call him?'

'Yeah, the guy did. Gunn.'

McCaleb tapped his finger on the copy of the booking slip.

'It says here that when he got his call he called this number. It's his sister.'

'Then she must've called Rudy for him.'

'So nobody gets two calls.'

'Nope, 'round here we're usually so busy they're lucky if they get the one.'

McCaleb nodded. He folded the photocopies and was about to put them back in his pocket when Winston took them from his hand.

'I'll hang on to those,' she said.

She slipped the folded copies into a back pocket of her black jeans.

'Sergeant Zucker,' she said. 'You wouldn't be the kind of nice guy who would call Tafero, being that he's former LAPD, and tip him that he had a potential fish over here in the tank, would you?'

Zucker stared at her for a moment, his face a stone.

'It's very important, Sergeant. If you don't tell us, it could come back on you.'

The stone cracked into a humorless smile.

'No, I'm not that kind of nice guy,' Zucker said. 'And I don't have any nice guys like that on A.M. watch. And speaking of which, I just got off shift which means I don't have to be talking to you anymore. Have a nice day.'

He started to step away from the counter.

'One last thing,' Winston said quickly.

Zucker turned back to her.

'Were you the one who called Harry Bosch and told him Gunn was in the tank?'

Zucker nodded.

'I had a standing request from him. Any and every time Gunn was brought in here, Bosch wanted to know about it. He'd come in and talk to the guy, try to get him to say something about that old case. Bosch wouldn't give up on it.'

'It says Gunn wasn't booked until two-thirty,' McCaleb said. 'You called Bosch in the middle of the night?'

'That was part of the deal. Bosch didn't care what time it was. And actually, the procedure was that I would page him and then he'd call in.'

'And that's what happened that last night?'

'Yeah, I paged and Bosch called in. I told him we had Gunn again and he came down to try to talk to him. I tried to tell him to wait until morning 'cause the guy was on his ass drunk – Gunn, I mean – but Harry came down anyway. Why are you asking so much about Harry Bosch?'

Winston didn't answer so McCaleb jumped in.

'We're not. We're asking about Gunn.'

'Well, that's all I know. Can I go home now? It's been a long one.'

'Aren't they all,' Winston said. 'Thank you, Sergeant.'

They stepped away from the counter and walked out to the front steps.

'What do you think?' Winston asked.

'He sounded legit to me. But you know what, let's watch the employee lot for a few minutes.'

'Why?'

'Humor me. Let's see what the sergeant drives home.'

'You're wasting my time, Terry.'

They got into McCaleb's Cherokee anyway and drove around the block until they came to the entrance–exit of the Hollywood station employee parking lot. McCaleb drove fifty yards past it and parked in front of a fire hydrant. He adjusted the side-view mirror so he could see any car that left the lot. They sat and waited in silence for a couple of minutes until Winston spoke.

'So if we are what we drive, what's this make you?'

McCaleb smiled.

'Never thought about it. A Cherokee . . . I guess that makes me the last of a breed or something.'

He glanced at her then looked back at the mirror.

'Yeah, and what about this coating of dust on everything, what does that—'

'Here we go. Think it's him.'

McCaleb watched a car leave the exit and turn left in their direction.

'Coming this way.'

Neither of them moved. The car drove up and stopped right next to them. McCaleb looked over casually and his eyes met Zucker's. The cop lowered his passenger-side window. McCaleb had no choice. He lowered his.

'You're parked in front of a plug there, Detective. Don't get a ticket.'

McCaleb nodded. Zucker saluted with two fingers and drove off. McCaleb noted that he was driving a Crown Victoria with commercial bumpers and wheels. It was a secondhand patrol car, the kind you pick up at auction for four hundred bucks and slap on an $89.95 paint job.

'Don't we look like a couple of assholes,' Winston said.

'Yeah.'

'So what's your theory about *that* car?'

'He's either an honest man or he drives the beater to work because he doesn't want people to see the Porsche.'

He paused.

'Or the Z3.'

He turned to her and smiled.

'Funny, Terry. Now what? Eventually, I have to get some real work done today. And I'm supposed to meet with your bureau buddies this morning as well.'

'Stick with me – and they aren't my buddies.'

He started the Cherokee and pulled away from the curb.

'You really think this car's dirty?' he asked.

36

The post office on Wilcox was a large World War II-era building with twenty-five-foot-high ceilings and murals depicting bucolic scenes of brotherhood and good deeds covering the upper walls. As they walked in, McCaleb's eyes scanned the murals but not for their artistic or philosophic merit. He counted three small cameras mounted above the public areas of the office. He pointed them out to Winston. They had a chance.

They waited in line and when it was their turn Winston flashed her badge and asked for the on-site security officer. They were directed to a door next to a row of vending machines and they waited nearly five minutes before it was opened and a small black man with gray hair looked out.

'Mr. Lucas?' Winston asked.

'That's right,' he said with a smile.

Winston showed the badge once more and introduced McCaleb simply by name. McCaleb had told her on the way over from Hollywood station that calling him an associate wasn't working.

'We're working a homicide investigation, Mr. Lucas, and an important piece of evidence is a money order that was purchased here and probably mailed here on December twenty-second.'

'The twenty-second? That's right in the Christmas rush.'

'That's right, sir.'

Winston looked at McCaleb.

'We noticed your cameras out there on the walls, Mr. Lucas,' she said. 'We'd be interested in knowing if you have a videotape from the twenty-second.'

'Videotape,' Lucas said, as if the word was foreign to him.

'You are the security officer here, right?' Winston said impatiently.

'Yes, I'm the security man. I run the cameras.'

'Can you take us back and show us your surveillance system, Mr. Lucas?' McCaleb said in a gentler tone.

'Yup, sure can. Just as soon as you get authorization I'll take you on back.'

'And how and where do we get authorization?' Winston asked.

'From L.A. Regional. Downtown.'

'Is there a specific person we talk to? We're on a homicide investigation, Mr. Lucas. Time is of the essence.'

'That would be Mr. Preechnar – he's a postal inspector – you would talk to. Yes.'

'Do you mind if we come back to your office and we call Mr. Preechnar together?' McCaleb asked. 'It would save us a lot of time and then Mr. Preechnar could just talk directly to you.'

Lucas thought about this for a moment and decided it was a good idea. He nodded.

'Let's see what we can do.'

Lucas opened the door and led them through a warren of huge mail baskets to a cubbyhole office with two desks squeezed together. On one of the desks was a video monitor with its screen cut into four camera views of the public area of the post office. McCaleb realized he had missed one of the cameras when he had searched the walls earlier.

Lucas ran his finger down a list of phone numbers taped to the top of the desk and made the call. Once he got ahold of his supervisor he explained the situation and then turned the phone over to Winston. She went through their explanation again and then turned the phone back over to Lucas. She nodded to McCaleb. They got the approval.

'Okay, then,' Lucas said after hanging up. 'Let's see what we've got here.'

He reached to his hip and pulled up a ring of keys on a retractable wire attached to his belt. He went to the other side of the office and unlocked a closet door which he opened to reveal a rack of video recorders and four upper shelves of videotapes marked with the numbers one through thirty-one on each shelf. On the floor were two cartons containing fresh videotapes.

McCaleb saw all of this and suddenly realized it was January 22, exactly one month from the day the money order was purchased.

'Mr. Lucas, stop the machines,' he said.

'Can't do that. The machines always gotta roll. If we're open for business, then the tapes are rolling.'

'You don't understand. December twenty-second is the day we want. We're taping over the day we want to look at.'

'Hold your horses, Detective McCallan. I have to explain the setup.'

McCaleb didn't bother correcting him on the name. There wasn't time.

'Then hurry, please.'

McCaleb looked at his watch. It was eight forty-eight. The post office had been open for forty-eight minutes. That was forty-eight minutes of the December 22 tape erased with forty-eight minutes of the current day's taping.

Lucas started explaining the taping procedure. One VCR for each of the four cameras. One tape in each machine at the start of each day. The cameras were set at thirty frames a minute, allowing one tape to cover the entire day. The tape for an individual day was held for a month and used again if not reserved because of an investigation by the postal inspectors service.

'We get a lot of scam artists and whatnot. You know how it is in Hollywood. We end up with a lot of tapes on reserve. The inspectors come in and get 'em. Or we send 'em on down in dispatch.'

'We understand, Mr. Lucas,' said Winston, an urgent tone in her voice as she apparently came to the same realization as McCaleb. 'Can you please turn off the machines or replace the tapes in them. We are taping over what could be valuable evidence.'

'Right away,' Lucas said.

But he proceeded to reach into the carton of new tapes and take out four cassettes. He then peeled labels off a dispenser roll and put them on the tapes. He took a pen from behind his ear and wrote the date and some sort of coding on the labels. Then, finally, he started popping tapes out of the VCRs and replacing them with the new cassettes.

'Now, how do you want to do this? These tapes are post office property. They are not leaving the premises. I can set you up over here at the desk. I've got a portable TV with built-in VCR if you want to use it.'

'Are you sure we just can't borrow them for the day?' Winston said. 'I could have them back by—'

'Not without a court order. That's what Mr. Preechnar told me. That's what I'm going to do.'

'Then I guess we don't have a choice,' Winston said, looking at McCaleb and shaking her head in frustration.

While Lucas went to get the TV, McCaleb and Winston decided that McCaleb would stay and watch the videotape while Winston went to her office for an 11 A.M. meeting with the bureau men, Twilley and Friedman. She said she would not be mentioning McCaleb's new investigation or the possibility that his earlier focus on Bosch might have been in error. She would return the copied murder book and crime scene tape.

'I know you don't believe in coincidences but that's all you have at the moment, Terry. You come up with something on the tape and I'll bring it to the captain and we'll blow Twilley and Friedman out of the water. But until you have it . . . I'm still in the doghouse and need something more than a coincidence to look anywhere other than at Bosch.'

'What about the call to Tafero?'

'What call?'

'Somehow he knew Gunn was in the tank and he came and bailed him out – so they could kill him that night and pin it on Bosch.'

'I don't know about the call – if it wasn't Zucker, it was probably somebody else in the station he's got a sweetheart deal with. And the rest of what you just said is pure speculation without a single fact backing it up.'

'I think it's—'

'Stop, Terry. I don't want to hear it until you have something backing it up. I'm going to work.'

As if on cue, Lucas came back pushing a cart with a small television on top of it.

'I'll set you up with this,' he said.

'Mr. Lucas, I need to go to an appointment,' Winston said. 'My colleague is going to look at the tapes. Thank you for your cooperation.'

'Happy to be of service, ma'am.'

Winston looked at McCaleb.

'Call me.'

'You want me to drive you back to your car?'

'It's just a few blocks. I'll walk it.'

He nodded.

'Happy hunting,' she said.

McCaleb nodded. She had said that to him once before on a case that had not turned out so happily for him.

37

Langwiser and Kretzler told Bosch they were going ahead with the plan to rest their case by the close of the day.

'We got him,' Kretzler said, smiling and enjoying the adrenaline ride that came with making the decision to pull the trigger. 'By the time we're done he'll be tied down nine ways till Sunday. We've got Hendricks and Crowe today. We've got everything we need.'

'Except motive,' Bosch said.

'Motive is not going to be important with a crime that is obviously the work of a psychopath,' Langwiser said. 'Those jurors aren't going to go back into their little room at the end of this and say, "Yeah, but what was his motive?" They're going to say this guy is a sick fuck and—'

Her voice dropped to a whisper when the judge entered the courtroom through the door behind the bench.

'– we're going to put him away.'

The judge called for the jury and after a few minutes the prosecutors were putting on their last witnesses of the trial.

The first three witnesses were film business people who had attended the premiere party on the night of Jody Krementz's death. Each testified to having seen David Storey at the film premiere and the following party with a woman they identified from exhibit photos as Jody Krementz. The fourth witness, a screenwriter named Brent Wiggan, testified that he left the premiere party a few minutes before midnight and that he waited at the valet stand for his car along with David Storey and a woman he also identified as Jody Krementz.

'Why are you so sure it was just a few minutes before midnight, Mr. Wiggan?' Kretzler asked. 'It was, after all, a party. Were you watching the clock?'

'One question at a time, Mr. Kretzler,' the judge barked.

'Sorry, Your Honor. Why are you so sure it was a few minutes before midnight, Mr. Wiggan?'

'Because I *was* watching the clock, actually,' Wiggan said. 'My watch, that is. I do my writing at night. I am most productive from midnight until six. So I was watching the clock, knowing I had to get back to my house at close to midnight or I would fall behind in my work.'

'Would that also mean you were not drinking alcoholic beverages at the premiere party?'

'That is correct. I wasn't drinking because I didn't want to become tired or have my creativity dampened. People don't usually drink before they go to work at a bank or as a plane pilot – well, I guess most of them don't.'

He paused until the titters of laughter subsided. The judge looked annoyed but didn't say anything. Wiggan looked like he was enjoying his moment of attention. Bosch started feeling uneasy.

'I don't drink before I go on the job,' Wiggan finally continued. 'Writing is a craft but it is also a job and I treat it as such.'

'So are you crystal clear in your memory and identification of who David Storey was with at a few minutes before midnight?'

'Absolutely.'

'And David Storey, you personally already knew him, correct?'

'Yes, that's true. For several years.'

'Have you ever worked for David Storey on a film project?'

'No, I haven't. But not for lack of trying.'

Wiggan smiled ruefully. This part of the testimony, right down to the self-deprecating comment, had been carefully planned by Kretzler earlier. He needed to limit the potential for damage to Wiggan's testimony by walking him through the weak spots on direct.

'What do you mean by that, Mr. Wiggan?'

'Oh, I would say that in the last five years or so I have pitched film projects to David directly or to people in his production company maybe six or seven times. He never bought any of them.'

He hiked his shoulders in a sheepish gesture.

'Would you say this created a sense of animosity between you two?'

'No, not at all – at least not on my part. That's the way the Hollywood game is played. You keep pitching and pitching and hopefully somebody eventually bites. It helps to have a thick skin, though.'

He smiled and nodded to the jury. He was giving Bosch a full set of the creeps. He wished Kretzler would end it before they lost the jury.

'Thank you, that's all, Mr. Wiggan,' Kretzler said, apparently getting the same vibes as Bosch.

Wiggan's face seemed to fall as he realized his moment was ending.

But then Fowkkes, who had passed on cross-examining the first three witnesses of the day, stood up and went to the lectern.

'Good morning, Mr. Wiggan.'

'Good morning.'

Wiggan raised his eyebrows in a what-do-we-have-here look.

'Just a few questions. Could you list for the jury the titles of films that you have written that have been produced?'

'Well . . . so far, nothing's been made. I've got some options and I think in a few—'

'I understand. Would you be surprised to know that in the last four years you have pitched Mr. Storey or submitted film treatments to him on a total of twenty-nine occasions, all of which were rejected?'

Wiggan's face flushed with embarrassment.

'Well, I . . . I guess that could be true. I . . . don't really know. I don't keep a record of my rejections, as Mr. Storey apparently does.'

He delivered the last line in a snippish manner and Bosch almost winced. There was nothing worse than a witness on the stand who is caught in a lie and then gets defensive about it. Bosch glanced at the jury. Several of them were not looking at the witness, a sign that they were as uncomfortable as Bosch.

Fowkkes moved in for the kill.

'You were rejected by the defendant on twenty-nine occasions and yet you say to the jury that you bear him no malice, is that correct, sir?'

'That's just business as usual in Hollywood. Ask anyone.'

'Well, Mr. Wiggan, I am asking you. Are you telling this jury that you bear this man no ill will when he is the same man who has constantly and repeatedly said to you your work is not good enough?'

Wiggan almost mumbled his answer into the microphone.

'Yes, that is true.'

'Well, you're a better man than me, Mr. Wiggan,' Fowkkes said. 'Thank you, Your Honor. Nothing further at this time.'

Bosch could feel a good bit of the air go out of the prosecution's balloon. With four questions and less than two minutes Fowkkes had put Wiggan's entire credibility into question. And what was so absolutely perfect about the defense attorney's skillful surgery was that there was little Kretzler could do on redirect to resuscitate Wiggan. The prosecutor at least knew better than to try to perhaps dig the hole deeper. He dismissed the witness and the judge called for the mid-morning break of fifteen minutes.

After the jury was out and people started working their way out of the courtroom, Kretzler leaned across Langwiser to whisper to Bosch.

'We should've known that this guy was going to blow up,' he said angrily.

Bosch just looked around to make sure no reporters were within earshot. He leaned toward Kretzler.

'You're probably right,' he said. 'But six weeks ago you were the one who said he would do the vetting on Wiggan. He was your responsibility, not mine. I'm going to get coffee.'

Bosch got up and left the two prosecutors sitting there.

After the break the prosecutors decided they needed to come back strong immediately after the disastrous cross-examination of Wiggan. They dropped plans to have another witness testify about seeing Storey and the victim together at the premiere party and Langwiser called a home security technician named Jamal Hendricks to the stand.

Bosch walked Hendricks in from the hallway. He was a black man wearing blue pants and a light blue uniform top, his first name embroidered over one pocket and the Lighthouse Security emblem over the other. He was planning to go to work following his testimony.

As they went through the first set of doors to the courtroom Bosch asked Hendricks in a whisper if he was nervous.

'Nah, man, piece of cake,' Hendricks replied.

On the stand Langwiser took Hendricks through his pedigree as a service technician for the home security company. She then moved specifically to his work on the security system at David Storey's house. Hendricks said that eight months earlier he had installed a deluxe Millennium 21 system in the house on Mulholland.

'Can you tell us what some of the features are on the deluxe Millennium Twenty-one system?'

'Well, it's top of the line. It's got everything. Remote sensing and operation, voice recognition command software, automatic sensor polling, an innkeeper program . . . you name it and Mr. Storey got it.'

'What is an innkeeper program?'

'Essentially, it's operation recording software. It lets you know what doors or windows have been opened and when, when the system has been turned on and off, what personal codes were used and whatnot. It keeps track of the whole system. It's primarily used in commercial-industrial applications but Mr. Storey wanted a commercial system and it came included.'

'So he didn't specifically ask for the innkeeper program?'

'I don't know about that. I didn't sell him the system. I only installed it.'

'But he could have had this program and not known about it.'

'Anything's possible, I guess.'

'Now did there come a time when Detective Bosch called Lighthouse Security and asked for a technician to meet him at Mr. Storey's home?'

'Yeah, he made the call and it was given to me because I had installed the system. I met him there at the house. This was after Mr. Storey had been arrested and was in lockup. Mr. Storey's lawyer was there, too.'

'When was that exactly?'

'That was November eleventh.'

'What did Detective Bosch ask you to do?'

'Well, first he showed me a search warrant. It allowed him to collect information from the system's chip.'

'And did you help him with that?'

'Yeah. I downloaded the innkeeper data file and printed it out for him.'

Langwiser first introduced the search warrant – the third executed during the investigation – as an exhibit, then she introduced the printout Hendricks had just testified about.

'Now Detective Bosch was interested in the innkeeper records for the evening of October twelfth going into the morning of October thirteenth, is that correct, Mr. Hendricks?'

'Right.'

'Can you look at the printout and read the entries for that time period?'

Hendricks studied the printout for several seconds before speaking.

'Well, it says the interior door leading to the garage was opened and the alarm system was engaged by Mr. Storey's voiceprint at seven-oh-nine the night of the twelfth. Then nothing happened until the next day, the thirteenth. At twelve-twelve A.M. the alarm system was disengaged by Mr. Storey's voiceprint and the interior garage door was opened again. He then put the alarm back on – once he was in the house.'

Hendricks studied the printout before continuing.

'The system remained at status until three-nineteen, when the alarm was shut off. The interior garage door was then opened and the alarm system was engaged once more by Mr. Storey's voiceprint. Then, forty-two minutes later, at four-oh-one A.M., the alarm was disengaged by Mr. Storey's voiceprint, the garage door was opened and the alarm system was engaged again. There was no other activity until eleven A.M., when the alarm was disengaged by the voice print of Betilda Lockett.'

'Do you know who Betilda Lockett is?'

'Yes, when I installed the system I set up her voice acceptance program. She's Mr. Storey's executive assistant.'

Langwiser asked permission to set up an easel with a board displaying the times and activities Hendricks had just testified to. It was approved over objection and Bosch helped Langwiser set up the display. The poster board had two columns on it showing the record of the house alarm's engagement and the usage of the door between the house and the garage.

	ALARM	INTERIOR GARAGE DOOR
10/12	7:09 P.M. – engaged by D. Storey	opened/closed
10/13	12:12 A.M. – disengaged by D. Storey	opened/closed
10/13	12:12 A.M. – engaged by D. Storey	
10/13	3:19 A.M. – disengaged by D. Storey	opened/closed
10/13	3:19 A.M. – engaged by D. Storey	
10/13	4:01 A.M. – disengaged by D. Storey	opened/closed
10/13	4:01 P.M. – engaged by D. Storey	

Langwiser continued her questioning of Hendricks.

'Does this illustration accurately reflect your testimony about the alarm system in David Storey's home on the evening of October twelfth going into October thirteenth?'

The technician looked at the poster carefully and then nodded.

'Is that a yes?'

'It's a yes.'

'Thank you. Now, because these activities were instigated with the system's recognition and approval of David Storey's voiceprint, are you telling the jury that this is the record of David Storey's comings and goings during the time period in question?'

Fowkkes objected, saying the question assumed facts not in evidence. Houghton agreed and told Langwiser to rephrase or ask another question. Her point made with the jury, she moved on.

'Mr. Hendricks, if I had a tape-recording of David Storey's voice, could I play it into the Millennium Twenty-one's station microphone and receive clearance to engage or disengage the alarm?'

'No. There are two fail-safe mechanisms. You must use a password recognized by the computer and you must say the date. So you need voice, password, correct date or the system won't accept the command.'

'What was David Storey's password?'

'I don't know. It's private. The system is set so that he can change his password as often as he likes.'

Langwiser looked at the poster on the easel. She went up and took a pointer off the easel's ledge and used it to underline the entries for 3:19 and 4:01 in the morning.

'Can you tell from these entries whether someone with Mr. Storey's voice left the house at three-nineteen and returned at four-oh-one, or if it was the other way around; someone came in at three-nineteen and then left at four-oh-one?'

'Yes, I can.'

'How is that?'

'The system also records which transmitter stations are used to engage and disengage the system. In this house the stations are set on either side of three doors – you know, outside and inside the door. The three are the front door, the door to the garage and one of the doors to the rear deck. The transmitters are on the outside and the inside of each door. Whatever one is used gets recorded in the innkeeper program.'

'Can you look at the printout from Mr. Storey's system that you looked at earlier and tell us what transmitters were used during the three-nineteen and four-oh-one entries?'

Hendricks studied his paperwork before answering.

'Uh, yes. At three-nineteen the exterior transmitter was used. That means somebody was in the garage when they turned the alarm on in the house. Then at four-oh-one the same exterior transmitter was used to turn the alarm off. The door was then opened and closed, then the alarm was turned back on from the inside.'

'So someone came home at four-oh-one, is that what you are saying?'

'Yes. Right.'

'And the system computer registered this someone as David Storey, correct?'

'It identified his voice, yes.'

'And this person would have to have used Mr. Storey's password and given the correct date as well?'

'Yes, that's right.'

Langwiser said she had no further questions. Fowkkes told the judge he had a quick cross-examination. He bounded to the lectern and looked at Hendricks.

'Mr. Hendricks, how long have you worked for Lighthouse?'

'Three years next month.'

'So you were employed by Lighthouse on January first a year ago, the so-called Y-two-K changeover?'

'Yes,' Hendricks said hesitantly.

'Can you tell us what happened to many of Lighthouse's clients on that day?'

'Uh, we had a few problems.'

'A *few* problems, Mr. Hendricks?'

'We had system failures.'

'What system in particular?'

'The Millennium Twos had a program malfunction. But it was minor. We were able to—'

'How many clients with Millennium Twos were affected in the Los Angeles area?'

'All of them. But we found the bug and—'

'That's all, sir. Thank you.'

'We got it fixed.'

'Mr. Hendricks,' the judge barked. 'That's enough. The jury will disregard the last statement.'

He looked at Langwiser.

'Redirect, Ms. Langwiser?'

Langwiser said she had a few quick questions. Bosch had known about the Y2K problems and reported them to the prosecutors. Their hope had been that the defense would not learn of them or raise them.

'Mr. Hendricks, did Lighthouse fix the bug that infected the systems after Y-two-K?'

'Yes, we did. It was fixed right away.'

'Would it in any way have affected data gathered from the defendant's system a full ten months after Y-two-K?'

'Not at all. The problem was resolved. The system was repaired.'

Langwiser said that was all she had for the witness and sat down. Fowkkes then rose for re-cross.

'The bug that was fixed, Mr. Hendricks, that was the bug they knew about, correct?'

Hendricks gave a confused look.

'Yeah, that was the one that caused the problem.'

'So what you're saying is that you only know about these "bugs" when they cause a problem.'

'Uh, usually.'

'So there could be a program bug in Mr. Storey's security system and you wouldn't know about it until it creates a problem, correct?'

Hendricks shrugged his shoulders.

'Anything's possible.'

Fowkkes sat down and the judge asked Langwiser if she had anything else. The prosecutor hesitated a moment but then said she had nothing further. Hendricks was dismissed by Houghton, who then suggested an early break for lunch.

'Our next witness will be very brief, Your Honor. I'd like to get him in before the break. We plan to concentrate on one witness during the afternoon session.'

'Very well, go on.'

'We recall Detective Bosch.'

Bosch got up and went to the witness stand, carrying the murder book. This time he did not touch the microphone. He settled in and was reminded by the judge that he was still under oath.

'Detective Bosch,' Langwiser began. 'At some point during your investigation of the murder of Jody Krementz were you directed to drive from the defendant's home to the victim's home and then back again?'

'Yes, I was. By you.'

'And did you follow that direction?'

'Yes.'

'When?'

'On November sixteenth at three-nineteen A.M.'

'Did you time your drive?'

'Yes, I did. Both ways.'

'And can you tell us those times? You can refer to your notes, if you wish.'

Bosch opened the binder to a previously marked page. He took a moment to study the notations even though he knew them by heart.

'From Mr. Storey's house to Jody Krementz's house it took eleven minutes and twenty-two seconds, driving within posted speed limits. Coming back it took eleven minutes and forty-eight seconds. The round trip was twenty-three minutes, ten seconds.'

'Thank you, Detective.'

That was it. Fowkkes passed again on cross-examination, reserving the right to call Bosch back to the stand during the defense phase. Judge Houghton recessed the trial for lunch and the crowded courtroom slowly drained into the outside hallway.

Bosch was pushing and moving through the crowd of lawyers, spectators and reporters in the hallway and looking for Annabelle Crowe when a hand strongly grabbed his upper arm from behind. He swung around and looked into the face of a black man he didn't recognize. Another man, this one white, came up to them. The two men had on almost identical gray suits. Bosch knew they were bureau men before the first man said his first word.

'Detective Bosch, I'm Special Agent Twilley with the FBI. This is Special Agent Friedman. Can we talk to you somewhere privately?'

38

It took three hours to go carefully through the videotape. At the end of it McCaleb had nothing to show for his time except a parking ticket. Tafero had appeared nowhere in the video of the post office on the day the money order was purchased. Neither had Harry Bosch, for that matter. The missing forty-eight minutes of video, which had been taped over before McCaleb and Winston got there, now haunted him. If they had gone to the post office first and Hollywood station second, they might have had the killer on tape. Those forty-eight minutes might be the difference in the case, the difference in being able to clear Bosch or convict him.

McCaleb was thinking about what-if scenarios when he got to the Cherokee and found the parking ticket under the wiper. He cursed and pulled it off and looked at it. He had been so absorbed in watching the tape he had forgotten he had parked in a fifteen-minute zone in front of the post office. The ticket would cost him forty dollars and that stung. With few fishing charters in the winter months, his family had been living mostly off Graciela's small paycheck and his monthly pension from the bureau. There wasn't a lot of leeway with expenses for the two kids. This, coupled with Saturday's canceled charter, would hurt.

He slipped the ticket back into place on the windshield and started walking down the sidewalk. He decided he wanted to go into Valentino Bonds, even if he knew Rudy Tafero would likely be up in Van Nuys in court. It was in keeping with his practice of viewing the target subject in comfortable surroundings. The target might not be there this time, but the surroundings where he felt safe would.

As he walked he took out his cell phone and called Jaye Winston but got her machine. He hung up without leaving a message and paged her. Four blocks later, when he was almost to Valentino Bonds, she called back.

'I got nothing,' he reported.

'Nothing?'

'No Tafero and no Bosch.'

'Damn.'

'It had to have been on that missing forty-eight minutes.'

'We should have—'

'Gone to the post office first. I know. My fault. The one thing I did get was a parking ticket.'

'Sorry, Terry.'

'Which at least gives me an idea. It was right before Christmas and crowded. If he was in a fifteen-minute zone he might have gone over while waiting in line. The parking enforcement goons in this city are like Nazis. They wait in the shadows. There's always a chance there was a ticket. It should be checked.'

'Son of Sam?'

'Right.'

She was referring to the New York City serial killer who was tripped up in the 1970s by a parking ticket.

'I'll take a shot at it. See what I can do. What are you going to do?'

'I'm about to check out Valentino Bonds.'

'Is he there?'

'He's probably up in court. I'm going to go up there next, see if I can talk to Bosch about all of this.'

'Better be careful. Your colleagues from the bureau said they were going up to see him at lunch. They might still be around when you get there.'

'What, they're expecting Bosch to be so impressed by their suits that he confesses or something?'

'I don't know. Something like that. They were going to brace him. Get some stuff on the record and then go find the contradictions. You know, routine word trap.'

'Harry Bosch is not routine. They're wasting their time.'

'I know. I told 'em. But you can't tell an FBI agent anything, you know that.'

He smiled.

'Hey, if this goes the other way and we take down Tafero, I want the sheriff to pay for this ticket.'

'Hey, you're not working for me. You're working for Bosch, remember? He pays parking tickets. The sheriff only pays for pancakes.'

'All right. I'm gonna go.'

'Call me.'

He slid the phone into the pocket of his windbreaker and opened the glass door of Valentino Bonds.

It was a small white room with a waiting couch and a counter. It reminded McCaleb of a motel office. There was a calendar on the wall depicting a beach scene from Puerta Vallarta. Behind the counter a man sat with his head down, filling in a crossword puzzle. Behind him was a closed door to what was probably a rear office. McCaleb put a smile on his face and started walking with purpose around the counter before the man there even looked up.

'Rudy? Hey, Rudy, come on outta there!'

The man looked up as McCaleb passed him and opened the door. He stepped into an office that was more than twice the size of the front room.

'Rudy?'

The man from the counter came in right behind him.

'Hey, man, what are you doing?'

McCaleb turned, scanning the room.

'Looking for Rudy. Where is he?'

'He's not here. Now, if you would step—'

'He told me he'd be here, that he didn't have to be in court until later.'

Scanning the office, he saw the rear wall was covered with framed photos. He took a step closer. Most of them were shots of Tafero with celebrities he had either bailed out or worked with as a security consultant. Some of the photos were clearly from his days working across the street at the cop shop.

'Excuse me, just who are you?'

McCaleb looked at the man as if insulted. He looked like he might be Tafero's younger brother. The same dark hair and eyes with rough good looks.

'I'm a friend. Terry. We used to work together when he was across the street.'

McCaleb pointed to a group photo that was on the wall. It showed several men in suits and a few women standing in front of the brick facade of the Hollywood Division station. The detective squad. McCaleb saw both Harry Bosch and Rudy Tafero in the back row. Bosch's face was turned slightly away from the camera. There was a cigarette in his mouth and smoke rising from it partially obscured his face.

The man turned and started looking at the photo.

McCaleb's eyes took another swing around the office. The room was nicely appointed with a desk to the left and a sitting area to the right with two short couches and an oriental rug. He stepped closer to the desk to look at a file sitting at center on the blotter but the file, though an inch thick with documents, had nothing written on the tab.

'What the fuck, you're not on here.'

'Yes, I am,' McCaleb said without turning from the desk. 'I was smoking. You can't see my face.'

There was a file tray to the right of the blotter that was stacked with folders. McCaleb leaned his head at an angle to check the tabs. He saw an assortment of names, some of them recognizable as entertainers or actors but none of them correlating to his investigation.

'Bullshit, man, that ain't you. That's Harry Bosch.'

'Really? You know Harry?'

The man didn't answer. McCaleb turned around. The man was looking at him with angry, suspicious eyes. For the first time McCaleb saw that he held an old billyclub down at his side.

'Let me see.'

He walked over and looked at the framed photo.

'You know, you're right, that's Harry. I must've been in the one they took the year before. I was working undercover when they took this one and couldn't be in the picture.'

McCaleb nonchalantly took a step toward the door. Inside he was bracing to get hit with the bat.

'Just tell him I was here, okay? Tell him Terry stopped by.'

He made it to the door but one last framed photo caught his eye. It showed Tafero and another man side by side, jointly holding a polished wood plaque in their hands. The picture was old, Tafero looked almost ten years younger. His eyes were brighter and his smile seemed genuine. The plaque itself was hanging on the wall next to the photo. McCaleb leaned closer and read the brass plate attached at the bottom.

RUDY TAFERO
HOLLYWOOD BOOSTERS DETECTIVE OF THE MONTH
FEBRUARY 1995

He glanced back at the photo again and then moved through the door to the front room.

'Terry what?' the man said as he passed.

McCaleb walked to the front door before turning back to him.

'Just tell him it was Terry, the undercover guy.'

He left the office and walked back up the street without looking back.

McCaleb sat in his car in front of the post office. He felt uneasy, the way he always did when he knew the answer was within reach but he just couldn't quite see it. His gut told him he was on the right track. Tafero, the PI who hid his upscale Hollywood practice behind a bail bonds shack, was the key. McCaleb just couldn't find the door.

He realized he was very hungry. He started the car and thought about a place to eat. He was a few blocks from Musso's but had eaten there too recently. He wondered if they served food at Nat's but figured if they did that it would be dangerous to the stomach. Instead, he drove over to the In 'n Out on Sunset and ordered at the drive-through.

While he was eating his hamburger over the to-go box in the Cherokee, his phone chirped. He put the burger down in the box, wiped his hands on a napkin and opened the phone.

'You're a genius.'

It was Jaye Winston.

'What?'

'Tafero got a ticket on his Mercedes. A black four-thirty CLK. He was in the fifteen-minute zone right in front of the post office. The ticket was written at eight-nineteen A.M. on the twenty-second. He hasn't paid it yet. He has till five today and then it's overdue.'

McCaleb was silent as he considered this. He felt nerve synapses firing like dominoes running up his backbone. The ticket was a hell of a break. It proved absolutely nothing but it told him that he was following the correct path. And sometimes knowing you were on the right path was better than having the proof.

His thoughts jumped to his visit to Tafero's office and the photographs he had seen.

'Hey, Jaye, did you get a chance to look up anything on the case with Bosch's old lieutenant?'

'I didn't have to go looking. Twilley and Friedman already had a file on it with them today. Lieutenant Harvey Pounds. Somebody beat him to death about four weeks after he had that altercation with Bosch over Gunn. Because of the bad blood Bosch was a likely suspect. But he apparently was cleared – by the LAPD at least. The case is open but inactive. The bureau kind of watched from afar and has kept an open file, too. Twilley told me today that there are some people in the LAPD who think Bosch was cleared on it a little too quickly.'

'Oh, and I bet Twilley loves that.'

'He does. He already has Bosch down for it. He thinks Gunn is only the tip of the iceberg with Harry.'

McCaleb shook his head but immediately moved on. He couldn't dwell on other peoples' foibles and motivations. There was a lot to think about and plan for with the investigation at hand.

'By the way, do you have a copy of the parking ticket?' he asked.

'Not yet. It was all phone work. But it's being faxed. The thing is, you and I know what it means but it's a long way off from being proof of anything.'

'I know. But it will make a good prop when the time comes.'

'When the time comes for what?'

'To make our play. We'll use Tafero to get to Storey. You know that's where this is heading.'

'We? You've got it all planned out, don't you, Terry?'

'Not quite but I'm working on it.'

He didn't want to have an argument with her about his role in the investigation.

'Listen, my lunch is getting cold here,' he said.

'Well, excuse me. Go ahead and eat.'

'Call me later. I'm going up to see Bosch later on. Anything from Twilley and Friedman on that?'

'I think they're still up there with him.'

'All right. Check you later.'

He closed the phone, got out of the car and carried the food box to a trash can. He then jumped back in and started the engine. On the way back to the post office on Wilcox he opened all the windows to air the smell of greasy food out of the car.

39

Annabelle Crowe walked to the witness stand, drawing all eyes in the courtroom. She was stunningly attractive but there was an almost awkward quality about her movements. This mixture made her seem old and young at the same time and even more attractive. Langwiser would do the questioning. She waited until Crowe was seated before disturbing the room's vibe and getting up to go to the lectern.

Bosch had barely noticed the entrance of the final witness for the prosecution. He sat at the prosecution table with his eyes down, deep in thought about his visit from the two FBI agents. He had sized them up quickly. They smelled blood in the water and knew if they bagged Bosch on the Gunn case that there would be no end to the media ride they would get from it. He expected them to make their move at any moment.

Langwiser quickly moved through a series of general questions with Crowe, establishing that she was a neophyte actress with a few plays and commercials on her resume as well as one line in a feature film that had yet to be released. Her story seemed to confirm the difficulties of making it in Hollywood – a knock-down beauty who was only one in a town full of them. She still lived on stipends sent from her parents in Albuquerque.

Langwiser moved on to more salient testimony, keying in on the night of April 14 of the previous year when Annabelle Crowe went out on a date with David Storey. After quickly drawing brief descriptions of the dinner and drinks the couple enjoyed at Dan Tana's in West Hollywood, Langwiser moved to the latter half of the evening, when Annabelle accompanied Storey to his home on Mulholland Drive.

Crow testified that she and Storey shared a whole pitcher of margaritas on the back deck of his house before they went to his bedroom.

'And did you go willingly, Ms. Crowe?'

'Yes, I did.'

'You engaged in sexual relations with the defendant?'

'Yes, I did.'

'And this was consensual sexual intercourse?'

'Yes, it was.'

'Did anything happen that was unusual once you began having sexual relations with the defendant?'

'Yes, he started to choke me.'

'He started to choke you. How did that occur?'

'Well, I guess I closed my eyes at one point and it felt like he was changing positions or moving. He was on top of me and I felt his hand slide behind my neck and he sort of lifted my head off the pillow. Then I felt him slide something down . . .'

She stopped and put her hand to her mouth as she appeared to fight to maintain her composure.

'Take your time, Ms. Crowe.'

The witness looked as though she was genuinely trying to hold back tears. She finally dropped her hand and picked up her cup of water. She sipped from it and then looked up at Langwiser, a new resolve in her eyes.

'I felt him slide something down over my head and around my neck. I opened my eyes and he was tightening a necktie around my neck.'

She stopped and took another sip of water.

'Can you describe this necktie?'

'It had a pattern. It was blue diamonds on a field of purple. I remember it exactly.'

'What happened when the defendant pulled the tie tightly around your neck?'

'It was choking me!' Crowe replied shrilly, as if the question was stupid and the answer was obvious. 'He was choking me. And he kept . . . moving in me . . . and I tried to fight him but he was too strong for me.'

'Did he say anything at this time?'

'He just kept saying, "I have to do this, I have to do this," and he was breathing really hard and he kept on having sex with me. His teeth were clenched tight when he said it. I . . .'

She stopped again and this time single tears slid down both her cheeks, one slightly behind the other. Langwiser went to the prosecution table and took a box of tissues from her spot. She held them up and said, 'Your Honor, may I?'

The judge allowed her to approach the witness with the tissues. Langwiser made the delivery and then went back to the lectern. The courtroom was silent save for the crying sounds of the witness. Langwiser broke the moment.

'Ms. Crowe, do you need a minute?'

'No, I'm fine. Thank you.'

'Did you pass out when the defendant choked you?'

'Yes.'

'What do you remember next?'

'I woke up in his bed.'

'Was he there?'

'No, but I could hear the shower running. In the bathroom next to the bedroom.'

'What did you do?'

'I got up to get dressed. I wanted to leave before he came out of the shower.'

'Were your clothes where you had left them?'

'No. I found them in a bag – like a grocery bag – by the bedroom door. I put on my underwear.'

'Did you have a purse with you that night?'

'Yes. That was in the bag, too. But it was opened. I looked inside and he had taken the keys out. I—'

Fowkkes objected, saying the answer assumed facts not in evidence and the judge sustained it.

'Did you see the defendant take your keys out of your purse?' Langwiser asked.

'Well, no. But they had been inside my purse. I didn't take them out.'

'Okay, then someone – someone you didn't see because you were unconscious on the bed – took your keys out, is that correct?'

'Yes.'

'Okay, where did you find your keys after you realized they were not in your purse?'

'They were on his bureau next to his own keys.'

'Did you finish getting dressed and leave?'

'Actually, I was so scared I just grabbed my clothes and my keys and my purse and I ran out of there. I finished getting dressed when I got outside. I then ran down the street.'

'How did you get home?'

'I got tired of running and so I walked on Mulholland for a long time until I came to a fire station with a pay phone out front. I used it to call a cab, then I went home.'

'Did you call the police when you got home?'

'Um, I didn't.'

'Why not, Ms. Crowe?'

'Well, two things. When I got home David was leaving a message on my machine and I picked up. He apologized and said he got carried away. He told me he thought that the choking was going to increase my satisfaction while we had sex.'

'Did you believe him?'

'I don't know. I was confused.'

'Did you ask him why he had put your clothes in a bag?'

'Yes. He said he thought he was going to have to take me to the hospital if I didn't wake up by the time he was out of the shower.'

'Did you ask him why he thought he should take a shower before taking an unconscious woman in his bed to the hospital?'

'I didn't ask that.'

'Did you ask him why he didn't call for paramedics?'

'No, I didn't think of that.'

'What was the other reason you did not call the police?'

The witness looked down at her hands, which were grasping each other in her lap.

'Well, I was embarrassed. After he called I wasn't sure anymore what had happened. You know, whether he had tried to kill me or was . . . trying to satisfy me more. I don't know. You always hear about Hollywood people and weird sex. I thought maybe I was . . . I don't know, just being uncool and square about it.'

She kept her eyes down and two more tears went down the slopes of her cheeks. Bosch saw a drop hit the collar of her chiffon blouse and leave a wet mark. Langwiser continued in a very soft tone.

'When did you contact the police about what happened that night with you and the defendant?'

Annabelle Crowe responded in a softer tone.

'When I read about him being arrested for killing Jody Krementz the same way.'

'You talked to Detective Bosch then?'

She nodded.

'Yes. And I knew that if I'd . . . I'd called the police that night that maybe she'd still . . .'

She didn't finish. She grabbed tissues out of the box and started a full force cry. Langwiser told the judge she was finished with her examination. Fowkkes said there would be a cross-examination but suggested that it should follow a break during which time the defendant could compose herself. Judge Houghton said that was a good idea and called a fifteen-minute break.

Bosch stayed in the courtroom watching over Annabelle Crowe as she went through the box of tissues. When she was done her face was no longer as beautiful. It was distorted and red, her eye sockets swollen. Bosch thought she had been convincing but he knew she hadn't faced Fowkkes yet. How she fared during the cross would determine whether the jury believed anything she had said on direct.

When Langwiser came back in she told Bosch there was someone at the outer door of the courtroom who wanted to speak to him.

'Who is it?'

'I didn't ask. I just overheard him talking to the deputies as I went in. They wouldn't let him in.'

'Was he in a suit? A black guy?'

'No, street clothes. A windbreaker.'

'Keep an eye on Annabelle. And you better find another box of tissues.'

He got up and went to the courtroom doors, working his way past all of the people coming back in at the end of the break. At one point he came face-to-face with Rudy Tafero. Bosch moved to his right to go around him but Tafero moved to his left. They danced back and forth a couple of times and Tafero smiled broadly. Bosch finally stopped and didn't move until Tafero pushed by him.

In the hall he looked around but didn't see anyone he recognized. Then Terry McCaleb walked out of the men's room and they nodded to each other. Bosch walked over to the railing in front of one of the floor-to-ceiling windows that looked out on the plaza below. McCaleb walked up.

'I've got about two minutes, then I've got to get back in there.'

'I just want to know if we can talk after court today. Things are happening and I need some time with you.'

'I know things are happening. Two agents showed up here today.'

'What did you tell them?'

'To fuck off. It made them mad.'

'Federal agents don't take that sort of language that well, you should know that, Bosch.'

'Yeah, well, I'm a slow learner.'

'What about after?'

'I'll be around. Unless Fowkkes creams this wit. Then I don't know, my team might have to retreat somewhere to lick our wounds.'

'All right, then I'll hang out, watch it on TV.'

'Later.'

Bosch went back into the courtroom, wondering what McCaleb had come up with so quickly. The jury was back and the judge was giving Fowkkes the go-ahead. The defense attorney waited politely as Bosch moved by him to get to the prosecution table. Then he began.

'Now Ms. Crowe, is acting your full-time occupation?'

'Yes.'

'Have you been acting here today?'

Langwiser immediately objected, angrily accusing Fowkkes of harassing the witness. Bosch thought her reaction was a bit extreme but knew she was sending a message to Fowkkes that she was going to defend her witness tooth and nail. The judge overruled the objection, saying Fowkkes was within bounds in cross-examining a witness hostile to his client.

'No, I am not acting,' Crowe answered forcefully.

Fowkkes nodded.

'You testified that you have been in Hollywood three years.'

'Yes.'

'I counted five paying jobs you spoke of. Anything else?'

'Not yet.'

Fowkkes nodded.

'Good to be hopeful. It's very difficult to break in, isn't it?'

'Yes, very difficult, very discouraging.'

'But you are on TV right now, aren't you?'

She hesitated a moment, the realization that she had walked into a trap showing on her face.

'And so are you,' she said.

Bosch almost smiled. It was the best answer she could have given.

'Let's talk about this . . . event that allegedly took place between you and Mr. Storey,' Fowkkes said. 'This event is, in fact, something you concocted from newspaper stories following David Storey's arrest, correct?'

'No, not correct. He tried to kill me.'

'So you say.'

Langwiser stood up to object but before she did the judge admonished Fowkkes to keep such editorial comments to himself. The defense lawyer moved on.

'Now, after Mr. Storey supposedly choked you to the point of unconsciousness, did you develop bruises on your neck?'

'Yes, I had a bruise for almost a week. I had to stay inside. I couldn't go to auditions or anything.'

'And you took photographs of the bruise to document its existence, correct?'

'No, I didn't.'

'But you showed the bruise to your agent and friends, did you not?'

'No.'

'And why is that?'

'Because I didn't think it would ever come to this, where I would have to try to prove what he did. I just wanted it to go away and I didn't want anyone to know.'

'So we only have your word for the bruise, is that correct?'

'Yes.'

'Just as we only have your word for the entire alleged incident, correct?'

'He tried to kill me.'

'And you testified that when you got home that evening David Storey happened at that very moment to be leaving a message on your phone machine, correct?'

'Absolutely.'

'And you picked that call up – a call from the man you say tried to kill you. Do I have that right?'

Fowkkes gestured as if grabbing a telephone. He held his hand up until she answered.

'Yes.'

'And you saved that message on that tape to document his words and what had happened to you, correct?'

'No, I taped over it. By mistake.'

'By mistake. You mean you left it in the machine and eventually taped over it?'

'Yes. I didn't want to but I forgot and it got taped over.'

'You mean you forgot that someone tried to kill you and taped over it?'

'No, I didn't forget that he tried to kill me. I'll never forget that.'

'So as far as this tape goes, we only have your word for it, correct?'

'That's right.'

There was a measure of defiance in her voice. But in a way it seemed pitiful to Bosch. It was like yelling, 'Fuck you' into a jet engine. He sensed that she was about to be thrown into that jet engine and torn apart.

'Now, you testified that you are supported in part by your parents and that you have earned some monies as an actress. Is there any other source of income you haven't told us about?'

'Well . . . not really. My grandmother sends me money. But not too often.'

'Anything else?'

'Not that I can think of.'

'Do you take money from men on occasion, Ms. Crowe?'

There was an objection from Langwiser and the judge called the lawyers to a sidebar. Bosch watched Annabelle Crowe the whole time the lawyers whispered. He studied her face. There was still a brushstroke of defiance but it was being crowded by fear. She knew something was coming. Bosch decided that Fowkkes had something legitimate that he was going after. It was something that was going to hurt her and thereby hurt the case.

When the sidebar broke up Kretzler and Langwiser returned to their seats at the prosecution table. Kretzler leaned over to Bosch.

'We're fucked,' he whispered. 'He's got four men that will testify they paid her for sex. Why didn't we know about this?'

Bosch didn't answer. She had been assigned to him for vetting. He had questioned her at length about her personal life and had run her prints for an arrest record. Her answers and the computer run were clean. If she'd never been popped for prostitution and she denied any criminal activities to Bosch, there wasn't much else he could have done.

Back at the lectern, Fowkkes rephrased the question.

'Ms. Crowe, have you ever taken money from men in exchange for sex?'

'No, absolutely not. That is a lie.'

'Do you know a man named Andre Snow?'

'Yes, I do.'

'If he were to testify under oath that he paid you for sexual relations, would he be lying?'

'Yes, he would.'

Fowkkes named three other men and they went through the same loop of Crowe acknowledging that she knew them but denying she had ever sold them sex.

'Then have you ever taken money from these men, but not for sex?' Fowkkes asked in a false tone of exasperation.

'Yes, on occasion. But it had nothing to do with whether we had sex or not.'

'Then what did it have to do with?'

'Them wanting to help me. I considered them friends.'

'Did you ever have sex with them?'

Annabelle Crowe looked down at her hands and shook her head.

'Are you saying no, Ms. Crowe?'

'I am saying that I didn't have sex with them every time they gave me money. They didn't give me money every time we had sex. One thing had nothing to do with the other. You are trying to make it look like something it's not.'

'I'm just asking questions, Ms. Crowe. As it is my job to do. As it is your job to tell this jury the truth.'

After a long pause Fowkkes said he had no further questions.

Bosch realized that he had been gripping the arms of his chair so tightly that his knuckles were white and had gone numb. He rubbed his hands together and tried to relax but he couldn't. He knew that Fowkkes was a master, a cut-and-run artist. He was brief and to the point and as devastating as a stiletto. Bosch realized that his discomfort was not only for Annabelle Crowe's helpless position and public humiliation, but for his own position. He knew the stiletto would be pointed at him next.

40

They settled into a booth at Nat's after getting bottles of Rolling Rock from the bartender with the tattoo of the barbed-wire-wrapped heart. While she pulled the bottles from the cold case and opened them, the woman hadn't said anything about McCaleb having come in the other night asking questions about the man he had now returned with. It was early and the place was empty except for groups of hard-cores at the bar and crowded into the booth all the way to the rear. Bruce Springsteen was on the jukebox singing, 'There's a darkness on the edge of town.'

McCaleb studied Bosch. He thought he looked pre-occupied by something, probably the trial. The last witness had been a wash at best. Good on direct, bad on cross. The kind of witness you don't use – if you have the choice.

'Looked like you guys got sandbagged there with your wit.'

Bosch nodded.

'My fault. I should've seen it coming. I looked at her and thought she was so beautiful she couldn't possibly . . . I just believed her.'

'I know what you mean.'

'Last time I trust a face.'

'You guys still look like you're in good shape. What else you got coming?'

Bosch smirked.

'That's it. They were going to rest today but decided to wait until the morning so Fowkkes wouldn't have the night to get ready. But we've fired all the bullets in the gun. Starting tomorrow we see what they've got.'

McCaleb watched Bosch take down almost half the bottle in one long pull. He decided he'd better get to the real questions while Bosch was still sharp.

'So tell me about Rudy Tafero.'

Bosch shrugged his shoulders in a gesture of ambivalence.

'What about him?'

'I don't know. How well do you know him? How well *did* you know him?'

'Well, I knew him when he was on *our* team. He worked Hollywood detectives about five years while I was there. Then he pulled the pin, got his twenty-year pension and moved across the street. Started working on getting people we put in the bucket out of the bucket.'

'When you were both on the same team, both in Hollywood, were you close?'

'I don't know what close means. We weren't friends, we weren't drinking buddies, he worked burglaries and I worked homicides. What are you asking so much about him for? What's he got to do with—'

He stopped and looked at McCaleb, the wheels obviously turning inside. Rod Stewart was now singing 'Twisting the Night Away.'

'Are you fucking kidding me?' Bosch finally asked. 'You're looking at—'

'Let me just ask some questions,' McCaleb interjected. 'Then you can ask yours.'

Bosch drained his bottle and held it up until the bartender noticed.

'No table service, guys,' she called over. 'Sorry.'

'Fuck that,' Bosch said.

He slid out of the booth and went to the bar. He came back with four more Rocks, though McCaleb had barely begun to drink his first one.

'Ask away,' Bosch said.

'Why weren't you two close?'

Bosch put both elbows on the table and held a fresh bottle with both hands. He looked out of the booth and then at McCaleb.

'Five, ten years ago there were two groups in the bureau. And to a large extent it was this way in the department, too. It was like the saints and the sinners – two distinct groups.'

'The born agains and the born againsts?'

'Something like that.'

McCaleb remembered. It had become well known in local law enforcement circles a decade earlier that a group within the LAPD known as the 'born agains' had members in key positions and was holding sway over promotions and choice assignments. The group's numbers – several hundred officers of all ranks – were members of a church in the San Fernando Valley where the department's deputy chief in charge of operations was a lay preacher. Ambitious officers joined the church in droves, in hopes of impressing the deputy chief and enhancing their career prospects. How much spirituality was involved was in question. But when the deputy chief delivered his sermon every Sunday at the eleven o'clock service, the church would be packed to standing room only with off-duty cops casting their eyes fervently on the pulpit. McCaleb had once heard a story about a car alarm going off in the parking lot during an eleven o'clock service. The hapless hype rummaging through the vehicle's glove compartment soon found himself surrounded by a hundred guns pointed by off-duty cops.

'I take it you were on the sinners' team, Harry.'

Bosch smiled and nodded.

'Of course.'

'And Tafero was on the saints'.'

'Yeah. And so was our lieutenant at the time. A paper pusher named Harvey Pounds. He and Tafero had their little church thing going and so they were tight. I think anybody who was tight with Pounds, whether because of church or not, wasn't somebody I was going to gravitate toward, if you know what I mean. And they weren't going to gravitate toward me.'

McCaleb nodded. He knew more than he was letting on.

'Pounds was the guy who messed up the Gunn case,' he said. 'The one you pushed through the window.'

'He's the one.'

Bosch dropped his head and shook it in self-disgust.

'Was Tafero there that day?'

'Tafero? I don't know, probably.'

'Well, wasn't there an IAD investigation with witness reports?'

'Yeah, but I didn't look at it. I mean, I pushed the guy through a window in front of the squad. I wasn't going to deny it.'

'And later – what, a month or so? – Pounds ends up dead in the tunnel up in the hills.'

'Griffith Park, yeah.'

'And it's still open . . .'

Bosch nodded.

'Technically.'

'You said that before. What does that mean?'

'It means it's open but nobody's working it. The LAPD has a special classification for cases like it, cases they don't want to touch. It's what is called closed by circumstances other than arrest.'

'And you know those circumstances?'

Bosch finished his second bottle, slid it to the side and pulled a fresh bottle in front of him.

'You're not drinking,' he said.

'You're doing enough for both of us. Do you know those circumstances?'

Bosch leaned forward.

'Listen, I'm going to tell you something very few people know about, okay?'

McCaleb nodded. He knew better than to ask a question now. He would just let Bosch tell it.

'Because of that window thing I went on suspension. When I got tired of walking around my house staring at the walls, I started investigating an old case. A cold case. A murder case. I went freelancing on it and I ended up following a blind trail to some very powerful people. But at the time I had no badge, no real standing. So a few times, when I made some calls, I used Pounds's name. You know, I was trying to hide what I was doing.'

'If the department found out you were working a case while on suspension things would've gotten worse for you.'

'Exactly. So I used his name when I made what I thought were some routine, innocuous calls. But then one night somebody called Pounds up and told him that they had something for him, some urgent information. He went to the meet. By himself. Then they found him later in that tunnel. He'd been beaten pretty bad. Like they had tortured him. Only he couldn't answer their questions because he was the wrong guy. I was the one who had used his name. I was the one they wanted.'

Bosch dropped his chin to his chest and was silent for a long moment.

'I got him killed,' he said without looking up. 'The guy was a pure-bred asshole but my actions got him killed.'

Bosch suddenly jerked his head up and drank from his bottle. McCaleb saw his eyes were dark and shiny. They looked weary.

'Is that what you wanted to know, Terry? Does that help you?'

McCaleb nodded.

'How much of this would Tafero have known?'

'Nothing.'

'Could he have thought you were the one who called Pounds out that night?'

'Maybe. There were people who did and probably still do. But what does it mean? What's it got to do with Gunn?'

McCaleb took his first long drink of beer. It was cold and he felt the chill in his chest. He put the bottle down and decided it was time to give something back to Bosch.

'I need to know about Tafero because I need to know about reasons, motives. I have no proof of anything – yet – but I think Tafero killed Gunn. He did it for Storey. He set you in the frame.'

'Jesus . . .'

'Nice perfect frame. The crime scene is connected to the painter Hieronymus Bosch, the painter is connected to you as his namesake and then you are connected to Gunn. And you know when Storey probably got the idea for it?'

Bosch shook his head. He looked too stunned to talk.

'The day you tried to interview him in his office. You played the tape in court last week. You identified yourself on it by your full first name.'

'I always do. I . . .'

'He then connects with Tafero and Tafero has the perfect victim to put in the frame. Gunn – a man he knew walked away from you and a murder charge six years ago.'

Bosch lifted his bottle a couple of inches off the table and brought it back down hard.

'I think the plan was twofold. If they got lucky the connection would be made quickly and you'd be fighting a murder charge before Storey's trial even started. If that didn't happen, then Plan B. They would still have it to crush you with at trial. Destroy you, they destroy the case. Fowkkes already took out that woman today and potshotted a few of the other wits. What does the case rest on? You, Harry. They knew it would come down to you.'

Bosch turned his head slightly and his eyes seemed to go blank as he stared at the scarred table top while considering what McCaleb had said.

'I needed to know your background with Tafero. Because that's a question; why would *he* do this? Yes, there probably is money in it and a hook into Storey if he walks. But there had to be something more. And I think you just told me what it was. He's probably hated you for a long time.'

Bosch looked up from the table and directly at McCaleb.

'It's a payback.'

McCaleb nodded.

'For Pounds. And unless we get the proof of it, it might just work.'

Bosch was silent. He stared down at the table. He looked tired and washed out to McCaleb.

'Still want to shake his hand?' McCaleb asked.

Bosch raised his eyes.

'Sorry, Harry, that was a cheap shot.'

Bosch shook his head, shrugging it off.

'I deserve it. So tell me, what *do* you have?'

'Not a lot. But you were right. I missed something. Tafero bailed Gunn out on New Year's Eve. I think the plan was to kill him that night, set the scene and let things take their course. The Hieronymus Bosch connection would come to light – either through Jaye Winston or a bureau VICAP inquiry – and you'd become a natural target. But then Gunn went and got himself drunk in here.'

He raised his bottle and gestured to the bar.

'And then he got himself duiced while driving home. Tafero had to get him out so they could stay with the plan. So he could kill him. That bail slip is the one direct link we have.'

Bosch nodded. McCaleb could tell he was seeing the scheme.

'They leaked it to that reporter,' Bosch said. 'Once it hit the media they could jump on it and use it and act like it was news to them, like they were behind the curve when all along they were bending the goddamn curve.'

McCaleb nodded hesitantly. He didn't bring up Buddy Lockridge's admission because it threw a jam into the working theory.

'What?' Bosch asked.

'Nothing. I'm just thinking.'

'You've got nothing other than Tafero posting the bail?'

'A traffic ticket and that's it for now.'

In detail McCaleb described his morning's visits to Valentino Bonds and the post office and how his being forty-eight minutes late at the post office might be the difference in being able to clear Bosch and take down Tafero.

Bosch winced and picked up his bottle, but then put it down without drinking from it.

'The parking ticket puts him at the post office,' McCaleb offered.

'It's nothing. He's got an office five blocks away. He could claim it was the only parking place he could find. He could say he lent his car to somebody. It's nothing.'

McCaleb didn't want to concentrate on what they didn't have. He wanted to fill in pieces.

'Listen, the morning watch sergeant told us you had a standing request to be notified every time Gunn was brought in. Would Tafero have known about it? Either from before when he was still in the squad or some other way?'

'He could have. It wasn't a secret. I was working on Gunn. Someday I was going to break him.'

'By the way, what did Pounds look like?'

Bosch gave him a confused look.

'Short, wide and balding with a mustache?'

Bosch nodded and was about to ask a question when McCaleb answered it.

'His picture is on the wall in Tafero's office. Pounds giving him the detective-of-the-month plaque. I bet you never got one of those, Harry.'

'Not with Pounds making the pick.'

McCaleb looked up and saw that Jaye Winston had entered the bar. She was carrying a briefcase. He nodded to her and she started toward the booth, walking with her shoulders up as though she were carefully stepping through a landfill.

McCaleb moved over and she slid into the booth next to him.

'Nice place.'

'Harry,' McCaleb said, 'I believe you know Jaye Winston.'

Bosch and Winston looked at each other.

'First thing,' Winston said, 'I'm sorry about the thing with Kiz. I hope—'

'We do what we have to do,' Bosch said. 'You want a drink? They don't come to the table here.'

'I'd be shocked if they did. Maker's Mark, rocks, if they have it.'

'Terry, you cool?'

'Cool.'

Bosch slid out to get the drink. Winston turned to look at McCaleb.

'How is it going?'

'Little pieces, here and there.'

'How's he taking it?'

'Not bad, I guess, for a guy who's been put into a pretty big box. How'd you do?'

She smiled in a way that McCaleb could tell meant she had come up with something.

'I got you the photo and a couple other . . . interesting . . . pieces.'

Bosch put Winston's drink down in front of her and slid back into the booth.

'She laughed when I said Maker's Mark,' he said. 'That's the house swill there.'

'Wonderful. Thank you.'

Winston moved her glass to the side and brought her briefcase up onto the table. She opened it, removed a file and then closed the briefcase and put it back on the floor next to the booth. McCaleb watched Bosch watching her. There was an expectant look on his face.

Winston opened the file and slid a five-by-eight photo of Rudy Tafero over to McCaleb.

'That's from his bonding license. It's eleven months old.'

She then referred to a page of typed notes.

'I went to county lockup and pulled everything on Storey. He was held there until they transferred him to Van Nuys jail for the trial. During his stay in county he had nineteen visits from Tafero. The first twelve visits coming during the first three weeks he was in there. During that same period, Fowkkes only visited him four times. A lawyer in Fowkkes's office visited an additional four times and Storey's executive assistant, a woman named Betilda Lockett, visited six times. That's it. He was meeting with his investigator more often than his lawyers.'

'That's when they planned it,' McCaleb said.

She nodded and then smiled in that same way again.

'What?' McCaleb asked.

'Just saving the best for last.'

She brought her briefcase back up and opened it.

'The jail keeps records of all property and possessions of inmates – things that were brought in with them, things approved and passed to them by visitors. There is a notation in Storey's records that his assistant, Betilda Lockett, was allowed to give him a book during the second of her six visits. According to the property report, it was called *The Art of Darkness*. I went to the downtown library and checked it out.'

From her briefcase she took a large, heavy book with a blue cloth cover. She started opening it on the table. There was a yellow Post-it sticking out as a marker.

'It's a study of artists who used darkness as a vital part of the visual medium, according to the introduction.'

She looked up and smiled as she got to the Post-it.

'It has a rather long chapter on Hieronymus Bosch. Complete with illustrations.'

McCaleb lifted his empty bottle and clicked against her glass, which she still hadn't touched. He then leaned in, along with Bosch, to look at the pages.

'Beautiful,' he said.

Winston turned the pages. The book's illustrations of Bosch's work included all of the paintings from which pieces of the crime scene could be traced: *The Stone Operation, The Seven Deadly Sins* with the eye of God, *The Last Judgment* and *The Garden of Earthly Delights.*

'He planned the thing right there from his cell,' McCaleb marveled.

'Looks like it,' Winston said.

They both looked at Bosch, who was nodding his head almost imperceptibly.

'Now your turn, Harry,' McCaleb said.

Bosch looked perplexed.

'My turn at what?'

'At making good luck.'

McCaleb slid the picture of Tafero across the table and nodded toward the bartender. Bosch slid out and took the photo to the bar.

'We're still just dancing around the edges,' Winston said as they both watched Bosch question the bartender about the photo. 'We've got little pieces but that's it.'

'I know,' McCaleb said. He couldn't hear what was being said at the bar. The music was too loud, Van Morrison singing, 'The wild night is coming.'

Bosch nodded to the bartender and came back to the booth.

'She recognizes him – drinks Kahlúa and cream of all things. She can't put him here with Gunn, though.'

McCaleb shrugged his shoulders in a no-big-deal gesture.

'It was worth the shot.'

'You know where this is going, don't you?' Bosch said, his eyes shifting from McCaleb's to Winston's and then back. 'You're going to have to make a play. It's going to be the only way. And it's gotta be a damn good play because my ass is on the line.'

McCaleb nodded.

'We know,' he said.

'When? I'm running out of time.'

McCaleb looked at Winston. It was her call.

'Soon,' she said. 'Maybe tomorrow. I haven't gone into the office with this yet. I have to finesse my captain on it because last he knew, Terry here was banished and I was working with the bureau on you. I also have to get a DA involved because when we make the move we'll have to move fast. If it all works out I say we take Tafero in tomorrow night and make the play to him.'

Bosch looked down at the table with a rueful smile. He slid an empty bottle back and forth between his hands.

'I met those guys today. The agents.'

'I heard. You didn't exactly assure them of your innocence. They came back all hot and bothered.'

Bosch looked up.

'So what do you need from me on this?'

'We need you to sit tight,' Winston said. 'We'll let you know about tomorrow night.'

Bosch nodded.

'There is one thing,' McCaleb said. 'The exhibits from the trial, do you have access to them?'

'During court, yeah. Otherwise they stay with the clerk. Why?'

'Because Storey obviously had existing knowledge of the painter Hieronymus Bosch. He had to have recognized your name during that interview and known what he could do with it. So I'm thinking that book his assistant brought him in jail had to be his own. He told her to bring it to him.'

Bosch nodded.

'The picture of the bookcase.'

McCaleb nodded.

'You got it.'

'I'll let you know.' Bosch looked around the place. 'Are we done here?'

'We're done,' Winston said. 'We'll be in touch.'

She slid out of the booth, followed by Bosch and McCaleb. They left two beers and a whiskey rocks untouched on the table. At the door, McCaleb glanced back and saw a couple of the hard-cores moving in on the treasure. From the jukebox John Fogerty was singing, 'There's a bad moon on the rise . . .'

41

The chill off the water worked its way into McCaleb's bones. He shoved his hands deep into the pockets of his windbreaker and turtled his neck as far down into the collar as he could as he carefully made his way down the ramp to the Cabrillo Marina docks.

Though his chin was down his eyes were alert and scanning the docks for unusual movement. Nothing caught his attention. He glanced at Buddy Lockridge's sailboat as he passed. Despite all the junk – surfboards, bikes, gas grill, an ocean kayak and other assorted equipment and debris – crowding the deck, he could see the cabin lights were on. He walked quietly on the wood planking. He decided that whether Buddy was awake or not it was too late and McCaleb was too tired and cold to deal with his supposed partner. Still, as he approached *The Following Sea,* he couldn't help but move his mind over the sharp-edged anomaly in his working theory on the case. Back at the bar Bosch had been correct when he deduced that someone from the Storey camp had to have leaked the story of the Gunn investigation to the *New Times.* McCaleb knew that the only way the current case theory hung together was if Tafero, or maybe Fowkkes or even Storey from jail, had been Jack McEvoy's source. The problem was that Buddy Lockridge had told McCaleb that he had leaked the investigation to the weekly tabloid.

Now the only way, at least as it appeared to McCaleb, that this could work would be if both Buddy and someone in Storey's defense group leaked the same information to the same media source. And this, of course, was a coincidence that even a believer in coincidence would have a difficult time accepting.

McCaleb tried to put it out of his mind for the moment. He got to the boat, looked around again, and stepped down into the cockpit. He unlocked the slider and went in, turning on the lights. He decided that in the morning he would go over and question Buddy more carefully about what he had done and who he had talked to.

He locked the door and put his keys and the videotape he'd been carrying down on the chart table. He immediately went to the galley and poured a large glass of orange juice. He then turned the upper deck lights off and took the juice with him down to the lower deck where he went into the head and quickly began his evening pill ritual. As he swallowed the pills and orange juice he looked at himself in the small mirror over the sink. He thought about what Bosch had looked like. The weariness clearly set deep in his eyes. McCaleb wondered if he would get the same look in a few years, after a few more cases.

When he was finished with his medicine routine he stripped off his clothes and took a quick shower, the water feeling ice cold because the water heater hadn't been on since he had crossed in the boat the day before.

Shivering, he went into the master cabin and put on a pair of boxer shorts and a sweatshirt. He was dead tired but once he got into the bed he decided he should write a few notes about his thoughts on how Jaye Winston should run the play with Tafero. He reached down to the nightstand's drawer, where he kept pens and scratch pads. When he opened it he found a folded newspaper crammed into the small drawer space. He pulled it out, unfolded it and found it was the previous week's issue of *New Times.* The pages had been folded backward so that the rear advertising section was at the front. McCaleb was looking at a page full of matchbook-sized ads under a heading that said OUTCALL MASSAGE.

McCaleb got up quickly and went to his windbreaker, which he had tossed onto a chair. He pulled the cell phone out of the pocket and went back to the bed with it. Though McCaleb had been carrying the phone with him in recent days, it usually stayed in its charger on the boat. It was paid for out of charter funds and was carried as a business expense. It was used by clients during charter trips and by Buddy Lockridge while confirming reservations and running credit card authorizations.

The phone had a small digital screen with a menu he scrolled through. He opened the call log program and began scrolling through the last hundred numbers the phone had been used to call. Most of the numbers he quickly identified and eliminated. But every time he did not recognize a number he compared it to the phone numbers at the bottom of the ads on the massage page. The fourth unrecognized number he compared to the ads was a match. The number was for a woman who advertised herself as an 'Exotic Japanese-Hawaiian Beauty' named Leilani. Her ad said she specialized in 'full-service relaxation' and was not associated with any massage agency.

McCaleb closed the phone and got off the bed again. He started pulling on a pair of sweatpants as he tried to recall exactly what had been said when he had accused Buddy Lockridge of leaking the case information to the *New Times.*

By the time he was dressed, McCaleb realized he had never specifically accused Buddy of leaking information to the newspaper. He had only mentioned the *New Times* and Buddy had immediately begun to apologize.

McCaleb now understood that Buddy's apology and embarrassment could have been over his using *The Following Sea* the week before when it was in the marina as a rendezvous point with the full-service masseuse. It explained why he had asked if McCaleb was going to tell Graciela what he had done.

McCaleb looked at his watch. It was ten after eleven. He grabbed the newspaper and went topside. He didn't want to wait until the morning to confirm this. He guessed that Buddy had used *The Following Sea* to meet the woman because his own boat was so small and cramped and looked like a forbidding floating rat trap. There was no master cabin – just one open space that was as crowded with junk as the deck above. If Buddy had *The Following Sea* available to him, he would have used it.

In the salon he didn't bother turning on the lights. He leaned over the couch and looked out the window to the boat's left. Buddy's boat, the *Double Down,* was four slips away and he could see the cabin lights were still on. Buddy was still awake, unless he had passed out with the lights on.

McCaleb went to the slider and was about to unlock it when he realized it was already open a half inch. He realized someone was on the boat, probably having entered while he had been in the shower and unable to hear the lock pop or feel the added weight on the boat. He quickly slid the door all the way open in an effort to escape. He was just stepping through when he was grabbed from behind. An arm came over his right shoulder and across the front of his neck. It bent at the elbow and his neck was shoved into the V it formed. His attacker's other forearm closed the triangle behind his neck. The hold closed like a vise on both sides of his neck, compressing the carotid arteries that carried oxygenated blood to his brain. McCaleb had an almost clinical understanding of what was happening. He was caught in a textbook choke hold. He began to struggle. He brought his arms up and tried to dig his fingers under the forearm and biceps on either side of his neck but it was no use. He was already weakening.

He was dragged back away from the door and into the darkness of the salon. He reached his left hand back to the point where his attacker's right hand gripped his left forearm – the weak point of the triangle. But he had no leverage and was losing power quickly. He tried to yell. Maybe Buddy would hear. But his voice was gone and nothing came out.

He remembered another defensive measure. He raised his right foot up and drove it down, heel first, toward his attacker's foot, with the last strength he could muster. But he missed. His heel hit the floor ineffectively and his attacker took another step backward, violently pulling McCaleb off balance and unable to attempt the kick release again.

McCaleb was quickly losing consciousness. His vision of the marina lights through the salon door was being crowded by a closing blackness with a reddish outline. His last thoughts were that he was in the grip of a classic choke hold, the kind taught at police departments across the country until too many deaths resulted from its use.

Soon even that thought drifted away and he saw no lights. The darkness moved in and took him.

42

McCaleb came awake to tremendous muscular pain in his shoulders and upper legs. When he opened his eyes he realized he was lying chest down across the master cabin's bed. His head was lying flat on the mattress, his left cheek down, and he was staring at the headboard. It took him a moment before he remembered that he had been on his way to visit Buddy Lockridge when he was attacked from behind.

He became completely conscious and tried to relax his aching muscles but realized he could not move. His wrists were bound behind his back and his legs were bent backward at the knees and were being held in that position by someone's hand.

He lifted his head off the mattress and tried to turn. He couldn't get the angle. He dropped back to the mattress and turned his head to the left. He lifted up once again and turned to see Rudy Tafero, standing next to the bed, smiling at him. With one gloved hand he was holding McCaleb's feet, which were bound at the ankles and folded back toward his thighs.

Comprehension rushed over him. McCaleb realized he was naked and that he was bound and held in the same posture as he had seen the body of Edward Gunn. The reverse fetal pose from the painting by Hieronymus Bosch. The cold chill of terror exploded in his chest. He instinctively flexed his leg muscles. Tafero was ready for it. His feet barely moved. But he heard three clicks behind his head and became aware of the ligature around his neck.

'Easy,' Tafero said. 'Easy now. Not yet.'

McCaleb stopped his movement. Tafero continued to press his ankles down toward the back of his thighs.

'You've seen the setup before,' Tafero said matter of factly. 'This one's a little different. I strung together a bunch of snap-cuffs, like every L.A. cop carries around in the trunk of his car.'

McCaleb understood the message. The plastic strips first invented to bundle cables together but found to be useful by police agencies faced with occasional social unrest and the need to make mass arrests. A cop can carry one set of handcuffs but hundreds of snap cuffs. String them around the wrists, slide the end through the lock. Tiny grooves in the plastic strip click and lock as the tie gets tighter. The only way to remove it is to cut it off. McCaleb realized that the clicking sound he had just heard had been a snap cuff tightening around his neck.

'So you be careful now,' Tafero said. 'Hold real steady.'

McCaleb put his face down into the mattress. His mind was racing, looking for the way out. He thought if he could engage Tafero he might buy some time. But time for what?

'How'd you find me?' he spoke into the mattress.

'Easy enough. My little brother followed you from my shop and got your plate. You should look around more often, make sure you aren't being followed.'

'I'll remember that.'

He understood the plan. It would look as if Gunn's killer had gotten McCaleb when he had come too close. He turned his head again so he could see Tafero.

'It's not going to work, Tafero,' he said. 'People know. They're not going to buy that it was Bosch.'

Tafero smiled down at him.

'You mean Jaye Winston? Don't worry about her. I'm going to go pay her a visit when I'm done here with you. Eighty-eight-oh-one Willoughby, apartment six, West Hollywood. She was easy to find, too.'

He raised his free hand and waved the fingers as though he were playing the piano or typing.

'Let your fingers do the walking through the voters registration – I've got it on CD-ROM. She's a registered Democrat, if you can believe it. A homicide cop who votes Democrat. Wonders never cease.'

'There are others. The FBI's on this. You—'

'They're on Bosch. Not me. I saw them today at the courthouse.'

He reached down and ticked one of the snap cuffs strung from McCaleb's legs to his neck.

'And these, I'm sure, will help bring them directly to Detective Bosch.'

He smiled at the genius of his own plan. And McCaleb knew his thinking was sound. Twilley and Friedman would go after Bosch like a pair of dogs chasing either side of a car.

'Hold steady now.'

Tafero let go of his feet and moved out of his sight. McCaleb strained to keep his legs from unfolding. Almost immediately he felt the muscles in his legs start to burn. He knew he didn't have the strength to hold them for long.

'Please . . .'

Tafero returned to view. He was holding a plastic owl in both hands, a delighted smile on his face.

'Took this off one of the boats down the dock. A little weathered but it'll work out nice. Gonna get another one for Winston.'

He looked around the room as if looking for a place for the owl. He settled on a shelf above the built-in bureau. He placed the owl there, looked back at McCaleb once and then adjusted it so the plastic bird's gaze was upon him.

'Perfect,' he said.

McCaleb closed his eyes. He could feel his muscles vibrating with the strain. An image of his daughter appeared in his mind. She was in his arms, her eyes were watching him over the bottle and telling him not to worry or be afraid. It soothed him. He concentrated on her face and somehow thought he could even smell her hair. He felt tears going down his face and his legs started to give way. He heard the clicking of the cuffs and –

Tafero grabbed his legs and held them.

'Not yet.'

Something hard banged off McCaleb's head and thudded on the mattress next to him. He turned his face and opened his eyes and saw it was the videotape he had gone back to borrow from Lucas, the post office security officer. He looked at the post office emblem of the flying eagle on the sticker Lucas had put on the tape for him.

'I hope you don't mind but while you were sleeping off the choke hold I took a look at the tape on your VCR. I couldn't find anything on it. It's blank. Why is that?'

McCaleb felt a pang of hope. He realized that the only reason he wasn't already dead was because of the tape. Tafero had found it and it raised too many questions. It was a break. McCaleb tried to think of a way to turn it further to his advantage. The tape was supposed to be blank. They had planned to use it as a prop when they brought Tafero in and tried to play him. It would have been part of a bluff. They would hold it up and tell him they had him on tape sending the money order. But they wouldn't actually play it. Now McCaleb thought he might be able to still use it – but in reverse.

Tafero shoved down hard on his ankles, so hard they came close to touching McCaleb's buttocks. McCaleb groaned from the stress on his muscles. Tafero eased back.

'I asked you a question, motherfucker. Now you fucking answer it.'

'It's nothing. It's supposed to be blank.'

'Bullshit. The label says "December twenty-second." It says "Wilcox surveillance." Why is it blank?'

He increased the pressure on McCaleb's legs but not to the point of a few moments before.

'Okay, I'll tell you the truth. I'll tell you.'

McCaleb took a deep breath and tried to relax. In the moment his body was still, when the air was held in his lungs, he thought he detected a movement of the boat that was out of rhythm with the gentle rise-and-fall cycle of the marina's wake. Somebody had stepped onto the boat. He could only think of Buddy Lockridge. And if it was him then he was most likely walking into his own doom. McCaleb started to speak quickly and loudly, hoping his voice would warn Lockridge off.

'It's just a prop, that's all. We were going to bluff you, tell you we had you on tape buying the money order that bought the owl. The plan, the plan was to get you to turn on Storey. We know it was his plan from the jail. You just followed orders. They want Storey more than they want you. I was going to—'

'All right, shut up!'

McCaleb was quiet. He wondered if Tafero had felt the boat move unusually or if he had heard something. But then McCaleb watched as the tape was lifted off the bed. He realized he had Tafero thinking. After a long moment of silence Tafero finally spoke.

'I think you are full of shit, McCaleb. I think this tape is out of one of those multiplex surveillance systems they use. It won't read on a regular VCR.'

If it didn't seem that every muscle in his body was screaming in pain, McCaleb might have smiled. He had Tafero. He was helplessly hogtied on the bed but he was playing his captor. Tafero was second-guessing his own plan.

'Who else has copies?' Tafero asked.

McCaleb didn't answer. He started thinking that he had been wrong about the boat's movement. Too much time had gone by. There was no one else onboard.

Tafero rapped the tape hard on the back of McCaleb's head.

'I said who else has copies?'

There was a new note in the tone of his voice. One part confidence had been removed and replaced with one equal part fear that there was a flaw in his perfect plan.

'Fuck you,' McCaleb said. 'You do what you have to do with me. Either way, you'll be finding out who's got copies soon enough.'

Tafero pushed down on his legs and leaned over him. McCaleb could feel his breath close to his ear.

'Listen to me, you fucking—'

There was a sudden loud crash from behind McCaleb.

'Don't fucking move!' a voice called.

In the same instant Tafero stood up and let go of McCaleb's legs. The sudden release of pressure coupled with the jarring noise made McCaleb startle and involuntarily flex his muscles at once. He heard the zipping sound of snap cuffs clicking in several places of his bindings. In chain reaction, the cuff around his neck pulled tight and locked. He tried to raise his legs but it was too late, the cuff was set. It was biting into his neck. He had no air. He opened his mouth but not a sound came out.

43

Harry Bosch stood in the doorway of the boat's downstairs cabin and pointed his gun at Rudy Tafero. His eyes widened as he took in the whole room. Terry McCaleb was naked on the bed, his arms and legs bound behind him. Bosch saw that several snap cuffs had been linked together and used to bind his wrists and ankles while a leader ran from his ankles and under his wrists to a loop around his neck. He couldn't see McCaleb's face but saw the plastic was digging tightly into his neck and the skin was a dark rouge. He was strangling.

'Turn around,' he yelled at Tafero. 'Get back against the wall.'

'He needs help, Bosch. You—'

'I said get back against the fucking wall! Now!'

He raised the gun to Tafero's chest level to drive home the order. Tafero raised his hands and started turning to the wall.

'Okay, okay, I'm turning around.'

As soon as Tafero had turned Bosch moved quickly into the room and shoved the big man up against the wall. He glanced at McCaleb. He could see his face now. It was getting redder. His eyes were opened and bugged. His mouth was opened in a desperate but fruitless bid for air.

Bosch pushed the barrel of his gun into Tafero's back and reached his other hand around him to check for a weapon. He pulled a handgun out of Tafero's belt and then stepped back. He looked at McCaleb again and knew he didn't have any time. The problem was controlling Tafero and getting to McCaleb to cut him free. He suddenly knew what needed to be done. He stepped back and brought his hands together so that the guns were side by side. He raised them over his head and brought the butts of both guns down violently into the back of Tafero's head. The big man pitched forward, going face-first into the wood-paneled wall and then dropping to the floor motionless.

Bosch turned and dropped both guns onto the bed and quickly pulled out his keys.

'Hold on, hold on, hold on.'

His fingers scrabbling, he pulled the blade out of the penknife attached to the key chain. He reached to the plastic cuff embedded around

McCaleb's neck but couldn't get his fingers underneath it. He shoved McCaleb onto his side and quickly worked his fingers under the cuff at the front of his neck. He slipped the blade in and sliced through the cuff, the point of the knife just nicking the skin beneath it.

A horrible sound came from McCaleb's throat as he gulped air into his lungs and tried to speak at the same time. The words were unintelligible, lost in the instinctive urgency for oxygen intake.

'Shut up and breathe!' Bosch yelled. 'Just breathe!'

There came an interior rattling sound with each breath McCaleb took. Bosch saw a vibrant red line running the circumference of his neck. He gently touched McCaleb's neck, wanting to feel for possible damage to the trachea or larynx or the arteries. McCaleb roughly turned his head on the mattress and tried to move away.

'Just . . . cut me loose.'

The words made him cough violently into the mattress, his whole body shaking from the trauma.

Bosch used the knife to cut his hands free and then his ankles. He saw red ligature marks on both sets of limbs. He pulled all the snap cuffs away and threw them on the floor. He looked around and saw the sweatpants and shirt on the floor. He picked them up and threw them onto the bed. McCaleb was slowly turning back to face him, his face still red.

'You . . . you . . . saved . . .'

'Don't talk.'

There was a groan from the floor and Bosch saw Tafero start moving as he began to regain consciousness. Bosch stepped over and stood straddling him. He took his handcuffs off his belt, bent down and then violently pulled Tafero's arms behind his back to cuff him. While he worked he talked to McCaleb.

'Hey, you want to take this guy out, tie him to the anchor and drop him over the side, it'd be fine by me. I wouldn't even blink about it.'

McCaleb didn't respond. He was pulling himself into a sitting position. Finished with the cuffing process, Bosch straightened up and looked down at Tafero, who had now opened his eyes.

'Stay still, shithead. And get used to those cuffs. You are under arrest for murder, attempted murder and general conspiracy to be an asshole. I think you know your rights but do yourself a favor and don't say a word until I get the card out and read it to you.'

The moment he was done speaking Bosch became aware of a creaking sound coming from the hallway. In that second he realized someone had used his words as cover to get close to the doorway.

Things seemed to drop into a slow-motion sense of clarity. Bosch instinctively brought his left hand up to his hip but realized his gun was not there. He had left it on the bed. He started to turn to the bed but saw

McCaleb sitting up, still naked, and already pointing one of the guns at the doorway.

Bosch's eyes followed the aim of the gun to the door. A man was swinging into the opening in a crouched position, two hands on a pistol. He was taking aim at Bosch. There was a shot and wood splintered from the doorjamb. The gunman flinched and squinted his eyes. He recovered and started to level the aim of his gun. There was another shot and another and then another. The noise was deafening in the confines of the wood-paneled room. Bosch watched one bullet hit the wall and two hit the gunman in the chest, throwing him backward into the hallway wall. He sank to the floor but was still visible from the bedroom.

'No!' Tafero shouted from the floor. 'Jesse, no!'

The wounded gunman was still moving but having difficulty with motor controls. With one hand he awkwardly raised the gun again and made a pathetic attempt to aim it once more at Bosch.

There was another shot and Bosch saw the gunman's cheek explode with blood. His head snapped back against the wall behind him and he became still.

'No!' Tafero cried out again.

And then there was silence.

Bosch looked at the bed. McCaleb still held the gun aimed at the door. A cloud of blue gunpowder smoke was rising into the center of the room. The air smelled acrid and burned.

Bosch picked his gun up off the bed and went out to the hallway. He squatted down next to the gunman but didn't need to touch him to know he was dead. During the shooting he had thought he recognized him as Tafero's younger brother who worked in the bail bonds office. Now most of his face was gone.

Bosch got up and went into the head to grab a tissue, which he then used to take the gun out of the dead man's grip. He carried it back into the master cabin and put it down on the nightstand. The gun McCaleb had used was now lying on the bed. McCaleb stood on the other side of the bed. He had the sweatpants on and was pulling the shirt over his head. Once his head came through he looked at Bosch.

Their eyes held for a long moment. They had saved each other. Bosch finally nodded.

Tafero worked his way up into a sitting position against the wall. Blood had run out of his nose and down around both sides of his mouth. It looked like a grotesque Fu Manchu mustache. Bosch guessed that his nose had been broken when he'd gone face-first into the wall. He sat slumped against the wall, his eyes staring in horror through the doorway to the body in the hallway.

Bosch used the tissue to pick the gun up off the bed and put it next to the other one on the nightstand. He then took a cell phone out of his pocket and punched in a number. While he waited for the call to connect he looked at Tafero.

'You got your little brother killed, Rudy,' he said. 'That's too bad.'

Tafero lowered his eyes and started crying.

Bosch's call was answered at central dispatch. He gave the address of the marina and said he was going to need a homicide team from the officer involved–shooting unit. He would need a coroner's crew and techs from Scientific Investigation Division to respond as well. He told the dispatcher to make all notifications by landline. He didn't want the media to get wind of the incident from a police scanner until the time was right.

He closed the phone and held it up for McCaleb to see.

'You want an ambulance? You should get checked out.'

'I'm fine.'

'Your neck looks like it could—'

'I said I'm fine.'

Bosch nodded.

'Suit yourself.'

He came around the bed and stood in front of Tafero.

'I'm going to get him out of here, put him in the car.'

He dragged Tafero to his feet and pushed him to the door. As he passed his brother's body in the hallway Tafero let out a loud animal-like wail, a kind of sound Bosch was surprised to hear coming from such a big man.

'Yeah, it's too bad,' Bosch said without a note of sympathy in his voice. 'The kid had a bright future helping you kill people and getting people out of jail.'

He shoved Tafero toward the steps up to the salon.

On the way up the gangway to the parking lot Bosch saw a man standing on the deck of a sailboat cluttered with rafts and surfboards and other junk. The man looked at Bosch and then Tafero and then back to Bosch. His eyes were wide and it was clear he recognized them, probably from the trial coverage on TV.

'Hey, I heard shots. Is Terry okay?'

'He's going to be fine.'

'Can I go talk to him?'

'Better not. The cops are coming. Let them handle it.'

'Hey, you're Bosch, aren't you? From the trial?'

'Yeah. I'm Bosch.'

The man said nothing else. Bosch kept moving with Tafero.

When Bosch came back onto the boat a few minutes later McCaleb was in the galley drinking a glass of orange juice. Behind him and down the steps the splayed legs of the dead man were visible.

'A neighbor of yours out there asked about you.'

McCaleb nodded.

'Buddy.'

That's all he said.

Bosch looked out the window and back up at the parking lot. He thought he could hear sirens in the distance but thought it might just be the wind playing sound games.

'They're going to be here any minute,' he said. 'How's the throat? I hope you can talk, 'cause we're going to have a lot of explaining to do.'

'It's fine. Why were you here, Harry?'

Bosch put his car keys down on the countertop. He didn't answer for a long moment.

'I just sort of guessed you might be drawing a bead, that's all.'

'How so?'

'You busting in on his brother at the office this morning. I figured that if he followed you, he might've gotten a plate or something they could trace to you here.'

McCaleb looked pointedly at him.

'And what, you were hanging out in the marina and saw Rudy but not the little brother?'

'No, I just drove down and cruised around a little. I saw Rudy's old Lincoln parked up there in the lot and figured something was going on. I never saw the little brother – he must've been hiding somewhere and watching.'

'I'm thinking he was on the docks looking for an owl he could take off a boat to use at Winston's. They were improvising tonight.'

Bosch nodded.

'Anyway, I was looking around and saw the door open on your boat and decided to check it out. I thought it was too cold a night and you were too careful a guy to sleep with the door open like that.'

McCaleb nodded.

Bosch now heard the unmistakable sound of approaching sirens and looked out the window and across the docks to the parking lot. He saw two patrol cars glide in and stop near his slickback where Tafero was locked in the back. They killed the sirens but left the blue lights flashing.

'I better go meet the boys in blue,' he said.

44

For most of the night they were separated and questioned and then questioned again. Then the interrogators switched rooms and they heard the same questions once more from different mouths. Five hours after the shooting on *The Following Sea* the doors were opened and McCaleb and Bosch stepped out into a hallway at Parker Center. Bosch came up to McCaleb then.

'You okay?'

'Tired.'

'Yeah.'

McCaleb watched him put a cigarette in his mouth but not light it.

'I'm heading out to the sheriff's,' Bosch said. 'I want to be there.'

McCaleb nodded.

'I'll see you there.'

They stood side by side behind the one-way glass, squeezed in next to the videographer. McCaleb was close enough to smell Bosch's menthol cigarette breath and the glove-box cologne he had seen him put on in his car while driving behind him out to Whittier. He could see the faint reflection of Bosch's face in the glass and he realized he was looking through it into what was happening in the next room.

On the other side of the glass was a conference table with Rudy Tafero seated next to a public defender named Arnold Prince. Tafero had white tape spread across his nose and cotton in both nostrils. He had six stitches in the crown of his head which could not be seen because of his full head of hair. Paramedics had treated him for a broken nose and the head laceration at Cabrillo Marina.

Across from Tafero sat Jaye Winston. To her right was Alice Short, from the DA's office. To her left were Deputy Chief Irvin Irving of the LAPD and Donald Twilley of the FBI. The early morning hours had been spent with all law enforcement agencies remotely involved in the investigation jockeying for the best position to take advantage of what all players knew to be a major case. It was now six-thirty in the morning and time to question the suspect.

It had been decided that Winston would handle the questioning – it being her case from the beginning – while the other three looked on and were available to her for advice. She began the interview by stating the date, time and identities of those in the room. She then read Tafero his constitutional rights and had him sign an acknowledgment form. His attorney said that Tafero would not be making a statement at the present time.

'That's fine,' Winston said, her eyes on Tafero. 'I don't need him to talk to me. I want to talk to him. I want to give him an idea of what he is facing here. I don't want there to be any regrets down the line over miscommunications or his passing up the one opportunity to cooperate that he'll be given.'

She looked down at the file in front of her and opened it. McCaleb recognized the top sheet as a DA's office complaint form.

'Mr. Tafero,' Winston began, 'I want you to know that this morning we are charging you with the first-degree murder of Edward Gunn on January first of this year, the attempted murder of Terrell McCaleb on this date, and the murder of Jesse Tafero, also on this date. I know you know the law but I am compelled to explain the last charge. Your brother's death occurred during the commission of a felony. Therefore, under California law you, as his co-conspirator, are held responsible for his death.'

She waited a beat, staring into Tafero's seemingly dead eyes. She went back to reading the complaint.

'Further, you should know that the district attorney's office has agreed to file a count of special circumstances in regard to the murder of Edward Gunn. To wit, murder for hire. The addition of special circumstances will make it a death penalty case. Alice?'

Short leaned forward. She was an attractive, petite woman in her late thirties with big, engaging eyes. She was the deputy chief in charge of major trials. It was a lot of power in such a small body – especially when contrasted with the size of the man across the table from her.

'Mr. Tafero, you were a policeman for twenty years,' she said. 'You more than most know the gravity of your actions. There is not a case I can think of that cries out more for the death penalty. We will ask a jury for it. And I have no doubt we will get it.'

Her rehearsed part of the play finished, Short leaned back in her chair and deferred to Winston. There was a long silence while Winston stared at Tafero and waited for him to look back at her. Eventually, his eyes came up and held on hers.

'Mr. Tafero, you've been around and you've even been in the opposite position in rooms just like this before. I don't think we could play a game on you if we had a year to work it out. So no game. Just the offer. A one-time offer that will be rescinded, permanently, when we walk out of this room. It comes down to this.'

The focus of Tafero's eyes had dropped to the table again. Winston leaned forward and looked up into them.

'Do you want to live or do you want to take your chances with the jury? It's as simple as that. And before you answer, there are a few things to consider. Number one, the jurors are going to see photographic evidence of what you did to Edward Gunn. Two, they are going to hear Terry McCaleb describe what it was like to be so helpless and to feel his own life being choked away by your design. You know, I don't usually bet on such things but I'd give it less than an hour. My bet is that it will be one of the quickest death verdicts ever returned in the state of California.'

Winston pulled back and closed the file in front of her. McCaleb found himself nodding. She was doing very well.

'We want your employer,' Winston said. 'We want physical evidence that will link him to the Gunn case. I have a feeling that someone like you would take precautions before carrying out such a scheme. Whatever it is, we want what you have.'

She looked at Short and the prosecutor nodded, her way of saying well done.

Almost half a minute went by. Finally, Tafero turned to his attorney and was about to whisper a question. Then he turned back to Winston.

'Fuck it, I'll ask myself. Without acknowledging a fucking thing here, what if you drop the special circumstances? What am I facing?'

Winston immediately burst out laughing and shook her head. McCaleb smiled.

'Are you kidding?' Winston asked. '"What am I facing?" Man, you are going to be buried in concrete and steel. That's what you are facing. You are never, *ever* going to see the light of day again. Deal, no deal, that is a given and non-negotiable.'

Tafero's attorney cleared his throat.

'Ms. Winston, this is hardly a professional manner in which—'

'I don't give a shit about my manner. This man is a killer. He's no different from a hit man except, no, he's worse. He used to carry a badge and that makes it all the more despicable. So this is what we'll do for your client, Mr. Prince. We'll take guilty pleas to the murder of Edward Gunn and the attempted on Terry McCaleb. Life without on both counts. Non-negotiable. We'll no-bill the charge on his brother. Maybe it will help him live with it better if he doesn't carry the charge. I don't really care. What I care about is that he understands that his life as he knows it is over. He's gone. And he can either go to death row or super max, but he's going to one of them and not coming back.'

She looked at her watch.

'You've got about five minutes and then we're out of here. You don't want the deal, fine, we'll take both of them to trial. Storey might be a long shot but there's no question about Mr. Tafero here. Alice is going to have prosecutors knocking down her door, sending her flowers and chocolates. Every day's going to be Valentine's Day – or Valentino's day, as the case may be. This one's a ticket to prosecutor of the year.'

Prince brought a slim briefcase up onto the table and slid his legal pad into it. He hadn't written a word on it.

'Thank you for your time,' he said. 'I think what we'll do is proceed to a bail hearing and go from there with discovery and other matters.'

He pushed his chair back and stood up.

Tafero slowly raised his head and looked at Winston, his eyes badly bloodshot from the hemorrhaging of his nose.

'It was his idea to make it look like a painting,' he said. 'David Storey's idea.'

There was a moment of stunned silence and then the defense attorney sat down heavily and closed his eyes in pain.

'Mr. Tafero,' Prince said. 'I am strongly advising—'

'Shut up,' Tafero barked. 'You little pissant. You're not the one facing the needle.'

He looked back at Winston.

'I'll take the deal. As long as I don't get charged with my brother.'

Winston nodded.

Tafero turned to Short and pointed his finger and waited. She nodded.

'Deal,' she said.

'One thing,' Winston said quickly. 'We're not going into this with your word against his. What else have you got?'

Tafero looked at her and a thin, dead smile cracked across his face.

In the viewing room, Bosch stepped closer to the glass. McCaleb saw his reflection more clearly on the glass. His eyes stared unblinking.

'I've got pictures,' Tafero said.

Winston hooked her hair behind her ear and narrowed her eyes. She leaned across the table.

'Pictures? What do you mean, photographs? Photographs of what?'

Tafero shook his head.

'No. Pictures. He drew pictures for me while we were in the attorney visiting room in the jail. Drawings of what he wanted the scene to look like. So it would look like the painting.'

McCaleb gripped his hands into fists at his sides.

'Where are the drawings?' Winston said.

Tafero smiled again.

'Safe-deposit box. City National Bank, Sunset and Doheny. The key's on the ring that was in my pocket.'

Bosch brought his hands up and slapped them together.

'Bang!' he exclaimed, loud enough that Tafero turned and looked toward the glass.

'Please!' the videographer whispered. 'We're taping.'

Bosch went to the door of the little room and stepped out. McCaleb followed. Bosch turned and looked at him. He nodded.

'Storey goes down,' he said. 'The monster goes back into the darkness from which it came.'

They looked at each other silently for a moment and then Bosch broke it away.

'I gotta go,' he said.

'Where?'

'Get ready for court.'

He turned and started walking through the deserted bullpen of the sheriff's department homicide squad. McCaleb saw him bang a fist on a desk and then punch it into the air above him.

McCaleb went back into the viewing room and watched the interview continue. Tafero was telling the assemblage in the interview room that David Storey had demanded that the killing of Edward Gunn take place on the first morning of the new year.

McCaleb listened for a while and then thought of something. He stepped out of the observation room and into the bullpen. Detectives were now filtering in to start the day of work. He went to an empty desk and tore a page off a notepad on its top. He wrote, 'Ask about the Lincoln' on it. He folded it and took it to the door of the interview room.

He knocked and after a moment Alice Short opened the door. He handed her the folded note.

'Give this to Jaye before the interview is over,' he whispered.

She nodded and closed the door. McCaleb went back into the observation room to watch.

45

Freshly showered and shaved, Bosch stepped off the elevator and headed toward the doors to the Division N courtroom. He walked with purpose. He felt like a true prince of the city. He had taken only a few strides when he was accosted by McEvoy, who stepped out of an alcove like a coyote that had been waiting in a cave for his unsuspecting prey. But nothing could dent Bosch's demeanor. He smiled as the reporter fell into stride with him.

'Detective Bosch, have you thought any more about what we talked about? I've got to start writing my story today.'

Bosch didn't slow his pace. He knew that once he got into the courtroom he wouldn't have a lot of time.

'Rudy Tafero,' he said.

'Excuse me?'

'He was your source. Rudy Tafero. I figured it out this morning.'

'Detective, I told you that I can't reveal—'

'Yeah, I know. But, see, I'm the one who's revealing it. Anyway, it doesn't matter.'

'Why not?'

Bosch suddenly stopped. McEvoy walked a few steps past and then came back.

'Why not?' he asked again.

'Today's your lucky day, Jack. I've got two good tips for you.'

'Okay. What?'

McEvoy started pulling a notebook from his back pocket. Bosch put his hand on his arm to stop him.

'Don't take that out. The other reporters see that, they'll think I'm telling you something.'

He gestured up the hall to the open door of the media room where a handful of reporters were loitering and waiting for the day's court session to begin.

'Then they'll come over and I'll have to tell them.'

McEvoy left the notebook in place.

'Okay. What are the tips?'

'First of all, you're full of shit on that story. In fact, your source was arrested this morning for the murder of Edward Gunn as well as the attempted murder of Terry McCaleb.'

'What? He got—'

'Wait. Let me talk. I don't have a lot of time.'

He waited and McEvoy nodded.

'Yeah, Rudy got popped. He killed Gunn. The plan was to put it on me and spring it on the world during the defense case.'

'Are you saying that Storey was a part of—'

'Exactly. Which brings me to tip number two. And that is, if I were you, I would be in that courtroom today long before the judge comes in and starts things. You see those guys standing down there? They're going to miss it, Jack. You don't want to be like them.'

Bosch left him there. He nodded to the deputy on the courtroom door and was allowed in.

Two deputies were walking David Storey to his place at the defense table as Bosch came into the courtroom. Fowkkes was already there and Langwiser and Kretzler were seated at the prosecution table. Bosch looked at his watch as he came through the gate. He had about fifteen minutes before the judge would take the bench and call for the jury.

He went to the prosecution table but remained standing. He leaned down and put both palms on the table and looked at the two prosecutors.

'Harry, you ready?' Langwiser began. 'Today's the day.'

'Today's the day but not because of what you think. You two would take a plea on this wouldn't you? If he copped to Jody Krementz *and* Alicia Lopez, you wouldn't go for the needle, right?'

They both looked at him with blank stares of confusion.

'Come on, we don't have a lot of time before the judge comes out. What if I could go over there and in five minutes get you two murder ones? Alicia Lopez's family would love you for it. You told them you didn't have a case.'

'Harry, what are you talking about?' Langwiser said. 'We floated a plea. Twice. Fowkkes shot it down both times.'

'And we don't have the evidence on Lopez,' Kretzler added. 'You know that – the grand jury passed. Nobody, no—'

'Listen, you want the plea or not? I think I can go over there and get it. I arrested Rudy Tafero for murder this morning. It was a setup orchestrated by Storey to get to me. It backfired and Tafero is taking a deal. He's talking.'

'Jesus Christ!' Kretzler said.

He said it too loudly. Bosch turned and looked over at the defense table. Both Fowkkes and Storey were looking at them. Just past the defense table he saw McEvoy take a seat in the media gallery that was closest to the defense table. No other reporters had come in and sat down yet.

'Harry, what are you talking about?' Langwiser said. 'What murder?'

Bosch ignored the questions.

'Let me go over there,' Bosch said. 'I want to look in Storey's eyes when I tell him.'

Kretzler and Langwiser looked at each other. Langwiser shrugged her shoulders and waved her hands in exasperation.

'Worth a try. We were only holding death as an ace in the hole.'

'Okay then,' Bosch said. 'See if you can get the clerk to buy me some time with the judge.'

Bosch stepped around the defense table and stood in front of it so he could look equally at Fowkkes and Storey. Fowkkes was writing something on a legal pad. Bosch cleared his throat and after a few moments the defense attorney slowly looked up.

'Yes, Detective? Shouldn't you be at your table preparing for—'

'Where's Rudy Tafero?'

Bosch looked at Storey as he asked it.

Fowkkes looked behind him to the seat against the rail where Tafero normally sat during court sessions.

'I'm sure he's on his way,' he said. 'We have a few minutes.'

Bosch smiled.

'On his way? Yeah, he's on his way. Up to super max at Corcoran, maybe Pelican Cove if he's lucky. I really wouldn't want to be a former cop doing my time in Corcoran.'

Fowkkes seemed unimpressed.

'Detective, I don't know what you are talking about. I am trying to prepare a defense strategy here because I think the prosecution is going to fold its tent today. So, if you don't mind.'

Bosch looked at Storey when he responded.

'There is no strategy. There is no defense. Rudy Tafero was arrested this morning. He's been charged with murder and attempted murder. I'm sure your client can tell you all about it, Counselor. That is, if you didn't know already.'

Fowkkes stood up abruptly as though he were making an objection.

'Sir, it is highly irregular for you to come to the defense table and—'

'He cut a deal about two hours ago. He's laying it all out.'

Again Bosch ignored Fowkkes and looked at Storey.

'So here's the deal. You've got about five minutes to go over there to Langwiser and Kretzler and agree to plead to murder one on Krementz *and* Lopez.'

'This is preposterous. I am going to complain to the judge about this.'

Bosch now looked at Fowkkes.

'You do that. But it doesn't change things. Five minutes.'

Bosch stepped away but went to the clerk's desk in front of the judge's bench. The exhibits were lying stacked on a side table. Bosch looked through them until he found the poster he wanted. He slid it out and carried it with him back to the defense table. Fowkkes was still standing but bending down so Storey could whisper in his ear. Bosch dropped the poster, containing the blowup photo of the bookcase in Storey's house, on the table. He tapped his finger on two of the books on an upper shelf. The titles on the spines were clearly readable. One title was *The Art of Darkness* and the other book was merely titled *Bosch.*

'There's your prior knowledge right there.'

He left the exhibit on the defense table and started to walk back to the prosecution table. But after two steps he came back and put his palms down flat on the defense table. He looked directly at Storey. He spoke in a voice that he knew would be loud enough for McEvoy to hear in the media gallery.

'You know what your big mistake was, David?'

'No,' Storey said, a sneer in his voice. 'Why don't you tell me?'

Fowkkes immediately grabbed his client's arm in a silencing gesture.

'Drawing out the scene for Tafero,' Bosch said. 'What he did was, he went and put those pretty pictures you made right into his safe-deposit box at City National. He knew they might come in handy and they sure did. He used them this morning to buy *his* way out of a death sentence. What are you going to use?'

Bosch saw the falter in Storey's eyes, the tell. For just a moment his eyes blinked without really blinking. But in that moment Bosch knew it was over because Storey knew it was over.

Bosch straightened up and casually looked at his watch, then at Fowkkes.

'About three minutes now, Mr. Fowkkes. Your client's life is on the line.'

He returned to the defense table and sat down. Kretzler and Langwiser leaned toward him and urgently whispered questions but Bosch ignored them.

'Let's just see what happens.'

Over the next five minutes he never once looked over at the defense table. He could hear muffled words and whispers but couldn't make out any of it. The courtroom filled with spectators and members of the media.

Nothing came from the defense table.

At precisely 9 A.M. the door behind the bench opened and Judge Houghton bounded up the steps to his spot. He took his seat and glanced at both the prosecution and defense tables.

'Ladies and gentlemen, are we ready for the jury?'

'Yes, Your Honor,' Kretzler said.

Nothing came from the defense table. Houghton looked over, a curious smile on his face.

'Mr. Fowkkes? Can I bring in our jury?'

Now Bosch leaned back so he could look past Langwiser and Kretzler at the defense table. Fowkkes sat slouched in his chair, a posture he had never exhibited in the courtroom before. He had an elbow on the arm of the chair and his hand up. He was wagging a pen in his fingers and seemed to be lost in deep, depressing thought. His client sat rigid next to him, face forward.

'Mr. Fowkkes? I'm waiting for an answer.'

Fowkkes finally looked up at the judge. Very slowly he rose from the seat and went to the lectern.

'Your Honor, may we approach at sidebar for a moment?'

The judge looked both curious and annoyed. It had been the routine of the trial to submit all non-public conference requests by 8:30 A.M. so that they could be considered and argued in chambers without cutting into court time.

'This can't be handled in open court, Mr. Fowkkes?'

'No, Your Honor. Not at this time.'

'Very well. Come on up.'

Houghton signaled the lawyers forward with both hands as though he were giving signals to a truck backing up.

The attorneys approached the side of the bench and huddled with the judge. From his angle Bosch could see all of their faces and he didn't need to hear what was being whispered. Fowkkes looked ashen and after a few words Kretzler and Langwiser seemed to grow in stature. Langwiser even glanced over at Bosch and he could read the victory message in her eyes.

He turned and looked over at the defendant. He waited and David Storey slowly turned and their eyes locked one final time. Bosch didn't smile. He didn't blink. He didn't do anything but hold the stare. Eventually, it was Storey who looked away and down at his hands lying in his lap. Bosch felt a trilling sensation move over his scalp. He'd felt it before, times when he had glimpsed the normally hidden face of the monster.

The sidebar conference broke up and the two prosecutors came back quickly to the table, excitement clearly showing in their strides and on their faces. By contrast J. Reason Fowkkes moved slowly to the defense table.

'That's all, Fowkkes,' Bosch said under his breath.

Langwiser grabbed Bosch by the shoulder as she sat down.

'He's going to plead,' she whispered excitedly. 'Krementz *and* Lopez. When you went over there, did you say consecutive or concurrent sentencing?'

'I didn't say either.'

'Okay. We just agreed on concurrent but we're going into chambers to work it out. We need to formally charge Storey with Lopez first. You want to come in and make the arrest?'

'Whatever. If you want me to.'

Bosch knew it was just a legal formality. Storey was already in custody.

'You deserve it, Harry. We want you to be there.'

'Fine.'

The judge tapped his gavel once and drew the courtroom's attention. The reporters in the media gallery were all leaning forward in their seats. They knew something big was going on.

'We'll stand in recess until ten o'clock,' the judge announced. 'I'll see all parties in chambers now.'

He stood up and quickly went down the three stairs to the rear door before the deputy had time to call, 'All rise.'

46

McCaleb stayed away from *The Following Sea*, even after the last detective and forensic technician had finished with it. From early afternoon until dark the boat was staked out by reporters and television news crews. The coupling of the shooting aboard the boat plus the arrest of Tafero and abrupt guilty pleas from David Storey had turned the boat into the central image of a story that had developed quickly through the day. Every local channel plus the networks shot their stand-up reports from the marina, *The Following Sea* serving as the backdrop with its yellow police tape strung across the salon door.

McCaleb hid out for most of the afternoon in Buddy Lockridge's boat, staying below decks and donning one of Buddy's floppy fishing hats if he poked his head up through a hatch to see what was going on outside. The two were talking again. Soon after leaving the sheriff's department and getting to the marina ahead of the media, McCaleb had sought out Buddy and apologized for assuming that his charter partner had leaked the story. Buddy in turn apologized for using *The Following Sea* – and McCaleb's cabin – as a rendezvous point for encounters with erotic masseuses. McCaleb agreed to tell Graciela he had been wrong about Buddy being the leak. He also agreed not to tell her about the masseuses. Buddy had explained that he didn't want Graciela thinking less of him than she probably already did.

While they hid out in the boat, they watched Buddy's little twelve-inch TV and remained up-to-the-minute with the day's developments. Channel 9, which had been carrying the Storey trial live, remained most current, staying on live and continuously reporting from the Van Nuys courthouse and the sheriff's Star Center.

McCaleb was left stunned and in awe by the day's events. David Storey abruptly filed guilty pleas in Van Nuys to two murders as he was simultaneously charged in the downtown Los Angeles courthouse with being a conspirator in the Gunn case. The movie director had avoided the death penalty in the first cases but still would face it in the Gunn case if he did not make another plea arrangement with prosecutors.

A televised news conference at the Star Center had featured Jaye

Winston prominently. She answered questions from reporters after the sheriff, flanked by LAPD and FBI brass, read a statement announcing the day's events from an investigative standpoint. McCaleb's name was mentioned numerous times in the discussion of the investigation and subsequent shooting aboard *The Following Sea.* Winston also mentioned it at the end of the news conference when she expressed her thanks to him, saying it was his volunteer work on the case that broke it open.

Bosch was also prominently mentioned but took no part in any press conferences. After Storey's guilty verdicts were entered in the Van Nuys court, Bosch and the lawyers involved in the case were mobbed outside the doors to the courtroom. But McCaleb had seen video on one channel of Bosch pushing his way through the reporters and cameras and refusing to comment as he moved to a fire escape and disappeared down the stairs.

The only reporter who got to McCaleb was Jack McEvoy, who still had his cell phone number. McCaleb talked to him briefly but declined to comment on what had happened in the master cabin of *The Following Sea* and how close he had come to death. His thoughts about that were too personal and he would never share them with any reporter.

McCaleb had also talked to Graciela, calling her and filling her in on the events before she saw them on the news. He told her he probably wouldn't get home until the next day because he was sure the media pack would be watching the boat until well after dark. She said she was glad it was over and that he'd be coming home. He sensed there was still a high level of stress in her voice and knew it was something he would have to address when he got back to the island.

Late in the day McCaleb was able to slip out of Buddy's boat unnoticed when the media pack was distracted by activity in the marina parking lot. The LAPD was towing off the old Lincoln Continental that the Tafero brothers had been using the night before when they had come to the marina to kill McCaleb. While the news crews filmed and watched the mundane task of a car being hooked up and towed away, McCaleb was able to get to his Cherokee without being spotted. He started the car and drove out of the lot ahead of the tow truck. Not a single reporter followed.

It was fully dark by the time he got to Bosch's house. The front door was open as it had been the time before, the screen door in place. McCaleb rapped on the wooden frame and peered through the mesh into the darkness of the house. There was a single light – a reading light – on in the living room. He could hear music and thought it was the same Art Pepper CD that had been playing during his last visit. But he didn't see Bosch.

McCaleb looked away from the door to check the street and when he looked back Bosch was standing at the screen and it startled him. Bosch unhooked a latch and opened the screen. He was wearing the same suit

McCaleb had seen him in on the news. He was holding a bottle of Anchor Steam down at his side.

'Terry. Come on in. I thought maybe you were a reporter. Bugs the hell out of me when they come to your house. Seems like there should be one place they can't go.'

'Yeah, I know what you mean. They're all over the boat. I had to get away.'

McCaleb passed by Bosch in the entrance hallway and stepped into the living room.

'So reporters aside, how's it going, Harry?'

'Never better. A good day for our side. How's your neck doing?'

'Sore as hell. But I'm alive.'

'Yeah, that's what's important. Want a beer?'

'Uh, that would be good.'

While Bosch got the beer McCaleb went out to the rear deck.

Bosch had the deck lights off, making the lights of the city more brilliant in the distance. McCaleb could hear the ever-present sound of the freeway at the bottom of the pass. Searchlights cut across the sky from three different locations on the valley floor. Bosch came out and handed him a beer.

'No glass, right?'

'No glass.'

They looked out into the night and drank their beers silently for a little while. McCaleb thought about how he should say what he wanted to say. He was still working on it.

'The last thing they were doing before I left was hooking up Tafero's car,' he said after some time.

Bosch nodded.

'What about the boat? They finished with it?'

'Yeah, they're done.'

'Is it a mess? They always leave things a mess.'

'Probably. I haven't been inside. I'll worry about it tomorrow.'

Bosch nodded. McCaleb took a long draw on his beer and put the bottle down on the railing. He had taken too much. It backed up in his throat and burned his sinuses.

'Okay?' Bosch asked.

'Yeah, fine.' He wiped his mouth with the back of his hand. 'Harry, I came up to tell you I'm not going to be your friend anymore.'

Bosch started to laugh but then stopped.

'What?'

McCaleb looked at him. Bosch's eyes were still piercing in the darkness. They had caught a speck of reflected light from somewhere and McCaleb could see the two pinpoints holding on him.

'You should've hung around a little longer this morning while Jaye interviewed Tafero.'

'I didn't have the time.'

'She asked him about the Lincoln and he said it was his undercover car. He said he used it on jobs when he didn't want there to be any chance of a trace. It has stolen plates on it. And the registration is phony.'

'Makes sense, a guy like that, having a car for the wet work.'

'You don't get it, do you?'

Bosch had finished his beer. He was leaning with his elbows on the railing. He was peeling the label off the bottle and dropping the little pieces into the darkness below.

'No, I don't get it, Terry. Why don't you tell me what you're talking about?'

McCaleb picked up his beer but then put it back down without drinking any more.

'His real car, the one he used every day, is a Mercedes 430 CLK. That was the one he caught the ticket with. For parking at the post office when he sent the money order.'

'Okay, the guy had two cars. His secret car and his show car. What does it mean?'

'It means you knew something you shouldn't have known.'

'What are you talking about? Knew what?'

'Last night I asked you why you came onto my boat. You said you saw Tafero's Lincoln and knew there was something wrong. How did you know that Lincoln was his?'

Bosch was silent for a long moment. He looked out into the night and nodded.

'I saved your life,' he said.

'I saved yours.'

'So we're even. Leave it at that, Terry.'

McCaleb shook his head. It felt like there was a fist in his stomach pushing up into his chest, trying to get to his new heart.

'I think you knew that Lincoln and knew it meant trouble for me because you had watched Tafero before. Maybe on a night he was using the Lincoln. Maybe on a night he was watching Gunn and setting up the hit. Maybe on the night he made the hit. You saved my life because you knew something, Harry.'

McCaleb was quiet for a moment, giving Bosch an opportunity to say something in his defense.

'That's a lot of maybes, Terry.'

'Yeah. A lot of maybes and one guess. My guess is that somehow you knew or you figured out back when Tafero hooked up with Storey that they would have to come after you in court. So you watched Tafero and you saw him draw the bead on Gunn. You knew what was going to happen and you let it happen.'

McCaleb took another long drink of beer and put the bottle back down on the railing.

'A dangerous game, Harry. They almost pulled it off. But I guess if I hadn't come along you would've figured out some way of pointing it back at them.'

Bosch continued to stare out into the darkness and say nothing.

'The one thing I hope is that you weren't the one who tipped Tafero that Gunn was in the tank that night. Tell me you didn't make that call, Harry. Tell me you didn't help get him out so they could kill him like that.'

Again Bosch said nothing. McCaleb nodded.

'You want to shake somebody's hand, Harry, shake your own.'

Bosch dropped his gaze and looked down into the darkness below the deck. McCaleb watched him closely and saw him slowly shake his head.

'We do what we have to do,' Bosch said quietly. 'Sometimes you have choices. Sometimes there is no choice, only necessity. You see things happening and you know they're wrong but somehow they're also right.'

He was silent for a long moment and McCaleb waited.

'I didn't make that call,' Bosch said.

He turned and looked at McCaleb. Again McCaleb could see the shining points of light in the blackness of his eyes.

'Three people – three monsters – are gone.'

'But not that way. We don't do it that way.'

Bosch nodded.

'What about your play, Terry? Pushing past the little brother into the office. Like you didn't think that would start some shit. You pushed the action with that little move and you know it.'

McCaleb felt his face growing hot under Bosch's stare. He didn't answer. He didn't know what to say.

'You had your own plan, Terry. So what's the difference?'

'The difference? If you don't see it, then you have completely fallen. You are lost.'

'Yeah, well, maybe I'm lost and maybe I've been found. I'll have to think about it. Meantime, why don't you just go home now. Go back to your little island and your little girl. Hide behind what you think you see in her eyes. Pretend the world is not what you know it to be.'

McCaleb nodded. He'd said what he wanted to say. He stepped away from the railing, leaving his beer, and walked toward the door to the house. But Bosch hit him with more words as he entered the house.

'You think naming her after a girl nobody cared about or loved can make up for that lost girl? Well, you're wrong, man. Just go home and keep dreaming.'

McCaleb hesitated in the doorway and looked back.

'Good-bye, Harry.'

'Yeah, good-bye.'

McCaleb walked through the house. When he passed the reading chair where the light was on he saw the printout of his profile of Bosch sitting on the arm of the chair. He kept going. When he got to the front door he pulled it closed behind him.

47

Bosch stood with his arms folded on the deck railing and his head down. He thought about McCaleb's words, both spoken and printed. They were pieces of hot shrapnel ripping through him. He felt a deep tearing of his interior lining. It felt as though something within had seized him and was pulling him into a black hole, that he was imploding into nothingness.

'What did I do?' he whispered. 'What did I do?'

He straightened up and saw the bottle on the railing, its label gone. He grabbed it and threw it as far as he could out into the darkness. He watched its trajectory, able to follow its flight because of moonlight reflecting off the brown glass. The bottle exploded in the brush on the rocky hillside below.

He saw McCaleb's half-finished beer and grabbed it. He pulled his arm back, wanting to throw this one all the way to the freeway. Then he stopped. He put the bottle back on the railing and went inside.

He grabbed the printed profile off the arm of the chair and started ripping the two pages apart. He went to the kitchen, turned the water on and put the pieces into the sink. He flicked on the garbage disposal and pushed the pieces of paper into the drain. He waited until he could tell by the sound that the paper had been chewed into nothing and was gone. He turned off the disposal and just watched the water running into the drain.

Slowly, his eyes came up and he looked through the kitchen window and out through the Cahuenga Pass. The lights of Hollywood glimmered in the cut, a mirror reflection of the stars of all galaxies everywhere. He thought about all that was bad out there. A city with more things wrong than right. A place where the earth could open up beneath you and suck you into the blackness. A city of lost light. His city. It was all of that and, still, always still, a place to begin again. His city. The city of the second chance.

Bosch nodded and bent down. He closed his eyes, put his hands under the water and brought them up to his face. The water was cold and bracing, as he thought any baptism, the start of any second chance, should be.

48

He could still smell burned gunpowder. McCaleb stood in the master cabin and looked around. There were rubber gloves and other debris scattered on the floor. Black fingerprint dust was everywhere, on everything. The door to the room was gone and so was the doorjamb, cut right out of the wall. In the hallway an entire wall panel had been removed as well. McCaleb walked over and looked down at the floor where the little brother had died from the bullets he had fired. The blood had dried brown and would permanently stain the alternating light and dark wood strips in the floor. It would always be there to remind him.

Staring at the blood, he replayed the shots he had fired at the man, the images in his mind moving much slower than real time. He thought about what Bosch had said to him, out on the deck. About letting the little brother follow him. He considered his own culpability. Could his guilt be any less than Bosch's? They had both set things in motion. For every action there is an equal and opposite reaction. You don't go into the darkness without the darkness going into you.

'We do what we have to do,' he said out loud.

He went up into the salon and looked out the door at the parking lot. The reporters were still up there with their vans. He had sneaked in. Parked at the far end of the marina and then borrowed a skiff from somebody's boat to get to *The Following Sea.* He had climbed aboard and slipped in without anyone seeing him.

He noticed that the vans had their microwave towers cranked up and each crew was getting ready for the eleven o'clock report, the camera angles set so that *The Following Sea* would once more be in all the shots. McCaleb smiled and opened his phone. He hit a number on speed dial and Buddy Lockridge answered.

'Buddy, it's me. Listen, I'm on the boat and I gotta go home. I want you to do me a favor.'

'You gotta go tonight? Are you sure?'

'Yeah, this is what I want you to do. When you hear me turn the Pentas over, you come over and untie me. Do it fast. I'll do the rest.'

'You want me to go with you?'

'No, I'll be fine. Catch an *Express* over on Friday. We've got the charter on Saturday morning.'

'All right, Terror. I heard on the radio it's pretty flat out there tonight and no fog, but be careful.'

McCaleb closed the phone and went to the salon door. Most of the reporters and their crews were preoccupied and not looking at the boat because they had already assured themselves it was empty. He slid open the door and stepped out, shut the door and then quickly climbed the ladder to the bridge. He unzipped the plastic curtain that enclosed the bridge and slipped in. Making sure both throttles were in neutral, he engaged the choke and slid his key into the ignition.

He turned the key and the starters began to whine loudly. Looking back through the plastic curtain he saw the reporters had all turned to the boat. The engines finally turned over and he worked the throttles, revving the engines into a quick-start warm-up. He glanced back again and saw Buddy coming down the dock to the boat's stern. A couple of the reporters were hurrying down the gangway to the dock behind him.

Buddy quickly uncleated the two stern lines and threw them into the cockpit. He then moved down the side pier to get the bow line. McCaleb lost sight of him but then heard his call.

'Clear!'

McCaleb took the throttles out of neutral and moved the boat out of the slip. As he made the turn into the fairway he looked back and saw Buddy standing on the side pier and the reporters behind him on the dock.

Once he was away from the cameras he unzipped the curtains and took them down. The cool air swept into the bridge and braced him. He sighted the flashing red lights of the channel markers and put the boat on course. He looked ahead, past the markers, into the darkness but saw nothing. He turned on the Raytheon and saw that which he could not see ahead. The island was there on the radar screen.

Ten minutes later, after he had cleared the harbor break line, McCaleb pulled the phone out of his jacket and speed-dialed home. He knew it was too late to call and that he was risking waking the children. Graciela answered in a whispered urgency.

'Sorry, it's just me.'

'Terry, are you all right?'

'I am now. I'm coming home.'

'You're crossing in the dark?'

McCaleb thought a moment about the question.

'I'll be all right. I can see in the dark.'

Graciela didn't say anything. She had an ability to know when he was saying one thing and talking about something else.

'Put the deck light on,' he said. 'I'll look for it when I get close.'

He closed the phone and pushed the throttles up. The bow started to rise and then leveled off. He passed the last channel marker twenty yards to his left. He was right on course. A three-quarter moon was high in the sky ahead and laying down a shimmering path of liquid silver for him to follow home. He held on tightly to the wheel and thought about the moment when he had truly thought he was going to die. He remembered the image of his daughter that had come to him and had comforted him. Tears started to roll down his cheeks. Soon the wind off the water dried them on his face.

City of Bones

This is for John Houghton,
for the help, the friendship and the stories

1

The old lady had changed her mind about dying but by then it was too late. She had dug her fingers into the paint and plaster of the nearby wall until most of her fingernails had broken off. Then she had gone for the neck, scrabbling to push the bloodied fingertips up and under the cord. She broke four toes kicking at the walls. She had tried so hard, shown such a desperate will to live, that it made Harry Bosch wonder what had happened before. Where was that determination and will and why had it deserted her until after she had put the extension cord noose around her neck and kicked over the chair? Why had it hidden from her?

These were not official questions that would be raised in his death report. But they were the things Bosch couldn't avoid thinking about as he sat in his car outside the Splendid Age Retirement Home on Sunset Boulevard east of the Hollywood Freeway. It was 4:20 p.m. on the first day of the year. Bosch had drawn holiday call-out duty.

The day more than half over and that duty consisted of two suicide runs – one a gunshot, the other the hanging. Both victims were women. In both cases there was evidence of depression and desperation. Isolation. New Year's Day was always a big day for suicides. While most people greeted the day with a sense of hope and renewal, there were those who saw it as a good day to die, some – like the old lady – not realizing their mistake until it was too late.

Bosch looked up through the windshield and watched as the latest victim's body, on a wheeled stretcher and covered in a green blanket, was loaded into the coroner's blue van. He saw there was one other occupied stretcher in the van and knew it was from the first suicide – a thirty-four-year-old actress who had shot herself while parked at a Hollywood overlook on Mulholland Drive. Bosch and the body crew had followed one case to the other.

Bosch's cell phone chirped and he welcomed the intrusion into his thoughts on small deaths. It was Mankiewicz, the watch sergeant at the Hollywood Division of the Los Angeles Police Department.

'You finished with that yet?'

'I'm about to clear.'

'Anything?'

'A changed-my-mind suicide. You got something else?'

'Yeah. And I didn't think I should go out on the radio with it. Must be a slow day for the media – getting more what's happening calls from reporters than I am getting service calls from citizens. They all want to do something on the first one, the actress on Mulholland. You know, a death-of-a-Hollywood-dream story. And they'd probably jump all over this latest call, too.'

'Yeah, what is it?'

'A citizen up in Laurel Canyon. On Wonderland. He just called up and said his dog came back from a run in the woods with a bone in its mouth. The guy says it's human – an arm bone from a kid.'

Bosch almost groaned. There were four or five call outs like this a year. Hysteria always followed by simple explanation: animal bones. Through the windshield he saluted the two body movers from the coroner's office as they headed to the front doors of the van.

'I know what you're thinking, Harry. Not another bone run. You've done it a hundred times and it's always the same thing. Coyote, deer, whatever. But listen, this guy with the dog, he's an MD. And he says there's no doubt. It's a humerus. That's the upper arm bone. He says it's a child, Harry. And then, get this. He said . . . '

There was silence while Mankiewicz apparently looked for his notes. Bosch watched the coroner's blue van pull off into traffic. When Mankiewicz came back he was obviously reading.

'The bone's got a fracture clearly visible just above the medial epicondyle, whatever that is.'

Bosch's jaw tightened. He felt a slight tickle of electric current go down the back of his neck.

'That's off my notes, I don't know if I am saying it right. The point is, this doctor says it was just a kid, Harry. So could you humor us and go check out this humerus?'

Bosch didn't respond.

'Sorry, had to get that in.'

'Yeah, that was funny, Mank. What's the address?'

Mankiewicz gave it to him and told him he had already dispatched a patrol team.

'You were right to keep it off the air. Let's try to keep it that way.'

Mankiewicz said he would. Bosch closed his phone and started the car. He glanced over at the entrance to the retirement home before pulling away from the curb. There was nothing about it that looked splendid to him. The woman who had hung herself in the closet of her tiny bedroom had no next of kin, according to the operators of the home. In death, she would be treated the way she had been in life, left alone and forgotten.

Bosch pulled away from the curb and headed toward Laurel Canyon.

2

Bosch listened to the Lakers game on the car radio while he made his way into the canyon and then up Lookout Mountain to Wonderland Avenue. He wasn't a religious follower of professional basketball but wanted to get a sense of the situation in case he needed his partner, Jerry Edgar. Bosch was working alone because Edgar had lucked into a pair of choice seats to the game. Bosch had agreed to handle the call outs and to not bother Edgar unless a homicide or something Bosch couldn't handle alone came up. Bosch was alone also because the third member of his team, Kizmin Rider, had been promoted nearly a year earlier to Robbery-Homicide Division and still had not been replaced.

It was early third quarter, and the game with the Trail Blazers was tied. While Bosch wasn't a hardcore fan he knew enough from Edgar's constant talking about the game and begging to be left free of call-out duty that it was an important matchup with one of the Los Angeles team's top rivals. He decided not to page Edgar until he had gotten to the scene and assessed the situation. He turned the radio off when he started losing the AM station in the canyon.

The drive up was steep. Laurel Canyon was a cut in the Santa Monica Mountains. The tributary roads ranged up toward the crest of the mountains. Wonderland Avenue dead-ended in a remote spot where the half-million-dollar homes were surrounded by heavily wooded and steep terrain. Bosch instinctively knew that searching for bones in the area would be a logistical nightmare. He pulled to a stop behind a patrol car already at the address Mankiewicz had provided and checked his watch. It was 4:38, and he wrote it down on a fresh page of his legal pad. He figured he had less than an hour of daylight left.

A patrol officer he didn't recognize answered his knock. Her nameplate said Brasher. She led him back through the house to a home office where her partner, a cop whom Bosch recognized and knew was named Edgewood, was talking to a white-haired man who sat behind a cluttered desk. There was a shoe box with the top off on the desk.

Bosch stepped forward and introduced himself. The white-haired man said he was Dr. Paul Guyot, a general practitioner. Leaning forward Bosch could see that the shoe box contained the bone that had drawn them all together. It was dark brown and looked like a gnarled piece of driftwood.

He could also see a dog lying on the floor next to the doctor's desk chair. It was a large dog with a yellow coat.

'So this is it,' Bosch said, looking back down into the box.

'Yes, Detective, that's your bone,' Guyot said. 'And as you can see . . . '

He reached to a shelf behind the desk and pulled down a heavy copy of *Gray's Anatomy*. He opened it to a previously marked spot. Bosch noticed he was wearing latex gloves.

The page showed an illustration of a bone, anterior and posterior views. In the corner of the page was a small sketch of a skeleton with the humerus bone of both arms highlighted.

'The humerus,' Guyot said, tapping the page. 'And then we have the recovered specimen.'

He reached into the shoe box and gently lifted the bone. Holding it above the book's illustration he went through a point-by-point comparison.

'Medial epicondyle, trochlea, greater and lesser tubercle,' he said. 'It's all there. And I was just telling these two officers, I know my bones even without the book. This bone is human, Detective. There's no doubt.'

Bosch looked at Guyot's face. There was a slight quiver, perhaps the first showing of the tremors of Parkinson's.

'Are you retired, Doctor?'

'Yes, but it doesn't mean I don't know a bone when I see—'

'I'm not challenging you, Dr. Guyot.' Bosch tried to smile. 'You say it is human, I believe it. Okay? I'm just trying to get the lay of the land here. You can put that back into the box now if you want.'

Guyot replaced the bone in the shoe box.

'What's your dog's name?'

'Calamity.'

Bosch looked down at the dog. It appeared to be sleeping.

'When she was a pup she was a lot of trouble.'

Bosch nodded.

'So, if you don't mind telling it again, tell me what happened today.'

Guyot reached down and ruffled the dog's collar. The dog looked up at him for a moment and then put its head back down and closed its eyes.

'I took Calamity out for her afternoon walk. Usually when I get up to the circle I take her off the leash and let her run up into the woods. She likes it.'

'What kind of dog is she?' Bosch asked.

'Yellow Lab,' Brasher answered quickly from behind him.

Bosch turned and looked at her. She realized she had made a mistake by intruding and nodded and stepped back toward the door of the room where her partner was.

'You guys can clear if you have other calls,' Bosch said. 'I can take it from here.'

Edgewood nodded and signaled his partner out.

'Thank you, Doctor,' he said as he went.

'Don't mention it.'

Bosch thought of something.

'Hey, guys?'

Edgewood and Brasher turned back.

'Let's keep this off the air, okay?'

'You got it,' said Brasher, her eyes holding on Bosch's until he looked away.

After the officers left, Bosch looked back at the doctor and noticed that the facial tremor was slightly more pronounced now.

'They didn't believe me at first either,' he said.

'It's just that we get a lot of calls like this. But I believe you, Doctor, so why don't you continue with the story?'

Guyot nodded.

'Well, I was up on the circle and I took off the leash. She went up into the woods like she likes to do. She's well trained. When I whistle she comes back. Trouble is, I can't whistle very loud anymore. So if she goes where she can't hear me, then I have to wait, you see.'

'What happened today when she found the bone?'

'I whistled and she didn't come back.'

'So she was pretty far up there.'

'Yes, exactly. I waited. I whistled a few more times, and then finally she came down out of the woods next to Mr. Ulrich's house. She had the bone. In her mouth. At first I thought it was a stick, you see, and that she wanted to play fetch with it. But as she came to me I recognized the shape. I took it from her – had a fight over that – and then I called you people after I examined it here and was sure.'

You people, Bosch thought. It was always said like that, as if the police were another species. The blue species which carried armor that the horrors of the world could not pierce.

'When you called you told the sergeant that the bone had a fracture.'

'Absolutely.'

Guyot picked up the bone again, handling it gently. He turned it and ran his finger along a vertical striation along the bone's surface.

'That's a break line, Detective. It's a healed fracture.'

'Okay.'

Bosch pointed to the box, and the doctor returned the bone.

'Doctor, do you mind putting your dog on a leash and taking a walk up to the circle with me?'

'Not at all. I just need to change my shoes.'

'I need to change, too. How about if I meet you out front?'

'Right away.'

'I'm going to take this now.'

Bosch put the top back on the shoe box and then carried it with two hands, making sure not to turn the box or jostle its contents in any way.

Outside, Bosch noticed the patrol car was still in front of the house. The two officers sat inside it, apparently writing out reports. He went to his car and placed the shoe box on the front passenger seat.

Since he had been on call out he had not dressed in a suit. He had on a sport coat with blue jeans and a white oxford shirt. He stripped off his coat, folded it inside out and put it on the backseat. He noticed that the trigger from the weapon he kept holstered on his hip had worn a hole in the lining and the jacket wasn't even a year old. Soon it would work its way into the pocket and then all the way through. More often than not he wore out his coats from the inside.

He took his shirt off next, revealing a white T-shirt beneath. He then opened the trunk to get out the pair of work boots from his crime scene equipment box. As he leaned against the rear bumper and changed his shoes he saw Brasher get out of the patrol car and come back toward him.

'So it looks legit, huh?'

'Think so. Somebody at the ME's office will have to confirm, though.'

'You going to go up and look?'

'I'm going to try to. Not much light left, though. Probably be back out here tomorrow.'

'By the way, I'm Julia Brasher. I'm new in the division.'

'Harry Bosch.'

'I know. I've heard of you.'

'I deny everything.'

She smiled at the line and put her hand out but Bosch was right in the middle of tying one of the boots. He stopped and shook her hand.

'Sorry,' she said. 'My timing is off today.'

'Don't worry about it.'

He finished tying the boot and stood up off the bumper.

'When I blurted out the answer in there, about the dog, I immediately realized you were trying to establish a rapport with the doctor. That was wrong. I'm sorry.'

Bosch studied her for a moment. She was mid-thirties with dark hair in a tight braid that left a short tail going over the back of her collar. Her eyes were dark brown. He guessed she liked the outdoors. Her skin had an even tan.

'Like I said, don't worry about it.'

'You're alone?'

Bosch hesitated.

'My partner's working on something else while I check this out.'

He saw the doctor coming out the front door of the house with the dog on a leash. He decided not to get out his crime scene jumpsuit and put it on. He glanced over at Julia Brasher, who was now watching the approaching dog.

'You guys don't have calls?'

'No, it's slow.'

Bosch looked down at the MagLite in his equipment box. He looked at her and then reached into the trunk and grabbed an oil rag, which he threw over the flashlight. He took out a roll of yellow crime scene tape and the Polaroid camera, then closed the trunk and turned to Brasher.

'Then do you mind if I borrow your Mag? I, uh, forgot mine.'

'No problem.'

She slid the flashlight out of the ring on her equipment belt and handed it to him.

The doctor and his dog came up then.

'Ready.'

'Okay, Doctor, I want you to take us up to the spot where you let the dog go and we'll see where she goes.'

'I'm not sure you'll be able to stay with her.'

'I'll worry about that, Doctor.'

'This way then.'

They walked up the incline toward the small turnaround circle where Wonderland reached a dead end. Brasher made a hand signal to her partner in the car and walked along with them.

'You know, we had a little excitement up this way a few years ago,' Guyot said. 'A man was followed home from the Hollywood Bowl and then killed in a robbery.'

'I remember,' Bosch said.

He knew the investigation was still open but didn't mention it. It wasn't his case.

Dr. Guyot walked with a strong step that belied his age and apparent condition. He let the dog set the pace and soon moved several paces ahead of Bosch and Brasher.

'So where were you before?' Bosch asked Brasher.

'What do you mean?'

'You said you were new in Hollywood Division. What about before?'

'Oh. The academy.'

He was surprised. He looked over at her, thinking he might need to reassess his age estimate.

She nodded and said, 'I know, I'm old.'

Bosch got embarrassed.

'No, I wasn't saying that. I just thought that you had been somewhere else. You don't seem like a rookie.'

'I didn't go in until I was thirty-four.'

'Really? Wow.'

'Yeah. Got the bug a little late.'

'What were you doing before?'

'Oh, a bunch of different things. Travel mostly. Took me a while to figure out what I wanted to do. And you want to know what I want to do the most?'

Bosch looked at her.

'What?'

'What you do. Homicide.'

He didn't know what to say, whether to encourage her or dissuade her.

'Well, good luck,' he said.

'I mean, don't you just find it to be the most fulfilling job ever? Look at what you do, you take the most evil people out of the mix.'

'The mix?'

'Society.'

'Yeah, I guess so. When we get lucky.'

They caught up to Dr. Guyot, who had stopped with the dog at the turnaround circle.

'This the place?'

'Yes. I let her go here. She went up through there.'

He pointed to an empty and overgrown lot that started level with the street but then quickly rose into a steep incline toward the crest of the hills. There was a large concrete drainage culvert, which explained why the lot had never been built on. It was city property, used to funnel storm water runoff away from the homes on the street. Many of the streets in the canyon were former creek and river beds. When it rained they would return to their original purpose if not for the drainage system.

'Are you going up there?' the doctor asked.

'I'm going to try.'

'I'll go with you,' Brasher said.

Bosch looked at her and then turned at the sound of a car. It was the patrol car. It pulled up and Edgewood put down the window.

'We got a hot shot, partner. Double D.'

He nodded toward the empty passenger seat. Brasher frowned and looked at Bosch.

'I hate domestic disputes.'

Bosch smiled. He hated them too, especially when they turned into homicides.

'Sorry about that.'

'Well, maybe next time.'

She started around the front of the car.

'Here,' Bosch said, holding out the MagLite.

'I've got an extra in the car,' she said. 'You can just get that back to me.'

'You sure?'

He was tempted to ask for a phone number but didn't.

'I'm sure. Good luck.'

'You too. Be careful.'

She smiled at him and then hurried around the front of the car. She got in and the car pulled away. Bosch turned his attention back to Guyot and the dog.

'An attractive woman,' Guyot said.

Bosch ignored it, wondering if the doctor had made the comment based on seeing Bosch's reaction to Brasher. He hoped he hadn't been that obvious.

'Okay, Doctor,' he said, 'let the dog go and I'll try to keep up.'

Guyot unhooked the leash while patting the dog's chest.

'Go get the bone, girl. Get a bone! Go!'

The dog took off into the lot and was gone from sight before Bosch had taken a step. He almost laughed.

'Well, I guess you were right about that, Doc.'

He turned to make sure the patrol car was gone and Brasher hadn't seen the dog take off.

'You want me to whistle?'

'Nah. I'll just go in and take a look around, see if I can catch up to her.'

He turned the flashlight on.

3

The woods were dark long before the sun disappeared. The overhead canopy created by a tall stand of Monterey pines blocked out most of the light before it got to the ground. Bosch used the flashlight and made his way up the hillside in the direction in which he had heard the dog moving through the brush. It was slow moving and hard work. The ground contained a foot-thick layer of pine needles that gave way often beneath Bosch's boots as he tried for purchase on the incline. Soon his hands were sticky with sap from grabbing branches to keep himself upright.

It took him nearly ten minutes to go thirty yards up the hillside. Then the ground started to level off and the light got better as the tall trees thinned. Bosch looked around for the dog but didn't see her. He called down to the street, though he could no longer see it or Dr. Guyot.

'Dr. Guyot? Can you hear me?'

'Yes, I hear you.'

'Whistle for your dog.'

He then heard a three-part whistle. It was distinct but very low, having the same trouble getting through the trees and underbrush as the sunlight had. Bosch tried to repeat it and after a few tries thought he had it right. But the dog didn't come.

Bosch pressed on, staying on the level ground because he believed that if someone was going to bury or abandon a body, then it would be done on even ground as opposed to the steep slope. Following a path of least resistance, he moved into a stand of acacia trees. And here he immediately came upon a spot where the earth had recently been disturbed. It had been overturned, as if a tool or an animal had been randomly rooting in the soil. He used his foot to push some of the dirt and twigs aside and then realized they weren't twigs.

He dropped to his knees and used the light to study the short brown bones scattered over a square foot of dirt. He believed he was looking at the disjointed fingers of a hand. A small hand. A child's hand.

Bosch stood up. He realized that his interest in Julia Brasher had distracted him. He had brought no means with him for collecting the bones. Picking them up and carrying them down the hill would violate every tenet of evidence collection.

The Polaroid camera hung on a shoelace around his neck. He raised it now and took a close-up shot of the bones. He then stepped back and took a wider shot of the spot beneath the acacia trees.

In the distance he heard Dr. Guyot's weak whistle. Bosch went to work with the yellow plastic crime scene tape. He tied a short length of it around the trunk of one of the acacia trees and then strung a boundary around the trees. Thinking about how he would work the case the following morning, he stepped out of the cover of the acacia trees and looked for something to use as an aerial marker. He found a nearby growth of sagebrush. He wrapped the crime scene tape around and over the top of the bush several times.

When he was finished it was almost dark. He took another cursory look around the area but knew that a flashlight search was useless and the ground would need to be exhaustively covered in the morning. Using a small penknife attached to his key chain, he began cutting four-foot lengths of the crime scene tape off the roll.

Making his way back down the hill, he tied the strips off at intervals on tree branches and bushes. He heard voices as he got closer to the street and used them to maintain his direction. At one point on the incline the soft ground suddenly gave way and he fell, tumbling hard into the base of a pine tree. The tree impacted his midsection, tearing his shirt and badly scratching his side.

Bosch didn't move for several seconds. He thought he might have cracked his ribs on the right side. His breathing was difficult and painful. He groaned loudly and slowly pulled himself up on the tree trunk so that he could continue to follow the voices.

He soon came back down into the street where Dr. Guyot was waiting with his dog and another man. The two men looked shocked when they saw the blood on Bosch's shirt.

'Oh my, what happened?' Guyot cried out.

'Nothing. I fell.'

'Your shirt is . . . there's blood!'

'Comes with the job.'

'Let me look at your chest.'

The doctor moved in to look but Bosch held his hands up.

'I'm okay. Who is this?'

The other man answered.

'I'm Victor Ulrich. I live there.'

He pointed to the house next to the lot. Bosch nodded.

'I just came out to see what was going on.'

'Well, nothing is going on at the moment. But there is a crime scene up there. Or there will be. We probably won't be back to work it until tomorrow morning. But I need both you men to keep clear of it and not to tell anybody about this. All right?'

Both of the neighbors nodded.

'And Doctor, don't let your dog off the leash for a few days. I need to go back down to my car to make a phone call. Mr. Ulrich, I am sure we will want to talk to you tomorrow. Will you be around?'

'Sure. Anytime. I work at home.'

'Doing what?'

'Writing.'

'Okay. We'll see you tomorrow.'

Bosch headed back down the street with Guyot and the dog.

'You really need me to take a look at your injury,' Guyot insisted.

'It'll be fine.'

Bosch glanced to his left and thought he saw a curtain quickly close behind a window of the house they were passing.

'The way you are holding yourself when you walk – you've damaged a rib,' Guyot said. 'Maybe you've broken it. Maybe more than one.'

Bosch thought of the small, thin bones he had just seen beneath the acacia trees.

'There's nothing you can do for a rib, broken or not,' he said.

'I can tape it. You'll breathe a hell of a lot easier. I can also take care of that wound.'

Bosch relented.

'Okay, Doc, you get out your black bag. I'm going to get my other shirt.'

Inside Guyot's house a few minutes later, the doctor cleaned the deep scratch on the side of Bosch's chest and taped his ribs. It did feel better, but it still hurt. Guyot said he could no longer write a prescription but suggested Bosch not take anything more powerful than aspirin anyway.

Bosch remembered that he had a prescription bottle with some Vicodin tablets left over from when he'd had a wisdom tooth removed a few months earlier. They would smooth out the pain if he wanted to go that way.

'I'll be fine,' Bosch said. 'Thanks for fixing me up.'

'Don't mention it.'

Bosch pulled on his good shirt and watched Guyot as he closed up his first-aid kit. He wondered how long it had been since the doctor had used his skills on a patient.

'How long have you been retired?' he asked.

'Twelve years next month.'

'You miss it?'

Guyot turned from the first-aid kit and looked at him. The tremor was gone.

'Every day. I don't miss the actual work – you know, the cases. But it was a job that made a difference. I miss that.'

Bosch thought about how Julia Brasher had described homicide work earlier. He nodded that he understood what Guyot was saying.

'You said there was a crime scene up there?' the doctor asked.

'Yes. I found more bones. I've got to make a call, see what we're going to do. Can I borrow your phone? I don't think my cell will work around here.'

'No, they never do in the canyon. Use the phone on the desk there and I'll give you some privacy.'

He headed out, carrying the first-aid kit with him. Bosch went behind the desk and sat down. The dog was on the ground next to the chair. The animal looked up and seemed startled when she saw Bosch in the master's spot.

'Calamity,' he said. 'I think you lived up to your name today, girl.'

Bosch reached down and rubbed the scruff of the dog's neck. The dog growled and he quickly took his hand away, wondering if it was the dog's training or something about himself that had caused the hostile response.

He picked up the phone and called the home of his supervisor, Lt. Grace Billets. He explained what had happened on Wonderland Avenue and his findings up on the hill.

'Harry, how old do these bones look?' Billets asked.

Bosch looked at the Polaroid he had taken of the small bones he had found in the dirt. It was a bad photo, the flash overexposing it because he was too close.

'I don't know, they look old to me. I'd say we're talking years here.'

'Okay, so whatever's there at the scene isn't fresh.'

'Maybe freshly uncovered, but no, it's been there.'

'That's what I'm saying. So I think we should stick a pin in it and gear up for tomorrow. Whatever is up there on that hill, it's not going anywhere tonight.'

'Yeah,' Bosch said. 'I'm thinking the same thing.'

She was silent a moment before speaking.

'These kind of cases, Harry . . . '

'What?'

'They drain the budget, they drain manpower . . . and they're the hardest to close, *if* you can close them.'

'Okay, I'll climb back up there and cover the bones up. I'll tell the doctor to keep his dog on a leash.'

'Come on, Harry, you know what I mean.' She exhaled loudly. 'First day of the year and we're going to start in the hole.'

Bosch was silent, letting her work through her administrative frustrations. It didn't take long. It was one of the things he liked about her.

'Okay, anything else happen today?'

'Not too much. A couple suicides, that's it so far.'

'Okay, when are you going to start tomorrow?'

'I'd like to get out there early. I'll make some calls and see what I can get going. And get the bone the dog found confirmed before we start anything.'

'Okay, let me know.'

Bosch agreed and hung up the phone. He next called Teresa Corazon, the county medical examiner, at home. Though their relationship outside of work had ended years before and she had moved at least two times since, she had always kept the same number and Bosch knew it by heart. It came in handy now. He explained what he had going and that he needed an official confirmation of the bone as human before he set other things in motion. He also told her that if it was confirmed he would need an archeological team to work the crime scene as soon as possible.

Corazon put him on hold for almost five minutes.

'Okay,' she said when she came back on the line. 'I couldn't get Kathy Kohl. She's not home.'

Bosch knew that Kohl was the staff archeologist. Her real expertise and reason for her inclusion as a full-time employee was retrieving bones from the body dump sites up in the desert of the north county, which was a weekly occurrence. But Bosch knew she would be called in to handle the search for bones off Wonderland Avenue.

'So what do you want me to do? I want to get this confirmed tonight.'

'Just hold your horses, Harry. You are always so impatient. You're like a dog with a bone, no pun intended.'

'It's a kid, Teresa. Can we be serious?'

'Just come here. I'll look at this bone.'

'And what about tomorrow?'

'I'll get things in motion. I left a message for Kathy and as soon as we hang up here I'll call the office and have her paged. She'll head up the dig as soon as the sun is up and we can get in there. Once the bones are recovered, there is a forensic anthropologist at UCLA we have on retainer and I can bring him in if he's in town. And I'll be there myself. Are you satisfied?'

This last part gave Bosch pause.

'Teresa,' he finally said, 'I want to try to keep this as low profile as I can for as long as I can.'

'And what are you implying?'

'That I'm not sure that *the* medical examiner for Los Angeles County needs to be there. And that I haven't seen you at a crime scene without a cameraman in tow for a long time.'

'Harry, he is a private videographer, okay? The film he takes is for future use by me and controlled solely by me. It doesn't end up on the six o'clock news.'

'Whatever. I just think we need to avoid any complications on this one. It's a child case. You know how they get.'

'Just get over here with that bone. I'm leaving in an hour.'

She abruptly hung up.

Bosch wished he had been a little more politic with Corazon but was glad he'd made his point. Corazon was a personality, regularly appearing on Court TV and network shows as a forensic expert. She had also taken to having a cameraman follow her so that her cases could be turned into documentaries for broadcast on any of the cop and legal shows on the vast cable and satellite spectrum. He could not and would not let her goals as a celebrity coroner interfere with his goals as an investigator of what might be the homicide of a child.

He decided he'd make the calls to the department's Special Services and K-9 units after he got confirmation on the bone. He got up and left the room, looking for Guyot.

The doctor was in the kitchen, sitting at a small table and writing in a spiral-bound notebook. He looked up at Bosch.

'Just writing a few notes on your treatment. I've kept notes on every patient I've ever treated.'

Bosch just nodded, even though he thought it was odd for Guyot to be writing about him.

'I'm going to go, Doctor. We'll be back tomorrow. In force, I'd expect. We might want to use your dog again. Will you be here?'

'I'll be here and be glad to help. How are the ribs?'

'They hurt.'

'Only when you breathe, right? That'll last about a week.'

'Thanks for taking care of me. You don't need that shoe box back, do you?'

'No, I wouldn't want that back now.'

Bosch turned to head toward the front door but then turned back to Guyot.

'Doctor, do you live alone here?'

'I do now. My wife died two years ago. A month before our fiftieth anniversary.'

'I'm sorry.'

Guyot nodded and said, 'My daughter has her own family up in Seattle. I see them on special occasions.'

Bosch felt like asking why only on special occasions but didn't. He thanked the man again and left.

Driving out of the canyon and toward Teresa Corazon's place in Hancock Park, he kept his hand on the shoe box so that it would not be jostled or slide off the seat. He felt a deep sense of dread rising from within. He knew it was because fate had certainly not smiled on him this day. He had caught the worst kind of case there was to catch. A child case.

Child cases haunted you. They hollowed you out and scarred you. There was no bulletproof vest thick enough to stop you from being pierced. Child cases left you knowing the world was full of lost light.

4

Teresa Corazon lived in a Mediterranean-style mansion with a stone turnaround circle complete with koi pond in front. Eight years earlier, when Bosch had shared a brief relationship with her, she had lived in a one-bedroom condominium. The riches of television and celebrity had paid for the house and the lifestyle that came with it. She was not even remotely like the woman who used to show up at his house unannounced at midnight with a cheap bottle of red wine from Trader Joe's and a video of her favorite movie to watch. The woman who was unabashedly ambitious but not yet skilled at using her position to enrich herself.

Bosch knew he now served as a reminder of what she had been and what she had lost in order to gain all that she had. It was no wonder their interactions were now few and far between but as tense as a visit to the dentist when they were unavoidable.

He parked on the circle and got out with the shoe box and the Polaroids. He looked into the pond as he came around the car and could see the dark shapes of the fish moving below the surface. He smiled, thinking about the movie *Chinatown* and how often they had watched it the year they were together. He remembered how much she enjoyed the portrayal of the coroner. He wore a black butcher's apron and ate a sandwich while examining a body. Bosch doubted she had the same sense of humor about things anymore.

The light hanging over the heavy wood door to the house went on, and Corazon opened it before he got there. She was wearing black slacks and a cream-colored blouse. She was probably on her way to a New Year's party. She looked past him at the slickback he had been driving.

'Let's make this quick before that car drips oil on my stones.'

'Hello to you, too, Teresa.'

'That's it?'

She pointed at the shoe box.

'This is it.'

He handed her the Polaroids and started taking the lid off the box. It was clear she was not asking him in for a glass of New Year's champagne.

'You want to do this right here?'

'I don't have a lot of time. I thought you'd be here sooner. What moron took these?'

'That would be me.'

'I can't tell anything from these. Do you have a glove?'

Bosch pulled a latex glove out of his coat pocket and handed it to her. He took the photos back and put them in an inside pocket of his jacket. She expertly snapped the glove on and reached into the open box. She held the bone up and turned it in the light. He was silent. He could smell her perfume. It was strong as usual, a holdover from her days when she spent most of her time in autopsy suites.

After a five-second examination she put the bone back down in the box.

'Human.'

'You sure?'

She looked up at him with a glare as she snapped off the glove.

'It's the humerus. The upper arm. I'd say a child of about ten. You may no longer respect my skills, Harry, but I do still have them.'

She dropped the glove into the box on top of the bone. Bosch could roll with all the verbal sparring from her, but it bothered him that she did that with the glove, dropping it on the child's bone like that.

He reached into the box and took the glove out. He remembered something and held the glove back out to her.

'The man whose dog found this said there was a fracture on the bone. A healed fracture. Do you want to take a look and see if you—'

'No. I'm late for an engagement. What you need to know right now is if it is human. You now have that confirmation. Further examination will come later under proper settings at the medical examiner's office. Now, I really have to go. I'll be there tomorrow morning.'

Bosch held her eyes for a long moment.

'Sure, Teresa, have a good time tonight.'

She broke off the stare and folded her arms across her chest. He carefully put the top back on the shoe box, nodded to her and headed back to his car. He heard the heavy door close behind him.

Thinking of the movie again as he passed the koi pond, he spoke the film's final line quietly to himself.

'Forget it, Jake, it's Chinatown.'

He got in the car and drove home, his hand holding the shoe box secure on the seat next to him.

5

By nine o'clock the next morning the end of Wonderland Avenue was a law enforcement encampment. And at its center was Harry Bosch. He directed teams from patrol, K-9, the Scientific Investigation Division, the medical examiner's office and the Special Services unit. A department helicopter circled above and a dozen police academy cadets milled about, waiting for orders.

Earlier, the aerial unit had locked in on the sagebrush Bosch had wrapped in yellow crime scene tape and used it as a base point to determine that Wonderland offered the closest access to the spot where Bosch had found the bones. The Special Services unit then swung into action. Following the trail of crime scene tape up the hillside, the six-man team hammered and strung together a series of wooden ramps and steps with rope guidelines that led up the hillside to the bones. Accessing and exiting the site would now be much easier than it had been for Bosch the evening before.

It was impossible to keep such a nest of police activity quiet. Also by 9 a.m. the neighborhood had become a media encampment. The media trucks were stacked behind the roadblocks set a half block from the turnaround circle. The reporters were gathering into press conference-sized groups. And no fewer than five news helicopters were circling at an altitude above the department's chopper. It all created a background cacophony that had already resulted in numerous complaints from residents on the street to police administrators at Parker Center downtown.

Bosch was getting ready to lead the first group up to the crime scene. He first conferred with Jerry Edgar, who had been apprised of the case the night before.

'All right, we're going to take the ME and SID up first,' he said, pronouncing the acronyms as Emmy and Sid. 'Then we'll take the cadets and the dogs up. I want you to oversee that part of it.'

'No problem. You see your pal the ME's got her damn cameraman with her?'

'Nothing we can do about it at the moment. Let's just hope she gets bored and goes back downtown, where she belongs.'

'You know, for all we know, these could be old Indian bones or something.'

Bosch shook his head.

'I don't think so. Too shallow.'

Bosch walked over to the first group: Teresa Corazon, her videographer and her four-person dig team, which consisted of archeologist Kathy Kohl and three investigators who would do the spadework. The dig team members were dressed in white jumpsuits. Corazon was in an outfit similar to what she was wearing the night before, including shoes with two-inch heels. Also in the group were two criminalists from SID.

Bosch signaled the group into a tighter circle so he could speak privately to them and not be overheard by all the others milling about.

'Okay, we're going to go up and start the documentation and recovery. Once we have all of you in place we'll bring up the dogs and the cadets to search the adjacent areas and possibly expand the crime scene. You guys—'

He stopped to reach his hand up to Corazon's cameraman.

'Turn that off. You can film her but not me.'

The man lowered his camera, and Bosch gave Corazon a look and then continued.

'You all know what you are doing so I don't need to brief you. The one thing I do want to say is that it is tough going getting up there. Even with the ramps and the stairs. So be careful. Hold on to the ropes, watch your footing. We don't want anybody hurt. If you have heavy equipment, break it up and make two or three trips. If you still need help I'll have the cadets bring it up. Don't worry about time. Worry about safety. All right, everybody cool?'

He got simultaneous nods from everybody. Bosch signaled Corazon away from the others and into a private conversation.

'You're not dressed right,' he said.

'Look, don't you start telling—'

'You want me to take my shirt off so you can see my ribs? The side of my chest looks like blueberry pie because I fell up there last night. Those shoes you've got on aren't going to work. It might look good for the camera but not—'

'I'm fine. I'll take my chances. Anything else?'

Bosch shook his head.

'I warned you,' he said. 'Let's go.'

He headed toward the ramp, and the others followed. Special Services had constructed a wooden gateway to be used as a checkpoint. A patrol officer stood there with a clipboard. He took each person's name and affiliation before they were allowed through.

Bosch led the way. The climbing was easier than the day before but his chest burned with pain as he pulled himself along on the rope guides and negotiated the ramps and steps. He said nothing and tried not to show it.

When he got to the acacia trees he signaled the others to hold back while he went under the crime scene tape to check first. He found the area of overturned earth and the small, brown bones he had seen the night before. They appeared undisturbed.

'Okay, come on in here and have a look.'

The group members came under the tape and stood over the bones in a semicircle. The camera started rolling and Corazon now took charge.

'All right, the first thing we're going to do is back out and take photos. Then we're going to set up a grid and Dr. Kohl will supervise the excavation and recovery. If you find anything, photograph it nine ways from Sunday before you collect it.'

She turned to one of the investigators.

'Finch, I want you to handle the sketches. Standard grid. Document everything. Don't assume we will be able to rely on photos.'

Finch nodded. Corazon turned to Bosch.

'Detective, I think we've got it. The less people in here the better.'

Bosch nodded and handed her a two-way radio.

'I'll be around. If you need me use the rover. Cell phones don't work up here. But be careful what you say.'

He pointed up at the sky, where the media helicopters were circling.

'Speaking of which,' Kohl said, 'I think we're going to string a tarp up off these trees so we can have some privacy as well as cut down on the sun glare. Is that okay with you?'

'It's your crime scene now,' Bosch said. 'Run with it.'

He headed back down the ramp with Edgar behind him.

'Harry, this could take days,' Edgar said.

'And maybe then some.'

'Well, they're not going to give us days. You know that, right?'

'Right.'

'I mean, these cases . . . we'll be lucky if we even come up with an ID.'

'Right.'

Bosch kept moving. When he got down to the street he saw that Lt. Billets was on the scene with her supervisor, Capt. LeValley.

'Jerry, why don't you go get the cadets ready?' Bosch said. 'Give them the crime scene one-oh-one speech. I'll be over in a minute.'

Bosch joined Billets and LeValley and updated them on what was happening, detailing the morning's activities right down to the neighborhood complaints about noise from the hammers, saws and helicopters.

'We've got to give something to the media,' LeValley said. 'Media Relations wants to know if you want them to handle it from downtown or you want to take it here.'

'I don't want to take it. What does Media Relations know about it?'

'Almost nothing. So you have to call them and they'll work up the press release.'

'Captain, I'm kind of busy here. Can I—'

'Make the time, Detective. Keep them off our backs.'

When Bosch looked away from the captain to the reporters gathered a half block away at the roadblock, he noticed Julia Brasher showing her badge to a patrol officer and being allowed through. She was in street clothes.

'All right. I'll make the call.'

He started down the street to Dr. Guyot's home. He was headed toward Brasher, who smiled at him as she approached.

'I've got your Mag. It's in my car down here. I have to go down to Dr. Guyot's house anyway.'

'Oh, don't worry about it. That's not why I'm here.'

She changed direction and continued with Bosch. He looked at her attire: faded blue jeans and a T-shirt from a 5K charity run.

'You're not on the clock, are you?'

'No, I work the three-to-eleven. I just thought you might need a volunteer. I heard about the academy call out.'

'You want to go up there and look for bones, huh?'

'I want to learn.'

Bosch nodded. They walked up the path to Guyot's door. It opened before they got there and the doctor invited them in. Bosch asked if he could use the phone in his office again and Guyot showed him the way even though he didn't have to. Bosch sat down behind the desk.

'How are the ribs?' the doctor asked.

'Fine.'

Brasher raised her eyebrows and Bosch picked up on it.

'Had a little accident when I was up there last night.'

'What happened?'

'Oh, I was just sort of minding my own business when a tree trunk suddenly attacked me for no reason.'

She grimaced and somehow managed to smile at the same time.

Bosch dialed Media Relations from memory and told an officer about the case in very general terms. At one point he put his hand over the phone and asked Guyot if he wanted his name put in the press release. The doctor declined. A few minutes later Bosch was finished and hung up. He looked at Guyot.

'Once we clear the scene in a few days the reporters will probably stick around. They'll be looking for the dog that found the bone, is my guess. So if you want to stay out of it, keep Calamity off the street or they'll put two and two together.'

'Good advice,' Guyot said.

'And you might want to call your neighbor, Mr. Ulrich, and tell him not to mention it to any reporters, either.'

On the way out of the house Bosch asked Brasher if she wanted her flashlight and she said she didn't want to bother carrying it while she was helping search the hillside.

'Get it to me whenever,' she said.

Bosch liked the answer. It meant he would get at least one more chance to see her.

Back at the circle Bosch found Edgar lecturing the academy cadets.

'The golden rule of the crime scene, people, is don't touch anything until it has been studied, photographed and charted.'

Bosch walked into the circle.

'Okay, we ready?'

'They're ready,' Edgar said. He nodded toward two of the cadets, who were holding metal detectors. 'I borrowed those from SID.'

Bosch nodded and gave the cadets and Brasher the same safety speech he had given the forensic crew. They then headed up to the crime scene, Bosch introducing Brasher to Edgar and then letting his partner lead the way through the checkpoint. He took up the rear, walking behind Brasher.

'We'll see if you want to be a homicide detective by the end of the day,' he said.

'Anything's got to be better than chasing the radio and washing puke out of the back of your car at the end of every shift.'

'I remember those days.'

Bosch and Edgar spread the twelve cadets and Brasher out in the areas adjacent to the stand of acacia trees and had them begin conducting side-by-side searches. Bosch then went down and brought up the two K-9 teams to supplement the search.

Once things were under way he left Edgar with the cadets and went back to the acacias to see what progress had been made. He found Kohl sitting on an equipment crate and supervising the placement of wooden stakes into the ground so that strings could be used to set the excavation grid.

Bosch had worked one prior case with Kohl and knew she was very thorough and good at what she did. She was in her late thirties with a tennis player's build and tan. Bosch had once run across her at a city park, where she was playing tennis with a twin sister. They had drawn a crowd. It looked like somebody hitting the ball off a mirrored wall.

Kohl's straight blonde hair fell forward and hid her eyes as she looked down at the oversized clipboard on her lap. She was making notations on a piece of paper with a grid already printed on it. Bosch looked over her shoulder at the chart. Kohl was labeling the individual blocks with letters of the alphabet as the corresponding stakes were placed in the ground. At the top of the page she had written 'City of Bones.'

Bosch reached down and tapped the chart where she had written the caption.

'Why do you call it that?'

She shrugged her shoulders.

'Because we're setting out the streets and the blocks of what will become a city to us,' she said, running her fingers over some of the lines on the chart in illustration. 'At least while we're working here it will feel like it. Our little city.'

Bosch nodded.

'In every murder is the tale of a city,' he said.

Kohl looked up at him.

'Who said that?'

'I don't know. Somebody did.'

He turned his attention to Corazon, who was squatting over the small bones on the surface of the soil, studying them while the lens of the video camera studied her. He was thinking of something to say about it when his rover was keyed and he took it off his belt.

'Bosch here.'

'Edgar. Better come on back over here, Harry. We already have something.'

'Right.'

Edgar was standing in an almost level spot in the brush about forty yards from the acacia trees. A half dozen of the cadets and Brasher had formed a circle and were looking down at something in the two-foot-high brush. The police chopper was circling in a tighter circle above.

Bosch got to the circle and looked down. It was a child's skull partially submerged in the soil, its hollow eyes staring up at him.

'Nobody touched it,' Edgar said. 'Brasher here found it.'

Bosch glanced at her and the humor she seemed to carry in her eyes and mouth were gone. He looked back at the skull and pulled the radio off his belt.

'Dr. Corazon?' he said into it.

It was a long moment before her voice came back.

'Yes, I'm here. What is it?'

'We are going to have to widen the crime scene.'

6

With Bosch acting as the general overseeing the small army that worked the expanded crime scene, the day progressed well. The bones came out of the ground and the hillside brush easily, as if they had been impatiently waiting a very long time. By noon, three blocks in the grid were being actively excavated by Kathy Kohl's team, and dozens of bones emerged from the dark soil. Like their archeological counterparts who unearthed the artifacts of the ancients, the dig team used small tools and brushes to bring these bones gently to light. They also used metal detectors and vapor probes. The process was painstaking yet it was moving at an even faster pace than Bosch had hoped for.

The finding of the skull had set this pace and brought a sense of urgency to the entire operation. It was removed from its location first, and the field examination conducted on camera by Teresa Corazon found fracture lines and surgical scarring. The record of surgery assured them they were dealing with relatively contemporary bones. The fractures in and of themselves were not definitive in the indication of homicide, but when added to the evidence that the body had been buried they gave a clear sense that the tale of a murder was unfolding.

By two o'clock, when the hillside crews broke for lunch, almost half of the skeleton had already been recovered from the grid. A small scattering of other bones had been found in the nearby brush by the cadets. Additionally, Kohl's crew had unearthed fragments of deteriorated clothing and a canvas backpack of a size most likely used by a child.

The bones came down the hillside in square wooden boxes with rope handles attached on the sides. By lunch, a forensic anthropologist was examining three boxes of bones in the medical examiner's office. The clothing, most of it rotten and unrecognizable, and the backpack, which had been left unopened, were transported to LAPD's Scientific Investigation Division lab for the same scrutiny.

A metal detector scan of the search grid produced a single coin – a quarter minted in 1975 – found at the same depth as the bones and approximately two inches from the left wing of the pelvis. It was assumed that the quarter had been in the left front pocket of pants that had rotted away along with the body's tissue. To Bosch, the coin gave one of the key parameters of time of death: If the assumption that the coin had been buried with the body was correct, the death could not have happened before 1975.

Patrol had arranged for two construction site lunch wagons to come to the circle to feed the small army working the crime scene. Lunch was late and people were hungry. One truck served hot lunches while the other served sandwiches. Bosch waited at the end of the line for the sandwich truck with Julia Brasher. The line was moving slowly but he didn't mind. They mostly talked about the investigation on the hillside and gossiped about department brass. It was get-to-know-you conversation. Bosch was attracted to her, and the more he heard her talk about her experiences as a rookie and a female in the department, the more he was intrigued by her. She had a mixture of excitement and awe and cynicism about the job that Bosch remembered clearly from his own early days on the job.

When he was about six people from the order window of the lunch truck, Bosch heard someone in the truck asking one of the cadets questions about the investigation.

'Are they bones from a bunch of different people?'

'I don't know, man. We just look for them, that's all.'

Bosch studied the man who had asked the question.

'Were they all cut up?'

'Hard to tell.'

Bosch broke from his spot with Brasher and walked to the back of the truck. He looked through the open door at-the back and saw three men wearing aprons working in the truck. Or appearing to work. They did not notice Bosch watching. Two of the men were making sandwiches and filling orders. The man in the middle, the one who had asked the cadet questions, was moving his arms on the prep counter below the order window. He wasn't making anything, but from outside the truck it would appear he was creating a sandwich. As Bosch watched, he saw the man to the right slice a sandwich in half, put it on a paper plate and slide it to the man in the middle. The middle man then held it out through the window to the cadet who ordered it.

Bosch noticed that while the two real sandwich makers wore jeans and T-shirts beneath their aprons, the man in the middle had on cuffed slacks and a shirt with a button-down collar. Protruding from the back pocket of his pants was a notebook. The long, thin kind that Bosch knew reporters used.

Bosch stuck his head in the door and looked around. On a shelf next to the doorway he saw a sport jacket rolled into a ball. He grabbed it and stepped back away from the door. He went through the pockets of the jacket and found an LAPD-issued press pass on a neck chain. It had a picture of the middle sandwich maker on it. His name was Victor Frizbe and he worked at the *New Times.*

Holding the jacket to the side of the door, Bosch rapped on the outside of the truck, and when all three men turned to look he signaled Frizbe over. The reporter pointed to his chest with a *Who, me?* look and Bosch nodded. Frizbe came to the door and bent down.

'Yes?'

Bosch reached up and grabbed him by the top bib on the apron and jerked him out of the truck. Frizbe landed on his feet but had to run several steps to stop from falling. As he turned around to protest, Bosch hit him in the chest with the balled-up jacket.

Two patrol officers – they always ate first – were dumping paper plates into a nearby trash can. Bosch signaled them over.

'Take him back to the perimeter. If you see him crossing it again, arrest him.'

Each officer took Frizbe by an arm and started marching him down the street to the barricades. Frizbe started protesting, his face growing as red as a Coke can, but the patrol officers ignored everything about him but his arms and marched him toward his humiliation in front of the other reporters. Bosch watched for a moment and then took the press card out of his back pocket and dropped it in the trash can.

He rejoined Brasher in line. Now they were just two cadets away from being served.

'What was that all about?' Brasher asked.

'Health-code violation. Didn't wash his hands.'

She started laughing.

'I'm serious. The law's the law as far as I'm concerned.'

'God, I hope I get my sandwich before you see a roach or something and close the whole thing down.'

'Don't worry, I think I just got rid of the roach.'

Ten minutes later, after Bosch lectured the truck owner about smuggling the media into the crime scene, they took their sandwiches and drinks to one of the picnic tables Special Services had set up on the circle. It was a table that had been reserved for the investigative team, but Bosch didn't mind allowing Brasher to sit there. Edgar was there along with Kohl and one of the diggers from her crew. Bosch introduced Brasher to those who didn't know her and mentioned she had taken the initial call on the case and helped him the night before.

'So where's the boss?' Bosch asked Kohl.

'Oh, she already ate. I think she went off to tape an interview with herself or something.'

Bosch smiled and nodded.

'I think I'm going to get seconds,' Edgar said as he climbed over the bench and left with his plate.

Bosch bit into his BLT and savored its taste. He was starved. He wasn't planning to do anything but eat and rest during the break but Kohl asked if it was all right if she gave him some of her initial conclusions on the excavation.

Bosch had his mouth full. After he swallowed he asked her to wait until his partner came back. They talked in generalities about the condition of the bones and how Kohl believed that the shallow nature of the grave had allowed animals to disinter the remains and scatter the bones – possibly for years.

'We're not going to get them all,' she said. 'We won't come close. We're going to quickly reach a point where the expense and the effort won't be worth the return.'

Edgar returned with another plate of fried chicken. Bosch nodded to Kohl, who looked down at a notepad she had on the table to her left. She checked some of her notations and started talking.

'The things I want you to be mindful of are the grave depth and location terrain. I think these are key things. They're going to have to play somehow into who this child was and what happened to him.'

'Him?' Bosch asked.

'The hip spacing and the waistband of the underwear.'

She explained that included in the rotten and decomposed clothing was the rubber waistband, which was all that was left of the underwear that had been on the body when it was buried. Decomposition fluids from the body had led to the deterioration of the clothing. But the rubber waistband was largely intact and appeared to have come from a style of underwear made for males.

'Okay,' Bosch said. 'You were saying about grave depth?'

'Yes, well, we think that the hip assembly and lower spinal column were in undisturbed position when we uncovered them. Going on that, we're talking about a grave that wasn't more than six inches to a foot deep. A grave this shallow reflects speed, panic, a host of things indicative of poor planning. But—' she held up a finger '—by the same token, the location – very remote, very difficult – reflects the opposite. It shows careful planning. So you have some kind of contradiction going on here. The location appears to have been chosen because it was damn hard to get to, yet the burial appears to have been fast and furious. This person was literally just covered with loose topsoil and pine needles. I know pointing all of this out isn't necessarily going to help you catch the bad guy but I want you to see what I'm seeing here. This contradiction.'

Bosch nodded.

'It's all good to know. We'll keep it in mind.'

'Okay, good. The other contradiction – the smaller one – is the backpack. Burying it with the body was a mistake. The body decomposes at a much faster rate than the canvas. So if you get identifiers off the bag or its contents, it becomes a mistake made by the bad guy. Again poor planning in the midst of good planning. You're smart detectives, I'm sure you'll figure all this out.'

She smiled at Bosch and then studied her pad again, lifting the top page to look beneath it.

'I think that's it. Everything else we talked about up at the site. I think things are going very well up there. By the end of the day we'll have the main grave done. Tomorrow we'll do some sampling in the other grids. But this should probably wrap by tomorrow. Like I said, we're not going to get everything but we should get enough to do what we need to do.'

Bosch suddenly thought of Victor Frizbe's question to the cadet at the lunch wagon and realized that the reporter might have been thinking ahead of Bosch.

'Sampling? You think there's more than one body buried up there?'

Kohl shook her head.

'I have no indication of that at all. But we should make sure. We'll do some sampling, sink some gas probes. It's routine. The likelihood – especially in light of the shallow grave – is that this is a singular case, but we should be sure about it. As sure as we can be.'

Bosch nodded. He was glad he had eaten most of his sandwich because he was suddenly not hungry. The prospect of mounting an investigation with multiple victims was daunting. He looked at the others at the table.

'That doesn't leave this table. I already caught one reporter sniffing around for a serial killer, we don't want media hysteria here. Even if you tell them what we're doing is routine and just to make sure, it will be the top of the story. All right?'

Everyone nodded, including Brasher. Bosch was about to say something when there was a loud banging from the row of portable toilets on the Special Services trailer on the other side of the circle. Someone was inside one of the phone booth-sized bathrooms pounding on its thin aluminum skin. After a moment Bosch could hear a woman's voice behind the sharp banging. He recognized it and jumped up from the table.

Bosch ran across the circle and up the steps to the truck's platform. He quickly determined which toilet the banging-was coming from and went to the door. The exterior hasp – used for securing the toilet for transport – had been closed over the loop and a chicken bone had been used to secure it.

'Hold on, hold on,' Bosch yelled.

He tried to pull the bone out but it was too greasy and slipped from his grip. The pounding and screaming continued. Bosch looked around for a tool of some kind but didn't see anything. Finally, he took his pistol out of his holster, checked the safety and used the butt of the weapon to hammer the bone through the hasp, careful all the time to aim the barrel of the gun at a downward angle.

When the bone finally popped out he put the gun away and flipped the hasp open. The door burst outward and Teresa Corazon charged out, almost knocking him over. He grabbed her to maintain his balance but she roughly pushed him away.

'You did that!'

'What? No, I didn't! I was over there the whole—'

'I want to know who did it!'

Bosch lowered his voice. He knew everyone in the encampment was probably looking at them. The media down the street as well.

'Look, Teresa, calm down. It was a joke, okay? Whoever did it did it as a joke. I know you don't like confined spaces but they didn't know that. Somebody just wanted to ease the tension around here a little bit, and you just happened to be—'

'It's because they're jealous, that's why.'

'What?'

'Of who I am, what I've done.'

Bosch was nonplussed by that.

'Whatever.'

She headed for the stairs, then abruptly turned around and came back to him.

'I'm leaving, you happy now?'

Bosch shook his head.

'Happy? That has nothing to do with anything here. I'm trying to conduct an investigation, and if you want to know the truth, not having the distraction of you and your cameraman around might be a help.'

'Then you've got it. And you know that phone number you called me on the other night?'

Bosch nodded. 'Yeah, what about—'

'Burn it.'

She walked down the steps, angrily hooked a finger at her cameraman and headed toward her official car. Bosch watched her go.

When he got back to the picnic table, only Brasher and Edgar remained. His partner had reduced his second order of fried chicken to bones. He sat with a satisfied smirk on his face.

Bosch dropped the bone he had knocked out of the hasp onto Edgar's plate.

'That went over real well,' he said.

He gave Edgar a look that told him he knew he had been the one who did it. But Edgar revealed nothing.

'The bigger the ego the harder they fall,' Edgar said. 'I wonder if her cameraman got any of that action on tape.'

'You know, it would have been good to keep her as an ally,' Bosch said. 'To just put up with her so that she was on our side when we needed her.'

Edgar picked up his plate and struggled to slide his large body out of the picnic table.

'I'll see you up on the hill,' he said.

Bosch looked at Brasher. She raised her eyebrows.

'You mean he was the one who did it?'

Bosch didn't answer.

7

The work in the city of bones lasted only two days. As Kohl had predicted, the majority of the pieces of the skeleton had been located and removed from the spot beneath the acacia trees by the end of the first day. Other bones had been found nearby in the brush in a scatter pattern indicative of disinterment over time by foraging animals. On Friday the searchers and diggers returned, but a daylong search of the hillside by fresh cadets and further excavation of the main squares of the grid found no more bones. Vapor probes and sample digs in all the remaining squares of the grid turned up no bones or other indications that other bodies had been buried beneath the acacia trees.

Kohl estimated that sixty percent of the skeleton had been collected. On her recommendation and with Teresa Corazon's approval the excavation and search were suspended pending further developments at dusk on Friday.

Bosch had not objected to this. He knew they were facing limited returns for a large amount of effort and he deferred to the experts. He was also anxious to proceed with the investigation and identification of the bones – elements which were largely stalled as he and Edgar had worked exclusively on Wonderland Avenue during the two days, supervising the collection of evidence, canvassing the neighborhood and putting together the initial reports on the case. It was all necessary work but Bosch wanted to move on.

On Saturday morning he and Edgar met in the lobby of the medical examiner's office and told the receptionist they had an appointment with Dr. William Golliher, the forensic anthropologist on retainer from UCLA.

'He's waiting for you in suite A,' the receptionist said after making a call to confirm. 'You know which way that is?'

Bosch nodded and they were buzzed through the gate. They took an elevator down to the basement level and were immediately greeted by the smell of the autopsy floor when they stepped out. It was a mixture of chemicals and decay that was unique in the world. Edgar immediately took a paper breathing mask out of a wall dispenser and put it on. Bosch didn't bother.

'You really ought to, Harry,' Edgar said as they walked down the hall. 'Do you know that all smells are particulate?'

Bosch looked at him.

'Thanks for that, Jerry.'

They had to stop in the hallway as a gurney was pushed out of an autopsy suite. There was a body on it, wrapped in plastic.

'Harry, you ever notice that they wrap 'em up the same way they do the burritos at Taco Bell?'

Bosch nodded at the man pushing the gurney.

'That's why I don't eat burritos.'

'Really?'

Bosch moved on down the hall without answering.

Suite A was an autopsy room reserved for Teresa Corazon for the infrequent times she actually left her administrative duties as chief medical examiner and performed an autopsy. Because the case had initially garnered her hands-on attention she had apparently authorized Golliher to use her suite. Corazon had not returned to the crime scene on Wonderland Avenue after the portable toilet incident.

They pushed through the double doors of the suite and were met by a man in blue jeans and a Hawaiian shirt.

'Please call me Bill,' Golliher said. 'I guess it's been a long two days.'

'Say that again,' Edgar said.

Golliher nodded in a friendly manner. He was about fifty with dark hair and eyes and an easy manner. He gestured toward the autopsy table that was in the center of the room. The bones that had been collected from beneath the acacia trees were now spread across the stainless steel surface.

'Well, let me tell you what's been going on in here,' Golliher said. 'As the team in the field has been collecting the evidence, I've been here examining the pieces, doing the radiograph work and generally trying to put the puzzle of all of this together.'

Bosch stepped over to the stainless steel table. The bones were laid out in place so as to form a partial skeleton. The most obvious pieces missing were the bones of the left arm and leg and the lower jaw. It was presumed that these were the pieces that had long ago been taken and scattered distantly by animals that had rooted in the shallow grave.

Each of the bones was marked, the larger pieces with stickers and the smaller ones with string tags. Bosch knew that notations on these markers were codes by which the location of each bone had been charted on the grid Kohl had drawn on the first day of the excavation.

'Bones can tell us much about how a person lived and died,' Golliher said somberly. 'In cases of child abuse, the bones do not lie. The bones become our final evidence.'

Bosch looked back at him and realized his eyes were not dark. They actually were blue but they were deeply set and seemed haunted in some way. He was staring past Bosch at the bones on the table. After a moment he broke from this reverie and looked at Bosch.

'Let me start by saying that we are learning quite a bit from the recovered artifacts,' the anthropologist said. 'But I have to tell you guys, I've consulted on a lot of cases but this one blows me away. I was looking at these bones and taking notes and I looked down and my notebook was smeared. I was crying, man. I was crying and I didn't even know it at first.'

He looked back at the outstretched bones with a look of tenderness and pity. Bosch knew that the anthropologist saw the person who was once there.

'This one is bad, guys. Real bad.'

'Then give us what you've got so we can go out there and do our job,' Bosch said in a voice that sounded like a reverent whisper.

Golliher nodded and reached back to a nearby counter for a spiral notebook.

'Okay,' Golliher said. 'Let's start with the basics. Some of this you may already know but I'm just going to go over all of my findings, if you don't mind.'

'We don't mind,' Bosch said.

'Good. Then here it is. What you have here are the remains of a young male Caucasoid. Comparisons to the indices of Maresh growth standards put the age at approximately ten years old. However, as we will soon discuss, this child was the victim of severe and prolonged physical abuse. Histologically, victims of chronic abuse often suffer from what is called growth disruption. This abuse-related stunting serves to skew age estimation. What you often get is a skeleton that looks younger than it is. So what I am saying is that this boy looks ten but is probably twelve or thirteen.'

Bosch looked over at Edgar. He was standing with his arms folded tightly across his chest, as if bracing for what he knew was ahead. Bosch took a notebook out of his jacket pocket and started writing notes in shorthand.

'Time of death,' Golliher said. 'This is tough. Radiological testing is far from exact in this regard. We have the coin which gives us the early marker of nineteen seventy-five. That helps us. What I am estimating is that this kid has been in the ground anywhere from twenty to twenty-five years. I'm comfortable with that and there is some surgical evidence we can talk about in a few minutes that adds support to that estimation.'

'So we've got a ten- to thirteen-year-old kid killed twenty to twenty-five years ago,' Edgar summarized, a note of frustration in his voice.

'I know I am giving you a wide set of parameters, Detective,' Golliher said. 'But at the moment it's the best the science can do for you.'

'Not your fault, Doc.'

Bosch wrote it all down. Despite the wide spread of the estimation, it was still vitally important to set a time frame for the investigation. Golliher's estimation put the time of death into the late seventies to early eighties. Bosch momentarily thought of Laurel Canyon in that time frame. It had been a rustic, funky enclave, part bohemian and part upscale, with cocaine dealers and users, porno purveyors and burned out rock-and-roll hedonists on almost every street. Could the murder of a child have been part of that mix?

'Cause of death,' Golliher said. 'Tell you what, let's get to cause of death last. I want to start with the extremities and the torso, give you guys an idea of what this boy endured in his short lifetime.'

His eyes locked on Bosch's for a moment before returning to the bones. Bosch breathed in deeply, producing a sharp pain from his damaged ribs. He knew his fear from the moment he had looked down at the small bones on the hillside was now going to be realized. He instinctively knew all along that it would come to this. That a story of horror would emerge from the overturned soil.

He started scribbling on the pad, running the ballpoint deep into the paper, as Golliher continued.

'First of all, we only have maybe sixty percent of the bones here,' he said. 'But even still, we have incontrovertible evidence of tremendous skeletal trauma and chronic abuse. I don't know what your level of anthropological expertise is but I'm going to assume much of this will be new to you. I'm going to give you the basics. Bones heal themselves, gentlemen. And it is through the study of bone regeneration that we can establish a history of abuse. On these bones there are multiple lesions in different stages of healing. There are fractures old and new. We only have two of the four extremities but both of these show multiple instances of trauma. In short, this boy spent pretty much most of his life either healing or being hurt.'

Bosch looked down at the pad and pen clutched tightly in his hands. His hands were turning white.

'You will be getting a written report from me by Monday, but for now, if you want a number, I will tell you that I found forty-four distinct locations indicating separate trauma in various stages of healing. And these were just his bones, Detectives. It doesn't cover the damage that could have been inflicted on vital organs and the tissue. But it is without a doubt that this boy lived probably day in and day out with a lot of pain.'

Bosch wrote the number down on the pad. It seemed like a meaningless gesture.

'Primarily, the injuries I have catalogued can be noted on the artifacts by subperiosteal lesions,' Golliher said. 'These lesions are thin layers of new bone that grow beneath the surface in the area of trauma or bleeding.'

'Subperi – how do you spell that?' Bosch asked.

'What does it matter? It will be in the report.'

Bosch nodded.

'Take a look at this,' Golliher said.

Golliher went to the X-ray box on the wall and flipped on the light. There was already film on the box. It showed an X-ray of a long thin bone. He ran his finger along the stem of the bone, pointing out a slight demarcation of color.

'This is the one femur that was collected,' he said. 'The upper thigh. This line here, where the color changes, is one of the lesions. This means that this area – the boy's upper leg – had suffered a pretty strong blow in the weeks before his death. A crushing blow. It did not break the bone but it damaged it. This kind of injury would no doubt have caused surface bruising and I think affected the boy's walk. What I am telling you is that it could not have gone unnoticed.'

Bosch moved forward to study the X-ray. Edgar stayed back. When he was finished Golliher removed the X-ray and put up three more, covering the entire light box.

'We also have periosteal shearing on both of the limbs present. This is the stripping of the bone's surface, primarily seen in child abuse cases when the limb is struck violently by the adult hand or other instrument. Recovery patterns on these bones show that this particular type of trauma occurred repeatedly and over years to this child.'

Golliher paused to look at his notes, then he glanced at the bones on the table. He picked up the upper arm bone and held it up while he referred to his notes and spoke. Bosch noticed he wore no gloves.

'The humerus,' Golliher said. 'The right humerus shows two separate and healed fractures. The breaks are longitudinal. This tells us the fractures are the result of the twisting of the arm with great force. It happened to him once and then it happened again.'

He put the bone down and picked up one of the lower arm bones.

'The ulna shows a healed latitudinal fracture. The break caused a slight deviation in the attitude of the bone. This was because the bone was allowed to heal in place after the injury.'

'You mean it wasn't set?' Edgar asked. 'He wasn't taken to a doctor or an emergency room?'

'Exactly. This kind of injury, though commonly accidental and treated every day in every emergency room, can also be a defensive injury. You hold your arm up to ward off an attack and take the blow across the forearm. The fracture occurs. Because of the lack of indication of medical attention paid to this injury, my supposition is that this was not an accidental injury and was part of the abuse pattern.'

Golliher gently returned the bone to its spot and then leaned over the examination table to look down at the rib cage. Many of the rib bones had been detached and were lying separated on the table.

'The ribs,' Golliher said. 'Nearly two dozen fractures in various stages of healing. A healed fracture on rib twelve I believe may date to when the boy was only two or three. Rib nine shows a callus indicative of trauma only a few weeks old at the time of death. The fractures are primarily consolidated near the angles. In infants this is indicative of violent shaking. In older children this is usually indicative of blows to the back.'

Bosch thought of the pain he was in, of how he had been unable to sleep well because of the injury to his ribs. He thought of a young boy living with that kind of pain year in and year out.

'I gotta go wash my face,' he suddenly said. 'You can continue.'

He walked to the door, shoving his notebook and pen into Edgar's hands. In the hallway he turned right. He knew the layout of the autopsy floor and knew there were rest rooms around the next turn of the corridor.

He entered the rest room and went right to an open stall. He felt nauseous and waited but nothing happened. After a long moment it passed.

Bosch came out of the stall just as the door opened from the hallway and Teresa Corazon's cameraman walked in. They looked warily at each other for a moment.

'Get out of here,' Bosch said. 'Come back later.'

The man silently turned and walked out.

Bosch walked to the sink and looked at himself in the mirror. His face was red. He bent down and used his hands to cup cold water against his face and eyes. He thought about baptisms and second chances. Of renewal. He raised his face until he was looking at himself again.

I'm going to get this guy.

He almost said it out loud.

When Bosch returned to suite A all eyes were on him. Edgar gave him his notebook and pen back and Golliher asked if he was all right.

'Yeah, fine,' he said.

'If it is any help to you,' Golliher said, 'I have consulted on cases all over the world. Chile, Kosovo, even the World Trade Center. And this case . . . '

He shook his head.

'It's hard to comprehend,' he added. 'It's one of those where you have to think that maybe the boy was better off leaving this world. That is, if you believe in a God and a better place than this.'

Bosch walked over to a counter and pulled a paper towel out of a dispenser. He started wiping his face again.

'And what if you don't?'

Golliher walked over to him.

'Well, you see, this is why you must believe,' he said. 'If this boy did not go from this world to a higher plane, to something better, then . . . then I think we're all lost.'

'Did that work for you when you were picking through the bones at the World Trade Center?'

Bosch immediately regretted saying something so harsh. But Golliher seemed unfazed. He spoke before Bosch could apologize.

'Yes, it did,' he said. 'My faith was not shaken by the horror or the unfairness of so much death. In many ways it became stronger. It brought me through it.'

Bosch nodded and threw the towel into a trash can with a foot-pedal device for opening it. It closed with an echoing slam when he took his foot off the pedal.

'What about cause of death?' he said, getting back to the case.

'We can jump ahead, Detective,' Golliher said. 'All injuries, discussed and not discussed here, will be outlined in my report.'

He went back to the table and picked up the skull. He brought it over to Bosch, holding it in one hand close to his chest.

'In the skull we have the bad – and possibly the good,' Golliher said. 'The skull exhibits three distinct cranial fractures showing mixed stages of healing. Here is the first.'

He pointed to an area at the lower rear of the skull.

'This fracture is small and healed. You can see here that the lesions are completely consolidated. Then, next we have this more traumatic injury on the right parietal extending to the frontal. This injury required surgery, most likely for a subdural hematoma.'

He outlined the injury area with a finger, circling the forward top of the skull. He then pointed to five small and smooth holes which were linked by a circular pattern on the skull.

'This is a trephine pattern. A trephine is a medical saw used to open the skull for surgery or to relieve pressure from brain swelling. In this case it was probably swelling due to the hematoma. Now the fracture itself and the surgical scar show the beginning of bridging across the lesions. New bone. I would say this injury and subsequent surgery occurred approximately six months prior to the boy's death.'

'It's not the injury causing death?' Bosch asked.

'No. This is.'

Golliher turned the skull one more time and showed them another fracture. This one in the lower left rear of the skull.

'Tight spider web fracture with no bridging, no consolidation. This injury occurred at the time of death. The tightness of the fracture indicates a blow with tremendous force from a very hard object. A baseball bat, perhaps. Something like that.'

Bosch nodded and stared down at the skull. Golliher had turned it so that its hollow eyes were focused on Bosch.

'There are other injuries to the head, but not of a fatal nature. The nose bones and the zygomatic process show new bone formation following trauma.'

Golliher returned to the autopsy table and gently placed the skull down.

'I don't think I need to summarize for you, Detectives, but in short, somebody beat the shit out of this boy on a regular basis. Eventually, they went too far. It will all be in the report to you.'

He turned from the autopsy table and looked at them.

'There is a glimmer of light in all of this, you know. Something that might help you.'

'The surgery,' Bosch said.

'Exactly. Opening a skull is a very serious operation. There will be records somewhere. There had to be follow-up. The roundel is held back in place with metal clips after surgery. There were none found with the skull. I would assume they were removed in a second procedure. Again, there will be records. The surgical scar also helps us date the bones. The trephine holes are too large by today's standards. By the mid-eighties the tools were more advanced than this. Sleeker. The perforations were smaller. I hope this all helps you.'

Bosch nodded and said, 'What about the teeth? Anything there?'

'We are missing the lower mandible,' Golliher said. 'On the upper teeth present there is no indication of any dental work despite indication of antemortem decay. This in itself is a clue. I think it puts this boy in the lower levels of social classification. He didn't go to the dentist.'

Edgar had pulled his mask down around his neck. His expression was pained.

'When this kid was in the hospital with the hematoma, why wouldn't he tell the doctors what was happening to him? What about his teachers, his friends?'

'You know the answers to that as well as me, Detective,' Golliher said. 'Children are reliant on their parents. They are scared of them and they love them, don't want to lose them. Sometimes there is no explanation for why they don't cry out for help.'

'What about all these fractures and such? Why didn't the doctors see it and do something?'

'That's the irony of what I do. I see the history and tragedy so clearly. But with a living patient it might not be apparent. If the parents came in with a plausible explanation for the boy's injury, what reason would a doctor have to X-ray an arm or a leg or a chest? None. And so the nightmare goes unnoticed.'

Unsatisfied, Edgar shook his head and walked to the far corner of the room.

'Anything else, Doctor?' Bosch asked.

Golliher checked his notes and then folded his arms.

'That's it on a scientific level – you'll get the report. On a purely personal level, I hope you find the person who did this. They will deserve whatever they get, and then some.'

Bosch nodded.

'We'll get him,' Edgar said. 'Don't you worry about that.'

They walked out of the building and got into Bosch's car. Bosch just sat there for a moment before starting the engine. Finally, he hit the steering wheel hard with the heel of his palm, sending a shock down the injured side of his chest.

'You know it doesn't make me believe in God like him,' Edgar said. 'Makes me believe in aliens, little green men from outer space.'

Bosch looked over at him. Edgar was leaning his head against the side window, looking down at the floor of the car.

'How so?'

'Because a human couldn't have done this to his own kid. A spaceship must've come down and abducted the kid and done all that stuff to him. Only explanation.'

'Yeah, I wish that was on the checklist, Jerry. Then we could all just go home.'

Bosch put the car into drive.

'I need a drink.'

He started driving out of the lot.

'Not me, man,' Edgar said. 'I just want to go see my kid and hug him until this gets better.'

They didn't speak again until they got over to Parker Center.

8

Bosch and Edgar rode the elevator to the fifth floor and went into the SID lab, where they had a meeting set up with Antoine Jesper, the lead criminalist assigned to the bones case. Jesper met them at the security fence and took them back. He was a young black man with gray eyes and smooth skin. He wore a white lab coat that swayed and flapped with his long strides and always moving arms.

'This way, guys,' he said. 'I don't have a lot but what I got is yours.'

He took them through the main lab, where only a handful of other criminalists were working, and into the drying room, a large climate-controlled space where clothing and other material evidence from cases were spread on stainless steel drying tables and examined. It was the only place that could rival the autopsy floor of the medical examiner's office in the stench of decay.

Jesper led them to two tables where Bosch saw the open backpack and several pieces of clothing blackened with soil and fungus. There was also a plastic sandwich bag filled with an unrecognizable lump of black decay.

'Water and mud got into the backpack,' Jesper said. 'Leached in over time, I guess.'

Jesper took a pen out of the pocket of his lab coat and extended it into a pointer. He used it to help illustrate his commentary.

'We've got your basic backpack containing three sets of clothes and what was probably a sandwich or some kind of food item. More specifically, three T-shirts, three underwear, three sets of socks. And the food item. There was also an envelope, or what was left of an envelope. You don't see that here because documents has it. But don't get your hopes up, guys. It was in worse shape than that sandwich – *if* it was a sandwich.'

Bosch nodded. He made a list of the contents in his notebook.

'Any identifiers?' he asked.

Jesper shook his head.

'No personal identifiers on the clothing or in the bag,' he said. 'But two things to note. First, this shirt here has a brand name identifier. 'Solid Surf.' Says it across the chest. You can't see it now but I picked it up with the black light. Might help, might not. If you are not familiar with the term 'Solid Surf,' I can tell you that it is a skateboarding reference.'

'Got it,' Bosch said.

'Next is the outside flap of the bag.'

He used his pointer to flip over the flap.

'Cleaned this up a little bit and came up with this.'

Bosch leaned over the table to look. The bag was made of blue canvas. On the flap was a clear demarcation of color forming a large letter B at the center.

'It looks like there was some kind of adhesive applicate at one time on the bag,' Jesper said. 'It's gone now and I don't really know if that occurred before or after this thing was put in the ground. My guess is before. It looks like it was peeled off.'

Bosch stepped back from the table and wrote a few lines in his notebook. He then looked at Jesper.

'Okay, Antoine, good stuff. Anything else?'

'Not on this stuff.'

'Then let's go to documents.'

Jesper led the way again through the central lab and then into a sub-lab where he had to enter a combination into a door lock to enter.

The documents lab contained two rows of desks that were all empty. Each desk had a horizontal light box and a magnifying glass mounted on a pivot. Jesper went to the middle desk in the second row. The nameplate on the desk said Bernadette Fornier. Bosch knew her. They had worked a case previously in which a suicide note had been forged. He knew she did good work.

Jesper picked up a plastic evidence pouch that was sitting in the middle of the desk. He unzipped it and removed two plastic viewing sleeves. One contained an unfolded envelope that was brown and smeared with black fungus. The other contained a deteriorated rectangular piece of paper that was broken into three parts along the folds and was also grossly discolored by decay and fungus.

'This is what happens when stuff gets wet, man,' Jesper said. 'It took Bernie all day just to unfold the envelope and separate the letter. As you can see, it came apart at the folds. And as far as whether we'll ever be able to tell what was in the letter, it doesn't look good.'

Bosch turned on the light box and put the plastic sleeves down on it. He swung the magnifier over and studied the envelope and the letter it had once contained. There was nothing remotely readable on either document. One thing he noted was that it looked like there was no stamp on the envelope.

'Damn,' he said.

He flipped the sleeves over and kept looking. Edgar came over next to him as if to confirm the obvious.

'Woulda been nice,' he said.

'What will she do now?' Bosch asked Jesper.

'Well, she'll probably try some dyes, some different lights. Try to get something that reacts with the ink, brings it up. But she wasn't too optimistic yesterday. So like I said, I wouldn't be getting my hopes up about it.'

Bosch nodded and turned off the light.

9

Near the back entrance to the Hollywood Division station was a bench with large sand-filled ashtrays on either side. It was called the Code 7, after the radio call for out-of-service or on break. At 11:15 p.m. on Saturday night Bosch was the only occupant on the Code 7 bench. He wasn't smoking, though he wished he was. He was waiting. The bench was dimly lit by the lights over the station's back door and had a view of the parking lot jointly shared by the station and the firehouse on the back end of the city complex.

Bosch watched as the patrol units came in from the three-to-eleven shift and the officers went into the station to change out of uniforms, shower and call it a night, if they could. He looked down at the MagLite he held in his hands and rubbed his thumb over the end cap and felt the scratchings where Julia Brasher had etched her badge number.

He hefted the light and then flipped it in his hand, feeling its weight. He flashed on what Golliher had said about the weapon that had killed the boy. He could add flashlight to the list.

Bosch watched a patrol car come into the lot and park by the motor pool garage. A cop he recognized as Julia Brasher's partner, Edgewood, emerged from the passenger side and headed into the station carrying the car's shotgun. Bosch waited and watched, suddenly unsure of his plan and wondering if he could abandon it and get into the station without being seen.

Before he decided on a move Brasher got out of the driver's side and headed toward the station door. She walked with her head down, the posture of someone tired and beat from a long day. Bosch knew the feeling. He also thought something might be wrong. It was a subtle thing, but the way Edgewood had gone in and left her behind told Bosch something was off. Since Brasher was a rookie, Edgewood was her training officer, even though he was at least five years younger than her. Maybe it was just an awkward situation because of age and gender. Or maybe it was something else.

Brasher didn't notice Bosch on the bench. She was almost to the station door before he spoke.

'Hey, you forgot to wash the puke out of the back seat.'

She looked back while continuing to walk until she saw it was him. She stopped then and walked over to the bench.

'I brought you something,' Bosch said.

He held out the flashlight. She smiled tiredly as she took it.

'Thank you, Harry. You didn't have to wait here to—'

'I wanted to.'

There was an awkward silence for a moment.

'Were you working the case tonight?' she asked.

'More or less. Started the paperwork. And we sort of got the autopsy earlier today. If you could call it an autopsy.'

'I can tell by your face it was bad.'

Bosch nodded. He felt strange. He was still sitting and she was still standing.

'I can tell by the way you look that you had a tough one, too.'

'Aren't they all?'

Before Bosch could say anything two cops, fresh from showers and in street clothes, came out of the station and headed toward their personal cars.

'Cheer up, Julia,' one of them said. 'We'll see you over there.'

'Okay, Kiko,' she said back.

She turned and looked back down at Bosch. She smiled.

'Some people from the shift are getting together over at Boardner's,' she said. 'You want to come?'

'Um . . . '

'That's okay. I just thought maybe you could use a drink or something.'

'I could. I need one. Actually, that's why I was waiting here for you. I just don't know if I want to get into a group thing at a bar.'

'Well, what were you thinking, then?'

Bosch checked his watch. It was now eleven-thirty.

'Depending on how long you take in the locker room, we could probably catch the last martini call at Musso's.'

She smiled broadly now.

'I love that place. Give me fifteen minutes.'

She headed toward the station door without waiting for a reply from him.

'I'll be here,' he called after her.

10

Musso and Frank's was an institution that had been serving martinis to the denizens of Hollywood – both famous and infamous – for a century. The front room was all red leather booths and quiet conversation with ancient waiters in red half-coats moving slowly about. The back room contained the long bar, where most nights it was standing room only while patrons vied for the attention of bartenders who could have been the fathers of the waiters. As Bosch and Brasher came into the bar two patrons slipped off their stools to leave. Bosch and Brasher quickly moved in, beating two black-clad studio types to the choice spots. A bartender who recognized Bosch came over and they both ordered vodka martinis, slightly dirty.

Bosch was already feeling at ease with her. They had spent lunch together at the crime scene picnic tables the last two days and she had never been far from his sight during the hillside searches. They had ridden over to Musso's together in his car and it seemed like a third or fourth date already. They small-talked about the division and the details Bosch was willing to part with about his case. By the time the bartender put down their martini glasses along with the sidecar carafes, he was ready to forget about bones and blood and baseball bats for a while.

They clinked glasses and Brasher said, 'To life.'

'Yeah,' Bosch said. 'Getting through another day.'

'Just barely.'

Bosch knew that now was the time to talk to her about what was troubling her. If she didn't want to talk, he wouldn't press it.

'That guy you called Kiko in the back lot, why'd he tell you to cheer up?'

She slumped a little and didn't answer at first.

'If you don't want to talk about—'

'No, it's not that. It's more like I don't want to *think* about it.'

'I know the feeling. Forget I asked.'

'No, it's okay. My partner's going to write me up and since I'm on probation, it could cost me.'

'Write you up for what?'

'Crossing the tube.'

It was a tactical expression, meaning to walk in front of the barrel of a shotgun or other weapon held by a fellow officer.

'What happened? I mean, if you want to talk about it.'

She shrugged and they both took long drinks from their glasses.

'Oh, it was a domestic – I hate domestics – and the guy locked himself in the bedroom with a gun. We didn't know if he was going to use it on himself, his wife or us. We waited for backup and then we were going to go in.'

She took another drink. Bosch watched her. Her inner turmoil showed clearly in her eyes.

'Edgewood had shotgun. Kiko had the kick. Fennel, Kiko's partner, and I had the door. So we did the deed. Kiko's big. He opened the door with one kick. Fennel and I went in. The guy was passed out on the bed. Seemed like no problem but Edgewood had a big problem with me. He said I crossed the tube.'

'Did you?'

'I don't think so. But if I did, then so did Fennel, and he didn't say jack to him.'

'You're the rookie. You're the one on probation.'

'Yeah, and I'm getting tired of it, that's for sure. I mean, how did you make it through, Harry? Right now you've got a job that makes a difference. What I do, just chasing the radio all day and night, going from dirtbag to dirtbag, it's like spitting on a house fire. We're not making any headway out there and on top of that I've got this uptight male asshole telling me every two minutes how I fucked up.'

Bosch knew what she was feeling. Every cop in a uniform went through it. You wade through the cesspool every day and soon it seems that that is all there is. An abyss. It was why he could never go back to working patrol. Patrol was a Band-Aid on a bullet hole.

'Did you think it would be different? When you were in the academy, I mean.'

'I don't know what I thought. I just don't know if I can make it through to a point where I think I'm making any difference.'

'I think you can. The first couple years are tough. But you dig in and you start seeing the long view. You pick your battles and you pick your path. You'll do all right.'

He didn't feel confident giving her the rah-rah speech. He had gone through long stretches of indecision about himself and his choices. Telling her to stick it out made him feel a little false.

'Let's talk about something else,' she said.

'Fine with me,' he said.

He took a long drink from his glass, trying to think of how to turn the conversation in another direction. He put his glass down, turned and smiled at her.

'So there you were, hiking in the Andes and you said to yourself, "Gee, I wanna be a cop."'

She laughed, seemingly shaking off the blues of her earlier comments.

'Not quite like that. And I've never been in the Andes.'

'Well, what about the rich, full life you lived before putting on the badge? You said you were a world traveler.'

'Never made it to South America.'

'Is that where the Andes are? All this time I thought they were in Florida.'

She laughed again and Bosch felt good about successfully changing the subject. He liked looking at her teeth when she laughed. They were just a little bit crooked and in a way that made them perfect.

'So seriously, what did you do?'

She turned in the stool so they were shoulder to shoulder, looking at each other in the mirror behind all the colored bottles lined along the back wall of the bar.

'Oh, I was a lawyer for a while – not a defense lawyer, so don't get excited. Civil law. Then I realized that was bullshit and quit and just started traveling. I worked along the way. I made pottery in Venice, Italy. I was a horse guide in the Swiss Alps for a while. I was cook on a day-trip tourist boat in Hawaii. I did other things and I just saw a lot of the world – except for the Andes. Then I came home.'

'To L.A.?'

'Born and raised. You?'

'Same. Queen of Angels.'

'Cedars.'

She held out her glass and they clinked.

'To the few, the proud, the brave,' she said.

Bosch finished off his glass and poured in the contents of his sidecar. He was way ahead of Brasher but didn't care. He was feeling relaxed. It was good to forget about things for a while. It was good to be with somebody not directly related to the case.

'Born at Cedars, huh?' he asked. 'Where'd you grow up?'

'Don't laugh. Bel Air.'

'Bel Air? I guess somebody's daddy isn't too happy about her joining the cops.'

'Especially since his was the law firm she walked out of one day and wasn't heard from for two years.'

Bosch smiled and raised his glass. She clicked hers off it.

'Brave girl.'

After they put their glasses down, she said, 'Let's stop all the questions.'

'Okay,' Bosch said. 'And do what?'

'Just take me home, Harry. To your place.'

He paused for a moment, looking at her shiny blue eyes. Things were moving lightning fast, greased on the smooth runners of alcohol. But that was often the way it was between cops, between people who felt they were part of a closed society, who lived by their instincts and went to work each day knowing that how they made their living could kill them.

'Yeah,' he finally said, 'I was just thinking the same thing.'

He leaned over and kissed her on the mouth.

11

Julia Brasher stood in the living room of Bosch's house and looked at the CDs stored in the racks next to the stereo.

'I love jazz.'

Bosch was in the kitchen. He smiled when he heard her say it. He finished pouring the two martinis out of a shaker and came out to the living room and handed her a glass.

'Who do you like?'

'Ummm, lately Bill Evans.'

Bosch nodded, went to the rack and came up with *Kind of Blue.* He loaded it into the stereo.

'Bill and Miles,' he said. 'Not to mention Coltrane and a few other guys. Nothing better.'

As the music began he picked up his martini and she came over and tapped it with her glass. Rather than drink, they kissed each other. She started laughing halfway through the kiss.

'What?' he said.

'Nothing. I'm just feeling reckless. And happy.'

'Yeah, me too.'

'I think it was you giving me the flashlight.'

Bosch was puzzled.

'What do you mean?'

'You know, it's so phallic.'

The look on Bosch's face made her laugh again and she spilled some of her drink on the floor.

Later, when she was lying face down on his bed, Bosch was tracing the outline of the flaming sun tattooed on the small of her back and thinking about how comfortable and yet strange she felt to him. He knew almost nothing about her. Like the tattoo, there seemed to be a surprise from every angle of view he had on her.

'What are you thinking about?' she asked.

'Nothing. Just wondering about the guy who got to put this on your back. I wish it had been me, I guess.'

'How come?'

'Because there will always be a piece of him with you.'

She turned on her side, revealing her breasts and her smile. Her hair was out of its braid and down around her shoulders. He liked that, too. She reached up and pulled him down into a long kiss. Then she said, 'That's the nicest thing that's been said to me in a long time.'

He put his head down on her pillow. He could smell the sweet scent of perfume and sex and sweat.

'You don't have any pictures on your walls,' she said. 'Photos, I mean.'

He shrugged his shoulders.

She turned over so her back was to him. He reached under her arm and cupped one of her breasts and pulled her back into him.

'Can you stay till the morning?' he asked.

'Well . . . my husband will probably wonder where I am, but I guess I could call him.'

Bosch froze. Then she started laughing.

'Don't scare me like that.'

'Well, you never even asked me if I was involved with anyone.'

'You didn't ask me.'

'You were obvious. The lone detective type.' And then in a deep male voice: 'Just the facts, ma'am. No time for dames. Murder is my business. I have a job to do and I am—'

He ran his thumb down her side, over the indentations of her ribs. She cut off her words with laughter.

'You lent me your flashlight,' he said. 'I didn't think an "involved" woman would have done that.'

'And I've got news for you, tough guy. I saw the Mag in your trunk. In the box before you covered it up. You weren't fooling anybody.'

Bosch rolled back on the other pillow, embarrassed. He could feel his face getting red. He brought his hands up to hide it.

'Oh, God . . . Mr. Obvious.'

She rolled over to him and peeled back his hands. She kissed him on the chin.

'I thought it was nice. Kinda made my day and gave me something to maybe look forward to.'

She turned his hands back and looked at the scarring across the knuckles. They were old marks and not very noticeable anymore.

'Hey, what is this?'

'Just scars.'

'I know that. From what?'

'I had tattoos. I took them off. It was a long time ago.'

'How come?'

'They made me take them off when I went into the army.'

She started to laugh.

'Why, what did it say, Fuck the army or something?'

'No, nothing like that.'

'Then what? Come on, I want to know.'

'It said H-O-L-D on one hand and F-A-S-T on the other.'

'Hold fast? What does "hold fast" mean?'

'Well, it's kind of a long story . . . '

'I have time. My husband doesn't mind.'

She smiled.

'Come on, I want to know.'

'It's not a big deal. When I was a kid, one of the times I ran away I ended up down in San Pedro. Down around the fishing docks. And a lot of those guys down there, the fishermen, the tuna guys, I saw they had this on their hands. Hold fast. And I asked one of them about it and he told me it was like their motto, their philosophy. It's like when they were out there in those boats, way out there for weeks, and the waves got huge and it got scary, you just had to grab on and hold fast.'

Bosch made two fists and held them up.

'Hold fast to life . . . to everything that you have.'

'So you had it done. How old were you?'

'I don't know, sixteen, thereabouts.'

He nodded and then he smiled.

'What I didn't know was that those tuna guys got it from some navy guys. So a year later I go waltzing into the army with "Hold Fast" on my hands and the first thing my sergeant told me was to get rid of it. He wasn't going to have any squid tattoo on one of his guys' hands.'

She grabbed his hands and looked closely at the knuckles.

'This doesn't look like laser work.'

Bosch shook his head.

'They didn't have lasers back then.'

'So what did you do?'

'My sergeant, his name was Rosser, took me out of the barracks and over to the back of the administration building. There was a brick wall. He made me punch it. Until every one of my knuckles was cut up. Then after they were scabbed up in about a week he made me do it again.'

'Jesus fucking Christ, that's barbaric.'

'No, that's the army.'

He smiled at the memory. It wasn't as bad as it sounded. He looked down at his hands. The music stopped and he got up and walked through the house naked to change it. When he came back to the bedroom, she recognized the music.

'Clifford Brown?'

He nodded and came toward the bed. He didn't think he had ever known a woman who could identify jazz music like that.

'Stand there.'

'What?'

'Let me look at you. Tell me about those other scars.'

The room was dimly lit by a light from the bathroom but Bosch became conscious of his nakedness. He was in good shape but he was more than fifteen years older than her. He wondered if she had ever been with a man so old.

'Harry, you look great. You totally turn me on, okay? What about the other scars?'

He touched the thick rope of skin above his left hip.

'This? This was a knife.'

'Where'd that happen?'

'A tunnel.'

'And your shoulder?'

'Bullet.'

'Where?'

He smiled.

'A tunnel.'

'Ouch, stay out of tunnels.'

'I try.'

He got into the bed and pulled the sheet up. She touched his shoulder, running her thumb over the thick skin of the scar.

'Right in the bone,' she said.

'Yeah, I got lucky. No permanent damage. It aches in the winter and when it rains, that's about it.'

'What did it feel like? Being shot, I mean.'

Bosch shrugged his shoulders.

'It hurt like hell and then everything sort of went numb.'

'How long were you down?'

'About three months.'

'You didn't get a disability out?'

'It was offered. I declined.'

'How come?'

'I don't know. I like the job, I guess. And I thought that if I stuck with it, someday I'd meet this beautiful young cop who'd be impressed by all my scars.'

She jammed him in the ribs and the pain made him grimace.

'Oh, poor baby,' she said in a mocking voice.

'That hurt.'

She touched the tattoo on his shoulder.

'What's that supposed to be, Mickey Mouse on acid?'

'Sort of. It's a tunnel rat.'

Her face lost all trace of humor.

'What's the matter?'

'You were in Vietnam,' she said, putting things together. 'I've been in those tunnels.'

'What do you mean?'

'When I was on the road. I spent six weeks in Vietnam. The tunnels, they're like a tourist thing now. You pay your money and you can go down into them. It must've been . . . what you had to do must've been so frightening.'

'It was more scary afterward. Thinking about it.'

'They have them roped off so they can sort of control where you go. But nobody really watches you. So I went under the rope and went further in. It got so dark in there, Harry.'

Bosch studied her eyes.

'And did you see it?' he asked quietly. 'The lost light?'

She held his eyes for a moment and nodded.

'I saw it. My eyes adjusted and there was light. Almost like a whisper. But it was enough for me to find my way.'

'Lost light. We called it lost light. We never knew where it came from. But it was down there. Like smoke hanging in the dark. Some people said it wasn't light, that it was the ghosts of everybody who died in those things. From both sides.'

They spoke no more after that. They held each other and soon she was asleep.

Bosch realized he had not thought about the case for more than three hours. At first this made him feel guilty but then he let it go and soon he too was asleep. He dreamed he was moving through a tunnel. But he wasn't crawling. It was as if he were underwater and moving like an eel through the labyrinth. He came to a dead end and there was a boy sitting against the curve of the tunnel's wall. He had his knees up and his face down, buried in his folded arms.

'Come with me,' Bosch said.

The boy peeked his eyes over one arm and looked up at Bosch. A single bubble of air rose from his mouth. He then looked past Bosch as if something was coming up behind him. Bosch turned around but there was only the darkness of the tunnel behind him.

When he looked back at the boy, he was gone.

12

Late Sunday morning Bosch drove Brasher to the Hollywood station so she could get her car and he could resume work on the case. She was off duty Sundays and Mondays. They made plans to meet at her house in Venice that night for dinner. There were other officers in the parking lot when Bosch dropped her next to her car. Bosch knew that word would get around quickly that it appeared they had spent the night together.

'I'm sorry,' he said. 'I should have thought it out better last night.'

'I don't really care, Harry. I'll see you tonight.'

'Hey, look, you should care. Cops can be brutal.'

She made a face.

'Oh, police brutality, yeah, I've heard of it.'

'I'm serious. It's also against regs. On my part. I'm a D-three. Supervisor level.'

She looked at him a moment.

'Well, that's your call, then. I'll see you tonight. I hope.'

She got out and closed the door. Bosch drove on to his assigned parking slot and went into the detective bureau, trying not to think of the complications he might have just invited into his life.

It was deserted in the squad room, which was what he was hoping for. He wanted time alone with the case. There was still a lot of office work to do but he also wanted to step back and think about all the evidence and information that had been accumulated since the discovery of the bones.

The first thing to do was put together a list of what needed to be done. The murder book – the blue binder containing all written reports pertaining to the case – had to be completed. He had to draw up search warrants seeking medical records of brain surgeries at local hospitals. He had to run routine computer checks on all the residents living in the vicinity of the crime scene on Wonderland. He also had to read through all the call-in tips spawned by the media coverage of the bones on the hill and start gathering missing person and runaway reports that might match the victim.

He knew it was more than a day's work if he labored by himself but decided to keep with his decision to allow Edgar the day off. His partner, the father of a thirteen-year-old boy, had been greatly upset by Golliher's report the day before and Bosch wanted him to take a break. The days ahead would likely be long and just as emotionally upsetting.

Once Bosch had his list together he took his cup out of a drawer and went back to the watch office to get coffee. The smallest he had on him was a five-dollar bill but he put it in the coffee fund basket without taking any change. He figured he'd be drinking more than his share through the day.

'You know what they say?' someone said behind him as he was filling the cup.

Bosch turned. It was Mankiewicz, the watch sergeant.

'About what?'

'Fishing off the company dock.'

'I don't know. What do they say?'

'I don't know either. That's why I was asking you.'

Mankiewicz smiled and moved toward the machine to warm up his cup.

So already it was starting to get around, Bosch thought. Gossip and innuendo – especially anything with a sexual tone – moved through a police station like a fire racing up a hill in August.

'Well, let me know when you find out,' Bosch said as he started for the door of the watch office. 'Could be useful to know.'

'Will do. Oh, and one other thing, Harry.'

Bosch turned, ready for another shot from Mankiewicz.

'What?'

'Just stop fooling around and wrap up your case. I'm tired of my guys having to take all the calls.'

There was a facetious tone in his voice. In his humor and sarcasm was a legitimate complaint about his officers on the desk being tied up by the tip calls.

'Yeah, I know. Any good ones today?'

'Not that I could tell, but you'll get to slog through the reports and use your investigative wiles to decide that.'

'Wiles?'

'Yes, wiles. Like Wile E. Coyote. Oh, and CNN must've had a slow morning and picked up the story – good video, all you brave guys on the hill with your makeshift stairs and little boxes of bones. So now we're getting the long-distance calls. Topeka and Providence so far this morning. It's not going to end until you clear it, Harry. We're all counting on you back here.'

Again there was a smile – and a message – behind what he was saying.

'All right, I'll use all my wiles. I promise, Mank.'

'That's what we're counting on.'

Back at the table Bosch sipped his coffee and let the details of the case move through his mind. There were anomalies, contradictions. There were the conflicts between location choice and method of burial noticed by

Kathy Kohl. But the conclusions made by Golliher added even more to the list of questions. Golliher saw it as a child abuse case. But the backpack full of clothes was an indication that the victim, the boy, was possibly a runaway.

Bosch had spoken to Edgar about it the day before when they returned to the station from the SID lab. His partner was not as sure of the conflict as Bosch but offered a theory that perhaps the boy was the victim of child abuse both at the hands of his parents and then an unrelated killer. He rightfully pointed out that many victims of abuse run away only to be drawn into another form of abusive relationship. Bosch knew the theory was legitimate but tried not to let himself go down that road because he knew it was even more depressing than the scenario Golliher had spun.

His direct line rang and Bosch answered, expecting it to be Edgar or Lt. Billets checking in. It was a reporter from the *L.A. Times* named Josh Meyer. Bosch barely knew him and was sure he'd never given him the direct line. He didn't let on that he was annoyed, however. Though tempted to tell the reporter that the police were running down leads extending as far as Topeka and Providence, he simply said there was no further update on the investigation since Friday's briefing from the Media Relations office.

After he hung up he finished his first cup of coffee and got down to work. The part of an investigation Bosch enjoyed the least was the computer work. Whenever possible he gave it to his partners to handle. So he decided to put the computer runs at the end of his list and started with a quick look through the accumulated tip sheets from the watch office.

There were about three dozen more sheets since he had last looked through the pile on Friday. None contained enough information to be helpful or worth pursuing at the moment. Each was from a parent or sibling or friend of someone who had disappeared. All of them permanently forlorn and seeking some kind of closure to the most pressing mystery of their lives.

He thought of something and rolled his chair over to one of the old IBM Selectrics. He inserted a sheet of paper and typed out four questions.

Do you know if your missing loved one underwent any kind of surgical procedure in the months before his disappearance?
If so, what hospital was he treated at?
What was the injury?
What was the name of his physician?

He rolled the page out and took it to the watch office. He gave it to Mankiewicz to be used as a template of questions to be asked of all callers about the bones.

'That wily enough for you?' Bosch asked.

'No, but it's a start.'

While he was there Bosch took a plastic cup and filled it with coffee and then came back to the bureau and dumped it into his cup. He made a note to ask Lt. Billets on Monday to procure some help in contacting all the callers of the last few days to ask the same medical questions. He then thought of Julia Brasher. He knew she was off on Mondays and would volunteer if needed. But he quickly dismissed it, knowing that by Monday the whole station would know about them and bringing her into the case would make matters worse.

He started the search warrants next. It was a matter of routine in homicide work to need medical records in the course of an investigation. Most often these records came from physicians and dentists. But hospitals were not unusual. Bosch kept a file with search warrant templates for hospitals as well as a listing of all twenty-nine hospitals in the Los Angeles area and the attorneys who handled legal filings at each location. Having all of this handy allowed him to draw up twenty-nine search warrants in a little over an hour. The warrants sought the records of all male patients under the age of sixteen who underwent brain surgery entailing the use of a trephine drill between 1975 and 1985.

After printing out the requests he put them in his briefcase. While normally it was proper on a weekend to fax a search warrant to a judge's home for approval and signature, it would certainly not be acceptable to fax twenty-nine requests to a judge on a Sunday afternoon. Besides, the hospital lawyers would not be available on a Sunday anyway. Bosch's plan was to take the warrants to a judge first thing Monday morning, then divide them with Edgar and hand-deliver them to the hospitals, thereby being able to push the urgency of the matter with the lawyers in person. Even if things went according to plan, Bosch didn't expect to start receiving returns of records from the hospitals until mid-week or later.

Bosch next typed out a daily case summary as well as a recap of the anthropological information from Golliher. He put these in the murder book and then typed up an evidence report detailing the preliminary SID findings on the backpack.

When he was finished Bosch leaned back and thought about the unreadable letter that had been found in the backpack. He did not anticipate that the documents section would have any success with it. It would forever be the mystery shrouded in the mystery of the case. He gulped the last of his second cup of coffee and opened the murder book to the page containing a copy of the crime scene sketch and chart. He studied the chart and noted that the backpack had been found right next to the spot Kohl had marked as the probable original location of the body.

Bosch wasn't sure what it all meant but instinctively he knew that the questions he now had about the case should be kept foremost in his mind as new evidence and details continued to be gathered. They would be the screen through which everything would be sifted.

He put the report into the murder book and then finished the updating of the paperwork by bringing the investigator's log – an hour-by-hour time chart with small entry blocks – up to date. He then put the murder book in his briefcase.

Bosch took his coffee cup to the sink in the rest room and washed it out. He then returned it to its drawer, picked up his briefcase and headed out the back door to his car.

13

The basement of Parker Center, the headquarters of the Los Angeles Police Department, serves as the record archives for every case the department has taken a report on in the modern era. Until the mid-nineties records were kept on paper for a period of eight years and then transferred to microfiche for permanent storage. The department now used computers for permanent storage and was also moving backward, putting older files into digital storage banks. But the process was slow and had not gone further back than the late eighties.

Bosch arrived at the counter in archives at one o'clock. He had two containers of coffee with him and two roast beef sandwiches from Philippe's in a paper bag. He looked at the clerk and smiled.

'Believe it or not I need to see the fiche on missing person reports, nineteen seventy-five to 'eighty-five.'

The clerk, an old guy with a basement pallor, whistled and said, 'Look out, Christine, here they come.'

Bosch smiled and nodded and didn't know what the man was talking about. There appeared to be no one else behind the counter.

'The good news is they break up,' the clerk said. 'I mean, I think it's good news. You looking for adult or juvy records?'

'Juveniles.'

'Then that cuts it up a bit.'

'Thanks.'

'Don't mention it.'

The clerk disappeared from the counter and Bosch waited. In four minutes the man came back with ten small envelopes containing microfiche sheets for the years Bosch requested. Altogether the stack was at least four inches thick.

Bosch went to a microfiche reader and copier, set out a sandwich and the two coffees and took the second sandwich back to the counter. The clerk refused the first offer but then took the sandwich when Bosch said it was from Philippe's.

Bosch went back to the machine and started fiche-ing, wading first into the year 1985. He was looking for missing person and runaway reports of young males in the age range of the victim. Once he got proficient with the machine he was able to move quickly through the reports. He would scan first for the 'closed' stamp that indicated the missing individual had returned home or been located. If there was no stamp his eyes would immediately go to the age and sex boxes on the form. If they fit the profile of his victim, he'd read the summary and then push the photocopy button on the machine to get a hard copy to take with him.

The microfiche also contained records of missing person reports forwarded to the LAPD by outside agencies seeking people believed to have gone to Los Angeles.

Despite his speed at the task, it took Bosch more than three hours to go through all the reports for the ten years he had requested. He had hard copies of more than three hundred reports in the tray to the side of the machine when he was finished. And he had no idea whether his effort had been worth the time or not.

Bosch rubbed his eyes and pinched the bridge of his nose. He had a headache from staring at the machine's screen and reading tale after tale of parental anguish and juvenile angst. He looked over and realized he hadn't eaten his sandwich.

He returned the stack of microfiche envelopes to the clerk and decided to do the computer work in Parker Center rather than drive back to Hollywood. From Parker Center he could jump on the 10 Freeway and shoot out to Venice for dinner at Julia Brasher's house. It would be easier.

The squad room of the Robbery-Homicide Division was empty except for the two on-call detectives who were sitting in front of a television watching a football game. One of them was Bosch's former partner, Kizmin Rider. The other Bosch didn't recognize. Rider stood up smiling when she saw it was Bosch.

'Harry, what are you doing here?' she asked.

'Working a case. I want to use a computer, that all right?'

'That bone thing?'

He nodded.

'I heard about it on the news. Harry, this is Rick Thornton, my partner.'

Bosch shook his hand and introduced himself.

'I hope she makes you look as good as she did me.'

Thornton just nodded and smiled and Rider looked embarrassed.

'Come on over to my desk,' she said. 'You can use my computer.'

She showed him the way and let him sit in her seat.

'We're just twiddling our thumbs here. Nothing happening. I don't even like football.'

'Don't complain about the slow days. Didn't anybody ever tell you that?'

'Yeah, my old partner. Only thing he ever said that made any sense.'

'I bet.'

'Anything I can do to help?'

'I'm just running the names – the usual.'

He opened his briefcase and took out the murder book. He opened it to a page where he had listed the names, addresses and birth dates of residents on Wonderland Avenue who had been interviewed during the neighborhood canvas. It was a matter of routine and due diligence to run the name of every person investigators came across in an investigation.

'You want a coffee or something?' Rider asked.

'Nah, I'm fine. Thanks, Kiz.'

He nodded in the direction of Thornton, who had his back to them and was on the other side of the room.

'How are things going?'

She shrugged her shoulders.

'Every now and then he lets me do some real detective work,' she said in a whisper.

'Well, you can always come back to Hollywood,' he whispered back with a smile.

He started typing in the commands for entering the National Crime Index Computer. Immediately, Rider made a sound of derision.

'Harry, you're still typing with two fingers?'

'It's all I know, Kiz. I've been doing it this way for almost thirty years. You expect me to suddenly know how to type with ten fingers? I'm still not fluent in Spanish and don't know how to dance, either. You've only been gone a year.'

'Just get up, dinosaur. Let me do it. You'll be here all night.'

Bosch raised his hands in surrender and stood up. She sat down and went to work. Behind her back Bosch secretly smiled.

'Just like old times,' he said.

'Don't remind me. I always get the shit work. And stop smiling.'

She hadn't looked up from her typing. Her fingers were a blur above the keyboard. Bosch watched in awe.

'Hey, it's not like I planned this. I didn't know you were going to be here.'

'Yeah, like Tom Sawyer didn't know he had to paint a fence.'

'What?'

'Never mind. Tell me about the boot.'

Bosch was stunned.

'What?'

'Is that all you can say? You heard me. The rookie you're, uh . . . seeing.'

'How the hell do you know about it already?'

'I'm a highly skilled gatherer of information. And I still have sources in Hollywood.'

Bosch stepped away from her cubicle and shook his head.

'Well, is she nice? That's all I wanted to know. I don't want to pry.'

Bosch came back.

'Yes, she's nice. I hardly know her. You seem to know more about her and me *than* me.'

'You havin' dinner with her tonight?'

'Yeah, I'm having dinner with her.'

'Hey, Harry?'

Rider's voice had lost any note of humor.

'What?'

'You got a pretty good hit here.'

Bosch leaned down and looked at the screen. After digesting the information he said, 'I don't think I'm going to make it to dinner tonight.'

14

Bosch pulled to a stop in front of the house and studied the darkened windows and porch.

'Figures,' Edgar said. 'The guy ain't even going to be home. Probably already in the wind.'

Edgar was annoyed with Bosch, who had called him in from home. The way he figured it, the bones had been in the ground twenty years, what was the harm of waiting until Monday morning to talk to this guy? But Bosch said he was going by himself if Edgar didn't come in.

Edgar came in.

'No, he's home,' Bosch said.

'How d'you know?'

'I just know.'

He looked at his watch and wrote the time and address down on a page in his small notebook. It occurred to him then that the house they were at was the one where he had seen the curtain pulled closed behind a window on the evening of the first call out.

'Let's go,' he said. 'You talked to him the first time, so you take the lead. I'll jump in when it feels right.'

They got out and walked up the driveway to the house. The man they were visiting was named Nicholas Trent. He lived alone in the house, which was across the street and two houses down from the hillside where the bones had been found. Trent was fifty-seven years old. He had told Edgar during his initial canvas of the neighborhood that he was a set decorator for a studio in Burbank. He was unmarried and had no children. He knew nothing about the bones on the hill and could offer no clues or suggestions that were helpful.

Edgar knocked hard on the front door and they waited.

'Mr. Trent, it's the police,' he said loudly. 'Detective Edgar. Answer your door, please.'

He had raised his fist to hit the door again when the porch light went on. The door was then opened and a white man with a shaved scalp stood in the darkness within. The light from the porch slashed across his face.

'Mr. Trent? It's Detective Edgar. This is my partner, Detective Bosch. We have a few follow-up questions for you. If you don't mind.'

Bosch nodded but didn't offer his hand. Trent said nothing and Edgar forced the issue by putting his hand against the door and pushing it open.

'All right if we come in?' he asked, already halfway across the threshold.

'No, it's not all right,' Trent said quickly.

Edgar stopped and put a puzzled look on his face.

'Sir, we just have a few more questions we'd like to ask.'

'Yeah, and that's bullshit!'

'Excuse me?'

'We all know what is going on here. I talked to my attorney already. Your act is just that, an act. A bad one.'

Bosch could see they were not going to get anywhere with the trick-or-treat strategy. He stepped up and pulled Edgar back by the arm. Once his partner had cleared the threshold he looked at Trent.

'Mr. Trent, if you knew we'd be back, then you knew we'd find out about your past. Why didn't you tell Detective Edgar about it before? It could have saved us some time. Instead, it gives us suspicion. You can understand that, I'm sure.'

'Because the past is the past. I didn't bring it up. I buried the past. Leave it that way.'

'Not when there are bones buried in it,' Edgar said in an accusatory tone.

Bosch looked back at Edgar and gave him a look that said use some finesse.

'See?' Trent said. 'This is why I am saying, 'Go away.' I have nothing to tell you people. Nothing. I don't know anything about it.'

'Mr. Trent, you molested a nine-year-old boy,' Bosch said.

'The year was nineteen sixty-six and I was punished for it. Severely. It's the past. I've been a perfect citizen ever since. I had nothing to do with those bones up there.'

Bosch waited a moment and then spoke in a calm and quieter tone.

'If that is the truth, then let us come in and ask our questions. The sooner we clear you, the sooner we move on to other possibilities. But you have to understand something here. The bones of a young boy were found about a hundred yards from the home of a man who molested a young boy in nineteen sixty-six. I don't care what kind of citizen he's been since then, we need to ask him some questions. And we *will* ask those questions. We have no choice. Whether we do it in your home right now or with your lawyer at the station with all of the news cameras waiting outside, that's going to be your choice.'

He paused. Trent looked at him with scared eyes.

'So you can understand our situation, Mr. Trent, and we can certainly understand yours. We are willing to move quickly and discreetly but we can't without your cooperation.'

Trent shook his head as though he knew that no matter what he did now, his life as he knew it was in jeopardy and probably permanently altered. He finally stepped back and signaled Bosch and Edgar in.

Trent was barefoot and wearing baggy black shorts that showed off thin ivory legs with no hair on them. He wore a flowing silk shirt over his thin upper body. He had the same build as a ladder, all hard angles. He led them to a living room cluttered with antiques. He sat down in the center of a couch. Bosch and Edgar took the two leather club chairs opposite. Bosch decided to keep the lead. He didn't like the way Edgar had handled the door.

'To be cautious and careful, I am going to read you your constitutional rights,' he said. 'Then I'll ask you to sign a waiver form. This protects you as well as us. I am also going to record our conversation so that nobody ends up putting words in anybody else's mouth. If you want a copy of the tape I will make it available.'

Trent shrugged and Bosch took it as reluctant agreement. When Bosch had the form signed he slipped it into his briefcase and took out a small recorder. Once he started it and identified those present as well as the time and date, he nodded to Edgar to assume the lead again. This was because Bosch thought that observations of Trent and his surroundings were going to be more important than his answers now.

'Mr. Trent, how long have you lived in this house?'

'Since nineteen eighty-four.'

He then laughed.

'What is funny about that?' Edgar asked.

'Nineteen eighty-four. Don't you get it? George Orwell? Big Brother?'

He gestured toward Bosch and Edgar as the front men of Big Brother. Edgar apparently didn't follow the statement and continued with the interview.

'Rent or own?'

'Own. Uh, at first I rented, then I bought the house in 'eighty-seven from the landlord.'

'Okay, and you are a set designer in the entertainment industry?'

'Set decorator. There is a difference.'

'What is the difference?'

'The designer plans and supervises the construction of the set. The decorator then goes in and puts in the details. The little character strokes. The characters' belongings or tools. Like that.'

'How long have you done this?'

'Twenty-six years.'

'Did you bury that boy up on the hillside?'

Trent stood up indignantly.

'Absolutely not. I've never even set foot on that hill. And you people are making a big mistake if you waste your time on me when the true killer of that poor soul is still out there somewhere.'

Bosch leaned forward in his chair.

'Sit down, Mr. Trent,' he said.

The fervent way in which Trent delivered the denial made Bosch instinctively think he was either innocent or one of the better actors he had come across on the job. Trent slowly sat down on the couch again.

'You're a smart guy,' Bosch said, deciding to jump in. 'You know exactly what we're doing here. We have to bag you or clear you. It's that simple. So why don't you help us out? Instead of dancing around with us, why don't you tell us how to clear you?'

Trent raised his hands wide.

'I don't know how! I don't know anything about the case! How can I help you when I don't know the first thing about it?'

'Well, right off the bat, you can let us take a look around here. If I can start to get comfortable with you, Mr. Trent, then maybe I can start seeing it from your side of things. But right now . . . like I said, I've got you with your record and I've got bones across the street.'

Bosch held up his two hands as if he was holding those two things in them.

'It doesn't look that good from where I'm looking at things.'

Trent stood up and threw one hand out in a gesture toward the interior of the house.

'Fine! Be my guest. Look around to your heart's content. You won't find a thing because I had nothing to do with it. Nothing!'

Bosch looked at Edgar and nodded, the signal being that he should keep Trent occupied while Bosch took a look around.

'Thank you, Mr. Trent,' Bosch said as he stood up.

As he headed into a hallway that led to the rear of the house, he heard Edgar asking if Trent had ever seen any unusual activity on the hillside where the bones had been found.

'I just remember kids used to play up—'

He stopped, apparently when he realized that any mention he made of kids would only further suspicion about him. Bosch glanced back to make sure the red light of the recorder was still on.

'Did you like watching the kids play up there in the woods, Mr. Trent?' Edgar asked.

Bosch stayed in the hallway, out of sight but listening to Trent's answer.

'No, I couldn't see them if they were up in the woods. On occasion I would be driving up or walking my dog – when he was alive – and I would see the kids climbing up there. The girl across the street. The Fosters next door. All the kids around here. It's a city-owned right-of-way – the only undeveloped land in the neighborhood. So they went up there to play.

Some of the neighbors thought the older ones went up there to smoke cigarettes, and the concern was they would set the whole hillside on fire.'

'How long ago are you talking about?'

'Like when I first moved here. I didn't get involved. The neighbors who had been here took care of it.'

Bosch moved down the hall. It was a small house, not much bigger than his own. The hallway ended at a conjunction of three doors. Bedrooms on the right and left and a linen closet in the middle. He checked the closet first, found nothing unusual, and then moved into the bedroom on the right. It was Trent's bedroom. It was neatly kept but the tops of the twin bureaus and bed tables were cluttered with knickknacks that Bosch assumed Trent used on the job in helping to turn sets into real places for the camera.

He looked in the closet. There were several shoe boxes on the upper shelf. Bosch started opening them and found they contained old, worn-out shoes. It was apparently Trent's habit of buying new shoes and putting his old ones in the box, then shelving them. Bosch guessed that these, too, became part of his work inventory. He opened one box and found a pair of work boots. He noticed that dirt had dried hard in some of the treads. He thought about the dark soil where the bones had been found. Samples of it had been collected.

He put the boots back and made a mental note of it for the search warrant. His current search was just a cursory look around. If they moved to the next step with Trent and he became a full-fledged suspect, then they would come back with a search warrant and literally tear the place apart looking for evidence tying him to the bones. The work boots might be a good place to start. He was already on tape saying he had never been up on that hillside. If the dirt in the treads matched the soil samples from the excavation, then they'd have Trent caught in a lie. Most of what sparring with suspects was about was the locking in of a story. It was then that the investigator looked for the lies.

There was nothing else in the closet that warranted Bosch's attention. Same with the bedroom or the attached bathroom. Bosch, of course, knew that if Trent was the killer, he'd had many years to cover his tracks. He would also have had the last three days – since Edgar first questioned him during the canvas – to double-check his trail and be ready.

The other bedroom was used as an office and a storage room for his work. On the walls hung framed one-sheets advertising the films Bosch assumed Trent had worked on. Bosch had seen some of them on television but rarely went to theaters to see movies. He noticed that one of the frames held the one-sheet for a film called *The Art of the Cape*. Years before, Bosch had investigated the murder of that film's producer. He had heard that after that, the one-sheets from the movie had become collector items in underground Hollywood.

When he was finished looking around the rear of the house, Bosch went through a kitchen door into the garage. There were two bays, one containing Trent's minivan. The other was stacked with boxes with markings on them corresponding to rooms in a house. At first Bosch was shocked at the thought that Trent had still not completely unpacked after moving in nearly twenty years before. Then he realized the boxes were work related and used in the process of set decoration.

When he turned around he was looking at an entire wall hung with the heads of wild game, their black marble eyes staring at him. Bosch felt a nerve tickle run down his spine. All of his life he had hated seeing things like that. He wasn't sure why.

He spent another few minutes in the garage, mostly going through a box in the stack that was marked 'boy's room 9–12.' It contained toys, airplane models, a skateboard, and a football. He took the skateboard out for a few moments and studied it, all the while thinking about the shirt from the backpack with 'Solid Surf' printed on it. After a while he put the skateboard back in the box and closed it.

There was a side door to the garage that led to a path that went to the backyard. A pool took up most of the level ground before the yard rose into the steep, wooded hillside. It was too dark to see much and Bosch decided he would have to do the exterior look during daylight hours.

Twenty minutes after he left to begin the search Bosch returned to the living room empty-handed. Trent looked up at him expectantly.

'Satisfied?'

'I'm satisfied for now, Mr. Trent. I appreciate your—'

'You see? It never ends. 'Satisfied for now.' You people will never let it go, will you? I mean, if I was a drug dealer or a bank robber, my debt would be cleared and you people would leave me alone. But because I touched a boy almost forty years ago I am guilty for life.'

'I think you did more than touch him,' Edgar said. 'But we'll get the records. Don't worry.'

Trent put his face in his hands and mumbled something about it being a mistake to have cooperated. Bosch looked at Edgar, who nodded that he was finished and ready to go. Bosch stepped over and picked up his recorder. He slid it into the breast pocket of his jacket but didn't turn it off. He'd learned a valuable lesson on a case the year before – sometimes the most important and telling things are said after an interview is supposedly over.

'Mr. Trent, thank you for your cooperation. We're going to go. But we might need to talk to you tomorrow. Are you working tomorrow?'

'God, no, don't call me at work! I need this job and you'll ruin it. You'll ruin everything.'

He gave Bosch his pager number. Bosch wrote it down and headed toward the front door. He looked back at Edgar.

'Did you ask him about trips? He's not planning to go anywhere, is he?'

Edgar looked at Trent.

'Mr. Trent, you work on movies, you know how the dialogue goes. You call us if you plan to go out of town. If you don't and we have to find you . . . you're not going to like it very much.'

Trent spoke in a flat-line monotone, his eyes focused forward, somewhere far away.

'I'm not going anywhere at all. Now please leave. Just leave me alone.'

They walked out the door and Trent closed it hard behind them. At the bottom of the driveway was a large bougainvillea bush in full bloom. It blocked Bosch's view of the left side of the street until he got there.

A bright light suddenly flashed on and in Bosch's face. A reporter with a cameraman in tow moved in on the two detectives. Bosch was blinded for a few moments until his eyes started to adjust.

'Hi, Detectives. Judy Surtain, Channel Four news. Is there a break in the bones case?'

'No comment,' Edgar barked. 'No comment and turn that damn light off.'

Bosch finally saw her in the glare of the light. He recognized her from TV and from the gathering at the roadblock earlier in the week. He also recognized that a 'no comment' was not the way to leave this situation. He needed to defuse it and keep the media away from Trent.

'No,' he said. 'No breakthrough. We're just following routine procedures.'

Surtain shoved the microphone she was carrying toward Bosch's face.

'Why are you out here in the neighborhood again?'

'We're just finishing the routine canvas of the residents here. I hadn't had a chance to talk to the resident here before. We just finished up, that's all.'

He was talking with a bored tone in his voice. He hoped she was buying it.

'Sorry,' he added. 'No big story tonight.'

'Well, was this neighbor or any of the neighbors helpful to the investigation?'

'Well, everyone here has been very cooperative with us but as far as investigative leads go it has been difficult. Most of these people weren't even living in the neighborhood when the bones were buried. That makes it tough.'

Bosch gestured toward Trent's house.

'This gentleman, for example. We just found out that he didn't buy his home here until nineteen eighty-seven and we're pretty sure those bones were already up there by then.'

'So then it's back to the drawing board?'

'Sort of. And that's really all I can tell you. Good night.'

He pushed past her toward his car. A few moments later Surtain was on him at the car door. Without her cameraman.

'Detective, we need to get your name.'

Bosch opened his wallet and took out a business card. The one with the general station number printed on it. He gave it to her and said good night again.

'Look, if there is anything you can tell me, you know, off the record, I would protect you,' Surtain said. 'You know, off camera like this, whatever you want to do.'

'No, there is nothing,' Bosch said as he opened the door. 'Have a good night.'

Edgar cursed the moment the doors of the car were closed.

'How the hell did she know we were here?'

'Probably a neighbor,' Bosch said. 'She was out here the whole two days of the dig. She's a celebrity. She made nice with the residents. Made friends. Plus, we're sitting in a goddamn Shamu. Might as well have called a press conference.'

Bosch thought of the inanity of trying to do detective work in a car painted black and white. Under a program designed to make cops more visible on the street, the department had assigned detectives in the divisions to black-and-whites that didn't carry the emergency lights on top but were just as noticeable.

They watched as the reporter and her cameraman went to Trent's door.

'She's going to try to talk to him,' Edgar said.

Bosch quickly went into his briefcase and got out his cell-phone. He was about to dial Trent's number and tell him not to answer when he realized he couldn't get a cell signal.

'Goddammit,' he said.

'Too late anyway,' Edgar said. 'Let's just hope he plays it smart.'

Bosch could see Trent at his front door, totally bathed in the white light from the camera. He said a few words and then made a waving gesture and closed the door.

'Good,' Edgar said.

Bosch started the car, turned it around and headed back through the canyon to the station.

'So what's next?' Edgar asked.

'We have to pull the records on his conviction, see what it was about.'

'I'll do that first thing.'

'No. First thing I want to deliver the search warrants to the hospitals. Whether Trent fits our picture or not, we need to ID the kid in order to connect him to Trent. Let's meet at Van Nuys Courthouse at eight. We get them signed and then split 'em up.'

Bosch had picked Van Nuys court because Edgar lived nearby and they could separate and go from there in the morning after the warrants had been approved by a judge.

'What about a warrant on Trent's place?' Edgar said. 'You see anything while you were looking around?'

'Not much. He's got a skateboard in a box in the garage. You know, with his work stuff. For putting on a set. I was thinking of our victim's shirt when I saw that. And there were some work boots with dirt in the treads. It might match the samples from the hill. But I'm not counting on a search coming through for us. The guy has had twenty years to make sure he's clear. *If* he's the guy.'

'You don't think so?'

Bosch shook his head.

'Timing's wrong. 'Eighty-four is on the late side. The far edge of our window.'

'I thought we were looking at 'seventy-five to 'eighty-five.'

'We are. In general. But you heard Golliher – twenty to twenty-five years ago. That's early eighties on the high side. I don't know about 'eighty-four being early eighties.'

'Well, maybe he moved to that house *because* of the body. He buried the kid there before and wanted to be close by so he moves into the neighborhood. I mean, Harry, these are sick fucks, these guys.'

Bosch nodded.

'There's that. But I just wasn't getting the vibe from the guy. I believed him.'

'Harry, your mojo's been wrong before.'

'Oh, yeah . . . '

'I think it's him. He's the guy. Hear how he said, 'just because I touched a boy.' Probably to him, sodomizing a nine-year-old is reaching out and touching somebody.'

Edgar was being reactionary but Bosch didn't call him on it. He was a father; Bosch wasn't.

'We'll get the records and we'll see. We also have to go to the Hall to check the reverses, see who was on that street back then.'

The reverses were phone books that listed residents by address instead of by name. A collection of the books for every year was kept in the Hall of Records. They would allow the detectives to determine who was living on the street during the 1975 to 1985 range they were looking at as the boy's time of death.

'That's going to be a lot of fun,' Edgar said.

'Oh, yeah,' Bosch said. 'I can't wait.'

They drove in silence the rest of the way. Bosch became depressed. He was disappointed with himself for how he had run the investigation so far. The bones were discovered Wednesday, and the full investigation took off on Thursday. He knew he should have run the names – a basic part of the investigation – sooner than Sunday. By delaying it he had given Trent the advantage. He'd had three days to expect and prepare for their questions. He had even been briefed by an attorney. He could have even been practicing his responses and looks in a mirror. Bosch knew what his internal lie detector said. But he also knew that a good actor could beat it.

15

Bosch drank a beer on the back porch with the sliding door open so he could hear Clifford Brown on the stereo. Almost fifty years before, the trumpet player made a handful of recordings and then checked out in a car crash. Bosch thought about all the music that had been lost. He thought about young bones in the ground and what had been lost. And then he thought about himself and what he had lost. Somehow the jazz and the beer and the grayness he was feeling about the case had all mixed together in his mind. He felt on edge, like he was missing something that was right in front of him. For a detective it was just about the worst feeling in the world.

At 11 p.m. he came inside and turned the music down so he could watch the news on Channel 4. Judy Surtain's report was the third story after the first break. The anchor said, 'New developments in the Laurel Canyon bone case. We go to Judy Surtain at the scene.'

'Ah, shit,' Bosch said, not liking the sound of the introduction.

The program cut to a live shot of Surtain on Wonderland Avenue, standing on the street in front of a house Bosch recognized as Trent's.

'I'm here on Wonderland Avenue in Laurel Canyon, where four days ago a dog brought home a bone that authorities say was human. The dog's find led to the discovery of more bones belonging to a young boy who investigators believe was murdered and then buried more than twenty years ago.'

Bosch's phone started ringing. He picked it up off the arm of the TV chair and answered it.

'Hold on,' he said and then held the phone down by his side while he watched the news report.

Surtain said, 'Tonight the lead investigators on the case returned to the neighborhood to speak to one resident who lives less than one hundred yards from the place where the boy was buried. That resident is Nicholas Trent, a fifty-seven-year-old Hollywood set decorator.'

The program cut to tape of Bosch being questioned by Surtain that night. But it was used as visual filler while Surtain continued her report in a voice-over dub.

'Investigators declined to comment on their questioning of Trent, but Channel Four news has learned—'

Bosch sat down heavily on the chair and braced himself.

'—-that Trent was once convicted of molesting a young boy.'

The sound was then brought up on the street interview just as Bosch said, 'That's really all I can tell you.'

The next jump was to video of Trent standing in his doorway and waving the camera off and closing the door.

'Trent declined to comment on his status in the case. But neighbors in the normally quiet hillside neighborhood expressed shock upon learning of Trent's background.'

As the report shifted to a taped interview of a resident Bosch recognized as Victor Ulrich, Bosch hit the mute button on the TV remote and brought the phone up. It was Edgar.

'You watching this shit?' he asked.

'Oh, yeah.'

'We look like shit. We look like we told her. They used your quote out of context, Harry. We're going to be fucked by this.'

'Well, you didn't tell her, right?'

'Harry, you think I'd tell some—'

'No, I don't. I was confirming. You didn't tell her, right?'

'Right.'

'And neither did I. So, yeah, we're going to take some shit but we're clear on it.'

'Well, who else knew? I doubt Trent was the one who told her. About a million people now know he's a child molester.'

Bosch realized the only people who knew were Kiz, who had gotten the records flag while doing the computer work, and Julia Brasher, whom Bosch told while he was making his excuse for missing dinner. Suddenly a vision of Surtain standing at the roadblock on Wonderland came to him. Brasher had volunteered her help during both days of the hillside search and excavation. It was entirely possible that she had connected with Surtain in some way. Was she the reporter's source, the leak?

'There didn't have to be a leak,' Bosch said to Edgar. 'All she needed was Trent's name. She could have gotten any cop she knew to run it on the box for her. Or she could have looked it up on the sexual offenders CD. It's public record. Hold on.'

He had gotten a call-waiting beep on the phone. He switched over and learned it was Lt. Billets calling. He told her to hold while he got off the other line. He clicked over.

'Jerry, it's Bullets. I gotta call you back.'

'It's still me,' Billets said.

'Oh, sorry. Hold on.'

He tried again and this time made the switch back. He told Edgar he'd call him back if Billets said anything he needed to know right away.

'Otherwise, go with the plan,' he added. 'See you at Van Nuys at eight.'

He switched back over to Billets.

'Bullets?' she said. 'Is that what you guys call me?'

'What?'

'You said 'Bullets.' When you thought I was Edgar you called me "Bullets."'

'You mean just now?'

'Yes, just now.'

'I don't know. I don't know what you're talking about. You mean when I was switching over to—'

'Never mind, it doesn't matter. I assume you saw Channel Four?'

'Yeah, I saw it. And all I can tell you is that it wasn't me and it wasn't Edgar. That woman got a tip that we were out there and we "no comment"-ed our way out of there. How she came up with his—'

'Harry, you didn't "no comment" your way out of there. They have you on tape, your mouth moving, and then I hear you say, "that's all I can say." If you say "that's all," that means you gave her something.'

Bosch shook his head, even though he was on the phone.

'I didn't give her shit. I just bullshitted my way by. I told her we were just finishing up the routine canvas of the neighborhood and I hadn't talked to Trent before.'

'Was that true?'

'Not really, but I wasn't going to say we were there because the guy's a child molester. Look, she didn't know about Trent when we were there. If she did, she would have asked me. She found out later, and how I don't know. That's what Jerry and I were just talking about.'

There was silence for a moment before Billets continued.

'Well, you better have your shit together on this tomorrow because I want a written explanation from you that I can send up the line. Before that report on Four was even over I got a call from Captain LeValley and she said she had already gotten a call from Deputy Chief Irving.'

'Yeah, yeah, typical. Right on down the food chain.'

'Look, you know that leaking the criminal record of a citizen is against departmental policy, whether that citizen is the target of an investigation or not. I just hope you have your story straight on this. I don't need to tell you that there are people in the department just waiting for you to make a mistake they can sink their teeth into.'

'Look, I'm not trying to downplay the leak. It was wrong and it was bad. But I'm trying to solve a murder here, Lieutenant, and now I've got a whole new obstacle to overcome. And that's what's typical. There is always something thrown in the way.'

'Then you should be more careful next time.'

'Careful of what? What did I do wrong? I'm following leads where they go.'

Bosch immediately regretted the explosion of frustration and anger. Of those people in the department waiting for his self-destruction, Billets certainly wasn't on the list. She was only the messenger here. In the same moment, he realized his anger was also self-directed because he knew Billets was right. He should have handled Surtain differently.

'Look, I'm sorry,' he said in a low, even tone. 'It's just the case. It's got its hooks, you know?'

'I think I do,' Billets answered just as quietly. 'And speaking of the case, what exactly is going on? This whole thing with Trent came out of left field for me. I thought you were going to keep me up to date.'

'It all came up today. Late. I was just going to fill you in in the morning. I didn't know Channel Four would be doing it for me. And doing it for LeValley and Irving as well.'

'Never mind them for now. Tell me about Trent.'

16

It was well after midnight by the time Bosch got to Venice. Parking on the little streets near the canals was nonexistent. He drove around looking for ten minutes and ended up parking in the lot by the library out on Venice Boulevard and then walking back in.

Not all of the dreamers drawn to Los Angeles came to make movies. Venice was the century-old dream of a man named Abbot Kinney. Before Hollywood and the film industry barely had a pulse, Kinney came to the marshlands along the Pacific. He envisioned a place built on a network of canals with arched bridges and a town center of Italian architecture. It would be a place emphasizing cultural and artistic learning. And he would call it Venice of America.

But like most of the dreamers who come to Los Angeles his vision was not uniformly shared or realized. Most financiers and investigators were cynical and passed on the opportunity to build Venice, putting their money into projects of less grand design. Venice of America was dubbed 'Kinney's Folly.'

But a century later many of the canals and the arched bridges reflected in their waters remained while the financiers and doomsayers and their projects were long swept away by time. Bosch liked the idea of Kinney's Folly outlasting them all.

Bosch had not been to the canals in many years, though for a short period in his life after returning from Vietnam he had lived there in a bungalow with three other men he knew from overseas. In the years since, many of the bungalows had been erased and modern two- and three-story homes costing a million dollars or more had replaced them.

Julia Brasher lived in a house at the corner of the Howland and Eastern canals. Bosch expected it to be one of the new structures. He guessed she probably used her law-firm money to buy it or even build it. But as he came to the address he saw that he was wrong. Her house was a small bungalow made of white clapboard with an open front porch overlooking the joining of the two canals.

Bosch saw lights on behind the windows of her house. It was late but not that late. If she worked the three-to-eleven shift, then it was unlikely she was used to going to bed before two.

He stepped up onto the porch but hesitated before knocking on the door. Until the doubts of the last hour had crept in, he had gotten only good feelings about Brasher and their fledgling relationship. He knew he now had to be careful. There could be nothing wrong and yet he could spoil everything if he misstepped here.

Finally, he raised his arm and knocked. Brasher answered right away.

'I was wondering if you were going to knock or stand out there all night.'

'You knew I was standing here?'

'The porch is old. It creaks. I heard it.'

'Well, I got here and then figured it was too late. I should have called first.'

'Just come in. Is anything wrong?'

Bosch came in and looked around. He didn't answer the question.

The living room had an unmistakable beach flavor to it, right down to the bamboo-and-rattan furniture and the surfboard leaning in one corner. The only deviation was her equipment belt and holster hanging on a wall rack near the door. It was a rookie mistake leaving it out like that, but Bosch assumed she was proud of her new career choice and wanted to remind friends outside the cop world of it.

'Sit down,' she said. 'I have some wine open. Would you like a glass?'

Bosch thought a moment about whether mixing wine with the beer he'd had an hour earlier would lead to a headache the next day when he knew he'd have to be focused.

'It's red.'

'Uh, I'll take just a little bit.'

'Got to be sharp tomorrow, huh?'

'I guess.'

She went into the kitchen while he sat down on the couch. He looked around the room and now saw a mounted fish with a long sharp point hanging over the white brick fireplace. The fish was a brilliant blue shading to black with a white and yellow underside. Mounted fish didn't bother him the way the heads of mounted game did but he still didn't like the eye of the fish always watching.

'You catch this thing?' he called out.

'Yeah. Off Cabo. Took me three and a half hours to bring it in.'

She then appeared with two glasses of wine.

'On fifty-pound test line,' she said. 'That was a workout.'

'What is it?'

'Black marlin.'

She toasted the fish with her glass and then toasted Bosch.

'Hold fast.'

Bosch looked at her.

'That's my new toast,' she said. 'Hold fast. It seems to cover everything.'

She sat down on the chair closest to Bosch. Behind her was the surfboard. It was white with a rainbow design in a border running along the edges. It was a short board.

'So you surf the wild waves, too.'

She glanced back at the board and then at Bosch and smiled.

'I try to. Picked it up in Hawaii.'

'You know John Burrows?'

She shook her head.

'Lot of surfers in Hawaii. What beach does he surf?'

'No, I mean here. He's a cop. He works Homicide out of Pacific Division. Lives on a walk street by the beach. Not too far from here. He surfs. On his board it says "To Protect and Surf."'

She laughed.

'That's cool. I like that. I'll have to get that put on my board.'

Bosch nodded.

'John Burrows, huh? I'll have to look him up.'

She said it with just a touch of teasing in her voice.

Bosch smiled and said, 'And maybe not.'

He liked the way she kidded him like that. It all felt good to Bosch, which made him feel all the more out of sorts because of his reason for being there. He looked at his wine glass.

'I've been fishing all day and didn't catch a thing,' he said. 'Microfiche mostly.'

'I saw you on the news tonight,' she said. 'Are you trying to put the squeeze on that guy, the child molester?'

Bosch sipped his wine to give himself time to think. She had opened the door. He now just had to step through very carefully.

'What do you mean?' he asked.

'Well, giving that reporter his criminal background. I figured you must be making some kind of play. You know, turning up the heat on him. To make him talk or something. It seems kind of risky.'

'Why?'

'Well, first of all, trusting a reporter is always risky. I know that from back when I was a lawyer and got burned. And second . . . and second, you never know how people are going to react when their secrets are no longer secrets.'

Bosch studied her for a moment and then shook his head.

'I didn't give it to her,' he said. 'Somebody else did.'

He studied her eyes for any kind of tell. There was nothing.

'There's going to be trouble over it,' he added.

She raised her eyebrows in surprise. Still no tell.

'Why? If you didn't give her the information, why would there . . . '

She stopped and now Bosch could see her put it together. He saw the disappointment fill her eyes.

'Oh, Harry . . . '

He tried to back out through the door.

'What? Don't worry about it. I'll be fine.'

'It wasn't me, Harry. Is that what you're here about? To see if I'm the leak or the source or whatever you'd call it?'

She abruptly put her wine glass down on the coffee table. Red wine lapped over the edge and onto the table. She didn't do anything about it. Bosch knew there was no use trying to avoid the collision. He had screwed up.

'Look, only four people knew . . . '

'And I was one of them. So you thought you'd come here undercover and find out if it was me.'

She waited for a response. Finally, all Bosch could do was nod.

'Well, it wasn't me. And I think you should go now.'

Bosch nodded and put down his glass. He stood up.

'Look, I'm sorry. I screwed it up. I thought the best way to not mess anything up, you know, between you and me, was to . . . '

He made a helpless gesture with his hands as he headed to the door.

'Was to do the undercover thing,' he continued. 'I just didn't want to mess it up, that's all. But I had to know. I think if you were me you would've felt the same way about it.'

He opened the door and looked back at her.

'I'm sorry, Julia. Thanks for the wine.'

He turned to go.

'Harry.'

He turned back. She came to him and reached up and grabbed the lapels of his jacket with both hands. She slowly pulled him forward and then pushed him backward, as if roughing up a suspect in slow motion. Her eyes dropped to his chest as her mind worked and she came to a decision.

She stopped shaking him but kept her grasp on his jacket.

'I can get over it,' she said. 'I think.'

She looked up to his eyes and pulled him forward. She kissed him hard on the mouth for a long time and then pushed him back. She let go.

'I hope. Call me tomorrow.'

Bosch nodded and stepped through the door. She closed it.

Bosch went down the porch to the sidewalk next to the canal. He looked at the reflection of the lights of all the houses on the water. An arched footbridge, lighted by the moon and nothing else, crossed the canal twenty yards away, its reflection perfect on the water. He turned and walked back up the steps to the porch. He hesitated at the door again and soon Brasher opened it.

'The porch creaks, remember?'

He nodded and she waited. He wasn't sure how to say what he wanted to say. Finally, he just began.

'One time when I was in one of those tunnels we were talking about last night I came up head-on with some guy. He was VC. Black pajamas, greased face. We sort of looked at each other for a split second and I guess instincts took over. We both raised up and fired at the same time. Simultaneous. And then we fucking ran in opposite directions. Both of us scared shitless, screaming in the dark.'

He paused as he thought about the story, seeing it more than remembering it.

'Anyway, I thought he had to have hit me. It was almost point-blank, too close to miss. I thought my gun had backfired and jammed or something. The kick had felt wrong. When I got up top the first thing I did was check myself. No blood, no pain. I took all of my clothes off and checked myself. Nothing. He had missed. Point-blank and somehow the guy had missed.'

She stepped over the door's threshold and leaned against the front wall beneath the porch light. She didn't say anything and he pressed on.

'Anyway, then I checked my forty-five for a jam and I found out why he hadn't hit me. The guy's bullet was in the barrel of my gun. With mine. We had pointed at each other and his shot went right up the barrel of my gun. What were the chances of that? A million to one? A billion?'

As he spoke he held his empty hand out as a gun pointing at her. His hand was extended directly in front of his chest. The bullet that day in the tunnel had been meant for his heart.

'I guess I just want you to know that I know how lucky I was with you tonight.'

He nodded and then turned and went down the steps.

17

Death investigation is a pursuit with countless dead ends, obstacles and colossal chunks of wasted time and effort. Bosch knew this every day of his existence as a cop but was reminded of it once again when he got to the homicide table shortly before noon Monday and found his morning's time and effort had most likely been wasted while a brand-new obstacle awaited him.

The homicide squad had the area at the rear corner of the detective bureau. The squad consisted of three teams of three. Each team had a table consisting of the three detectives' desks pushed together, two facing each other, the third along one side. Sitting at Bosch's table, in the slot left vacant by Kiz Rider's departure, was a young woman in a business suit. She had dark hair and even darker eyes. They were eyes sharp enough to peel a walnut and they held on Bosch his whole way through the squad room.

'Can I help you?' he asked when he got to the table.

'Harry Bosch?'

'That's me.'

'Detective Carol Bradley, IAD. I need to take a statement from you.'

Bosch looked around. There were several people in the squad room trying to act busy while surreptitiously watching.

'Statement about what?'

'Deputy Chief Irving asked our division to determine if the criminal record of Nicholas Trent was improperly divulged to the media.'

Bosch still hadn't sat down. He put his hands on the top of his chair and stood behind it. He shook his head.

'I think it's pretty safe to assume it was improperly divulged.'

'Then I need to find out who did it.'

Bosch nodded.

'I'm trying to run an investigation here and all anybody cares about is—'

'Look, I know you think it's bullshit. And I may think it's bullshit. But I've got the order. So let's go into one of the rooms and put your story on tape. It won't take long. And then you can go back to your investigation.'

Bosch put his briefcase on the table and opened it. He took out his tape recorder. He had remembered it while driving around all morning delivering search warrants at the local hospitals.

'Speaking of tape, why don't you take this into one of the rooms and listen to it first? I had it on last night. It should end my involvement in this pretty quick.'

She hesitantly took the recorder, and Bosch pointed to the hallway that led to the three interview rooms.

'I'm still going to need to—'

'Fine. Listen to the tape, then we'll talk.'

'Your partner, too.'

'He should be in anytime now.'

Bradley went down the hall with the recorder. Bosch finally sat down and didn't bother to look at any of the other detectives.

It wasn't even noon but he felt exhausted. He had spent the morning waiting for a judge in Van Nuys to sign the search warrants for medical records and then driving across the city delivering them to the legal offices of nineteen different hospitals. Edgar had taken ten of the warrants and headed off on his own. With fewer to deliver, he was then going downtown to conduct record searches on Nicholas Trent's criminal background and to check the reverse directories and property records for Wonderland Avenue.

Bosch noticed that waiting for him was a stack of phone messages and the latest batch of call-in tips from the front desk. He took the phone messages first. Nine out of twelve of them were from reporters, all no doubt wanting to follow up on Channel 4's report on Trent the night before and then rebroadcast during the morning news program. The other three were from Trent's lawyer, Edward Morton. He had called three times between 8 and 9:30 a.m.

Bosch didn't know Morton but expected he was calling to complain about Trent's record being given to the media. He normally wasn't quick to return calls to lawyers but decided it would be best to get the confrontation over with and to assure Morton that the leak had not come from the investigators on the case. Even though he doubted that Morton would believe anything he said, he picked up the phone and called back. A secretary told him that Morton had gone to a court hearing but was due to check in at any moment. Bosch said he would be waiting for him to call again.

After hanging up Bosch dropped the pink slips with the reporters' numbers on them into the trash can next to his spot at the table. He started going through the call-in sheets and quickly noticed that the desk officers were now asking the questions he had typed out the morning before and given to Mankiewicz.

On the eleventh report in the pile he came across a direct hit. A woman named Sheila Delacroix had called at 8:41 a.m. that morning and said she had seen the Channel 4 report that morning. She said her younger brother Arthur Delacroix disappeared in 1980 in Los Angeles. He was twelve years old at the time and was never heard from since.

In answer to the medical questions, she responded that her brother had been injured during a fall from a skateboard a few months before his disappearance. He suffered a brain injury that required hospitalization and neurosurgery. She did not remember the exact medical details but was sure the hospital was Queen of Angels. She could not recall the name of any of the doctors who treated her brother. Other than an address and call-back number for Sheila Delacroix, that was all the information on the report.

Bosch circled the word 'skateboard' on the sheet. He opened his briefcase and got out a business card Bill Golliher had given him. He called the first number and got a machine at the anthropologist's office at UCLA. He called the second and got Golliher while he was eating lunch in Westwood Village.

'Got a quick question. The injury that required surgery on the skull.'

'The hematoma.'

'Right. Could that have been caused by a fall from a skateboard?'

There was silence and Bosch let Golliher think. The clerk who took the calls to the general lines in the squad room came up to the homicide table and shot Bosch a peace sign. Bosch covered his receiver.

'Who is it?'

'Kiz Rider.'

'Tell her to hold.'

He uncovered the receiver.

'Doc, you there?'

'Yes, I'm just thinking. It might be possible, depending on what it was he hit. But a fall just to the ground, I would say it's not likely. You had a tight fracture pattern, which indicates a small area of surface-to-surface contact. Also, the location is high up on the cranium. It's not the back of the head, which you would normally associate with fall injuries.'

Bosch felt some of the wind going out of his sails. He had thought he might have an ID on the victim.

'Is this a particular person you are talking about?' Golliher asked.

'Yeah, we just got a tip.'

'Are there X-rays, surgical records?'

'I'm working on it.'

'Well, I'd like to see them to make a comparison.'

'As soon as I get them. What about the other injuries? Could they be from skateboarding?'

'Of course some of them could be from that,' Golliher said. 'But I would say not all. The ribs, the twist fractures – also, some of these injuries dated to very early childhood, Detective. There aren't many three-year-olds on skateboards, I would think.'

Bosch nodded and tried to think if there was anything else to ask.

'Detective, you do know that in abuse cases the reported cause of injury and the true cause are not often the same?'

'I understand. Whoever brought the kid into the emergency room wouldn't volunteer he hit him with a flashlight or whatever.'

'Right. There would be a story. The child would adhere to it.'

'Skateboard accident.'

'It's possible.'

'Okay, Doc, I gotta go. I'll get you the X-rays as soon as I get them. Thanks.'

He punched line two on the phone.

'Kiz?'

'Harry, hi, how're you doing?'

'Busy. What's up?'

'I feel awful, Harry. I think I fucked up.'

Bosch leaned back in his chair. He would have never guessed it was her.

'Channel Four?'

'Yeah. I, uh . . . yesterday after you left Parker and my partner stopped watching the football game, he asked what was up with you being in there. So I told him. I'm still trying to establish the relationship, Harry, you know? I told him I ran the names for you and there was a hit. One of the neighbors had a molestation record. That's all I told him, Harry. I swear.'

Bosch breathed out heavily. He actually felt better. His instinct about Rider had been right on. She was not the leak. She had simply trusted someone she should have been able to trust.

'Kiz, I got IAD sitting up here waiting to talk to me about this. How do you know Thornton gave it to Channel Four?'

'I saw the report on TV this morning when I was getting ready. I know Thornton knows that reporter. Surtain. Thornton and I worked a case a few months ago – an insurance murder on the Westside. It got some media play and he was feeding her stuff off the record. I saw them together. Then yesterday, after I told him about the hit, he said he had to go to the can. He picked the sports page up and went down the hall. But he didn't go to the can. We got a call out and I went down and banged on the door to tell him we were rolling. He didn't answer. I didn't really think anything about it until I saw the news today. I think he didn't go to the can because he went into another office or down to the lobby to use a phone to call her.'

'Well, it explains a lot.'

'I'm really sorry, Harry. That TV report didn't make you look good at all. I'm going to talk to IAD.'

'Just hold on to that, Kiz. For now. I'll let you know if I need you to talk to IAD. But what are *you* going to do?'

'Get a new partner. I can't work with this guy.'

'Be careful. You start jumping partners and pretty soon you'll be all alone.'

'I'd rather work alone than with some asshole I can't trust.'

'There's that.'

'What about you? The offer still stand?'

'What, I'm an asshole you can trust?'

'You know what I mean.'

'The offer stands. All you have to do is—'

'Hey, Harry, I gotta go. Here he comes.'

'Okay, bye.'

Bosch hung up and rubbed his mouth with his hand as he thought about what to do about Thornton. He could tell Kiz's story to Carol Bradley. But there was still too much room in it for error. He wouldn't feel comfortable going to IAD with it unless he was sure. The actual idea of going to IAD about anything repulsed him, but in this instance someone was harming Bosch's investigation.

And that was something he could not let pass.

After a few minutes he came up with a plan and checked his watch. It was ten minutes before noon. He called Kiz Rider back.

'It's Harry. Is he there?'

'Yeah, why?'

'Repeat after me, in a sort of excited voice. "You did, Harry? Great! Who was he?"'

'You did, Harry? That's great! Who was he?'

'Okay, now you're listening, listening, listening. Now say, "How did a ten-year-old get here from New Orleans?"'

'How did a ten-year-old get all the way here from New Orleans?'

'Perfect. Now hang up and don't say anything. If Thornton asks you, tell him we ID'd the kid through dental records. He was a ten-year-old runaway from New Orleans last seen in nineteen seventy-five. His parents are on a plane heading here now. And the chief is going to have a press conference about it all today at four.'

'Okay, Harry, good luck.'

'You, too.'

Bosch hung up and looked up. Edgar was standing across the table from him. He had heard the last part of the conversation and his eyebrows were up.

'No, it's all bullshit,' Bosch said. 'I'm setting up the leak. And that reporter.'

'The leak? Who is the leak?'

'Kiz's new partner. We think.'

Edgar slid into his chair and just nodded.

'But we do have a possible ID on the bones,' Bosch said.

He told Edgar about the call-in sheet on Arthur Delacroix and his subsequent conversations with Bill Golliher.

'Nineteen eighty? That's not going to work with Trent. I checked the reverses and property records. He wasn't on that street until 'eighty-four. Like he said last night.'

'Something tells me he isn't our guy.'

Bosch thought about the skateboard again. It wasn't enough to alter his gut feeling.

'Tell that to Channel Four.'

Bosch's phone rang. It was Rider.

'He just went to the can.'

'You tell him about the press conference?'

'I told him everything. He kept asking questions, the dipshit.'

'Well, if he tells her that everybody will have it at four, she'll go out with the exclusive on the noon news. I'm going to go watch.'

'Let me know.'

He hung up and checked his watch. He still had a few minutes. He looked at Edgar.

'By the way, IAD is in one of the rooms back there. We're under investigation.'

Edgar's jaw dropped. Like most cops, he resented Internal Affairs because even when you did a good and honest job, the IAD could still be on you for any number of things. It was like the Internal Revenue Service, the way just seeing a letter with the IRS return address in the corner was enough to pull your guts into a knot.

'Relax. It's about the Channel Four thing. We should be clear of it in a few minutes. Come with me.'

They went into Lt. Billets's office, where there was a small television on a stand. She was doing paperwork at her desk.

'You mind if we check out Channel Four's noon report?' Bosch asked.

'Be my guest. I'm sure Captain LeValley and Chief Irving are going to be watching as well.'

The news program opened with a report on a sixteen-car pileup in the morning fog on the Santa Monica Freeway. It wasn't that significant a story – no one was killed – but they had good video, so it led the program. But the 'dog bone' case had moved up to second billing. The anchor said they were going to Judy Surtain with another exclusive report.

The program cut to Surtain sitting at a desk in the Channel 4 newsroom.

'Channel Four has learned that the bones found in Laurel Canyon have been identified as those of a ten-year-old runaway from New Orleans.'

Bosch looked at Edgar and then at Billets, who was rising from her seat with an expression of surprise on her face. Bosch put out his hand as if to signal her to wait a moment.

'The parents of the boy, who reported him missing more than twenty-five years ago, are en route to Los Angeles to meet with police. The remains were identified through dental records. Later today, the chief of police is expected to hold a press conference where he will identify the boy and discuss the investigation. As reported by Channel Four last night, police are focusing on—'

Bosch turned the TV off.

'Harry, Jerry, what's going on?' Billets asked immediately.

'All of that was bogus. I was smoking out the leak.'

'Who?'

'Kiz's new partner. A guy named Rick Thornton.'

Bosch explained what Rider had explained to him earlier. He then outlined the scam he had just pulled.

'Where's the IAD detective?' Billets asked.

'One of the interview rooms. She's listening to a tape I had of me and the reporter last night.'

'A tape? Why didn't you tell me about it last night?'

'I forgot about it last night.'

'All right, I'll take it from here. You feel Kiz is clean on this?'

Bosch nodded.

'She has to trust her partner enough to tell him anything. He took that trust and gave it to Channel Four. I don't know what he's getting in return but it doesn't matter. He's fucking with my case.'

'All right, Harry, I said I would handle it. You go back to the case. Anything new I should know about?'

'We've got a possible ID – this one legit – that we'll be running down today.'

'What about Trent?'

'We're letting that sit until we find out if this is the kid. If it is, the timing is wrong. The kid disappeared in nineteen eighty. Trent didn't move into the neighborhood until four years later.'

'Great. Meantime, we've taken his buried secret and put it on TV. Last I heard from patrol, the media was camped in his driveway.'

Bosch nodded.

'Talk to Thornton about it,' he said.

'Oh, we will.'

She sat down behind her desk and picked up the phone. It was their cue to leave. On the way back to the table Bosch asked Edgar if he had pulled the file on Trent's conviction.

'Yeah, I got it. It was a weak case. Nowadays the DA probably wouldn't have even filed on it.'

They went to their respective spots at the table and Bosch saw that he had missed a callback from Trent's lawyer. He reached for the phone but then waited until Edgar finished his report.

'The guy worked as a teacher at an elementary school in Santa Monica.

He was caught by another teacher in a stall in the bathroom holding an eight-year-old's penis while he urinated. He said he was teaching the kid how to aim it, that the kid kept pissing on the floor. What it came down to is the kid's story was all over the place but didn't back his. And the parents said the boy already knew how to aim by the time he was four. Trent was convicted and got a two plus one. He served fifteen months of it up at Wayside.'

Bosch thought about all of this. His hand was still on the phone.

'It's a long ass jump from that to beating a kid to death with a baseball bat.'

'Yeah, Harry, I'm beginning to like your mojo better all the time.'

'I wish I did.'

He picked up the phone and punched in the number for Trent's attorney, Edward Morton. He was transferred to the lawyer's cell phone. He was on his way to lunch.

'Hello?'

'Detective Bosch.'

'Bosch, yes, I want to know where he is.'

'Who?'

'Don't play this game, Detective. I've called every holding jail in the county. I want to be able to speak to my client. Right now.'

'I'm assuming you are speaking about Nicholas Trent. Have you tried his job?'

'Home and work, no answer. Pager, too. If you people have him, he's entitled to representation. And I am entitled to know. I'm telling you now, if you fuck with me on this, I will go right to a judge. And the media.'

'We don't have your man, counselor. I haven't seen him since last night.'

'Yes, he called me after you left. Then again after watching the news. You people fucked him over – you should be ashamed of yourself.'

Bosch's face burned with the rebuke but he didn't respond to it. If he didn't personally deserve it, then the department did. He'd take the bullet for now.

'Do you think he ran, Mr. Morton?'

'Why run if you are innocent?'

'I don't know. Ask O.J.'

A horrible thought suddenly shot into Bosch's gut. He stood up, the phone still pressed to his ear.

'Where are you now, Mr. Morton?'

'Sunset heading west. Near Book Soup.'

'Turn around and come back. Meet me at Trent's house.'

'I have a lunch. I'm not going—'

'Meet me at Trent's house. I'm leaving now.'

He put the phone in its cradle and told Edgar it was time to go. He'd explain on the way.

18

There was a small gathering of television reporters in the street in front of Nicholas Trent's house. Bosch parked behind the Channel 2 van and he and Edgar got out. Bosch didn't know what Edward Morton looked like but didn't see anyone in the group who looked like an attorney. After more than twenty-five years on the job, he had unerring instincts that allowed him to identify lawyers and reporters. Over the top of the car, Bosch spoke to Edgar before the reporters could hear them.

'If we have to go in, we'll do it around back – without the audience.'

'I gotya.'

They walked up to the driveway and were immediately accosted by the media crews, who turned on cameras and threw questions that went unanswered. Bosch noticed that Judy Surtain of Channel 4 was not among the reporters.

'Are you here to arrest Trent?'

'Can you tell us about the boy from New Orleans?'

'What about the press conference? Media Relations doesn't know anything about a press conference.'

'Is Trent a suspect or not?'

Once Bosch was through the crowd and on Trent's driveway, he suddenly turned back and faced the cameras. He hesitated a moment as if composing his thoughts. What he really was doing was giving them time to focus and get ready. He didn't want anyone to miss this.

'There is no press conference scheduled,' Bosch said. 'There has been no identification of the bones yet. The man who lives in this house was questioned last night as was every resident of this neighborhood. At no time was he called a suspect by the investigators on this case. Information leaked to the media by someone outside of the investigation and then broadcast without being checked first with the actual investigators has been completely wrong and damaging to the ongoing investigation. That's it. That's all I'm going to say. When there is some real and accurate information to report, we will give it to you through Media Relations.'

He turned back around and headed up the driveway to the house with

Edgar. The reporters threw more questions at them but Bosch gave no indication of even hearing them.

At the front door Edgar knocked sharply and called out to Trent, telling him it was the police. After a few moments he knocked again and made the same announcement. They waited again and nothing happened.

'The back?' Edgar asked.

'Yeah, or the garage has a door on the side.'

They walked across the driveway and started heading down the side of the house. The reporters yelled more questions. Bosch guessed they were so used to throwing questions that were not answered at people that it simply became natural for them to do it and natural for them to know they would not be answered. Like a dog barking in the backyard long after the master has left for work.

They passed the side door to the garage, and Bosch noted that he was correct in remembering that there was only a single key lock on the knob. They continued into the backyard. There was a kitchen door with a dead bolt and a key lock on the knob. There was also a sliding door, which would be easy to pop open. Edgar stepped over to it but looked down through the glass to the interior sliding track and saw that there was a wooden dowel in place that would prevent the door from being opened from the outside.

'This won't work, Harry,' he said.

Bosch had a small pouch containing a set of lock picks in his pocket. He didn't want to have to work the dead bolt on the kitchen door.

'Let's do the garage, unless ... '

He walked over to the kitchen door and tried it. It was unlocked and he opened the door. In that moment he knew they would find Trent dead inside. Trent would be the helpful suicide. The one who leaves the door open so people don't have to break in.

'Shit.'

Edgar came over, pulling his gun from its holster.

'You're not going to need that,' Bosch said.

He stepped into the house and they moved through the kitchen.

'Mr. Trent?' Edgar yelled. 'Police! Police in the house! Are you here, Mr. Trent?'

'Take the front,' Bosch said.

They split up and Bosch went down the short hallway to the rear bedrooms. He found Trent in the walk-in shower of the master bath. He had taken two wire hangers and fashioned a noose which he had attached to the stem pipe of the shower. He had then leaned back against the tiled wall and dropped his weight and asphyxiated himself. He was still dressed in the clothes he had worn the night before. His bare feet were on the floor tiles. There were no indications at all that Trent had had second thoughts about killing himself. Being that it was not a suspension hanging, he could have stopped his death at any time. He didn't.

Bosch would have to leave it for the coroner's people but he judged by the darkening of the body's tongue, which was distended from the mouth, that Trent had been dead at least twelve hours. That would put his death in the vicinity of the very early morning, not long after Channel 4 had first announced his hidden past to the world and labeled him a suspect in the bones case.

'Harry?'

Bosch nearly jumped. He turned around and looked at Edgar.

'Don't do that to me, man. What?'

Edgar was staring at the body as he spoke.

'He left a three-page note out on the coffee table.'

Bosch stepped out of the shower and pushed past Edgar. He headed toward the living room, taking a pair of latex gloves from his pocket and blowing into them to expand the rubber before snapping them on.

'Did you read the whole thing?'

'Yeah, he says he didn't do the kid. He says he's killing himself because the police and reporters have destroyed him and he can't go on. Like that. There's some weird stuff, too.'

Bosch went into the living room. Edgar was a few steps behind him. Bosch saw three handwritten pages spread side by side on the coffee table. He sat down on the couch in front of them.

'This how they were?'

'Yup. I didn't touch them.'

Bosch started reading the pages. What he presumed were Trent's last words were a rambling denial of the murder of the boy on the hillside and a purging of anger over what had been done to him.

> *Now EVERYBODY will know! You people have ruined me, KILLED me. The blood is on you, not on me! I didn't do it, I didn't do it, no, no, NO! I never hurt anyone. Never, never, never. Not a soul on this earth. I love the children. LOVE!!!! No, it was you who hurt me. You. But it is I who can't live with the pain of what you have ruthlessly caused. I can't.*

It was repetitive and almost as if someone had written down an extemporaneous diatribe rather than sat down with pen and paper and wrote out their thoughts. The middle of the second page was blocked off and inside the box were names under a heading of 'Those Found Responsible.' The list started with Judy Surtain, included the anchor on the Channel 4 nightly news, and listed Bosch, Edgar and three names Bosch didn't recognize. Calvin Stumbo, Max Rebner and Alicia Felzer.

'Stumbo was the cop and Rebner was the DA on the first case,' Edgar said. 'In the sixties.'

Bosch nodded.

'And Felzer?'

'Don't know that one.'

The pen with which the pages were apparently written was on the table next to the last page. Bosch didn't touch it because he planned to have it checked for Trent's fingerprints.

As he continued to read, Bosch noticed that each page was signed at the bottom with Trent's signature. At the end of the last page, Trent made an odd plea that Bosch didn't readily understand.

My one regret is for my children. Who will care for my children? They need food and clothes. I have some money. The money goes to them. Whatever I have. This is my last will and testament signed by me. Give the money to the children. Have Morton give the money and don't charge me anything. Do it for the children.

'His children?' Bosch asked.

'Yeah, I know,' Edgar said. 'Weird.'

'What are you doing here? Where is Nicholas?'

They looked at the doorway from the kitchen to the living room. A short man in a suit who Bosch guessed was a lawyer and had to be Morton stood there. Bosch stood up.

'He's dead. It looks like a suicide.'

'Where?'

'Master bath, but I wouldn't—'

Morton was already gone, heading to the bathroom. Bosch called after him.

'Don't touch anything.'

He nodded to Edgar to follow and make sure. Bosch sat back down and looked at the pages again. He wondered how long it took Trent to decide that killing himself was all that he had left and then to labor over the three-page note. It was the longest suicide note he had ever encountered.

Morton came back into the living room, Edgar just behind him. His face was ashen and his eyes held on the floor.

'I tried to tell you not to go back there,' Bosch said.

The lawyer's eyes came up and fixed on Bosch. They filled with anger, which seemed to restore some color to Morton's face.

'Are you people happy now? You completely destroyed him. Give a man's secret to the vultures, they put it on the air and this is what you get.'

He gestured with a hand in the direction of the bathroom.

'Mr. Morton, you've got your facts wrong, but essentially it looks like that's what happened. In fact, you'd probably be surprised by how much I agree with you.'

'Now that he's dead, that must be very easy for you to say. Is that a note? Did he leave a note?'

Bosch got up and gestured for him to take his spot on the couch in front of the three pages.

'Just don't touch the pages.'

Morton sat down, unfolded a pair of reading glasses and started studying the pages.

Bosch walked over to Edgar and said in a low voice, 'I'm going to use the phone in the kitchen to make the calls.'

Edgar nodded.

'Better get Media Relations on it. The shit is going to hit that fan.'

'Yeah.'

Bosch picked up the wall phone in the kitchen and saw it had a redial button. He pushed it and waited. He recognized the voice that answered as Morton's. It was an answering machine. Morton said he wasn't home and to leave a message.

Bosch called Lt. Billets's direct line. She answered right away and Bosch could tell she was eating.

'Well, I hate to break this to you while you're eating, but we're up here at Trent's place. It looks like he killed himself.'

There was silence for a long moment and then she asked Bosch if he was sure.

'I'm sure he's dead and I'm pretty sure he did it himself. Hung himself with a couple of wire hangers in the shower. There's a three-page note here. He denies anything to do with the bones. He blames his death on Channel Four and the police mostly – me and Edgar in particular. You're the first one I've called.'

'Well, we all know it wasn't you who—'

'That's okay, Lieutenant, I don't need the absolution. What do you want me to do here?'

'You handle the routine call outs. I'll call Chief Irving's office and tell him what has transpired. This is going to get hot.'

'Yes. What about Media Relations? There's already a gang of reporters out on the street.'

'I'll call them.'

'Did you do anything about Thornton yet?'

'Already in the pipeline. The woman from IAD, Bradley, is running with it. With this latest thing, I'd bet Thornton not only leaked his way out of a job, but they might want to go after him with a charge of some kind.'

Bosch nodded. Thornton deserved it. He still had no second thoughts about the scam he had devised.

'All right, well, we'll be here. For a while, at least.'

'Let me know if you find anything there that connects him to the bones.'

Bosch thought of the boots with the dirt in the treads and the skateboard.

'You got it,' he said.

Bosch clicked off the call and then immediately made calls to the coroner's office and SID.

In the living room Morton had finished reading the note.

'Mr. Morton, when was the last time you talked to Mr. Trent?' Bosch asked.

'Last night. He called me at home after the news on Channel Four. His boss had seen it and called him.'

Bosch nodded. That accounted for the last call.

'You know his boss's name?'

Morton pointed to the middle page on the table.

'Right here on the list. Alicia Felzer. She told him she was going to seek his termination. The studio makes movies for children. She couldn't have him on a set with a child. You see? The leaking of his record to the media destroyed this man. You recklessly took a man's existence and—'

'Let me ask the questions, Mr. Morton. You can save your outrage for when you go outside and talk to the reporters yourself, which I know you'll do. What about that last page? He mentions the children. His children. What does that mean?'

'I have no idea. He obviously was emotionally distraught when he wrote this. It may mean nothing.'

Bosch remained standing, studying the attorney.

'Why did he call you last night?'

'Why do you think? To tell me you had been here, that it was all over the news, that his boss had seen it and wanted to fire him.'

'Did he say whether he buried that boy up there on the hill?'

Morton put on the best indignant look he could muster.

'He certainly said that he did not have a thing to do with it. He believed he was being persecuted for a past mistake, a very distant mistake, and I'd say he was correct about that.'

Bosch nodded.

'Okay, Mr. Morton, you can leave now.'

'What are you talking about? I'm not going to—'

'This house is now a crime scene. We are investigating your client's death to confirm or deny it was by his own hand. You are no longer welcome here. Jerry?'

Edgar stepped over to the couch and waved Morton up.

'Come on. Time to go out there and get your face on TV. It'll be good for business, right?'

Morton stood up and left in a huff. Bosch walked over to the front windows and pulled the curtain back a few inches. When Morton came down the side of the house to the driveway, he immediately walked to the center of the knot of reporters and started talking angrily. Bosch couldn't hear what was said. He didn't need to.

When Edgar came back into the room, Bosch told him to call the watch office and get a patrol car up to Wonderland for crowd control. He had a feeling that the media mob, like a virus replicating itself, was going to start growing bigger and hungrier by the minute.

19

They found Nicholas Trent's children when they searched his home following the removal of his body. Filling the entire two drawers of a small desk in the living room, a desk Bosch had not searched the night before, were files, photographs and financial records, including several thick bank envelopes containing canceled checks. Trent had been sending small amounts of money on a monthly basis to a number of charitable organizations that fed and clothed children. From Appalachia to the Brazilian rain forest to Kosovo, Trent had been sending checks for years. Bosch found no check for an amount higher than twelve dollars. He found dozens and dozens of photographs of the children he was supposedly helping as well as small handwritten notes from them.

Bosch had seen any number of public-service ads for the charities on late-night television. He had always been suspicious. Not about whether a few dollars could keep a child from going hungry and unclothed, but about whether the few dollars would actually get to them. He wondered if the photos Trent kept in the drawers of his desk were the same stock shots sent to everybody who contributed. He wondered if the thank-you notes in childish printing were fake.

'Man,' Edgar said as he surveyed the contents of the desk. 'This guy, it's like I think he was paying a penance or something, sending all his cash to these outfits.'

'Yeah, a penance for what?'

'We may never know.'

Edgar went back to searching the second bedroom. Bosch studied some of the photos he had spread on the top of the desk. There were boys and girls, none looking older than ten, though this was hard to estimate because they all had the hollow and ancient eyes of children who have been through war and famine and indifference. He picked up one shot of a young white boy and turned it over. The information said the boy had been orphaned during the fighting in Kosovo. He had been injured in the mortar blast that killed his parents. His name was Milos Fidor and he was ten years old.

Bosch had been orphaned at age eleven. He looked into the boy's eyes and saw his own.

At 4 p.m. they locked Trent's home and took three boxes of seized materials to the car. A small group of reporters lingered outside during the whole afternoon, despite word from Media Relations that all information on the day's events would be distributed through Parker Center.

The reporters approached them with questions but Bosch quickly said that he was not allowed to comment on the investigation. They put the boxes in the trunk and drove off, heading downtown, where a meeting had been called by Deputy Chief Irvin Irving.

Bosch was uncomfortable with himself as he drove. He was ill at ease because Trent's suicide – and he had no doubts now that it was – had served to deflect the forward movement of the investigation of the boy's death. Bosch had spent half the day going through Trent's belongings when what he had wanted to be doing was nailing down the ID of the boy, running out the lead he had received in the call-in reports.

'What's the matter, Harry?' Edgar asked at one point on the drive.

'What?'

'I don't know. You're acting all morose. I know that's probably your natural disposition, but you usually don't show it so much.'

Edgar smiled but didn't get one in return from Bosch.

'I'm just thinking about things. This guy might be alive today if we had handled things differently.'

'Come on, Harry. You mean like if we didn't investigate him? There was no way. We did our job and things ran their course. Nothing we could do. If anybody's responsible it's Thornton, and he's gonna get his due. But if you ask me, the world's better off without somebody like Trent in it anyway. My conscience is clear, man. Crystal clear.'

'Good for you.'

Bosch thought about his decision to give Edgar the day off on Sunday. If he hadn't done that, Edgar might have been the one to make the computer runs on the names. Kiz Rider would've been out of the loop and the information would have never gotten to Thornton.

He sighed. Everything always seemed to work on a domino theory. If, then, if, then, if, then.

'What's your gut say on this guy?' he asked Edgar.

'You mean, like did he do the boy on the hill?'

Bosch nodded.

'I don't know,' Edgar said. 'Have to see what the lab says about the dirt and the sister says about the skateboard. If it is the sister and we get an ID.'

Bosch didn't say anything. But he always felt uncomfortable about relying on lab reports in determining which way to go with an investigation.

'What about you, Har?'

Bosch thought of the photos of all the children Trent thought he was caring for. His act of contrition. His chance at redemption.

'I'm thinking we're spinning our wheels,' he said. 'He isn't the guy.'

20

Deputy Chief Irvin Irving sat behind his desk in his spacious office on the sixth floor of Parker Center. Also seated in the room were Lt. Grace Billets, Bosch and Edgar and an officer from the Media Relations unit named Sergio Medina. Irving's adjutant, a female lieutenant named Simonton, stood in the open doorway of the office in case she was needed.

Irving had a glass-topped desk. There was nothing on it except for two pieces of paper with printing on them that Bosch could not read from his spot in front of Irving's desk and to the left.

'Now then,' Irving began. 'What do we know as fact about Mr. Trent? We know he was a pedophile with a criminal record of abusing a child. We know that he lived a stone's throw from the burial site of a murdered child. And we know that he committed suicide on the evening he was questioned by investigators in regard to the first two points just stated.'

Irving picked up one of the pages on his desk and studied it without sharing its contents with the room. Finally, he spoke.

'I have here a press release that states those same three facts and goes on to say, "Mr. Trent is the subject of an ongoing investigation. Determination of whether he was responsible for the death of the victim found buried near his home is pending lab work and follow-up investigation."'

He looked at the page silently again and then finally put it down.

'Nice and succinct. But it will do little to quell the thirst of the media for this story. Or to help us avert another troubling situation for this department.'

Bosch cleared his throat. Irving seemed to ignore it at first but then spoke without looking at the detective.

'Yes, Detective Bosch?'

'Well, it sort of seems as though you're not satisfied with that. The problem is, what is on that press release is exactly where we stand. I'd love to tell you I think the guy did the kid on the hill. I'd love to tell you I *know* he did it. But we are a long way from that and, if anything, I think we're going to end up concluding the opposite.'

'Based on what?' Irving snapped.

It was becoming clear to Bosch what the purpose of the meeting was. He guessed that the second page on Irving's desk was the press release the deputy chief wanted to put out. It probably pinned everything on Trent and called his suicide the result of his knowing he would be found out. This would allow the department to handle Thornton, the leaker, quietly outside of the magnifying glass of the press. It would spare the department the humiliation of acknowledging that a leak of confidential information from one of its officers caused a possibly innocent man to kill himself. It would also allow them to close the case of the boy on the hill.

Bosch understood that everyone sitting in the room knew that closing a case of this nature was the longest of long shots. The case had drawn growing media attention, and Trent with his suicide had now presented them with a way out. Suspicions could be cast on the dead pedophile, and the department could call it a day and move on to the next case – hopefully one with a better chance of being solved.

Bosch could understand this but not accept it. He had seen the bones. He had heard Golliher run down the litany of injuries. In that autopsy suite Bosch had resolved to find the killer and close the case. The expediency of department politics and image management would be second to that.

He reached into his coat pocket and pulled out his notebook. He opened it to a page with a folded corner and looked at it as if he was studying a page full of notes. But there was only one notation on the page, written on Saturday in the autopsy suite.

44 separate indications of trauma

His eyes held on the number he had written until Irving spoke again.

'Detective Bosch? I asked, "Based on what?"'

Bosch looked up and closed the notebook.

'Based on the timing – we don't think Trent moved into that neighborhood until after that boy was in the ground – and on the analysis of the bones. This kid was physically abused over a long period of time – from when he was a small child. It doesn't add up to Trent.'

'Analysis of both the timing and the bones will not be conclusive,' Irving said. 'No matter what they tell us, there is still a possibility – no matter how slim – that Nicholas Trent was the perpetrator of this crime.'

'A very slim possibility.'

'What about the search of Trent's home today?'

'We took some old work boots with dried mud in the treads. It will be compared to soil samples taken where the bones were found. But they'll be just as inconclusive. Even if they match up, Trent could have picked up the dirt hiking behind his house. It's all part of the same sediment, geologically speaking.'

'What else?'

'Not much. We've got a skateboard.'

'A skateboard?'

Bosch explained about the call-in tip he had not had time to follow up on because of the suicide. As he told it, he could see Irving warming to the possibility that a skateboard in Trent's possession could be linked to the bones on the hill.

'I want that to be your priority,' he said. 'I want that nailed down and I want to know it the moment you do.'

Bosch only nodded.

'Yes, sir,' Billets threw in.

Irving went silent and studied the two pages on his desk. Finally, he picked up the one he had not read from – the page Bosch guessed was the loaded press release – and turned at his desk. He slid it into a shredder, which whined loudly as it destroyed the document. He then turned back to his desk and picked up the remaining document.

'Officer Medina, you may put this out to the press.'

He handed the document to Medina, who stood up to receive it. Irving checked his watch.

'Just in time for the six o'clock news,' he said.

'Sir?' Medina said.

'Yes?'

'Uh, there have been many inquiries about the erroneous reports on Channel Four. Should we—'

'Say it is against policy to comment on any internal investigation. You may also add that the department will not condone or accept the leaking of confidential information to the media. That is all, Officer Medina.'

Medina looked like he had another question to ask but knew better. He nodded and left the office.

Irving nodded to his adjutant and she closed the office door, remaining in the anteroom outside. The deputy chief then turned his head, looking from Billets to Edgar to Bosch.

'We have a delicate situation here,' he said. 'Are we clear on how we are proceeding?'

'Yes,' Billets and Edgar said in unison.

Bosch said nothing. Irving looked at him.

'Detective, do you have something to say?'

Bosch thought a moment before answering.

'I just want to say that I am going to find out who killed that boy and put him up in that hole. If it's Trent, fine. Good. But if it's not him, I'm going to keep going.'

Irving saw something on his desk. Something small like a hair or other near-microscopic particle. Something Bosch couldn't see. Irving picked it up with two fingers and dropped it into the trash can behind him. As he brushed his fingers together over the shredder, Bosch looked on and wondered if the demonstration was some sort of threat directed at him.

'Not every case is solved, Detective, not every case is solvable,' he said. 'At some point our duties may require us to move on to more pressing matters.'

'Are you giving me a deadline?'

'No, Detective. I am saying I understand you. And I just hope you understand me.'

'What's going to happen with Thornton?'

'It's under internal review. I can't discuss it with you at this time.'

Bosch shook his head in frustration.

'Watch yourself, Detective Bosch,' Irving said curtly. 'I've shown a lot of patience with you. On this case and others before it.'

'What Thornton did jammed up this case. He should—'

'If he is responsible he will be dealt with accordingly. But keep in mind he was not operating in a vacuum. He needed to get the information in order to leak it. The investigation is ongoing.'

Bosch stared at Irving. The message was clear. Kiz Rider could go down with Thornton if Bosch didn't fall into step with Irving's march.

'You read me, Detective?'

'I read you. Loud and clear.'

21

Before taking Edgar back to Hollywood Division and then heading out to Venice, Bosch got the evidence box containing the skateboard out of the trunk and took it back inside Parker Center to the SID lab. At the counter he asked for Antoine Jesper. While he waited, he studied the skateboard. It appeared to be made out of laminated plywood. It had a lacquered finish to which several decals had been applied, most notably a skull and crossbones located in the middle of the top surface of the board.

When Jesper came to the counter, Bosch presented him with the evidence box.

'I want to know who made this, when it was made and where it was sold,' he said. 'It's priority one. I got the sixth floor riding my back on this case.'

'No problem. I can tell you the make right now. It's a Boney board. They don't make 'em anymore. He sold out and moved, I think, to Hawaii.'

'How do you know all of that?'

''Cause when I was a kid I was a boarder and this was what I wanted but never had the dough for. Pretty ironic, huh?'

'What is?'

'A Boney board and the case. You know, bones.'

Bosch nodded.

'Whatever. I want whatever you can get me by tomorrow.'

'Um, I can try. I can't prom—'

'Tomorrow, Antoine. The sixth floor, remember? I'll be talking to you tomorrow.'

Jesper nodded.

'Give me the morning, at least.'

'You got it. Anything happening with documents?'

Jesper shook his head.

'Nothing yet. She tried the dyes and nothing came up. I don't think you should count on anything there, Harry.'

'All right, Antoine.'

Bosch left him there holding the box.

On the way back to Hollywood he let Edgar drive while he pulled the tip sheet out of his briefcase and called Sheila Delacroix on his cell phone. She answered promptly and Bosch introduced himself and said her call had been referred to him.

'Was it Arthur?' she asked urgently.

'We don't know, ma'am. That's why I'm calling.'

'Oh.'

'Will it be possible for me and my partner to come see you tomorrow morning to talk about Arthur and get some information? It will help us to be better able to determine if the remains are those of your brother.'

'I understand. Um, yes. You can come here, if that is convenient.'

'Where is there, ma'am?'

'Oh. My home. Off Wilshire in the Miracle Mile.'

Bosch looked at the address on the call-in sheet.

'On Orange Grove.'

'Yes, that's correct.'

'Is eight-thirty too early for you?'

'That would be fine, Officer. If I can help I would like to. It just bothers me to think that that man lived there all those years after doing something like this. Even if the victim wasn't my brother.'

Bosch decided it wasn't worth telling her that Trent was probably completely innocent in terms of the bone case. There were too many people in the world who believed everything they saw on television.

Instead, Bosch gave her his cell phone number and told her to call it if something came up and eight-thirty the next morning turned out to be a bad time for her.

'It won't be a bad time,' she said. 'I want to help. If it's Arthur, I want to know. Part of me wants it to be him so I know it is over. But the other part wants it to be somebody else. That way I can keep thinking he is out there someplace. Maybe with a family of his own now.'

'I understand,' Bosch said. 'We'll see you in the morning.'

22

It was a brutal drive to Venice and Bosch arrived more than a half hour late. His lateness was then compounded by his fruitless search for a parking space before he went back to the library lot in defeat. His delay was no bother to Julia Brasher, who was in the critical stage of putting things together in the kitchen. She instructed him to go to the stereo and put on some music, then pour himself a glass of wine from the bottle that was already open on the coffee table. She did not make a move to touch him or kiss him, but her manner was completely warm. He thought things seemed good, that maybe he had gotten past the gaffe of the night before.

He chose a CD of live recordings of the Bill Evans Trio at the Village Vanguard in New York. He had the CD at home and knew it would make for quiet dinner music. He poured himself a glass of red wine and casually walked around the living room, looking at the things she had on display.

The mantel of the white brick fireplace was crowded with small framed photos he hadn't gotten a chance to look at the night before. Some were propped on stands and displayed more prominently than others. Not all were of people. Some photos were of places he assumed she had visited in her travels. There was a ground shot of a live volcano billowing smoke and spewing molten debris in the air. There was an underwater shot of the gaping mouth and jagged teeth of a shark. The killer fish appeared to be launching itself right at the camera – and whoever was behind it. At the edge of the photo Bosch could see one of the iron bars of the cage the photographer – who he assumed was Brasher – had been protected by.

There was a photo of Brasher with two Aboriginal men on either side of her standing somewhere, Bosch assumed, in the Australian outback. And there were several other photos of her with what appeared to be fellow backpackers in other locations of exotic or rugged terrain that Bosch could not readily identify. In none of the photos in which Julia was a subject was she looking at the camera. Her eyes were always staring off in the distance or at one of the other individuals posed with her.

In the last position on the mantel, as if hidden behind the other photos, was a small gold-framed shot of a much younger Julia Brasher with a slightly older man. Bosch reached behind the photos and lifted it out so he could see it better. The couple was sitting at a restaurant or perhaps a wedding reception. Julia wore a beige gown with a low-cut neckline. The man wore a tuxedo.

'You know, this man is a god in Japan,' Julia called from the kitchen.

Bosch put the framed photo back in its place and walked to the kitchen. Her hair was down and he couldn't decide which way he liked it best.

'Bill Evans?'

'Yeah. It seems like they have whole channels of the radio dedicated to playing his music.'

'Don't tell me, you spent some time in Japan, too.'

'About two months. It's a fascinating place.'

It looked to Bosch like she was making a risotto with chicken and asparagus in it.

'Smells good.'

'Thank you. I hope it is.'

'So what do you think you were running from?'

She looked up at him from her work at the stove. A hand held a stirring spoon steady.

'What?'

'You know, all the travel. Leaving Daddy's law firm to go swim with sharks and dive into volcanoes. Was it the old man or the law firm the old man ran?'

'Some people would look at it as maybe I was running toward something.'

'The guy in the tuxedo?'

'Harry, take your gun off. Leave your badge at the door. I always do.'

'Sorry.'

She went back to work at the stove and Bosch came up behind her. He put his hands on her shoulders and pushed his thumbs into the indentations of her upper spine. She offered no resistance. Soon he felt her muscles begin to relax. He noticed her empty wine glass on the counter.

'I'll go get the wine.'

He came back with his glass and the bottle. He refilled her glass and she picked it up and clicked it off the side of his.

'Whether to something or away from something, here's to running,' she said. 'Just running.'

'What happened to 'Hold fast'?'

'There's that, too.'

'Here's to forgiveness and reconciliation.'

They clicked glasses again. He came around behind her and started working her neck again.

'You know, I thought about your story all last night after you left,' she said.

'My story?'

'About the bullet and the tunnel.'

'And?'

She shrugged her shoulders.

'Nothing. It's just amazing, that's all.'

'You know, after that day, I wasn't afraid anymore when I was down in the darkness. I just knew that I was going to make it through. I can't explain why, I just knew. Which, of course, was stupid, because there are no guarantees of that – back then and there or anywhere else. It made me sort of reckless.'

He held his hands steady for a moment.

'It's not good to be too reckless,' he said. 'You cross the tube too often, you'll eventually get burned.'

'Hmm. Are you lecturing me, Harry? You want to be my training officer now?'

'No. I checked my gun and my badge at the door, remember?'

'Okay, then.'

She turned around, his hands still on her neck, and kissed him. Then she pulled back away.

'You know, the great thing about this risotto is that it can keep in the oven as long as we need it to.'

Bosch smiled.

Later on, after they had made love, Bosch got up from her bed and went out to the living room.

'Where are you going?' she called after him.

When he didn't answer she called out to him to turn the oven up. He came back into the room carrying the gold-framed photo. He got into the bed and turned on the light on the bed table. It was a low-wattage bulb beneath a heavy lamp shade. The room still was cast in shadow.

'Harry, what are you doing?' Julia said in a tone that warned he was treading close to her heart. 'Did you turn the oven up?'

'Yeah, three-fifty. Tell me about this guy.'

'Why?'

'I just want to know.'

'It's a private story.'

'I know. But you can tell me.'

She tried to take the photo away but he held it out of her reach.

'Is he the one? Did he break your heart and send you running?'

'Harry. I thought you took your badge off.'

'I did. And my clothes, everything.'

She smiled.

'Well, I'm not telling you anything.'

She was on her back, head propped on a pillow. Bosch put the picture on the bed table and then turned back and moved in next to her. Under the sheet he put his arm across her body and pulled her tightly to him.

'Look, you want to trade scars again? I got my heart broken twice by the same woman. And you know what? I kept her picture on a shelf in my living room for a long time. Then on New Year's Day I decided it had been a long enough time. I put her picture away. Then I got called out to work and I met you.'

She looked at him, her eyes moving slightly back and forth as she seemed to be searching his face for something, maybe the slightest hint of insincerity.

'Yes,' she finally said. 'He broke my heart. Okay?'

'No, not okay. Who is the creep?'

She started laughing.

'Harry, you're my knight in tarnished armor, aren't you?'

She pulled herself up into a sitting position, the sheet falling away from her breasts. She folded her arms across them.

'He was in the firm. I really fell for him – right down the old elevator shaft. And then . . . then he decided it was over. And he decided to betray me and to tell secret things to my father.'

'What things?'

She shook her head.

'Things I will never tell a man again.'

'Where was that picture taken?'

'Oh, at a firm function – probably the New Year's banquet, I don't remember. They have a lot of them.'

Bosch had become angled behind her. He leaned down and kissed her back, just above the tattoo.

'I couldn't be there anymore while he was there. So I quit. I said I wanted to travel. My father thought it was a midlife crisis because I had turned thirty. I just let him think it. But then I had to do what I said I wanted to do – travel. I went to Australia first. It was the farthest place I could think of.'

Bosch pulled himself up and stacked two pillows behind his back. He then pulled her back against his chest. He kissed the top of her head and kept his nose in her hair.

'I had a lot of money from the firm,' she said. 'I didn't have to worry. I just kept traveling, going wherever I wanted, working odd jobs when I felt like it. I didn't come home for almost four years. And when I did, that's when I joined the academy. I was walking along the boardwalk and saw the little Venice community service office. I went in and picked up a pamphlet. It all happened pretty fast after that.'

'Your history shows impulsive and possibly reckless decision-making processes. How did that get by the screeners?'

She gently elbowed him in the side, setting off a flare of pain from his ribs. He tensed.

'Oh, Harry, sorry. I forgot.'

'Yeah, sure.'

She laughed.

'I guess all you old guys know that the department's been pushing big time for what they term "mature" women cadets the last few years. To smooth off all the hard testosterone edges of the department.'

She rocked her hips back against Bosch's genitals to underline the point.

'And speaking of testosterone,' she said, 'you never told me how it went with old bullet head himself today.'

Bosch groaned but didn't answer.

'You know,' she said, 'Irving came to address our class one day on the moral responsibilities that come with carrying the badge. And everybody sitting there knew the guy probably makes more backroom deals up there on the sixth floor than there are days in the year. The guy's the classic fixer. You could practically cut the irony in the auditorium with a knife.'

Her use of the word 'irony' made Bosch flash on what Antoine Jesper had said about coupling the bones found on the hill with the bones on the skateboard. He felt his body tensing as thoughts of the case started encroaching on what had been an oasis of respite from the investigation.

She sensed his tightness.

'What is it?'

'Nothing.'

'You got all tense all of a sudden.'

'The case, I guess.'

She was quiet a moment.

'I think it's kind of amazing,' she then said. 'Those bones being up there all of these years and then coming up out of the ground. Like a ghost or something.'

'It's a city of bones. And all of them are waiting to come up.'

He paused.

'I don't want to talk about Irving or the bones or the case or anything else right now.'

'Then what do you want?'

He didn't answer. She turned to face him and started pushing him down off the pillows until he was flat on his back.

'How about a mature woman to smooth off all the hard edges again?'

It was impossible for Bosch not to smile.

23

Before dawn Bosch was on the road. He left Julia Brasher sleeping in her bed and started on his way to his home, after first stopping at Abbot's Habit for a coffee to go. Venice was like a ghost town, with the tendrils of the morning fog moving across the streets. But as he got closer to Hollywood the lights of cars on the streets multiplied and Bosch was reminded that the city of bones was a twenty-four-hour city.

At home he showered and put on fresh clothes. He then climbed back into his car and went down the hill to Hollywood Division. It was 7:30 when he got there. Surprisingly, a number of detectives were already in place, chasing paperwork and cases. Edgar wasn't among them. Bosch put his briefcase down and walked to the watch office to get coffee and to see if any citizen had brought in doughnuts. Almost every day a John Q who still kept the faith brought in doughnuts for the division. A little way of saying there were still those out there who knew or at least understood the difficulties of the job. Every day in every division cops put on the badge and tried to do their best in a place where the populace didn't understand them, didn't particularly like them and in many instances outright despised them. Bosch always thought it was amazing how far a box of doughnuts could go in undoing that.

He poured a cup and dropped a dollar in the basket. He took a sugar doughnut out of a box on the counter that had already been decimated by the patrol guys. No wonder. They were from Bob's Donuts in the farmers' market. He noticed Mankiewicz sitting at his desk, his dark eyebrows forming a deep V as he studied what looked like a deployment chart.

'Hey, Mank, I think we pulled a grade A lead off the call-in sheets. Thought you'd want to know.'

Mankiewicz answered without looking up.

'Good. Let me know when my guys can give it a rest. We're going to be short on the desk the next few days.'

Bosch knew this meant he was juggling personnel. When there weren't enough uniforms to put in cars – due to vacations, court appearances or sick-outs – the watch sergeant always pulled people off the desk and put them on wheels.

'You got it.'

Edgar still wasn't at the table when Bosch got back to the detective squad room. Bosch put his coffee and doughnut down next to one of the Selectrics and went to get a search warrant application out of a community file drawer. For the next fifteen minutes he typed out an addendum to the search warrant he had already delivered to the records custodian at Queen of Angels. It asked for all records from the care of Arthur Delacroix circa 1975 to 1985.

When he was finished he took it to the fax machine and sent it to the office of Judge John A. Houghton, who had signed all the hospital search warrants the day before. He added a note requesting that the judge review the addendum application as soon as possible because it might lead to the positive identification of the bones and therefore swing the investigation into focus.

Bosch returned to the table and from a drawer pulled out the stack of missing person reports he had gathered while fiche-ing in the archives. He started looking through them quickly, glancing only at the box reserved for the name of the missing individual. In ten minutes he was finished. There had been no report in the stack about Arthur Delacroix. He didn't know what this meant but he planned to ask the boy's sister about it.

It was now eight o'clock and Bosch was ready to leave to visit the sister. But still no Edgar. Bosch ate the remainder of his doughnut and decided to give his partner ten minutes to show before he would leave on his own. He had worked with Edgar for more than ten years and still was bothered by his partner's lack of punctuality. It was one thing to be late for dinner. It was another to be late for a case. He had always taken Edgar's tardiness as a lack of commitment to their mission as homicide investigators.

His direct line rang and Bosch answered it with an annoyed rasp, expecting it to be Edgar announcing he was running late. But it wasn't Edgar. It was Julia Brasher.

'So, you just leave a woman high and dry in bed, huh?'

Bosch smiled and his frustration with Edgar quickly drained away.

'I got a busy day here,' he said. 'I had to get going.'

'I know but you could've said good-bye.'

Bosch saw Edgar making his way through the squad room. He wanted to get going before Edgar started his coffee, doughnut and sports-page ritual.

'Well, I'm saying good-bye now, okay? I'm in the middle of something here and I gotta run.'

'Harry . . . '

'What?'

'I thought you were going to hang up on me or something.'

'I'm not, but I gotta go. Look, come by before you go up for roll call, okay? I'll probably be back by then.'

'All right. I'll see you.'

Bosch hung up and stood up just as Edgar got to the homicide table and dropped the folded sports page at his spot.

'You ready?'

'Yeah, I was just going to get—'

'Let's go. I don't want to keep the lady waiting. And she'll probably have coffee there.'

On the way out Bosch checked the incoming tray on the fax machine. His search warrant addendum had been signed and returned by Judge Houghton.

'We're in business,' Bosch said to Edgar, showing him the warrant as they walked to the car. 'See? You come in early, you get stuff done.'

'What's that supposed to mean? Is that a crack on me?'

'It means what it means, I guess.'

'I just want some coffee.'

24

Sheila Delacroix lived in a part of the city called the Miracle Mile. It was a neighborhood south of Wilshire that wasn't quite up to the standards of nearby Hancock Park but was lined with nicely kept homes and duplexes with modest stylistic adjustments to promote individuality.

Delacroix's home was the second floor of a duplex with pseudo-Beaux Arts styling. She invited the detectives into her home in a friendly manner, but when the first question Edgar asked was about coffee, she said it was against her religion. She offered tea, and Edgar reluctantly accepted. Bosch passed. He wondered which religion outlawed coffee.

They took seats in the living room while the woman made Edgar his tea in the kitchen. She called out to them, saying she only had an hour and then had to leave for work.

'What is it you do?' Bosch asked as she came out with a mug of hot tea, the tag from the tea bag looped over the side. She put it down on a coaster on a side table next to Edgar. She was a tall woman. She was slightly overweight with blonde hair cut short. Bosch thought she wore too much makeup.

'I'm a casting agent,' she said as she took a seat on the couch. 'Mostly independent films, some episodic television. I'm actually casting a cop show this week.'

Bosch watched Edgar sip some tea and make a face. He then held the mug so he could read the tea bag tag.

'It's a blend,' Delacroix said. 'Strawberry and Darjeeling. Do you like it?'

Edgar put the mug down on its coaster.

'It's fine.'

'Ms. Delacroix? If you're in the entertainment business, did you by any chance know Nicholas Trent?'

'Please, just call me Sheila. Now, that name, Nicholas Trent. It sounds familiar but I can't quite place it. Is he an actor or is he in casting?'

'Neither. He's the man who lived up on Wonderland. He was a set designer – I mean, decorator.'

'Oh, the one on TV, the man who killed himself. Oh, no wonder it was familiar.'

'So you didn't know him from the business, then?'

'No, not at all.'

'Okay, well I shouldn't have asked that. We're out of order here. Let's just start with your brother. Tell us about Arthur. Do you have a picture we can look at?'

'Yes,' she said, as she stood up and walked behind his chair. 'Here he is.'

She went to a waist-high cabinet Bosch hadn't noticed behind him. There were framed photos on it displayed in much the same way he had seen the photos on Julia Brasher's mantel. Delacroix chose one and turned around and handed it to Bosch.

The frame contained a photo of a boy and a girl sitting on a set of stairs Bosch recognized as the stairs they had climbed before knocking on her door. The boy was much smaller than the girl. Both were smiling at the camera and had the smiles of children who have been told to smile – a lot of teeth but not a legitimately turned-up mouth.

Bosch handed the photo to Edgar and looked at Delacroix, who had returned to the couch.

'Those stairs . . . was that taken here?'

'Yes, this is the home we grew up in.'

'When he disappeared, it was from here?'

'Yes.'

'Are any of his belongings still here in the house?'

Delacroix smiled sadly and shook her head.

'No, it's all gone. I gave his things to the charity rummage sale at church. That was a long time ago.'

'What church is that?'

'The Wilshire Church of Nature.'

Bosch just nodded.

'They're the ones who don't let you have coffee?' Edgar asked.

'Nothing with caffeine.'

Edgar put the framed photo down next to his tea.

'Do you have any other photos of him?' he asked.

'Of course, I have a box of old photos.'

'Can we look at those? You know, while we talk.'

Delacroix's eyebrows came together in confusion.

'Sheila,' Bosch said. 'We found some clothing with the remains. We would like to look at the photos to see if any of it matches. It will help the investigation.'

She nodded.

'I see. Well, then I'll be right back. I just need to go to the closet in the hallway.'

'Do you need help?'

'No, I can manage.'

After she was gone Edgar leaned over to Bosch and whispered, 'This Church of Nature tea tastes like piss water.'

Bosch whispered back, 'How would you know what piss water tastes like?'

The skin around Edgar's eyes drew tight with embarrassment as he realized he had walked into that one. Before he could muster a response Sheila Delacroix came back into the room carrying an old shoe box. She put it down on the coffee table and removed the lid. The box was filled with loose photographs.

'These aren't in any order or anything. But he should be in a lot of them.'

Bosch nodded to Edgar, who reached into the box for the first stack of photos.

'While my partner looks through these, why don't you tell me about your brother and when he disappeared?'

Sheila nodded and composed her thoughts before beginning.

'May fourth, nineteen eighty. He didn't come home from school. That's it. That's all. We thought he had run away. You said you found clothes with the remains. Well, my father looked in his drawers and said that Arthur had taken clothes. That was what made us think he had run away.'

Bosch wrote a few notes down in a notebook he had pulled from his coat pocket.

'You mentioned that he had been injured a few months before on a skateboard.'

'Yes, he hit his head and they had to operate.'

'When he disappeared, did he take his skateboard?'

She thought about this for a long moment.

'It was so long ago . . . all I know is that he loved that board. So I think he probably took it. But I just remember the clothes. My father found some of his clothes missing.'

'Did you report him missing?'

'I was sixteen years old at the time, so I didn't do anything. My father talked to the police though. I'm sure of it.'

'I couldn't find any record of Arthur being reported missing. Are you sure he reported him missing?'

'I drove with him to the police station.'

'Was it Wilshire Division?'

'I would assume but I don't really remember.'

'Sheila, where is your father? Is he still alive?'

'He's alive. He lives in the Valley. But he's not well these days.'

'Where in the Valley?'

'Van Nuys. In the Manchester Trailer Park.'

There was silence while Bosch wrote the information down. He had been to the Manchester Trailer Park before on investigations. It wasn't a pleasant place to live.

'He drinks ... '

Bosch looked at her.

'Ever since Arthur ... '

Bosch nodded that he understood. Edgar leaned forward and handed him a photograph. It was a yellowed 3 × 5. It showed a young boy, his arms raised in an effort to maintain balance, gliding on the sidewalk on a skateboard. The angle of the photograph showed little of the skateboard other than its profile. Bosch could not tell if it carried a bone design on it or not.

'Can't see much there,' he said as he started to hand the photo back.

'No, the clothes – the shirt.'

Bosch looked at the photo again. Edgar was right. The boy in the photo wore a gray T-shirt with solid surf printed across the chest.

Bosch showed the photo to Sheila.

'This is your brother, right?'

She leaned forward to look at the photo.

'Yes, definitely.'

'That shirt he is wearing, do you remember if it is one of the pieces of clothing your father found missing?'

Delacroix shook her head.

'I can't remember. It's been – I just remember that he liked that shirt a lot.'

Bosch nodded and gave the photo back to Edgar. It wasn't the kind of solid confirmation they could get from X-rays and bone comparison but it was one more notch. Bosch was feeling more and more sure that they were about to identify the bones. He watched Edgar put the photo in a short stack of pictures he intended to borrow from Sheila's collection.

Bosch checked his watch and looked back at Sheila.

'What about your mother?'

Sheila immediately shook her head.

'Nope, she was long gone by the time all of this happened.'

'You mean she died?'

'I mean she took a bus the minute the going got tough. You see, Arthur was a difficult child. Right from the beginning. He needed a lot of attention and it fell to my mother. After a while she couldn't take it any longer. One night she went out to get some medicine at the drugstore and she never came back. We found little notes from her under our pillows.'

Bosch dropped his eyes to his notebook. It was hard to hear this story and keep looking at Sheila Delacroix.

'How old were you? How old was your brother?'

'I was six, so that would make Artie two.'

Bosch nodded.

'Did you keep the note from her?'

'No. There was no need. I didn't need a reminder of how she supposedly loved us but not enough to stay with us.'

'What about Arthur? Did he keep his?'

'Well, he was only two, so my father kept it for him. He gave it to him when he was older. He may have kept it, I don't know. Because he never really knew her, he was always very interested in what she was like. He asked me a lot of questions about her. There were no photos of her. My father had gotten rid of them all so he wouldn't have any reminders.'

'Do you know what happened to her? Or if she's still alive?'

'I haven't the faintest idea. And to tell you the truth, I don't care if she is alive or not.'

'What is her name?'

'Christine Dorsett Delacroix. Dorsett was her maiden name.'

'Do you know her birth date or Social Security number?'

Sheila shook her head.

'Do you have your own birth certificate handy here?'

'It's somewhere in my records. I could go look for it.'

She started to get up.

'No, wait, we can look for that at the end. I'd like to keep talking here.'

'Okay.'

'Um, after your mother was gone, did your father remarry?'

'No, he never did. He lives alone now.'

'Did he ever have a girlfriend, someone who might have stayed in the house?'

She looked at Bosch with eyes that seemed almost lifeless.

'No,' she said. 'Never.'

Bosch decided to move on to an area of discussion that would be less difficult for her.

'What school did your brother go to?'

'At the end he was going to The Brethren.'

Bosch didn't say anything. He wrote the name of the school down on his pad and then a large letter *B* beneath it. He circled the letter, thinking about the backpack. Sheila continued unbidden.

'It was a private school for troubled boys. My dad paid to send him there. It's off of Crescent Heights near Pico. It's still there.'

'Why did he go there? I mean, why was he considered troubled?'

'Because he got kicked out of his other schools for fighting mostly.'

'Fighting?' Edgar said.

'That's right.'

Edgar picked the top photograph off of his keeper file and studied it for a moment.

'This boy looks like he was as light as smoke. Was he the one starting these fights?'

'Most times. He had trouble getting along. All he wanted to do was be on his skateboard. I think that by today's standards he would be diagnosed as having attention deficit disorder or something similar. He just wanted to be by himself all the time.'

'Did he get hurt in these fights?' Bosch asked.

'Sometimes. Black and blue mostly.'

'Broken bones?'

'Not that I remember. Just schoolyard fights.'

Bosch felt agitated. The information they were getting could point them in many different directions. He had hoped a clear-cut path might emerge from the interview.

'You said your father searched the drawers in your brother's room and found clothes missing.'

'That's right. Not a lot. Just a few things.'

'Any idea what was missing specifically?'

She shook her head.

'I can't remember.'

'What did he take the clothes in? Like a suitcase or something?'

'I think he took his schoolbag. Took out the books and put in some clothes.'

'Do you remember what that looked like?'

'No. Just a backpack. Everybody had to use the same thing at The Brethren. I still see kids walking on Pico with them, the backpacks with the *B* on the back.'

Bosch glanced at Edgar and then back at Delacroix.

'Let's go back to the skateboard. Are you sure he took it with him?'

She paused to think about this, then slowly nodded.

'Yes, I'm pretty sure he took it with him.'

Bosch decided to cut off the interview and concentrate on completing the identification. Once they confirmed the bones came from Arthur Delacroix, then they could come back to his sister.

He thought about Golliher's take on the injuries to the bones. Chronic abuse. Could it all have been injuries from schoolyard fights and skateboarding? He knew he needed to approach the issue of child abuse but did not feel the time was appropriate. He also didn't want to tip his hand to the daughter so that she could turn around and possibly tell the father. What Bosch wanted was to back out and come back in later when he felt he had a tighter grasp on the case and a solid investigative plan to go with.

'Okay, we're going to wrap things up here pretty quickly, Sheila. Just a few more questions. Did Arthur have some friends? Maybe a best friend, someone he might confide in?'

She shook her head.

'Not really. He mostly was by himself.'

Bosch nodded and was about to close his notebook when she continued.

'There was one boy he'd go boarding with. His name was Johnny Stokes. He was from somewhere down near Pico. He was bigger and a little bit older than Arthur but they were in the same class at The Brethren. My father was pretty sure he smoked pot. So we didn't like Arthur being friends with him.'

'By "we," you mean your dad and you?'

'Yes, my father. He was upset about it.'

'Did either of you talk to Johnny Stokes after Arthur went missing?'

'Yes, that night when he didn't come home my father called Johnny Stokes, but he said he hadn't seen Artie. The next day when Dad went to the school to ask about him, he told me he talked to Johnny again about Artie.'

'And what did he say?'

'That he hadn't seen him.'

Bosch wrote down the friend's name in his notebook and underlined it.

'Any other friends you can think of?'

'No, not really.'

'What's your father's name?'

'Samuel. Are you going to talk to him?'

'Most likely.'

Her eyes dropped to the hands clasped in her lap.

'Is that a problem if we talk to him?'

'Not really. He's just not well. If those bones turn out to be Arthur . . . I was thinking it would be better if he didn't ever know.'

'We'll keep that in mind when we talk to him. But we won't do it until we have a positive identification.'

'But if you talk to him, then he'll know.'

'It may be unavoidable, Sheila.'

Edgar handed Bosch another photo. It showed Arthur standing next to a tall blond man who looked faintly familiar to Bosch. He showed the photo to Sheila.

'Is this your father?'

'Yes, it's him.'

'He looks familiar. Was he ever—'

'He's an actor. Was, actually. He was on some television shows in the sixties and a few things after that, some movie parts.'

'Not enough to make a living?'

'No, he always had to work other jobs. So we could live.'

Bosch nodded and handed the photo back to Edgar but Sheila reached across the coffee table and intercepted it.

'I don't want that one to leave, please. I don't have many photos of my father.'

'Fine,' Bosch said. 'Could we go look for the birth certificate now?'

'I'll go look. You can stay here.'

She got up and left the room again, and Edgar took the opportunity to show Bosch some of the other photos he had taken to keep during the investigation.

'It's him, Harry,' he whispered. 'I got no doubt.'

He showed him a photo of Arthur Delacroix that had apparently been taken for school. His hair was combed neatly and he wore a blue blazer and tie. Bosch studied the boy's eyes. They reminded him of the photo of the boy from Kosovo he had found in Nicholas Trent's house. The boy with the thousand-yard stare.

'I found it.'

Sheila Delacroix came into the room carrying an envelope and unfolding a yellowed document. Bosch looked at it for a moment and then copied down the names, birth dates and Social Security numbers of her parents.

'Thanks,' he said. 'You and Arthur had the same parents, right?'

'Of course.'

'Okay, Sheila, thank you. We're going to go. We'll call you as soon as we know something for sure.'

He stood up and so did Edgar.

'All right if we borrow these photos?' Edgar asked. 'I will personally see that you get them back.'

'Okay, if you need them.'

They headed to the door and she opened it. While still on the threshold Bosch asked her one last question.

'Sheila, have you always lived here?'

She nodded.

'All my life. I've stayed here in case he comes back, you know? In case he doesn't know where to start and comes here.'

She smiled but not in any way that imparted humor. Bosch nodded and stepped outside behind Edgar.

25

Bosch walked up to the museum ticket window and told the woman sitting behind it his name and that he had an appointment with Dr. William Golliher in the anthropology lab. She picked up a phone and made a call. A few minutes later she rapped on the glass with her wedding band until it drew the attention of a nearby security guard. He came over and the woman instructed him to escort Bosch to the lab. He did not have to pay the admission.

The guard said nothing as they walked through the dimly lit museum, past the mammoth display and the wall of wolf skulls. Bosch had never been inside the museum, though he had gone to the La Brea Tar Pits often on field trips when he was a child. The museum was built after that, to house and display all of the finds that bubbled up out of the earth in the tar pits.

When Bosch had called Golliher's cell phone after receiving the medical records on Arthur Delacroix, the anthropologist said he was already working on another case and couldn't get downtown to the medical examiner's office until the next day. Bosch had said he couldn't wait. Golliher said he did have copies of the X-rays and photographs from the Wonderland case with him. If Bosch could come to him, he could make the comparisons and give an unofficial response.

Bosch took the compromise and headed to the tar pits while Edgar remained at Hollywood Division working the computer to see if he could locate Arthur and Sheila Delacroix's mother as well as run down Arthur's friend Johnny Stokes.

Now Bosch was curious as to what the new case was that Golliher was working. The tar pits were an ancient black hole where animals had gone to their death for centuries. In a grim chain reaction, animals caught in the miasma became prey for other animals, who in turn were mired and slowly pulled down. In some form of natural equilibrium the bones now came back up out of the blackness and were collected for study by modern man. All of this took place right next to one of the busiest streets in Los Angeles, a constant reminder of the crushing passage of time.

Bosch was led through two doors and into the crowded lab where the bones were identified, classified, dated and cleaned. There appeared to be boxes of bones everywhere on every flat surface. A half dozen people in white lab coats worked at stations, cleaning and examining the bones.

Golliher was the only one not in a lab coat. He had on another Hawaiian shirt, this one with parrots on it, and was working at a table in the far corner. As Bosch approached, he saw there were two wooden bone boxes on the worktable in front of him. In one of the boxes was a skull.

'Detective Bosch, how are you?'

'Doing okay. What's this?'

'This, as I'm sure you can tell, is a human skull. It and some other human bones were collected two days ago from asphalt that was actually excavated thirty years ago to make room for this museum. They've asked me to take a look before they make the announcement.'

'I don't understand. Is it . . . old or . . . from thirty years ago?'

'Oh, it's quite old. It was carbon-dated to nine thousand years ago, actually.'

Bosch nodded. The skull and the bones in the other box looked like mahogany.

'Take a look,' Golliher said and he lifted the skull out of the box.

He turned it so that the rear of the skull faced Bosch. He moved his finger in a circle around a star fracture near the top of the skull.

'Look familiar?'

'Blunt force fracture?'

'Exactly. Much like your case. Just goes to show you.'

He gently replaced the skull in the wooden box.

'Show me what?'

'Things don't change that much. This woman – at least we think it was a woman – was murdered nine thousand years ago, her body probably thrown into the tar pit as a means of covering the crime. Human nature, it doesn't change.'

Bosch stared at the skull.

'She's not the first.'

Bosch looked up at Golliher.

'In nineteen fourteen the bones – a more complete skeleton, actually – of another woman were found in the tar. She had the same star fracture in the same spot on her skull. Her bones were carbon-dated as nine thousand years old. Same time frame as her.'

He nodded to the skull in the box.

'So, what are you saying, Doc, that there was a serial killer here nine thousand years ago?'

'It's impossible to know that, Detective Bosch. All we have are the bones.'

Bosch looked down at the skull again. He thought about what Julia Brasher had said about his job, about his taking evil out of the world. What she didn't know was a truth he had known for too long. That true evil could never be taken out of the world. At best he was wading into the dark waters of the abyss with two leaking buckets in his hands.

'But you have other things on your mind, don't you?' Golliher said, interrupting Bosch's thoughts. 'Do you have the hospital records?'

Bosch brought his briefcase up onto the worktable and opened it. He handed Golliher a file. Then, from his pocket he pulled the stack of photos he and Edgar had borrowed from Sheila Delacroix.

'I don't know if these help,' he said. 'But this is the kid.'

Golliher picked up the photos. He went through them quickly, stopping at the posed close-up of Arthur Delacroix in a jacket and tie. He went over to a chair where a backpack was slung over the armrest. He pulled out his own file and came back to the worktable. He opened the file and took out an 8 × 10 photo of the skull from Wonderland Avenue. For a long moment he held the photos of Arthur Delacroix and the skull side by side and studied them.

Finally, he said, 'The malar and superciliary ridge formation look similar.'

'I'm not an anthropologist, Doc.'

Golliher put the photos down on the table. He then explained by running his finger across the left eyebrow of the boy and then down around the outside of his eye.

'The brow ridge and the exterior orbit,' he said. 'It's wider than usual on the recovered specimen. Looking at this photo of the boy, we see his facial structure is in line with what we see here.'

Bosch nodded.

'Let's look at the X-rays,' Golliher said. 'There's a box back here.'

Golliher gathered the files and led Bosch to another worktable, where there was a light box built into the surface. He opened the hospital file, picked up the X-rays and began reading the patient history report.

Bosch had already read the document. The hospital reported that the boy was brought into the emergency room at 5:40 p.m. on February 11, 1980, by his father, who said he was found in a dazed and unresponsive state following a fall from a skateboard in which he struck his head. Neurosurgery was performed in order to relieve pressure inside the skull caused by swelling of the brain. The boy remained in the hospital under observation for ten days and was then released to his father. Two weeks later he was readmitted for follow-up surgery to remove the clips that had been used to hold his skull together following the neurosurgery.

There was no report anywhere in the file of the boy complaining about being mistreated by his father or anyone else. While recovering from the initial surgery he was routinely interviewed by an on-site social worker. Her report was less than half a page. It reported that the boy said he had hurt himself while skateboarding. There was no follow-up questioning or referral to juvenile authorities or the police.

Golliher shook his head while he finished his scan of the document.

'What is it?' Bosch asked.

'It's nothing. And that's the problem. No investigation. They took the boy at his word. His father was probably sitting right there in the room with him when he was interviewed. You know how hard it would have been for him to tell the truth? So they just patched him up and sent him right back to the person who was hurting him.'

'Hey, Doc, you're getting a little bit ahead of us. Let's get the ID, if it's there, and then we'll figure out who was hurting the kid.'

'Fine. It's your case. It's just that I've seen this a hundred times.'

Golliher dropped the reports and picked up the X-rays. Bosch watched him with a bemused smile on his face. It seemed that Golliher was annoyed because Bosch had not jumped to the same conclusions he had with the same speed he had.

Golliher put two X-rays down on the light box. He then went to his own file and brought out X-rays he had taken of the Wonderland skull. He flipped the box's light on and three X-rays glowed before them. Golliher pointed to the X-ray he had taken from his own file.

'This is a radiological X-ray I took to look inside the bone of the skull. But we can use it here for comparison purposes. Tomorrow when I get back to the medical examiner's office I will use the skull itself.'

Golliher leaned over the light box and reached for a small glass eyepiece that was stored on a nearby shelf. He held one end to his eye and pressed the other against one of the X-rays. After a few moments he moved to one of the hospital X-rays and pressed the eyepiece to the same location on the skull. He went back and forth numerous times, making comparison after comparison.

When he was finished, Golliher straightened up, leaned back against the next worktable and folded his arms.

'Queen of Angels was a government-subsidized hospital. Money was always tight. They should have taken more than two pictures of this kid's head. If they had, they might have seen some of his other injuries.'

'Okay. But they didn't.'

'Yeah, they didn't. But based on what they did do and what we've got here, I was able to make several comparison points on the roundel, the fracture pattern and along the squamous suture. There is no doubt in my mind.'

He gestured toward the X-rays still glowing on the light box.

'Meet Arthur Delacroix.'

Bosch nodded.

'Okay.'

Golliher stepped over to the light box and started collecting the X-rays.

'How sure are you?'

'Like I said, there's no doubt. I'll look at the skull tomorrow when I'm downtown, but I can tell you now, it's him. It's a match.'

'So, if we get somebody and go into court with it, there aren't going to be any surprises, right?'

Golliher looked at Bosch.

'No surprises. These findings can't be challenged. As you know, the challenge lies in the interpretation of the injuries. I look at this boy and see something horribly, horribly wrong. And I will testify to that. Gladly. But then you have these official records.'

He gestured dismissively to the open file of hospital records.

'They say skateboard. That's where the fight will be.'

Bosch nodded. Golliher put the two X-rays back into the file and closed it. Bosch put it back in his briefcase.

'Well, Doctor, thanks for taking the time to see me here. I think—'

'Detective Bosch?'

'Yes?'

'The other day you seemed very uncomfortable when I mentioned the necessity of faith in what we do. Basically, you changed the subject.'

'Not really a subject I feel comfortable talking about.'

'I would think that in your line of work it would be paramount to have a healthy spirituality.'

'I don't know. My partner likes blaming aliens from outer space for everything that's wrong. I guess that's healthy, too.'

'You're avoiding the question.'

Bosch grew annoyed and the feeling quickly slipped toward anger.

'What is the question, Doc? Why do you care so much about me and what I believe or don't believe?'

'Because it is important to me. I study bones. The framework of life. And I have come to believe that there is something more than blood and tissue and bone. There is something else that holds us together. I have something inside, that you'll never see on any X-ray, that holds me together and keeps me going. And so, when I meet someone who carries a void in the place where I carry my faith, I get scared for him.'

Bosch looked at him for a long moment.

'You're wrong about me. I have faith and I have a mission. Call it blue religion, call it whatever you like. It's the belief that this won't just go by. That those bones came out of the ground for a reason. That they came out of the ground for me to find, and for me to do something about. And that's what holds me together and keeps me going. And it won't show up on any X-ray either. Okay?'

He stared at Golliher, waiting for a reply. But the anthropologist said nothing.

'I gotta go, Doctor,' Bosch finally said. 'Thanks for your help. You've made things very clear for me.'

He left him there, surrounded by the dark bones the city had been built on.

26

Edgar was not at his spot at the homicide table when Bosch got back to the squad room.

'Harry?'

Bosch looked up and saw Lt. Billets standing in the doorway to her office. Through the glass window Bosch could see Edgar in there sitting in front of her desk. Bosch put his briefcase down and headed over.

'What's up?' he said as he entered the office.

'No, that's my question,' Billets said as she closed the door. 'Do we have an ID?'

She went around behind her desk and sat down as Bosch took the seat next to Edgar.

'Yes, we have an ID. Arthur Delacroix, disappeared May fourth, nineteen eighty.'

'The ME is sure of this?'

'Their bone guy says there is no doubt.'

'How close are we on time of death?'

'Pretty close. The bone guy said before we knew anything that the fatal impact to the skull came about three months after the kid had the earlier skull fracture and surgery. We got the records on that surgery today. February eleven, nineteen eighty at Queen of Angels. You add three months and we're almost right on the button – Arthur Delacroix disappeared May fourth, according to his sister. The point is, Arthur Delacroix was dead four years before Nicholas Trent moved into that neighborhood. I think that puts him in the clear.'

Billets reluctantly nodded.

'I've had Irving's office and Media Relations on my ass all day about this,' she said. 'They're not going to like it when I call them back with this.'

'That's too bad,' Bosch said. 'That's the way the case shakes out.'

'Okay, so Trent wasn't in the neighborhood in nineteen eighty. Do we have anything yet on where he was?'

Bosch blew out his breath and shook his head.

'You're not going to let this go, are you? We need to concentrate on the kid.'

'I'm not letting go because they're not. Irving called me himself this morning. He was very clear without having to say the words. If it turns out an innocent man killed himself because a cop leaked information to the media that held him up to public ridicule, then it's one more black eye for the department. Haven't we had enough humiliation in the last ten years?'

Bosch smiled without a hint of humor.

'You sound just like him, Lieutenant. That's really good.'

It was the wrong thing to say. He could see that it hurt her.

'Yeah, well, maybe I sound like him because I agree with him, for once. This department has had nothing but scandal after scandal. Like most of the decent cops around here, I for one am sick of it.'

'Good. So am I. But the solution is not to bend things to fit our needs. This is a homicide case.'

'I know that, Harry. I'm not saying bend anything. I'm saying we have to be sure.'

'We're sure. I'm sure.'

They were silent for a long moment, everyone's eyes avoiding the others'.

'What about Kiz?' Edgar finally asked.

Bosch sneered.

'Irving won't do a thing to Kiz,' he said. 'He knows it will make him look even worse if he touches her. Besides, she's probably the best cop they got down there on the third floor.'

'You're always so sure, Harry,' Billets said. 'It must be nice.'

'Well, I'm sure about this.'

He stood up.

'And I'd like to get back to it. We've got stuff happening.'

'I know all about it. Jerry was just telling me. But sit down and let's get back to this for one minute, okay?'

Bosch sat back down.

'I can't just talk to Irving the way I let you talk to me,' Billets said. 'This is what I am going to do. I am going to update him on the ID and everything else. I am going to say you are pursuing the case as is. I will then invite him to assign IAD to the background investigation of Trent. In other words, if he remains unconvinced by the circumstances of the ID, then he can have IAD or whoever he can find run the background on Trent to see where he was in nineteen eighty.'

Bosch just looked at her, giving no indication of approval or disapproval of her plan.

'Can we go now?'

'Yes, you can go.'

When they got back to the homicide table and sat down Edgar asked Bosch why he hadn't mentioned the theory that maybe Trent moved into the neighborhood because he knew the bones were up on the hillside.

'Because your "sick fuck" theory is too farfetched to go beyond this table for the time being. If that gets to Irving, next thing you know it's in a press release and is the official line. Now, did you get anything on the box or not?'

'Yeah, I got stuff.'

'What?'

'First of all, I confirmed Samuel Delacroix's address at the Manchester Trailer Park. So he's there when we want to go see him. In the last ten years he's had two DUIs. He drives on a restricted license at the moment. I also ran his Social and came up with a hit – he works for the city.'

Bosch's face showed his surprise.

'Doing what?'

'He works part-time at a driving range at the municipal golf course right next to the trailer park. I made a call to Parks and Recs – discreetly. Delacroix drives the cart that collects all the balls. You know, out on the range. The guy everybody tries to hit when he's out there. I guess he comes over from the trailer park and does it a couple times a day.'

'Okay.'

'Next, Christine Dorsett Delacroix, the name of the mother on Sheila's birth certificate. I ran her Social and got her now listed as a Christine Dorsett Waters. Address is in Palm Springs. Must've gone there to re-invent herself. New name, new life, whatever.'

Bosch nodded.

'You pull the divorce?'

'Got it. She filed on Samuel Delacroix in 'seventy-three. The boy would've been about five at the time. Cited mental and physical abuse. Details of what that abuse consisted of were not included. It never went to trial, so the details never came out.'

'He didn't contest it?'

'It looks like a deal was made. He got custody of the two kids and didn't contest. Nice and clean. The file's about twelve pages thick. I've seen some that are twelve inches. My own, for example.'

'If Arthur was five . . . some of those injuries predate that, according to the anthropologist.'

Edgar shook his head.

'The extract says the marriage had ended three years prior and they were living separately. So it looks like she split when the boy was about two – like Sheila said. Harry, you usually don't refer to the vic by name.'

'Yeah, so?'

'Just pointing it out.'

'Thank you. Anything else in the file?'

'That's about it. I got copies if you want it.'

'Okay, what about the skateboard friend?'

'Got him, too. Still alive, still local. But there's a problem. I ran all the usual data banks and came up with three John Stokes in L.A. that fall into the right age range. Two are in the Valley, both clean. The third's a player. Multiple arrests for petty theft, auto theft, burglary and possession going back to a full juvy jacket. Five years ago he finally ran out of second chances and got sent to Corcoran to iron out a nickel. Did two and a half to parole.'

'You talk to his agent? Is Stokes still on the line?'

'Talked to his agent, yes. No, Stokes isn't on the hook. He cleared parole two months ago. The agent doesn't know where he is.'

'Damn.'

'Yeah, but I got him to pull a look at the client bio. It has Stokes growing up mostly in Mid-Wilshire. In and out of foster homes. In and out of trouble. He's gotta be our guy.'

'The agent think he's still in L.A.?'

'Yeah, he thinks so. We just gotta find him. I already had patrol go by his last known – he moved out of there as soon as he cleared parole.'

'So he's in the wind. Beautiful.'

Edgar nodded.

'We have to put him on the box,' Bosch said. 'Start with—'

'Did it,' Edgar said. 'I also typed up a roll-call notice and gave it to Mankiewicz a while ago. He promised to get it read at all calls. I'm having a batch of visor photos made, too.'

'Good.'

Bosch was impressed. Getting photos of Stokes to clip to the sun visors of every patrol car was the sort of extra step Edgar usually didn't bother to make.

'We'll get him, Harry. I'm not sure what good he'll do us, but we'll get him.'

'He could be a key witness. If Arthur – I mean, the vic – ever told him his father was beating him, then we've got something.'

Bosch looked at his watch. It was almost two. He wanted to keep things moving, keep the investigation focused and urgent. For him the most difficult time was waiting. Whether it was for lab results or other cops to make moves, it was always when he became most agitated.

'What do you have going tonight?' he asked Edgar.

'Tonight? Nothing much.'

'You got your kid tonight?'

'No, Thursdays. Why?'

'I'm thinking about going out to the Springs.'

'Now?'

'Yeah, talk to the ex-wife.'

He saw Edgar check his watch. He knew that even if they left that moment, they still wouldn't get back until late.

'It's all right. I can go by myself. Just give me the address.'

'Nah, I'm going with you.'

'You sure? You don't have to. I just don't like waitin' around for something to happen, you know?'

'Yeah, Harry, I know.'

Edgar stood up and took his jacket off the back of his chair.

'Then I'll go tell Bullets,' Bosch said.

27

They were more than halfway across the desert to Palm Springs before either one of them spoke.

'Harry,' Edgar said, 'you're not talking.'

'I know,' Bosch said.

The one thing they had always had as partners was the ability to share long silences. Whenever Edgar felt the need to break the silence, Bosch knew there was something on his mind he wanted to talk about.

'What is it, J. Edgar?'

'Nothing.'

'The case?'

'No, man, nothing. I'm cool.'

'All right, then.'

They were passing a windmill farm. The air was dead. None of the blades were turning.

'Did your parents stay together?' Bosch asked.

'Yeah, all the way,' Edgar said, then he laughed. 'I think they wished sometimes they didn't but, yeah, they stuck it out. That's how it goes, I guess. The strong survive.'

Bosch nodded. They were both divorced but rarely talked about their failed marriages.

'Harry, I heard about you and the boot. It's getting around.'

Bosch nodded. This is what Edgar had wanted to bring up. Rookies in the department were often called 'boots.' The origin of the term was obscure. One school of thought was that it referred to boot camp, another that it was a sarcastic reference to rookies being the new boots of the fascist empire.

'All I'm saying, man, is be careful with that. You got rank on her, okay?'

'Yeah, I know. I'll figure something out.'

'From what I hear and have seen, she's worth the risk. But you still gotta be careful.'

Bosch didn't say anything. After a few minutes they passed a road sign that said Palm Springs was coming up in nine miles. It was nearing dusk.

Bosch was hoping to knock on the door where Christine Waters lived before it got dark.

'Harry, you going to take the lead on this, when we get there?'

'Yeah, I'll take it. You can be the indignant one.'

'That will be easy.'

Once they crossed the city boundary into Palm Springs they picked up a map at a gas station and made their way through the town until they found Frank Sinatra Boulevard and took it up toward the mountains. Bosch pulled the car up to the gate house of a place called Mountaingate Estates. Their map showed the street Christine Waters lived on was within Mountaingate.

A uniformed rent-a-cop stepped out of the gate house, eying the slickback they were in and smiling.

'You guys are a little ways off the beat,' he said.

Bosch nodded and tried to give a pleasant smile. But it only made him look like he had something sour in his mouth.

'Something like that,' he said.

'What's up?'

'We're going to talk to Christine Waters, three-twelve Deep Waters Drive.'

'Mrs. Waters know you're coming?'

'Not unless she's a psychic or you tell her.'

'That's my job. Hold on a second.'

He returned to the gate house and Bosch saw him pick up a phone.

'Looks like Christine Delacroix seriously traded up,' Edgar said.

He was looking through the windshield at some of the homes that were visible from their position. They were all huge with manicured lawns big enough to play touch football on.

The guard came out, put both hands on the window sill of the car and leaned down to look in at Bosch.

'She wants to know what it's about.'

'Tell her we'll discuss it with her at her house. Privately. Tell her we have a court order.'

The guard shrugged his shoulders in a have-it-your-way-gesture and went back inside. Bosch watched him speaking on the phone for a few more moments. After he hung up, the gate started to open slowly. The guard stood in the open doorway and waved them in. But not without the last word.

'You know that tough-guy stuff probably works real well for you in L.A. Out here in the desert it's just—'

Bosch didn't hear the rest. He drove through the gate while putting the window up.

They found Deep Waters Drive at the far extreme of the development.

The homes here looked to be a couple million dollars more opulent than those built near the entrance to Mountaingate.

'Who would name a street in the desert Deep Waters Drive?' Edgar mused.

'Maybe somebody named Waters.'

It dawned on Edgar then.

'Damn. You think? Then she really has traded up.'

The address Edgar came up with for Christine Waters corresponded with a mansion of contemporary Spanish design that sat at the end of a cul-de-sac at the terminus of Mountaingate Estates. It was most definitely the development's premier lot. The house was positioned on a promontory that afforded it a view of all the other homes in the development as well as a sweeping view of the golf course that surrounded it.

The property had its own gated drive but the gate was open. Bosch wondered if it always stood open or had been opened for them.

'This is going to be interesting,' Edgar said as they pulled into a parking circle made of interlocking paving stones.

'Just remember,' Bosch said, 'people can change their addresses but they can't change who they are.'

'Right. Homicide one-oh-one.'

They got out and walked under the portico that led to the double-wide front door. It was opened before they got to it by a woman in a black-and-white maid's uniform. In a thick Spanish accent the woman told them that Mrs. Waters was waiting in the living room.

The living room was the size and had the feel of a small cathedral, with a twenty-five-foot ceiling with exposed roof beams. High on the wall facing the east were three large stained-glass windows, a triptych depicting a sunrise, a garden and a moonrise. The opposite wall had six side-by-side sliding doors with a view of a golf course putting green. The room had two distinct groupings of furniture, as if to accommodate two separate gatherings at the same time.

Sitting in the middle of a cream-colored couch in the first grouping was a woman with blonde hair and a tight face. Her pale blue eyes followed the men as they entered and took in the size of the room.

'Mrs. Waters?' Bosch said. 'I am Detective Bosch and this is Detective Edgar. We're from the Los Angeles Police Department.'

He held out his hand and she took it but didn't shake it. She just held it for a moment and then moved on to Edgar's outstretched hand. Bosch knew from the birth certificate that she was fifty-six years old. But she looked close to a decade younger, her smooth tan face a testament to the wonders of modern medical science.

'Please have a seat,' she said. 'I can't tell you how embarrassed I am to have that car sitting in front of my house. I guess discretion is not the better part of valor when it comes to the LAPD.'

Bosch smiled.

'Well, Mrs. Waters, we're kind of embarrassed about it, too, but that's what the bosses tell us to drive. So that's what we drive.'

'What is this about? The guard at the gate said you have a court order. May I see it?'

Bosch sat down on a couch directly opposite her and across a black coffee table with gold designs inlaid on it.

'Uh, he must have misunderstood me,' he said. 'I told him we could get a court order, if you refused to see us.'

'I'm sure he did,' she replied, the tone of her voice letting them know she didn't believe Bosch at all. 'What do you want to see me about?'

'We need to ask you about your husband.'

'My husband has been dead for five years. Besides that, he rarely went to Los Angeles. What could he possibly—'

'Your first husband, Mrs. Waters. Samuel Delacroix. We need to talk to you about your children as well.'

Bosch saw a wariness immediately enter her eyes.

'I . . . I haven't seen or spoken to them in years. Almost thirty years.'

'You mean since you went out for medicine for the boy and forgot to come back home?' Edgar asked.

The woman looked at him as though he had slapped her. Bosch had hoped Edgar was going to use a little more finesse when he acted indignant with her.

'Who told you that?'

'Mrs. Waters,' Bosch said. 'I want to ask questions first and then we can get to yours.'

'I don't understand this. How did you find me? What are you doing? Why are you here?'

Her voice rose with emotion from question to question. A life she had put aside thirty years before was suddenly intruding into the carefully ordered life she now had.

'We are homicide investigators, ma'am. We are working on a case that may involve your husband. We—'

'He's *not* my husband. I divorced him twenty-five years ago, at least. This is crazy, you coming here to ask about a man I don't even know anymore, that I didn't even know was still alive. I think you should leave. I want you to leave.'

She stood up and extended her hand in the direction they had come in.

Bosch glanced at Edgar and then back at the woman. Her anger had turned the tan on her sculptured face uneven. There were blotches beginning to form, the tell of plastic surgery.

'Mrs. Waters, sit down,' Bosch said sternly. 'Please try to relax.'

'Relax? Do you know who I am? My husband built this place. The houses, the golf course, everything. You can't just come in here like this. I could pick up the phone and have the chief of police on the line in two—'

'Your son is dead, lady,' Edgar snapped. 'The one you left behind thirty years ago. So sit down and let us ask you our questions.'

She dropped back onto the couch as if her feet had been kicked out from beneath her. Her mouth opened and then closed. Her eyes were no longer on them, they were on some distant memory.

'Arthur . . . '

'That's right,' Edgar said. 'Arthur. Glad you at least remember it.'

They watched her in silence for a few moments. All the years and all the distance wasn't enough. She was hurt by the news. Hurt bad. Bosch had seen it before. The past had a way of coming back up out of the ground. Always right below your feet.

Bosch took his notebook out of his pocket and opened it to a blank page. He wrote 'Cool it' on it and handed the notebook to Edgar.

'Jerry, why don't you take some notes? I think Mrs. Waters wants to cooperate with us.'

His speaking drew Christine Waters out of her blue reverie. She looked at Bosch.

'What happened? Was it Sam?'

'We don't know. That's why we're here. Arthur has been dead a long time. His remains were found just last week.'

She slowly brought one of her hands to her mouth in a fist. She lightly started bumping it against her lips.

'How long?'

'He had been buried for twenty years. It was a call from your daughter that helped us identify him.'

'Sheila.'

It was as if she had not spoken the name in so long she had to try it out to see if it still worked.

'Mrs. Waters, Arthur disappeared in nineteen eighty. Did you know about that?'

She shook her head.

'I was gone. I left almost ten years before that.'

'And you had no contact with your family at all?'

'I thought . . . '

She didn't finish. Bosch waited.

'Mrs. Waters?'

'I couldn't take them with me. I was young and couldn't handle . . . the responsibility. I ran away. I admit that. I ran away. I thought that it would be best for them to not hear from me, to not even know about me.'

Bosch nodded in a way he hoped conveyed that he understood and agreed with her thinking at the time. It didn't matter that he did not. It didn't matter that his own mother had faced the same hardship of having a child too soon and under difficult circumstances but had clung to and protected him with a fierceness that inspired his life.

'You wrote them letters before you left? Your children, I mean.'

'How did you know that?'

'Sheila told us. What did you say in the letter to Arthur?'

'I just . . . I just told him I loved him and I'd always think about him, but I couldn't be with him. I can't really remember everything I said. Is it important?'

Bosch shrugged his shoulders.

'I don't know. Your son had a letter with him. It might have been the one from you. It's deteriorated. We probably won't ever know. In the divorce petition you filed a few years after leaving home, you cited physical abuse as a cause of action. I need you to tell us about that. What was the physical abuse?'

She shook her head again, this time in a dismissive way, as if the question was annoying or stupid.

'What do you think? Sam liked to bat me around. He'd get drunk and it was like walking on eggshells. Anything could set him off, the baby crying, Sheila talking too loud. And I was always the target.'

'He would hit you?'

'Yes, he would hit me. He'd become a monster. It was one of the reasons I had to leave.'

'But you left the kids with the monster,' Edgar said.

This time she didn't react as if struck. She fixed her pale eyes on Edgar with a deathly look that made Edgar turn his indignant eyes away. She spoke very calmly to him.

'Who are you to judge anyone? I had to survive and I could not take them with me. If I had tried none of us would have survived.'

'I'm sure they understood that,' Edgar said.

The woman stood up again.

'I don't think I am going to talk to you anymore. I'm sure you can find your way out.'

She headed toward the arched doorway at the far end of the room.

'Mrs. Waters,' Bosch said. 'If you don't talk to us now, we will go get that court order.'

'Fine,' she said without looking back. 'Do it. I'll have one of my attorneys handle it.'

'And it will become public record at the courthouse in town.'

It was a gamble but Bosch thought it might stop her. He guessed that her life in Palm Springs was built squarely atop her secrets. And that she wouldn't want anybody going down into the basement. The social gossips might, like Edgar, have a hard time viewing her actions and motives the way she did. Deep inside, she had a hard time herself, even after so many years.

She stopped under the archway, composed herself and came back to the couch. Looking at Bosch, she said, 'I will only talk to you. I want him to leave.'

Bosch shook his head.

'He's my partner. It's our case. He stays, Mrs. Waters.'

'I will still answer questions from you only.'

'Fine. Please sit down.'

She did so, this time sitting on the side of the couch farthest from Edgar and closest to Bosch.

'I know you want to help us find your son's killer. We'll try to be as fast as we can here.'

She nodded once.

'Just tell us about your ex-husband.'

'The whole sordid story?' she asked rhetorically. 'I'll give you the short version. I met him in an acting class. I was eighteen. He was seven years older, had already done some film work and to top it off was very, very handsome. You could say I quickly fell under his spell. And I was pregnant before I was nineteen.'

Bosch checked Edgar to see if he was writing any of this down. Edgar caught the look and started writing.

'We got married and Sheila was born. I didn't pursue a career. I have to admit I wasn't that dedicated. Acting just seemed like something to do at the time. I had the looks but soon I found out every girl in Hollywood had the looks. I was happy to stay at home.'

'How did your husband do at it?'

'At first, very well. He got a recurring role on *First Infantry*. Did you ever watch it?'

Bosch nodded. It was a World War II television drama that ran in the mid to late sixties, until public sentiment over the Vietnam War and war in general led to declining ratings and it was cancelled. The show followed an army platoon as it moved behind German lines each week. Bosch had liked the show as a kid and always tried to watch it, whether he was in a foster home or the youth hall.

'Sam was one of the Germans. His blond hair and Aryan looks. He was on it the last two years. Right up until I got pregnant with Arthur.'

She let some silence punctuate that.

'Then the show got cancelled because of that stupid war in Vietnam. It got cancelled and Sam had trouble finding work. He was typecast as this German. He really started drinking then. And hitting me. He'd spend his days going to casting calls and getting nothing. He'd then spend his nights drinking and being angry at me.'

'Why you?'

'Because I was the one who had gotten pregnant. First with Sheila and then with Arthur. Neither was planned and it all added up to too much pressure on him. He took it out on whoever was close.'

'He assaulted you.'

'Assaulted? It sounds so clinical. But yes, he assaulted me. Many times.'

'Did you ever see him strike the children?'

It was the key question they had come to ask. Everything else was window dressing.

'Not specifically,' she said. 'When I was carrying Arthur he hit me once. In the stomach. It broke my water. I went into labor about six weeks before my due date. Arthur didn't even weigh five pounds when he was born.'

Bosch waited. She was talking in a way that hinted she would say more as long as he gave her the space. He looked out through the sliding door behind her at the golf course. There was a deep sand trap guarding a putting green. A man in a red shirt and plaid pants was in the trap, flailing with a club at an unseen ball. Sprays of sand were flying up out of the trap onto the green. But no ball.

In the distance three other golfers were getting out of two carts parked on the other side of the green. The lip of the sand trap shielded them from view of the man in the red shirt. As Bosch watched, the man checked up and down the fairway for witnesses, then reached down and grabbed his ball. He threw it up onto the green, giving it the nice arc of a perfectly hit shot. He then climbed out of the trap, holding his club with both hands still locked in their grip, a posture that suggested he had just hit the ball.

Finally, Christine Waters began to talk again and Bosch looked back at her.

'Arthur only weighed five pounds when he was born. He was small right up through that first year and very sickly. We never talked about it but I think we both knew that what Sam had done had hurt that boy. He just wasn't right.'

'Aside from that incident when he struck you, you never saw him strike Arthur or Sheila?'

'He might have spanked Sheila. I don't really remember. He never hit the children. I mean, he had me there to hit.'

Bosch nodded, the unspoken conclusion being that once she was gone, who knows who became the target? Bosch thought of the bones laid out on the autopsy table and all the injuries Dr. Golliher had catalogued.

'Is my hus – is Sam under arrest?'

Bosch looked at her.

'No. We're in the fact-finding stage here. The indication from your son's remains is that there is a history of chronic physical abuse. We're just trying to figure things out.'

'And Sheila? Was she . . . ?'

'We haven't specifically asked her. We will. Mrs. Waters, when you were struck by your husband, was it always with his hand?'

'Sometimes he would hit me with things. A shoe once, I remember. He held me on the floor and hit me with it. And once he threw his briefcase at me. It hit me in the side.'

She shook her head.

'What?'

'Nothing. Just that briefcase. He carried it with him to all his auditions. Like he was so important and had so much going on. And all he ever had in it were a few head shots and a flask.'

Bitterness burned in her voice, even after so many years.

'Did you ever go to a hospital or an emergency room? Is there any physical record of the abuse?'

She shook her head.

'He never hurt me enough that I had to go. Except when I had Arthur, and then I lied. I said I fell and my water broke. You see, Detective, it wasn't something I wanted the world to know about.'

Bosch nodded.

'When you left, was that planned? Or did you just go?'

She didn't answer for a long moment as she watched the memory first on her inside screen.

'I wrote the letters to my children long before I left. I carried them in my purse and waited for the right time. On the night I left, I put them under their pillows and left with my purse and only the clothes I was wearing. And my car that my father had given us when we got married. That was it. I'd had enough. I told him we needed medicine for Arthur. He had been drinking. He told me to go out and get it.'

'And you never went back.'

'Never. About a year later, before I came out to the Springs, I drove by the house at night. Saw the lights on. I didn't stop.'

Bosch nodded. He couldn't think of anything else to ask. While the woman's memory of that early time in her life was good, what she was remembering wasn't going to help make a case against her ex-husband for a murder committed ten years after she had last seen him. Maybe Bosch had known that all along – that she wouldn't be a vital part of the case. Maybe he had just wanted to take the measure of a woman who had abandoned her children, leaving them with a man she believed was a monster.

'What does she look like?'

Bosch was momentarily taken aback by her question.

'My daughter.'

'Um, she's blonde like you. A little taller, heavier. No children, not married.'

'When will Arthur be buried?'

'I don't know. You would have to call the medical examiner's office. Or you could probably check with Sheila to see if . . . '

He stopped. He couldn't get involved in mending the thirty-year gaps in people's lives.

'I think we're finished here, Mrs. Waters. We appreciate your cooperation.'

'Definitely,' Edgar said, the sarcasm in his tone making its mark.

'You came all this way to ask so few questions.'

'I think that's because you have so few answers,' Edgar said.

They walked to the door and she followed a few paces behind. Outside, under the portico, Bosch looked back at the woman standing in the open doorway. They held each other's eyes for a moment. He tried to think of something to say. But he had nothing for her. She closed the door.

28

They pulled into the station lot shortly before eleven. It had been a sixteen-hour day that had netted very little in terms of evidence that could carry a case toward prosecution. Still, Bosch was satisfied. They had the identification and that was the center of the wheel. All things would come from that.

Edgar said good night and went straight to his car without going inside the station. Bosch wanted to check with the watch sergeant to see if anything had come up with Johnny Stokes. He also wanted to check for messages and knew that if he hung around until eleven he might see Julia Brasher when she got off shift. He wanted to talk to her.

The station was quiet. The midnight shift cops were up in roll call. The incoming and outgoing watch sergeants would be up there as well. Bosch went down the hallway to the detective bureau. The lights were out, which was in violation of an order from the Office of the Chief of Police. The chief had mandated that the lights in Parker Center and every division station should never be off. His goal was to let the public know that the fight against crime never slept. The result was that the lights glowed brightly every night in empty police offices across the city.

Bosch flicked on the row of lights over the homicide table and went to his spot. There were a number of pink phone message slips and he looked through these, but all were from reporters or related to other cases he had pending. He tossed the reporters' messages in the trash can and put the others in his top drawer to follow up on the next day.

There were two department dispatch envelopes waiting on the desk for him. The first contained Golliher's report and Bosch put it aside for reading later. He picked up the second envelope and saw it was from SID. He realized he had forgotten to call Antoine Jesper about the skateboard.

He was about to open the envelope when he noticed it had been dropped on top of a folded piece of paper on his calendar blotter. He unfolded it and read the short message. He knew it was from Julia, though she had not signed it.

Where are you, tough guy?

He had forgotten that he had told her to come by the squad room before she started her shift. He smiled at the note but felt bad about forgetting. He also thought once more about Edgar's admonishment to be careful with the relationship.

He refolded the page and put it in his drawer. He wondered how Julia would react to what he wanted to talk about. He was dead tired from the long hours but didn't want to wait until the next day.

The dispatch envelope from SID contained a one-page evidence analysis report from Jesper. Bosch read the report quickly. Jesper had confirmed that the board was made by Boneyard Boards Inc., a Huntington Beach manufacturer. The model was called a 'Boney Board.' The particular model at hand was made from February 1978 until June 1986, when design variations created a slight change in the board's nose.

Before Bosch could get excited by the implications of a match between the board and the time frame of the case, he read the last paragraph of the report, which put any match in doubt.

> *The trucks (wheel assemblies) are of a design first implemented by Boneyard in May* 1984. The graphite wheels also indicate a later manufacture. Graphite wheels did not become commonplace in the industry until the mid-80s. However, because trucks and wheels are interchangeable and often are traded out or replaced by boarders, it is impossible to determine the exact date of manufacture of the skateboard in evidence. Best estimate pending additional evidence is manufacture between February 1978 and June 1986.

Bosch slid the report back into the dispatch envelope and dropped it on the desk. The report was inconclusive but to Bosch the factors Jesper had outlined leaned toward the skateboard not having been Arthur Delacroix's. In his mind the report tilted toward clearing rather than implicating Nicholas Trent in the boy's death. In the morning he would type up a report with his conclusions and give it to Lt. Billets to send up the chain to Deputy Chief Irving's office.

As if to punctuate the end of this line of investigation, the sound of the back door to the station banging open echoed down the hallway. Several loud male voices followed, all heading out into the night. Roll call was over and fresh troops were taking the field, their voices full of us-versus-them bravado.

The police chief's wishes notwithstanding, Bosch flicked off the light and headed back down the hallway to the watch office. There were two sergeants in the small office. Lenkov was going off duty, while Renshaw was just starting her shift. They both registered surprise at Bosch's appearance so late at night but then didn't ask him what he was doing in the station.

'So,' Bosch said, 'anything on my guy, Johnny Stokes?'

'Nothing yet,' Lenkov said. 'But we're looking. We're putting it out at all roll calls and we've got the pictures in the cars now. So ... '

'You'll let me know.'

'We'll let you know.'

Renshaw nodded her agreement.

Bosch thought about asking if Julia Brasher had come in to end her shift yet but thought better of it. He thanked them and stepped back into the hallway. The conversation had felt odd, like they couldn't wait for him to get out of there. He sensed it was because of the word getting around about him and Julia. Maybe they knew she was coming off of shift and wanted to avoid seeing them together. As supervisors they would then be witnesses to what was an infraction of department policy. As minor and rarely enforced as the rule was, things would be better all the way around if they didn't see the infraction and then have to look the other way.

Bosch walked out the back door and into the parking lot. He had no idea whether Julia was in the station locker room, still out on patrol or had come and gone already. Mid-shifts were fluid. You didn't come in until the watch sergeant sent your replacement out.

He found her car in the parking lot and knew he hadn't missed her. He walked back toward the station to sit down on the Code 7 bench. But when he got to it, Julia was already sitting there. Her hair was slightly wet from the locker room shower. She wore faded blue jeans and a long-sleeved pullover with a high neck.

'I heard you were in the house,' she said. 'I checked and saw the light out and thought maybe I'd missed you.'

'Just don't tell the chief about the lights.'

She smiled and Bosch sat down next to her. He wanted to touch her but didn't.

'Or us,' he said.

She nodded.

'Yeah. A lot of people know, don't they?'

'Yeah. I wanted to talk to you about that. Can you get a drink?'

'Sure.'

'Let's walk over to the Cat and Fiddle. I'm tired of driving today.'

Rather than walk through the station together and out the front door, they took the long way through the parking lot and around the station. They walked two blocks up to Sunset and then another two down to the pub. Along the way Bosch apologized for missing her in the squad room before her shift and explained he had driven to Palm Springs. She was very quiet as they walked, mostly just nodding her head at his explanations. They didn't talk about the issue at hand until they reached the pub and slid into one of the booths by the fireplace.

They both ordered pints of Guinness and then Julia folded her arms on the table and fixed Bosch with a hard stare.

'Okay, Harry, I've got my drink coming. You can give it to me. But I have to warn you, if you are going to say you want to just be friends, well, I already have enough friends.'

Bosch couldn't help but break into a broad smile. He loved her boldness, her directness. He started shaking his head.

'Nah, I don't want to be your friend, Julia. Not at all.'

He reached across the table and squeezed her forearm. Instinctively, he glanced around the pub to make sure no one from the cop shop had wandered over for an after-shift drink. He didn't recognize anyone and looked back at Julia.

'What I want is to be with you. Just like we've been.'

'Good. So do I.'

'But we have to be careful. You haven't been around the department long enough. I have and I know how things get around, and so it's my fault. We should've never left your car in the station lot that first night.'

'Oh, fuck 'em if they can't take a joke.'

'No, it's—'

He waited while the barmaid put their beers down on little paper coasters with the Guinness seal on them.

'It's not like that, Julia,' he said when they were alone again. 'If we're going to keep going, we need to be more careful. We have to go underground. No more meeting at the bench, no more notes, no more anything like that. We can't even go here anymore because cops come here. We have to be totally underground. We meet outside the division, we talk outside the division.'

'You make it sound like we're a couple of spies or something.'

Bosch picked up his glass, clicked it off hers and drank deeply from it. It tasted so good after such a long day. He immediately had to stifle a yawn, which Julia caught and repeated.

'Spies? That's not too far off. You forget, I've been in this department more than twenty-five years. You're just a boot, a baby. I've got more enemies inside the wire than you've got arrests under your belt. Some of these people would take any opportunity to put me down if they could. It sounds like I'm just worrying about myself here, but the thing is if they need to go after a rookie to get to me, they'll do it in a heartbeat. I mean that. A heartbeat.'

She turtled her head down and looked both ways.

'Okay, Harry – I mean, Secret Agent double-oh-forty-five.'

Bosch smiled and shook his head.

'Yeah, yeah, you think it's all a joke. Wait until you get your first IAD jacket. Then you'll see the light.'

'Come on, I don't think it's a joke. I'm just having fun.'

They both drank from their beers, and Bosch leaned back and tried to relax. The heat from the fireplace felt good. The walk over had been brisk. He looked at Julia and she was smiling like she knew a secret about him.

'What?'

'Nothing. You just get so worked up.'

'I'm trying to protect you, that's all. I'm plus-twenty-five, so it doesn't matter as much to me.'

'What does that mean? I've heard people say that – 'plus-twenty-five' – like they're untouchable or something.'

Bosch shook his head.

'Nobody's untouchable. But after you hit twenty-five years in, you top out on the pension scale. So it doesn't matter if you quit at twenty-five years or thirty-five years, you get the same pension. So 'plus-twenty-five' means you have some fuck-you room. You don't like what they're doing to you, you can always pull the pin and say have a nice day. Because you're not in it for the check and the bennies anymore.'

The waitress came back to the table and put down a basket of popcorn. Julia let some time go by and then leaned across the table, her chin almost over the mouth of her pint.

'Then what are you in it for?'

Bosch shrugged his shoulders and looked down at his glass.

'The job, I guess ... Nothing big, nothing heroic. Just the chance to maybe make things right every now and then in a fucked-up world.'

He used his thumb to draw patterns on the frosted glass. He continued speaking without taking his eyes off the glass.

'This case, for example ... '

'What about it?'

'If we can just figure it out and put it together ... we can maybe make up a little bit for what happened to that kid. I don't know, I think it might mean something, something really small, to the world.'

He thought about the skull Golliher had held up to him that morning. A murder victim buried in tar for 9,000 years. A city of bones, and all of them waiting to come up out of the ground. For what? Maybe nobody cares anymore.

'I don't know,' he said. 'Maybe it doesn't mean anything in the long run. Suicide terrorists hit New York and three thousand people are dead before they've finished their first cup of coffee. What does one little set of bones buried in the past matter?'

She smiled sweetly and shook her head.

'Don't go existential on me, Harry. The important thing is that it means something to you. And if it means something to you, then it is important to do what you can. No matter what happens in the world, there will always be the need for heroes. I hope someday I get a chance to be one.'

'Maybe.'

He nodded and kept his eyes from hers. He played some more with his glass.

'Do you remember that commercial that used to be on TV, where there's this old lady who's on the ground or something and she says, 'I've fallen and I can't get up,' and everybody used to make fun of it?'

'I remember. They sell T-shirts that say that on Venice Beach.'

'Yeah, well . . . sometimes I feel like that. I mean, plus twenty-five. You can't go the distance without screwing up from time to time. You fall down, Julia, and sometimes you feel like you can't get up.'

He nodded to himself.

'But then you get lucky and a case comes along and you say to yourself, this is the one. You just feel it. This is the one I can get back up with.'

'It's called redemption, Harry. What's that song say, 'Everybody wants a shot at it'?'

'Something like that. Yeah.'

'And maybe this case is your shot?'

'Yeah, I think it is. I hope so.'

'Then here's to redemption.'

She picked up her glass for a toast.

'Hold fast,' he said.

She banged it off of his. Some of her beer sloshed into his almost empty glass.

'Sorry. I need to practice that.'

'It's okay. I needed a refill.'

He raised his glass and drained it. He put it back down and wiped his mouth with the back of his hand.

'So are you coming home with me tonight?' he asked.

She shook her head.

'No, not with you.'

He frowned and started to wonder if his directness had offended her.

'I'm *following* you home tonight,' she said. 'Remember? Can't leave the car at the division. Everything's got to be top secret, hush-hush, eyes only from now on.'

He smiled. The beer and her smile were like magic on him.

'You got me there.'

'I hope in more ways than one.'

29

Bosch came in late to the meeting in Lt. Billets's office. Edgar was already there, a rarity, as well as Medina from Media Relations. Billets pointed him to a seat with a pencil she was holding, then picked up her phone and punched in a number.

'This is Lieutenant Billets,' she said when her call was answered. 'You can tell Chief Irving that we are all here now and ready to begin.'

Bosch looked at Edgar and raised his eyebrows. The deputy chief was still keeping his hand directly in the case.

Billets hung up and said, 'He's going to call back and I'll put him on the speaker.'

'To listen or to tell?' Bosch asked.

'Who knows?'

'While we're waiting,' Medina said, 'I've started getting a few calls about a BOLO you guys put out. A man named John Stokes? How do you want me to handle that? Is he a new suspect?'

Bosch was annoyed. He knew the Be on the Lookout flier distributed at roll calls would eventually leak to the media. He didn't anticipate it happening so quickly.

'No, he's not a suspect at all,' he said to Medina. 'And if the reporters screw that up like they did Trent, we'll never find him. He's just somebody we want to talk to. He was an acquaintance of the victim. Many years ago.'

'Then you have the victim's ID?'

Before Bosch could answer, the phone buzzed. Billets answered and put Deputy Chief Irving on the speaker.

'Chief, we have Detectives Bosch and Edgar here, along with Officer Medina from Media Relations.'

'Very good,' Irving's voice boomed from the phone's speaker. 'Where are we at?'

Billets started tapping a button on the phone to turn down the volume.

'Uh, Harry, why don't you take that?' she said.

Bosch reached into his inside coat pocket and took out his notebook. He took his time about it. He liked the idea of Irving sitting behind his spotless glass desk in his office at Parker Center, waiting for voices over the phone.

He opened the notebook to a page full of jottings he had made that morning while eating breakfast with Julia.

'Detective, are you there?' Irving said.

'Uh, yes, sir, I'm right here. I was just going through some notes here. Um, the main thing is we have made a positive identification of the victim. His name is Arthur Delacroix. He disappeared from his home in the Miracle Mile area on May fourth, nineteen eighty. He was twelve years old.'

He stopped there, anticipating questions. He noticed that Medina was writing the name down.

'I'm not sure we want to put that out yet,' Bosch said.

'Why is that?' Irving asked. 'Are you saying the identification is not positive?'

'No, we're positive on it, Chief. It's just that if we put the name out, we might be telegraphing which way we're moving here.'

'Which is?'

'Well, we are very confident that Nicholas Trent was clear on this. So we are looking elsewhere. The autopsy – the injuries to the bones – indicate chronic child abuse, dating to early childhood. The mother was out of the picture, so we are looking at the father now. We haven't approached him yet. We're gathering string. If we were to announce that we have an ID and the father saw it, we would be putting him on notice before we need to.'

'If he buried the kid there, then he already is on notice.'

'To a degree. But he knows if we can't come up with a legit ID we'll never link it to him. The lack of an ID is what keeps him safe. And it gives us time to look at him.'

'Understood,' Irving said.

They sat in silence for a few moments, Bosch expecting Irving to say something else. But he didn't. Bosch looked at Billets and spread his hands in a what gives gesture. She shrugged her shoulders.

'So then . . .,' Bosch began, 'we're not putting it out, right?'

Silence. Then:

'I think that is the prudent course to follow,' Irving said.

Medina tore the page he had written on out of his notebook, crumpled it and tossed it into a trash can in the corner.

'Is there anything we *can* put out?' he asked.

'Yes,' Bosch said quickly. 'We can clear Trent.'

'Negative,' Irving said just as quickly. 'We do that at the end. When and if you make a case, then we will clean up the rest.'

Bosch looked at Edgar and then at Billets.

'Chief,' he said. 'If we do it that way, we could be hurting our case.'

'How so?'

'It's an old case. The older the case, the longer the shot. We can't take chances. If we don't go out there and tell them Trent is clear, we'll be giving the guy we eventually take down a defense. He'll be able to point at Trent and say he was a child molester, he did it.'

'But he will be able to do that, whether we clear Trent now or later.'

Bosch nodded.

'True. But I am looking at it from the standpoint of testifying at trial. I want to be able to say we checked Trent out and quickly dismissed him. I don't want some lawyer asking me why, if we so quickly dismissed him, we waited a week or two weeks to announce it. Chief, it will look like we were hiding something. It's going to be subtle but it will have an impact. People on juries look for any reason not to trust cops in general and the LAPD in par—'

'Okay, Detective, you have made your point. My decision still stands. There will be no announcement on Trent. Not at this time, not until we have a solid suspect we can come forward with.'

Bosch shook his head and slumped a bit in his seat.

'What else?' Irving said. 'I have a briefing with the chief in two minutes.'

Bosch looked at Billets and shook his head again. He had nothing else he wanted to share. Billets spoke up.

'Chief, at this time I think that's pretty much where we stand.'

'When do you plan to approach the father, Detectives?'

Bosch poked his chin at Edgar.

'Uh, Chief, Detective Edgar here. We are still looking for a witness that could be important to talk to before approaching the father. That would be a boyhood friend of the victim. We're thinking he might have knowledge of the abuse the boy suffered. We're planning to give it the day. We believe he's here in Hollywood and we have a lot of eyes out there on the—'

'Yes, that is fine, Detective. We will reconvene this conversation tomorrow morning.'

'Yes, Chief,' Billets said. 'At nine-thirty again?'

There was no answer. Irving was already gone.

30

Bosch and Edgar spent the rest of the morning updating reports and the murder book and calling hospitals all over the city to cancel the records searches they had requested by warrant on Monday morning. But by noon Bosch had had enough of the office work and said he had to get out of the station.

'Where you want to go?' Edgar asked.

'I'm tired of waiting around,' Bosch said. 'Let's go take a look at him.'

They used Edgar's personal car because it was unmarked and there were no undercover units left in the motor pool. They took the 101 up into the Valley and then the 405 north before exiting in Van Nuys. The Manchester Trailer Park was on Sepulveda near Victory. They drove by it once before coming back and driving in.

There was no gate house, just a yellow-striped speed bump. The park road circled the property, and Sam Delacroix's trailer was at the rear of the tract, where it bumped up against a twenty-foot-high sound-retention wall next to the freeway. The wall was designed to knock down the nonstop roar of the freeway. All it did was redirect and change its tone, but it was still there.

The trailer was a single-wide with rust stains dripping down the aluminum skin from most of the steel rivet seams. There was an awning with a picnic table and a charcoal grill beneath it. A clothesline ran from one of the awning's support poles to a corner of the next trailer in line. Near the back of the narrow yard an aluminum storage shed about the size of an outhouse was pushed up against the sound wall.

The windows and door of the trailer were closed. There was no vehicle in the lone parking spot. Edgar kept the car going by at an even five miles an hour.

'Looks like nobody's home.'

'Let's try the driving range,' Bosch said. 'If he's over there, maybe you can hit a bucket of balls or something.'

'Always like to practice.'

The range had few customers when they got there but it looked like it had been a busy morning. Golf balls littered the entire range, which was three hundred yards deep, extending to the same sound wall that backed the trailer park. At the far end of the property, netting was erected on high utility poles to protect the freeway drivers from long balls. A small tractor with ball harvesters attached at the rear was slowly traversing the far end of the range, its driver secured in a safety cage.

Bosch watched for a few moments alone until Edgar came up with a half bucket of balls and his golf bag, which had been in the trunk of his car.

'I guess that's him,' Edgar said.

'Yeah.'

Bosch went over to a bench and sat down to watch his partner hit some balls from a little square of rubber grass. Edgar had taken off his tie and jacket. He didn't look that much out of place. Hitting balls a few green squares down from him were two men wearing suit pants and button-down shirts, obviously using their lunch break from the office to fine-tune their game.

Edgar propped his bag on a wooden stand and chose one of the irons. He put on a glove, which he had taken from the bag, took a few warm-up swings and then started striking balls. The first few were grounders that made him curse. Then he started getting some air underneath them and he seemed pleased with himself.

Bosch was amused. He had never played golf a single time in his life and couldn't understand the draw it had for many men – in fact, most of the detectives in the squad room played religiously, and there was a whole network of police tournaments around the state. He enjoyed watching Edgar get worked up even though hitting range balls didn't count.

'Take a shot at him,' he instructed after he thought Edgar was fully warmed up and ready.

'Harry,' Edgar said. 'I know you don't play but I got news for you. In golf you hit the ball at the pin – the flag. No moving targets in golf.'

'Then how come the ex-presidents are always hitting people?'

'Because they're allowed to.'

'Come on, you said everybody tries to hit the guy in the tractor. Take a shot.'

'Everybody but the serious golfers.'

But he angled his body so that Bosch could tell he was going to take a shot at the tractor as it came to the end of a crossing and was making the U-turn to go back the other way. Judging by the yardage markers, the tractor was a hundred forty yards out.

Edgar swung but the ball was another grounder.

'Dammit! See, Harry? This could hurt my game.'

Bosch started laughing.

'What are you laughing at?'

'It's just a game, man. Take another shot.'

'Forget it. It's childish.'

'Take the shot.'

Edgar didn't say anything. He angled his body again, taking aim at the tractor, which was now in the middle of the range. He swung and hit the ball, sending it screaming down the middle but a good twenty feet over the tractor.

'Nice shot,' Bosch said. 'Unless you were aiming for the tractor.'

Edgar gave him a look but didn't say anything. For the next five minutes he hit ball after ball at the range tractor but never came closer to it than ten yards. Bosch never said anything but Edgar's frustrations increased until he turned and angrily said, 'You want to try?'

Bosch feigned confusion.

'Oh, you're still trying to hit him? I didn't realize.'

'Come on, let's go.'

'You still have half your balls there.'

'I don't care. This will set my game back a month.'

'That's all?'

Edgar angrily shoved the club he had been using into his bag and gave Bosch his dead-eye look. It was all Bosch could do not to burst into laughter.

'Come on, Jerry, I want to get a look at the guy. Can't you hit a few more? It looks like he's gotta be done soon.'

Edgar looked out at the range. The tractor was now near the fifty-yard markers. Assuming he had started back at the sound wall, he would be finished soon. There weren't enough new balls out there – just Edgar's and the two business guys' – to warrant going back over the entire range.

Edgar silently relented. He took out one of his woods and went back to the green square of fake grass. He hit a beautiful shot that almost carried to the sound wall.

'Tiger Woods, kiss my ass,' he said.

The next shot he put into the real grass ten feet from the tee.

'Shit.'

'When you play for real, do you hit off that fake grass?'

'No, Harry, you don't. This is practice.'

'Oh, so in practice you don't re-create the actual playing situation.'

'Something like that.'

The tractor pulled off the range and up to a shed behind the concession stand where Edgar had paid for his bucket of balls. The cage door opened and a man in his early sixties got out. He started pulling wire-mesh baskets full of balls out of the harvester and carrying them into the shed. Bosch told Edgar to keep hitting balls so that they wouldn't be obvious. Bosch nonchalantly walked toward the concession stand and bought another half bucket of balls. This put him no more than twenty feet from the man who had been driving the tractor.

It was Samuel Delacroix. Bosch recognized him from a driver's license photo Edgar had pulled and shown him. The man who once played a blond, blue-eyed Aryan soldier and had put a spell on an eighteen-year-old girl was now about as distinguished as a ham sandwich. He was still blond but it obviously came from a bottle and he was bald to the crown of his head. He had day-old whiskers that shone white in the sun. His nose was swollen by time and alcohol and pinched by a pair of ill-fitting glasses. He carried a beer paunch that would've been a ticket to a discharge in anybody's army.

'Two-fifty.'

Bosch looked at the woman behind the cash register.

'For the balls.'

'Right.'

He paid her and picked up the bucket by the handle. He took a last glance at Delacroix, who suddenly looked over at Bosch at the same time. Their eyes locked for a moment and Bosch casually looked away. He headed back toward Edgar. That was when his cell phone started to chirp.

He quickly handed the bucket to Edgar and pulled the phone out of his back pocket. It was Mankiewicz, the day-shift watch sergeant.

'Hey, Bosch, what are you doing?'

'Just hitting some balls.'

'Figures. You guys fuck off while we do all the work.'

'You found my guy?'

'We think so.'

'Where?'

'He's working at the Washateria. You know, picking up some tips, loose change.'

The Washateria was a car wash on La Brea. It employed day laborers to vacuum and wipe down cars. They worked mostly for tips and what they could steal out of the cars without getting caught.

'Who spotted him?'

'Couple guys from vice. They're eighty percent sure. They want to know if you want them to make the move or do you want to be on scene.'

'Tell them to sit tight and that we're on the way. And you know what, Mank? We think this guy's a rabbit. You got a unit we can use as an extra backup in case he runs?'

'Um . . . '

There was silence and Bosch guessed that Mankiewicz was checking his deployment chart.

'Well, you're in luck. I got a couple three-elevens starting early. They should be out of roll call in fifteen. That work for you?'

'Perfect. Tell them to meet us in the parking lot of the Checkers at La Brea and Sunset. Have the vice guys meet us there, too.'

Bosch signaled to Edgar that they were going to roll.

'Uh, one thing,' Mankiewicz said.

'What's that?'

'On the backup, one of them's Brasher. Is that going to be a problem?'

Bosch was silent a moment. He wanted to tell Mankiewicz to put somebody else on it but knew it was not his place to. If he tried to influence deployment or anything else based on his relationship with Brasher, then he could leave himself open to criticism and the possibility of an IAD investigation.

'No, no problem.'

'Look, I wouldn't do it but she's green. She's made a few mistakes and needs this kind of experience.'

'I said no problem.'

31

They planned the takedown of Johnny Stokes on the hood of Edgar's car. The vice guys, Eyman and Leiby, drew the layout of the Washateria on a legal pad and circled the spot where they had spotted Stokes working under the waxing canopy. The car wash was surrounded on three sides by concrete walls and other structures. The area fronting La Brea was almost fifty yards, with a five-foot retention wall running the border except for entry and exit lanes at each corner of the property. If Stokes decided to run, he could go to the retention wall and climb it, but it was more likely that he would go for one of the open lanes.

The plan was simple. Eyman and Leiby would cover the car wash entrance, and Brasher and her partner, Edgewood, would cover the exit. Bosch and Edgar would drive Edgar's car in as customers and make the move on Stokes. They switched their radios to a tactical unit and worked out a code; red meant Stokes had rabbitted, and green meant he had been taken peaceably.

'Remember something,' Bosch said. 'Almost every wiper, rubber, soaper and vacuum guy on that lot is probably running from something – even if it's just *la migra.* So even if we take Stokes without a problem, the others may rumble. Cops showing up at a car wash is like yelling fire in a theater. Everybody scatters till they see who's the one who's it.'

Everybody nodded and Bosch looked pointedly at Brasher, the rookie. In keeping with the plan agreed to the night before, they made no showing of knowing each other as anything other than fellow cops. But now he wanted to make sure she understood just how fluid a takedown like this could become.

'You got that, boot?' he said.

She smiled.

'Yeah, I got it.'

'All right, then let's concentrate. Let's go.'

He thought he saw the smile stay on Brasher's face as she and Edgewood walked to their patrol car.

He and Edgar walked to Edgar's Lexus. Bosch stopped when he got to it and realized that it looked like it had just been washed and waxed.

'Shit.'

'What can I say, Harry? I take care of my car.'

Bosch looked around. Behind the fast-food restaurant was an open Dumpster in a concrete alcove that had recently been washed down. There was a puddle of black water pooling on the pavement.

'Drive through that puddle a couple times,' he said. 'Get it on your car.'

'Harry, I'm not going to get that shit on my car.'

'Come on, your car has to look like it needs to be washed or it might be a tell. You said yourself, the guy's a rabbit. Let's not give him a reason.'

'But we're not actually going to get the car washed. I splash that shit on there, it stays there.'

'Tell you what, Jerry. If we get this guy, I'll have Eyman and Leiby drive him in while you get your car washed. I'll even pay for it.'

'Shit.'

'Come on, just drive through the puddle. We're wasting time.'

After messing up Edgar's car they made the drive to the car wash in silence. As they came up on it, Bosch could see the vice car parked at the curb a few car lengths from the car wash entrance. Further down the block past the car wash, the patrol unit was stopped in a lane of parked cars. Bosch went to his rover.

'Okay, everybody set?'

He got two return clicks on the mike from the vice guys. Brasher responded by voice.

'All ready.'

'Okay. We're going in.'

Edgar pulled into the car wash and drove into the service lane, where customers delivered their cars to the vacuum station and ordered the kind of wash or wax they wanted. Bosch's eyes immediately started moving among the workers, all of whom were dressed in identical orange jumpsuits and baseball caps. It slowed the identification process but Bosch soon saw the blue wax canopy and picked out Johnny Stokes.

'He's there,' he said to Edgar. 'On the black Beemer.'

Bosch knew that once they stepped out of the car most of the cons on the lot would be able to identify them as cops. In the same way Bosch could spot a con ninety-eight percent of the time, they in turn could spot a cop. He would have to move swiftly in on Stokes.

He looked over at Edgar.

'Ready?'

'Let's do it.'

They cracked the doors at the same time. Bosch got out and turned toward Stokes, who was twenty-five yards away with his back turned. He was crouched down and spraying something on the wheels of a black BMW. Bosch heard Edgar tell someone to skip the vacuum and that he'd be right back.

Bosch and Edgar had covered half the distance to their target when they were made by other workers on the lot. From somewhere behind him, Bosch heard a voice call out, 'Five-oh, five-oh, five-oh.'

Immediately alerted, Stokes stood up and started turning. Bosch started running.

He was fifteen feet from Stokes when the ex-con realized he was the target. His obvious escape was to his left and then out through the car wash entrance but the BMW was blocking him. He made a move to his right but then seemed to stop when he realized it was a dead end.

'No, no!' Bosch called out. 'We just want to talk, we just want to talk.'

Stokes visibly slumped. Bosch moved directly toward him while Edgar moved out to the right in case the ex-con decided to make a break.

Bosch slowed and opened his hands wide as he got close. One hand held his rover.

'LAPD. We just want to ask you a few questions, nothing else.'

'Man, about what?'

'About—'

Stokes suddenly raised his arm and sprayed Bosch in the face with the tire cleaner. He then bolted to his right, seemingly toward the dead end, where the high rear wall of the car wash joined the side wall of a three-story apartment building.

Bosch instinctively brought his hands up to his eyes. He heard Edgar yell at Stokes and then the scuffling sound of his shoes on concrete as he gave chase. Bosch couldn't open his eyes. He put his mouth to the radio and yelled, 'Red! Red! Red! He's heading toward the back corner.'

He then dropped the radio to the concrete, using his shoe to break its fall. He used the sleeves of his jacket to wipe at his burning eyes. He finally could open them for brief moments at a time. He spotted a hose coiled on a faucet near the rear of the BMW. He made his way to it, turned it on and doused his face and eyes, not caring how wet his clothes got. His eyes felt like they had been dropped in boiling water.

After a few moments the water eased the burning sensation and he dropped the hose without turning it off and went back to get the radio. His vision was blurred at the edges but he could see well enough to get moving. As he bent down for the radio he heard laughter from some of the other men in orange jumpsuits.

Bosch ignored it. He switched the rover to the Hollywood patrol channel and spoke into it.

'Hollywood units, officers in pursuit of assault suspect, La Brea and Santa Monica. Suspect white male, thirty-five YOA, dark hair, orange jumpsuit. Suspect in the vicinity of Hollywood Washateria.'

He couldn't remember the exact address of the car wash but wasn't worried. Every cop on patrol would know it. He switched the rover to the department's main communication channel and requested that a paramedic unit respond as well to treat an injured officer. He had no idea what had been sprayed into his eyes. They were beginning to feel better but he didn't want to take a chance on long-term injury.

Lastly, he switched back to the tactical channel and asked for the others' locations. Only Edgar came back up on the radio.

'There was a hole in the back corner. He went through to the alley. He's in one of these apartment complexes on the north side of the car wash.'

'Where are the others?'

Edgar's return was broken up. He was moving into a radio void.

'They're back . . . spread out. I think . . . garage. You . . . ight, Harry?'

'I'll make it. Backup's on the way.'

He didn't know if Edgar had heard that. He put the rover in his pocket and hustled to the back corner of the car-wash lot, where he found the hole Stokes had slipped through. Behind a two-high pallet of fifty-five-gallon drums of liquid soap, the concrete wall was broken in. It appeared that at one time a car in the alley on the other side had struck the wall, creating the hole. Intentionally done or not, it was probably a well-known escape hatch for every wanted man who worked at the car wash.

Bosch crouched down and slipped through, momentarily catching his jacket on a rusty piece of rebar protruding from the broken wall. On the other side he got up in an alley that ran behind rows of apartment buildings on either side for the length of the block.

The patrol car was stopped at an angle forty yards down the alley. It was empty, both doors open. Bosch could hear the sound of the main communications channel playing over the dash radio. Further down, at the end of the block, the vice car was parked across the alley.

He quickly moved down the alley toward the patrol car, looking and listening for anything. When he got to the car he pulled the rover out again and tried to raise someone on tactical. He got no response.

He saw the patrol car was parked in front of a ramp that dipped down into an underground garage beneath the largest of the apartment complexes on the alley. Remembering auto theft was in Edgar's recitation of Stokes's criminal record, Bosch suddenly knew that Stokes would go for the garage. His only way out was to get a car.

He trotted down the garage ramp into the dark.

The garage was huge and appeared to follow the imprint of the building above. There were three parking lanes and a ramp leading to an even lower level. Bosch saw no one. The only sound he heard was a dripping from the overhead pipes. He moved swiftly down the middle lane, drawing his weapon for the first time. Stokes had already fashioned a weapon out of a spray bottle. There was no telling what he might find in the garage to also use as a weapon.

As he moved, Bosch checked the few vehicles in the garage – everyone was at work, he guessed – for signs of break-in. He saw nothing. He was raising the rover to his mouth when he heard the sound of running footsteps echo up the ramp from the lower level of the garage. He quickly moved to the ramp and descended, careful to keep the rubber soles of his shoes as quiet as he could.

The lower garage was even darker, with less natural light finding its way down. As the incline leveled, his eyes adjusted. He saw no one, but the ramp structure blocked his view of half of the space. As he began his way around the ramp he suddenly heard a high and taut voice coming from the far end. It was Brasher's.

'Right there! Right there! Don't move!'

Bosch followed the sound, moving in tight to the side of the ramp and holding his weapon up. His training told him to call out, to alert the other officer to his presence. But he knew that if Brasher was alone with Stokes his calling might distract her and give Stokes another chance to break or make a move on her.

As he cut beneath the underside of the ramp, Bosch saw them at the far wall, no more than fifty feet away. Brasher had Stokes up against the wall, legs and arms spread. She held him there with one hand pressed against his back. Her flashlight was on the ground next to her right foot, its beam lighting the wall on which Stokes leaned.

It was perfect. Bosch felt relief flood his body and almost immediately he understood it was relief that she had not been hurt. He came out of the semi-crouch he was in and started toward them, lowering his weapon.

He was directly behind them. After he had taken only a few steps he saw Brasher take her hand off Stokes and step back from him, glancing to either side as she did it. This immediately registered with Bosch as the wrong thing to do. It was completely out of training. It would allow Stokes to make another run if he wanted to.

Things seemed to slow down then. Bosch started to yell to her but the garage suddenly filled with the flash and shattering blast of a gunshot. Brasher went down, Stokes remained up. The blast echo reverberated through the concrete structure, obscuring its origin.

All Bosch could think was, where is the gun?

He raised his weapon while lowering his body into a combat crouch. He started to turn his head to look for the gun. But he saw Stokes start turning from the wall. He then saw Brasher's arm rising up from the ground, her gun pointed at Stokes's turning body.

Bosch aimed his Glock at Stokes.

'Freeze!' he yelled. 'Freeze! Freeze! Freeze!'

In a second he was on them.

'Don't shoot, man,' Stokes yelled. 'Don't shoot!'

Bosch kept his eyes unwavering on Stokes. They still burned and needed relief but he knew even one blink now could be a fatal mistake.

'Down! Get on the ground. Now!'

Stokes dropped onto his stomach and spread his arms at ninety-degree angles to his body. Bosch stepped over him and with a move performed a thousand times before quickly cuffed his wrists behind his back.

He then holstered his weapon and turned to Brasher. Her eyes were wide and moving in a back-and-forth pattern. Blood had spattered onto her neck and had already soaked the front of her uniform shirt. He knelt over her and ripped open her shirt. Still, there was so much blood it took him a moment to find the wound. The bullet had entered her left shoulder, just an inch or so from the Velcro shoulder strap of her Kevlar vest.

The blood was flowing freely from the wound, and Bosch could see Brasher's face was losing color quickly. Her lips were moving but not making any sound. He looked around for something and saw a car wash rag poking out of Stokes's back pocket. He yanked it out and pressed it down on the wound. Brasher moaned in pain.

'Julia, this is going to hurt but I have to stop the bleeding.'

With one hand he stripped off his tie and pushed it under her shoulder and then over the top. He tied a knot that was just tight enough to keep the rag compress in place.

'Okay, hang on, Julia.'

He grabbed his rover off the ground and quickly switched the frequency knob to the main channel.

'CDC, officer down, lower-level garage at the La Brea Park apartments, La Brea and Santa Monica. We need paramedics right NOW! Suspect in custody. Confirm CDC.'

He waited for what seemed to be an interminable time before a CDC dispatcher came on the air to say he was breaking up and needed to repeat his call. Bosch clicked the call button and yelled, 'Where's my paramedics? Officer DOWN!'

He switched to tactical.

'Edgar, Edgewood, we're in the lower level of the garage. Brasher is down. I've got Stokes controlled. Repeat, Brasher is down.'

He dropped the radio and yelled Edgar's name as loud as he could. He took off his jacket and balled it together.

'Man, I didn't do it,' Stokes yelled. 'I don't know what—'

'Shut up! Shut the fuck up!'

Bosch put his jacket under Brasher's head. Her teeth were clenched in pain, her chin jutting upward. Her lips were almost white.

'Paramedics are coming, Julia. I called 'em before this even went down. I must be psychic or something. You just gotta hold on, Julia. Hold on.'

She opened her mouth, though it looked like a terrible struggle. But before she could say anything Stokes yelled out again in a voice now tinged with fear bordering on hysteria.

'I did not do that, man. Don't let them kill me, man. I didn't DO it!'

Bosch leaned over, putting his weight on Stokes's back. He bent down and spoke in a loud voice directly into his ear.

'Shut the fuck up or I'll kill you myself!'

He turned his attention back to Brasher. Her eyes were still open. Tears were going down her cheeks.

'Julia, just a few more minutes. You've got to hang on.'

He pulled the gun out of her right hand and put it on the ground, far away from Stokes. He then held her hand in both of his.

'What happened? What the hell happened?'

She opened and then closed her mouth again. Bosch could hear running feet on the ramp. He heard Edgar call his name.

'Over here!'

In a moment both Edgar and Edgewood were there.

'Julia!' Edgewood cried out. 'Oh, shit!'

Without a moment's hesitation Edgewood stepped forward and delivered a vicious kick to Stokes's side.

'You motherfucker!'

He readied himself to do it again when Bosch yelled.

'No! Get back! Get away from him!'

Edgar grabbed Edgewood and pulled him away from Stokes, who had let out a hurt animal cry at the impact of the kick and was now murmuring and moaning in fear.

'Take Edgewood up and get the paramedics down here,' Bosch said to Edgar. 'The rovers aren't for shit down here.'

Both of them seemed frozen.

'Go! Now!'

As if on cue, the sound of sirens could be heard in the distance.

'You want to help her? Go get them!'

Edgar turned Edgewood around and they both ran back toward the ramp.

Bosch turned back to Brasher. Her face was now the color of death. She was going into shock. Bosch didn't understand. It was a shoulder wound. He suddenly wondered if he had heard two shots. Had the blast and echo obscured a second shot? He checked her body again but found nothing. He didn't want to turn her to check her back for fear of causing more damage. But there was no blood coming from beneath her.

'Come on, hang in there, Julia. You can do it. You hear that? The paramedics are just about here. Just hang in there.'

She opened her mouth again, jutted her chin and started to speak.

'He ... he grabbed ... he went for ... '

She clenched her teeth and rocked her head back and forth on his coat. She tried to talk again.

'It wasn't ... I'm not ... '

Bosch leaned his face close to hers and lowered his voice to an urgent whisper.

'Shhhh, shhhh. Don't talk. Just stay alive. Concentrate, Julia. Hold fast. Stay alive. Please, stay alive.'

He could feel the garage rumble with noise and vibration. In a moment red lights were bouncing off the walls and then a paramedic truck was pulling up next to them. A patrol cruiser was behind it and other uniformed officers, as well as Eyman and Leiby, were running down the ramp and flooding the garage.

'Oh God, oh please,' Stokes mumbled. 'Don't let it happen ... '

The first paramedic reached them and the first thing he did was put a hand on Bosch's shoulder and gently push him back. Bosch went willingly, realizing he was only complicating things now. As he moved backward away from Brasher, her right hand suddenly grasped his forearm and pulled him back toward her. Her voice was now as thin as paper.

'Harry, don't let them—'

The paramedic put a breathing mask over her face and her words were lost.

'Officer, please get back,' the paramedic said firmly.

As Bosch crawled backward on hands and knees he reached over and gripped Brasher's ankle for a moment and squeezed it.

'Julia, you'll be all right.'

'Julia?' said the second paramedic as he crouched next to her with a large equipment case.

'Julia.'

'Okay, Julia,' the paramedic said. 'I'm Eddie and that there's Charlie. We're going to fix you up here. Like your buddy just said, you're going to be all right. But you gotta be tough for us. You gotta want it, Julia. You gotta fight.'

She said something that was garbled through the mask. Just one word but Bosch thought he recognized it. *Numb.*

The paramedics started stabilizing procedures, the one called Eddie talking to her all the while. Bosch got up and moved over to Stokes. He pulled him up into a standing position and pushed him away from the rescue scene.

'My ribs are broken,' Stokes complained. 'I need the paramedics.'

'Trust me, Stokes, there's nothing they can do about it. So just shut the fuck up.'

Two uniforms came up to them. Bosch recognized them from the other night when they had told Julia they would meet her at Boardner's. Her friends.

'We'll take him to the station for you.'

Bosch pushed Stokes past them without hesitation.

'No, I got him.'

'You need to stay here for OIS, Detective Bosch.'

They were right. The Officer Involved Shooting team would soon descend on the scene and Bosch would be questioned as a primary witness. But he wasn't putting Stokes into any hands he did not explicitly trust.

He walked Stokes up the ramp toward the light.

'Listen, Stokes, you want to live?'

The younger man didn't answer. He was walking with his upper body hunched forward because of the injury to his ribs. Bosch tapped him lightly in the spot Edgewood had kicked him. Stokes groaned loudly.

'Are you listening?' Bosch asked. 'Do you want to stay alive?'

'Yes! I want to stay alive.'

'Then you listen to me. I'm going to put you in a room and you don't talk to anybody but me. You understand that?'

'I understand. Just don't let them hurt me. I didn't do anything. I don't know what happened, man. She said get against the wall and I did what I was told. I swear to God all I did was—'

'Shut up!' Bosch ordered.

More cops were coming down the ramp and he just wanted to get Stokes out of there.

When they got to daylight, Bosch saw Edgar standing on the sidewalk talking on his cell phone and using his other hand to signal a transport ambulance into the parking garage. Bosch pushed Stokes toward him. As they approached, Edgar closed the phone.

'I just talked to the lieutenant. She's on the way.'

'Great. Where's your car?'

'Still at the car wash.'

'Go get it. We're taking Stokes to the division.'

'Harry, we can't just leave the scene of a—'

'You saw what Edgewood did. We need to get this shitbag to a place of safety. Go get your car. If we get any shit for it, I'll take it.'

'You got it.'

Edgar started running in the direction of the car wash.

Bosch saw a utility pole near the corner of the apartment building. He walked Stokes to it and recuffed him with his arms around it.

'Wait here,' he said.

He then stepped away and ran a hand through his hair.

'What the hell happened back there?'

He didn't realize he had spoken out loud until Stokes started answering the question, stammering about him not doing anything wrong.

'Shut up,' Bosch said. 'I wasn't talking to you.'

32

Bosch and Edgar walked Stokes through the squad room and down the short hallway leading to the interview rooms. They took him into room 3 and cuffed him to the steel ring bolted to the middle of the table.

'We'll be back,' Bosch said.

'Hey, man, don't leave me in here,' Stokes began. 'They'll come in here, man.'

'Nobody's coming in but me,' Bosch said. 'Just sit tight.'

They left the room and locked it. Bosch went to the homicide table. The squad room was completely empty. When a cop went down in the division everybody responded. It was part of keeping the faith in the blue religion. If it was you who went down, you'd want everybody coming. So you responded in kind.

Bosch needed a smoke, he needed time to think and he needed some answers. His mind was crowded with thoughts about Julia and her condition. But he knew it was out of his hands and the best way to control his thoughts was to concentrate on something still in his hands.

He knew he had little time before the OIS detail would pick up the trail and come for him and Stokes. He picked up the phone and called the watch office. Mankiewicz answered. He was probably the last cop in the station.

'What's the latest?' Bosch asked. 'How is she?'

'I don't know. I hear it's bad. Where are you?'

'In the squad. I've got the guy here.'

'Harry, what are you doing? OIS is all over this. You should be at the scene. Both of you.'

'Let's just say I was fearful of a deteriorating situation. Listen, let me know the minute you hear something about Julia, okay?'

'You got it.'

Bosch was about to hang up when he remembered something.

'And Mank, listen. Your guy Edgewood tried to kick the shit out of the suspect. He was cuffed and on the ground at the time. He's probably got four or five broken ribs.'

Bosch waited. Mankiewicz didn't say anything.

'Your choice. I can go formal with it or I can let you take care of it your way.'

'I'll take care of it.'

'All right. Remember, let me know what you know.'

He hung up and looked at Edgar, who nodded his approval on the way Bosch was handling the Edgewood matter.

'What about Stokes?' Edgar said. 'Harry, what the fuck happened in that garage?'

'I'm not sure. Listen, I'm going to go in there and talk to him about Arthur Delacroix, see what I can get before OIS storms the place and takes him away. When they get here, see if you can stall them.'

'Yeah, and this Saturday I'm planning to kick Tiger Woods's ass on Riviera.'

'Yeah, I know.'

Bosch went into the rear hallway and was about to enter room 3 when he realized he had not gotten his recorder back from Detective Bradley of IAD. He wanted to record his interview with Stokes. He walked past the door to room 3 and stepped into the adjoining video room. He turned on the room 3 camera and auxiliary recorder and then went back to room 3.

Bosch sat across from Stokes. The life appeared drained from the younger man's eyes. Less than an hour before he had been waxing a BMW, picking up a few bucks. Now he was looking at a return to prison – if he was lucky. He knew cop blood in the water brought out the blue sharks. Many were the suspects who were shot trying to escape or inexplicably hung themselves in rooms just like this. Or so it was explained to the reporters.

'Do yourself a big favor,' Bosch said. 'Calm the fuck down and don't do anything stupid. Don't do anything with these people that gets you killed. You understand me?'

Stokes nodded.

Bosch saw the package of Marlboros in the breast pocket of Stokes's jumpsuit. He reached across the table, causing Stokes to flinch.

'Relax.'

He took the pack of cigarettes and fired one up with a match from a book slipped behind the cellophane. From the corner of the room he pulled a small trash can next to his chair and dropped in the match.

'If I wanted to hurt you I would've done it in the garage. Thanks for the smoke.'

Bosch savored the smoke. It had been at least two months since he'd had a cigarette.

'Can I have one?' Stokes asked.

'No, you don't deserve one. You don't deserve shit. But I'm going to make a little deal with you here.'

Stokes raised his eyes to Bosch's.

'You know that little kick in the ribs you got back there? I'll trade you. You forget about it and take it like a man and I'll forget about you spraying me in the face with that shit.'

'My ribs are broke, man.'

'My eyes still burn, man. That was a commercial cleaning chemical. The DA will be able to get assault on a police officer out of that faster than you can say five to ten in Corcoran. You remember being in the Cork, don't you?'

Bosch let that sink in for a long moment.

'So do we have a deal?'

Stokes nodded but said, 'What difference is it going to make? They're going to say I shot her. I—'

'But I know you didn't.'

Bosch saw a glimmer of hope returning to Stokes's eyes.

'And I will tell them exactly what I saw.'

'Okay.'

Stokes's voice was barely a whisper.

'So let's start at the start. Why'd you run?'

Stokes shook his head.

'Because it's what I do, man. I run. I'm a convict and you're the Man. I run.'

Bosch realized that in all of the confusion and haste, nobody had searched Stokes. He told him to stand up, which could only be accomplished by Stokes leaning over the table because of his shackled wrists. Bosch moved around behind him and started checking his pockets.

'You got any needles?'

'No, man, no needles.'

'Good, I don't want to get stuck. I get stuck and all deals are off.'

As he searched he held the cigarette in his lips. The smoke stung his already burning eyes. Bosch took out a wallet, a set of keys and roll of cash totaling $27 in ones. Stokes's tips for the day. There was nothing else. If Stokes had been carrying drugs for sale or personal use, he had tossed them while trying to make his escape.

'They'll be out there with dogs,' Bosch said. 'If you tossed a stash, they'll find it and there won't be anything I can do about it.'

'I didn't toss anything. If they find something, they planted it.'

'Yeah. Just like O.J.'

Bosch sat back down.

'What was the first thing I said to you? I said, 'I just want to talk.' It was the truth. All of this . . . '

Bosch made a sweeping gesture with his hands.

'It could have all been avoided if you had just listened.'

'Cops never want to talk. They always want something more.'

Bosch nodded. He had never been surprised by how accurate the street knowledge of ex-convicts was.

'Tell me about Arthur Delacroix.'

Confusion tightened Stokes's eyes.

'What? Who?'

'Arthur Delacroix. Your skateboard buddy. From the Miracle Mile days. Remember?'

'Jesus, man, that was—'

'A long time ago. I know. That's why I'm asking.'

'What about him? He's long gone, man.'

'Tell me about him. Tell me about when he disappeared.'

Stokes looked down at his cuffed hands and slowly shook his head.

'That was a long time ago. I can't remember that.'

'Try. Why did he disappear?'

'I don't know. He just couldn't take no more of the shit and ran away.'

'Did he tell you he was running away?'

'No, man, he just left. One day he was just gone. And I never saw him again.'

'What shit?'

'What do you mean?'

'You said he couldn't take any more of the shit and ran away. That shit. What are you talking about?'

'Oh, you know, like all the shit in his life.'

'Did he have trouble at home?'

Stokes laughed. He mocked Bosch in an imitation.

"Did he have trouble at home?' Like, who didn't, man?'

'Was he abused – physically abused – at home? is what I mean.'

Again, laughter.

'Who wasn't? My old man, he'd rather take a shot at me than talk to me about anything. When I was twelve he hit me from across the room with a full can of beer. Just because I ate a taco he wanted. They took me away from him for that.'

'You know, that's a real shame, but we're talking about Arthur Delacroix here. Did he ever tell you his father hit him?'

'He didn't have to, man. I saw the bruises. The guy always had a black eye is what I remember.'

'That was from skateboarding. He fell a lot.'

Stokes shook his head.

'Fuck that, man. Artie was the best. That's all he did. He was too good to get hurt.'

Bosch's feet were flat on the floor. He could tell by the sudden vibrations through his soles that there were people in the squad room now. He reached over and pushed the button lock on the doorknob.

'You remember when he was in the hospital? He'd hurt his head. Did he tell you that it was from a skateboarding accident?'

Stokes knitted his brow and looked down. Bosch had jogged loose a direct memory. He could tell.

'I remember he had a shaved head and stitches like a fucking zipper. I can't remember what he—'

Someone tried the door from the outside and then there was a harsh banging on the door. A muffled voice came through.

'Detective Bosch, this is Lieutenant Gilmore, OIS. Open the door.'

Stokes suddenly reared back, panic filling his eyes.

'No! Don't let them—'

'Shut up!'

Bosch leaned across the table, grabbed Stokes by the collar and pulled him forward.

'Listen to me, this is important.'

There was another knock on the door.

'Are you saying that Arthur never told you his father hurt him?'

'Look, man, take care of me here and I'll say whatever the fuck you want me to say. Okay? His father was an asshole. You want me to say Artie told me his father beat him with the goddamn broomstick, I'll say it. You want it to be a baseball bat? Fine, I'll say—'

'I don't want you to say anything but the truth, goddammit. Did he ever tell you that or not?'

The door came open. They had gotten a key from the drawer at the front desk. Two men in suits came in. Gilmore, whom Bosch recognized, and another OIS detective Bosch didn't recognize.

'All right, this is over,' Gilmore announced. 'Bosch, what the fuck are you doing?'

'Did he?' Bosch said to Stokes.

The other OIS detective took keys from his pocket and started taking the cuffs off of Stokes's wrists.

'I didn't do anything,' Stokes started to protest. 'I didn't—'

'Did he ever tell you?' Bosch yelled.

'Get him out of here,' Gilmore barked to the other detective. 'Put him in another room.'

The detective physically lifted Stokes from his seat and half carried, half pushed him out of the room. Bosch's cuffs remained on the table. Bosch stared blankly at them, thinking of the answers Stokes had given him and feeling a terrible weight on his chest from the knowledge that the whole thing had been a dead end. Stokes added nothing to the case. Julia had been shot and it was for nothing.

He finally looked up at Gilmore, who closed the door and then turned to face Bosch.

'Now, like I said, what the fuck were you doing, Bosch?'

33

Gilmore twiddled a pencil in his fingers, drumming the eraser on the table. Bosch never trusted an investigator who took notes in pencil. But that's what the Officer Involved Shooting team was all about, making stories and facts fit the picture the department wanted to present to the public. It was a pencil squad. To get it right often meant using the pencil and eraser, never ink, never a tape recorder.

'So we're going to go over this again,' he said. 'Tell me once more, what did Officer Brasher do?'

Bosch looked past him. He had been moved to the suspect's chair in the interview room. He was facing the mirror – the one way glass behind which he was sure there were at least a half dozen people, probably including Deputy Chief Irving. He wondered if anybody had noticed that the video had been running. If they had, it would have immediately been shut off.

'Somehow she shot herself.'

'And you saw this.'

'Not exactly. I saw it from the rear. Her back was to me.'

'Then how do you know she shot herself?'

'Because there was no one else there but her, me and Stokes. I didn't shoot her and Stokes didn't shoot her. She shot herself.'

'During the struggle with Stokes.'

Bosch shook his head.

'No, there was no struggle at the moment of the shooting. I don't know what happened before I got there, but at the moment of the shooting Stokes had both hands flat on the wall and his back to her when the gun went off. Officer Brasher had her hand on his back, holding him in place. I saw her step back from him and drop her hand. I didn't see the gun but I then heard the shot and saw the flash originate in front of her. And she went down.'

Gilmore drummed his pencil loudly on the table.

'That's probably messing up the recording,' Bosch said. 'Oh, that's right, you guys never put anything on tape.'

'Never mind that. Then what happened?'

'I started moving toward them at the wall. Stokes started to turn to see what had happened. From the ground Officer Brasher raised her right arm and took aim with her weapon at Stokes.'

'But she didn't fire, did she?'

'No. I yelled 'Freeze!' to Stokes and she did not fire and he did not move. I then moved to the scene and put Stokes on the ground. I handcuffed him. I then used the radio to call for help and tried to tend to Officer Brasher's wound as best I could.'

Gilmore was also chewing gum in a loud way that annoyed Bosch. He worked it for several chews before speaking.

'See, what I'm not getting here is why would she shoot herself?'

'You'll have to ask her that. I'm only telling you what I saw.'

'Yeah, but I'm asking you. You were there. What do you think?'

Bosch waited a long moment. Things had happened so fast. He had put off thinking about the garage by concentrating on Stokes. Now the images of what he had seen kept replaying in his mind. He finally shrugged.

'I don't know.'

'I'll tell you what, let's go your way with it for a minute. Let's assume she was re-holstering her weapon – which would have been against procedures, but let's assume it for the sake of argument. She's reholstering so she can cuff the guy. Her holster is on her right hip and the entry wound is on the left shoulder. How does that happen?'

Bosch thought about Brasher's questioning him a few nights earlier about the scar on his left shoulder. About being shot and what it had felt like. He felt the room closing in, getting tight on him. He started sweating.

'I don't know,' he said.

'You don't know very much, do you, Bosch?'

'I only know what I saw. I told you what I saw.'

Bosch wished they hadn't taken away Stokes's pack of cigarettes.

'What was your relationship with Officer Brasher?'

Bosch looked down at the table.

'What do you mean?'

'From what I hear you were fucking her. That's what I mean.'

'What's it have to do with anything?'

'I don't know. Maybe you tell me.'

Bosch didn't answer. He worked hard not to show the fury building inside.

'Well, first off, this relationship of yours was a violation of department policy,' Gilmore said. 'You know that, don't you?'

'She's in patrol. I'm in detective services.'

'You think that matters? That doesn't matter. You're a D-three. That's supervisor level. She's a grunt and a rookie no less. If this was the military you'd get a dishonorable just for starters. Maybe even some custody time.'

'But this is the LAPD. So what's it get me, a promotion?'

That was the first offensive move Bosch had made. It was a warning to Gilmore to go another way. It was a veiled reference to several well-known and not so well-known dalliances between high-ranking officers and members of the rank and file. It was known that the police union, which represented the rank and file to the level of sergeant, was waiting with the goods ready to challenge any disciplinary action taken under the department's so-called sexual harassment policy.

'I don't need any smart remarks from you,' Gilmore said. 'I'm trying to conduct an investigation here.'

He followed this with an extended drum roll while he looked at the few notes he had written on his pad. What he was doing, Bosch knew, was conducting a reverse investigation. Start with a conclusion and then gather only the facts that support it.

'How are your eyes?' Gilmore finally asked without looking up.

'One of them still stings like a son of a bitch. They feel like poached eggs.'

'Now, you say that Stokes hit you in the face with a shot from his bottle of cleaner.'

'Correct.'

'And it momentarily blinded you.'

'Correct.'

Now Gilmore stood up and started pacing in the small space behind his chair.

'How long between the moment you were blinded and when you were down in that dark garage and supposedly saw her shoot herself?'

Bosch thought for a moment.

'Well, I used a hose to wash my eyes, then I followed the pursuit. I would say not more than five minutes. But not too much less.'

'So you went from blind man to eagle scout – able to see everything – inside of five minutes.'

'I wouldn't characterize it like that but you have the time right.'

'Well, at least I got something right. Thank you.'

'No problem, Lieutenant.'

'So you're saying you didn't see the struggle for control of Officer Brasher's gun before the shot occurred. Is that correct?'

He had his hands clasped behind his back, the pencil between two fingers like a cigarette. Bosch leaned across the table. He understood the game of semantics Gilmore was playing.

'Don't play with the words, Lieutenant. There was no struggle. I saw no struggle because there was no struggle. If there had been a struggle I would have seen it. Is that clear enough for you?'

Gilmore didn't respond. He kept pacing.

'Look,' Bosch said, 'why don't you just go do a GSR test on Stokes? His hands, his jumpsuit. You won't find anything. That should end this pretty quick.'

Gilmore came back to his chair and leaned down on it. He looked at Bosch and shook his head.

'You know, Detective, I would love to do that. Normally in a situation like this, first thing we'd do is look for gunshot residue. The problem is, you broke the box. You took it upon yourself to take Stokes out of the crime scene and bring him back here. The chain of evidence was broken, you understand that? He could've washed himself, changed his clothes, I don't know what else, because you took it upon yourself to take him from the crime scene.'

Bosch was ready for that.

'I felt there was a safety issue there. My partner will back me on that. So will Stokes. And he was never out of my custody and control until you came busting in here.'

'That doesn't change the fact that you thought your case was more important than us getting the facts about a shooting of an officer of this department, does it?'

Bosch had no answer for that. But he was now coming to a full understanding of what Gilmore was doing. It was important for him and the department to conclude and be able to announce that Brasher was shot during a struggle for control of her gun. It was heroic that way. And it was something the department public relations machine could take advantage of and run with. There was nothing like the shooting of a good cop – a female rookie, no less – in the line of duty to help remind the public of all that was good and noble about their police department and all that was dangerous about the police officer's duty.

The alternative, to announce that Brasher had shot herself accidentally – or even something worse – would be an embarrassment for the department. One more in a long line of public relations fiascos.

Standing in the way of the conclusion Gilmore – and therefore Irving and the department brass – wanted was Stokes, of course, and then Bosch. Stokes was no problem. A convicted felon facing prison time for shooting a cop, whatever he said would be self-serving and unimportant. But Bosch was an eyewitness with a badge. Gilmore had to change his account or failing that, taint it. The first soft spot to attack was Bosch's physical condition – considering what had been thrown in his eyes, could he actually have seen what he claimed to have seen? The second move was to go after Bosch the detective. In order to preserve Stokes as a witness in his murder case, would Bosch go so far as to lie about seeing Stokes shoot a cop?

To Bosch, it was so outlandish as to be bizarre. But over the years he had seen even worse things happen to cops who had stepped in front of the machinery that produced the image of the department that was delivered to the public.

'Wait a minute, you—' Bosch said, able to hold himself from calling a superior officer an expletive. 'If you're trying to say I would lie about Stokes shooting Julia – uh, Officer Brasher – so he would stay in the clear for my case, then you – with all due respect – are out of your fucking mind.'

'Detective Bosch, I am exploring all possibilities here. It is my job to do so.'

'Well, you can explore them without me.'

Bosch stood up and went to the door.

'Where are you going?'

'I'm done with this.'

He glanced at the mirror and opened the door, then looked back at Gilmore.

'I got news for you, Lieutenant. Your theory is for shit. Stokes is nothing to my case. A zero. Julia getting shot, it was for nothing.'

'But you didn't know that until you got him in here, did you?'

Bosch looked at him and then slowly shook his head.

'Have a good day, Lieutenant.'

He turned to go through the door and almost stepped into Irving. The deputy chief stood ramrod straight in the hallway outside the room.

'Step back inside for a moment, Detective,' he said calmly. 'Please.'

Bosch backed into the room. Irving followed him in.

'Lieutenant, give us some space here,' the deputy chief said. 'And I want everyone out of the viewing room as well.'

He pointed at the mirror as he said this.

'Yes, sir,' Gilmore said and he left the room, closing the door behind him.

'Take your seat again,' Irving said.

Bosch moved back to the seat facing the mirror. Irving remained standing. After a moment he also started pacing, moving back and forth in front of the mirror, a double image for Bosch to track.

'We are going to call the shooting accidental,' Irving said, not looking at Bosch. 'Officer Brasher apprehended the suspect and while reholstering her weapon inadvertently fired the shot.'

'Is that what she said?' Bosch asked.

Irving looked momentarily confused, then shook his head.

'As far as I know, she only spoke to you and you said she didn't say anything specifically in regard to the shooting.'

Bosch nodded.

'So that's the end of it?'

'I don't see why it should go any further.'

Bosch thought of the photo of the shark on Julia's mantel. About what he knew about her in such a short time with her. Again the images of what he saw in the garage played back in slow motion. And things didn't add up.

'If we can't be honest with ourselves, how can we ever tell the truth to the people out there?'

Irving cleared his throat.

'I am not going to debate things with you, Detective. The decision has been made.'

'By you.'

'Yes, by me.'

'What about Stokes?'

'That will be up to the District Attorney's Office. He could be charged under the felony-murder law. His action of fleeing ultimately led to the shooting. It will get technical. If it is determined he was already in custody when the fatal shot occurred, then he might be able to—'

'Wait a minute, wait a minute,' Bosch said, coming out of his chair. 'Felony-*murder* law? Did you say *fatal* shot?'

Irving turned to face him.

'Lieutenant Gilmore did not tell you?'

Bosch dropped back into the chair and put his elbows on the table. He covered his face with his hands.

'The bullet hit a bone in her shoulder and apparently ricocheted inside her body. It cut through her chest. Pierced her heart. And she was dead on arrival.'

Bosch lowered his face so that his hands were now on top of his head. He felt himself get dizzy and he thought he might fall out of the chair. He tried to breathe deeply until it passed. After a few moments Irving spoke into the darkness of his mind.

'Detective, there are some officers in this department they call 'shit magnets.' I am sure you have heard the term. Personally, I find the phrase distasteful. But its meaning is that things always seem to happen to these particular officers. Bad things. Repeatedly. Always.'

Bosch waited in the dark for what he knew was coming.

'Unfortunately, Detective Bosch, you are one of those officers.'

Bosch unconsciously nodded. He was thinking about the moment that the paramedic put the breathing mask over Julia's mouth as she was speaking.

Don't let them—

What did she mean? Don't let them what? He was beginning to put things together and to know what she was going to say.

'Detective,' Irving said, his strong voice cutting through Bosch's thoughts. 'I have shown tremendous patience with you over the cases and over the years. But I have grown tired of it. So has this department. I want you to start thinking about retirement. Soon, Detective. Soon.'

Bosch kept his head down and didn't respond. After a moment he heard the door open and close.

34

In keeping with the wishes of Julia Brasher's family that she be buried in accordance with her faith, her funeral was late the next morning at Hollywood Memorial Park. Because she had been killed accidentally while in the line of duty, she was accorded the full police burial ceremony, complete with motorcycle procession, honor guard, twenty-one-gun salute and a generous showing of the department's brass at graveside. The department's aero squadron also flew over the cemetery, five helicopters flying in 'missing man' formation.

But because the funeral was not even twenty-four hours after her death it was not well attended. Line-of-duty deaths routinely bring at least token representations of officers from departments all over the state and the southwest. It was not to be with Julia Brasher. The quickness of the ceremony and the circumstances of her death added up to it being a relatively small affair – by police burial standards. A death in a gun battle would have crowded the small cemetery from stone to stone with the trappings of the blue religion. A cop killing herself while holstering her weapon did not engender much of the mythology and danger of police work. The funeral simply wasn't a draw.

Bosch watched from the outer edges of the funeral group. His head was throbbing from a night of drinking and trying to dull the guilt and pain he felt. Bones had come out of the ground and now two people were dead for reasons that made little sense to him. His eyes were badly bloodshot and swollen but he knew he could pass that off, if he had to, to being sprayed with the tire cleaner by Stokes the day before.

He saw Teresa Corazon, for once without her videographer, seated in the front row line of brass and dignitaries, what few of them there were in attendance. She wore sunglasses but Bosch could tell when she had noticed him. Her mouth seemed to settle into a hard, thin line. A perfect funeral smile.

Bosch was the first to look away.

It was a beautiful day for a funeral. Brisk overnight winds from the Pacific had temporarily cleared the smog out of the sky. Even the view of the Valley from Bosch's home had been clear that morning. Cirrus clouds scudded across the upper reaches of the sky along with contrails left by high-flying jets. The air in the cemetery smelled sweet from all the flowers arranged near the grave. From his standpoint, Bosch could see the crooked letters of the Hollywood sign, high up on Mount Lee, presiding over the service.

The chief of police did not deliver the eulogy as was his custom in line-of-duty deaths. Instead, the academy commander spoke, using the moment to talk about how danger in police work always comes from the unexpected corner and how Officer Brasher's death might save other cops by being a reminder never to let down the guard of caution. He never called her anything but Officer Brasher during his ten-minute speech, giving it an embarrassingly impersonal touch.

During the whole thing Bosch kept thinking about photos of sharks with open mouths and volcanoes disgorging their molten flows. He wondered if Julia had finally proven herself to the person she believed she needed to.

Amidst the blue uniforms surrounding the silver casket was a swath of gray. The lawyers. Her father and a large contingent from the firm. In the second row behind Brasher's father Bosch could see the man from the photo on the mantel of the Venice bungalow. For a while Bosch fantasized about going up to him and slapping him or bringing a knee up into his genitals. Doing it right in the middle of the service for all to see, then pointing to the casket and telling the man that he sent her on the path to this.

But he let it go. He knew that explanation and assignment of blame was too simple and wrong. Ultimately, he knew, people chose their own path. They can be pointed and pushed, but they always get the final choice. Everybody's got a cage that keeps out the sharks. Those who open the door and venture out do so at their own risk.

Seven members of Brasher's rookie class were chosen for the salute. They pointed rifles toward the blue sky and fired three rounds of blanks each, the ejected brass jackets arcing through the light and falling to the grass like tears. While the shots were still echoing off the stones, the helicopters made their pass overhead and then the funeral was over.

Bosch slowly made his way toward the grave, passing people heading away. A hand tugged his elbow from behind and he turned around. It was Brasher's partner, Edgewood.

'I, uh, just wanted to apologize about yesterday, about what I did,' he said. 'It won't happen again.'

Bosch waited for him to make eye contact and then just nodded. He had nothing to say to Edgewood.

'I guess you didn't mention it to OIS and I, uh, just want to say I appreciate it.'

Bosch just looked at him. Edgewood became uncomfortable, nodded once and walked away. When he was gone Bosch found himself looking at a woman who had been standing right behind the cop. A Latina with silver hair. It took Bosch a moment to recognize her.

'Dr. Hinojos.'

'Detective Bosch, how are you?'

It was the hair. Almost seven years earlier, when Bosch had been a regular visitor to Hinojos's office, her hair had been a deep brown without a hint of gray. She was still an attractive woman, gray or brown. But the change was startling.

'I'm doing okay. How're things in the psych shop?'

She smiled.

'They're fine.'

'I hear you run the whole show now.'

She nodded. Bosch felt himself getting nervous. When he had known her before, he had been on an involuntary stress leave. In twice-a-week sessions he had told her things he had never told anyone before or since. And once he was returned to duty he had never spoken to her again.

Until now.

'Did you know Julia Brasher?' he asked.

It wasn't unusual for a department shrink to attend a line-of-duty funeral; to offer on-the-spot counseling to those close to the deceased.

'No, not really. Not personally. As head of the department I reviewed her academy application and screening interview. I signed off on it.'

She waited a moment, studying Bosch for a reaction.

'I understand you were close to her. And that you were there. You were the witness.'

Bosch nodded. People leaving the funeral were passing on both sides of them. Hinojos took a step closer to him so that she would not be overheard.

'This is not the time or place but, Harry, I want to talk to you about her.'

'What's there to talk about?'

'I want to know what happened. And why.'

'It was an accident. Talk to Chief Irving.'

'I have and I'm not satisfied. I doubt you are, either.'

'Listen, Doctor, she's dead, okay? I'm not going to—'

'I signed off on her. My signature put that badge on her. If we missed something – if I missed something – I want to know. If there were signs, we should have seen them.'

Bosch nodded and looked down at the grass between them.

'Don't worry, there were signs I should've seen. But I didn't put it together either.'

She took another step closer. Now Bosch could look nowhere but directly at her.

'Then I am right. There is something more to this.'

He nodded.

'Nothing overt. It's just that she lived close to the edge. She took risks – she crossed the tube. She was trying to prove something. I don't think she was even sure she wanted to be a cop.'

'Prove something to who?'

'I don't know. Maybe herself, maybe somebody else.'

'Harry, I knew you as a man of great instincts. What else?'

Bosch shrugged.

'It's just things she did or said . . . I have a scar on my shoulder from a bullet wound. She asked me about it. The other night. She asked how I got shot and I told her how I had been lucky that it hit me where it did because it was all bone. Then . . . where she shot herself, it's the same spot. Only with her . . . it ricocheted. She didn't expect that.'

Hinojos nodded and waited.

'What I've been thinking I can't stand thinking, know what I mean?'

'Tell me, Harry.'

'I keep replaying it in my head. What I saw and what I know. She pointed her gun at him. And I think if I hadn't been there and yelled that maybe she would have shot him. Once he was down she would have wrapped his hands around the gun and fired a shot into the ceiling or maybe a car. Or maybe into him. It wouldn't matter as long as he ended up dead with paraffin on his hands and she could claim he went for her gun.'

'What are you suggesting, that she shot herself in order to kill him and make herself look like a hero?'

'I don't know. She talked about the world needing heroes. Especially now. She said she hoped to get a chance to be a hero one day. But I think there was something else in all of this. It was like she wanted the scar, the experience of it.'

'And she was willing to kill for it?'

'I don't know. I don't know if I'm even right about any of this. All I know is that she might have been a rookie but she had already reached the point where there was a line between us and them, where everybody without a badge is a scumbag. She saw it happening to herself. She might have been just looking for a way out . . . '

Bosch shook his head and looked off to the side. The cemetery was almost deserted now.

'I don't know. Saying it out loud makes it sound . . . I don't know. It's a crazy world.'

He took a step back from Hinojos.

'I guess you never really know anybody, do you?' he asked. 'You might think you do. You might be close enough to sleep with somebody but you'll never know what's really going on inside.'

'No, you won't. Everybody's got secrets.'

Bosch nodded and was about to step away.

'Wait, Harry.'

She lifted her purse and opened it. She started digging through it.

'I still want to talk about this,' she said as she came out with a business card and handed it to him. 'I want you to call me. Completely unofficial, confidential. For the good of the department.'

Bosch almost laughed.

'The department doesn't care about it. The department cares about the image, not the truth. And when the truth endangers the image, then fuck the truth.'

'Well, I care, Harry. And so do you.'

Bosch looked down at the card and nodded and put it in his pocket.

'Okay, I'll call you.'

'My cell phone's on there. I carry it with me all the time.'

Bosch nodded. She stepped forward and reached out. She grasped his arm and squeezed it.

'What about you, Harry? Are you okay?'

'Well, other than losing her and being told by Irving to start thinking about retiring, I'm doing okay.'

Hinojos frowned.

'Hang in there, Harry.'

Bosch nodded, thinking about how he had used the same words with Julia at the end.

Hinojos went off and Bosch continued his trek to the grave. He thought he was alone now. He grabbed a handful of dirt from the fill mound and walked over and looked down. A whole bouquet and several single flowers had been dropped on top of the casket. Bosch thought about holding Julia in his bed just two nights before. He wished he had seen what was coming. He wished he had been able to take the hints and put them into a clear picture of what she was doing and where she was going.

Slowly, he raised his hand out and let the dirt slide through his fingers.

'City of bones,' he whispered.

He watched the dirt fall into the grave like dreams disappearing.

'I assume you knew her.'

Bosch quickly turned. It was her father. Smiling sadly. They were the only two left in the cemetery. Bosch nodded.

'Just recently. I got to know her. I'm sorry for your loss.'

'Frederick Brasher.'

He put out his hand. Bosch started to take it but then held up.

'My hand's dirty.'

'Don't worry. So is mine.'

They shook hands.

'Harry Bosch.'

Brasher's hand stopped its shaking movement for a moment as the name registered.

'The detective,' he said. 'You were there yesterday.'

'Yes. I tried . . . I did what I could to help her. I . . . '

He stopped. He didn't know what to say.

'I'm sure you did. It must've been an awful thing to be there.'

Bosch nodded. A wave of guilt passed through him like an X-ray lighting his bones. He had left her there, thinking she would be all right. Somehow it hurt almost as bad as the fact she had died.

'What I don't understand is how it happened,' Brasher said. 'A mistake like that, how could it kill her? And then the District Attorney's Office today saying this man Stokes would not face any charge in the shooting. I'm a lawyer but I just don't understand. They are letting him go.'

Bosch studied the older man, saw the misery in his eyes.

'I'm sorry, sir. I wish I could tell you. I have the same questions as you.'

Brasher nodded and looked into the grave.

'I'm going now,' he said after a long moment. 'Thank you for coming, Detective Bosch.'

Bosch nodded. They shook hands again and Brasher started to walk away.

'Sir?' Bosch asked.

Brasher turned back.

'Do you know when someone from the family will be going to her house?'

'Actually, I was given her keys today. I was going to go now. Take a look at things. Try to get a sense of her, I guess. In recent years we hadn't . . . '

He didn't finish. Bosch stepped closer to him.

'There's something that she had. A picture in a frame. If it's not . . . if it's okay with you, I'd like to keep it.'

Brasher nodded.

'Why don't you come now? Meet me there. Show me this picture.'

Bosch looked at his watch. Lt. Billets had scheduled a one-thirty meeting to discuss the status of the case. He probably had just enough time to make it to Venice and back to the station. There would be no time for lunch but he couldn't see himself eating anything anyway.

'Okay, I will.'

They parted and headed toward their cars. On the way Bosch stopped on the grass where the salute had been fired. Combing the grass with his foot, he looked until he saw the glint of brass and bent down to pick up one of the ejected rifle shells. He held it on his palm and looked at it for a few moments, then closed his hand and dropped it into his coat pocket. He had picked up a shell from every cop funeral he had ever attended. He had a jar full of them.

He turned and walked out of the cemetery.

35

Jerry Edgar had a warrant knock that sounded like no other Bosch had ever heard. Like a gifted athlete who can focus the forces of his whole body into the swinging of a bat or the dunking of a basketball, Edgar could put his whole weight and six-foot-four frame into his knock. It was as though he could call down and concentrate all the power and fury of the righteous into the fist of his large left hand. He'd plant his feet firmly and stand sideways to the door. He'd raise his left arm, bend the elbow to less than thirty degrees and hit the door with the fleshy side of his fist. It was a backhand knock, but he was able to fire the pistons of this muscle assembly so quickly that it sounded like the staccato bark of a machine gun. What it sounded like was Judgment Day.

Samuel Delacroix's aluminum-skinned trailer seemed to shudder from end to end when Edgar hit its door with his fist at 3:30 on Thursday afternoon. Edgar waited a few seconds and then hit it again, this time announcing 'POLICE!' and then stepping back off the stoop, which was a stack of unconnected concrete blocks.

They waited. Neither had a weapon out but Bosch had his hand under his jacket and was gripping his gun in its holster. It was his standard procedure when delivering a warrant on a person not believed to be dangerous.

Bosch listened for movements from inside but the hiss from the nearby freeway was too loud. He checked the windows; none of the closed curtains were moving.

'You know,' Bosch whispered, 'I'm starting to think it comes as a relief when you yell it's just the cops after that knock. At least then they know it's not an earthquake.'

Edgar didn't respond. He probably knew it was just nervous banter from Bosch. It wasn't anxiety about the door knock – Bosch fully expected Delacroix to be easy. He was anxious because he knew the case was all coming down to the next few hours with Delacroix. They would search the trailer and then have to make a decision, largely communicated in partners' code, on whether to arrest Delacroix for his son's murder. Somewhere in that process they would need to find the evidence or elicit the confession that would change a case largely built on theory into one built on lawyer-resistant fact.

So in Bosch's mind they were quickly approaching the moment of truth, and that always made him nervous.

Earlier, in the case status meeting with Lt. Billets, it had been decided that it was time to talk to Sam Delacroix. He was the victim's father, he was the chief suspect. What little evidence they had still pointed to him. They spent the next hour typing up a search warrant for Delacroix's trailer and taking it to the downtown criminal courts building to a judge who was normally a soft touch.

But even this judge took some convincing. The problem was the case was old, the evidence directly linking the suspect was thin and the place Bosch and Edgar wanted to search was not where the homicide could have occurred and was not even occupied by the suspect at the time of the death.

What the detectives had in their favor was the emotional impact that came from the list in the warrant of all the injuries that the boy's bones indicated he had sustained over his short life. In the end, it was all those fractures that won the judge over and he signed the warrant.

They had gone to the driving range first but were informed that Delacroix was finished driving the tractor for the day.

'Give him another shot,' Bosch told Edgar outside the trailer.

'I think I can hear him coming.'

'I don't care. I want him rattled.'

Edgar stepped back up onto the stoop and hit the door again. The concrete blocks wobbled and he didn't plant his feet firmly. The resulting knock didn't carry the power and terror of the first two assaults on the door.

Edgar stepped back down.

'That wasn't the police,' Bosch whispered. 'That was a neighbor complaining about the dog or something.'

'Sorry, I—'

The door came open and Edgar shut up. Bosch went into high alert. Trailers were tricky. Unlike most structures, their doors opened outward so that the interior space didn't have to accommodate the swing. Bosch was positioned on the blind side, so that whoever answered was looking at Edgar but couldn't see Bosch. The problem was Bosch couldn't see whoever had opened the door either. If there was trouble Edgar's job was to yell a warning to Bosch and get himself clear. Without hesitation Bosch would empty his gun into the door of the trailer, the bullets tearing through the aluminum and whoever was on the other side like they were paper.

'What?' a man's voice said.

Edgar held up his badge. Bosch studied his partner for any warning sign of trouble.

'Mr. Delacroix, police.'

Seeing no sign of alarm, Bosch stepped forward and grabbed the knob and pulled the door all the way open. He kept his jacket flipped back and his hand on the grip of his gun.

The man he had seen on the golf range the day before was standing there. He wore an old pair of plaid shorts and a washed-out maroon T-shirt with permanent stains under the arms.

'We have a warrant allowing us to search these premises,' Bosch said. 'Can we come in?'

'You guys,' Delacroix said. 'You guys were at the range yesterday.'

'Sir,' Bosch said forcefully, 'I said that we have a search warrant for this trailer. Can we come in and conduct the search?'

Bosch took the folded warrant out of his pocket and held it up, but not within Delacroix's reach. That was the trick. To get the warrant they had to show all their cards to a judge. But they didn't want to show the same cards to Delacroix. Not just yet. So while Delacroix was entitled to read and study the warrant before granting the detectives entrance, Bosch was hoping to get inside the trailer without that happening. Delacroix would soon know the facts of the case, but Bosch wanted to control the delivery of information to him so that he could take readings and make judgments based on the suspect's reactions.

Bosch started putting the warrant back into his inside coat pocket.

'What's this about?' Delacroix asked in muted protest. 'Can I at least see that thing?'

'Are you Samuel Delacroix?' Bosch replied quickly.

'Yes.'

'This is your trailer, correct, sir?'

'It's my trailer. I lease the spot. I want to read the—'

'Mr. Delacroix,' Edgar said. 'We'd rather not stand out here in the view of your neighbors discussing this. I'm sure you don't want that either. Are you going to allow us to lawfully execute the search warrant or not?'

Delacroix looked from Bosch to Edgar and then back to Bosch. He nodded his head.

'I guess so.'

Bosch was first onto the stoop. He entered, squeezing by Delacroix on the threshold and picking up the odor of bourbon and bad breath and cat urine.

'Starting early, Mr. Delacroix?'

'Yeah, I've had a drink,' Delacroix said with a mixture of so what and self-loathing in his voice. 'I'm done my work. I'm entitled.'

Edgar came in then, a much tighter squeeze past Delacroix, and he and Bosch scanned what they could see of the dimly lit trailer. To the right from the doorway was the living room. It was wood paneled and had a green Naugahyde couch and a coffee table with pieces of the wood veneer scraped off, exposing the particleboard beneath. There was a matching lamp table with no lamp on it and a television stand with a TV awkwardly stacked on top of a videocassette recorder. There were several videotapes stacked on top of the television. Across from the coffee table was an old recliner with its shoulders torn open – probably by a cat – and stuffing leaking out. Under the coffee table was a stack of newspapers, most of them gossip tabloids with blaring headlines.

To the left was a galley-style kitchen with sink, cabinets, stove, oven and refrigerator on one side and a four-person dining booth on the right. There was a bottle of Ancient Age bourbon on the table. On the floor under the table were a few crumbs of cat food on a plate and an old plastic margarine tub half full of water. There was no sign of the cat, other than the smell of its urine.

Beyond the kitchen was a narrow hallway leading back to one or two bedrooms and a bathroom.

'Let's leave the door open and open up a few windows,' Bosch said. 'Mr. Delacroix, why don't you sit down on the couch there?'

Delacroix moved toward the couch and said, 'Look, you don't have to search the place. I know why you're here.'

Bosch glanced at Edgar and then at Delacroix.

'Yeah?' Edgar said. 'Why are we here?'

Delacroix dropped himself heavily into the middle of the couch. The springs were shot. He sank into the midsection, and the ends of the cushion on either side of him rose into the air like the bows of twin *Titanics* going down.

'The gas,' Delacroix said. 'And I hardly used any of it. I don't go anywhere but back and forth from the range. I have a restricted license because of my DUI.'

'The gas?' Edgar asked. 'What are—'

'Mr. Delacroix, we're not here about you stealing gas,' Bosch said.

He picked up one of the videotapes off the stack on the television. There was tape on the spine with writing on it. *First Infantry, episode 46.* He put it back down and glanced at the writing on some of the other tapes. They were all episodes of the television show Delacroix had worked on as an actor more than thirty years before.

'That's not really our gig,' he added, without looking at Delacroix.

'Then what? What do you want?'

Now Bosch looked at him.

'We're here about your son.'

Delacroix stared at him for a long moment, his mouth slowly coming open and exposing his yellowed teeth.

'Arthur,' he finally said.

'Yeah. We found him.'

Delacroix's eyes dropped from Bosch's and seemed to leave the trailer as he studied a far-off memory. In his look was knowledge. Bosch saw it. His instincts told him that what they would tell Delacroix next he would already know. He glanced over at Edgar to see if he had seen it. Edgar gave a single short nod.

Bosch looked back at the man on the couch.

'You don't seem very excited for a father who hasn't seen his son in more than twenty years,' he said.

Delacroix looked at him.

'I guess that's because I know he's dead.'

Bosch studied him for a long moment, his breath holding in his lungs.

'Why would you say that? What would make you think that?'

'Because I know. I've known all along.'

'What have you known?'

'That he wasn't coming back.'

This wasn't going the way of any of the scenarios Bosch had imagined. It seemed to him that Delacroix had been waiting for them, expecting them, maybe for years. He decided that they might have to change the strategy and arrest Delacroix and advise him of his rights.

'Am I under arrest?' Delacroix asked, as if he had joined Bosch in his thoughts.

Bosch glanced at Edgar again, wondering if his partner had sensed how their plan was now slipping away from them.

'We thought we might want to talk first. You know, informally.'

'You might as well arrest me,' Delacroix said quietly.

'You think so? Does that mean you don't want to talk to us?'

Delacroix shook his head slowly and went into the long-distance stare again.

'No, I'll talk to you,' he said. 'I'll tell you all about it.'

'Tell us about what?'

'How it happened.'

'How what happened?'

'My son.'

'You know how it happened?'

'Sure I know. I did it.'

Bosch almost cursed out loud. Their suspect had literally just confessed before they had advised him of his rights, including the right to avoid giving self-incriminating statements.

'Mr. Delacroix, we're going to cut this off right here. I am going to advise you of your rights now.'

'I just want to—'

'No, please, sir, don't say anything else. Not yet. Let's get this rights thing taken care of and then we'll be more than happy to listen to anything you want to tell us.'

Delacroix waved a hand like it didn't matter to him, like nothing mattered.

'Jerry, where's your recorder? I never got mine back from IAD.'

'Uh, in the car. I don't know about the batteries, though.'

'Go check.'

Edgar left the trailer and Bosch waited in silence. Delacroix put his elbows on his knees and his face in his hands. Bosch studied his posture. It didn't happen often, but it wouldn't be the first time he had scored a confession during his first meeting with a suspect.

Edgar came back in with a tape recorder but shook his head.

'Batteries are dead. I thought you had yours.'

'Shit. Then take notes.'

Bosch took out his badge case and took out one of his business cards. He'd had them made with the Miranda rights advisory printed on the back, along with a signature line. He read the advisory statement and asked Delacroix if he understood his rights. Delacroix nodded his head.

'Is that a yes?'

'Yes, it's a yes.'

'Then sign on the line beneath what I just read to you.'

He gave Delacroix the card and a pen. Once it was signed, Bosch returned the card to his badge wallet. He stepped over and sat on the edge of the recliner chair.

'Now, Mr. Delacroix, do you want to repeat what you just said to us a few minutes ago?'

Delacroix shrugged like it was no big deal.

'I killed my son. Arthur. I killed him. I knew you people would show up someday. It took a long time.'

Bosch looked over at Edgar. He was writing in a notebook. They would have some record of Delacroix's admission. He looked back at the suspect and waited, hoping the silence would be an invitation for Delacroix to say more. But he didn't. Instead, the suspect buried his face in his hands again. His shoulders soon began shaking as he started to cry.

'God help me . . . I did it.'

Bosch looked back at Edgar and raised his eyebrows. His partner gave a quick thumbs-up sign. They had more than enough to move to the next stage; the controlled and recorded setting of an interview room at the police station.

'Mr. Delacroix, do you have a cat?' Bosch asked. 'Where's your cat?'

Delacroix peeked his wet eyes through his fingers.

'He's around. Probably sleepin' in the bed. Why?'

'Well, we're going to call Animal Control and they'll come get him to take care of him. You're going to have to come with us. We're going to place you under arrest now. And we'll talk more at the police station.'

Delacroix dropped his hands and seemed upset.

'No. Animal Control won't take care of him. They'll gas him the minute they find out I won't be coming back.'

'Well, we can't just leave him here.'

'Mrs. Kresky will take care of him. She's next door. She can come in and feed him.'

Bosch shook his head. The whole thing was foundering because of a cat.

'We can't do that. We have to seal this place until we can search it.'

'What do you have to search it for?' Delacroix said, real anger in his voice now. 'I'm telling you what you need to know. I killed my son. It was an accident. I hit him too hard, I guess. I . . . '

Delacroix put his face back into his hands and tearfully mumbled, 'God . . . what did I do?'

Bosch checked Edgar; he was writing. Bosch stood up. He wanted to get Delacroix to the station and into one of the interview rooms. His anxiety was gone now, replaced by a sense of urgency. Attacks of conscience and guilt were ephemeral. He wanted to get Delacroix locked down on tape – video and audio – before he decided to talk to a lawyer and before he realized that he was talking himself into a 9 × 6 room for the rest of his life.

'Okay, we'll figure out the cat thing later,' he said. 'We'll leave enough food for now. Stand up, Mr. Delacroix, we're going to go.'

Delacroix stood up.

'Can I change into something nicer? This is just old stuff I was wearing around here.'

'No, don't worry about that,' Bosch said. 'We'll bring you clothes to wear later on.'

He didn't bother telling him that those clothes wouldn't be his. What would happen was that he'd be given a county jail-issued jumpsuit with a number across the back. His jumpsuit would be yellow, the color given to custodies on the high-power floor – the murderers.

'Are you going to handcuff me?' Delacroix asked.

'It's department policy,' Bosch said. 'We have to.'

He came around the coffee table and turned Delacroix so he could cuff his hands behind his back.

'I was an actor, you know. I once played a prisoner in an episode of *The Fugitive.* The first series, with David Janssen. It was just a small role. I sat on a bench next to Janssen. That's all I did. I was supposed to be on drugs, I think.'

Bosch didn't say anything. He gently pushed Delacroix toward the trailer's narrow door.

'I don't know why I just remembered that,' Delacroix said.

'It's all right,' Edgar said. 'People remember the strangest things at a time like this.'

'Just be careful on these steps,' Bosch said.

They led him out, Edgar in front and Bosch behind him.

'Is there a key?' Bosch asked.

'On the kitchen counter there,' Delacroix said.

Bosch went back inside and found the keys. He then started opening cabinets in the kitchenette until he found the box of cat food. He opened it and dumped it out onto the paper plate under the table. There was not very much food. Bosch knew he would have to do something about the animal later.

When Bosch came out of the trailer Edgar had already put Delacroix into the rear of the slickback. He saw a neighbor watching from the open front door of a nearby trailer. He turned and closed and locked Delacroix's door.

36

Bosch stuck his head into Lt. Billets's office. She was turned sideways at her desk and working on a computer at a side table. Her desk had been cleared. She was about to go home for the day.

'Yes?' she said without looking to see who it was.

'Looks like we got lucky,' Bosch said.

She turned from the computer and saw it was Bosch.

'Let me guess. Delacroix invites you in and just sits down and confesses.'

Bosch nodded.

'Just about.'

Her eyes grew wide in surprise.

'You are fucking kidding me.'

'He says he did it. We had to shut him up so we could get him back here on tape. It was like he had been waiting for us to show up.'

Billets asked a few more questions and Bosch ended up recapping the entire visit to the trailer, including the problem they had in not having a working tape recorder with which to take Delacroix's confession. Billets grew concerned and annoyed, equally with Bosch and Edgar for not being prepared and Bradley of IAD for not returning Bosch's tape recorder.

'All I can say is that this better not put hair on the cake, Harry,' she said, referring to the possibility of a legal challenge to any confession because Delacroix's initial words were not on tape. 'If we lose this one because of a screwup on our part . . . '

She didn't finish but didn't need to.

'Look, I think we'll be all right. Edgar got everything he said down verbatim. We stopped as soon as we got enough to hook him up and now we'll lock it all down with sound and video.'

Billets seemed barely placated.

'And what about Miranda? You're confident we will not have a Miranda situation,' she said, the last part not a question but an order.

'I don't see it. He started spouting off before we had a chance to advise him. Then he kept talking afterward. Sometimes it goes like that. You're ready to go with the battering ram and they just open the door for you.

Whoever he gets as a lawyer might have a heart attack and start screaming about it but nothing's going to come of it. We're clean, Lieutenant.'

Billets nodded, a sign that Bosch was convincing her.

'I wish they were all this easy,' she said. 'What about the DA's office?'

'I'm calling them next.'

'Okay, which room if I want to take a look?'

'Three.'

'Okay, Harry, go wrap him up.'

She turned back to her computer. Bosch threw a salute at her and was about to duck out of the doorway when he stopped. She sensed he had not left and turned back to him.

'What is it?'

Bosch shrugged his shoulders.

'I don't know. The whole way in I was thinking about what could have been avoided if we just went to him instead of dancing around him, gathering string.'

'Harry, I know what you're thinking and there's no way in the world you could have known that this guy – after twenty-some years – was just waiting for you to knock on his door. You handled it the right way and if you had it to do again you would still do it the same way. You circle the prey. What happened with Officer Brasher had nothing to do with how you ran this case.'

Bosch looked at her for a moment and then nodded. What she said would help ease his conscience.

Billets turned back to her computer.

'Like I said, go wrap him up.'

Bosch went back to the homicide table to call the District Attorney's Office to advise that an arrest had been made in a murder case and that a confession was being taken. He talked to a supervisor named O'Brien and told her that either he or his partner would be coming in to file charges by the end of the day. O'Brien, who was familiar with the case only through media reports, said she wanted to send a prosecutor to the station to oversee the handling of the confession and the forward movement of the case at this stage.

Bosch knew that with rush hour traffic out of downtown it would still be a minimum of forty-five minutes before the prosecutor got to the station. He told O'Brien the prosecutor was welcome but that he wasn't going to wait for anyone before taking the suspect's confession. O'Brien suggested he should.

'Look, this guy wants to talk,' Bosch said. 'In forty-five minutes or an hour it could be a different story. We can't wait. Tell your guy to knock on the door at room three when he gets here. We'll bring him into it as soon as we can.'

In a perfect world the prosecutor would be there for an interview but

Bosch knew from years working cases that a guilty conscience doesn't always stay guilty. When someone tells you they want to confess to a killing, you don't wait. You turn on the tape recorder and say, 'Tell me all about it.'

O'Brien reluctantly agreed, citing her own experiences, and they hung up. Bosch immediately picked the phone back up and called Internal Affairs and asked for Carol Bradley. He was transferred.

'This is Bosch, Hollywood Division, where's my damn tape recorder?'

There was silence in response.

'Bradley? Hello? Are you—'

'I'm here. I have your recorder here.'

'Why did you take it? I told you to listen to the tape. I didn't say take my machine, I don't need it anymore.'

'I wanted to review it and have the tape checked, to make sure it was continuous.'

'Then open it up and take the tape. Don't take the machine.'

'Detective, sometimes they need the original recorder to authenticate the tape.'

Bosch shook his head in frustration.

'Jesus, why are you doing this? You know who the leak is, why are you wasting time?'

Again there was a pause before she answered.

'I needed to cover all bases. Detective, I need to run my investigation the way I see fit.'

Now Bosch paused for a moment, wondering if he was missing something, if there was something else going on. He finally decided he couldn't worry about it. He had to keep his eyes on the prize. His case.

'Cover the bases, that's great,' he said. 'Well, I almost lost a confession today because I didn't have my machine. I would appreciate it if you would get it back to me.'

'I'm finished with it and am putting it in inter-office dispatch right now.'

'Thank you. Good-bye.'

He hung up, just as Edgar showed up at the table with three cups of coffee. It made Bosch think of something they should do.

'Who's got the watch down there?' he asked.

'Mankiewicz was in there,' Edgar said. 'So was Young.'

Bosch poured the coffee from the Styrofoam container into the mug he got out of his drawer. He then picked up the phone and dialed the watch office. Mankiewicz answered.

'You got anybody in the bat cave?'

'Bosch? I thought you might take some time off.'

'You thought wrong. What about the cave?'

'No, nobody till about eight today. What do you need?'

'I'm about to take a confession and don't want any lawyer to be able to open the box once I wrap it. My guy smells like Ancient Age but I think he's straight. I'd like to make a record of it, just the same.'

'This the bones case?'

'Yeah.'

'Bring him down and I'll do it. I'm certified.'

'Thanks, Mank.'

He hung up and looked at Edgar.

'Let's take him down to the cave and see what he blows. Just to be safe.'

'Good idea.'

They took their coffees into interview room 3, where they had earlier shackled Delacroix to the table's center ring. They released him from the cuffs and let him take a few gulps of his coffee before walking him down the back hallway to the station's small jail facility. The jail essentially consisted of two large holding cells for drunks and prostitutes. Arrestees of a higher order were usually transported to the main city or county jail. There was a small third cell that was known as the bat cave, as in blood alcohol testing.

They met Mankiewicz in the hallway and followed him to the cave, where he turned on the Breathalyzer and instructed Delacroix to blow into a clear plastic tube attached to the machine. Bosch noticed that Mankiewicz had a black mourning ribbon across his badge for Brasher.

In a few minutes they had the result. Delacroix blew a .003, not even close to the legal limit for driving. There was no standard set for giving a confession to murder.

As they took Delacroix out of the tank Bosch felt Mankiewicz tap his arm from behind. He turned to face him while Edgar headed back up the hallway with Delacroix.

Mankiewicz nodded.

'Harry, I just wanted to say I'm sorry. You know, about what happened out there.'

Bosch knew he was talking about Brasher. He nodded back.

'Yeah, thanks. It's a tough one.'

'I had to put her out there, you know. I knew she was green but—'

'Hey, Mank, you did the right thing. Don't second guess anything.'

Mankiewicz nodded.

'I gotta go,' Bosch said.

While Edgar returned Delacroix to his spot in the interview room Bosch went into the viewing room, focused the video camera through the one-way glass and put in a new cassette he took from the supply cabinet. He then turned on the camera as well as the backup sound recorder. Everything was set. He went back into the interview room to finish wrapping the package.

37

Bosch identified the three occupants of the interview room and announced the date and time, even though both of these would be printed on the lower frame of the video being recorded of the session. He put a rights waiver form on the table and told Delacroix he wanted to advise him one more time of his rights. When he was finished he asked Delacroix to sign the form and then moved it to the side of the table. He took a gulp of coffee and started.

'Mr. Delacroix, earlier today you expressed to me a desire to talk about what happened to your son, Arthur, in nineteen eighty. Do you still wish to speak to us about that?'

'Yes.'

'Let's start with the basic questions and then we can go back and cover everything else. Did you cause the death of your son, Arthur Delacroix?'

'Yes, I did.'

He said it without hesitation or emotion.

'Did you kill him?'

'Yes, I did. I didn't mean to, but I did. Yes.'

'When did this occur?'

'It was in May, I think, of nineteen eighty. I think that's when it was. You people probably know more about it than me.'

'Please don't assume that. Please answer each question to the best of your ability and recollection.'

'I'll try.'

'Where was your son killed?'

'In the house where we lived at the time. In his room.'

'How was he killed? Did you strike him?'

'Uh, yes. I . . . '

Delacroix's businesslike approach to the interview suddenly eroded and his face seemed to close in on itself. He used the heels of his palms to wipe tears from the corners of his eyes.

'You struck him?'

'Yes.'

'Where?'

'All over, I guess.'

'Including the head?'

'Yes.'

'This was in his room, you said?'

'Yes, his room.'

'What did you hit him with?'

'What do you mean?'

'Did you use your fists or an object of some kind?'

'Yes, both. My hands and an object.'

'What was the object you struck your son with?'

'I really can't remember. I'll have to . . . it was just something he had there. In his room. I have to think.'

'We can come back to it, Mr. Delacroix. Why on that day did you – first of all, when did it happen? What time of day?'

'It was in the morning. After Sheila – she's my daughter – had gone to school. That's really all I remember, Sheila was gone.'

'What about your wife, the boy's mother?'

'Oh, she was long gone. She's the reason I started—'

He stopped. Bosch assumed he was going to lay blame for his drinking on his wife, which would conveniently blame her for everything that came out of the drinking, including murder.

'When was the last time you talked to your wife?'

'Ex-wife. I haven't talked to her since the day she left. That was . . . '

He didn't finish. He couldn't remember how long.

'What about your daughter? When did you talk to her last?'

Delacroix looked away from Bosch and down at his hands on the table.

'Long time,' he said.

'How long?'

'I don't remember. We don't talk. She helped me buy the trailer. That was five or six years ago.'

'You didn't talk to her this week?'

Delacroix looked up at him, a curious look on his face.

'This week? No. Why would—'

'Let me ask the questions. What about the news? Did you read any newspapers in the last couple weeks or watch the news on TV?'

Delacroix shook his head.

'I don't like what's on television now. I like to watch tapes.'

Bosch realized he had gotten off track. He decided to get back to the basic story. What was important for him to achieve here was a clear and simple confession to Arthur Delacroix's death. It needed to be solid and detailed enough to stand up. Without a doubt Bosch knew that at some point after Delacroix got a lawyer, the confession would be withdrawn. They always were. It would be challenged on all fronts – from the procedures followed to the suspect's state of mind – and Bosch's duty was not only to take the confession but to make sure it survived and could eventually be delivered to twelve jurors.

'Let's get back to your son, Arthur. Do you remember what the object was you struck him with on the day of his death?'

'I'm thinking it was this little bat he had. A miniature baseball bat that was like a souvenir from a Dodgers game.'

Bosch nodded. He knew what he was talking about. They sold bats at the souvenir stands that were like the old billy clubs cops carried until they went to metal batons. They could be lethal.

'Why did you hit him?'

Delacroix looked down at his hands. Bosch noticed his fingernails were gone. It looked painful.

'Um, I don't remember. I was probably drunk. I . . . '

Again the tears came in a burst and he hid his face in his tortured hands. Bosch waited until he dropped his hands and continued.

'He . . . he should have been in school. And he wasn't. I came in the room and there he was. I got mad. I paid good money – money I didn't have – for that school. I started to yell. I started to hit and then . . . then I just picked up the little bat and I hit him. I hit him too hard, I guess. I didn't mean to.'

Bosch waited again but Delacroix didn't go on.

'He was dead then?'

Delacroix nodded.

'That means yes?'

'Yes. Yes.'

There was a soft knock on the door. Bosch nodded to Edgar, who got up and went out. Bosch assumed it was the prosecutor but he wasn't going to interrupt things now to make introductions. He pressed on.

'What did you do next? After Arthur was dead.'

'I took him out the back and down the steps to the garage. Nobody saw me. I put him in the trunk of my car. I then went back to his room, I cleaned up and put some of his clothes in a bag.'

'What kind of bag?'

'It was his school bag. His backpack.'

'What clothes did you put into it?'

'I don't remember. Whatever I grabbed out of the drawer, you know?'

'All right. Can you describe this backpack?'

Delacroix shrugged his shoulders.

'I don't remember. It was just a normal backpack.'

'Okay, after you put clothes in it, what did you do?'

'I put it in the trunk. And I closed it.'

'What car was that?'

'That was my 'seventy-two Impala.'

'You still have it?'

'I wish; it'd be a classic. But I wrecked it. That was my first DUI.'

'What do you mean "wrecked"?'

'I totaled it. I wrapped it around a palm tree in Beverly Hills. It was taken to a junkyard somewhere.'

Bosch knew that tracing a thirty-year-old car would be difficult, but news that the vehicle had been totaled ended all hope of finding it and checking the trunk for physical evidence.

'Then let's go back to your story. You had the body in the trunk. When did you dispose of it?'

'That night. Late. When he didn't come home from school that day we started looking for him.'

'We?'

'Sheila and me. We drove around and we looked. We went to all the skateboard spots.'

'And all the time Arthur's body was in the trunk of the car you were in?'

'That's right. You see, I didn't want her to know what I had done. I was protecting her.'

'I understand. Did you make a missing person report with the police?'

Delacroix shook his head.

'No. I went to the Wilshire station and talked to a cop. He was right there where you walk in. At the desk. He told me Arthur probably ran away and he'd be back. To give it a few days. So I didn't make out the report.'

Bosch was trying to cover as many markers as he could, going over story facts that could be verified and therefore used to buttress the confession when Delacroix and his lawyer withdrew it and denied it. The best way to do this was with hard evidence or scientific fact. But cross-matching stories was also important. Sheila Delacroix had already told Bosch and Edgar that she and her father had driven to the police station on the night Arthur didn't come home. Her father went in while she waited in the car. But Bosch found no record of a missing person report. It now seemed to fit. He had a marker that would help validate the confession.

'Mr. Delacroix, are you comfortable talking to me?'

'Yeah, sure.'

'You are not feeling coerced or threatened in any way?'

'No, I'm fine.'

'You are talking freely to me, right?'

'That's right.'

'Okay, when did you take your son's body from the trunk?'

'I did that later. After Sheila went to sleep I went back out to the car and I took it to where I could hide the body.'

'And where was that?'

'Up in the hills. Laurel Canyon.'

'Can you remember more specifically where?'

'Not too much. I went up Lookout Mountain past the school. Up in around there. It was dark and I . . . you know, I was drinking because I felt so bad about the accident, you know.'

'Accident?'

'Hitting Arthur too hard like I did.'

'Oh. So up past the school, do you remember what road you were on?'

'Wonderland.'

'Wonderland? Are you sure?'

'No, but that's what I think it was. I've spent all these years . . . I tried to forget as much about this as I could.'

'So you're saying you were intoxicated when you hid the body?'

'I was drunk. Don't you think I'd have to be?'

'It doesn't matter what I think.'

Bosch felt the first tremor of danger go through him. While Delacroix was offering a complete confession, Bosch had elicited information that might be damaging to the case as well. Delacroix being drunk could explain why the body had apparently been hurriedly dropped in the hillside woods and quickly covered with loose soil and pine needles. But Bosch recalled his own difficult climb up the hill and couldn't imagine an intoxicated man doing it while carrying or dragging the body of his own son along with him.

Not to mention the backpack. Would it have been carried along with the body or did Delacroix climb back up the hill a second time with the bag, somehow finding the same spot in the dark where he had left the body?

Bosch studied Delacroix, trying to figure out which way to go. He had to be very careful. It would be case suicide to bring out a response that a defense attorney could later exploit for days in court.

'All I remember,' Delacroix suddenly said unbidden, 'is that it took me a long time. I was gone almost all night. And I remember that I hugged him as tight as I could before I put him down in the hole. It was like I had a funeral for him.'

Delacroix nodded and searched Bosch's eyes as if looking for an acknowledgment that he had done the right thing. Bosch returned nothing with his look.

'Let's start with that,' he said. 'The hole you put him into, how deep was it?'

'It wasn't that deep, maybe a couple feet at the most.'

'How did you dig it? Did you have tools with you?'

'No, I didn't think about that. So I had to dig with my hands. I didn't get very far either.'

'What about the backpack?'

'Um, I put it there, too. In the hole. But I'm not sure.'

Bosch nodded.

'Okay. Do you remember anything else about this place? Was it steep or flat or muddy?'

Delacroix shook his head.

'I can't remember.'

'Were there houses there?'

'There was some right nearby, yeah, but nobody saw me, if that's what you mean.'

Bosch finally concluded that he was going too far down a path of legal peril. He had to stop and go back and clean up a few details.

'What about your son's skateboard?'

'What about it?'

'What did you do with it?'

Delacroix leaned forward to consider this.

'You know, I don't really remember.'

'Did you bury it with him?'

'I can't . . . I don't remember.'

Bosch waited a long moment to see if something would come out. Delacroix said nothing.

'Okay, Mr. Delacroix, we're going to take a break here while I go talk to my partner. I want you to think about what we were just talking about. About the place where you took your son. I need you to remember more about it. And about the skateboard, too.'

'Okay, I'll try.'

'I'll bring you back some more coffee.'

'That would be good.'

Bosch got up and took the empties from the room. He immediately went to the viewing room and opened the door. Edgar and another man were in there. The man, whom Bosch didn't know, was looking at Delacroix through the one-way glass. Edgar was reaching to the video to turn it off.

'Don't turn it off,' Bosch said quickly.

Edgar held back.

'Let it run. If he starts remembering more stuff I don't want anybody to try to say we gave it to him.'

Edgar nodded. The other man turned from the window and put out his hand. He looked like he was no more than thirty. He had dark hair that was slicked back and very white skin. He had a broad smile on his face.

'Hi, George Portugal, deputy district attorney.'

Bosch put the empty cups down on a table and shook his hand.

'Looks like you've got an interesting case here,' Portugal said.

'And getting more so all the time,' Bosch said.

'Well, from what I've seen in the last ten minutes, you don't have a worry in the world. This is a slam dunk.'

Bosch nodded but didn't return the smile. What he wanted to do was laugh at the inanity of Portugal's statement. He knew better than to trust the instincts of young prosecutors. He thought of all that had happened before they had gotten Delacroix into the room on the other side of the glass. And he knew there was no such thing as a slam dunk.

38

At 7 p.m. Bosch and Edgar drove Samuel Delacroix downtown to be booked at Parker Center on charges of murdering his son. With Portugal in the interview room taking part in the questioning, they had interrogated Delacroix for almost another hour, gleaning only a few new details about the killing. The father's memory of his son's death and his part in it had been eroded by twenty years of guilt and whiskey.

Portugal left the room still believing the case was a slam dunk. Bosch, on the other hand, was not so sure. He was never as welcoming of voluntary confessions as other detectives and prosecutors were. He believed true remorse was rare in the world. He treated the unanticipated confession with extreme caution, always looking for the play behind the words. To him, every case was like a house under construction. When a confession came into play, it became the concrete slab the house was built upon. If it was mixed wrong or poured wrong, the house might not withstand the jolt of the first earthquake. As he drove Delacroix toward Parker Center, Bosch couldn't help but think there were unseen cracks in this house's foundation. And that the earthquake was coming.

Bosch's thoughts were interrupted by his cell phone chirping. It was Lt. Billets.

'You guys slipped out of here before we had a chance to talk.'

'We're taking him down to booking.'

'You sound happy about it.'

'Well . . . I can't really talk.'

'You're in the car with him?'

'Yeah.'

'Is it serious or are you just playing mother hen?'

'I don't know yet.'

'I've got Irving and Media Relations calling me. I guess word is already out through the DA's press office that charges are coming. How do you want me to handle it?'

Bosch looked at his watch. He figured that after booking Delacroix they could get to Sheila Delacroix's house by eight. The trouble was that an announcement to the media might mean that reporters would get to her before that.

'Tell you what, we want to get to the daughter first. Can you get to the DA's office and see if they can hold it till nine? Same with Media Relations.'

'No problem. And look, after you dump the guy, call me when you can talk. At home. If there's a problem, I want to know about it.'

'You got it.'

He closed the phone and looked over at Edgar.

'First thing Portugal must've done was call his press office.'

'Figures. Probably his first big case. He's going to milk it for all he can.'

'Yeah.'

They drove in silence for a few minutes. Bosch thought about what he had insinuated to Billets. He couldn't quite place his reason for discomfort. The case was now moving from the realm of the police investigation to the realm of the court system. There was still a lot of investigative work to be done, but all cases changed once a suspect was charged and in custody and the prosecution began. Most times Bosch felt a sense of relief and fulfillment at the moment he was taking a killer to be booked. He felt as though he was a prince of the city, that he had made a difference in some way. But not this time and he wasn't sure why.

He finally tied off his feelings on his own missteps and the uncontrollable movements of the case. He decided he could not celebrate or feel much like a prince of the city when the case had cost so much. Yes, they had the admitted killer of a child in the car with them and they were taking him to jail. But Nicholas Trent and Julia Brasher were dead. The house he had built of the case would always have rooms containing their ghosts. They would always haunt him.

'Was that my daughter you were talking about? You're going to talk to her?'

Bosch looked up into the rearview mirror. Delacroix was hunched forward because his hands were cuffed behind his back. Bosch had to adjust the mirror and turn on the dome light to see his eyes.

'Yeah. We're going to give her the news.'

'Do you have to? Do you have to bring her into this?'

Bosch watched him in the mirror for a moment. Delacroix's eyes were shifting back and forth.

'We've got no choice,' Bosch said. 'It's her brother, her father.'

Bosch put the car onto the Los Angeles Street exit. They would be at the booking entrance at the back of Parker Center in five minutes.

'What are you going to tell her?'

'What you told us. That you killed Arthur. We want to tell her before the reporters get to her or she sees it on the news.'

He checked the mirror. He saw Delacroix nod his approval. Then the man's eyes came up and looked at Bosch's in the mirror.

'Will you tell her something for me?'

'Tell her what?'

Bosch reached inside his coat pocket for his recorder but then realized he didn't have it with him. He silently cursed Bradley and his own decision to cooperate with IAD.

Delacroix was quiet for a moment. He moved his head as he looked from side to side as if searching for the thing he wanted to say to his daughter. Then he looked back up at the mirror and spoke.

'Just tell her that I'm sorry for everything. Just like that. Sorry for everything. Tell her that.'

'You're sorry for everything. I got it. Anything else?'

'No, just that.'

Edgar shifted in his seat so he could look back at Delacroix.

'You're sorry, huh?' he said. 'Seems kind of late after twenty years, don't you think?'

Bosch turned right onto Los Angeles Street. He couldn't check the mirror for Delacroix's reaction.

'You don't know anything,' Delacroix angrily retorted. 'I've been crying for twenty years.'

'Yeah,' Edgar threw back. 'Crying in your whiskey. But not enough to do anything about it until we showed up. Not enough to crawl out of your bottle and turn yourself in and get your boy out of the dirt while there was still enough of him for a proper burial. All we have is bones, you know. Bones.'

Bosch now checked the mirror. Delacroix shook his head and leaned even further forward, until his head was against the back of the front seat.

'I couldn't,' he said. 'I didn't even—'

He stopped himself and Bosch watched the mirror as Delacroix's shoulders started to shake. He was crying.

'Didn't even what?' Bosch asked.

Delacroix didn't respond.

'Didn't even what?' Bosch asked louder.

Then he heard Delacroix vomit onto the floor of the back compartment.

'Ah, shit!' Edgar yelled. 'I knew this was going to happen.'

The car filled with the acrid smell of a drunk tank. Alcohol-based vomit. Bosch lowered his window all the way despite the brisk January air. Edgar did the same. Bosch turned the car into Parker Center.

'It's your turn, I think,' Bosch said. 'I got the last one. That wit we pulled out of Bar Marmount.'

'I know, I know,' Edgar said. 'Just what I wanna be doing before dinner.'

Bosch pulled into one of the spaces near the intake doors that were reserved for vehicles carrying prisoners. A booking officer standing by the door started heading toward the car.

Bosch recalled Julia Brasher's complaint about having to clean vomit out of the back of patrol cars. It was almost like she was jabbing him in the sore ribs again, making him smile despite the pain.

39

Sheila Delacroix answered the door of the home where she and her brother had lived but only one of them had grown up. She was wearing black leggings and a long T-shirt that went almost to her knees. Her face was scrubbed of makeup and Bosch noticed for the first time that she had a pretty face when it was not hidden by paint and powder. Her eyes grew wide when she recognized Bosch and Edgar.

'Detectives? I wasn't expecting you.'

She made no move to invite them in. Bosch spoke.

'Sheila, we have been able to identify the remains from Laurel Canyon as those of your brother, Arthur. We are sorry to have to tell you this. Can we come in for a few minutes?'

She nodded as she received the information and leaned for just a moment on the door frame. Bosch wondered if she would leave the place now that there was no chance of Arthur ever coming back.

She stepped aside and waved them in.

'Please,' she said, signaling them to sit down as they moved to the living room.

Everybody took the same seats as they had before. Bosch noticed the box of photos she had retrieved the other day was still on the coffee table. The photos were neatly stacked in rows in the box now. Sheila noticed his glance.

'I kind of put them in order. I had been meaning to get around to it for a long time.'

Bosch nodded. He waited until she took her seat before sitting down last and continuing. He and Edgar had worked out how the visit should go on the way over. Sheila Delacroix was going to be an important component of the case. They had her father's confession and the evidence of the bones. But what would pull it all together would be her story. They needed her to tell what it was like growing up in the Delacroix house.

'Uh, there's more, Sheila. We wanted to talk to you before you saw it on the news. Late today your father was charged with Arthur's murder.'

'Oh, my God.'

She leaned forward and brought her elbows down to her knees. She clasped her hands into fists and held them tight against her mouth. She closed her eyes and her hair fell forward, helping to hide her face.

'He's being held down at Parker Center pending his arraignment tomorrow and a bail hearing. I would say that from the looks of things – his lifestyle, I mean – I don't think he'll be able to make the kind of bail they're going to be talking about.'

She opened her eyes.

'There must be some kind of mistake. What about the man, the man across the street? He killed himself, he must be the one.'

'We don't think so, Sheila.'

'My father couldn't have done this.'

'Actually,' Edgar said softly, 'he confessed to it.'

She straightened herself, and Bosch saw the true surprise on her face. And this surprised him. He thought she would have always harbored the idea, the suspicion about her father.

'He told us that he hit him with a baseball bat because he skipped school,' Bosch said. 'Your father said he was drinking at the time and that he just lost it and he hit him too hard. An accident, according to him.'

Sheila stared back at him as she tried to process this information.

'He then put your brother's body in the trunk of the car. He told us that when you two drove around looking for him that night, he was in the trunk all along.'

She closed her eyes again.

'Then, later that night,' Edgar continued, 'while you were sleeping, he snuck out and drove up into the hills and dumped the body.'

Sheila started shaking her head like she was trying to fend off the words.

'No, no, he . . . '

'Did you ever see your father strike Arthur?' Bosch asked.

Sheila looked at him, seemingly coming out of her daze.

'No, never.'

'Are you sure about that?'

She shook her head.

'Nothing more than a swat on the behind when he was small and being a brat. That's all.'

Bosch looked over at Edgar and then back at the woman, who was leaning forward again, looking down at the floor by her feet.

'Sheila, I know we're talking about your father here. But we're also talking about your brother. He didn't get much of a chance at life, did he?'

He waited and after a long moment she shook her head without looking up.

'We have your father's confession and we have evidence. Arthur's bones tell us a story, Sheila. There are injuries.

A lot of them. From his whole life.'

She nodded.

'What we need is another voice. Someone who can tell us what it was like for Arthur to grow up in this house.'

'To try to grow up,' Edgar added.

Sheila straightened herself and used her palms to smear tears across her cheeks.

'All I can tell you is that I never saw him hit my brother. Never once.'

She wiped more tears away. Her face was becoming shiny and distorted.

'This is unbelievable,' she said. 'All I did . . . all I wanted was to see if that was Arthur up there. And now . . . I should have never called you people. I should've . . . '

She didn't finish. She pinched the bridge of her nose in an effort to stop the tears.

'Sheila,' Edgar said. 'If your father didn't do it, why would he tell us he did?'

She sharply shook her head and seemed to grow agitated.

'Why would he tell us to tell you he said he was sorry?'

'I don't know. He's sick. He drinks. Maybe he wants the attention, I don't know. He was an actor, you know. '

Bosch pulled the box of photos across the coffee table and used his finger to go through one of the rows. He saw a photo of Arthur as maybe a five-year-old. He pulled it out and studied it. There was no hint in the picture that the boy was doomed, that the bones beneath the flesh were already damaged.

He slid the photo back into its place and looked up at the woman. Their eyes held.

'Sheila, will you help us?'

She looked away from him.

'I can't.'

40

Bosch pulled the car to a stop in front of the drainage culvert and quickly cut the engine. He didn't want to draw any attention from the residents on Wonderland Avenue. Being in a slickback exposed him. But he hoped it was late enough that all the curtains would be drawn across all the windows.

Bosch was alone in the car, his partner having gone home for the night. He reached down and pushed the trunk release button. He leaned to the side window and looked up into the darkness of the hillside. He could tell that the Special Services unit had already been out and removed the network of ramps and staircases that led to the crime scene. This was the way Bosch wanted it. He wanted it to be as close as possible to the way it was when Samuel Delacroix had dragged his son's body up the hillside in the dead of night.

The flashlight came on and momentarily startled Bosch. He hadn't realized he had his thumb on the button. He turned it off and looked out at the quiet houses on the circle. Bosch was following his instincts, returning to the place where it had all begun. He had a guy in lockup for a murder more than twenty years old but it didn't feel good to him. Something wasn't right and he was going to start here.

He reached up and switched the dome light off. He quietly opened the door and got out with the flashlight.

At the back of the car he looked around once more and raised the lid. Lying in the trunk was a test dummy he had borrowed from Jesper at the SID lab. Dummies were used on occasion in the restaging of crimes, particularly suspicious suicide jumps and hit-and-runs. The SID had an assortment ranging in size from infant to adult. The weight of each dummy could be manipulated by adding or removing one-pound sandbags from zippered pockets on the torso and limbs.

The dummy in Bosch's trunk had SID stenciled across the chest. It had no face. In the lab Bosch and Jesper had used sandbags to make it weigh seventy pounds, the estimated weight Golliher had given to Arthur Delacroix based on bone size and the photos of the boy. The dummy wore a store-bought backpack similar to the one recovered during the excavation. It was stuffed with old rags from the trunk of the slickback in an approximation of the clothing found buried with the bones.

Bosch put the flashlight down and grabbed the dummy by its upper arms and pulled it out of the trunk. He hefted it up and over his left shoulder. He stepped back to get his balance and then reached back into the trunk for the flashlight. It was a cheap drugstore light, the kind Samuel Delacroix told them he had used the night he buried his son. Bosch turned it on, stepped over the curb and headed for the hillside.

Bosch started to climb but immediately realized he needed both his hands to grab tree limbs to help pull him up the incline. He shoved the flashlight into one of his front pockets and its beam largely illuminated the upper reaches of the trees and was useless to him.

He fell twice in the first five minutes and quickly exhausted himself before getting thirty feet up the steep slope. Without the flashlight illuminating his path he didn't see a small leafless branch he was passing and it raked across his cheek, cutting it open. Bosch cursed but kept going.

At fifty feet up Bosch took his first break, dropping the dummy next to the trunk of a Monterey pine and then sitting down on its chest. He pulled his T-shirt up out of his pants and used the cloth to help stanch the flow of blood on his cheek. The wound stung from the sweat that was dripping down his face.

'Okay, Sid, let's go,' he said when he had caught his breath.

For the next twenty feet he pulled the dummy up the slope. The progress was slower but it was easier than carrying the full weight and it was also the way Delacroix told them he remembered doing it.

After one more break Bosch made it the last thirty feet to the level spot and dragged the dummy into the clearing beneath the acacia trees. He dropped to his knees and sat back on his heels.

'Bullshit,' he said while gulping breath. 'This is bullshit.'

He couldn't see Delacroix doing it. He was maybe ten years older than Delacroix had been when he had supposedly accomplished the same feat but Bosch was in good shape for a man his age. He was also sober, something Delacroix claimed he had not been.

Even though Bosch had been able to get the body to the burial spot, his gut instinct told him Delacroix had lied to them. He had not done it the way he claimed. He either didn't take the body up the hill or he'd had help. And there was a third possibility, that Arthur Delacroix had been alive and climbed up the hill by himself.

His breathing finally returned to normal. Bosch leaned his head back and looked up through the opening in the canopy of the trees. He could see the night sky and a partial piece of the moon behind a cloud. He realized he could smell burning wood from a fireplace in one of the houses on the circle below.

He pulled the flashlight from his pocket and reached down to a strap sewn onto the back of the dummy. Since taking the dummy down the hill was not part of the test, he intended to pull it by the carrying strap. He was about to get up when he heard movement in the ground cover about thirty feet to his left.

Bosch immediately extended the flashlight in the direction of the noise and caught a fleeting glimpse of a coyote moving in the brush. The animal quickly moved out of the light beam and disappeared. Bosch swept the light back and forth but couldn't find it. He got up and started dragging the dummy toward the slope.

The law of gravity made going down easier but just as treacherous. As he carefully and slowly chose his steps, Bosch wondered about the coyote. He wondered how long coyotes lived and if the one he had seen tonight could have watched another man twenty years before as he buried a body in the same spot.

Bosch made it down the hill without falling. When he carried the dummy out to the curb he saw Dr. Guyot and his dog standing next to the slickback. The dog was on a leash. Bosch quickly went to the trunk, dumped in the dummy and then slammed it closed. Guyot came around to the back of his car.

'Detective Bosch.'

He seemed to know better than to ask what Bosch was doing.

'Dr. Guyot. How are you?'

'Better than you, I'm afraid. You've hurt yourself again. That looks like a nasty laceration.'

Bosch touched his cheek. It still stung.

'It's all right. Just a scratch. You better keep Calamity on the leash. I just saw a coyote up there.'

'Yes, I never take her off the leash at night. The hills are full of roaming coyotes. We hear them at night. You better come with me to the house. I can butterfly that. If you don't do it right it will scar.'

A memory of Julia Brasher asking about his scars suddenly came into Bosch's mind. He looked at Guyot.

'Okay.'

They left the car on the circle and walked down to Guyot's house. In the back office Bosch sat on the desk while the doctor cleaned the cut on his cheek and then used two butterfly bandages to close it.

'I think you'll recover,' Guyot said as he closed his first-aid kit. 'I don't know if your shirt will, though.'

Bosch looked down at his T-shirt. It was stained with his blood at the bottom.

'Thanks for fixing me up, Doc. How long do I have to leave these things on?'

'Few days. If you can stand it.'

Bosch gently touched his cheek. It was swelling slightly but the wound was no longer stinging. Guyot turned from his first-aid kit and looked at him and Bosch knew he wanted to say something. He guessed he was going to ask about the dummy.

'What is it, Doctor?'

'The officer that was here that first night. The woman. She was the one who got killed?'

Bosch nodded.

'Yes, that was her.'

Guyot shook his head in genuine sadness. He slowly stepped around the desk and sank into the chair.

'It's funny sometimes how things go,' he said. 'Chain reaction. Mr. Trent across the street. That officer. All because a dog fetched a bone. A most natural thing to do.'

All Bosch could do was nod. He started tucking in his shirt to see if it would hide the part with blood stains.

Guyot looked down at his dog, who was lying in the spot next to the desk chair.

'I wish that I'd never taken her off that leash,' he said. 'I really do.'

Bosch slid off the desk and stood up. He looked down at his midsection. The blood stain could not be seen but it didn't matter because the shirt was stained with his sweat.

'I don't know about that, Dr. Guyot,' he said. 'I think if you start thinking that way, then you'll never be able to come out your door again.'

They looked at each other and exchanged nods. Bosch pointed to his cheek.

'Thanks for this,' he said. 'I can find my way out.'

He turned toward the door. Guyot stopped him.

'On television there was a commercial for the news. They said the police announced an arrest in the case. I was going to watch it at eleven.'

Bosch looked back at him from the doorway.

'Don't believe everything you see on TV.'

41

The phone rang just as Bosch had finished watching the first session of Samuel Delacroix's confession. He picked up the remote and muted the sound on his television and then answered the call. It was Lieutenant Billets.

'I thought you were going to call me.'

Bosch took a pull from the bottle of beer he was holding and put it down on the table next to his television chair.

'Sorry, I forgot.'

'Still feeling the same way about things?'

'More so.'

'Well, what is it, Harry? I don't think I've ever seen a detective more upset about a confession before.'

'It's a lot of things. Something's going on.'

'What do you mean?'

'I mean I'm beginning to think that maybe he didn't do it. That maybe he's setting something up and I don't know what.'

Billets was quiet a long moment, probably not sure how to respond.

'What does Jerry think?' she finally asked.

'I don't know what he thinks. He's happy to clear the case.'

'We all are, Harry. But not if he's not the guy. Do you have anything concrete? Anything to back up these doubts you are having?'

Bosch gently touched his cheek. The swelling had gone down but the wound itself was sore to the touch. He couldn't stop himself from touching it.

'I went up to the crime scene tonight. With a dummy from SID. Seventy pounds. I got it up there but it was a hell of a fight.'

'Okay, so you proved it could be done. Where's the problem?'

'I hauled a dummy up there. This guy was dragging his dead son's body. I was straight; Delacroix says he was looped. I had been up there before; he hadn't. I don't think he could've done it. At least not alone.'

'You think he had help? The daughter maybe?'

'Maybe he had help and maybe he was never there. I don't know. We talked to the daughter tonight and she won't come across on the father.

Won't say a word. So you start to think, maybe it was the two of them. But then, no. If she was involved, why would she call us and give us the ID on the bones? Doesn't make sense.'

Billets didn't respond. Bosch looked at his watch and saw it was eleven o'clock. He wanted to watch the news. He used the remote to turn off the VCR and put the TV on Channel 4.

'You got the news on?' he asked Billets.

'Yes. Four.'

It was the lead story – father kills son and then buries the body, arrested twenty-some years later because of a dog. A perfect L.A. story. Bosch watched silently and so did Billets on her end. The report by Judy Surtain had no inaccuracies that Bosch picked up on. He was surprised.

'Not bad,' he said when it was over. 'They finally get it right.'

He muted the television again just as the anchor segued to the next story. He was silent for a moment as he watched the television. The story was about the human bones found at the La Brea Tar Pits. Golliher was shown at a press conference, standing in front of a cluster of microphones.

'Harry, come on,' Billets said. 'What else is bugging you? There's got to be more than just your feeling that he couldn't have done it. And as far as the daughter goes, it doesn't bug me that she made the call with the ID. She saw it on the news, right? The story about Trent. Maybe she thought she could just pin it on Trent. After twenty years of worrying, she had a way to put it on somebody else.'

Bosch shook his head, though he knew she could not see this. He just didn't think Sheila would call the tip line if she had been involved in her brother's death.

'I don't know,' he said. 'It doesn't really work for me.'

'Then what are you going to do?'

'I'm going through everything now. I'll start over.'

'When's the arraignment, tomorrow?'

'Yup.'

'You don't have enough time, Harry.'

'I know. But I'm doing it. I already picked up a contradiction I didn't see before.'

'What?'

'Delacroix said he killed Arthur in the morning after he discovered the boy hadn't gone to school. When we interviewed the daughter the first time, she said Arthur didn't come home from school. There's a difference there.'

Billets made a chortling sound in the phone.

'Harry, that's minor. It's been more than twenty years and he's a drunk. I assume you are going to check the school's records?'

'Tomorrow.'

'Then you get it ironed out then. But how would the sister know for sure whether he went to school or not? All she knows is that he wasn't home afterward. You're not convincing me of anything.'

'I know. I'm not trying to. I'm just telling you about the things I'm looking at.'

'Did you guys find anything when you searched his trailer?'

'We didn't search it yet. He started talking almost as soon as we got in there. We're going tomorrow after the arraignment.'

'What's the window on the warrant?'

'Forty-eight hours. We're all right.'

Talking about the trailer made Bosch suddenly remember Delacroix's cat. They had gotten so involved in the suspect's confession that Bosch had forgotten to make arrangements for the animal.

'Shit.'

'What?'

'Nothing. I forgot about the guy's cat. Delacroix has a cat. I said I'd get a neighbor to take care of it.'

'Should've called Animal Control.'

'He was on to us about that. Hey, you have cats, right?'

'Yeah, but I'm not taking in this guy's.'

'No, I don't mean that. I just want to know, like, how long do they last without food and some water?'

'You mean you didn't leave any food for the cat?'

'No, we did, but it's probably gone by now.'

'Well, if you fed it today it can probably last until tomorrow. But it won't be too happy about it. Maybe tear the place up a little bit.'

'Looked like it already had. Listen, I gotta go. I want to watch the rest of the tape and see how we sit.'

'All right, I'll let you go. But, Harry, don't kick a gift horse in the mouth. You know what I mean?'

'I think so.'

They hung up then and Bosch started the videotape of the confession again. But almost immediately he turned it back off. The cat was bugging him. He should have made arrangements for it to be taken care of. He decided to go back out.

42

As Bosch approached Delacroix's trailer he saw light behind every curtain of every window. There had been no lights on when they left with Delacroix twelve hours earlier. He drove on by and pulled into the open parking space of a lot several trailers away. He left the box of cat food in the car, walked back to Delacroix's trailer and watched it from the same position where he had stood when Edgar had hit the door with his warrant knock. Despite the late hour the freeway's hiss was ever present and hindered his ability to hear sounds or movement from within the trailer.

He slipped his gun out of its holster and went to the door. He carefully and quietly stepped up onto the cinder blocks and tried the doorknob. It turned. He leaned to the door and listened but still could hear nothing from within. He waited another moment, slowly and silently turned the knob and then pulled the door open while raising his weapon.

The living room was empty. Bosch stepped in and swept the trailer with his eyes. No one. He pulled the door closed without a sound.

He looked through the kitchen and down the hallway to the bedroom. The door was partially closed and he could not see anyone, but he heard banging sounds, like somebody closing drawers. He started moving through the kitchen. The smell of cat urine was horrible. He noticed the plate on the floor under the table was clean, the water bowl almost empty. He moved into the hallway and was six feet from the bedroom door when it opened and a head-down figure came toward him.

Sheila Delacroix screamed when she looked up and saw Bosch. Bosch raised his gun and then immediately lowered it when he recognized who it was. Sheila raised her hand to her chest, her eyes growing wide.

'What are you doing here?' she said.

Bosch holstered his weapon.

'I was going to ask you the same thing.'

'It's my father's place. I have a key.'

'And?'

She shook her head and shrugged.

'I was . . . I was worried about the cat. I was looking for the cat. What happened to your face?'

Bosch moved past her in the tight space and stepped into the bedroom.

'Had an accident.'

He looked around the room and saw no cat or anything else that drew his attention.

'I think he's under the bed.'

Bosch looked back at her.

'The cat. I couldn't get him out.'

Bosch came back to the door and touched her shoulder, directing her to the living room.

'Let's go sit down.'

In the living room she sat down in the recliner while Bosch remained standing.

'What were you looking for?'

'I told you, the cat.'

'I heard you opening and closing drawers. The cat like to hide in drawers?'

Sheila shook her head as if to say he was bothering over nothing.

'I was just curious about my father. While I was here I looked around, that's all.'

'And where's your car?'

'I parked it by the front office. I didn't know if there'd be any parking here, so I parked there and walked in.'

'And you were going to walk the cat back on a leash or something?'

'No, I was going to carry him. Why are you asking me all these questions?'

Bosch studied her. He could tell she was lying but he wasn't sure what he should or could do about it. He decided to throw her a fastball.

'Sheila, listen to me. If you were in any way involved with what happened to your brother, now's the time to tell me and to try to make a deal.'

'What are you talking about?'

'Did you help your father that night? Did you help him carry your brother up the hill and bury him?'

She brought her hands up to her face so quickly it was as if Bosch had thrown acid in her eyes. Through her hands she yelled, 'Oh my God, oh my God, I can't believe this is happening! What are you—'

She just as abruptly dropped her hands and stared at him with bewildered eyes.

'You think *I* had something to do with it? How could you think that?'

Bosch waited a moment for her to calm down before answering.

'I think you're not telling me the truth about what's going on here. So it makes me suspicious and it means I have to consider all possibilities.'

She abruptly stood up.

'Am I under arrest?'

Bosch shook his head.

'No, Sheila, you're not. But I would appreciate it if you'd tell me the—'

'Then I'm leaving.'

She stepped around the coffee table and headed for the door with a purposeful stride.

'What about the cat?' Bosch asked.

She didn't stop. She was through the door and into the night. Bosch heard her answer from outside.

'You take care of it.'

Bosch stepped to the door and watched her walking down the trailer park's access road, out toward the management building, where her car was parked.

'Yeah,' he said to himself.

He leaned against the door frame and breathed some of the untainted air from the outside. He thought about Sheila and what she might have been doing. After a while he checked his watch and looked back over his shoulder at the interior of the trailer. It was after midnight and he was tired. But he decided he was going to stay and look for whatever it was she had been looking for.

He felt something brush up against his leg and looked down to see a black cat rubbing up against him. He gently pushed it away with his leg. He didn't care much for cats.

The animal came back and insisted on rubbing its head against Bosch's leg again. Bosch stepped back into the trailer, causing the cat to make a cautionary retreat of a few feet.

'Wait here,' Bosch said. 'I've got some food in the car.'

43

Downtown arraignment court was always a zoo. When Bosch entered the courtroom at ten minutes before nine on Friday morning, he saw no judge yet on the bench but a flurry of lawyers conferring and moving about the front of the courtroom like ants on a kicked-over hill. It took a seasoned veteran to know and understand what was going on at any given time in arraignment court.

Bosch first scanned the rows of public seating for Sheila Delacroix but didn't see her. He next looked for his partner and Portugal, the prosecutor, but they weren't in the courtroom either. He did notice that two cameramen were setting up equipment next to the bailiff's desk. Their position would give them a clear view of the glass prisoner docket once court was in session.

Bosch moved forward and pushed through the gate. He took out his badge, palmed it and showed it to the bailiff, who had been studying a computer printout of the day's arraignment schedule.

'You got a Samuel Delacroix on there?' he asked.

'Arrested Wednesday or Thursday?'

'Thursday. Yesterday.'

The bailiff flipped the top sheet over and ran his finger down a list. He stopped at Delacroix's name.

'Got it.'

'When will he come up?'

'We've still got some Wednesdays to finish. When we get to Thursdays it will depend on who his lawyer is. Private or public?'

'It'll be a PD, I think.'

'They go in order. You're looking at an hour, at least. That's if the judge starts at nine. Last I heard he wasn't here yet.'

'Thanks.'

Bosch moved toward the prosecution table, having to weave around two groupings of defense lawyers telling war stories while waiting for the judge to take the bench. In the first position at the table was a woman Bosch didn't recognize. She would be the arraignments deputy assigned to the courtroom. She would routinely handle eighty percent of the arraignments, as most of the cases were minor in nature and had not yet been assigned to prosecutors. In front of her on the table was a stack of files – the morning's cases – half a foot high. Bosch showed her his badge, too.

'Do you know if George Portugal is coming down for the Delacroix arraignment? It's a Thursday.'

'Yes, he is,' she said, without looking up. 'I just talked to him.'

She now looked up and Bosch saw her eyes go to the cut on his cheek. He'd taken the butterfly bandages off before his shower that morning but the wound was still quite noticeable.

'It's not going to happen for an hour or so. Delacroix has a public defender. That looks like it hurts.'

'Only when I smile. Can I use your phone?'

'Until the judge comes out.'

Bosch picked up the phone and called the DA's Office, which was three floors above. He asked for Portugal and was transferred.

'Yeah, it's Bosch. All right if I come up? We've gotta talk.'

'I'm here until I'm called down to arraignments.'

'See you in five.'

On the way out Bosch told the bailiff that if a detective named Edgar checked in he should be sent up to the DA's Office. The bailiff said no problem.

The hallway outside the courtroom was teeming with lawyers and citizens, all with some business with the courts. Everybody seemed to be on a cell phone. The marble floor and high ceiling took all of the voices and multiplied them into a fierce cacophony of white noise. Bosch ducked into the little snack bar and had to wait more than five minutes in line just to buy a coffee. After he was out, he legged it up the fire exit stairs because he didn't want to lose another five minutes waiting for one of the horribly slow elevators.

When he stepped into Portugal's small office Edgar was already there.

'We were beginning to wonder where you were,' Portugal said.

'What the hell happened to you?' Edgar added after seeing Bosch's cheek.

'It's a long story. And I'm about to tell it.'

He took the other chair in front of Portugal's desk and put his coffee down on the floor next to him. He realized he should have brought cups for Portugal and Edgar, so he decided not to drink in front of them.

He opened his briefcase on his lap and took out a folded section of the *Los Angeles Times.* He closed the briefcase and put it on the floor.

'So what's going on?' Portugal said, clearly anxious about the reason Bosch had called the meeting.

Bosch started unfolding the newspaper.

'What's going on is we charged the wrong guy and we better fix it before he gets arraigned.'

'Whoa, shit. I knew you were going to say something like that,' Portugal said. 'I don't know if I want to hear this. You are messing up a good thing, Bosch.'

'I don't care what I'm doing. If the guy didn't do it, he didn't do it.'

'But he *told* us he did it. *Several* times.'

'Look,' Edgar said to Portugal. 'Let Harry say what he wants to say. We don't want to fuck this up.'

'It may be too late with Mr. Can't-Leave-A-Good-Thing-Alone here.'

'Harry, just go on. What's wrong?'

Bosch told them about taking the dummy up to Wonderland Avenue and re-creating Delacroix's supposed trek up the steep hillside.

'I made it – just barely,' he said, gently touching his cheek. 'But the point is, Del—'

'Yeah, you made it,' Portugal said. 'You made it, so Delacroix could have made it. What's the problem with that?'

'The problem is that I was sober when I did it and he says he wasn't. I also knew where I was going. I knew it leveled off up there. He didn't.'

'This is all minor bullshit.'

'No, what's bullshit is Delacroix's story. Nobody dragged that kid's body up there. He was alive when he was up there. Somebody killed him up there.'

Portugal shook his head in frustration.

'This is all wild conjecture, Detective Bosch. I'm not going to stop this whole process because—'

'It's conjecture. Not wild conjecture.'

Bosch looked over at Edgar but his partner didn't look back at him. He had a glum look on his face. Bosch looked back at Portugal.

'Look, I'm not done. There's more. After I got home last night I remembered Delacroix's cat. We left it in his trailer and told him we'd take care of it but we forgot. So I went back.'

Bosch could hear Edgar breathing heavily and he knew what the problem was. Edgar had been left out of the loop by his own partner. It was embarrassing for him to be getting this information at the same time as Portugal. In a perfect world Bosch would have told him what he had before going to the prosecutor. But there hadn't been time for that.

'All I was going to do was feed the cat. But when I got there somebody was already in the trailer. It was his daughter.'

'Sheila?' Edgar said. 'What was she doing there?'

The news was apparently surprising enough for Edgar to no longer care if Portugal knew he was out of the latest investigative moves.

'She was searching the place. She claimed she was there for the cat, too, but she was searching the place when I got there.'

'For what?' Edgar said.

'She wouldn't tell me. She claimed she wasn't looking for anything. But after she left I stayed. I found some things.'

Bosch held up the newspaper.

'This is Sunday's Metro section. It has a pretty big story on the case, mostly a generic feature about forensics on cases like this. But there's a lot of detail about our case from an unnamed source. Mostly about the crime scene.'

Bosch thought after reading the article the first time in Delacroix's trailer the night before that the source was probably Teresa Corazon, since she was quoted by name in the article in regard to generic information about bone cases. He was aware of the trading that went on between reporters and sources; direct attribution for some information, no attribution for other information. But the identity of the source wasn't important to the present discussion and he didn't bring it up.

'So there was an article,' Portugal asked. 'What does it mean?'

'Well, it reveals that the bones were in a shallow grave and that it appeared that the body was not buried with the use of any tools. It also says that a knapsack had been buried along with the body. A lot of other details. Also details left out, like no mention of the kid's skateboard.'

'Your point being?' Portugal asked with a bored tone in his voice.

'That if you were going to put together a false confession, a lot of what you'd need is right here.'

'Oh, come on, Detective. Delacroix gave us much more than the crime scene details. He gave us the killing itself, the driving around with the body, all of that.'

'All of that was easy. It can't be proved or disproved. There were no witnesses. We'll never find the car because it's been squashed to the size of a mailbox in some junkyard in the Valley. All we have is his story. And the only place where his story meets the physical evidence is the crime scene. And every marker he gave us he could have gotten from this.'

He tossed the newspaper onto Portugal's desk but the prosecutor didn't even look at it. He leaned his elbows on the desk and brought his hands flat against each other and spread his fingers wide. Bosch could see his muscles flexing under his shirtsleeves and realized he was doing some kind of an at-your-desk exercise. Portugal spoke while his hands pushed against each other.

'I work out the tension this way.'

He finally stopped, releasing his breath loudly and leaning back in his seat.

'Okay, he had the ability to concoct a confession if he wanted to do it. Why would he want to do it? We're talking about his own son. Why would he say he killed his own son if he didn't?'

'Because of these,' Bosch said.

He reached into his inside jacket pocket and took out an envelope that was folded in half. He leaned forward and gently put it down on top of the newspaper on Portugal's desk.

As Portugal picked up the envelope and started to open it, Bosch said, 'I think that was what Sheila was looking for in the trailer last night. I found it in the night table next to her father's bed. It was underneath the bottom drawer. A hiding place there. You had to take the drawer out to find it. She didn't do that.'

From the envelope Portugal took a stack of Polaroid photos. He started looking through them.

'Oh, God,' he said almost immediately. 'Is this her? The daughter? I don't want to look at these.'

He shuffled through the remaining photos quickly and put them down on the desk. Edgar got up and leaned over the desk. With one finger he spread the photos out on the desk so he could view them. His jaw drew tight but he didn't say anything.

The photos were old. The white borders were yellowed, the colors of the images almost washed out by time. Bosch used Polaroids on the job all the time. He knew by the degradation of the colors that the photos on the desk were far more than a decade old and some of them were older than others. There were fourteen photos in all. The constant in each was a naked girl. Based on physical changes to the girl's body and hair length, he had guessed that the photos spanned at least a five-year-period. The girl innocently smiled in some of the photos. In others there was sadness and maybe even anger evident in her eyes. It had been clear to Bosch from the moment he first looked at them that the girl in the photos was Sheila Delacroix.

Edgar sat back down heavily. Bosch could no longer tell if he was upset by being so far behind on the case or by the content of the photos.

'Yesterday this was a slam dunk,' Portugal said. 'Today it's a can of worms. I assume you are going to give me your theory on these, Detective Bosch?'

Bosch nodded.

'You start with a family,' he said.

As he spoke he leaned forward and collected the photos, squared the edges and put them back in the envelope. He didn't like them being on display. He held the envelope in his hand.

'For one reason or another, the mother's weak,' he said. 'Too young to marry, too young to have kids. The boy she has is too hard to handle. She sees where her life is going and she decides she doesn't want to go there. She ups and splits and that leaves Sheila . . . to pick up with the boy and to fend for herself with the father.'

Bosch glanced from Portugal to Edgar to see how he was playing so far. Both men seemed hooked by the story. Bosch held the envelope with the photos up.

'Obviously, a hellish life. And what could she do about it? She could blame her mother, her father, her brother. But who could she lash out against? Her mother was gone. Her father was big and overpowering. In control. That only left . . . Arthur.'

He noticed a subtle shake of Edgar's head.

'What are you saying, that she killed him? That doesn't make sense. She's the one who called us and gave us the ID.'

'I know. But her father doesn't know she called us.'

Edgar frowned. Portugal leaned forward and started doing his hand exercise again.

'I don't think I am following you, Detective,' he said. 'How does this have anything to do with whether or not he killed the son?'

Bosch also leaned forward and became more animated. He held the envelope up again, as if it was the answer to everything.

'Don't you see? The bones. All the injuries. We had it wrong. It wasn't the father who hurt him. It was her. Sheila. She was abused and she turned right around and became the abuser. To Arthur.'

Portugal dropped his hands to the desk and shook his head.

'So you *are* saying that she killed the boy and then twenty years later called up and gave you a key clue in the investigation. Don't tell me, you're going to say she has amnesia about killing him, right?'

Bosch let the sarcasm go.

'No, I'm saying she didn't kill him. But her record of abuse led her father to suspect she did. All these years Arthur's been gone, the father thought she did it. And he knew why.'

Once more Bosch proffered the envelope of photos.

'And so he carried the guilt of knowing his actions with Sheila caused it all. Then the bones come up, he reads it in the paper and puts two and two together. We show up and he starts confessing before we're three feet in the door.'

Portugal raised his hands wide.

'Why?'

Bosch had been turning it over in his mind ever since he had found the photos.

'Redemption.'

'Oh, please.'

'I'm serious. The guy's getting old, broken down. When you have more to look back at than forward to, you start thinking about the things you've done. You try making up for things. He thinks his daughter killed his son because of his own actions. So now he's willing to take the fall for her. After all, what's he got to lose? He lives in a trailer next to the freeway and works at a driving range. This is a guy who once had a shot at fame and fortune. Now look at him. He could be looking at this as his last shot at making up for everything.'

'And he's wrong about her but doesn't know it.'

'That's right.'

Portugal kicked his chair back from his desk. It was on wheels and he let it bang into the wall behind his desk.

'I got a guy waiting down there I could put in Q with one hand tied to my balls and you come in here and want me to kick him loose.'

Bosch nodded.

'If I'm wrong, you could always charge him again. But if I'm right, he's going to try to plead guilty down there. No trial, no lawyer, nothing. He wants to plead and if the judge lets him, then we're done. Whoever really killed Arthur is safe.'

Bosch looked over at Edgar.

'What do you think?'

'I think you got your mojo working.'

Portugal smiled but not because he found any humor in the situation.

'Two against one. That's not fair.'

'There's two things we can do,' Bosch said. 'To help be sure. He's probably down there in the holding tank by now. We can go down there, tell him it was Sheila who gave us the ID and flat out ask him if he's covering for her.'

'And?'

'Ask him to take a polygraph.'

'They're worthless. We can't admit them in—'

'I'm not talking about court. I'm talking about bluffing him. If he's lying, he won't take it.'

Portugal pulled his chair back to his desk. He picked up the paper and glanced at the story for a moment. His eyes then appeared to take a roving inventory of the desktop while he thought and came to a decision.

'Okay,' he finally said. 'Go do it. I'm dropping the charge. For now.'

44

Bosch and Edgar walked out to the elevator alcove and stood silently after Edgar pushed the down button.

Bosch looked at his blurred image reflected in the stainless steel doors of the elevator. He looked over at Edgar's reflection and then directly at his partner.

'So,' he said. 'How pissed off are you?'

'Somewhere between very and not too.'

Bosch nodded.

'You really left me with my dick in my hand in there, Harry.'

'I know. I'm sorry. You want to just take the stairs?'

'Have patience, Harry. What happened to your cell phone last night? You break it or something?'

Bosch shook his head.

'No, I just wanted to – I wasn't sure of what I was thinking and so I wanted to check things out on my own first. Besides, I knew you had the kid on Thursday nights. Then running into Sheila at the trailer, that was out of left field.'

'What about when you started searching the place? You coulda called. My kid was back home asleep by then.'

'Yeah, I know. I should have, Jed.'

Edgar nodded and that was the end of it.

'You know this theory of yours puts us at ground zero now,' he said.

'Yeah, ground zero. We're gonna have to start over, look at everything again.'

'You going to work it this weekend?'

'Yeah, probably.'

'Then call me.'

'I will.'

Finally, Bosch's impatience got the better of him.

'Fuck it. I'm taking the stairs. I'll see you down there.'

He left the alcove and went to the emergency stairwell.

45

Through an assistant in Sheila Delacroix's office Bosch and Edgar learned that she was working out of a temporary production office on the Westside, where she was casting a television pilot called *The Closers*.

Bosch and Edgar parked in a reserved lot full of Jaguars and BMWs and went into a brick warehouse that had been divided into two levels of offices. There were paper signs taped on the wall that said casting and showed arrows pointing the way. They went down a long hallway and then up a rear staircase.

When they reached the second floor they came into another long hallway that was lined with men in dark suits that were rumpled and out of style. Some of the men wore raincoats and fedoras. Some were pacing and gesturing and talking quietly to themselves.

Bosch and Edgar followed the arrows and turned into a large room lined with chairs holding more men in bad suits. They all stared as the partners walked to a desk at the far end of the room where a young woman sat, studying the names on a clipboard. There were stacks of 8 × 10 photos on the desk and script pages. From beyond a closed door behind the woman, Bosch could hear the muffled sounds of tense voices.

They waited until the woman looked up from her clipboard.

'We need to see Sheila Delacroix,' Bosch said.

'And your names?'

'Detectives Bosch and Edgar.'

She started to smile and Bosch took out his badge and let her see it.

'You guys are good,' she said. 'Did you get the sides already?'

'Excuse me?'

'The sides. And where are your head shots?'

Bosch put it together.

'We're not actors. We're real cops. Would you please tell her we need to see her right away?'

The woman continued to smile.

'Is that real, that cut on your cheek?' she said. 'It looks real.'

Bosch looked at Edgar and nodded toward the door. Simultaneously they went around both sides of her desk and approached the door.

'Hey! She's taking a reading! You can't—'

Bosch opened the door and stepped into a small room where Sheila Delacroix was sitting behind a desk watching a man seated on a folding chair in the middle of the room. He was reading from a page of script. A young woman was in the corner behind a video camera on a tripod. In another corner two men sat on folding chairs watching the reading.

The man reading the script didn't stop when Bosch and Edgar entered.

'The proof's in your pudding, you mutt!' he said. 'You left your DNA all over the scene. Now get up and get against—'

'Okay, okay,' Delacroix said. 'Stop there, Frank.'

She looked up at Bosch and Edgar.

'*What* is this?'

The woman from the desk roughly pushed past Bosch into the room.

'I'm sorry, Sheila, these guys just bullied their way in like they're real cops or something.'

'We need to talk to you, Sheila,' Bosch said. 'Right now.'

'I'm in the middle of a reading. Can't you see that I—'

'We're in the middle of a murder investigation. Remember?'

She threw a pen down on the desk and pushed her hands up through her hair. She turned to the woman on the video camera, which was now focused on Bosch and Edgar.

'Okay, Jennifer, turn that off,' she said. 'Everybody, I need a few minutes. Frank, I am very sorry. You were doing great. Can you stay and wait a few minutes? I promise to take you first, as soon as I am done.'

Frank stood up and smiled brilliantly.

'No problem, Sheila. I'll be right outside.'

Everybody shuffled out of the room, leaving Bosch and Edgar alone with Sheila.

'Well,' she said after the door closed. 'With an entrance like that, you really should be actors.'

She tried smiling but it didn't work. Bosch came over to the desk. He remained standing. Edgar leaned his back against the door. They had decided on the way over that Bosch would handle her.

She said, 'The show I'm casting is about two detectives called 'the closers' because they have a perfect record of closing cases nobody else seems able to. I guess there's no such thing in real life, is there?'

'Nobody's perfect,' Bosch said. 'Not even close.'

'What is so important that you had to come bursting in here, embarrassing me like that?'

'Couple things. I thought you might want to know that I found what you were looking for last night and—'

'I told you, I wasn't—'

'—your father was released from custody about an hour ago.'

'What do you mean *released*? You said last night he wouldn't be able to make bail.'

'He wouldn't have been able to. But he's not charged with the crime anymore.'

'But he confessed. You said he—'

'Well, he de-confessed this morning. That was after we told him we were going to put him on a polygraph machine and mentioned that it was you who called us up and gave us the tip that led to the ID of your brother.'

She shook her head slightly.

'I don't understand.'

'I think you do, Sheila. Your father thought you killed Arthur. You were the one who hit him all the time, who hurt him, who put him in the hospital that time after hitting him with the bat. When he disappeared your father thought maybe you'd finally gone all the way and killed him, then hidden the body. He even went into Arthur's room and got rid of that little bat in case you had used that again.'

Sheila put her elbows on the desk and hid her face in her hands.

'So when we showed up he started confessing. He was willing to take the fall for you to make up for what he did to you. For this.'

Bosch reached into his pocket and took out the envelope containing the photos. He dropped it onto the desk between her elbows. She slowly lowered her hands and picked it up. She didn't open the envelope. She didn't have to.

'How's that for a reading, Sheila?'

'You people . . . is this what you do? Invade people's lives like this? I mean, their secrets, everything?'

'We're the closers, Sheila. Sometimes we have to.'

Bosch saw a case of water bottles on the floor next to her desk. He reached down and opened a bottle for her. He looked at Edgar, who shook his head. Bosch got another bottle for himself, pulled the chair Frank had used close to her desk and sat down.

'Listen to me, Sheila. You were a victim. You were a kid. He was your father, he was strong and in control. There is no shame for you in being a victim.'

She didn't respond.

'Whatever baggage you carry with you, now is the time to lose it. To tell us what happened. Everything. I think there is more than what you told us before. We're back at square one and we need your help. This is your brother we're talking about.'

He opened the bottle and took a long draw of water. For the first time he noticed how warm it was in the room. Sheila spoke while he took his second drink from the bottle.

'I understand something now . . . '

'What is that?'

She was staring down at her hands. When she spoke it was like she was speaking to herself. Or to nobody.

'After Arthur was gone, my father never touched me again. I never . . . I thought it was because I had become undesirable in some way. I was overweight, ugly. I think now maybe it was because . . . he was afraid of what he thought I had done or what I might be able to do.'

She put the envelope back down on the desk. Bosch leaned forward again.

'Sheila, is there anything else about that time, about that last day, that you didn't tell us before? Anything that can help us?'

She nodded very slightly and then bowed her head, hiding her face behind her raised fists.

'I knew he was running away,' she said slowly. 'And I didn't do anything to stop him.'

Bosch moved forward on the edge of the seat. He spoke gently to her.

'How so, Sheila?'

There was a long pause before she answered.

'When I came home from school that day. He was there. In his room.'

'So he did come home?'

'Yes. For a little bit. His door was open a crack and I looked in. He didn't see me. He was putting things into his book bag. Clothes, things like that. I knew what he was doing. He was packing and was going to run. I just . . . I went into my room and closed the door. I wanted him to go. I guess I hated him, I don't know. But I wanted him gone. To me he was the cause of everything. I just wanted him to be gone. I stayed in my room until I heard the front door close.'

She raised her face and looked at Bosch. Her eyes were wet but Bosch had often before seen that in a purging of guilt and truth came a strength. He saw it in her eyes now.

'I could have stopped him but I didn't. And that's what I've had to live with. Now that I know what happened to him . . . '

Her eyes went off past Bosch, somewhere over his shoulder, where she could see the wave of guilt coming toward her.

'Thank you, Sheila,' Bosch said softly. 'Is there anything else you know that could help us?'

She shook her head.

'We'll leave you alone now.'

He got up and moved the chair back to the spot in the middle of the room. He then came back to the desk and picked up the envelope containing the Polaroids. He headed toward the office door and Edgar opened it.

'What will happen to him?' she asked.

They turned around and looked back. Edgar closed the door. Bosch knew she was talking about her father.

'Nothing,' he said. 'What he did to you is long past any statute of limitation. He goes back to his trailer.'

She nodded without looking up at Bosch.

'Sheila, he may have been a destroyer at one time. But time has a way of changing things. It's a circle. It takes power away and gives it to those who once had none. Right now your father is the one who is destroyed. Believe me. He can't hurt you anymore. He's nothing.'

'What will you do with the photographs?'

Bosch looked down at the envelope in his hand and then back up at her.

'They have to go into the file. Nobody will see them.'

'I want to burn them.'

'Burn the memories.'

She nodded. Bosch was turning to go when he heard her laugh and he looked back at her. She was shaking her head.

'What?'

'Nothing. It's just that I've got to sit here and listen to people trying to talk and sound like you all day. And I know right now nobody will come close. Nobody will get it right.'

'That's show business,' Bosch said.

As they headed back down the hallway to the stairs Bosch and Edgar passed by all the actors again. In the stairwell the one named Frank was saying his lines out loud. He smiled at the true detectives as they passed.

'Hey, guys, you guys are for real, right? How do you think I was doing in there?'

Bosch didn't answer.

'You were great, Frank,' Edgar said. 'You're a closer, man. The proof is in the pudding.'

46

At two o'clock Friday afternoon Bosch and Edgar made their way through the squad room to the homicide table. They had driven from the Westside to Hollywood in virtual silence. It was the tenth day of the case. They were no closer to the killer of Arthur Delacroix than they had been during all the years that Arthur Delacroix's bones had lain silently on the hillside above Wonderland Avenue. All they had to show for their ten days was a dead cop and the suicide of an apparently reformed pedophile.

As usual there was a stack of pink phone messages left for Bosch at his place. There was also an inter-office dispatch envelope. He picked up the envelope first, guessing he knew what was in it.

'About time,' he said.

He opened the envelope and slid his mini-cassette recorder out of it. He pushed the play button to check the battery. He immediately heard his own voice. He lowered the volume and turned off the device. He slipped it into his jacket pocket and dropped the envelope into the trash can by his feet.

He shuffled through the phone messages. Almost all were from reporters. Live by the media, die by the media, he thought. He would leave it to the Media Relations Office to explain to the world how a man who confessed to and was charged with a murder one day was exonerated and released the next.

'You know,' Bosch said to Edgar, 'in Canada the cops don't have to tell the media jack about a case until it's over. It's like a media blackout on every case.'

'Plus, they've got that round bacon up there,' Edgar replied. 'What're we doing here, Harry?'

There was a message from the family counselor at the medical examiner's office telling Bosch that the remains of Arthur Delacroix had been released to his family for burial on Sunday. Bosch put it aside so he could call back to find out about the funeral arrangements and which member of the family had claimed the remains.

He went back to the messages and came upon a pink slip that immediately gave him pause. He leaned back in his chair and studied it, a tightness coming over his scalp and going down the back of his neck. The message came in at ten-thirty-five and was from a Lieutenant Bollenbach in the Office of Operations – the O-3 as it was more popularly known by the rank and file. The O-3 was where all personnel assignments and transfers were issued. A decade before when Bosch was moved to the Hollywood Division he had gotten the word after a forthwith from the O-3. Same thing with Kiz Rider going to RHD the year before.

Bosch thought about what Irving had said to him in the interview room three days earlier. He guessed that the O-3 was now about to begin an effort to achieve the deputy chief's wish for Bosch's retirement. He took the message as a sign he was being transferred out of Hollywood. His new assignment would likely involve some freeway therapy – a posting far from his home and requiring long drives each day to and from work. It was a frequently used management tool for convincing cops they might be better off turning in the badge and doing something else.

Bosch looked at Edgar. His partner was going through his own collection of phone messages, none of which appeared to have stopped him the way the one in Bosch's hand had. He decided not to return the call yet or to tell Edgar about it. He folded the message and put it in his pocket. He took a look around the squad room, at all the bustling activity of the detectives. He would miss it if the new assignment wasn't a posting with the same kind of ebb and flow of adrenaline. He didn't care about freeway therapy. He could take the best punch they could give and not care. What he did care about was the job, the mission. He knew that without it he was lost.

He went back to the messages. The last one in the stack, meaning it was the first one received, was from Antoine Jesper in SID. He had called at ten that morning.

'Shit,' Bosch said.

'What?' Edgar said.

'I'm going to have to go downtown. I still have the dummy I borrowed last night in my trunk. I think Jesper needs it back.'

He picked up the phone and was about to call SID when he heard his and Edgar's names called from the far end of the squad room. It was Lieutenant Billets. She signaled them to her office.

'Here we go,' Edgar said as he got up. 'Harry, you can have the honors. You tell her where we're at on this thing. More like where we aren't at.'

Bosch did. In five minutes he brought Billets completely up to date on the case and its latest reversal and lack of progress.

'So where do we go from here?' she asked when he was finished.

'We start over, look at everything we've got, see what we missed. We go to the kid's school, see what records they have, look at yearbooks, try to contact classmates. Things like that.'

Billets nodded. If she knew anything about the call from the O-3, she wasn't letting on.

'I think the most important thing is that spot up there on the hill,' Bosch added.

'How so?'

'I think the kid was alive when he got up there. That's where he was killed. We have to figure out what or who brought him up there. We're going to have to go back in time on that whole street. Profile the whole neighborhood. It's going to take time.'

She shook her head.

'Well, we don't have time to work it full-time,' she said. 'You guys just sat out of the rotation for ten days. This isn't RHD. That's the longest I've been able to hold a team out since I got here.'

'So we're back in?'

She nodded.

'And right now it's your up – the next case is yours.'

Bosch nodded. He had assumed that was coming. In the ten days they'd been working the case, the two other Hollywood homicide teams had both caught cases. It was now their turn. It was rare to get such a long ride on a divisional case anyway. It had been a luxury. Too bad they hadn't turned the case, he thought.

Bosch also knew that by putting them back on the rotation Billets was making a tacit acknowledgment that she wasn't expecting the case to clear. With each day that a case stayed open, the chances of clearing it dropped markedly. It was a given in homicide and it happened to everybody. There were no closers.

'Okay,' Billets said. 'Anything else anybody wants to talk about?'

She looked at Bosch with a raised eyebrow. He suddenly thought maybe she did know something about the call from the O-3. He hesitated, then shook his head along with Edgar.

'Okay, guys. Thanks.'

They went back to the table and Bosch called Jesper.

'The dummy's safe,' he said when the criminalist picked up the phone. 'I'll bring it down later today.'

'Cool, man. But that wasn't why I called. I just wanted to tell you I can make a little refinement on that report I sent you on the skateboard. That is, if it still matters.'

Bosch hesitated for a moment.

'Not really, but what do you want to refine, Antoine?'

Bosch opened the murder book in front of him and leafed through it until he found the SID report. He looked at it as Jesper spoke.

'Well, in there I said we could put manufacture of the board between February of 'seventy-eight and June of 'eighty-six, right?'

'Right. I'm looking at it.'

'Okay, well, I can now cut more than half of that time period. This particular board was made between 'seventy-eight and 'eighty. Two years. I don't know if that means anything to the case or not.'

Bosch scanned the report. Jesper's amendment to the report didn't really matter, since they had dropped Trent as a suspect and the skateboard had never been linked to Arthur Delacroix. But Bosch was curious about it, anyway.

'How'd you cut it down? Says here the same design was manufactured until 'eighty-six.'

'It was. But this particular board has a date on it. Nineteen eighty.'

Bosch was puzzled.

'Wait a minute. Where? I didn't see any—'

'I took the trucks off – you know, the wheels. I had some time here between things and I wanted to see if there were any manufacture markings on the hardware. You know, patent or trademark coding. There weren't. But then I saw that somebody had scratched the date in the wood. Like carved it in on the underside of the board and then it was covered up by the truck assembly.'

'You mean like when the board was made?'

'No, I don't think so. It's not a professional job. In fact it was hard to read. I had to put it under glass and angled light. I just think it was the original owner's way of marking his board in a secret way in case there was ever a dispute or something over ownership. Like if somebody stole it from him. Like I said in the report, Boney boards were the choice board for a while there. They were hard to get – might've been easier to steal one than find one in a store. So the kid who had this one took off the back truck – this would have been the original truck, not the current wheels – and carved in the date. Nineteen eighty a.d.'

Bosch looked over at Edgar. He was on the phone speaking with his hand cupped over the mouthpiece. A personal call.

'You said A.D.?'

'Yeah, you know, as in anno Domini or however you say it. It's Latin. Means the year of our Lord. I looked it up.'

'No, it means Arthur Delacroix.'

'What? Who's that?'

'That's the vic, Antoine. Arthur Delacroix. As in A.D.'

'Damn! I didn't have the vic's name here, Bosch. You filed all of this evidence while he was still a John Doe and never amended it, man. I didn't even know you had an ID.'

Bosch wasn't listening to him. A surge of adrenaline was moving through his body. He knew his pulse was quickening.

'Antoine, don't move. I'm coming down there.'

'I'll be here.'

47

The freeway was crowded with people getting an early start on the weekend. Bosch couldn't keep his speed as he headed downtown. He had a feeling of pulsing urgency. He knew it was because of Jesper's discovery and the message from the O-3.

He turned his wrist on the wheel so he could see his watch and check the date. He knew that transfers usually took place at the end of a pay period. There were two pay periods a month – beginning the first and the fifteenth. If the transfer they were going to put on him was immediate, he knew that gave him only three or four days to wrap up the case. He didn't want to be taken off it, to leave it in Edgar's or anybody else's hands. He wanted to finish it.

Bosch reached into his pocket and brought out the phone slip. He unfolded it, driving with the heels of his palms on the wheel. He studied it for a moment and then got out his phone. He punched in the number from the message and waited.

'Office of Operations, Lieutenant Bollenbach speaking.'

Bosch clicked the phone off. He felt his face grow hot. He wondered if Bollenbach had caller ID on his phone. He knew that delaying the call was ridiculous because what was done was done whether he called in to get the news or not.

He put the phone and the message aside and tried to concentrate on the case, particularly the latest information Antoine Jesper had provided about the skateboard found in Nicholas Trent's house. Bosch realized that after ten days the case was wholly out of his grasp. A man he had fought with others in the department to clear was now the only suspect – with apparent physical evidence tying him to the victim. The thought that immediately poked through all of this was that maybe Irving was right. It was time for Bosch to go.

His phone chirped and he immediately thought it was Bollenbach. He was not going to answer but then decided his fate was unavoidable. He flipped open the phone. It was Edgar.

'Harry, what are you doing?'

'I told you. I had to go to SID.'

He didn't want to tell him about Jesper's latest discovery until he had seen it for himself.

'I could've gone with you.'

'Would've been a waste of your time.'

'Yeah, well, listen, Harry, Bullets is looking for you and, uh, there's a rumor floatin' around up here that you caught a transfer.'

'Don't know anything about it.'

'Well, you're going to let me know if something's happening, aren't you? We've been together a long time.'

'You'll be the first, Jerry.'

When Bosch got to Parker Center he had one of the patrolmen stationed in the lobby help him lug the dummy up to SID, where he returned it to Jesper, who took it and carried it easily to its storage closet.

Jesper led Bosch into a lab where the skateboard was on an examination table. He turned on a light that was mounted on a stand next to the board, then turned off the overhead light. He swung a mounted magnifying glass over the skateboard and invited Bosch to look. The angled light created small shadows in the etchings of the wood, allowing the letters to be clearly seen.

1980 A.D.

Bosch could definitely see why Jesper had jumped to the conclusion he did about the letters, especially since he did not have the case victim's name.

'It looks like somebody sanded it down,' Jesper said while Bosch continued to look. 'I bet what happened was that the whole board was rehabbed at one point. New trucks and new lacquer.'

Bosch nodded.

'All right,' he said after straightening up from the magnifying glass. 'I'm going to need to take this with me, maybe show it to some people.'

'I'm done with it,' Jesper said. 'It's all yours.'

He turned the overhead light back on.

'Did you check under these other wheels?'

''Course. Nothing there, though. So I put the truck back on.'

'You got a box or something?'

'Oh, I thought you were going to ride it out of here, Harry.'

Bosch didn't smile.

'That's a joke.'

'Yeah, I know.'

Jesper left the room and came back with an empty cardboard file box that was long enough to contain the skateboard. He put the skateboard in it along with the detached set of wheels and the screws, which were in a small plastic bag. Bosch thanked him.

'Did I do good, Harry?'

Bosch hesitated and then said, 'Yeah, I think so, Antoine.'

Jesper pointed to Bosch's cheek.

'Shaving?'

'Something like that.'

The drive back to Hollywood was even slower on the freeway. Bosch finally bailed at the Alvarado exit and worked his way over to Sunset. He took it the rest of the way in, not making any better time and knowing it.

As he drove he kept thinking about the skateboard and Nicholas Trent, trying to fit explanations into the framework of time and evidence that they had. He couldn't do it. There was a piece missing from the equation. He knew that at some level and at some place it all made sense. He was confident he would get there, if he had enough time.

At four-thirty Bosch banged through the back door into the station house carrying the file box containing the skateboard. He was heading quickly down the hallway to the squad room, when Mankiewicz ducked his head into the hallway from the watch office.

'Hey, Harry?'

Bosch looked back at him but kept walking.

'What's up?'

'I heard the news. We're gonna miss you around here.'

The word traveled fast. Bosch held the box with his right arm and raised his left hand palm down and made a sweeping gesture across the flat surface of an imaginary ocean. It was a gesture usually reserved for drivers of patrol cars passing on the street. It said, Smooth sailing to you, brother. Bosch kept going.

Edgar had a large white board lying flat across his desk and covering most of Bosch's as well. He had drawn what looked like a thermometer on it. It was Wonderland Avenue, the turnaround circle at the end being the bulb at the bottom of the thermometer. From the street there were lines drawn signifying the various homes. Extending from these lines were names printed in green, blue and black marker. There was a red X that marked the spot where the bones had been found.

Bosch stood and stared at the street diagram without asking a question.

'We should've done this from the start,' Edgar said.

'How's it work?'

'The green names are residents in nineteen eighty who moved sometime after. The blue names are anybody who came after 'eighty but has already left. The black names are current residents. Anywhere you see just a black name – like Guyot right here – that means they've been there the whole time.'

Bosch nodded. There were only two names in black. Dr. Guyot and someone named Al Hutter, who was at the end of the street farthest from the crime scene.

'Good,' Bosch said, though he didn't know what use the chart would be now.

'What's in the box?' Edgar asked.

'The skateboard. Jesper found something.'

Bosch put the box down on his desk and took off the top. He told and showed Edgar the scratched date and initials.

'We've got to start looking at Trent again. Maybe look at that theory you had about him moving into the neighborhood *because* he had buried the kid up there.'

'Jesus, Harry, I was almost joking about that.'

'Yeah, well, it's no joke now. We have to go back, put together a whole profile on Trent going all the way back to nineteen eighty, at least.'

'And meantime we catch the next case here. That's real sweet.'

'I heard on the radio it's supposed to rain this weekend. If we're lucky it will keep everybody inside and quiet.'

'Harry, inside is where most of the killing is done.'

Bosch looked across the squad room and saw Lt. Billets standing in her office. She was waving him in. He had forgotten that Edgar said she was looking for him. He pointed a finger at Edgar and then back at himself, asking if she wanted to see them both. Billets shook her head and pointed back only at Bosch. He knew what it was about.

'I gotta go see Bullets.'

Edgar looked up at him. He knew what it was about, too.

'Good luck, partner.'

'Yeah, partner. If that's still the case.'

He crossed the squad room to the lieutenant's office. She was now seated behind her desk. She didn't look at him when she spoke.

'Harry, you've got a forthwith from the Oh Three. Call Lieutenant Bollenbach before you do anything else. That's an order.'

Bosch nodded.

'Did you ask him where I'm going?'

'No, Harry, I'm too pissed off about it. I was afraid if I asked I'd get into it with him and it's got nothing to do with him. Bollenbach's just the messenger.'

Bosch smiled.

'You're pissed off?'

'That's right. I don't want to lose you. Especially because of some bullshit grudge somebody up top has against you.'

He nodded and shrugged.

'Thanks, Lieutenant. Why don't you call him on speakerphone? We'll get this over with.'

Now she looked up at him.

'You sure? I could go get a coffee so you can have the office to yourself if you want.'

'It's all right. Go ahead and make the call.'

She put the phone on speaker and called Bollenbach's office. He answered right away.

'Lieutenant, this is Lieutenant Billets. I have Detective Bosch in my office.'

'Very good, Lieutenant. Just let me find the order here.'

There was the sound of papers rustling, then Bollenbach cleared his throat.

'Detective High . . . Heronyim . . . is that—'

'Hieronymus,' Bosch said. 'Rhymes with anonymous.'

'Hieronymus then. Detective Hieronymus Bosch, you are ordered to report for duty at Robbery Homicide Division at oh-eight-hundred January fifteen. That is all. Are these orders clear to you?'

Bosch was stunned. RHD was a promotion. He had been demoted from RHD to Hollywood more than ten years earlier. He looked at Billets, who also had a look of suspicious surprise on her face.

'Did you say RHD?'

'Yes, Detective, Robbery Homicide Division. Are these orders clear?'

'What's my assignment?'

'I just told you. You report at—'

'No, I mean what do I do at RHD? What's my assignment there?'

'You'll have to get that from your new commanding officer on the morning of the fifteenth. That's all I have for you, Detective Bosch. You have your orders. Have a nice weekend.'

He clicked off and a dial tone came from the speaker.

Bosch looked at Billets.

'What do you think? Is this some kind of a joke?'

'If it is, it's a good one. Congratulations.'

'But three days ago Irving told me to quit. Then he turns around and sends me downtown?'

'Well, maybe it's because he wants to watch you more closely. They don't call Parker Center the glass house for nothing, Harry. You better be careful.'

Bosch nodded.

'On the other hand,' she said, 'we both know you should be down there. You should've never been taken out of there in the first place. Maybe it's just the circle closing. Whatever it is, we're going to miss you. I'll miss you, Harry. You do good work.'

Bosch nodded his thanks. He made a move toward leaving but then looked back up at her and smiled.

'You're not going to believe this, especially in light of what just happened, but we're looking at Trent again. The skateboard. SID found a link to the boy on it.'

Billets threw her head back and laughed loudly, loud enough to draw the attention of everyone in the squad room.

'Well,' she said, 'when Irving hears that, he's definitely going to change RHD to Southeast Division, for sure.'

Her reference was to the gang-infested district at the far end of the city. A posting that would be the pure-form example of freeway therapy.

'I wouldn't doubt it,' Bosch said.

Billets dropped the smile and got serious. She asked Bosch about the latest turn in the case and listened intently while he outlined the plan to put together what would basically be a full life profile on the dead set decorator.

'I'll tell you what,' she said when he was finished. 'I'll take you guys off rotation. No sense in you pulling a new case if you're splitting for RHD. I'm also authorizing weekend OT. So work on Trent and hit it hard and let me know. You've got four days, Harry. Don't leave this one on the table when you go.'

Bosch nodded and left the office. On his way back to his space he knew all eyes in the squad room were on him. He gave nothing away. He sat down at his space and kept his eyes down.

'So?' Edgar eventually whispered. 'What did you get?'

'RHD.'

'RHD?'

He had practically yelled it. It would now be known to all in the squad room. Bosch felt his face getting red. He knew everybody else would be looking at him.

'Jesus Christ,' Edgar said. 'First Kiz and now you. What am I, fucking chopped liver?'

48

Kind of Blue played on the stereo. Bosch held a bottle of beer and leaned back in the recliner with his eyes closed. It had been a confusing day at the end of a confusing week. He now just wanted to let the music move through him and clear out his insides. He felt sure that what he was looking for he already had in his possession. It was a matter of ordering things and getting rid of the unimportant things that cluttered the view.

He and Edgar had worked until seven before deciding on an early night. Edgar couldn't concentrate. The news of Bosch's transfer had affected him more deeply than it did Bosch. Edgar perceived it as a slight against him because he wasn't chosen to go to RHD. Bosch tried to calm him by assuring him that it was a pit of snakes that Bosch would be entering, but it was no use. Bosch pulled the plug and told his partner to go home, have a drink and get a good night's sleep. They would work through the weekend gathering information on Trent.

Now it was Bosch who was having the drink and falling asleep in his chair. He sensed he was at a threshold of some sort. He was about to begin a new and clearly defined time in his life. A time of higher danger, higher stakes and higher rewards. It made him smile, now that he knew no one was watching him.

The phone rang and Bosch bolted upright. He clicked off the stereo and went into the kitchen. When he answered, a woman's voice told him to hold for Deputy Chief Irving. After a long moment Irving's voice came on the line.

'Detective Bosch?'

'Yes?'

'You received your transfer orders today?'

'Yes, I did.'

'Good. I wanted to let you know that I made the decision to bring you back to Robbery Homicide Division.'

'Why is that, Chief?'

'Because I decided after our last conversation to hold out one last chance to you. This assignment is that chance. You will be in a position where I can watch your moves very closely.'

'What position is that?'

'You were not told?'

'I was just told to report to RHD next pay period. That was it.'

There was silence on the phone and Bosch thought now he would find the sand in the engine oil. He was going back to RHD, but as what? He tried to think, What was the worst assignment within the best assignment?

Irving finally spoke.

'You are getting your old job back. Homicide Special. An opening came up today when Detective Thornton turned in his badge.'

'Thornton.'

'That is correct.'

'I'll be working with Kiz Rider?'

'That will be up to Lieutenant Henriques. But Detective Rider is currently without a partner and you have an established working relationship with her.'

Bosch nodded. The kitchen was dark. He was elated but did not want to transmit his feelings over the phone to Irving.

As if knowing these thoughts, Irving said, 'Detective, you may feel as though you fell into the sewer but came out smelling like a rose. Do not think that. Do not make any assumptions. Do not make any mistakes. If you do, I will be there. Am I clear?'

'Crystal clear.'

Irving hung up without another word. Bosch stood there in the dark holding the phone to his ear until it started making a loud, annoying tone. He hung up and went back into the living room. He thought about calling Kiz and seeing what she knew but decided he would wait. When he sat back down on the recliner he felt something hard jab into his hip. He knew it wasn't his gun because he had already unclipped it. He reached into his pocket and came up with his mini-cassette recorder.

He turned it on and listened to his verbal exchange with Surtain, the TV reporter outside Trent's house on the night he killed himself. Filtering it through the history of what would happen, Bosch felt guilty and thought that maybe he should have done or said more in an effort to stop the reporter.

After he heard the car door slam on the tape he stopped it and hit the rewind button. He realized that he had not yet heard the whole interview with Trent because he had been out of earshot while searching some parts of the house. He decided he would listen to the interview now. It would be a starting point for the weekend's investigation.

As he listened, Bosch tried to analyze the words and sentences for new meanings, things that would reveal a killer. All the while he was warring with his own instincts. As he listened to Trent speak in almost desperate tones he still felt convinced the man was not the killer, that his protests of innocence had been true. And this of course contradicted what he now knew. The skateboard – found in Trent's house – had the dead boy's initials on it and the year he both got the skateboard and was killed. The skateboard now served as a tombstone of sorts. A marker for Bosch.

He finished the Trent interview, but nothing in it, including the parts he had not previously heard, sparked any ideas in him. He rewound the tape and decided to play it again. And it was early in the second go through that he picked up on something that made his face suddenly grow hot, almost with a feeling of being feverish. He quickly reversed the tape and replayed the exchange between Edgar and Trent that had drawn his attention. He remembered standing in the hallway in Trent's house and listening to this part of the interview. But he had missed its significance until this moment.

'Did you like watching the kids play up there in the woods, Mr. Trent?'

'No, I couldn't see them if they were up in the woods. On occasion I would be driving up or walking my dog – when he was alive – and I would see the kids climbing up there. The girl across the street. The Fosters next door. All the kids around here. It's a city owned right-of-way – the only undeveloped land in the neighborhood. So they went up there to play. Some of the neighbors thought the older ones went up there to smoke cigarettes, and the concern was they would set the whole hillside on fire.'

He turned off the tape and went back to the kitchen and the phone. Edgar answered after one ring. Bosch could tell he had not been asleep. It was only nine o'clock.

'You didn't bring anything home with you, did you?'

'Like what?'

'The reverse directory lists?'

'No, Harry, they're at the office. What's up?'

'I don't know. Do you remember when you were making that chart on the board today, was there anybody named Foster on Wonderland?'

'Foster. You mean last name of Foster?'

'Yeah, last name.'

He waited. Edgar said nothing.

'Jerry, you remember?'

'Harry, take it easy. I'm thinking.'

More silence.

'Um,' Edgar finally said. 'No Foster. None that I can remember.'

'How sure are you?'

'Well, Harry, come on. I don't have the board or the lists here. But I think I would've remembered that name. Why is it so important? What's going on?'

'I'll call you back.'

Bosch took the phone with him out to the dining room table where he had left his briefcase. He opened it and took out the murder book. He quickly turned to the page that listed the current residents of Wonderland Avenue with their addresses and phone numbers. There were no Fosters on the list. He picked up the phone and punched in a number. After four rings it was answered by a voice he recognized.

'Dr. Guyot, this is Detective Bosch. Am I calling too late?'

'Hello, Detective. No, it's not too late for me. I spent forty years getting phone calls at all hours of the night. Nine o'clock? Nine o'clock is for amateurs. How are your various injuries?'

'They're fine, Doctor. I'm in a bit of a hurry and I need to ask you a couple questions about the neighborhood.'

'Well, go right ahead.'

'Going way back, nineteen eighty or so, was there ever a family or a couple on the street named Foster?'

There was silence as Guyot thought over the question.

'No, I don't think so,' he finally said. 'I don't remember anybody named Foster.'

'Okay. Then can you tell me if there was anybody on the street that took in foster kids?'

This time Guyot answered without hesitation.

'Uh, yes, there was. That was the Blaylocks. Very nice people. They helped many children over the years, taking them in. I admired them greatly.'

Bosch wrote the name down on a blank piece of paper at the front of the murder book. He then flipped to the report on the neighborhood canvas and saw there was no one named Blaylock currently living on the block.

'Do you remember their first names?'

'Don and Audrey.'

'What about when they moved from the neighborhood? Do you remember when that was?'

'Oh, that would have been at least ten years ago. After the last child was grown, they didn't need that big house anymore. They sold it and moved.'

'Any idea where they moved to? Are they still local?'

Guyot said nothing. Bosch waited.

'I'm trying to remember,' Guyot said. 'I know I know this.'

'Take your time, Doctor,' Bosch said, even though it was the last thing he wanted Guyot to do.

'Oh, you know what, Detective?' Guyot said. 'Christmas. I saved all the cards I received in a box. So I know who to send cards to next year. My wife always did that. Let me put the phone down and get the box. Audrey still sends me a card every year.'

'Go get the box, Doctor. I'll wait.'

Bosch heard the phone being put down. He nodded to himself. He was going to get it. He tried to think about what this new information could mean but then decided to wait. He would gather the information and then sift through it after.

It took Guyot several minutes to come back to the phone. The whole time Bosch waited with his pen poised to write the address on the note page.

'Okay, Detective Bosch, I've got it here.'

Guyot gave him the address and Bosch almost sighed out loud. Don and Audrey Blaylock had not moved to Alaska or some other far reach of the world. They were still within a car drive. He thanked Guyot and hung up.

49

At 8 a.m. Saturday morning Bosch was sitting in his slickback watching a small wood-frame house a block off the main drag in the town of Lone Pine three hours north of Los Angeles in the foothills of the Sierra Nevadas. He was sipping cold coffee from a plastic cup and had another one just like it ready to take over when he was finished. His bones ached from the cold and a night spent driving and then trying to sleep in the car. He had made it to the little mountain town too late to find a motel open. He also knew from experience that coming to Lone Pine without a reservation on a weekend was not advisable anyway.

As dawn's light came up he saw the blue-gray mountain rising in the mist behind the town and reducing it to what it was; insignificant in the face of time and the natural pace of things. Bosch looked up at Mt. Whitney, the highest point in California, and knew it had been there long before any human eyes had ever seen it and would be there long after the last set was gone. Somehow it made it easier to know all that he knew.

Bosch was hungry and wanted to go over to one of the diners in town for steak and eggs. But he wouldn't leave his post. If you moved from L.A. to Lone Pine it wasn't just because you hated the crowds, the smog and the pace of the big city. It was because you also loved the mountain. And Bosch wasn't going to risk missing Don and Audrey Blaylock to a morning mountain hike while he was eating breakfast. He settled for turning the car on and running the heater for five minutes. He had been parceling out the heat and the gas that way all night.

Bosch watched the house and waited for a light to come on or someone to pick up the newspaper that had been dropped on the driveway from a passing pickup two hours earlier. It was a thin roll of newspaper. Bosch knew it wasn't the *L.A. Times.* People in Lone Pine didn't care about Los Angeles or its murders or its detectives.

At nine Bosch saw smoke start to curl out of the house's chimney. A few minutes later, a man of about sixty wearing a down vest came out and got the paper. After picking it up he looked a half block down the street to Bosch's car. He then went back inside.

Bosch knew his car stood out on the street. He hadn't been trying to hide himself. He was just waiting. He started the car and drove down to the Blaylocks' house and pulled into the driveway.

When Bosch got to the door the man he had seen earlier opened it before he had to knock.

'Mr. Blaylock?'

'Yeah, that's me.'

Bosch showed his badge and ID.

'I was wondering if I could talk to you and your wife for a few minutes. It's about a case I'm working.'

'You alone?'

'Yeah.'

'How long've you been out there?'

Bosch smiled.

'Since about four. Got here too late to get a room.'

'Come in. We have coffee on.'

'If it's hot, I'll take it.'

He led Bosch in and pointed him toward a seating arrangement of chairs and a couch near the fireplace.

'I'll get my wife and the coffee.'

Bosch stepped over to the chair nearest the fireplace. He was about to sit down when he noticed all the framed photographs on the wall behind the couch. He stepped over to study them. They were all of children and young adults. They were of all races. Two had obvious physical or mental handicaps. The foster children. He turned and took the seat closest to the fire and waited.

Soon Blaylock returned with a large mug of steaming coffee. A woman came into the room behind him. She looked a little bit older than her husband. She had eyes still creased by sleep but a kind face.

'This is my wife, Audrey,' Blaylock said. 'Do you take your coffee black? Every cop I ever knew took it black.'

The husband and wife sat next to each other on the couch.

'Black's fine. Did you know a lot of cops?'

'When I was in L.A. I did. I worked thirty years for the city fire department. Quit as a station commander after the 'ninety-two riots. That was enough for me. Came in right before Watts and left after 'ninety-two.'

'What is it you want to talk to us about?' Audrey asked, seemingly impatient with her husband's small talk.

Bosch nodded. He had his coffee and the introductions were over.

'I work homicide. Out of Hollywood Division. I'm on a—'

'I worked six years out of fifty-eights,' Blaylock said, referring to the fire station that was behind the Hollywood Division station house.

Bosch nodded again.

'Don, let the man tell us why he came all the way up here,' Audrey said.

'Sorry, go ahead.'

'I'm on a case. A homicide up in Laurel Canyon. Your old neighborhood, actually, and we're contacting people who lived on the street back in nineteen eighty.'

'Why then?'

'Because that is when the homicide took place.'

They looked at him with puzzled faces.

'Is this one of those cold cases?' Blaylock said. 'Because I don't remember anything like that happening in our neighborhood back then.'

'In a way it's a cold case. Only the body wasn't discovered until a couple weeks ago. It had been buried up in the woods. In the hills.'

Bosch studied their faces. No tells, just shock.

'Oh, my God,' Audrey said. 'You mean all that time we were living there, somebody was dead up there? Our kids used to play up there. Who was it who was killed?'

'It was a child. A boy twelve years old. His name was Arthur Delacroix. Does that name mean anything to either of you?'

The husband and wife first searched their own memory banks and then looked at each other and confirmed the results, each shaking their head.

'No, not that name,' Don Blaylock said.

'Where did he live?' Audrey Blaylock asked. 'Not in the neighborhood, I don't think.'

'No, he lived down in the Miracle Mile area.'

'It sounds awful,' Audrey said. 'How was he killed?'

'He was beaten to death. If you don't mind – I mean, I know you're curious about it, but I need to ask the questions starting out.'

'Oh, I'm sorry,' Audrey said. 'Please go on. What else can we tell you?'

'Well, we are trying to put together a profile of the street – Wonderland Avenue – at that time. You know, so we know who was who and who was where. It's really routine.'

Bosch smiled and knew right away it didn't come off as sincere.

'And it's been pretty tough so far. The neighborhood has sort of turned over a lot since then. In fact, Dr. Guyot and a man down the street named Hutter are the only residents still there since nineteen eighty.'

Audrey smiled warmly.

'Oh, Paul, he is such a nice man. We still get Christmas cards from him, even since his wife passed away.'

Bosch nodded.

'Of course, he was too expensive for us. We mostly took our kids to the clinics. But if there was ever an emergency on a weekend or when Paul was home, he never hesitated. Some doctors these days are afraid to do anything because they might get – I'm sorry, I'm going off like my husband, and that's not what you came here to hear.'

'It's all right, Mrs. Blaylock. Um, you mentioned your kids. I heard from some of the neighbors that you two had a foster home, is that right?'

'Oh, yes,' she said. 'Don and I took in children for twenty-five years.'

'That's a tremendous, uh, thing you did. I admire that. How many children was it?'

'It was hard to keep track of them. We had some for years, some for only weeks. A lot of it was at the whim of the juvenile courts. It used to break my heart when we were just getting started with a child, you know, making them feel comfortable and at home, and then the child would be ordered home or to the other parent or what have you. I always said that to do foster work you had to have a big heart with a big callus on it.'

She looked at her husband and nodded. He nodded back and reached over and took her hand. He looked back at Bosch.

'We counted it up once,' he said. 'We had a total of thirty-eight kids at one time or another. But realistically, we say we raised seventeen of them. These were kids that were with us long enough for it to have an impact. You know, anywhere from two years to – one child was with us fourteen years.'

He turned so he could see the wall over the couch and reached up and pointed to a picture of a boy in a wheelchair. He was slightly built and had thick glasses. His wrists were bent at sharp angles. His smile was crooked.

'That's Benny,' he said.

'Amazing,' Bosch said.

He took a notebook out of his pocket and flipped it open to a blank page. He took out a pen. Just then his cell phone started chirping.

'That's me,' he said. 'Don't worry about it.'

'Don't you want to answer it?' Blaylock asked.

'They can leave a message. I didn't even think there'd be clear service this close to the mountain.'

'Yeah, we even get TV.'

Bosch looked at him and realized he had somehow been insulting.

'Sorry, I didn't mean anything. I was wondering if you could tell me what children you had living in your home in nineteen eighty.'

There was a moment when everyone looked at one another and said nothing.

'Is one of our kids involved in this?' Audrey asked.

'I don't know, ma'am. I don't know who was living with you. Like I said, we're trying to put together a profile of that neighborhood. We need to know exactly who was living there. And then we'll go from there.'

'Well, I am sure the Division of Youth Services can help you.'

Bosch nodded.

'Actually, they changed the name. It's now called the Department of Children's Services. And they're not going to be able to help us until Monday at the earliest, Mrs. Blaylock. This is a homicide. We need this information now.'

Again there was a pause as they all looked at one another.

'Well,' Don Blaylock finally said, 'it's going to be kind of hard to remember exactly who was with us at any given time. There are some obvious ones. Like Benny and Jodi and Frances. But every year we'd have a few kids that, like Audrey said, would be dropped in and then taken out. They're the tough ones. Let's see, nineteen eighty . . . '

He stood up and turned so he could see the breadth of the wall of photos. He pointed to one, a young black boy of about eight.

'William there. He was nineteen eighty. He—'

'No, he wasn't,' Audrey said. 'He came to us in 'eighty-four. Don't you remember, the Olympics? You made him that torch out of foil.'

'Oh, yeah, 'eighty-four.'

Bosch leaned forward in his seat. The location near the fire was now getting too warm for him.

'Let's start with the three you mentioned. Benny and the two others. What were their full names?'

He was given their names, and when he asked how they could be contacted he was given phone numbers for two of them but not Benny.

'Benny passed away six years ago,' Audrey said. 'Multiple sclerosis.'

'I'm sorry.'

'He was very dear to us.'

Bosch nodded and waited for an appropriate silence to go by.

'Um, who else? Didn't you keep records of who came and for how long?'

'We did but we don't have them here,' Blaylock said. 'They're in storage in L.A.'

He suddenly snapped his fingers.

'You know, we have a list of the names of every child we tried to help or did help. It's just not by year. We could probably cut it down a little bit, but would that help you?'

Bosch noticed Audrey give her husband a momentary look of anger. Her husband didn't see it but Bosch did. He knew her instincts would be to protect her children from the threat, real or not, that Bosch represented.

'Yes, that would help a lot.'

Blaylock left the room and Bosch looked at Audrey.

'You don't want him to give me that list. Why is that, Mrs. Blaylock?'

'Because I don't think you are being honest with us. You are looking for something. Something that will fit your needs. You don't drive three hours in the middle of the night from Los Angeles for a 'routine questioning,' as you call it. You know these children come from tough backgrounds. They weren't all angels when they came to us. And I don't want any of them blamed for something just because of who they were or where they came from.'

Bosch waited to make sure she was done.

'Mrs. Blaylock, have you ever been to the McClaren Youth Hall?'

'Of course. Several of our children came from there.'

'I came from there, too. And an assortment of foster homes where I never lasted very long. So I know what these children were like because I was one myself, all right? And I know that some foster homes can be full of love and some can be just as bad as or worse than the place you were taken from. I know that some foster parents are committed to the children and some are committed to the subsistence checks from Children's Services.'

She was quiet a long moment before answering.

'It doesn't matter,' she said. 'You still are looking to finish your puzzle with any piece that fits.'

'You're wrong, Mrs. Blaylock. Wrong about that, wrong about me.'

Blaylock came back into the room with what looked like a green school folder. He placed it down on the square coffee table and opened it. Its pockets were stuffed with photos and letters. Audrey continued despite his return.

'My husband worked for the city like you do, so he won't want to hear me say this. But, Detective, I don't trust you or the reasons you say you are here. You are not being honest with us.'

'Audrey!' Blaylock yelped. 'The man is just trying to do his job.'

'And he'll say anything to do it. And he'll hurt any of our children to do it.'

'Audrey, please.'

He turned his attention back to Bosch and offered a sheet of paper. There was a list of handwritten names on it. Before Bosch could read them Blaylock took the page back and put it down on the table. He went to work on it with a pencil, putting check marks next to some of the names. He spoke as he worked.

'We made this list just so we could sort of keep track of everybody. You'd be surprised, you can love somebody to death but when it comes time to remember twenty, thirty birthdays you always forget somebody. The ones I'm checking off here are the kids that came in more recent than nineteen eighty. Audrey will double-check when I'm done.'

'No, I won't.'

The men ignored her. Bosch's eyes moved ahead of Blaylock's pencil and down the list. Before he was two-thirds to the bottom he reached down and put his finger on a name.

'Tell me about him.'

Blaylock looked up at Bosch and then over at his wife.

'Who is it?' she asked.

'Johnny Stokes,' Bosch said. 'You had him in your home in nineteen eighty, didn't you?'

Audrey stared at him for a moment.

'There, you see?' she said to her husband while looking only at Bosch. 'He already knew about Johnny when he came in here. I was right. He's not an honest man.'

50

By the time Don Blaylock went to the kitchen to brew a second pot of coffee Bosch had two pages of notes on Johnny Stokes. He had come to the Blaylock house through a DYS referral in January 1980 and was gone the following July, when he was arrested for stealing a car and going on a joyride through Hollywood. It was his second arrest for car theft. He was incarcerated at the Sylmar Juvenile Hall for six months. By the time his period of rehabilitation was completed he was returned by a judge to his parents. Though the Blaylocks heard from him on occasion and even saw him during his infrequent visits to the neighborhood, they had other children still in their care and soon drifted from contact with the boy.

When Blaylock went to make the coffee Bosch settled into what he thought would be an uncomfortable silence with Audrey. But then she spoke to him.

'Twelve of our children graduated from college,' she said. 'Two have military careers. One followed Don into the fire service. He works in the Valley.'

She nodded at Bosch and he nodded back.

'We've never considered ourselves to be one hundred percent successful with our children,' she continued. 'We did our best with each one. Sometimes the circumstances or the courts or the youth authorities prevented us from helping a child. John was one of those cases. He made a mistake and it was as if we were to blame. He was taken from us . . . before we could help him.'

All Bosch could do was nod.

'You seemed to know of him already,' she said. 'Have you already spoken to him?'

'Yes. Briefly.'

'Is he in jail now?'

'No, he's not.'

'What has his life been since . . . we knew him?'

Bosch spread his hands apart.

'He hasn't done well. Drugs, a lot of arrests, prison.'

She nodded sadly.

'Do you think he killed that boy in our neighborhood? While he was living with us?'

Bosch could tell by her face that if he were to answer truthfully he would knock down everything she had built out of what was good in what they had done. The whole wall of pictures, the graduation gowns and the good jobs would mean nothing next to this.

'I don't really know. But we do know he was a friend of the boy who was killed.'

She closed her eyes. Not tightly, just as if she were resting them. She said nothing else until Blaylock came back into the room. He went past Bosch and put another log on the fire.

'Coffee will be up in a minute.'

'Thank you,' Bosch said.

After Blaylock walked back to the couch, Bosch stood up.

'I have some things I would like you to look at, if you don't mind. They're in my car.'

He excused himself and went out to the slickback. He grabbed his briefcase from the front seat and then went to the trunk to get the file box containing the skateboard. He thought it might be worth a try showing it to the Blaylocks.

His phone chirped just as he closed the trunk and this time he answered it. It was Edgar.

'Harry, where are you?'

'Up in Lone Pine.'

'Lone Pine! What the fuck are you doing up there?'

'I don't have time to talk. Where are you?'

'At the table. Like we agreed. I thought you—'

'Listen, I'll call you back in an hour. Meantime, put out a new BOLO on Stokes.'

'What?'

Bosch checked the house to make sure the Blaylocks weren't listening or in sight.

'I said put out another BOLO on Stokes. We need him picked up.'

'Why?'

'Because he did it. He killed the kid.'

'What the fuck, Harry?'

'I'll call you in an hour. Put out the BOLO.'

He hung up and this time turned the phone off.

Inside the house Bosch put the file box down on the floor and then opened his briefcase on his lap. He found the envelope containing the family photos borrowed from Sheila Delacroix. He opened it and slid them out. He split the stack in two and gave one half to each of the Blaylocks.

'Look at the boy in these pictures and tell me if you recognize him, if he ever came to your house. With Johnny or anybody else.'

He watched as the couple looked at the photos and then exchanged stacks. When they were finished they both shook their heads and handed the photos back.

'Don't recognize him,' Don Blaylock said.

'Okay,' Bosch said as he put the photos back into the envelope.

He closed his briefcase and put it on the floor. He then opened the file box and lifted out the skateboard.

'Has either of you—'

'That was John's,' Audrey said.

'Are you sure?'

'Yes, I recognize it. When he was . . . taken from us, he left it behind. I told him we had it. I called his house but he never came for it.'

'How do you know that this is the one that was his?'

'I just remember. I didn't like the skull and crossbones. I remember those.'

Bosch put the skateboard back in the box.

'What happened to it if he never came for it?'

'We sold it,' Audrey said. 'When Don retired after thirty years and we decided to move up here, we sold all of our junk. We had a gigantic garage sale.'

'More like a house sale,' her husband added. 'We got rid of everything.'

'Not everything. You wouldn't sell that stupid fire bell we have in the backyard. Anyway, that was when we sold the skateboard.'

'Do you remember who you sold it to?'

'Yes, the man who lived next door. Mr. Trent.'

'When was this?'

'Summer of 'ninety-two. Right after we sold the house. We were still in escrow, I remember.'

'Why do you remember selling the skateboard to Mr. Trent? 'Ninety-two was a long time ago.'

'I remember because he bought half of what we were selling. The junky half. He gathered it all up and offered us one price for everything. He needed it all for his work. He was a set designer.'

'Set decorator,' her husband corrected. 'There is a difference.'

'Anyway, he used everything he bought from us on movie sets. I always hoped I would see something in a movie that I'd know came from our house. But I never did.'

Bosch scribbled some notes in his pad. He had just about everything he needed from the Blaylocks. It was almost time to head south, back to the city to put the case together.

'How did you get the skateboard?' Audrey asked him.

Bosch looked up from his notepad.

'Uh, it was in Mr. Trent's possessions.'

'He's still on the street?' Don Blaylock asked. 'He was a great neighbor. Never a problem at all with him.'

'He was until recently,' Bosch said. 'He passed away, though.'

'Oh, my gosh,' Audrey proclaimed. 'What a shame. And he wasn't that old a man.'

'I just have a couple more questions,' Bosch said. 'Did John Stokes ever tell either of you how he came to have the skateboard?'

'He told me that he had won it during a contest with some other boys at school,' Audrey said.

'The Brethren School?'

'Yes, that's where he went. He was going when he first came to us and so we continued it.'

Bosch nodded and looked down at his notes. He had everything. He closed the notebook, put it in his coat pocket and stood up to go.

51

Bosch pulled the car into a space in front of the Lone Pine Diner. The booths by all the windows were filled and almost all of the people in them looked out at the LAPD car two hundred miles from home.

He was starved but knew he needed to talk to Edgar before delaying any further. He took out the cell phone and made the call. Edgar answered after half a ring.

'It's me. Did you put the BOLO out?'

'Yeah, it's out. But it's a little hard to do when you don't know what the fuck is going on, *partner*.'

He said the last word as if it was a synonym for asshole. It was their last case together and Bosch felt bad that they were going to end their time this way. He knew it was his fault. He had cut Edgar out of the case for reasons Bosch wasn't even sure about.

'Jerry, you're right,' he said. 'I fucked up. I just wanted to keep things moving and that meant driving through the night.'

'I would've gone with you.'

'I know,' Bosch lied. 'I just didn't think. I just drove. I'm coming back now.'

'Well, start at the beginning so I know what the fuck is going on in our own case. I feel like a moron here, putting out a BOLO and not even knowing why.'

'I told you, Stokes is the guy.'

'Yeah, you told me that and you didn't tell me anything else.'

Bosch spent the next ten minutes watching diners eat their food while he recounted his moves for Edgar and brought him up to date.

'Jesus Christ, and we had him right here,' Edgar said when Bosch was finished.

'Yeah, well, it's too late to worry about that. We have to get him back.'

'So you're saying that when the kid packed up and ran away, he went to Stokes. Then Stokes leads him up there into the woods and just kills him.'

'More or less.'

'Why?'

'That's what we have to ask him. I've got a theory, though.'

'What, the skateboard?'

'Yeah, he wanted the skateboard.'

'He'd kill a kid over a skateboard?'

'We've both seen it done for less and we don't know if he intended to kill him or not. It was a shallow grave, dug by hand. Nothing premeditated about that. Maybe he just pushed him and knocked him down. Maybe he hit him with a rock. Maybe there was something else going on between them we don't even know about.'

Edgar didn't say anything for a long moment and Bosch thought maybe they were finished and he could get some food.

'What did the foster parents think about your theory?'

Bosch sighed.

'I didn't really spin it for them. But put it this way, they weren't too surprised when I started asking questions about Stokes.'

'You know something, Harry, we've been spinning our wheels is what we've been doing.'

'What do you mean?'

'This whole case. It comes down to what? – a thirteen-year-old killing a twelve-year-old over a fucking toy. Stokes was a juvy when this went down. Ain't nobody going to prosecute him now.'

Bosch thought about this for a moment.

'They might. Depends on what we get out of him after we pick him up.'

'You just said yourself there was no sign of premed. They're not going to file it, partner. I'm telling you. We've been chasing our tail. We close the case but nobody goes away for it.'

Bosch knew Edgar was probably right. Under the law, it was rare that adults were prosecuted for crimes committed while they were juveniles as young as thirteen. Even if they pulled a full confession out of Stokes he would probably walk.

'I should have let her shoot him,' he whispered.

'What's that, Harry?'

'Nothing. I'm going to grab something to eat and get on the road. You going to be there?'

'Yeah, I'm here. I'll let you know if anything happens.'

'All right.'

He hung up and got out of the car, thinking about the likelihood of Stokes walking away from his crime. As he entered the warm diner and was hit with the smells of grease and breakfast, he suddenly realized he had lost his appetite.

52

Bosch was just coming down out of the squiggle of treacherous freeway called The Grapevine when his phone chirped. It was Edgar.

'Harry, I've been trying to call you. Where y'at?'

'I was in the mountains. I'm less than an hour out. What's going on?'

'They've got a fix on Stokes. He's squatting in the Usher.'

Bosch thought about this. The Usher was a 1930s hotel a block off Hollywood Boulevard. For decades it was a weekly flophouse and prostitution center until redevelopment on the boulevard pushed up against it and suddenly made it a valuable property again. It was sold, closed and readied to go through a major renovation and restoration that would allow it to rejoin the new Hollywood as an elegant grande dame. But the project had been delayed by city planners who held final approval. And in that delay was an opportunity for the denizens of the night.

While the Hotel Usher awaited rebirth, the rooms on its thirteen floors became the homes of squatters who snuck past the fences and plywood barriers to find shelter. In the previous two months Bosch had been inside the Usher twice while searching for suspects. There was no electricity. There was no water, but the squatters used the toilets anyway and the place smelled like an aboveground sewer. There were no doors on any of the rooms and no furniture. People used rolled-up carpets in the rooms as their beds. It was a nightmare to try to search safely. You moved down the hall and every doorway was open and a possible blind for a gunman. You kept your eyes on the openings and you might step on a needle.

Bosch flipped on the car's emergency lights and put his foot hard on the pedal.

'How do we know he's in there?' he asked.

'From last week when we were looking for him. Some guys in narcs were working something in there and got a line on him squatting all the way up on the thirteenth floor. You gotta be scared of something to go all the way to the top in a place with the elevators shut down.'

'Okay, what's the plan?'

'We're going to go in big. Four teams from patrol, me and the narcs. We start at the bottom and work our way up.'

'When do you go?'

'We're about to go into roll call now and talk it out, then we go. We can't wait for you, Harry. We have to take this guy before he gets out and about.'

Bosch wondered for a moment if Edgar's hurry was legitimate or simply an effort to get even with Bosch for his cutting him out of several of the investigative moves on the case.

'I know,' he finally said. 'You going to have a rover with you?'

'Yeah, we're using channel two.'

'Okay, I'll see you there. Put your vest on.'

He said the last not because he was concerned about Stokes being armed, but because he knew a heavily armed team of cops in the enclosed confinement of a dark hotel hallway had danger written all over it.

Bosch closed the phone and pushed the pedal down even harder. Soon he crossed the northern perimeter of the city and was in the San Fernando Valley. Saturday traffic was light. He switched freeways twice and was cruising through the Cahuenga Pass into Hollywood a half hour after hanging up with Edgar. As he exited onto Highland he could see the Hotel Usher rising a few blocks to the south. Its windows were uniformly dark, the curtains stripped out in preparation for the work ahead.

Bosch had no rover with him and had forgotten to ask Edgar where the command post for the search would be located. He didn't want to simply drive up to the hotel in his slickback and risk exposing the operation. He took out his phone and called the watch office. Mankiewicz answered.

'Mank, you ever take a day off?'

'Not in January. My kids celebrate Christmas and Chanukah. I need the OT. What's up?'

'Can you get me the CP location on the thing at the Usher?'

'Yeah, it's the parking lot at Hollywood Presbyterian.'

'Got it. Thanks.'

Two minutes later Bosch pulled into the church parking lot. There were five squad cars parked there along with a slickback and a narc car. The cars were parked up close to the church so that they were shielded from view of the windows of the Usher, which rose into the sky on the other side of the church.

Two officers sat in one of the patrol cars. Bosch parked and walked over to the driver side window. The car was running. Bosch knew it was the pickup car. When the others grabbed Stokes in the Usher, a radio call would go out for the pickup. They would drive over and pick up the prisoner.

'Where are they?'

'Twelfth floor,' said the driver. 'Nothing yet.'

'Let me borrow your rover.'

The cop handed his radio out the window to Bosch. Bosch called Edgar on channel two.

'Harry, you here?'

'Yeah, I'm coming up.'

'We're almost done.'

'I'm still coming up.'

He gave the radio back to the driver and started walking out of the parking lot. When he got to the construction fence that surrounded the Usher property he went to the north end, where he knew he would find the seam in the fence the squatters used to get in. It was partially hidden behind a construction sign announcing the arrival soon of historic luxury apartments. He pulled back the loose fence and ducked through.

There were two main staircases at either end of the building. Bosch assumed there would be a team of uniform officers posted at the bottom of each in case Stokes somehow slipped through the search and tried to escape. Bosch took out his badge and held it up and out as he opened the exterior stairwell door on the east side of the building.

As he stepped into the stairwell he was met by two officers who held their weapons out and at their sides. Bosch nodded and the cops nodded back. Bosch started up the stairs.

He tried to pace himself. Each floor had two runners of stairs and a landing for the turn. He had twenty-four to climb. The smell from the overflowing toilets was stifling and all he could think about was what Edgar had told him about all odors being particulate. Sometimes knowledge was an awful thing.

The hallway doors had been removed and with them the floor markings. Though someone had taken it upon himself to paint numbers on the walls of the lower landings, as Bosch got higher the markings disappeared and he lost count and became unsure what floor he was on.

At either the ninth or tenth floor he took a breather. He sat down on a reasonably clean step and waited for his breathing to become more regular. The air was cleaner this high up. Fewer squatters used the upper floors of the building because of the climb.

Bosch listened but he heard no human sounds. He knew the search teams had to be on the top floor by now. He was wondering if the tip on Stokes had been wrong, or if the suspect had slipped out.

Finally, he stood and started up again. A minute later he realized he had counted wrong – but in his favor. He stepped up onto the last landing and the open door of the penthouse – the thirteenth floor.

He blew out his breath and almost smiled at the prospect of not having to climb another set of stairs when he heard shouts coming from the hallway.

'There! Right there!'

'Stokes, no! Police! Free—'

Two quick and brutally loud gunshots sounded and echoed down the hall, obliterating the voices. Bosch drew his gun and quickly moved to the doorway. As he began to peek around the jamb he heard two more shots and pulled back.

The echo prevented him from identifying the origin of the shots. He leaned around the jamb again and looked into the hallway. It was dark with light slashing through it from the doorways of the rooms on the west side. He saw Edgar standing in a combat crouch behind two uniformed officers. Their backs were to Bosch and their weapons were pointed at one of the open doorways. They were fifty feet down the hall from Bosch.

'Clear!' a voice yelled. 'We're clear in here!'

The men in the hall raised their weapons up in unison and moved toward the open doorway.

'LAPD in the back!' Bosch yelled and then stepped into the hallway.

Edgar glanced back at him as he followed the two uniforms into the room.

Bosch walked quickly down the hallway and was about to enter the room when he had to step back to let a uniform officer out. He was talking on his rover.

'Central, we need paramedics to forty-one Highland, thirteenth floor. Suspect down, gunshot wounds.'

As Bosch entered the room he looked back. The cop on the rover was Edgewood. Their eyes locked for just a moment and then Edgewood disappeared into the shadows of the hallway. Bosch turned back to view the room.

Stokes was sitting in a closet that had no door. He was leaning back against the rear wall. His hands were in his lap, one holding a small gun, a .25 caliber pocket rocket. He wore black jeans and a sleeveless T-shirt that was covered with his own blood. He had entry wounds on his chest and right below his left eye. His eyes were open but he was clearly dead.

Edgar was squatted in front of the body. He didn't touch it. There was no use trying for a pulse and everybody knew it. The smell of burnt cordite invaded Bosch's nose and it was a welcome relief from the smell outside the room.

Bosch turned around to take in the whole room. There were too many people in the small space. There were three uniforms, Edgar, and a plainclothes Bosch assumed was a narc. Two of the uniforms were huddled together at the far wall, studying two bullet holes in the plaster. One raised a finger and was about to probe one of the holes.

'Don't touch that,' Bosch barked. 'Don't touch anything. I want everybody to back out of here and wait for OIS. Who fired a weapon?'

'Edge did it,' said the narc. 'The guy was waitin' for us in the closet and we—'

'Excuse me, what's your name?'

'Phillips.'

'Okay, Phillips, I don't want to hear your story. Save it for OIS. Go get Edgewood and go back downstairs and wait. When the paramedics get here tell them never mind. Save them a trip up the steps.'

The cops reluctantly shuffled out of the room, leaving only Bosch and Edgar. Edgar got up and walked over to the window. Bosch went to the corner farthest from the closet and looked back at the body. He then approached the body and squatted down in the same spot where Edgar had been.

He studied the gun in Stokes's hand. He assumed that when it was removed from the hand OIS investigators would find the serial number had been burned away by acid.

He thought about the shots he had heard while on the stairway landing. Two and two. It was hard to judge them by memory, especially considering his position at the time. But he thought the first two rounds had been louder and heavier than the second two. If that was so it would mean Stokes had fired his little popper after Edgewood had fired his service weapon. It would mean Stokes had gotten off two shots after he had been hit in the face and chest – wounds that appeared instantly fatal to Bosch.

'What do you think?'

Edgar had come up behind him.

'It doesn't matter what I think,' Bosch said. 'He's dead. It's an OIS case now.'

'What it is is a closed case, partner. I guess we didn't have to worry about whether the DA would file the case after all.'

Bosch nodded. He knew there would be wrap-up investigation and paperwork, but the case was finished. It would ultimately be classified as 'closed by other means,' meaning no trial and no conviction but carried in the solved column just the same.

'Guess not,' he said.

Edgar swatted him on the shoulder.

'Our last case together, Harry. We go out on top.'

'Yeah. Tell me something, did you mention the DA and about it being a juvy case during the briefing in the roll-call room this morning?'

After a long moment Edgar said, 'Yeah, I might've mentioned something about it.'

'Did you tell them we were spinning our wheels, the way you said it to me? That the DA probably wouldn't even file a case on Stokes?'

'Yeah, I might've said it like that. Why?'

Bosch didn't answer. He stood up and walked over to the room's window. He could see the Capitol Records building and farther past it the Hollywood sign up on the crest of the hill. Painted on the side of a building a few blocks away was an anti-smoking sign showing a cowboy with a drooping cigarette in his mouth accompanied by a warning about cigarettes causing impotence.

He turned back to Edgar.

'You going to hold the scene until OIS gets here?'

'Yeah, sure. They're going to be pissed off about having to hump the thirteen floors.'

Bosch headed toward the door.

'Where are you going, Harry?'

Bosch walked out of the room without answering. He used the stairwell at the farthest end of the hallway so that he wouldn't catch up to the others as he was going down.

53

The living members of what had once been a family stood as points of a hard-edged triangle with the grave in the middle. They stood on a sloping hillside in Forest Lawn, Samuel Delacroix on one side of the coffin while his ex-wife stood across from him. Sheila Delacroix's spot was at the end of the coffin opposite the preacher. The mother and daughter had black umbrellas open against the light drizzle that had been falling since dawn. The father had none. He stood there getting wet, and neither woman made a move to share her protection with him.

The sound of the rain and the freeway hissing nearby drowned out most of what the rented preacher had to say before it got to Bosch. He had no umbrella either and watched from a distance and the protection of an oak tree. He thought that it was somehow appropriate that the boy should be formally buried on a hill and in the rain.

He had called the medical examiner's office to find out which funeral home was handling the service and it had led him to Forest Lawn. He had also learned that it had been the boy's mother who had claimed the remains and planned the service. Bosch came to the funeral for the boy, and because he wanted to see the mother again.

Arthur Delacroix's coffin looked like it had been made for an adult. It was polished gray with brushed chrome handles. As coffins went it was beautiful, like a newly waxed car. The rain beaded on its surface and then slid down into the hole beneath. But it was still too big for those bones and somehow that bothered Bosch. It was like seeing a child in ill-fitting clothes, obvious hand-me-downs. It always seemed to say something about the child. That they were wanting. That they were second.

When the rain started coming down harder the preacher raised an umbrella from his side and held his prayer book with one hand. A few of his lines managed to drift over to Bosch intact. He was talking about the greater kingdom that had welcomed Arthur. It made Bosch think of Golliher and his unfaltering faith in that kingdom despite the atrocities he studied and documented every day. For Bosch, though, the jury was still out on all of that. He was still a dweller in the lesser kingdom.

Bosch noticed that none of the three family members looked at one another. After the coffin was lowered and the preacher made the final sign of the cross, Sheila turned and started walking down the slope to the parking road. She had never once acknowledged her parents.

Samuel immediately followed and when Sheila looked back and saw him coming after her she picked up speed. Finally, she just dropped the umbrella and started running. She made it to her car and drove away before her father could catch up.

Samuel watched his daughter's car cutting through the vast cemetery until it disappeared through the gate. He then went back and picked up the discarded umbrella. He took it to his own car and left as well.

Bosch looked back at the burial site. The preacher was gone. Bosch looked about and saw the top of a black umbrella disappearing over the crest of the hill. Bosch didn't know where the man was going, unless he had another funeral to officiate on the other side of the hill.

That left Christine Waters at the grave. Bosch watched her say a silent prayer and then walk toward the two remaining cars on the road below. He chose an angle of intersection and headed that way. As he got close she calmly looked at him.

'Detective Bosch, I am surprised to see you here.'

'Why is that?'

'Aren't detectives supposed to be aloof, not get emotionally involved? Showing up at a funeral shows emotional attachment, don't you think? Especially rainy-day funerals.'

He fell into stride next to her and she gave him half of the umbrella's protection.

'Why did you claim the remains?' he asked. 'Why did you do this?'

He gestured back toward the grave on the hill.

'Because I didn't think anybody else would.'

They got to the road. Bosch's car was parked in front of hers.

'Good-bye, Detective,' she said as she broke from him, walked between the cars and went to the driver's door of hers.

'I have something for you.'

She opened the car door and looked back at him.

'What?'

He opened his door and popped the trunk. He walked back between the cars. She closed her umbrella and threw it into her car and then came over.

'Somebody once told me that life was the pursuit of one thing. Redemption. The search for redemption.'

'For what?'

'For everything. Anything. We all want to be forgiven.'

He raised the trunk lid and took out a cardboard box. He held it out to her.

'Take care of these kids.'

She didn't take the box. Instead she lifted the lid and looked inside.

There were stacks of envelopes held together by rubber bands. There were loose photos. On top was the photo of the boy from Kosovo who had the thousand-yard stare. She reached into the box.

'Where are they from?' she asked, as she lifted an envelope from one of the charities.

'It doesn't matter,' he said. 'Somebody has to take care of them.'

She nodded and carefully put the lid back on. She took the box from Bosch and walked it back to her car. She put it on the backseat and then went to the open front door. She looked at Bosch before getting in. She looked like she was about to say something but then she stopped. She got in the car and drove away. Bosch closed the trunk of his car and watched her go.

54

The edict of the chief of police was once again being ignored. Bosch turned on the squad room lights and went to his spot at the homicide table. He put down two empty cardboard boxes.

It was late Sunday, near midnight. He'd decided to come in and clear out his desk and files when no one else would be around to watch. He still had one more day in Hollywood Division but he didn't want to spend it packing boxes and exchanging insincere good-byes with anyone. His plan was to have a clean desk at the start of the day and a three-hour lunch at Musso & Frank's to end it. He'd say a few good-byes to those who mattered and then slip out the back door before anyone even knew he was gone. It was the only way to do it.

He started with his file cabinet, taking the murder books of the open cases that still kept him awake some nights. He wasn't giving up on them just yet. His plan was to work the cases during the downtimes in RHD. Or to work them at home alone.

With one box full he turned to his desk and started emptying the file drawers. When he pulled out the mason jar full of bullet shells, he paused. He had not yet put the shell collected at Julia Brasher's funeral into the jar. Instead he had put that one on a shelf in his home. Next to the picture of the shark he would always keep there as a reminder of the perils of leaving the safety cage. Her father had allowed him to take it.

He carefully put the jar into the corner of the second box and made sure it was held secure by the other contents. He then opened the middle drawer and started collecting all the pens and pads and other office supplies.

Old phone messages and business cards from people he had met on cases were scattered throughout the drawer. Bosch checked each one before deciding whether to keep it or drop it into the trash can. After he had a stack of keepers he put a rubber band around it and dropped it into the box.

When the drawer was almost clear, he pulled out a folded piece of paper and opened it. There was a message on it.

Where are you, tough guy?

Bosch studied it for a long time. Soon it made him think about all that had happened since he had pulled his car to a stop on Wonderland Avenue just thirteen days before. It made him think about what he was doing and where he was going. It made him think of Trent and Stokes and most of all Arthur Delacroix and Julia Brasher. It made him think about what Golliher had said while studying the bones of the murder victims from millenniums ago. And it made him know the answer to the question on the piece of paper.

'Nowhere,' he said out loud.

He folded the paper and put it in the box. He looked down at his hands, at the scars across the knuckles. He ran the fingers of one hand across the markings on the other. He thought about the interior scars left from punching all of the brick walls he couldn't see.

He had always known that he would be lost without his job and his badge and his mission. In that moment he came to realize that he could be just as lost with it all. In fact, he could be lost *because* of it. The very thing he thought he needed the most was the thing that drew the shroud of futility around him.

He made a decision.

He reached into his back pocket and took out his badge wallet. He slid the ID card out from behind the plastic window and then unclipped the badge. He ran his thumb along the indentations where it said *Detective.* It felt like the scars on his knuckles.

He put the badge and the ID card in the desk drawer. He then pulled his gun from its holster, looked at it for a long moment and put it in the drawer, too. He closed the drawer and locked it with a key.

He stood up and walked through the squad room to Billets's office. The door was unlocked. He put the key to his desk drawer and the key to his slickback down on her blotter. When he didn't show up in the morning he was sure she would get curious and check out his desk. She'd then understand that he wasn't coming back. Not to Hollywood Division and not to RHD. He was turning in his badge, going Code 7. He was done.

On the walk back through the squad room Bosch looked about and felt a wave of finality move through him. But he didn't hesitate. At his desk he put one box on top of the other and carried them out through the front hallway. He left the lights on behind him. After he passed the front desk he used his back to push open the heavy front door of the station. He called to the officer sitting behind the counter.

'Hey, do me a favor. Call a cab for me.'

'You got it. But with the weather it might be a while. You might want to wait in—'

The door closed, cutting off the cop's voice. Bosch walked out to the curb. It was a crisp, wet night. There was no sign of the moon beyond the cloud cover. He held the boxes against his chest and waited in the rain.

Lost Light

This is for
Noel
Megan
Sam
Devin
Maddie
Michael
Brendan
Connor
Callie
Rachel
Maggie
and
Katie

There is no end of things in the heart.

Somebody once told me that. She said it came from a poem she believed in. She understood it to mean that if you took something to heart, really brought it inside those red velvet folds, then it would always be there for you. No matter what happened, it would be there waiting. She said this could mean a person, a place, a dream. A mission. Anything sacred. She told me that it is all connected in those secret folds. Always. It is all part of the same and will always be there, carrying the same beat as your heart.

I am fifty-two years old and I believe it. At night when I try to sleep but can't, that is when I know it. It is when all the pathways seem to connect and I see the people I have loved and hated and helped and hurt. I see the hands that reach for me. I hear the beat and see and understand what I must do. I know my mission and I know there is no turning away or turning back. And it is in those moments that I know there is no end of things in the heart.

1

The last thing I expected was for Alexander Taylor to answer his own door. It belied everything I knew about Hollywood. A man with a billion-dollar box-office record answered the door for nobody. Instead, he would have a uniformed man posted full-time at his front door. And this doorman would only allow me entrance after carefully checking my identification and appointment. He would then hand me off to a butler or the first-floor maid, who would walk me the rest of the way in, footsteps falling as silent as snow as we went.

But there was none of that at the mansion on Bel-Air Crest Road. The driveway gate had been left open. And after I parked in the front turnaround circle and knocked on the door, it was the box-office champion himself who opened it and beckoned me into a home whose dimensions could have been copied directly from the international terminal at LAX.

Taylor was a large man. Over six feet and 250 pounds. He carried it well, though, with a full head of curly brown hair and contrasting blue eyes. The hair on his chin added the highbrow look of an artist to this image, though art had very little to do with the field in which he toiled.

He was wearing a soft-blue running suit that probably cost more than everything I was wearing. A white towel was wrapped tightly around his neck and stuffed into the collar. His cheeks were pink, his breathing heavy and labored. I had caught him in the middle of something and he seemed a little put out by it.

I had come to the door in my best suit, the ash gray single-breasted I had paid twelve hundred dollars for three years before. I hadn't worn it in over nine months and that morning I had needed to dust off the shoulders after taking it out of the closet. I was clean-shaven and I had purpose, the first I had felt since I put the suit on that hanger so many months before.

'Come in,' Taylor said. 'Everybody's off today and I was just working out. Lucky the gym's just down the hall or I probably wouldn't have even heard you. It's a big place.'

'Yes, that was lucky.'

He moved back into the house. He didn't shake my hand and I

remembered that from the time I first met him four years before. He led the way, leaving it to me to close the front door.

'Do you mind if I finish up on the bike while we talk?'

'No, that's fine.'

We walked down a marble hallway, Taylor staying three steps ahead of me as if I were part of his entourage. He was probably most comfortable that way and that was all right with me. It gave me time to look around.

The bank of windows on the left gave a view of the opulent grounds – a soccer-field-sized rectangle of rolling green that led to what I assumed was a guest house or a pool house or both. There was a golf cart parked outside of the distant structure and I could see tracks back and forth across the manicured green leading to the main house. I had seen a lot in L.A., from the poorest ghettos to mountaintop mansions. But it was the first time I had seen a homestead inside the city limits so large that a golf cart was necessary to get from one side to the other.

Along the wall on the right were framed one-sheets from the many films Alexander Taylor had produced. I had seen a few of them when they made it to television and seen commercials for the rest. For the most part they were the kind of action films that neatly fit into the confines of a thirty-second commercial, the kind that leave you no pressing need afterward to actually see the movie. None would ever be considered art by any meaning of the word. But in Hollywood they were far more important than art. They were profitable. And that was the bottom line of all bottom lines.

Taylor made a sweeping right and I followed him into the gym. The room brought new meaning to the idea of personal fitness. All manner of weight machines were lined against the mirrored walls. At center was what appeared to be a full-size boxing ring. Taylor smoothly mounted a stationary bike, pushed a few buttons on the digital display in front of him and started pedaling.

Mounted side by side and high on the opposite wall were three large flat-screen televisions tuned to competing twenty-four-hour news channels and the Bloomberg business report. The sound on the Bloomberg screen was up. Taylor lifted a remote control and muted it. Again, it was a courtesy I wasn't expecting. When I had spoken to his secretary to make the appointment, she had made it sound like I would be lucky to get a few questions in while the great man worked his cell phone.

'No partner?' Taylor asked. 'I thought you guys worked in pairs.'

'I like to work alone.'

I left it at that for the moment. I stood silently as Taylor got up to a rhythm on the cycle. He was in his late forties but he looked much younger. Maybe surrounding himself with the equipment and machinery of health and youthfulness did the trick. Then again maybe it was face peels and Botox injections, too.

‘I can give you three miles,’ he said, as he pulled the towel from around his neck and draped it over the handle-bars. ‘About twenty minutes.’

‘That’ll be fine.’

I reached for the notebook in my inside coat pocket. It was a spiral notebook and the wire coil caught on the jacket’s lining as I pulled. I felt like a jackass trying to get it loose and finally just jerked it free. I heard the lining tear but smiled away the embarrassment. Taylor cut me a break by looking away and up at one of the silent television screens.

I think it’s the little things I miss most about my former life. For more than twenty years I carried a small bound notebook in my coat pocket. Spiral notebooks weren’t allowed – a smart defense attorney could claim pages of exculpatory notes had been torn out. The bound notebooks took care of that problem and were easier on the jacket lining at the same time.

‘I was glad to hear from you,’ Taylor said. ‘It has always bothered me about Angie. To this day. She was a good kid, you know? And all this time, I thought you guys had just given up on it, that she didn’t matter.’

I nodded. I had been careful with my words when I spoke to the secretary on the phone. While I had not lied to her I had been guilty of leading her and letting her assume things. It was a necessity. If I had told her I was an ex-cop working freelance on an old case, then I was pretty sure I wouldn’t have gotten anywhere near the box-office champ for the interview.

‘Uh, before we start, I think there might have been a misunderstanding. I don’t know what your secretary told you, but I’m not a cop. Not anymore.’

Taylor coasted for a moment on the pedals but then quickly worked back into his rhythm. His face was red and he was sweating freely. He reached to a cup holder on the side of the digital control board and took out a pair of half glasses and a slim card that had his production company’s logo at the top – a square with a mazelike design of curls inside it – and several handwritten notations below it. He put on the glasses and squinted anyway as he read the card.

‘That’s not what I have here,’ he said. ‘I’ve got LAPD Detective Harry Bosch at ten. Audrey wrote this. She’s been with me for eighteen years – since I was making straight-to-video dreck in the Valley. She is very good at what she does. And usually very accurate.’

‘Well, that *was* me for a long time. But not since last year. I retired. I might not have been very clear about that on the phone. I wouldn’t blame Audrey if I were you.’

‘I won’t.’

He glanced down at me, tilting his head forward to see over the glasses.

‘So then what can I do for you, Detective – or I guess I should say Mr. – Bosch? I’ve got two and a half miles and then we’re finished here.’

There was a bench-press machine to Taylor’s right. I moved over and sat down. I took the pen out of my shirt pocket – no snags this time – and got ready to write.

'I don't know if you remember me but we have spoken, Mr. Taylor. Four years ago when the body of Angella Benton was found in the vestibule of her apartment building, the case was assigned to me. You and I spoke in your office over at Eidolon. On the Archway lot. One of my partners, Kiz Rider, was with me.'

'I remember. The black woman – she had known Angie, she said. From the gym, I think it was. I remember that at the time you two instilled a lot of confidence in me. But then you disappeared. I never heard from—'

'We were taken off the case. We were from Hollywood Division. After the robbery and shooting a few days later, the case was taken away. Robbery-Homicide Division took it.'

A low chime sounded from the stationary cycle and I thought maybe it meant Taylor had covered his first mile.

'I remember those guys,' Taylor said in a derisive voice. 'Tweedledumb and Tweedledumber. They inspired nothing in me. I remember one was more interested in securing a position as technical advisor to my films than he was in the real case, Angie. Whatever happened to them?'

'One's dead and one's retired.'

Dorsey and Cross. I had known them both. Taylor's description aside, both had been capable investigators. You didn't get to RHD by coasting. What I didn't tell Taylor was that Jack Dorsey and Lawton Cross became known in Detective Services as the partners who had the ultimate bad luck. While working an investigation they drew several months after the Angella Benton case, they stopped into a bar in Hollywood to grab lunch and a booster shot. They were sitting in a booth with their ham sandwiches and Bushmills when the place was hit by an armed robber. It was believed that Dorsey, who was sitting facing the door, made a move from the booth but was too slow. The gunman cut him down before he got the safety off his gun and he was dead before he hit the floor. A round fired at Cross creased his skull and a second hit him in the neck and lodged in his spine. The bartender was executed last at point-blank range.

'And then what happened to the case?' Taylor asked rhetorically, not an ounce of sympathy in his voice for the fallen cops. 'Not a damn thing happened. I guarantee it's been gathering dust like that cheap suit you pulled out of the closet before coming to see me.'

I took the insult because I had to. I just nodded as if I agreed with him. I couldn't tell if his anger was for the never-avenged murder of Angella Benton or for what happened after, the robbery and the next murder and the shutting down of his film.

'It was worked by those guys full-time for six months,' I said. 'After that there were other cases. The cases keep coming, Mr. Taylor. It's not like in your movies. I wish it was.'

'Yes, there are always other cases,' Taylor said. 'That's always the easy out, isn't it? Blame it on the workload. Meantime, the kid is still dead, the money's still gone and that's too bad. Next case. Step right up.'

I waited to make sure he was finished. He wasn't.

'But now it's four years later and you show up. What's your story, Bosch? You con her family into hiring you? Is that it?'

'No. All of her family was in Ohio. I haven't contacted them.'

'Then what is it?'

'It's unsolved, Mr. Taylor. And I still care about it. I don't think it is being worked with any kind of . . . dedication.'

'And that's it?'

I nodded. Then Taylor nodded to himself.

'Fifty grand,' he said.

'Excuse me?'

'I'll pay you fifty grand – if you solve the thing. There's no movie if you don't solve it.'

'Mr. Taylor, you somehow have the wrong impression. I don't want your money and this is no movie. All I want right now is your help.'

'Listen to me. I know a good story when I hear it. Detective haunted by the one that got away. It's a universal theme, tried and true. Fifty up front, we can talk about the back end.'

I gathered the notebook and pen from the bench and stood up. This wasn't going anywhere, or at least not in the direction I wanted.

'Thanks for your time, Mr. Taylor. If I can't find my way out I'll send up a flare.'

As I took my first step toward the door a second chime came from the exercise bike. Taylor spoke to my back.

'Home stretch, Bosch. Come back and ask me your questions. And I'll keep my fifty grand if you don't want it.'

I turned back to him but kept standing. I opened the notebook again.

'Let's start with the robbery,' I said. 'Who from your company knew about the two million dollars? I'm talking about who knew the specifics – when it was coming in for the shoot and how it was going to be delivered. Anything and anybody you can remember. I'm starting this from scratch.'

2

Angella Benton died on her twenty-fourth birthday. Her body was found crumpled on the Spanish tile in the vestibule of the apartment building where she lived on Fountain near La Brea. Her key was in her mailbox. Inside the mailbox were two birthday cards mailed separately from Columbus by her mother and father. It turned out they were not divorced. They each just wanted to write their own birthday wishes to their only daughter.

Benton had been strangled. Before or after death, but most likely after, her blouse had been torn open and her bra jerked up to expose her breasts. Her killer then apparently masturbated over the corpse, producing a small amount of ejaculate that was later collected by forensic technicians for DNA typing. Her purse was taken and never recovered.

Time of death was established as between 11 p.m. and midnight. Her body was found by another resident in the apartment building when he left his home at 12:30 a.m. to take his dog for a walk.

That was where I came in. At the time I was a detective third grade assigned to the Hollywood Division of the Los Angeles Police Department. I had two partners. We worked in threes instead of pairs back then as part of an experimental configuration designed to close cases quickly. Kizmin Rider and Jerry Edgar and I were alerted by pager and assigned the case at 1 a.m. We met at Hollywood Division, picked up two Crown Vics and then drove to the crime scene. We saw Angella Benton's body for the first time approximately two to three hours after she had been killed.

She lay on her side on brown tile that was the color of dried blood. Her eyes were open and bugged, distorting what I could tell had been a pretty face. The corneas were hemorrhaged. I noticed that her exposed chest was almost flat. It looked almost boyish and I thought maybe this had been a private embarrassment to her in a city where physical attributes seemed often to outweigh those on the inside. It made the tearing open of her blouse and lifting of her bra all the more of an attack, as if it were not enough to take her life, the killer also had to expose her most private vulnerability.

But it was her hands that I would remember the most. Somehow when her lifeless body was dropped to the tile, her hands fell together. Off to the left side of her body, they were directed upward from her head, as if she were reaching out to someone, almost beseechingly, begging for something. They looked like hands from a Renaissance painting, like the hands of the damned reaching heavenward for forgiveness. In my life I have worked almost a thousand homicides and no positioning of a fallen body ever gave me such pause.

Perhaps I saw too much in the vagaries of how she had fallen. But every case is a battle in a war that never ends. Believe me, you need something to carry with you every time you go into the fight. Something to hold on to, an edge that drives you or pulls you. And it was her hands that did it for me. I could not forget her hands. I believed they were reaching to me. I still do.

We got an immediate jump on the investigation because Kizmin Rider recognized the victim. They had been acquaintances. Rider knew her by first name from the gym on El Centro where they both worked out. Because of the irregular hours that came with her job on the homicide table Rider could not keep a regular workout schedule. She exercised at different times on different days, depending on her time and the case she was working. Often she had encountered Benton in the gym and they had struck up a conversational relationship while they worked side by side StairMasters.

Rider knew Benton was trying to establish a career in the film business on the production side. She worked as a production assistant for Eidolon Productions, the company headed by Alexander Taylor. Production schedules used all twenty-four hours on the clock, depending on the availability of locations and personnel. It meant that Benton had a gym schedule similar to Rider's. It also meant that Benton had little time for relationships. She told Rider that she'd had only two dates in the past year and that there was no man in her life.

It was only a surface friendship and Rider had never seen Benton outside of the gym. They were both young black women trying to keep their bodies from betraying them as they went about busy professional lives and attempted to scale steep ladders in different worlds.

Nevertheless, the fact Kiz knew her gave us a good jump. We knew right away who we were dealing with – a responsible and confident young woman who cared about both her health and her career. It eliminated a variety of lifestyle angles we might have mistakenly pursued. The negative from the break was that it was the first time Rider had ever come across someone she knew as the victim of a homicide she'd been assigned to investigate. I noticed right away at the scene that it put a pause in her step. She usually was quite vocal when breaking down a crime scene and developing an investigative theory. At this scene she was silent until spoken to.

There were no witnesses to the murder. The vestibule was hidden from street view and offered the killer a perfect blind. He would have been able to move into the small space and attack without fear of being seen from outside. Still, there had been a risk to the crime. At any moment another resident of the building could have come home or left and come upon Benton and her killer. If the dog walker had taken his pet out an hour earlier he possibly could have ventured into the crime in progress. He could have saved her, or possibly have become a victim himself.

Anomalies. So much of the work entailed study of the anomalies. The crime had the appearance of an attack of opportunity. The killer had followed Benton and waited for the moment she was in the blind. Yet there were aspects of the scene – its privacy, for example – that suggested that he already knew about the vestibule and may have been waiting there, like a hunter watching a bait trap.

Anomalies. Angella Benton was no more than five feet five but she was a strong young woman. Rider had witnessed her workout regimen and knew first-hand of her strength and stamina. Yet there was no sign of a struggle. Fingernail scrapings produced no skin or blood belonging to anyone else. Had she known her killer? Why hadn't she fought? The masturbation and the tearing open of the blouse suggested a crime of psychosexual motivation, a crime perpetrated alone. Yet the seeming lack of any fight for life suggested Benton had been completely and quickly overpowered. Had there been more than one killer?

In the first twenty-four hours our purpose had been to collect the evidence, make notifications and conduct first interviews of those immediately connected to the crime scene. It was in the second twenty-four that the sifting began and we began to work the anomalies, trying to crack them open like walnuts. And by the end of that second day we had concluded that it was a staged crime scene. That is, a scene designed by the perpetrator to convey false ideas about the crime. We concluded we had a killer who thought he was smarter than us, who was sending us down the psychosexual-predator road when the reality of the crime was something altogether different.

The thing that tilted us in this direction was the semen found on the body. In studying the crime scene photographs I noticed that drops of semen stretched across the victim's body in a line suggesting a trajectory. However, the individual drops were round. It was common investigative knowledge in regard to blood spatter evidence that round drops are formed when blood drops directly down to a surface. Elliptical-shaped drops occur when blood is spattered in a trajectory or at an angle to the surface. We consulted the department's blood spatter expert to see if the norms of blood evidence extended to other bodily fluids. We were told it did, and that for us cracked open an anomaly. We now theorized that the possibility was high that the killer or killers had planted the semen on the body. It had possibly been taken to the crime scene and then dripped onto the body as part of an intended misdirection.

We refocused the investigation. No longer did we view it as a case in which the victim wandered into the kill zone of a predator. Angella Benton was the kill zone. It had been something about her life and circumstances that had drawn the killer to her.

We attacked her life and work, looking for that hidden thing that had set the plan to kill her into motion. Someone had wanted her dead and thought they were clever enough to disguise it as the work of a hit-and-run psycho. While publicly we pumped the sex-slayer angle into the media machine, privately we began looking elsewhere.

On the third day of the investigation Edgar took the autopsy and the mounting paperwork duty while Rider and I took the field. We spent twelve hours in the offices of Eidolon Productions located at Archway Pictures on Melrose. Alexander Taylor had his moviemaking machine taking up nearly a third of the office space on the Archway lot. There were more than fifty employees. By virtue of her job as a production assistant, Angella Benton had interaction with them all. A PA stands at the bottom of the Hollywood totem pole. Benton had been a gofer, a runner. She had no office. She had a desk in the windowless mail room. But no matter, because she was always on the move, running between offices at Archway and back and forth from productions in the field. At that moment Eidolon had two movies and a television show shooting at separate locations in and around Los Angeles. Each one of those productions was a small city unto itself, a tent city that packed up and moved from location to location almost every night. A city with another hundred or more people who could have interacted with Angella Benton and needed to be interviewed.

The task we had was daunting. We asked for help – additional bodies to help with the interviews. The lieutenant could spare none. It took the whole day for Rider and me to cover the interviews at the company headquarters at Archway. And that was the one and only time I spoke to Alexander Taylor. Rider and I got a half hour with him and the conversation was perfunctory. He knew Benton, of course, but not well. While she was at the bottom of the totem pole, he was at the very top. Their interactions were infrequent and short. She had been with the company less than six months and he had not been the one who had hired her.

We got no hits during that first day of interviews. That is, no interview we conducted resulted in a new direction or focus for the investigation. We hit a wall. No one we talked to had an inkling of why someone would want to kill Angella Benton.

The following day we split up so each detective could visit a production location to conduct interviews. Edgar took the television production out in Valencia. It was a family-oriented comedy about a couple with an only child who connives to keep her parents from having more children. Rider took the movie production nearest her home in Santa Monica. It was a story about a man who takes credit for an anonymous valentine sent to a beautiful coworker and how their subsequent romance is built on a lie that grows inside him like a cancer. I had the second movie production, which was being shot in Hollywood. It was a high-action caper about a burglar who steals a suitcase with two million dollars in it, not knowing that the money belongs to the mob.

As a detective three I was the team leader. As such, I made the decision not to inform Taylor or any other administrators of his company that members of my team would be visiting the production locations. I didn't want advance notice to precede us. We simply split up the locations and the next morning we each arrived unannounced, using the power of the badge to force our way in.

What happened the next morning shortly after I arrived at the set is well documented. I sometimes review the moves of the investigation and wish I had gotten to the set one day sooner. I think that I would have heard somebody mention the money and that I would have been able to put it all together. But the truth is we handled the investigation appropriately. We made the right moves at the right time. I have no regrets about that.

But after that fourth morning the investigation was no longer mine. The Robbery-Homicide Division came in and bigfooted the case. Jack Dorsey and Lawton Cross ran with it. It had everything RHD likes in a case: movies, money and murder. But they got nowhere with it, moved on to other cases and then walked into Nat's for a ham sandwich and a jolt. The case more or less died with Dorsey. Cross lived but never recovered. He came out of a six-week coma with no memory of the shooting and no feeling below the neck. A machine did his breathing for him and a lot of people in the department figured his luck was worse than Dorsey's because he survived but was no longer really living.

Meantime, the Angella Benton case was gathering dust. Everything Dorsey and Cross touched was tainted by their luck. Haunted. Nobody worked the Benton case anymore. Every six months somebody in RHD would pull out the file and blow off the dust, write the date and 'No New Developments' on the investigative log, then slide it back into its place until the next time. In the LAPD that is what is called due diligence.

Four years went by and I was now retired. I was supposedly comfortable. I had a house with no mortgage and a car that I'd paid cash for. I had a pension that covered more than I needed covered. It was like being on vacation. No work, no worries, no problems. But something was missing and deep down I knew it. I was living like a jazz musician waiting for a gig. I was staying up late, staring at the walls and drinking too much red wine. I needed to either pawn my instrument or find a place to play it.

And then I got the call. It was Lawton Cross on the line. Word had finally gotten to him that I had pulled the pin. He got his wife to call and then she held the phone up so he could speak to me.

'Harry, do you ever think about Angella Benton?'

'All the time,' I told him.

'Me, too, Harry. My memory's come back, and I think about that one a lot.'

And that's all it took. When I walked out of the Hollywood Division for the last time, I thought I'd had enough, that I'd walked around my last body, conducted my last interview with somebody I knew was a liar. But I'd hedged my bet just the same. I walked out carrying a box full of files – copies of my open cases from twelve years in

Hollywood homicide.

Angella Benton's file had been in that box. I didn't have to open it to remember the details, to remember the way her body looked on the tile floor, so exposed and violated. It still drove the hook into me. It cut me that she had been lost in the fireworks that came after, that her life had not become important until after two million dollars was stolen.

I had never closed the case. It had been taken away from me by the big shots before I could. That was life in the LAPD. But that was then and this was now. The call from Lawton Cross changed all of that in me. It ended my extended vacation. It gave me a job.

3

I no longer carried a badge but I still carried a thousand different habits and instincts that came with the badge. Like a reformed smoker whose hand digs inside his shirt pocket for the fix that is no longer there, I constantly found myself reaching in some way for the comfort of my badge. For almost thirty years of my life I had been part of an organization that promoted isolation from the outside world, that cultivated the 'us versus them' ethic. I had been part of the cult of the blue religion and now I was out, excommunicated, part of the outside world. I had no badge. I was no longer part of us. I was one of them.

As the months passed, there was not a day that I did not alternately regret and revel in my decision to leave the department behind. It was a period in which my main work was to separate the badge and what it stood for from my own personal mission. For the longest time I believed the two were inextricably entwined. I could not have one without the other. But over the weeks and months came the realization that one identity was greater, that it superseded the other. My mission remained intact. My job in this world, badge or no badge, was to stand for the dead.

When I hung up the phone after talking to Lawton Cross I knew I was ready and that it was time to stand again. I went to the closet in the hallway and pulled out the box that contained the dusty files and all the voices of the dead. They spoke to me in memories. In crime scene visions. Of all of them I remembered Angella Benton the most. I remembered her body crumpled on the Spanish tile, her hands held out in such a way, as if reaching to me.

And I had my mission.

4

The morning after I spoke to Alexander Taylor I sat at the dining-room table in my house on Woodrow Wilson Drive. I had a pot of hot coffee in the kitchen. I had filled my five-disc changer with CDs chronicling some of Art Pepper's late work as a sideman. And I had the documents and photographs from the Angella Benton file spread in front of me.

The file was incomplete because the case was taken by RHD just as my investigation was beginning to come into focus and before many of the reports were written. It was merely a starting point. But after almost four years removed from a crime scene it was all I had. That and the list of names Alexander Taylor had given me the day before.

As I readied myself for a day of chasing down names and setting up interviews, my eyes were drawn to the small stack of newspaper clippings that had yellowed at the edges while closed in the file. I took these up and began looking through them.

Initially Angella Benton's murder rated only a short report in the *Los Angeles Times.* I remembered how this had frustrated me. We needed witnesses. Not only to the crime itself but possibly to the killer's car or getaway route. We needed to know the victim's movements before she was attacked. It had been her birthday. Where and with whom had she spent the evening before coming home? One of the best ways to stimulate citizen reports is through news stories. Because the *Times* decided to run only a short that was buried in the back of the B section, we got almost no help from the public. When I called the reporter to express my frustration, I was told that polling showed that customers were tired of stories about death and tragedy. The reporter said the news hole for crimes stories was shrinking and there was nothing she could do about it. As a consolation she wrote an update for the next day's edition which included a line about the police seeking the public's help in the case. But the story was even shorter than the first report and was buried deeper inside the paper. We got not one call from a citizen that day.

All of that changed three days later when the story hit the front page and was the lead story for every television station in the city. I picked up the first of the stories clipped from the front page and read it once again.

REAL-LIFE SHOOT-OUT ON FILM SET

1 DEAD, 1 HURT AS COPS AND ROBBERS INTERRUPT CELLULOID COUNTERPARTS

By Keisha Russell
Times *Staff Writer*

A deadly reality intruded on Hollywood fantasy Friday morning when Los Angeles police and security guards exchanged gunfire with armed robbers during a heist of $2 million in cash being used in the filming of a movie about a heist of $2-million in cash. Two bank employees were shot, one of them fatally.

The armed robbers escaped with the money after opening fire on security officers and a real-life police detective who happened to be on the set. Police said that blood found later in the abandoned getaway vehicle indicated that at least one of the robbers was also hit by gunfire.

The film's star, Brenda Barstow, was inside a nearby trailer at the time of the shooting. She was unhurt and did not witness the real-life shoot-out.

The incident occurred outside a bungalow on Selma Avenue shortly before 10 a.m., according to police spokesmen. An armored truck arrived at the filming location to deliver $2 million scheduled to be used as a prop in scenes to be shot inside the house. The film set was described as being under heavy security at the time, though the exact number of armed security guards and police on hand was not disclosed.

The victim who was fatally shot was identified as Raymond Vaughn, 43, director of security for BankLA, the bank that was delivering the money to the film set. Also shot was Linus Simonson, 27, another BankLA employee. He suffered a bullet wound to the lower torso and was listed late Friday in stable condition at Cedars-Sinai Medical Center.

LAPD Detective Jack Dorsey said that as two guards were moving the cash from the armored truck into the house, three heavily armed men jumped from a van parked nearby, while a fourth waited behind the wheel. The gunmen confronted the guards and took the money. As the suspects were retreating to the van with the four satchels containing the cash, one of them opened fire.

'That was when all hell broke loose,' Dorsey said. 'It turned into a firefight.'

It was unclear Friday why the shooting started. Witnesses told police that the robbers encountered no resistance from the security people on the scene.

'As far as we can tell, they just opened up and started firing,' said Detective Lawton Cross.

Police said several security guards returned fire, along with at least two off-duty patrol officers working as on-set security and a police detective, Harry Bosch, who had been inside a movie set trailer conducting a seemingly unrelated investigation.

Police yesterday estimated that more than a hundred gunshots were fired during the wild shoot-out.

Even so, the crossfire lasted no more than a minute, witnesses said. The robbers managed to get into the van and speed away. The van, riddled with bullet holes, was later found abandoned near the Sunset Boulevard entrance to the Hollywood Freeway. It was determined that it had been stolen from a movie studio equipment yard the night before.

'At this time we have no identities of the suspects,' Dorsey said. 'We are following a variety of leads that we think will prove useful to the investigation.'

The shoot-out brought a sobering dose of reality to the encampment of moviemakers.

'At first I thought it was the prop guys just shooting blanks,' said Sean O'Malley, a production assistant on the film project. 'I thought it was like a joke. Then I heard people screaming to get down and real bullets started hitting the house. I knew it was real. I hit the deck, man, and just prayed. It was scary.'

The untitled film is about a thief who steals a suitcase containing $2 million from the Las Vegas mob and runs to Los Angeles. According to experts, it is highly unusual for real money to be used in film productions, but the film's director, Wolfgang Haus, insisted on the use of real money because the scenes being shot in the Selma Avenue home entailed a variety of close-ups of the thief, played by Barstow, and the money.

Haus said the film's script called for the thief to dump the money on a bed and roll around in it, throwing it into the air and celebrating. Another scene involved the thief covering herself in a bathtub filled with the money. Haus said fake money would easily be noticeable in the finished film.

The German filmmaker also insisted that using real currency helped the actors perform better in scenes containing the money.

'If you are using play money, then you are playacting,' Haus said. 'We needed to get beyond that. I wanted this woman to feel she had stolen two million dollars. It would be impossible to do it any other way. My films rely on accuracy and truth. If we were to use Monopoly money, the film would be a lie and everybody who watched it would know it.'

The film's producers, Eidolon Productions, arranged for a one-day loan of the cash and a phalanx of security guards to go with it, police detectives told reporters. The armored car was scheduled to remain on the scene during shooting, and the money was to be returned immediately after filming was completed. The largesse was entirely comprised of one-hundred-dollar bills wrapped in $25,000 packets.

Alexander Taylor, owner of the film's production company, declined comment on the robbery or the decision to use real money during the filming. It was unclear if the money was insured against robbery.

Police also declined to reveal why Detective Bosch was on the set when the shoot-out erupted. But sources told the *Times* that Bosch was investigating the death of Angella Benton, who was found strangled in her Hollywood apartment building four days earlier. Benton, 24, was an employee of Eidolon Productions, and police are now investigating the possibility of a connection between her murder and the armed robbery.

In a statement released by her publicist, Brenda Barstow said, 'I am shocked by what has happened and my heart goes out to the family of the man who was killed.'

A spokesman for BankLA said that Raymond Vaughn had been employed by the bank for seven years. Formerly he was a police officer who worked for departments in New York and Pennsylvania. Simonson, the injured employee, is an assistant to bank vice-president Gordon Scaggs, who was in charge of the one-day cash loan to the movie set. Scaggs could not be reached for comment.

Production of the film was temporarily suspended. It was unclear Friday when the cameras would roll again, or if real currency would be used in the filming when it begins again.

I remembered the surreal scene of that day. The screaming, the cloud of smoke left after all of the shooting. People on the ground and me not knowing if they'd been hit or were just taking cover. No one got up for a long time, even after the getaway van was long gone.

I skimmed through a sidebar story that focused on how unusual it was to use real money – and so much of it – on a movie set, no matter what precautions had been taken. The story reported that the volume of the money took up four delivery satchels and correctly pointed out that it was unlikely that all $2 million would ever be contained in a single camera shot. Yet the producers of the film acceded to the director's demand that real money be used and that all $2 million be on hand for verisimilitude. But the unnamed insiders and Hollywood watchers quoted in the story seemed to suggest that it wasn't about the money or verisimilitude or even art. It was simply a power play. Wolfgang Haus did it because he could. The director was coming off of back-to-back films that had grossed more than $200 million each. In four short years he had risen from making small independent films to being a powerful Hollywood player. In demanding that $2 million in real cash be on hand for the filming of the rather routine scenes, he was exercising his newfound muscle. He had the power to ask for and get the $2 million on the set. Just another story about Hollywood ego. Only this time it involved murder.

I moved on to a follow-up story published two days after the robbery. It was a rehash of the first day's stories with little new information on the investigation. There were no arrests and no suspects. The most notable new information was that Warner Bros., the studio backing the film, had pulled the plug, canceling financing seven days into production after the film's star, Brenda Barstow, pulled out, citing safety concerns. The story cited unnamed sources within the production who suggested Barstow pulled out for other reasons but was using a personal safety clause in her contract to walk away. The other reasons suggested were her realization that a pall had been cast over the production that could shroud the film's box-office appeal as well, and her disappointment with the final script, which was finished after she signed on to the production.

The end of the follow-up story swung back to the investigation and reported that the investigation of the robbery and shooting had grown to encompass the murder of Angella Benton and that the Robbery-Homicide Division had taken over the case from Hollywood Division. I noticed that a paragraph had been circled near the bottom of the clip. Most likely by me four years before.

> Sources confirmed to the *Times* that the shipment of money stolen during the robbery was insured and contained marked bills. Investigators confided that tracing the cash may offer the best chance of identifying and capturing the suspects.

I didn't remember circling the paragraph four years before and wondered why I had – by the time the follow-up had been published I was off the case. I guessed that at the time I remained interested, whether on or off it, and was curious as to whether the reporter's source had given her accurate information or was simply hoping the robbers would read the story and panic over the possibility of the cash being traceable. Maybe it would make them hold onto it longer and increase the chance of a full recovery.

Wishful thinking. It didn't matter now. I folded the clips and put them aside. I thought about the trailer I was in that day when it began. The newspaper stories were just a blueprint, as distant as an aerial view. Like trying to figure out Vietnam in 1967 by watching Walter Cronkite at night. The stories carried none of the confusion, the smell of blood and fear, the searing charge of adrenaline dumping into the pipes like paratroopers going down the ramp of a C-130 over hostile territory, *'Go! Go! Go!'*

The trailer was parked on Selma. I was talking to Haus, the director, about Angella Benton. I was searching for anything to grab onto. I was obsessed with her hands, and suddenly in that trailer I thought maybe the hands had been part of the staging of the crime scene. Staged by a director. I was pressing Haus, pushing him, wanting to know his whereabouts on the night in question. And then there was a knock and the door opened and everything changed.

'Wolfgang,' a man in a baseball cap said. 'The armored truck's here with the money.'

I looked at Haus.

'What money?'

And then I knew, instinctively, what was about to happen.

I look back at the memory now and see everything in slow motion. I see all the moves, all the details. I came out of the director's trailer to see the red armored truck in the middle of the street two houses down. The back door was open and a man in uniform inside was handing money satchels to two men on the ground. Two men in suits, one much older than the other, stood nearby watching.

As the money carriers turned toward the house, the side door of a van parked across the street slid open and three armed men in ski masks emerged. Through the open door of the van I saw a fourth behind the wheel. My hand went inside my coat to the gun on my hip but I held it there. The situation was too volatile. Too many people around and in the possible crossfire. I let things go.

The robbers came up behind the money carriers, surprised them and took the satchels without a shot. Then, as they backed into the street toward the van, the inexplicable happened. The cover man not carrying a satchel stopped, spread his stance and leveled his weapon in a two-handed grip. I didn't get it. What had he seen? Where was the threat? Who had made a move? The gunman opened fire and the older man in the suit, his hands raised and no threat, went down backwards on the street.

In less than a second the full firefight erupted. The guard in the truck, the security men and the off-duty cops on the front lawn all opened up. I pulled my gun and moved down the lawn toward the van.

'Down! Everybody down!'

As crew members and technicians dove for ground cover I moved in closer. I heard someone start screaming and the van's engine begin revving. The smell of spent gunpowder invaded and burned my nostrils. By the time I had a clear, safe shot the robbers were to the van. One threw his satchels through the open door and then turned back, drawing two pistols from his belt.

He never got a shot off. I opened up and watched him fly backwards into the van. The others then dove in after him and the van took off, its tires screaming and the side door still open, the wounded man's feet protruding. I watched the van round the corner and head toward Sunset and the freeway. I had no chance of pursuit. My Crown Vic was parked more than a block away.

Instead, I opened up my cell phone and called it in. I told them to send ambulances and lots of people. I gave them the direction of the van and told them to get to the freeway.

The whole while the background screaming never stopped. I closed the phone and walked over to the screaming man. It was the younger man in the suit. He was on his side, his hand clamped over his left hip. Blood was leaking between his fingers. His day and his suit were ruined but I knew he was going to make it.

'I'm hit!' he yelled as he squirmed. 'I'm fucking hit!'

I came out of the memory and back to my dining-room table as Art Pepper started playing 'You'd Be So Nice to Come Home To,' with Jack Sheldon on trumpet. I had at least two or three versions of Pepper performing the Cole Porter standard on disc. On each one he always attacked it, tore its guts out. It was the only way he knew how to play and that relentlessness was what I liked best about him. It was the thing that I hoped I shared with him.

I opened my notebook to a fresh page and was about to write a note about something I had seen in my memory of the shoot-out, when someone knocked on the door.

5

I got up and went down the hall and looked through the peephole. I then quickly came back to the dining room and got a tablecloth from the cabinet against the wall. The tablecloth had never been used. It had been bought by my ex-wife and put in the cabinet for when we entertained. But we never entertained. I no longer had the wife but now the tablecloth would come in handy. There was another knock on the door. Louder this time. I quickly finished covering the photos and documents and went back to the door.

Kiz Rider had her back to me and was looking out at the street when I opened the door.

'Kiz, sorry. I was on the back deck and didn't hear the first knock. Come on in.'

She walked past me and down the short hallway toward the living and dining room areas. She probably saw that the sliding door to the deck was closed.

'Then how did you know there was a first knock?' she asked as she went by.

'I, uh, just thought that the knock I heard was so loud it must've meant that whoever was out there had—'

'Okay, okay, Harry, I got it.'

I hadn't seen her in almost eight months. Since my retirement party, which she had organized and held at Musso's, renting out the whole bar and inviting everybody from Hollywood Division.

She moved into the dining room and I saw her eyes run over the rumpled tablecloth. It was clear that I was covering something and I immediately regretted doing it.

She was wearing a charcoal-gray business suit with the skirt below the knee. The outfit took me by surprise. Ninety percent of the time we worked together as partners she wore black jeans and a blazer over a white blouse. It allowed her freedom to move, to run if necessary. In the suit she looked more like a bank vice-president than a homicide detective.

Her eyes still on the table, she said, 'Oh, Harry, you always set such a nice table. What's for lunch?'

'Sorry. I didn't know who was at the door and I just sort of threw that over some stuff I have out.'

She turned to face me.

'What stuff, Harry?'

'Just stuff. Old case stuff. So tell me, how are things down at RHD? Better than last time we talked?'

She had been promoted downtown about a year before I split the department. She'd had trouble with her new partner and others in RHD and had confided in me about it. I'd had a mentoring relationship with her that continued after she transferred to RHD. But it ended when I chose retirement over a reassignment that would have put us back together as partners in RHD. I knew it hurt her. Her organizing of the retirement party had been a nice gesture but it was also the big good-bye from her.

'RHD? RHD didn't work out.'

'What? What are you talking about?'

I was genuinely surprised. Rider had been the most skilled and intuitive partner I had ever worked with. She was made for the mission. The department needed more like her. I had thought for sure that she would be able to adjust to life in the department's highest profile squad and do good work.

'I transferred out at the beginning of the summer. I'm in the chief's office now.'

'You're kidding. Oh, man ... '

I was stunned. She had obviously chosen a career path through the department. If she was working for the chief as an adjutant or on special projects, then she was being groomed for command staff administration. There was nothing wrong with that. I knew Rider was as ambitious as the next cop. But homicide was a calling, not a career. I had always thought she understood and accepted that. She had heard the call.

'Kiz, I don't know what to say. I wish ... '

'What, that I had talked to you about it? You split the gig, Harry. Remember? What were you going to tell me, to tough it out in RHD when you bailed out yourself?'

'It was different for me, Kiz. I had built up too much resistance. I was pulling too much baggage. You were different. You were the star, Kiz.'

'Well, stars burn out. It was too petty and political on the third floor. I changed directions. I just took the lieutenant's exam. And the chief is a good man. He wants to do good things and I want to be right there with him. It's funny, things are less political on the sixth floor. You'd think it would be the other way around.'

It sounded as though she was trying to convince herself more than me. All I could do was nod as a sense of guilt and loss flooded me. If I had stayed and taken the RHD job, she would have stayed also. I went into the living room and dropped onto the couch. She followed me but remained standing.

I reached over to turn down the music but not too much. I liked the song. I stared out through the sliding doors and across the deck to the vista of mountains across the Valley. It was no smoggier out there than most days. But the overcast somehow seemed to fit as Pepper took up the clarinet to accompany Lee Konitz on 'The Shadow of Your Smile.' There was a sad wistfulness to it that I think even gave Rider pause. She stood silently listening.

I had been given the discs by a friend named Quentin McKinzie, who was an old jazzman who knew Pepper and had played with him decades earlier at Shelly Manne's and Donte's and some of the other long gone Hollywood jazz clubs spawned by the West Coast sound. McKinzie had told me to listen and study the discs. They were some of Pepper's last recordings. After years spent in jails and prisons because of his addictions, the artist was making up for lost time. Even in his work as a sideman. That relentlessness. He never stopped it until his heart stopped. There was a kind of integrity in that and the music that my friend admired. He gave me the discs and told me never to stop making up for lost time.

Soon the song ended and Kiz turned to me.

'Who was that?'

'Art Pepper, Lee Konitz.'

'White guys?'

I nodded.

'Damn. That was good.'

I nodded again.

'So what's under the tablecloth, Harry?'

I shrugged.

'First time you've come around in eight months, I suppose you know.'

She nodded.

'Yeah.'

'Let me guess. Alexander Taylor's tight with the chief or the mayor or both and he called to check me out.'

She nodded. I had gotten it right.

'And the chief knew you and I were close at one time, so . . . '

At one time. She seemed to stumble while saying that part.

'Anyhow, he sent me out to tell you that you're barking up the wrong tree.'

She sat down on the chair opposite the couch and looked out across the deck. I could tell she wasn't interested in what was out there. She just didn't want to look at me.

'So this is what you gave up homicide for, to run errands for the chief.'

She looked sharply at me and I saw the injury in her eyes. But I didn't regret what I said. I was just as angry with her as she was with me.

'It's easy for you to say that, Harry. You've already been through the war.'

'The war never ends, Kiz.'

I almost smiled at the coincidence of the song that was now playing while Rider was delivering her message. The piece was 'High Jingo,' with Pepper still accompanying Konitz. Pepper would be dead six months after laying down the track. The coincidence was that when I was young in the department, 'high jingo' was a way old guard detectives would describe a case that had taken on unusual interest from the sixth floor or carried other unseen political or bureaucratic dangers. When a case had high jingo on it, you had to be careful. You were in murky water. You had to watch your back because nobody else was watching it for you.

I got up and went to the window. The sun was reflecting off a billion particles that hung in the air. It was orange and pink and looked beautiful. It didn't seem like it could be poison.

'So what's the word from the chief – lay off it, Bosch? You're a citizen now. Leave it to the professionals?'

'More or less.'

'The case is gathering dust, Kiz. Why does he care that I'm poking around when nobody in his own department does? Is he afraid I'll embarrass him or something by closing it?'

'Who says it's gathering dust?'

I turned around and looked at her.

'Come on, don't give me the due diligence dance. I know how that goes. A signature every six months on the log, 'Uh yup, nothing new here.' I mean, don't you care about this, Kiz? You knew Angella Benton. Don't you want to see this thing cleared?'

'Of course I do. Don't think for one moment that I want anything less. But things are happening, Harry. I was sent out here as a courtesy to you. Don't get involved. You might wander into something you shouldn't. You might hurt rather than help.'

I sat back down and looked at her for a long moment as I tried to read between the lines. I wasn't convinced.

'If it is actively being worked, who is working it?'

She shook her head.

'I can't tell you that. I can only tell you to leave it alone.'

'Look, Kiz, this is me. Whatever anger you have because I pulled the pin shouldn't stop you—'

'From what? Doing what I am supposed to do? Following orders? Harry, you no longer have a badge. People with badges are actively working on this. Actively. You understand? Leave it at that.'

Before I could speak she fired another round at me.

'And don't trouble yourself about me, okay? I have no anger toward you anymore, Harry. You left me high and dry but that was a long time ago.

Yeah, I had anger but it's a long time gone. I didn't even want to be the one who came here today but he made me come. He thought I could convince you.'

He being the chief, I assumed. I sat silently for a moment, waiting to see if there was more. But that was all she had. I spoke quietly then, almost as if I was putting a confession through the screen to a priest.

'And what if I can't leave it alone? What if for reasons that have nothing to do with this case I need to work this? Reasons for myself. What happens then?'

She shook her head in annoyance.

'Then you are going to get hurt. These people, they don't fuck around. Find some other case or some other way to work out your demons.'

'What people?'

Rider stood up.

'Kiz, what people?'

'I've told you enough, Harry. Message delivered. Good luck.'

She headed toward the hallway and the door. I got up and followed, my mind churning through what I knew.

'Who is working the case?' I asked. 'Tell me.'

She glanced back at me but kept moving toward the door.

'Tell me, Kiz. Who?'

She stopped suddenly and turned to me. I saw anger and challenge in her eyes.

'For old time's sake, Harry? Is that what you want to say?'

I stepped back. Her anger was a force field around her body that was pushing me back. I held my hands out wide in surrender and didn't say anything. She waited a moment and then turned back to the door.

'Good-bye, Harry.'

She opened the door and stepped out, then pulled it closed behind her.

'Good-bye, Kiz.'

But she was already gone. For a long time I stood there thinking about what she had said and not said. There had been a message within a message but I couldn't yet read it. The water was too murky.

'High jingo, baby,' I said to myself as I locked the door.

6

The drive out to Woodland Hills took almost an hour. It used to be in this place that if you waited, picked your spots and went against the grain of traffic, you could get somewhere in a decent amount of time. Not anymore. It seemed to me that the freeways, no matter what time and what location, were always a nightmare. There was never any respite. And having done little long-distance driving in the past months, being re-immersed in the routine was an annoying and frustrating exercise. When I'd finally hit my limit, I got off the 101 at the Topanga Canyon exit and worked my way on surface streets the rest of the way. I was careful not to try to make up for lost time by speeding through the mostly residential districts. In my inside coat pocket was a flask. If I got pulled over, it could be a problem.

In fifteen minutes I got to the house on Melba Avenue. I pulled my car in behind the van and got out. I walked up the wooden ramp that started next to the van's side door and had been built over the front steps of the house.

At the door I was met by Danielle Cross, who beckoned me in silently.

'How's he doing today, Danny?'

'Same as always.'

'Yeah.'

I didn't know what else to say. I couldn't imagine what her view of the world was, how it had changed from one set of hopes and anticipations to something completely different overnight. I knew she couldn't be much older than her husband. Early forties. But it was impossible to tell. She had old eyes and a mouth that seemed permanently tight and turned down at the corners.

I knew my way and she let me go. Through the living room and down the hallway to the last room on the left. I walked in and saw Lawton Cross in his chair – the one bought along with the van after the fund-raiser run by the police union. He was watching CNN on a television mounted on a bracket hanging from the ceiling in the corner. Another report on the Mideast situation.

His eyes moved toward me but his face didn't. A strap crossed above his eyebrows and held his head to the cushion behind it. A network of tubes connected his right arm to a bag of clear fluid that hung from a utility tree attached to the back of his chair. His skin was sallow, he weighed no more than 125 pounds, his collarbones jutted out like shards of broken pottery. His lips were dry and cracked, his hair was an uncombed nest. I had been shocked by his appearance when I'd come by after his call to me. I tried not to show it again.

'Hey, Law, how are you doing?'

It was a question I hated to ask but felt I owed it to him to ask.

'About what you'd expect, Harry.'

'Yeah.'

His voice was a harsh whisper, like a college football coach's who has spent forty years screaming from the sidelines.

'Listen,' I said. 'I'm sorry to come back so soon but there were a few other things.'

'Did you go see the producer?'

'Yeah, I started with him yesterday. He gave me twenty minutes.'

There was a low hissing sound in the room that I had noticed when I came by earlier in the week. I think it was the ventilator, pumping air through the network of clear tubes that ran under Cross's shirt and out of his collar and up either side of his face before plugging into his nose.

'Anything?'

'He gave me some names. Everybody from Eidolon Productions who supposedly knew about the money. I haven't had a chance to run them down yet.'

'Did you ever ask him what Eidolon means?'

'No, I never thought to ask. What is it, like a family name or something?'

'No, it means phantom. That's one of the things that's come back to me. Just sort of popped into my head while I've been thinking about the case. I asked him once. He said it came from a poem. Something about a phantom sitting on a throne in the dark. I guess he figures that's him.'

'Strange.'

'Yeah. Hey, Harry, you can turn off the monitor. So we don't have to bother Danny.'

He had asked me to do the same thing on the first visit. I moved around his chair to a nearby bureau. On the top of it was a small plastic device with a small green light glowing on its face. It was an audio monitor manufactured for parents to listen in on their sleeping babies. It helped Cross call to his wife when he needed to change the channel or wanted anything else. I switched it off so we could speak privately and came back around to the front of the chair.

'Good,' Cross said. 'Why don't you close the door now.'

I did as instructed. I knew what this was leading to.

'Did you bring me something this time?' Cross said. 'Like I asked?'

'Uh, yeah, I did.'

'Good. Let's start with that. Go into the bathroom behind you and see if she left my bottle in there.'

In the bathroom the counter surrounding the sink was crowded with all manner of medicines and small medical equipment. Sitting on a soap dish was a plastic bottle with an open top. It looked like something normally found on a touring bike but a little different. The neck was wider and it was slightly curved. Probably to make the drinking angle a little more comfortable, I thought. I quickly took the flask out of my jacket and then poured a couple ounces of Bushmills into the bottle. When I took it out to the bedroom Cross's eyes widened in horror.

'No, not that! That's a piss bottle! It goes under the chair.'

'Ah, shit! Sorry.'

I turned around and went back to the bathroom, pouring the booze out into the sink just as Cross yelled, 'No, don't!'

I looked back out at him.

'I would've taken it.'

'Don't worry. I've got more.'

After the piss bottle was rinsed and returned to the soap dish I went back out to the bedroom.

'Law, there's no drinking bottle in there. What do you want me to do?'

'Goddamn, she probably took it. She knows what I'm up to. You have the flask?'

'Yeah, right here.'

I tapped it from the outside of my sport coat.

'Bring it out. Let me have a taste.'

I pulled the flask out and opened it. I brought the mouth to his and let him take a swallow. He coughed loudly and some of it spilled down his cheek and neck.

'Ah, Jesus!' he gasped.

'What?'

'Jesus . . . '

'What? Law, you all right? I'll get Danny.'

I made a move toward the door but he stopped me.

'No, no. I'm fine. I'm fine. I just . . . it's been a long time, is all. Give me another.'

'Law, we've got to talk.'

'I know that. Just give me another taste.'

I held the flask to his mouth again and poured in a good jolt. He took it down well this time and closed his eyes.

'Black Bush . . . Jesus, is that good.'

I smiled and nodded.

'Fuck the meds,' he said. 'Give me Bushmills anytime, Harry. Any fucking time.'

He was a man who couldn't move but I could still see the whiskey work into his eyes and soften them.

'She won't give me anything,' he said. 'Doctor's orders. Only time I get a nip is when one of you guys comes by and visits. And that ain't often. Who wants to come and see this sorry sight . . .

'You gotta keep coming, Harry. I don't care about the case, clear it, don't clear it, but keep comin' to see me.'

His eyes moved to the flask.

'And bring your friend there. Always bring a friend.'

It was beginning to dawn on me. Cross had held back on me. I had come to him the day before I went to Taylor. Cross had been the place to start. But he had held back in order to bring me back – with a flask. Maybe the whole thing, his call to reawaken the case in me had all been about one thing. The flask.

I held the wallet-size container up.

'You held back on me, Law, so I'd bring you this.'

'No. I was going to have Danny call you. There was something I forgot.'

'Yeah, well, I already know it. I go talk to Taylor and the next thing I know I get a visit from the sixth floor telling me to lay off, it's being worked. By people who don't fuck around.'

Cross's eyes were darting back and forth in his frozen face.

'No,' he said.

'Who came to see you before me, Law?'

'No one. Nobody's come about the case.'

'Who did you call before you called me?'

'Nobody, Harry, I promise.'

I must have raised my voice because the door to the bedroom suddenly opened and Cross's wife stood there.

'Is everything okay?'

'Everything is fine, Danny,' her husband said. 'Leave us alone.'

She stood in the doorway for a moment and I saw her eyes go to the flask in my hand. For a moment, I thought about taking a drink from it myself, so she might think it was there for me. But in her eyes I could see she knew exactly what was going on. She didn't move for a long moment and then her eyes came up to mine and held for a moment. She then took a step back and closed the door. I looked back at Cross.

'If she didn't know she knows now.'

'I don't care. What time is it, Harry? I can't see the screen too good.'

I looked up at the corner of the television screen where CNN always carried the time.

'It's eleven-eighteen. Who came out to see you, Law? I want to know who is working the case.'

'I'm telling you, Harry, nobody came. As far as I knew, the case was deader than these goddamn legs of mine.'

'Then what was it you didn't tell me when I was here before?'

His eyes went to the flask and he didn't have to ask. I held it to his chapped and peeling lips and he drank deeply from it. He closed his eyes.

'Ah, God . . .,' he said. 'I've got . . . '

His eyes opened and they jumped on me like wolves taking down a deer.

'She's keeping me alive,' he whispered desperately. 'You think this is what I want? Sitting in my own shit half the time? She's getting a full ride while I'm alive – full pay and medical. If I'm gone she gets the widow's pension. And I wasn't in that long, Harry. Fourteen years. It's about half of what she gets with me alive.'

I looked at him for a long moment, the whole time wondering if she was outside the door listening.

'So what do you want from me, Law? To pull the plug? I can't do that. I can get you a lawyer if you want, but I'm not—'

'And she doesn't treat me right, either.'

I paused again. I felt a tugging sensation in the pit of my guts. If what he was saying was true, then his life was more of a hell than I could imagine. I lowered my voice when I spoke.

'What does she do to you, Law?'

'She gets mad. She does things. I don't want to talk about it. It's not her fault.'

'Listen, you want me to get a lawyer in here? I could also get a social services investigator.'

'No, no lawyers. That'll take forever. No investigators. I don't want that. And I don't want you to get in any trouble, Harry, but what am I going to do? If I could pull the plug myself I would . . . '

He blew out a burst of air. The only gesture his body would allow him to make. I could only imagine his horrible frustration.

'This is no way to live, Harry. It isn't living.'

I nodded. None of this had come up on the first visit. We had talked about the case, what he could remember about it. His case memory was coming back in chunks. It had been a difficult interview but there was no sense of self-loathing or desperation. No more depression than would be expected. I wondered if it had been the alcohol that had suddenly brought it out.

'I'm sorry, Law.'

It was all I could say. His eyes looked away, up to the television screen which was over my left shoulder.

'What time is it now, Harry?'

This time I checked my watch.

'Twenty after. What's your hurry, Law? You expecting somebody else?'

'No, no, nothing like that. There's just a show I like to watch on Court TV. Comes on at twelve. Rikki Klieman. I like her.'

'Then you've still got time to talk to me. Why don't you get a bigger clock in here?'

'She won't give me one. She says the doctor says it's bad for me to be watching a clock.'

'She's probably right.'

It was the wrong thing to say. I saw anger flood his eyes and I immediately regretted the words.

'I'm sorry. I shouldn't—'

'You know what it's like not to be able to raise your own goddamn wrist to look at your fucking watch?'

'No, Law, I don't have any idea.'

'You know what it's like to shit in a bag and have your wife take it to the toilet? To have to ask her for every goddamn thing, including a taste of whiskey?'

'I'm sorry, Law.'

'Yeah, you're sorry. Everybody's fucking sorry but nobody's—'

He didn't finish. He seemed to bite off the end of the sentence like a dog getting a hold of raw meat. He looked away and was silent and I was silent for a long moment, until I thought the anger had drained back down his throat into the seemingly bottomless well of frustration and self-pity that was down there.

'Hey, Law?'

His eyes came back to me.

'What, Harry?'

He was calm. The moment had passed.

'Let's go back. You said you were going to call me because there was something you forgot. You know, when we went over the case before. What was it you forgot to tell me?'

'Nobody's come here and talked to me about the case, Harry. You're the only one. I mean that.'

'I believe you. I was wrong about that. But what was it that you forgot before? Why were you going to call me?'

He closed his eyes for a moment but then opened them. They were clear and focused.

'I told you that Taylor insured the money, right?'

'Right, you told me that.'

'What I forgot was that the insurance company – offhand I can't remember the name of—'

'Global Underwriters. You remembered the other day.'

'Right. Global Underwriters. As a condition of contract Global required that the lender – that was BankLA— scan all the bills.'

'Scan the bills? What do you mean?'

'Record the serial numbers.'

I remembered the paragraph I had circled on the newspaper clip. It had apparently been true. I started doing the math in my head. Two million divided by a hundred. I almost had it and then lost the number.

'That would be a lot of numbers.'

'I know. The bank balked – said it would take four people a week, something like that. So they negotiated and compromised. They sampled. They took ten numbers from every one of the stacks.'

I remembered from the *Times* story that the money was delivered in $25,000 bundles. That math I could do. Eighty bundles made $2 million.

'So they took eight hundred numbers. Still a lot.'

'Yeah, I remember the printout was like six pages long.'

'And what did you do with it?'

'Let me have another taste of that Black Bush, would you?'

I gave it to him. I could tell the flask was just about empty. I needed to get what he had and get out of there. I was getting sucked into his miserable world and I didn't like it.

'Did you put out the numbers?'

'Yeah, we put out the list. Gave it to the feds. And used the robbery guys to get the list out to all the banks in the county. I also sent it to Vegas Metro so they could get it into the casinos.'

I nodded, waiting for more.

'But you know how that goes, Harry. A list like that is only good if the people are checking it. Believe it or not, there are a hell of a lot of hundred-dollar bills out there, and if you use them in the right places people don't raise an eyebrow. They aren't going to take the time to run the number down a six-page list. They don't have the time or the inclination.'

It was true. Recorded money was most often used as evidence when it was found in the possession of a suspect in a financial crime such as a bank robbery. I could not remember working on or even hearing about a case where marked or recorded money was actually traced by transaction to a suspect.

'You were going to call me back because you forgot to tell me that?'

'No, not just that. There's more. Anything left in that little flask of yours?'

I shook the flask so he could hear that it was almost empty. I gave him what was left and then capped it and put it back in my pocket.

'That's it, Law. Until next time. Finish what you were going to tell me.'

His tongue poked out of his horrible hole of a mouth and licked a drop of whiskey from the corner. It was pathetic and I turned away as if to check the time on the television so he didn't have to know I saw it. On the tube was a financial news report. A graph with a red line trending down was on the screen to the side of the anchorman's concerned and puffy face.

I looked back at Cross and waited.

'Well,' he said, 'about, I don't know, ten months or so into the case, close to a year – this is after me and Jack had moved on and were working other things – Jack got a call from Westwood about the serial numbers. It all came back to me the other day after you left.'

I assumed Cross was talking about an FBI agent calling his partner. It was not an uncommon practice within the LAPD for investigators to never refer to FBI agents as FBI agents, as if denying them their title somehow knocked them down a notch or two. There had never been any love lost between the two competing organizations. But the main federal building in Los Angeles was on Wilshire Boulevard in Westwood and it housed the whole sandbox of federal law enforcement. All jurisdictional biases aside, I needed to be sure.

'An FBI agent?' I asked.

'Yeah, an agent. A woman, in fact.'

'Okay. What did she tell you guys?'

'She only spoke to Jack, and then Jack told me. The agent said that one of the serial numbers was wrong and Jack said, 'Is that right? How so?' And the agent told him that the list had wound through the building and eventually across her desk and she'd taken the time to scan the numbers into her computer and there was a problem with one of them.'

He stopped as if to catch his breath. He licked his lips again and it reminded me of some sort of underwater creature poking out of a crevice.

'I sure wish you had more in that flask, Harry.'

'Sorry, I don't. Next time. What was the problem with the number?'

'Well, as far as I remember, this gal, she told Jack that she collects numbers. Know what I mean? Whenever a flier comes across the desk with currency numbers on it, she puts them into her computer, adds them to the data bank. She can run cross-matches, things like that. It was a new program she was working on. She'd been doing it for a few years and had a lot of numbers in the box. Tell you what, I need some water. My throat – too much talking.'

'I'll go get Danny.'

'No, no, that's not – tell you what, just go to the sink and put some water in that thing you got and I can drink from that. That'll be fine. Don't bother Danny. She's been bothered enough.'

In the bathroom I filled the flask halfway with water from the faucet. I shook it and brought it out to him. He took it all. After a few moments he finally continued the story.

'She said one of the numbers on our list was on somebody else's list and that was impossible.'

'What do you mean? I'm not tracking this.'

'Let me see if I remember this right. She said that one of the hundreds that was on our list had a serial number that belonged to a hundred that was part of a bait packet taken in a bank robbery about six months before our movie set robbery went down.'

'Where was the bank robbery?'

'Marina del Rey, I think. I'm not sure about that, though.'

'Okay, so what was the problem? Why couldn't the hundred from the earlier bank robbery get recirculated, land back in a bank and then become part of the two million sent to the movie set?'

'That's what I said and Jack told me that it was impossible. He said the agent said the guy who took that bill in Marina del Rey in the first place got caught. He had the bait pack on him and he went to the federal clink and the bill was held as evidence.'

I nodded and thought about this, trying to get it right.

'You're saying that she was telling you that it would have been impossible for the hundred on your list to have been part of the movie delivery because at that time that hundred-dollar bill was in evidence lockup in regard to the Marina del Rey bank robbery.'

'Exactly. She even went in and checked the evidence to make sure the hundred was still there. It was.'

I tried to think about what this could mean, if it meant anything at all.

'What did you and Jack do?'

'Well, not much. There were a lot of numbers – six pages' worth. We figured maybe we just got a bad one. You know, maybe the guy who recorded it all had messed up, transposed a number or whatever. We were running on a new case by then. Jack said he'd make some calls to the bank and Global Underwriters. But I don't know if he did. Then, soon after that, we walked into the shit in that bar and everything else sort of drifted away . . . until I thought about Angella Benton and called you. Things are starting to come back to me now, you know?'

'I understand. Do you remember the agent's name?'

'Sorry, Harry, I don't remember the name. I might've never had it. I didn't talk to her and I don't think Jack even told me.'

I was silent while I considered whether this was a lead worth pursuing. I thought about what Kiz Rider had said about the case being worked. Maybe this was the angle. Maybe the people she told me about were FBI agents. While I was working it over, Cross started talking again.

'For what it's worth, I got the idea from Jack that this agent, whoever she was, sort of came up with this thing on her own. It was her own little program she was running. Almost like a hobby. Not on the official computer.'

'Okay. Do you remember if you ever got any other hits on the numbers? Before this one?'

'There was one but it didn't go anywhere. It came up pretty soon, in fact.'

'What was that?'

'It came up in a bank deposit. I think it was Phoenix. My memory's like Swiss cheese. A lot of holes.'

'You remember anything about that one at all?'

'Just that it was a deposit from a cash business. Like a restaurant. Something we weren't going to be able to trace any further back.'

'But it was pretty soon after the heist?'

'Yeah, I remember we jumped on it. Jack went out there. But it was a dead end.'

'How soon after the heist, can you remember?'

'Maybe a few weeks. I don't know for sure.'

I nodded. His memory was coming back but it still wasn't reliable. It served to remind me that without the murder book – the case documentation – I was severely handicapped.

'Okay, Law, thanks. If you remember or think of anything else, have Danny call me. And whether that happens or not I'll be back to see you.'

'And you'll bring the . . . '

He didn't finish and didn't need to.

'Yeah, I'll bring it. You sure you don't want me to bring somebody else? Maybe a lawyer that could talk to you about—'

'No, Harry, no lawyers, not yet.'

'You want me to talk to Danny?'

'No, Harry, don't talk to her.'

'You sure?'

'I'm sure.'

I nodded my good-bye and left the room. I wanted to get to my car so I could quickly write some notes about the call Jack Dorsey had gotten from the bureau agent. But when I came from the hallway into the living room Danielle Cross was sitting there waiting for me. She was on the couch and looked at me with accusing eyes. I threw the look right back at her.

'I think it's almost time for a show he wants to watch on Court TV.'

'I'll take care of it.'

'Okay. I'm leaving now.'

'I wish you would not come back.'

'Well, I may have to.'

'The man is on a delicate balance – mentally and physically. The alcohol upsets it. It takes days for him to recover.'

'Looked to me like it improved things for him.'

'Then come back tomorrow and have another look.'

I nodded. She was right. I spent a half hour with the man, not my life. I waited. I could tell she was working up toward something.

'I assume he told you that he wants to die and that I'm the one keeping him alive. For the money.'

I hesitated but then nodded.

'He said I mistreat him.'

I nodded again.

'He tells that to everybody that comes visit. All the cops.'

'Is it true?'

'The part about wanting to die? Some days. Some days it's not.'

'What about the part about being mistreated.'

She looked away from me.

'It's frustrating, dealing with him. He's not happy. He takes it out on me. One time I took it out on him. I turned off the television. He started crying like a baby.'

She looked up at me.

'That's all I've ever done but it was enough. I hate what I did, what I became in the moment. Everything got the better of me.'

I tried to read her eyes, the set of her jaw and mouth. She had her hands together in front of her, the fingers of one hand working the rings on the other set. A nervous gesture. I watched her chin start to quiver and then the tears started to come.

'What am I supposed to do?'

I shook my head. I didn't know. The only thing I knew was that I had to get out of there.

'I don't know, Danny. I don't know what any of us are supposed to do.'

It was all I could think of to say. I walked quickly to the front door and left. I felt like a coward walking away and leaving them alone together in that house.

7

Loose lips sink ships. The theory of the case pursued by Cross and Dorsey four years earlier was simple. They believed that Angella Benton had intimate knowledge through her job about the $2 million that was to be delivered to the film location and had set the robbery and her own death in motion by either intentionally or mistakenly talking about the money. Her loose lips planted the seed of the robbery and, consequently, her own demise. Being the inside link to the robbers, she had to be eliminated to cover their tracks. Because she was murdered four days before the robbery, it was believed by the two investigators that her involvement was unintentional. She had somehow furnished the information that led to the robbery and needed to be eliminated before she realized what she had done. She also needed to be eliminated in a way that would not draw suspicion to the impending cash delivery. Thus the psychosexual aspects of the crime scene – the tearing of the clothes and the evidence of masturbation – were in a way simply window dressing on the misdirection.

Conversely, if she had been a willing participant in the robbery scheme, it seemed likely to the investigators that her death would have come after the robbery had been successfully accomplished.

It seemed like a solid theory to me as Lawton Cross had recounted it during my first visit to his home. It was probably the way I would have gone if I had been allowed to stay on the case. But ultimately the theory didn't pay off. Cross told me that he and his partner had worked a full field investigation on Benton but never came across the one clue that opened up the case. They spent five solid months on her. They traced her movements, personal habits and daily-life routines. They studied her credit card, banking and telephone data. They interviewed and re-interviewed all family members and known friends and associates. They spent eight days in Columbus alone. Dorsey went to Phoenix to chase down a single hundred-dollar bill. They spent so much time at Eidolon Productions that for one month they were given their own office at Archway Pictures in which to conduct interviews.

And they got nothing.

As is often the case with a homicide, they amassed a wealth of knowledge about the victim but not the key piece of information that led to the identity of her killer. They ended up knowing who she had slept with in college but not where she had spent the last evening of her life. They knew her last meal had been Mexican – the corn tortillas and beans were still in her digestive tract – but not which one of the city's thousands of such establishments had served her.

And after six months on the case they found absolutely no link between Angella Benton and the robbery, aside from the surface connection of her job as a production assistant for the company that was making the film in which the cash was to play a starring role.

Six months in and they were at a dead end. What they did have in the way of evidence were the forty-six slugs and shell casings collected after the shoot-out, the blood collected from the getaway van and the semen collected from the murder scene. It was all good evidence to have; ballistics and DNA could tie a suspect to a crime with zero doubt – unless your lawyer was Johnnie Cochran. But it was the kind of evidence that was icing on a cake; the kind that links a suspect and weapon already identified and usually in custody. It didn't do much as far as getting you that suspect. After half a year on it they had the icing but no cake to put it on.

When they reached this dead end it was time to evaluate the case at the six-month mark. This is the point where hard choices are made. The probability of clearing the case is weighed against the need for the pair of investigators to work other cases and help shoulder the caseload of the division. Their supervisor took the case off full-time status and Dorsey and Cross went back into rotation at RHD. They were free to work the Benton case as often and as much as possible, but they also drew new investigations. As could be expected, the Benton case suffered for it. Cross had readily admitted this to me. He said it became a part-time investigation, with Dorsey doing most of the follow-up while Cross concentrated on the new cases they were assigned.

Then it all became academic when the pair got shot up in Nat's bar in Hollywood. The Benton case went into the OU files. Open-Unsolved. And it was orphaned. No detective likes a hand-me-down file, which the Benton case was. No one likes the idea of going into a file and proving his colleagues were wrong or misguided or possibly even incompetent or lazy. Added to this deterrent was the fact that the Benton case was now haunted. Cops are a superstitious species. The fate of the two original investigators – one dead, the other in a chair for life – was somehow inextricably bound to the cases they had worked, whether directly related or not. Nobody, and I mean nobody, was going to take on the Benton case now.

Except me. Now that I was out of the official game.

And four years later, I had to trust that Cross and Dorsey had done their job well in the investigation of Angella Benton's death and its connection to the robbery. I had no choice really. Covering the ground they had already trod to a dead end didn't seem to be the way to go. That was why I went to see Taylor. My plan was to accept their investigation as thorough if not flawless and approach it from a different direction. I was operating on the belief that Cross and Dorsey found nothing linking Benton to the robbery because there was nothing to find. Her death had been part of a plan, a carefully planned misdirection within a misdirection. I now had a list with nine names on it that had come out of my three-mile ride with Taylor. All the people involved in the planning of the money shoot. Everyone – as far as he knew – with knowledge that the cash was coming, when it was coming and who would bring it. I would go from there.

But now I had been thrown a curveball of sorts; what Cross had told me about the serial numbers and how at least one of them had been wrong. He said he had left it to Dorsey to pursue and didn't know what had happened. Shortly thereafter Dorsey was dead and the case died with him. But now I was interested. It was an anomaly and it had to be dealt with. Coupled with Kiz Rider's warning and oblique reference to 'these people,' I felt something stirring inside that had been absent for a long time. A small tug toward the darkness I one time knew so well.

8

I drove back into Hollywood and ate a late lunch at Musso's. A Ketel One martini for openers, followed by chicken pot pie, creamed spinach on the side. A good combination, but not good enough to make me forget about Lawton Cross and his situation. I asked for a second martini to help with that and tried to concentrate on other things.

I hadn't been back to Musso's since my retirement party and I missed the place. I had my head down and was reading and writing some notes when I heard a voice in the restaurant that I recognized. I looked up and saw Captain LeValley being led to a table with a man I didn't recognize. She was commander of the Hollywood Division, which was only a few blocks away. Three days after I'd left my badge in a desk drawer and walked out she called to ask me to reconsider. She almost convinced me but I said no. I told her to send in my papers and she did. She didn't come to my retirement party and we hadn't spoken since.

She didn't see me and sat with her back to me in a booth far enough away that I could not hear her conversation. I left by the back way without finishing the second martini. In the lot I paid the attendant and got in my car, a Mercedes Benz ML55 that I'd bought used from a guy moving to Florida. It had been the one big extravagance I allowed myself after retiring. In my mind the ML55 stood for Money Lost: $55,000, because that was what I paid for it. It was one of the fastest sport utility vehicles on the road. But that wasn't really why I bought it. The low mileage on it wasn't the reason either. I bought it because it was black and it blended in. Every fifth car in L.A. was a Mercedes, or so it seemed. And every fifth one of them was a black M-class SUV. I think maybe I knew where I was going long before I started the journey. Eight months before I would need it I'd bought an automobile that would serve me well as a private investigator. It had speed and comfort, it had dark smoked windows, and if you looked in your mirror and saw one of these behind you in L.A. it wouldn't cause a second thought.

The Mercedes took some getting used to. In terms of comfort as well as routine operation and maintenance. In fact, I had already run out of gas on the road twice. It was one of those little things that came with giving up the badge. For several years before my retirement I had been a detective third grade, a supervisory-level position that came with a take-home car. That car was a Ford Crown Victoria, the Police Interceptor model that rode like a tank, had vinyl wash-off seats, heavy-duty suspension and the expanded gas tank. I never needed gas when on the job. And the car was routinely refueled at the station by the guys from the motor pool. As a citizen I had to re-learn to watch the needle. Or else I found myself sitting on the side of the road.

From the center console I retrieved my cell phone and turned it on. I'd had little need for a cell phone but had kept the one I carried on the job. I don't know, maybe I thought somebody from the division would call and ask my advice on a case or something. For four months I kept it charged and turned it on every day. Nobody ever called. After the second time I ran out of gas I plugged it into the charger in the center console and left it there for the next time I would need roadside assistance.

Now I needed assistance but not of the roadside variety. I called information and got the number for the Federal Bureau of Investigation in Los Angeles. I called the number and asked for the supervisory agent in the bank squad. I figured the agent that had contacted Dorsey might have worked in the unit that handled bank robberies. It was the unit that most often dealt with currency numbers.

My call was transferred and picked up by someone who simply said, 'Nunez.'

'Agent Nunez?'

'Yes, what can I help you with?'

I knew that handling a supervising FBI agent would not be the same as handling the secretary of a movie mogul. I had to be as up-front as I could with Nunez.

'Yes, my name is Harry Bosch. I just retired from the LAPD after about thirty years and I—'

'Good for you,' he said curtly. 'What can I do for you?'

'Well, that's what I'm trying to tell you. About four years ago I was working a homicide case that was connected to a large cash robbery involving currency that had been recorded.'

'What case?'

'Well, you probably won't recognize it by case name but it was the murder of Angella Benton. The murder preceded the robbery, which took place on a movie set in Hollywood. It made a big splash. The bad guys got away with two million dollars. Eight hundred of the hundred-dollar bills had been recorded.'

'I remember it. But we did not work it. We had noth–'

'I know that. Like I told you, I worked the case.'

'Then go on, what can I do for you?'

'Several months into the case an agent from your office contacted the

LAPD to report an anomaly in the recorded numbers. She had received the list of serials because we had sent it all over.'

'An anomaly, what is that?'

'An anomaly is a deviation, something that doesn't—'

'I know what the word means. What anomaly are you talking about?'

'Oh, sorry. This agent called and said one of the numbers was a misprint or a couple of the numbers got inverted, something like that. But that's not what I'm calling about. She said she had a computer program that cross-referenced and cross-matched numbers from these sorts of cases. I think it was her own program, something that she worked up on her own. Does any of this ring a bell? Not the case but the agent. An agent who had this program. A female agent.'

'Why?'

'Well, because I have misplaced her name. Actually, I never got it because she spoke to one of the other investigators on the case. But I would like to speak to her, if I could.'

'Speak to her about what? You said you are retired.'

I knew it would come to this, and this is where I was weak. I had no station, no validity. You either had a badge that opened all doors or you didn't. I didn't.

'Some cases die hard, Agent Nunez. I'm still working it. Nobody else is, so I figured I'd take the shot. You know how it is.'

'No, actually, I don't. I'm not retired.'

A real hard-ass. He was silent after that and I found myself getting angry with this faceless man who was probably trying to balance a burdensome caseload with a lack of manpower and funding. L.A. was the bank robbery capital of the world. Three a day was the norm and the FBI had to respond to every one of them.

'Look, man,' I said. 'I don't want to waste your time. You can either help me or not. You either know who I am talking about or you don't.'

'Yeah, I know who you're talking about.'

But then he was silent. I tried one last angle. I had held it back because I wasn't sure I wanted it known in some circles what I was doing. But the visit from Kiz Rider sort of shot that down anyway.

'Look, you want a name, somebody you can check me out with? Call over to Hollywood detectives and ask for the lieutenant. Her name is Billets and she can vouch for me. She won't know anything about this though. As far as she knows, I'm swinging in a hammock.'

'All right, I'll do that. Why don't you call me back? Give me ten minutes.'

'Right. I will.'

I closed the phone and checked my watch. It was almost three. I started the Mercedes and drove down to Sunset and headed east. I turned on the radio but didn't like the fusion that was playing. I turned it back off. At the ten-minute mark I pulled to the curb in front of the Splendid Age Retirement Home. I picked up the phone to call Nunez back and it rang in my hand. I thought maybe Nunez had caller ID on his line and had gotten the number. But then I remembered I had been transferred to his line. I didn't think an ID record could jump with a transfer.

'Harry Bosch.'

'Harry, it's Jerry.'

Jerry Edgar. It was turning into old home week. First Kiz Rider and now Jerry Edgar.

'Jed, how you doing?'

'I'm fine, man. How's the retiring life?'

'It's very restful.'

'You don't sound like you're on the beach, Harry.'

He was right. The Splendid Age was just yards from the Hollywood Freeway and the din of gas-combustion machinery was ever present. Quentin McKinzie told me that they house the Splendid Age residents with hearing loss in the rooms on the west side because they are closer to the noise.

'I'm not a beach guy. What's up? Don't tell me that eight months after I'm gone you actually want to ask my advice on something?'

'Nah, it's not that. I just got a call from somebody who was checking you out.'

I was immediately embarrassed. My pride had led me to conclude that Edgar needed me on a case.

'Oh. Was it a bureau agent named Nunez?'

'Yeah, he didn't say what it was about, though. You starting a new career or something, Harry?'

'Thinking about it.'

'You ever get your private ticket?'

'Yeah, about six months ago, just in case. I stuck it in a drawer somewhere. What did you tell Nunez? I hope you said I was a man of high moral standing and courage.'

'Absolutely not. I gave him the straight dope. I said you could trust Harry Bosch about as far as you could throw him.'

I could hear the smile in his voice.

'Thanks, man. You're a pal.'

'I just thought you should know. You want to tell me what's going on?'

I was silent for a moment as I thought about this. I didn't want to tell Edgar what I was doing. Not that I didn't trust him. I did. But as a rule I operated under the belief that the fewer people who know your business the better.

'Not right now, Jed. I'm late for an appointment and have to get going. But I'll tell you what – you want to catch lunch one of these days? I'll tell you all about my exciting life as a pensioner.'

I sort of laughed as I said the last line and I think it worked. He agreed to lunch but said he'd have to call me back about it. I knew from experience it was difficult to schedule a lunch ahead of time when you were working homicide. What would happen was that he would call on the morning he had a lunch free. That was the way it worked. We said we'd stay in touch and ended the call. It was nice to know that he apparently wasn't carrying the same anger as Kiz Rider over my abrupt departure from our partnership and the department.

I called the bureau back and was put through to Nunez.

'You get a chance to make that call?'

'Yeah, but she wasn't there. I talked to your old partner.'

'Rider?'

'No, his name was Edgar.'

'Oh, yeah. Jerry. How is he doing?'

'I don't know. I didn't ask. I'm sure you did when he just called you.'

'Excuse me?'

He had nailed me.

'You can skip the bullshit, Bosch. Edgar told me he felt obligated to call you and let you know someone was checking you out. I said that was fine with me. I asked him for your number so that way I would know I was dealing with the real Harry Bosch. He gave it to me and when I tried to call a couple minutes ago it was busy. I figure you were talking to Edgar, so I don't appreciate your little dumb-guy dance.'

My embarrassment over being cornered turned to anger. Maybe it was the vodka in my stomach or the hammering reminder that I was an outsider now, but I was tired of dealing with this guy.

'Man, you are a great investigator,' I said into the phone. 'A brilliant deductive mind. Tell me, do you ever use it on cases or do you reserve it only for busting the chops of people who are just trying to get something done in the world?'

'I have to be careful about who I give information to. You understand that.'

'Yeah, I understand that. I also understand why law enforcement works about as well as the freeways in this town.'

'Hey, Bosch, don't go away mad. Just go away.'

I shook my head in frustration. I didn't know if I had blown it or if I was never going to get anything from him in the first place.

'So that's your little dance, huh? You call me on my act but you were acting the whole time, too. You never were going to give me the name, were you?'

He didn't answer.

'It's just a name, Nunez. No harm no foul.'

Still nothing from the agent.

'Well, I'll tell you what. You've got my name and number. And I think you know what agent I am talking about. So go to her and let her decide. Give her my name and number. I don't care what you think about me, Nunez. You owe it to your fellow agent to give it to her. Just like Edgar. He was obligated. So are you.'

That was it. That was my pitch. I waited in the silence, this time deciding not to speak again until Nunez did.

'Look, Bosch, I would tell her you were calling for her. I would have told her before I even talked to Edgar. But obligations only go so far. The agent you were asking about? She's not around anymore.'

'What do you mean not around? Where is she?'

Nunez said nothing. I sat up straight, my elbow hitting the wheel, drawing a blast from the horn. Something was in my memory, something about a female agent in the news. I couldn't quite get to it.

'Nunez, is she dead?'

'Bosch, I don't like this. This talking on the phone with somebody I've never met. Why don't you come in and maybe we can talk about this.'

'Maybe?'

'Don't worry, we'll talk. When can you come in?'

The dashboard clock said it was five after three. I looked at the front door of the retirement home.

'Four o'clock.'

'We'll be here.'

I closed the phone and sat there unmoving for a long moment, working at the memory. It was there, just out of reach.

I reopened the phone. I didn't have my phone book with me, and numbers I once knew by heart had washed away in the past eight months like they had been written in sand on the beach. I called information and got the number for the *Times* newsroom. I then was connected to Keisha Russell. She remembered me like I had never left the department. We'd had a good relationship. I fed a number of exclusives to her over the years and she returned the favor by helping me with clip searches and keeping stories in the paper when she could. The Angella Benton case had been one of the times she couldn't.

'Harry Bosch,' she said. 'How are you?'

I noticed that her Jamaican accent was now almost completely gone. I missed it. I wondered if that was intentional or just the product of living ten years in the so-called melting pot.

'I'm fine. You still on the beat?'

'Of course. Some things never change.'

She had once told me that the cop beat was an entry-level position in journalism but that she never wanted to leave it. She thought moving up to cover city hall or elections or almost anything else would be terminally boring compared with writing stories about life and death and crime and consequences. She was good and thorough and accurate. So much so she had been invited to my retirement party. It was a rarity for an outsider of any ilk, especially a journalist, to earn such an invitation.

'Unlike *you*, Harry Bosch. You, I thought, would always be there in Hollywood Division. Almost a year later now and I still can't believe it. You know, I called your number out of habit on a story a few months ago and a strange voice answered and I just had to hang up.'

'Who was it?'

'Perkins. They moved him over from autos.'

I hadn't kept up. I didn't know who had taken my slot. Perkins was good but not good enough. But I didn't tell Russell that.

'So what's up with you, mon?'

Every now and then she would turn on the accent and the patter. It was her way of making a transition, getting to the point.

'Sounds like you're busy.'

'A bit.'

'Then I won't bother you.'

'No, no, no. No bother. What can I do for you, Harry? You're not working a case are you? Have you gone private?'

'Nothing like that. I was just curious about something that's all. It can wait. I'll check you later, Keisha.'

'Harry, wait!'

'You sure?'

'I am not too busy for an old friend, you know? What are you curious about?'

'I was just wondering, remember a while back there was an FBI agent, a woman, who disappeared? I think it was in the Valley. She was last seen driving home from—'

'Martha Gessler.'

The name brought it all back. Now I remembered.

'Yeah, that's it. Whatever happened with her, do you know?'

'As far as I know she's still missing in action, presumed dead probably.'

'There hasn't been anything about her lately? I mean, any stories?'

'Nope, because I would've written them and I haven't written about her in, oh, two years at least.'

'Two years. Is that when it happened?'

'No, more like three. I think I did a one-year-later story. An update. That was the last time I wrote about her. But thanks for the reminder. It may be time for another look.'

'Hey, if you do that, hold off a few days, would you?'

'So you are working on something, Harry.'

'Sort of. I don't know if it's related to Martha Gessler or not. But give me till next week, okay?'

'No problem if you come clean and talk to me then.'

'Okay, give me a call. Meantime, could you pull the clips on her? I'd like to read what you wrote back then.'

I knew they still called it pulling clips even though it was all on computer now and actual newspaper clippings were a thing of the past.

'Sure, I can do that. You have a fax or an e-mail?'

I had neither.

'Maybe you can just mail them to me. Regular mail, I mean.'

I heard her laugh.

'Harry, you won't make it as a modern private detective like that. I bet all you have is a trench coat.'

'I've got a cell phone.'

'Well, that's a start then.'

I smiled and gave her my address. She said the clips would go out in the afternoon mail. She asked for my cell number so she could call me the following week and I gave her that, too.

Then I thanked her and closed the phone. I sat there for a moment considering things. I had taken an interest in the Martha Gessler case at the time. I didn't know her but my former wife had. They had worked together in the bureau's bank robbery unit many years before. Her disappearance had held in the news for several days, then the reports were more sporadic and then they just dropped off completely. I had forgotten about her until now.

I felt a burning in my chest and I knew it wasn't the midday martini backing up. I felt like I was closing in on something. Like when a child can't see something in the dark but is sure it is there just the same.

9

I got the instrument case out of the back of the Benz and carried it up the sidewalk to the double doors of the retirement home. I nodded to the woman behind the counter and walked by. She didn't stop me. She knew me by now. I went down the hallway to the right and opened the door to the music room. There was a piano and an organ at the front of the room and a small grouping of chairs lined up for watching performances, but I knew that those were few. Quentin McKinzie was sitting on a seat in the front row. He was slouched and his chin was down, his eyes closed. I gently nudged his shoulder and immediately his face and eyes came up.

'Sorry, I'm late, Sugar Ray.'

I think he liked that I called him by his stage name. He had been known professionally as Sugar Ray McK because when he played he would dodge and weave on the stage like Sugar Ray Robinson in the ring.

I pulled a chair out of the front row and brought it around so it faced him. I sat down and put the case on the ground. I flipped up the snaps and opened it, revealing the shining instrument held snug in its maroon velvet lining.

'This has got to be short today,' I said. 'I've got an appointment at four in Westwood.'

'Retired guys don't have appointments,' Sugar Ray said, his voice sounding like he grew up just down the street from Louis Armstrong. 'Retired guys have all the time in the world.'

'Well, I've got something working and I might . . . well, I'm going to try to keep our schedule but the next couple weeks might be tough. I'll call the desk and get a message to you if I can't make the next lesson.'

We had been meeting two afternoons a week for six months. I had first seen Sugar Ray play on a hospital ship in the South China Sea. He had been part of the Bob Hope entourage that came to entertain the wounded during Christmas time 1969. Many years later, in fact one of my last cases as a cop, I was working a homicide and came across a stolen saxophone with his name engraved inside the mouth. I tracked him to Splendid Age and returned it. But he was too old to play it anymore. His lungs no longer had the push.

Still, I had done the right thing. It was like returning a lost child to a parent. He invited me to Christmas dinner. We stayed in touch and after I pulled the pin I came back to him with a plan that would save his instrument from gathering dust.

Sugar Ray was a good teacher because he didn't know how to teach. He told me stories and told me how to love the instrument, how to draw from it the sounds of life. Any note I could sound could bring out a memory and a story. I knew I was never going to be any good at playing the sax but I came twice a week to spend an hour with him and hear his stories about jazz and feel the passion he still carried for his deathless art. Somehow it got inside me and came out in my own breath when I held the instrument to my mouth.

I lifted the saxophone out of the case and held it in position, ready to play. We always began each lesson with me trying to play 'Lullaby,' a song by George Cables that I had first heard on a Frank Morgan disc. It was a slow ballad and easier for me to play. But it was also a beautiful composition. It was sad and steadfast and uplifting all at the same time. The song wasn't even a minute and a half long but to me it said all that ever needed to be said about being alone in the world. Sometimes I believed that if I could learn to play this one song well, then that would be enough for me. I would not be wanting.

Today it felt like a funeral dirge. I thought about Martha Gessler the whole time I played. I remembered her picture in the paper and on the TV at eleven. I remembered my ex-wife talking about how they had been the only two females on the bank robbery squad at one time. They took a constant ration of abuse from the men until they proved themselves by working together and taking down a robber known as the Two Step Bandit because he always did a little dance as he left a bank with the loot.

As I played, Sugar Ray watched my finger work and nodded approvingly. Halfway through the ballad he closed his eyes and just listened, nodding his head with the beats. It was a high compliment. When I finished the piece he opened his eyes and smiled.

'Gettin' there,' he said.

I nodded.

'You still got to get the smoke out of your lungs. Get your capacity up.'

I nodded again. I hadn't had a cigarette in more than a year, but I had spent most of my life as a two-pack-a-day man and the damage was done. Sometimes putting air into the instrument was like pushing a boulder up a hill.

We talked and I played for another fifteen minutes, taking a hopeless shot at 'Soul Eyes,' the Coltrane standard, and then working the bridge of Sugar Ray's own signature song, 'The Sweet Spot.' It was a complicated riff but I had been working on it at home because I wanted to please the old man.

At the end of the abbreviated lesson I thanked Sugar Ray and asked if he needed anything.

'Just music,' he said.

He answered that way every time I asked. I put the instrument back into the case – he always insisted I keep it with me for practicing – and left him there in the music room.

As I was heading back down the hallway to the main entrance a woman named Melissa Royal was approaching from the other way. I smiled.

'Melissa.'

'Hi, Harry, how was the lesson?'

She was there to see her mother, an Alzheimer's victim who never knew who she was. We had met at the Christmas dinner and then had run into each other during our separate visits. She started timing her visits to her mother with my three o'clock lessons. She didn't tell me this but I knew. We had coffee a few times and then I asked her out to hear some jazz at the Catalina. She said she had fun but I knew she didn't know or care much about the music. She was just lonely and looking for someone. That was okay with me. We're all that way.

That was how it stood. Each of us waiting for the other to make the next move, though her showing up when she knew I was scheduled to be there was a move in some way. But seeing her now was a problem. I had to get rolling if I was going to make it to Westwood on time.

'Gettin' there,' I said. 'At least that's what my teacher tells me.'

She smiled.

'Great. Someday you're going to have to perform for us here.'

'Believe me, that day is a long way off.'

She nodded good-naturedly and waited. My turn now. She was in her early forties, divorced like me. She had light brown hair with lighter streaks in it that she told me she had added in the beauty shop. Her smile was the thing, though. It took over her whole face and was infectious. I could tell that being with her would mean working night and day to keep that smile going. And I didn't know if I could do it.

'How's your mother doing?'

'I'm about to go find out. Are you leaving? I thought maybe I could check in with her and we could get some coffee in the cafeteria.'

I put a pained look on my face and checked my watch.

'I can't. I have to be in Westwood at four.'

She nodded like she understood. But I could see in her eyes that she was taking it as a rejection.

'Well, don't let me hold you up. You'll probably be late as it is.'

'Yeah, I should go.'

But I didn't. I stood looking at her.

'What?' she finally asked.

'I don't know. I'm kind of involved in this case at the moment but I was trying to think of when we could get together.'

Suspicion entered her eyes and she gestured toward the saxophone case in my hand.

'You told me you were retired.'

'I am. I'm kind of working this on the side. Freelance, you could say. That's where I have to go now, to go talk to an investigator at the FBI.'

'Oh. Well, go. Be careful.'

'I will. So can we get together maybe one night next week or something?'

'Sure, Harry. I'd like that.'

'Okay, good. I want to, Melissa.'

I nodded and she nodded and then she made a move toward me and came up on her toes. She put one hand on my shoulder and kissed me on the cheek. Then she continued down the hallway. I turned and watched her go.

I walked out of that place wondering what I was doing. I was holding out hope of something to that woman that I knew deep down I could not deliver. It was a mistake that was born of good intentions but that would ultimately hurt her. As I got into the Mercedes I told myself I had to end it before it started. Next time I saw her I would have to tell her I was not the man she was looking for. I couldn't keep that smile on her face.

10

It was 4:15 by the time I got to the federal building in Westwood. As I was heading through the parking lot toward the security entrance my cell phone rang. It was Keisha Russell.

'Hey, Harry Bosch,' she said. 'Wanted to let you know, I printed out everything and put it in the mail. But I was wrong about something.'

'What was that?'

'There was an update on the case. It ran a couple months ago. I was on vacation. You stick around here long enough and they give you four weeks paid vacation. I took it all at once and went to London. While I was gone it was the third anniversary of Martha Gessler's disappearance. People were poaching on my beat right and left, I tell you. David Ferrell did an update. Nothing new, though. She's still in the wind.'

'In the wind? That suggests you – or the bureau – think she's still alive. Before, you said she was presumed dead.'

'Just an expression, mon. I don't think anybody's holding their breath for her, if you know what I mean.'

'Yeah. Did you put that update in the clips you're sending me?'

'It's all there. And you remember who sent it. Ferrell's a nice guy but I don't want you calling him if something you're doing breaks big.'

'Never happen, Keisha.'

'I know you are up to something. I did my homework on you.'

That made me pause as I was halfway across the building's front plaza. If she had called the bureau and spoken to Nunez, the agent wasn't going to be happy about me involving a nosy reporter.

'What do you mean?' I asked calmly. 'What did you do?'

'I did more than just check the clips. I called Sacramento. The state licensing board. I found out that you applied for and received a private investigator's license.'

'Yeah, so? Every cop who retires does that. It's part of the process of letting go of the badge. You think, *Oh, well, I'll just get a PI ticket and keep on catching the bad guys.* My ticket is in a drawer in my house, Keisha. I'm not in business and I'm not working for anybody.'

'Okay, Harry, okay.'

'Thanks for the clips. I've gotta go.'

'Bye, Harry.'

I closed the phone and smiled. I liked sparring with her. Ten years covering cops and she seemed no more cynical than the first day I talked to her. That was amazing for a journalist, even more so for a black journalist.

I looked up at the building. It was a concrete monolith that eclipsed the sun from the angle I had. I was thirty feet from the entrance. But I walked over to a row of benches to the right of the entranceway and sat down. I checked my watch and saw that I was very late for my appointment with Nunez. The trouble was I didn't know what I was walking into up there and that made me reluctant to go through the doors. The federals always had a way of putting you off balance, of making it clear that it was their world and you were only an invited visitor. I assumed that now without a badge I would be treated more like an uninvited visitor.

I opened the phone back up and called the general number for Parker Center, one of the few numbers I still remembered. I asked for Kiz Rider in the chief's office and was transferred. She picked up immediately.

'Kiz, it's me, Harry.'

'Hello, Harry.'

I tried to read something in her tone but she had flat-lined her response. I couldn't tell how much of the morning's anger and animosity remained.

'How are you doing? You feeling any . . . uh, better?'

'Did you get my message, Harry?'

'Message? No, what did it say?'

'I called your house a little while ago. I apologized. I shouldn't have let personal feelings get mixed in with the reason I had come out there. I'm sorry.'

'Hey, it's okay, Kiz. I apologize, too.'

'Really? For what?'

'I don't know. For the way I left, I guess. You and Edgar didn't deserve that. Especially you. I should have talked about it with you guys. That's what partners do. I guess I wasn't a very good partner at that moment.'

'Don't worry about it. That's what I said on the message. Water under the bridge. Let's just be friends now.'

'I'd like to. But . . . '

I waited for her to pick up the invitation.

'But what, Harry?'

'Well, I don't know how friendly you'll want to be after this because I've got to ask you a question and you're probably not going to like it.'

She groaned into the phone so loud that I had to hold it away from my ear.

'Harry, you're killing me. What is it?'

'I'm sitting outside the federal building in Westwood. I'm supposed to go in and see some guy named Nunez. A bureau man. And something's not feeling right about this. So I was wondering, are these the people you warned me were working the Angella Benton case? A guy named Nunez? Is it connected to Martha Gessler, the agent who disappeared a few years ago?'

There was a long silence on the phone. Too long.

'Kiz?'

'I'm here. Look, Harry, it's just like I told you at your house. I can't talk to you about the case. All I can tell you is what I *did* tell you. It is open and active and you should stay away from it.'

Now it was my turn not to respond. She was like a complete stranger. Less than a year earlier I would have gone into combat with her and trusted her to take my back while I took hers. Now I wasn't sure I could trust her to tell me if the sun was out, unless she cleared it first with the sixth-floor.

'Harry, you there?'

'Yeah, I'm here. I'm just kind of speechless, Kiz. I thought if there was somebody in the department who would always level with me, it was going to be you. That's all.'

'Look, Harry, have you done anything illegal while running this little freelance operation of yours?'

'No, but thanks for asking.'

'Then you have nothing to worry about with Nunez. Go in and see what they want. I don't know anything about Martha Gessler. And that's all I can tell you.'

'Okay, Kiz, thanks,' I said, putting my voice on a flat line now. 'You take care of yourself up there on the sixth floor. And I'll talk to you later.'

Before she could throw in the last word I closed the phone. I got up from the bench and headed to the building's entrance. Inside, I had to go through a metal detector, take off my shoes and spread my arms wide for a search with the magic wand. I could barely understand the man with the wand when he told me to raise my arms. He looked more like a terrorist than I did, but I didn't protest. You have to pick your battles. Finally, I got to the elevator and took it to the twelfth floor, which was really the thirteenth since the elevator didn't count the lobby. I stepped into a waiting area where there was a large glass and presumably bullet-proof window separating the public area from the bureau's inner sanctum. I said my name and who I wanted to see into a microphone and the woman on the other side of the glass told me to have a seat.

Instead I walked over to the window and looked down at the veterans cemetery across Wilshire Boulevard. I recalled that I was in the exact same position more than twelve years earlier when I first met the woman who would later become my wife, ex-wife and lasting infatuation.

I turned away from the window and sat down on the plastic couch. There was a magazine with Brenda Barstow's photo on its cover on a beat-up coffee table. Under the picture the caption read 'Brenda, America's Sweetheart.' I was reaching for the magazine when the door to the interior offices opened and a man with a white shirt and tie stepped out.

'Mr. Bosch?'

I stood up and nodded. He reached his right hand forward while he used the left to keep the security door from closing and locking.

'Ken Nunez, thanks for coming in.'

The handshake was quick and then Nunez turned and led the way inside. He said nothing as he walked. He wasn't what I had expected. On the phone he had sounded like a tired veteran who had seen it all twice. But he was young, just a year or two past thirty. And he didn't really walk down the hallway. He strode. He was a young go-getter, still out to prove something to himself and others. I wasn't sure which – old or new agent – I would have preferred.

He opened a door on the left and stepped back to allow me in. When I saw that the door opened outward and that there was a peephole I knew I was going into an interrogation room. And I knew then that this was not going to be a polite little meet-and-greet. More likely, I was about to get my ass kicked – federal style.

11

As I made the turn into the doorway I saw a square table positioned in the middle of the interrogation room. Sitting at the table, his back to me, was a man wearing a black shirt and jeans. He had close-cropped blond hair. As I entered I looked over his heavily muscled shoulder and saw he was reading an open investigative file. He closed it and looked up as I moved around the table to the other chair, opposite him.

It was Roy Lindell. He smiled at my reaction.

'Harry Bosch,' he said. 'Long time no see there, *podjo*.'

I paused for a moment but then pulled the chair out and sat down. Meantime, Nunez closed the door, leaving me alone with Lindell.

Roy Lindell was about forty now. The heavy muscles I remembered were still in place, pressing his shirt to its boundaries. He still had the Las Vegas tan and the bleached teeth to go with it. I had first met him on a case that took me to Vegas and right into the middle of an undercover FBI operation. Forced to work together, we had managed to put aside jurisdictional and agency animosities to a certain extent and we closed the case, the bureau taking all the credit of course. That had been six or seven years earlier. I ran into him on a case in L.A. once after that, but we never stayed in touch. Not because the bureau had thieved the credit on that first case. Because cops and feds just don't mix.

'Almost didn't recognize you without the ponytail, Roy.'

He stuck his big hand across the table and I slowly reached out and shook it. He had the confident demeanor that big men often have. And he had the rascal's smile that often comes with it. The ponytail line had been a crack. When I first met him – and before I knew his status as an undercover agent – I took the liberty of cutting the tail off the back of his head with a penknife.

'How you been? You told Nunez you're retired, huh? I hadn't heard about that.'

I nodded but otherwise didn't respond. This was his play. I wanted to let him make all the first moves.

'So what's it like being retired from the force?'

'I'm not complaining.'

'We ran a check. You're a licensed private eye now, huh?'

Big day in Sacramento.

'Yeah, I got a license. For the hell of it.'

I almost gave him the same story I gave Keisha Russell about it being part of the letting-go process but decided not to bother.

'Must be nice to have a little business, make your own hours, work for whoever you want to work for.'

That was enough for me as far as preliminaries went.

'Tell you what, let's not talk about me, Roy. Let's get to the point. What am I doing here?'

Lindell nodded as if to say fair enough.

'Well, what happened is that you called up and asked about an agent who used to work here, and doing that sort of raised a bunch of flags for us.'

'Martha Gessler.'

'That's right. Marty Gessler. So you knew who you were calling about when you told Nunez you didn't know who you were calling about?'

I shook my head.

'No. I put it together off his reaction. I remembered a female agent who went missing without a trace. Took me a while, then I remembered her name. What's the latest with her? Gone but not forgotten, I suppose.'

Lindell leaned forward and brought his massive arms together over the closed file. His wrists were as thick as the legs of the table. I remembered the struggle I had putting cuffs on them. Back in Vegas when he was under and I still didn't know it.

'Harry, I consider us to be like old friends. We haven't talked in a while but we've sort of been through a battle or two together so I don't want to jerk you around too bad here. But the way this is going to work is that I'm going to ask you the questions. That okay?'

'To a point.'

'We're talking about a missing agent here. A female.'

'And you're not fucking around.'

Paraphrasing the warning from Kiz Rider. Lindell didn't seem to appreciate it.

'Let's start with the reason you called,' he said. 'What are you up to?'

I waited for a long moment, trying to work out how I should handle this. I wasn't working for anybody other than myself. There was no confidentiality agreement. But I had always been resistant to bending over for the imperialist forces of the FBI. It had been part of the inbred LAPD culture. It wasn't going to change now. I respected Lindell – like he said, we had been in the trenches together and I knew he ultimately would deal fairly with me. But the agency he worked for liked to play with a marked deck. I had to be careful. I had to remember that.

'I told Nunez what I was doing when I called. I'm just checking out a case that I worked a few years back and that has always sort of stuck with me. There a problem with that?'

'Who's your client?'

'I don't have one. I got the private license right after I pulled the pin to keep my options open. But I started looking into this thing for myself.'

He didn't believe me. I could read it in his eyes.

'But this movie caper thing wasn't even your case.'

'It was. For about four days. Then I got pulled. But I still remember the girl. The victim. I didn't think anybody cared anymore so I started poking around.'

'So who told you to call the bureau?'

'Nobody.'

'You just thought it up on your own.'

'Not exactly. But you asked me who told me to call. Nobody told me to call. I did it all on my own, Roy. I learned about the call Gessler made to one of the detectives on the case. This was information that was new to me and I'm not sure it was ever followed up. It may have sort of fallen through the cracks. So I made a call to check it out. I didn't have a name at the time. I talked to Nunez and here I am.'

'How do you know that Gessler called one of the detectives on the case?'

It seemed to me that the answer would be obvious. It also would mean nothing to Lawton Cross if I told Lindell about something that he freely had told me and that was probably part of the official investigative file.

'I was told about your agent's call by Lawton Cross. He was one of the Robbery-Homicide guys who took the case from me once it blew up big. He told me his partner, Jack Dorsey, was the one who got the call from your agent.'

Lindell was writing the names down on a piece of paper he had pulled out of the file. I continued.

'This was well into the case when Gessler called him up. Months. Cross and Dorsey weren't even working it full-time at that point. And it didn't sound like they were too impressed with whatever it was Gessler had to say.'

'You talk to Dorsey about this?'

'No, Roy. Dorsey's dead. Killed in a robbery in a bar in Hollywood. Cross was hit, too. He's in a wheelchair with tubes in his arms and up his nose.'

'When was this?'

'About three years ago. It was big news.'

Lindell's eyes showed his mind working. He was doing the math, checking dates. It reminded me that I had to put together a timeline for the case. It was getting too unwieldy.

'What's the prevailing theory on Gessler? Dead or alive?'

Lindell looked down at the file on the table and shook his head.

'I can't answer that, Harry. You are not a cop, you have no standing. You're just some guy who can't let go of his badge and gun, out there running around like a loose cannon. I can't bring you into this.'

'Fine. Answer me one question then. And don't worry. It won't be giving anything away.'

He shrugged his shoulders. His answer would depend on the question.

'Was my call today the first connection you've come across between the movie money thing and Gessler?'

Lindell shrugged again and it seemed he was surprised by the question. It was as if he had been expecting something a little tougher.

'I'm not even saying there is a connection, you understand?' he said. 'But yes, this is the first time this came up. And that's exactly why I want you to back off and let us check it out. Just leave it to us, Harry.'

'Yeah, I've heard that before. I think it was the FBI who said it to me, too.'

Lindell nodded.

'Don't put us on a collision course. You'll regret it.'

Before I could come up with an answer he stood up. He reached into one of his pockets and pulled out a package of cigarettes and a yellow plastic lighter.

'I'm going to go down and have a smoke,' he said. 'That will give you a few minutes to think about things and remember anything else you forgot to tell me.'

I was about to take another verbal shot at him when I noticed that he was turning around and leaving without the file. It was left there on the table and I instinctively knew he was doing this on purpose. He wanted me to see the file.

I realized then that we were being taped. What he had been saying to me was for a record of some sort or perhaps a supervisor listening in. What he was allowing me to do was something different.

'Take your time,' I said. 'It's a lot to think about.'

'Fuckin' federal building. I have to go all the way downstairs.'

As he opened the door he looked back at me and gave me the wink. The moment the door was closed I slid the file across the table and opened it.

12

The file was marked with Martha Gessler's name on the tab. I took out my notebook and wrote that down at the top of a fresh page before opening the inch-thick file folder and seeing what Lindell had left me. I figured I had maybe fifteen minutes tops to look through the file.

On top of the documents stacked in the file was a single page with nothing on it but a phone number. I figured this was left specifically for me so I folded it and put it in my pocket. The rest of the file was a collection of investigative reports, most of which had Lindell's name and signature on them. It listed him as working for the OPR. I knew that was the Office of Professional Responsibility, the bureau's version of Internal Affairs.

The file contained the reports detailing the investigation into Special Agent Martha Gessler's disappearance without a trace on March 19, 2000. This date was immediately significant to me because I knew Angella Benton was murdered the night of May 16, 1999. This put Gessler's disappearance roughly ten months later, about the same time that Cross said the agent had called Dorsey about the currency number.

According to the investigative file, Gessler was working as a crime analyst, not a field agent, at the time of her disappearance. She had long since transferred from the bank robbery unit where she had known my wife and into a cyber unit. She worked Internet investigations and was developing computer programs for tracking criminal patterns. I assumed the program Cross told me about was something that came out of this assignment.

On the evening of March 19, 2000, Gessler left work in Westwood after a long day. Fellow agents remembered her being in the office until at least 8:30 p.m. But she apparently never made it to her home in Sherman Oaks. She was unmarried. Her disappearance was not discovered until the next day, when she did not show up for work and did not answer phone calls or pages. A fellow agent went to her home to check on her and discovered her missing. He found her home partially ransacked but later determined her two dogs, crazed with hunger and inattention, had spent the night tearing the place apart. I noticed in the incident report that the fellow agent who made this discovery happened to be Roy Lindell. I wasn't sure if this meant anything. Possibly as an agent assigned to the OPR he would be sent to check on a fellow agent's well-being. Nevertheless, I wrote his name under hers in my notebook.

Gessler's personal car, a 1998 Ford Taurus, was not found at the house. Eight days later it was located in a long-term parking lot at LAX. The key was left on top of one of the rear tires. The rear bumper showed an eighteen-inch surface scratch and a broken taillight, damages acquaintances of the agent said were new. Again, Lindell was listed in the reports as one of these acquaintances.

The trunk of the car was empty and the interior offered no immediate clues as to where Gessler was or what had happened. The briefcase containing her laptop computer that she was known to have left the office with was gone as well.

Forensic analysis of the entire car found no evidence of foul play. No record of Gessler taking any flight from LAX was ever found. Agents checked flights at Burbank, Long Beach, Ontario and Orange County airports and also found no flight with her name on the passenger list.

Gessler was known to carry an ATM card, two gas credit cards as well as American Express and Visa cards. On the night of her disappearance she used the Chevron card to buy gas and a Diet Coke at a station on Sepulveda Boulevard near the Getty Museum. The receipt indicated she purchased 12.4 gallons of midgrade unleaded gasoline at 8:53 p.m. Her car's tank held a maximum of 16 gallons.

The purchase was significant because it placed Gessler in the Sepulveda Pass – her normal route home from Westwood to Sherman Oaks – at a time that coordinated with her leaving the bureau offices in Westwood. The night-shift cashier at the Chevron also identified Gessler from a photo lineup as a regular customer who had bought gas on the night of March 19. Gessler was an attractive woman. He knew and remembered her. He had told her she didn't need to drink Diet Coke and she seemed pleased by the compliment.

This confirmed sighting was important for several reasons. First, if Gessler was going from Westwood to LAX, where her car was later found, it was unlikely that she would have traveled north into the Sepulveda Pass to buy gas. The airport was southwest of the bureau office. The service station was directly to the north.

The next significance was that Gessler's Chevron card was used a second time the same night at a Chevron service station off Highway 114 in the north county. The card was used at point of purchase to buy 29.1 gallons of gasoline, more than Gessler's and most other cars could hold. Highway 114 was the main route to the desert areas of the northeast county. It was also a major trucking route.

Last but not least in terms of significance was the fact that none of Gessler's credit cards were ever found or used again.

There was no summary or conclusion in the reports I scanned. This would be something the investigator— Lindell – would draw for himself and keep to himself. You don't write a report concluding that your fellow agent is dead. You don't say the obvious and you always speak about the missing agent in the present tense.

But it was clear to me from what I had read what the conclusion had to be. Sometime after Gessler pumped gas into her car in the Sepulveda Pass she was stopped and abducted and it didn't look like she was coming back. She had probably been rear-ended. She then pulled to the side of the road to check damage and possibly to exchange insurance information with the other driver.

What happened next was unknown. But she was likely abducted by force and her car was dumped at the LAX lot – a move that probably guaranteed it would not be located for several days, thereby allowing the trail to go cold and the memories of potential witnesses to fade.

The second gas purchase was the curiosity. Was it a mistake, a clue pointing to the direction of the agent's abductors? Or was it misdirection, an intentional move by the abductors to point the investigation the wrong way? And the amount of gasoline purchased raised a whole other question. What kind of vehicle were they looking for? A tow truck? A pickup? A moving van?

Bureau agents descended on the station but there were no exterior video cameras and no credible witnesses to the use of the credit card because it had been a pay-at-the-pump purchase. It was the last blip on the radar screen, but nothing more than that.

Nevertheless, an agent was still missing. There was no choice. The file contained the short summaries of three days of aerial searches over the desert of the northeast county. It was a needle-in-the-haystack operation but it had to be done. It proved fruitless.

Agents also spent several days on the likely routes that Gessler would have taken through the Sepulveda Pass on her way home. The Pass cut through the Santa Monica Mountains. While the south slope offered few choices besides the 405 Freeway and Sepulveda Boulevard, the northern slope offered a network of shortcuts pioneered over fifty years of rush hours. Agents traveled all of these roads looking for witnesses to an accident involving a blue Ford Taurus, an accident scene that might have seemed routine but was actually the abduction of a federal agent.

They got nothing.

The Sepulveda Pass had been the location of similar crimes in the past. The son of popular entertainer Bill Cosby had been robbed and murdered on the dark side of the road one night just a few years before. And over the last decade a handful of women had been abducted and raped, one of them stabbed to death, after pulling off the road when their vehicles were rear-ended or became disabled. These incidents were not thought to be the work of one person. But rather that the Pass, with its hillsides, dark, winding roads and anonymity, was a place that drew predators. Like lions keeping watch on a water hole, the human predators would not need to wait long in the Sepulveda Pass. The cut through the mountains was one of the busiest traffic corridors in the world.

It was possible Gessler was the victim of a random crime, the very thing she sought to categorize and make sense of in her job. She could have drawn a predator at the service station, maybe opening her purse too wide when she pulled out her credit card. Maybe drawing a tail for some other unknown reason. She was an attractive woman. If a service station attendant had noticed it and acted on it in a subtle way, a predator could have just as likely seen what he needed in her as well.

Still, the team of agents initially assigned to the case had doubts about Gessler falling into the profile of prior victims in the Pass. Gessler's car advertised no personal riches. And she would have been a formidable opponent. She was a highly trained federal agent after all. She was also tall, standing almost six feet tall and weighing a hundred and forty pounds. She worked out regularly at the L.A. Fitness Club on Sepulveda and had been taking Tai-Bo training for several years. Her charts at the club showed she had four percent body fat. She was mostly muscle and she knew how to use it.

Gessler was also known to wear her service weapon while off duty. On the night she disappeared she had been wearing black slacks and blazer with a white blouse. Her pistol, a Smith & Wesson 9mm, was holstered on her right hip. The service station attendant recalled seeing the weapon because Gessler was not wearing her blazer when she put gas in her car at the self-pump station. The blazer was later found on a hanger hooked above the rear driver's-side window in the Taurus.

All of this meant that when Gessler's car was rear-ended somewhere in the Pass that night, she got out of the car with a weapon clearly showing on her hip. She got out of that car a woman who was competent and confident in her physical skills. It was a combination that would have likely been a high deterrent to attack, that would seemingly convince any predator to find another victim.

So while the bureau never gave an inch on the possibility that Gessler was the randomly chosen victim of a crime, Lindell headed a parallel investigation into the possibility that Gessler had been specifically targeted because of her job as an FBI agent.

The reports on this branch of the investigation accounted for more than half of the documents in the file in front of me. Though I could tell that I did not have the complete investigative file, it was clear that agents on the case left no stone uncovered in seeking a possible link to Gessler's disappearance. Cases ranging back to Gessler's first years in the Los Angeles field office were examined for potential links to the investigation. Partners and colleagues from all her years in the bureau were questioned about potential enemies and threats she might have received. Among these reports was a summary of an interview with former agent Eleanor Wish, my former wife, conducted in Las Vegas. She had not spoken with Gessler in nearly ten years before the disappearance. She had no recollection of any threats or anything else that might help in the investigation.

Every criminal Gessler ever put in jail or testified against was run down and checked. Most were cleared through alibis. None surfaced as a prime suspect.

According to the reports, Gessler had become the go-to agent in the L.A. field office for any and all requests for computer-related searches and investigations. It was to be expected in a giant bureaucracy like the FBI. Most requests by L.A. agents for computer-based expertise would be shipped to bureau offices in Washington and Quantico, sometimes taking days before being approved and then weeks before any results were shipped back. But Gessler was part of a growing breed of agents with high computer skills who liked to do things for herself. The special agent in charge of the L.A. office became aware of this and, consequently, Gessler was taken off the street, where she had worked for several years in the bank robbery unit. She was placed in a newly formed computer unit, where she handled requests from street agents while developing her own computer programs.

This meant Gessler had her finger in a lot of investigative pies at the time she disappeared. I checked my watch and quickly skimmed through dozens of reports detailing work she had done on different cases in just the month before her disappearance. Lindell and other agents working for him backtracked on these jobs, looking for anything that was a clue to why Gessler had disappeared. The closest it appeared they came to finding something was when they reviewed Gessler's work on an investigation of an escort service that advertised women for hire on a website. Gessler's work was part of the organized crime unit's investigation into the eastern mob's ties to prostitution in Los Angeles.

According to what I read, Gessler was able to find Internet connections between websites advertising women in more than a dozen cities. Women were being moved from city to city and client to client. Money generated by the escort services flowed to Florida and then to New York. Seven weeks before Gessler disappeared a grand jury indicted nine men under the federal Racketeering Influenced and Corrupt Organization Act. Exactly one week before her disappearance, Gessler testified about her part in the investigation during a pretrial hearing in the case. Her testimony was described as effective and it was assumed she would testify when the case went to trial. She was not, however, a key witness. Her testimony was seemingly part of the linkage between the websites and the defendants. The key witness was one of the members of the ring who had cut a deal with prosecutors to escape a stiff sentence.

The possibility that Gessler was targeted because she was a witness was a long shot but it seemed to be the best thing going. Lindell worked it hard, judging by the number of reports and the details they contained. But apparently nothing came of it. The last report in the file pertaining to the RICO case described this branch of the investigation as 'open and active but without substantive leads at this time.' I recognized it as bureau-speak, meaning this path of investigation had hit a dead end.

I closed the file and checked my watch again. Lindell had been gone seventeen minutes. There was nothing in the file about Gessler filing a report or notifying a supervisor or colleague that she had run a computer cross-reference check on the currency numbers contained on the flier put out by Cross and Dorsey. Nothing that said she had gotten a hit and had called the LAPD to report that one of the numbers on the currency report was bad.

After putting away my notebook I stood up and stretched my back and paced a little bit in the small room. I checked the door and found it unlocked. That was good. They weren't holding me like a suspect. At least, not yet. After a few more minutes I got tired of waiting and stepped out into the hallway. I looked both ways and saw no one, not even Nunez. I went back into the room and picked up the file and then started walking out the way I had come in. I got all the way to the front waiting room without anyone stopping me or asking where I was going. I nodded to the receptionist through the glass and took the elevator down.

13

Roy Lindell was sitting on the same bench I had used before entering the building. There were three cigarettes crushed on the pavement between his feet. A fourth was between his fingers.

'You took your sweet-ass time,' he said.

I sat down next to him and put the file between us.

'Putting you in the OPR – isn't that like putting the fox in charge of the henhouse?'

I was thinking about the case I had met him on six years before. I'd had no clue he was law enforcement. This was mostly because he was running a strip club in Vegas and bedding the strippers two and three at a time. His front was so convincing that even after I learned he was an undercover I entertained the idea that he had crossed over. Eventually and completely, I was convinced otherwise.

'Once a smart-ass always a smart-ass, eh, Bosch?'

'Something like that, I guess. So who was listening to our little conversation up there?'

'I was told to tape it. That the tape would be forwarded.'

'To who?'

He didn't say anything. It was like he was still deciding something.

'Come on, Roy, you want to give me a clue about what's going on? I looked through your file. It's pretty thin, not much that helps me.'

'That's just the highlights – stuff I kept in a backup file. The real file used to fill a whole drawer.'

'Used to?'

Lindell looked around as if realizing for the first time he was sitting outside a building that housed more agents and spooks than anywhere west of Chicago. He looked down at the file lying there between us for the world to see.

'I don't like sitting out here. Where's your car? Let's take a ride.'

We walked out into the parking lot without talking. But seeing Lindell acting the way he was unnerved me and made me think again about Kiz Rider's warning about some sort of higher authority being involved in the case. Once we got inside the Benz, I put the file on the backseat and keyed the engine. I asked him where he wanted to go.

'I don't care, just drive.'

I went west on Wilshire, thinking I'd cut over to San Vicente and cruise through Brentwood. It would be a nice drive on a street lined with trees and joggers, even if the conversation wasn't nice.

'Were you being square on the tape?' Lindell asked. 'That's your real story about not working on this for anybody?'

'Yeah, that's the square story.'

'Well, you better watch your ass, *podjo.* There are larger forces at work here. People that don't—'

'Fuck around. Yeah, I know. I've been told that but nobody wants to tell me who this higher authority is and why this connects to Gessler or means anything to the movie money heist four years after it went down.'

'Well, I can't tell you because I don't know. All I know is that after you called today I made a few calls myself and the next thing I know the walls came down on me. Hard, man, they came down hard.'

'This came out of Washington?'

'No, right here.'

'Who, Roy? There's no use in us driving around and talking if you're not talking. What do we have here? Organized Crime? I read the report on Gessler's RICO case. It looked like the only thing you had going on it.'

Lindell laughed as though I had suggested something absurd.

'Organized crime. Shit, I wish this was just an OC deal.'

I pulled to the side of San Vicente. We were a couple blocks from where Marilyn Monroe had OD'd, one of the city's lasting scandals and mysteries.

'Then what, Roy? I'm tired of talking to myself.'

Lindell nodded and then looked over at me.

'Homeland security, baby.'

'What do you mean? Somebody thinks there's a terrorist connection to this?'

'I don't know what they think. I wasn't made privy. All I know is that I was told to shut you down, tape it and send it down to the ninth floor.'

'The ninth floor . . . '

I said it just to be saying something. I was trying to think. My mind scanned quickly through the images of the case, Angella Benton on the tile, the gunman waving weapons and firing, the impact of one of my shots catching one of them in the body and knocking him – at least I think it was a him – backward into the van. Nothing seemed to fit with what Lindell was telling me.

'The ninth is where they put the REACT squad,' Lindell said, pulling me out of the reverie. 'They're heavy hitters, Bosch. You walk out in front of them in the street and they won't stop. They won't even tap the brakes.'

'What's REACT?'

I knew it had to be another federal acronym. All law enforcement agencies are good for putting together acronyms. But the feds are the best at it.

'Regional Response . . . no, it's Rapid Enforcement Against something Terrorism. I forget the whole thing – oh, I got it, Rapid Response Enforcement And Counterterrorism. That's it.'

'That one must've come straight out of the director's office in D.C. That took some thought.'

'Funny. Basically, it's a multi-agency gang bang. You've got us, Secret Service, DEA, everybody.'

I figured that last 'everybody' was a catchall for the agencies that didn't like their initials bandied about. NSA, CIA, DIA and so on through the federal alphabet.

A man on a bike rode by the Benz and slapped the side view mirror hard, making Lindell jump. The biker kept going, keeping his gloved hand up and giving me the finger. I realized I had pulled over in the bike lane and pulled the Benz back out onto the street.

'These fucking bikers think they own the road,' Lindell said. 'Pull up next to him and I'll give *him* a whack.'

Ignoring the request, I sped past the biker, giving him a wide berth.

'I don't get it, Roy. What does the ninth floor have to do with my case?'

'First of all, it's not your case anymore. Secondly, I don't know. They ask me the questions. I don't get to ask them.'

'When did they start asking?'

'Today. You call up and ask about Marty Gessler and tell Nunez it has something to do with the movie money case. He comes to me and I tell him to have you come in. Meantime, I start doing some checking. Turns out, we've got the movie money caper listed on our computer. With a REACT flag on it. So I call down to the ninth and say, 'What's up, fellas?' and two seconds later I get crapped on pretty good.'

'You were told to find out what I know, then shut me down and send me on my way. Oh, and to tape it so they could listen and make sure you were a good little agent and did what you were told to do.'

'Yeah, something like that.'

'So why'd you let me read the file? And take it? Why are we driving around talking?'

Lindell took his time before responding. We had made the curve onto Ocean Boulevard in Santa Monica. I pulled off the road again next to the cliffs that look down to the beach and the Pacific. The horizon was blurred white by the marine layer. The Ferris wheel on the Pacific Park pier stood still, and without its neon blazing.

'I did it because Marty Gessler was a friend of mine.'

'Yeah, I could sort of tell from the file. Close friends?'

My meaning was obvious.

'Close,' he said.

'Wasn't that sort of a conflict, you leading the case?'

'Let's just say my relationship with her was not known until we were down the road a ways on the investigation. I then cashed in every chip I had to stay on it. Not that it did a hell of a lot of good. Here we are three-plus years later and I still have no idea what happened to her. Then you call up and tell me something that was brand-fucking-new to me.'

'So you were being square. There was no record of her talking to Dorsey about the currency number?'

'Nothing we found. But she kept a lot of stuff on her computer and that's gone, man. There had to be stuff she hadn't backed up on the office box. You know, the rule is back everything up every night before going home, but nobody does that. Nobody has the time.'

I nodded and thought about things. I was gathering a lot of information but had little time to process it. I tried to think about what else I needed to ask Lindell while I was with him.

'I'm still not tracking something,' I finally said. 'Why was it one way up in the interrogation room and another way out here? Why are you talking to me, Roy? Why let me see the file?'

'REACT is a BAM squad, Bosch. By Any Means. There are no rules with these guys. The rules went out the window September eleventh, two thousand one. The world changed, so did the bureau. The country sat back and let it happen. They were watching the war over there in Afghanistan when they were changing all the rules here. Homeland security is what it's all about now and everything else can take a back-fucking-seat. Including Marty Gessler. You think the ninth floor took over this case because an agent is missing? They couldn't care less. There is something else and whether or not they find out what happened to her doesn't matter. To them, that is. It's not the same for me.'

Lindell stared straight ahead as he spoke. I understood a little better what was happening now. The bureau told him to cease and desist. It could keep him in check but I was a free agent. Lindell would help me when and if he could.

'So you've got no idea what their interest is in this case.'

'Not a clue.'

'But you want me to keep going.'

'If you ever repeat it, I'll deny it. But the answer is yes. I want to be your client, *podjo*.'

I put the Benz in drive and pulled back onto the roadway. I headed back toward Westwood.

'I can't pay you, of course,' Lindell said. 'And I probably can't contact you after today, either.'

'Tell you what. Stop calling me *podjo* and we'll call it even.'

Lindell nodded as though I had been serious and to say that he had agreed to the deal. We drove in silence while I dropped down the California Incline to the coast highway and took it up to Santa Monica Canyon and then back up to San Vicente.

'So what did you think about what you read up there?' Lindell finally asked.

'Looked like you made all the right moves to me. What about the gas station guy who saw her that night? He checked out?'

'Yeah, we came down on him six ways till Sunday. He was clean. The place was busy and he was there till midnight. We have him on the security video. And he never left the booth after she came and went. His alibi for after midnight checked out, too.'

'Anything else from the video? I didn't see anything in the file.'

'Nah, the video was worthless. Other than the fact it shows her and it was the last time she was ever seen.'

He looked out the window. Three years later and Lindell was still hooked in deeply on this one. I had to remember that. I had to filter everything he said and did through that prism.

'What are the chances of me getting a look at the whole investigative file?'

'I'd say somewhere between zero and none.'

'The ninth floor?'

He nodded.

'They came up and popped the drawer out and took it. I won't see that stuff again. I probably won't even get the goddamn drawer back.'

'Why didn't they put the freeze on me? Why you?'

'Because I knew you. But mostly because you're not supposed to even know about them.'

I nodded as I turned onto Wilshire, the federal building in sight up ahead.

'Look, Roy, I don't know if the two things are connected, know what I mean? I'm talking about Martha Gessler and the thing in Hollywood. Angella Benton. Martha made a call on it but it doesn't mean that they are connected. I've got other things I'll be chasing down. This is just one of them. Okay?'

He looked out the window again and mumbled something I couldn't hear.

'What?'

'I said nobody ever called her Martha until she disappeared. Then it was in the papers and on TV that way. She hated that name, Martha.'

I just nodded because there was nothing else to do. I turned into the federal parking lot and drove up to the plaza to drop him off.

'That phone number in the file, it's okay to call you on that?'

'Yeah, anytime. Make sure your own phones are safe before you do.'

I thought about that until I brought the Benz to a stop at the curb in front of the plaza. Lindell looked out the window and surveyed the plaza as if he was judging whether it was safe to get out.

'You get back to Vegas much?' I asked him.

He answered without looking back at me. He kept his eyes on the plaza and the windows of the building looming above.

'Whenever I get the chance. Have to go in disguise. A lot of people over there don't like me.'

'I can imagine.'

His undercover work coupled with my team's homicide investigation had toppled a major underworld figure and most of his minions.

'I saw your wife over there about a month ago,' he said. 'Playing cards. I think it was at the Bellagio. She had a nice stack of chips in front of her.'

He knew Eleanor Wish from that first case in Vegas. That was when and where I had married her.

'Ex-wife,' I said. 'But that wasn't why I was asking.'

'Sure, I know.'

Seemingly satisfied with the view he opened the door and got out. He looked back in at me and waited for me to say something. I nodded.

'I'll take your case, Roy.'

He nodded back.

'Then call me anytime. And watch yourself out there, *podjo*.'

He gave me the rogue's got-you-last smile and closed the door before I could say anything.

14

Around the detective squad rooms of the LAPD's numerous stations the state of Idaho is called Blue Heaven. It's the goal line, the final destination for a good number of the detectives who go the distance, put in their twenty-five years and then cash out. I hear there are whole neighborhoods up there full of ex-cops from L.A. living side by side by side. Realtors from Coeur d'Alene and Sandpoint run business card-size ads in the police union newsletter. In every issue.

Of course some cops turn in the badge and set out for Nevada to bake in the desert and pick up part-time work in the casinos. Some disappear into northern California – there are more retired cops in the backwoods of Humboldt County than there are marijuana growers, only the growers don't know it. And some head south to Mexico, where there are still spots where an air-conditioned ranch house with an ocean view is affordable on an LAPD pension.

The point is, few stick around. They spend their adult lives trying to make sense of this place, trying to bring a small measure of order to it, and then can't stand to stay here once their job is done. The work does that to you. It robs you of the ability to enjoy your accomplishment. There is no reward for making it through.

One of the few men I knew who turned in the badge but not the city was named Burnett Biggar. He gave the city its twenty-five years – the last half of it in South Bureau homicide – and then retired to open up a small business with his son near the airport. Biggar & Biggar Professional Security was on Sepulveda near La Tijera. The building was nondescript, the offices unpretentious. Biggar's business was primarily geared toward providing security systems and patrols to the warehouse industries around the airport. The last time I had spoken to him – which was probably two years earlier – he had told me he had more than fifty employees and business was going good.

But out of the other side of his mouth he confided that he missed what he called the real work. The vital work, the work that made a difference. Protecting a warehouse full of blue jeans made in Taiwan could be profitable. But it didn't even begin to touch what you got out of putting a stone killer on the floor and the cuffs on his wrists. It wasn't even close, and that was what Biggar missed. It was because of that I thought I could approach him for help with what I wanted to do for Lawton Cross.

There was a small waiting room with a coffee machine but I wasn't there that long. Burnett Biggar came down a hallway and invited me back to his office. As befitting his name, he was a large man. I had to follow him down the hallway rather than walk next to him. His head was shaved, which was a new look for him as far as I knew.

'So Big, I see you traded the Julius for the Jordan, huh?'

He rubbed a hand over his polished scalp.

'Had to do it, Harry. It's the style. And I'm getting gray.'

'Aren't we all.'

He led me into his office. It wasn't small and it wasn't big. It was basic, with wood paneling and framed commendations, news clips and photos from his days with the department. It was probably all very impressive to the clients.

Biggar swung around behind a cluttered desk and pointed me to a chair in front of it. As I sat down I noticed a framed slogan on the wall behind him. It said 'Biggar & Biggar is getting Better & Better.'

Biggar leaned forward and folded his arms on his desk.

'So, Harry Bosch, I don't think I was expecting to see you maybe ever again. It's funny seeing you in that chair.'

'Funny seeing you, too. I don't think I was expecting it either.'

'You come here for a job? I heard you quit last year. You were the last guy I ever thought about quitting.'

'Nobody goes the distance, Big. And I appreciate the offer but I already have a job. I'm just looking for a little help.'

Biggar smiled, the skin pulling tight around his eyes. He was intrigued. He knew I wasn't ever going to be the corporate or industrial security type.

'I never heard you ask for help on a goddamn thing. What do you need?'

'I need a setup. Electronic surveillance. One room, nobody can know the camera is there.'

'How big's the room?'

'Like a bedroom. Maybe fifteen by fifteen.'

'Ah, man, Harry, don't go down that road. You start that sort of snooping and you'll lose sight of yourself. Come work for me. I can find some—'

'No, it's nothing like that. It's actually an offshoot of a homicide I'm working. The guy's in a wheelchair. He sits and watches TV all day. I just want to be able to make sure he's okay, you know? There's something going on with the wife. At least I think so.'

'You mean like abuse?'

'Maybe. I don't know. Something.'

'Does the guy know you're going to do this?'

'No.'

'But you've got access to the room?'

'Pretty much. Think you can help me out?'

'Well, we got cameras. But you have to understand most of our work is industrial application. Heavy-duty stuff. Sounds to me like all you need is a nanny cam, something that you can just pick up at Radio Shack.'

I shook my head.

'I don't want to be too obvious about it. The guy was a cop.'

Biggar nodded, digested it quickly and stood up.

'Well, come on back to the tech room and take a look at what we've got. Andre's back there and he can fix you up.'

He led me back into the hallway and toward the back of the building. We entered the tech room, which was about the size of a double garage and was crowded with workbenches and shelves of all manner of electronics equipment. There were three men gathered around one of the workbenches. They were looking at the screen of a small television. A grainy black-and-white surveillance tape was playing. I recognized one of the men, the largest, as Andre Biggar, Burnett's son. I had never met him but I knew it was him by his size and resemblance to Burnett. Right down to the shaved scalp.

Introductions were made and Andre explained that he was reviewing a tape showing a burglary of a client's warehouse. His father explained what I was looking for and the son led me to another workbench, where he could display and review equipment. He showed me cameras housed in a vase, a lamp, a picture frame and finally a clock. Thinking about how Lawton Cross had complained about not being able to see the time on his television, I stopped Andre right there.

'This will do. How does it work?'

It was a round clock about ten inches across.

'This is a classroom clock. You want to put this on the wall of a bedroom? It will stick out like tits on a—'

'Andre,' his father said.

'It's not being used as a bedroom,' I said. 'It's like a TV room. And the subject told me he can't see the time on the corner of the screen on CNN. So this will make sense when I bring it in.'

Andre nodded.

'Okay. You want sound? Color?'

'Sound, yes. Color would be good but not necessary.'

'All right. Are you going to transmit, or you want to go self-contained?'

I looked at him blankly and he knew I didn't understand.

'I build these two ways. One is you have a camera in the clock and you transmit picture and sound to a receiver that records it on video. You would have to find a secure place for the recorder within about a hundred feet to be sure. Are you going to be outside the house in a van or something?'

'I wasn't planning on it.'

'Okay, the second option is to go digital and put everything in the camera and record internally to a digital tape or memory card. The drawback is capacity. With a digital tape you get about two hours real time, then you have to change it out. With a card you get even less.'

'That won't work. I was only planning to check on it every few days.'

I started thinking of how I would be able to hide the receiver inside the house. Maybe the garage. I could pretend I was going to the garage to throw something away and I could hide the receiver somewhere Danny Cross wouldn't see it.

'Well, we can slow the recording down if we need to.'

'How?'

'A number of different ways. First off we put the camera on a clock. Turn it off, say, midnight to eight. We can also stagger the FPS and lengthen—'

'FPS?'

'The recorded frames per second. It makes the image jump, though.'

'What about sound? Does that jump, too?'

'No, sound is separate. You'd get full sound.'

I nodded but wasn't sure I wanted to lose any of the visual recording.

'We can also put it on a motion sensor. This guy you say is in a wheelchair, does he move around a lot?'

'No, he can't. He's paralyzed. Most of the time I think he just sits there staring at the TV.'

'Any pets?'

'I don't think so.'

'So the only time there is real movement in the room is when the caregiver comes in, and that's who you want to watch. Am I right?'

'Right.'

'No problem then. This will work. We put a motion sensor on it and a two-gig memory card and you'll probably stretch it out a couple days.'

'That'll work.'

I nodded and looked at Burnett. I was impressed with his son. Andre looked like he should be out breaking quarterbacks in half. But he had found a specialty in life dealing with circuits and microprocessors. I could see the pride in Burnett's eyes.

'Give me fifteen minutes to put it together and then I'll come show you how to install it and how to switch out the memory card.'

'Sounds good.'

I sat with Burnett in his office and we talked about the department and a couple of the cases that we had worked together. One case had involved a hired killer who had murdered both the intended target in South L.A. and then his employer in Hollywood when the employer failed to pay the second half of the agreed-upon fee. We had worked it together for a month, my team and Biggar and his partner, who was named Miles Manley. We broke it when Big and Manley, as the pair were called, came up with a witness in the target victim's neighborhood who remembered seeing a white man on the day of the shooting and could describe his car, a black Corvette with red leather interior. The car matched the vehicle used by the second victim's next-door neighbor. He confessed after a lengthy interrogation conducted alternately by Biggar and me.

'It's always something small like that,' Biggar said while leaning back behind his desk. 'That's what I loved best about it. Not knowing where that little break was going to come from.'

'I know what you mean.'

'So you miss it?'

'Yeah. But I'll get it back. I'm starting to now.'

'You mean the feeling, not the job.'

'Right. How about you, you still missing it?'

'I'm making more money than I need here but, yeah, I miss the juice. The job gave me the juice and I don't get it shuffling rent-a-cops around and setting up cameras. Be careful what you do, Harry. You might end up successful like me and then you sit around remembering the old days, thinking they were a lot better than they were.'

'I'll be careful, Big.'

Biggar nodded, pleased that he had dispensed his dose of advice for the day.

'You don't have to tell me if you don't want to, Harry, but I'm guessing this guy in the chair is Lawton Cross, huh?'

I hesitated but decided it didn't matter.

'Yeah, it's him. I'm working something else and it crossed his path. I went to see him and he said some stuff. I just want to make sure. You know.'

'Good luck with it. I remember his wife, saw her a couple times at things. She was a nice lady.'

I nodded. I knew what he was saying, that he hoped Cross wasn't being victimized by his wife.

'People can change,' I said. 'I'm going to find out.'

Andre Biggar came in a few minutes later carrying a toolbox, a laptop computer and the camera clock in a box. He took me to school on electronic surveillance. The clock was rigged and ready. All I needed to do was mount it on a wall and plug it in. When I adjusted the time, I would activate the surveillance by pushing the dial all the way in. To switch out the memory card I just had to remove the backing of the clock and pop the card out of the camera. Easy.

'Okay, so once I take the card out, how do I look at what I've got?'

Andre nodded and showed me how to plug the memory card into the side of the laptop computer. He then went through the keyboard commands that would bring up the surveillance recording on the computer's screen.

'It's simple. Just take care of the equipment and bring it all back. We've got a lot of bread invested in it.'

I didn't want to tell him that it wasn't simple enough for me. I seized on the financial side of the equation as a way of avoiding revealing my technical shortcomings.

'Tell you what,' I said. 'I think I'll leave your laptop here and just come back with the memory card when I want to look at it. I don't want to risk all your equipment. I like to travel light, anyway.'

'Whatever suits you. But the beauty of this setup is the immediacy. You can pull the card and watch it in your car right outside the guy's house if you want. Why come all the way back here?'

'I don't think there's that kind of urgency. I'll leave the laptop and bring you back the card, okay?'

'Whatever.'

Andre put the clock back in its cushioned box, then shook my hand and left the office, taking the laptop with him but leaving me the toolbox along with the clock. I looked at Burnett. It was time to go.

'He looks like he's more than helping you.'

'Andre's the heart of this place.'

He gestured toward the wall of framed memorabilia.

'I bring the clients in, impress them, sign them up. Andre's the one who gets it done. He figures out the needs and gets it done.'

I nodded and stood up.

'You want to charge me something for this?' I said, holding up the box with the clock in it.

Biggar smiled.

'Not if you bring it back.'

Then his face turned serious.

'It's the least I can do for Lawton Cross.'

'Yeah,' I said, knowing the feeling.

We shook hands and I went out, carrying the clock and the toolbox, hoping the hidden camera would be the piece of equipment that would show me the world wasn't as bad as I thought it could be.

15

From Biggar & Biggar I drove back to the Valley, taking the Sepulveda Pass and catching the first brutal wave of rush hour. It took me almost an hour just to get to Mulholland Drive. At that point I jumped off the freeway and drove west along the crest of the mountains. I watched the sun drop behind Malibu and leave a burning sky in its trail. At the low angles the sun often reflected off the smog caught in the bowl of the Valley and turned it brilliant shades of orange and pink and purple. It was like some sort of reward for putting up with having to breathe the poisoned air every day. This evening it was mostly a smooth orange color with wisps of white mixed in. It was what my ex-wife used to call a Creamsicle sky when she watched sunsets off the back deck of the house. She had a descriptive label for each one and that always made me smile.

The memory of her on the deck seemed like such a long time ago and such a different part of my life. I thought about what Roy Lindell had said about seeing her in Las Vegas. He knew I had been asking about her even though I told him I hadn't. If not a day then at least not a week went by that I didn't think about going out there, finding her and asking for another chance. A chance of making a go of it on her terms. I had no job holding me to L.A. anymore. I could go where I wanted. This time I could go to her and we could live there together in the city of sin. She could still be free to find what she needed on the blue-felt poker tables of the city's casinos. And at the end of each day she could come home to me. I could do whatever came up. There would always be something in Vegas for a person with my skills.

One time I had packed a box, put it in the back of the Benz and had gotten as far as Riverside before the familiar fears started rising in my chest and I pulled off the freeway. I ate a hamburger at an In-N-Out and then headed back home. I didn't bother unpacking the box when I got there. I put it on the floor in the bedroom and took out the clothes I had packed as I needed them over the next two weeks. The empty box was still there on the floor, ready for the next time I wanted to pack it and make that drive.

The fear. It was always there. Fear of rejection, fear of unrequited hope and love, fear of feelings still below the surface in me. It was all mixed in the blender and poured smooth as a milkshake into my cup until it was filled to the very edge. So full that if I were to move even a step it would spill over the sides. Therefore I couldn't move. I stood paralyzed. I stayed home and lived out of a box.

I'm a believer in the single-bullet theory. You can fall in love and make love many times but there is only one bullet with your name etched on the side. And if you are lucky enough to be shot with that bullet then the wound never heals.

Roy Lindell might have had Martha Gessler's name on a bullet. I don't know. What I do know is that Eleanor Wish had been my bullet. She had pierced me through and through. There were other women before and other women since but the wound she left was always there. It would not heal right. I was still bleeding and I knew I would always bleed for her. That was just the way it had to be. There is no end of things in the heart.

16

On the way into Woodland Hills I made a quick stop at a Vendome Liquors and then headed to the house on Melba Avenue. I didn't call ahead. With Lawton Cross I knew the chances were always good he'd be at home.

Danielle Cross answered the door after three knocks, and her already strained face took on a deeper scowl when she saw it was me.

'He's sleeping,' she said, holding her body tightly in the door's opening. 'He's still recovering from yesterday.'

'Then wake him up, Danny, because I need to talk to him.'

'Look, you can't just barge in here. You're not a cop anymore. You have no right.'

'Do you have the right to decide who he does and doesn't see?'

That seemed to stall her anger a little bit. She looked down at the toolbox in one hand and the box I had under my arm.

'What is all of that?'

'I got him a gift. Look, Danny, I need to talk to him. People are going to be coming to see him. I have to talk to him about it so he'll be ready.'

She relented. Without further word she stepped back and opened the door wide. She signaled me in with an outstretched arm and I stepped over the threshold. I found my way to the bedroom.

Lawton Cross was asleep in his chair, his mouth open and a spill of medicinal-looking drool curved down his cheek. I didn't want to look at him. He was too much of a reminder of what could happen. I put the toolbox and the clock box down on the bed. I went back to the door and closed it, making sure it banged in the jamb loud enough to hopefully startle Cross awake. I didn't want to have to touch him to wake him up.

When I turned back to the chair I noticed his eyes flutter and then go still at half mast.

'Hey, Law? It's me, Harry Bosch.'

I noticed the green light on the monitor on the bureau and moved behind the chair to turn it off.

'Harry?' he said. 'Where?'

I came back around the chair and looked down on him with a frozen smile on my face.

'Right here, man. You awake now?'

'Yeah . . . mmm 'wake.'

'Good. There's some stuff I need to tell you. And I got you something.'

I went to the bed and started pulling the clock out of the box Andre Biggar had packed for me.

'Black Bush?'

His voice was alert now. Once again I regretted my choice of words to him. I came back into his field of vision holding the clock up.

'I got you this clock for the wall. Now you'll be able to tell the time when you need it.'

He blew a burst of air out through his lips.

'She'll just take it down.'

'I'll tell her not to. Don't worry.'

I opened the toolbox and pulled out the hammer and a drywall nail from a plastic package that contained a variety of nails for different purposes. I surveyed the wall to the left of the television and picked a spot at center. There was an electrical outlet directly below. I held the nail up high on the wall and drove it halfway in with the hammer. I was hanging the clock when the door opened and Danny looked in.

'What are you doing? He doesn't want a clock in here.'

I finished hanging the clock, lowered my hands and looked at her.

'He told me he did want a clock.'

We both looked at Law to settle it. His eyes flitted from his wife to me and then back again.

'Let's try having a clock for a while,' he said. 'I'd like to know the time of day so I know when my shows are coming on.'

'Fine,' she said in a clipped tone. 'Whatever you want.'

She left the room, closing the door behind her. I leaned over and plugged the clock's line into the outlet. Then I checked my watch and reached up to set the time and turn on the camera. When I was finished I put the hammer back into the toolbox and snapped the latch.

'Harry?'

'What?' I asked, though I knew what the question would be.

'Did you bring me some?'

'A little.'

I reopened the toolbox and took out the flask I had filled in the parking lot at the Vendome.

'Danny said you're hung-over. You sure?'

''Course I'm sure. Give me a taste, Harry. I need it.'

I went through the same routine as the day before and then waited to see if he could tell I had watered down the whiskey.

'Ah, that's the good stuff, Harry. Give me another, would you?'

I did and then I closed the flask, feeling somehow guilty about giving this broken man the one joy he seemed to have left in life.

'Listen, Law, I'm here to give you a heads-up. I think I sort of kicked over a can of worms with this thing.'

'What happened?'

'I tried to run down that agent you said had called Jack Dorsey about the currency numbers. You know, about the problem?'

'Yeah, I know. Did you find her?'

'No, Law, I didn't. The agent was Martha Gessler. That ring a bell with you?'

His eyes moved across the ceiling as if that was where he kept his memory banks.

'No, should it?'

'I don't know. She's missing. She's been missing for three years, since right about the time she called Jack.'

'Holy shit, Harry.'

'Yeah. So I kind of walked into that when I called up to try to track that call.'

'They're going to come talk to me?'

'I don't know. But that's the heads-up. I think they might. Somehow, they've got this whole thing tied into a terrorism angle. It's one of these post-September eleven crews running with it now. And I hear they like to kick ass and read the rule book later.'

'I don't want them coming here, Harry. What did you start?'

'I'm sorry about that, Law. If they come, just let them ask their questions and you answer them the best you can. Get their names and tell Danny to call me after they leave.'

'I'll try. I just want to be left alone.'

'I know, Law.'

I moved closer to his chair and held the flask up into his field of vision.

'You want more?'

'Does the pope shit in the woods?'

I poured a good slug into his mouth, then a chaser. I waited for it to go down and then work its way back up into his eyes. They seemed to glaze over.

'You okay?'

'Fine.'

'There are a few more questions I have for you. They sort of came to me after I talked to the bureau.'

'Like what?'

'Like about the phone call Jack got. The FBI says there was no record of Gessler calling about the currency list.'

'That's simple. Maybe it wasn't her. Like I said, I didn't get a name from Jack. Or if I did it's gone. I don't remember it.'

'I'm pretty sure it was her. Everything else you described about it fits. She had a program like you described on her laptop. It went missing with her.'

'There you go. There probably was a record of her calling. It just disappeared with her.'

'I guess so. What about the time of the call? Can you remember anything more about that, about when it came in?'

'Ah, jeez, I don't know, Harry. It was just one of those things. It was just a call. I'm sure Jack put it on the log.'

He was talking about the chronological log. Everything was always entered on the log. Or was supposed to be.

'Yeah, I know,' I said. 'But I don't have access to that. I'm on the outside, remember?'

'Yeah.'

'You told me you thought it was ten or so months into the case, remember? You said you were working other cases by then and Jack took over lead on Angella Benton. Her murder was May sixteenth of 'ninety-nine. Martha Gessler disappeared the following March nineteenth. That's almost exactly ten months later.'

'So I remembered it right. What else you want from me?'

'It's just that . . . '

I didn't finish. I was trying to figure out what to ask and how to say it. Something wasn't right about the chronology.

'It's just what?'

'I don't know. It seems to me if Jack had recently talked to this agent he would have said something about it when she went missing. It was a big story, you know? In the papers and on the TV every night. Is there any way the call could have come earlier? Closer to the beginning of the case? That way Jack might have forgotten about it and her by the time she hit the news.'

Cross didn't say anything for a while as he considered this. I considered other possibilities, too, but kept hitting logic walls.

'Give me another shot of that stuff, would you, Harry?'

He tried to suck too much of it down and it backed up and burned his throat. When he spoke again his voice was hoarser than usual.

'I don't think so. I think it was ten months.'

'Close your eyes for a second, Law.'

'What are you talking about?'

'Just close your eyes and concentrate on that memory. Whatever it is that you have, that you're keying on, concentrate on that.'

'You trying to hypnotize me, Harry?'

'I'm just trying to focus your thoughts, help you remember what Jack said.'

'It won't work.'

'Not if you don't let it. Relax, Law. Relax and try to forget everything. Like your mind's a blackboard and you're erasing it. Think about what Jack said about the call.'

His eyes moved under the thin, pale eyelids but after a few moments they slowed and stopped. I watched his face and waited. It was years since I had tried any hypnotic techniques, and that had been to draw out visual descriptions of events and suspects. What I wanted from Cross now was a memory of a time and place and the dialogue that went with it.

'You see the blackboard, Law?'

'Yeah, I see it.'

'Okay, go to the board and write Jack's name on it. Write it at the top so you have room underneath it.'

'Harry, this is stupid. I—'

'Just humor me, Law. Write Jack's name at the top of the board.'

'Okay.'

'Okay, Law, that's good. Now look at the board and underneath Jack's name write the words 'phone call.' Okay?'

'Okay, did it.'

'Good. Now look at those three words and concentrate on them. Jack. Phone call. Jack. Phone call.'

The silence that followed my words was punctuated by the barely discernible ticking of the new clock.

'Now, Law, I want you to concentrate on the black around those words. Around those letters. Go through the letters, Law, into the black. Go through the letters.'

I waited and watched his eyelids. I saw the retinal movement begin again.

'Jack is talking to you, Law. He's telling you about the agent. He says she has new information on the movie set heist.'

I waited for a long moment, wondering if I should have mentioned Gessler by name, then deciding it was better that I hadn't.

'What is he saying to you, Law?'

'There's something wrong with the numbers. They don't match.'

'Did she call him?'

'She called him.'

'Where are you when he is telling you this, Law?'

'We're in the car. We've got court.'

'Is it a trial?'

'Yes.'

'Whose trial is it?'

'It's that little Mexican kid. The little gangbanger who killed the Korean jeweler on Western. Alejandro Penjeda. It's the verdict.'

'Penjeda is the defendant?'

'That's right.'

'And Jack got the call from the agent before you went to court to hear the verdict?'

'That's right.'

'Okay, Law.'

I had gotten what I wanted. I tried to think what else I could ask him.

'Law? Did Jack say what the agent's name was?'

'No, he didn't say.'

'Did he say he would check out the information she gave him?'

'He said he'd do some checking but that he thought it was a bullshit call. He said he didn't think it meant anything.'

'Did you believe him?'

'Yes.'

'Okay, Law, I'm going to tell you to open your eyes in a moment. And when you open them, I want you to feel like you just woke up but I want you to remember what we just talked about. Okay?'

'Okay, yes.'

'And the other thing is I want you to feel better. I want you to be . . . okay about things in your life. I want you to be as happy as you can be, Law. Okay?'

'Yes.'

'Okay, Law, open your eyes now.'

The eyelids fluttered once and then they were open. They strafed the ceiling and then came to me. They seemed brighter than before.

'Harry . . . '

'How do you feel, Law?'

'Okay.'

'You remember what we were talking about?'

'Yeah, that little Mex. Penjeda. We called him PinHeada. He didn't take the deal the DA floated. Life with. He took his chances with the jury and got snake eyes. Life without.'

'Live and learn.'

What sounded like what might have been a laugh gurgled from deep in his throat.

'Yeah, that was a good one,' he said. 'I remember when we were going over to court that day was when Jack told me about the call from Westwood.'

'Right. You remember when that verdict came in on Penjeda?'

'End of February, beginning of March. My last trial, Harry. A month later I took the bullet in that shithole bar and I was history. I remember watching PinHeada's face when he heard that verdict and knew he was facing life *without* parole. Fucker got what he deserved.'

The laugh came up again and then I saw the light go out of his eyes.

'What is it, Law?'

'He's up there at Corcoran playing handball in the yard or getting his ass rented out by the Mexican Mafia on an hourly basis. And I'm here. I got life without, too, I guess.'

His eyes looked into mine. I nodded because it was the only thing I could think of to do.

'It's not fair, Harry. Life isn't fair.'

17

The downtown library was on Flower and Figueroa. It was one of the oldest buildings in the whole city. Therefore it was dwarfed by the modern glass-and-steel structures that surrounded it. Inside it was a beauty, centered around a domed rotunda with 360-degree mosaics depicting the founding of the city by the *padres.* The place had been twice burned by arsonists and closed for years, then restored to its original beauty. I had come after the restoration was completed, the first time back since I was a child. And I continued to come. It brought me close to the Los Angeles I remembered. Where I felt comfortable. I would take my lunch in the book rooms or the upper-level patios while reading case files and writing notes. I got to know the security guards and a few of the librarians. I had a library card, though I rarely checked out a book.

I went to the library after leaving Lawton Cross because I no longer could call on Keisha Russell to help me with clip searches. Her call to Sacramento to run a check on me when I had asked her to simply run a clip search on Martha Gessler was the warning. Her journalistic curiosity would lead her further than my requests, to places I didn't want her to go.

The main reference desk was on the second floor. I recognized the woman behind the counter, though I had never spoken to her before. I could tell she recognized me as I approached. I used a library card where a police shield used to do. She read it and recognized the name.

'Do you know that you have the same name as a famous painter?' she asked.

'Yes, I know.'

Her face flushed. She was midthirties with an unattractive hairstyle. She wore a name tag that said Mrs. Molloy.

'Of course you do,' she said. 'You must know that. How can I help you?'

'I need to look for stories that were in the *Times* from about three years ago.'

'You want to do a key word search?'

'I guess so. What is that?'

She smiled.

'We have the *Los Angeles Times* on computer going back to nineteen eighty-seven. If what you are looking for was published after that, all you have to do is go online on one of our computers, type in a key word or phrase, like a name, for example, that you think is in the story and it will search for it. There is a five-dollar-per-hour fee for accessing the newspaper archives.'

'Fine, that's what I want to do.'

She smiled and reached beneath the counter. She handed me a white plastic device that was about a foot long. It looked like no computer I had ever seen.

'How do I use this?'

She almost laughed.

'It's a pager. All our computers are being used at the moment. I will page you as soon as one becomes available.'

'Oh.'

'The pager doesn't work outside of the building. It also does not emit an audible page. It vibrates. So keep it on your person.'

'I will. Any idea how long it will be?'

'We set one-hour use limits, which right now would mean one won't be available for another thirty minutes. However, people often don't require the full hour.'

'Okay, thank you. I'll be nearby.'

I found an empty table in one of the reading rooms and decided to work on the case chronology. I got out my notebook and on a fresh page wrote down the three key dates and events I knew.

Angella Benton – murdered – May 16, 1999
Movie set heist – May 19, 1999
Martha Gessler – missing – March 19, 2000

I then began adding the things I was missing.

Gessler/Dorsey – phone call – ?????

And after a few moments I thought of something else that might help explain something that bothered me.

Dorsey/Cross – murder/shooting – ?????

I looked around to see if anyone was using a cell phone. I wanted to make a call but wasn't sure it would be allowed in a library. When I turned and looked behind me I saw a man standing by a magazine rack quickly turn away and take a magazine off the display without seeming to look at what it was first. He was dressed in blue jeans and a flannel shirt. Nothing about him said FBI but it still seemed to me that he had been looking directly at me until I had looked at him. His reaction had been too quick, almost furtive. There had been no eye contact, nothing that suggested any sort of overture. The man clearly didn't want me to know he was watching me.

Putting my notebook away, I got up from the table and headed toward the magazine racks. I passed the man and noticed that the magazine he had grabbed was called

Parenting Today. It was another strike against him. He didn't look like the parenting type to me. I was pretty sure I was being watched.

Back at the reference desk I put my hands on the counter and leaned over to whisper to Mrs. Molloy.

'Can I ask you a question? Is it okay to use a cell phone in the library?'

'No, it's not. Is somebody bothering you by using a phone?'

'No, I was just wondering what the rule was. Thank you.'

Before I could turn away she said she was just about to page me because a computer was now available. I gave her back the pager and she led me to a cubicle where the glowing screen of a computer was waiting.

'Good luck,' she said as she headed back to the desk.

'Excuse me,' I said, beckoning her back. 'Um, I don't know how to get to the *Times* stuff on this.'

'There's an icon on the desktop.'

I turned back around and scanned the desk. There was nothing on it but the computer and the keyboard and the mouse. The librarian started to laugh behind me but then covered her mouth with her hand.

'I'm sorry,' she said. 'It's just . . . you don't know the first thing about how to do this, do you?'

'Or the second or the third. Can you just help get me started?'

'Hold on. Let me just go check the front desk and make sure there is no one waiting for me.'

'Fine. Thank you.'

She was gone thirty seconds and then came back and leaned over me to work the mouse and click through screens until she was inside the *Times* archives and at what she called the key word search template.

'So now you type in the key word for the story you are looking for.'

I nodded that I understood that much and typed in the name 'Alejandro Penjeda.' Mrs. Molloy reached across and hit the enter key and the search began. In about five seconds I had the results on the screen. There were five hits. The first two were from 1991 and 1994 and the final three were all from 2000. I dismissed the first two as being unrelated to the Penjeda I was interested in. The next three were all from March 2000. I moved the mouse to the first one – March 1, 2000 – and clicked on the read button. The story filled the top half of the screen. It was a short report on the opening of the trial of Alejandro Penjeda, who was charged with the murder of a Korean jeweler named Kyungwon Park.

The second story was also short and it was the one I wanted. It was the verdict story in the Penjeda case. It was dated March 14 and reported events from the day before. I took the notebook out of my pocket and completed that part of the chronology, putting the new information in the right time slot.

Angella Benton – murdered – May 16, 1999
Movie set heist – May 19, 1999
Gessler/Dorsey – phone call – March 13, 2000
Martha Gessler – missing – March 19, 2000

I looked at what I had. Martha Gessler disappeared and presumably was murdered six days after talking to Jack Dorsey about the currency list anomaly.

'If there isn't anything else, I'm going to go back up front.'

I had forgotten that Mrs. Molloy was still standing behind me. I stood up and signaled her to the seat.

'Actually, this might be faster if you could do it,' I said. 'I need to do a couple more searches.'

'We are not supposed to do the searches. You are supposed to be proficient with the computer if you are going to use it.'

'I understand. I am going to learn but at the moment I'm not that proficient and these searches are very important.'

She seemed to be wavering on whether to continue to help me. I wished I'd had the small wallet-size copy of the private investigator's license I had gotten from the state. Maybe that would have impressed her. She leaned backwards to look down the row of cubicles to the front desk to see if anyone was waiting for help. The *Parenting Today* guy was milling about, trying to act as though he was either waiting for someone or waiting for help.

'I'll come back after I ask this gentleman if he needs help,' Mrs. Molloy said.

She walked off without waiting for a response from me. I watched as she asked Parenting Today if he needed something and he shook his head and then glanced back at me before walking off. Mrs. Molloy then came back down the aisle to me. She took the seat in front of the computer.

'What is the next search?'

She moved the mouse smoothly and quickly and got back to the key word template.

'Try "John Dorsey," I said. 'And to narrow it down, can you also add "Nat's bar"?'

She typed in the information and started the search. It came back with thirteen hits and I asked her to bring up the first one. It was dated April 7, 2000, and reported events from the day before.

ONE COP DEAD, ONE HURT
IN HOLLYWOOD BAR SHOOTING

By Keisha Russell
Times *Staff Writer*

Two Los Angeles police detectives on a lunch break and a bartender were gunned down in a Hollywood bar yesterday when a man entered the establishment and attempted to rob it at gunpoint.

The 1 p.m. shooting at Nat's on Cherokee Avenue left Detective John H. Dorsey, 49, dead of multiple gunshot wounds and his partner, Lawton Cross Jr., 38, in critical condition with head and neck wounds. Donald Rice, 29, a bartender working in the lounge, was shot multiple times and also died at the scene.

The suspect, who wore a black ski mask, escaped with an undisclosed amount of cash from the cash register, said Lt. James Macy, of the Officer Involved Shooting unit.

'It appears this was about a few hundred dollars at most,' Macy said at a press conference staged outside of the bar where the shooting took place. 'We can find no reason for this guy to have started shooting.'

Macy went on to say that it was unclear whether Dorsey and Cross had attempted to stop the robbery, thereby causing the shooting to start. He said both detectives were shot while sitting in a booth in the dimly lit bar area. Neither had drawn his weapon.

The detectives had been conducting an interview in a business near Nat's bar when they decided to take a lunch break in the bar, according to Macy. There was no indication that either man had been consuming alcohol in the bar.

'They went there as a matter of convenience,' Macy said. 'It was the unluckiest decision they could have made.'

No other patrons or employees were in the bar at the time of the incident. A person who was not in the bar saw the gunman fleeing after the shooting and was able to provide police with a limited description of the suspect. As a safety precaution the witness was not identified by police.

I stopped reading to ask the librarian if I could simply print the story out.

'It's fifty cents a page,' she said. 'Cash only.'

'Okay, do it.'

She hit the print command and then leaned backwards in her seat to see if she could see down the aisle to the reference desk. Standing, I could see it better.

'You're still clear. Can you do one more for me?'

'If we hurry. What is it?'

I raced through my memory banks trying to come up with a name that would work for what I wanted to do next.

'How about the word "terrorism"?'

'Are you kidding me? Do you know how many stories that word's been used in during the last two years?'

'Right, right, what am I thinking? Let's cut it down. The search words don't have to be connected, like in a sentence, right?'

'No. Listen, I need to get back to my—'

'Okay, okay, how about the words "FBI" and "suspected terrorist" plus "Al Qaeda" and "cell" spelled with a "c." Could you try that?'

'That will probably break the bank, too.'

She typed in the information and we waited, and then the computer reported that there were 467 hits, all but six of them since September 11, 2001. Beneath this number the computer printed out the headline of each story. The screen displayed the first of forty-two pages of headline listings.

'You're going to have to look through this yourself,' Mrs. Molloy said. 'I need to go back to my post now.'

I had started the last search almost as a joke. My assumption was that Parenting Today would either interview Mrs. Molloy after I left or send another agent while he continued the tail. I wanted to add a terrorism angle to my search just so they would have something to puzzle over. Now I realized I might be able to find out about what the bureau was doing.

'Okay,' I said. 'That's fine. Thanks for all of your help.'

'Remember, we close the library at nine this evening. That gives you about twenty-five more minutes.'

'Okay, thanks. Where did that printout go, by the way?'

'The printer is at the front desk. Anything you print will come out there. You come to me and pay for it and I give it to you.'

'A well-oiled machine.'

She didn't answer. She walked off and left me alone with the computer. I took a look around and didn't see Parenting Today anywhere. I then dropped back down into the cubicle and began scrolling through the story list. I clicked on a few and started to read them but stopped each time I discerned that the story had not even a remote connection to Los Angeles. I realized I should have included Los Angeles in the key word search. I stood up to see if Mrs. Molloy was at the front desk but she was not there. The front desk was abandoned.

I went back to the computer and on the third page of the story list a headline caught my eye.

TERRORISM MONEY MAN CAPTURED
AT BORDER CROSSING

I clicked the READ button and pulled up the entire story. The box above the body of the story said it had been published a month earlier on page A13 of the newspaper. It was accompanied by a mugshot of a man with deeply tanned skin and wavy blond hair.

By Josh Meyer
Times *Staff Writer*

A suspected money courier for supporters of global terrorism was arrested yesterday as he attempted to cross the Mexican border at Calexico with a satchel of cash, the Justice Department reported.

Mousouwa Aziz, 39, who has been on the FBI's terrorist watch list for four years, was apprehended by Border Patrol agents as he attempted to cross from the United States into Mexico.

Aziz, who the FBI claims has ties to a Philippine cell of Al Qaeda terrorists, was carrying a large quantity of U.S. currency in a satchel found hidden under the seat of the car he was attempting to drive across the border. Aziz, who was alone in the car, was arrested without a struggle. He was being held in an unknown location under federal guidelines as an enemy combatant.

Agents said Aziz had attempted to disguise himself by dyeing his hair blond and shaving the beard he had been known to wear.

'This is a significant arrest,' said Abraham Klein, an assistant U.S. attorney in the Los Angeles anti-terrorism unit. 'Our efforts around the world have been geared toward cutting off funding for terrorists. This suspected terrorist is believed to be a person intimately involved in financing terrorist activities here and abroad.'

Klein and other sources said Aziz could be a key figure in efforts to stop the movement of money— the lifeblood of long-term terrorism activity – to those targeting American interests.

'Not only did we take away a good chunk of cash with this arrest but, perhaps more importantly, we took a person who was in the business of delivering money to terrorists out of circulation,' said a Justice source who spoke on the condition he would not be identified.

Aziz is a Jordanian national who attended high school in Cleveland, Ohio, and speaks fluent English, the Justice source said. He had a passport and an Alabama driver's license in his possession that both identified him as Frank Aiello.

Aziz's name was placed on an FBI watch list four years ago after information was developed that connected him to money deliveries made to terrorists involved in the bombings of U.S. embassies in Africa. Aziz was nicknamed 'Mouse' by federal agents because of his

> small stature, ability to stay hidden from authorities in recent months and the difficulty agents had in pronouncing his first name.
>
> After the terrorist attacks of September 11, 2001, a higher alert status was issued in regard to Aziz, though sources said there was no evidence directly linking Aziz to the 19 terrorists who carried out those suicide attacks.
>
> 'This guy is a money man,' the Justice source said. 'His job is to move money from point A to point B. The money is then used to buy materials to make bombs and weapons, to support the lifestyles of terrorists while they plan and carry out their operations.'
>
> It was unclear why Aziz was apparently attempting to take U.S. currency out of the country.
>
> 'The U.S. dollar is good anywhere,' Klein said. 'In fact, it is stronger than the currency in most of the countries where these terrorist cells exist. The U.S. dollar goes a lot further. It could be that this suspect was taking the money to the Philippines to simply help pay for an operation.'
>
> Klein also suggested that money could have been headed for terrorists planning to infiltrate the United States.
>
> Klein refused to say how much money Aziz was transporting or where it came from. In recent months federal investigators have suggested that a large source of financing of terrorists has come from illegal activities within the United States. For example, the FBI linked an Arizona drug operation last year to a terrorist financing network.
>
> Federal sources also told the *Times* last year that it was believed that desolate areas of Mexico might be the location of terrorist training camps linked to Al Qaeda. Klein refused to comment yesterday on the possibility that Aziz might have been headed to such a camp.

I sat there staring at the screen for a long moment, wondering if I had just stumbled onto something more significant than a way to take a jab at the feds. I wondered if what I had just read could in some way be connected to my own investigation. Could the agents on the ninth floor in Westwood have connected the movie money to this terrorist?

My thoughts were broken by a loudspeaker announcement that the library was closing in fifteen minutes. I clicked on the PRINT button for the story and went back to the story list. I scrolled through the headlines, looking for follow-ups to the Aziz arrest. I found only one, which was published two days after the first story. I called it up and found it to be only a short. It said that an arraignment for Aziz was postponed indefinitely while he was continuing to be debriefed by federal agents. The tone of the article indicated that Aziz was cooperating with investigators, though it did not specifically or clearly say that. The story said that changes in federal laws enacted after the September 11 attacks gave federal authorities wide leeway in holding suspected terrorists as enemy combatants. The rest of the story was background information already contained in the first story.

I went back to the list and continued to scroll through the headlines. It took nearly ten minutes but I never found another story about Mousouwa Aziz.

The loudspeaker announced that the library was closing. I looked around and saw Mrs. Molloy back at the front desk. She was putting things away in the drawers, getting ready to go home. I decided that I now didn't want Parenting Today to know what I had been looking up on the computer. At least not right away. So I stayed in the cubicle until after the next announcement that the library was closed. I stayed until Mrs. Molloy came to the cubicle and told me I had to leave. She had my printouts. I paid her then folded the printouts and put them in my coat pocket with my notebook. I thanked her and left the reference room.

On my way out I pretended that I was studying the mosaics and architecture of the building, turning several times in complete circles in the rotunda as I watched for the tail man. I never saw him and began to wonder if I was being overly paranoid.

It looked like I was the last to leave through the public exit. I thought about finding the employee exit and waiting for Mrs. Molloy to come out so I could ask her if she had been questioned about me and my research requests. But I thought maybe I would only end up scaring her and let it go.

Alone as I walked through the third level of the garage toward my car, I felt the faint chill of fear move down my spine. Whether I was being tailed or not, I had successfully spooked myself. I picked up my pace and was almost trotting by the time I got to the door of the Mercedes.

18

Paranoia is not always a bad thing. It can help you keep an edge and sometimes an edge is the difference. From the library I headed over to Broadway and then toward the Civic Center. It might seem normal enough, an ex-cop heading toward the police department. Nothing unusual about that. But as I got to the *Los Angeles Times* complex I yanked the wheel hard left without using the brakes or a turn signal and sliced through oncoming traffic into the Third Street tunnel. I pinned the accelerator and the Mercedes responded, the front end rising like a boat as it picked up speed and roared through the three-block tunnel.

As often as I could I checked the rearview mirror for a follower. The tiles on the rounded walls of the tunnel carried headlights like halos. Filmmakers rent it from the city all the time for that reason. Any car trying to keep pace with me would be advertising, unless the lights were turned off, and that would be just as obvious in the mirror.

I was smiling. I'm not sure why. Having a possible FBI tail isn't necessarily something to be happy about. And the FBI is generally humorless about it as well. But I felt all at once that I had made the right move with the Mercedes. The car was flying. I was up high – higher than in any police car I had ever been in – so I had a good view in the mirror. It was as if I had planned for this and the plan was working. And that brought the smile.

As I came out of the tunnel I hit the brakes and took a hard right. The thick tires held the pavement, and when I was clear of the mouth of the tunnel I stopped completely. I waited, my eyes on the mirror. Of the cars that came out of the tunnel none turned right behind me and none even braked as they went through the intersection. If I had a tail I had either lost it or the follower was proficient enough at the game to be willing to lose the target in order to avoid obvious exposure. The latter didn't fit with the way Parenting Today had been so obvious in the library.

The third possibility I had to now consider was electronic surveillance. The bureau could have easily tricked my car at almost any point during the day. In the garage at the library a tech could have slid under and wired it.

The same tech could have been waiting for me to show up at the federal building as well. This of course would mean that they already knew of my ride about town with Roy Lindell. I was tempted to call the agent and warn him but decided that I shouldn't use my cell phone to contact him.

I shook my head. Maybe paranoia was not such a good thing after all. It can help you keep an edge but it can also paralyze you. I pulled back into traffic and worked my way over to the Hollywood Freeway. I kept my eyes off the rear view as much as possible.

The freeway is elevated as it cuts through Hollywood and into the Cahuenga Pass. It offers a good view of the place where I spent the most significant part of my time as a cop. With just glancing looks I could pick out some of the buildings where I had worked cases. The Capitol Records building, designed to resemble a stack of records. The Usher Hotel, now being renovated as luxury apartments as part of the Hollywood core-area redesign and development. I could see the lighted homes rising up on the dark hillsides in Beechwood Canyon and Whitley Heights. I could see the ten-story image of a local basketball legend on the side of an otherwise nondescript office building. Smaller in stature but still covering the side of a building was a Marlboro Man with a drooping cigarette in his mouth, his steely coolness replaced by a symbol of impotence.

Hollywood was always best viewed at night. It could only hold its mystique in darkness. In sunlight the curtain comes up and the intrigue is gone, replaced by a sense of hidden danger. It was a place of takers and users, of broken sidewalks and dreams. You build a city in the desert, water it with false hopes and false idols, and eventually this is what happens. The desert reclaims it, turns it arid, leaves it barren. Human tumbleweeds drift across its streets, predators hide in the rocks.

I took the Mulholland exit and crossed over the freeway, then at the split took Woodrow Wilson on up the side of the mountain. My house was dark. The only light I saw when I came through the carport door was the red glow from the answering machine on the kitchen counter. I hit a light switch and then pushed the playback button on the phone.

There were two messages. The first was from Kiz Rider and she had already told me about that. The second was from Lawton Cross. He had held back on me once again. He said he had something, his voice croaking into the phone like static. I pictured his wife holding the phone to his mouth.

The message had been left two hours before. It was getting late but I called back. The man lived in a chair. What was late to him? I had no idea.

Danny Cross answered. She must have had caller ID on the phone because her hello was clipped and carried an edge of malice in it. Or was I reading too much into it?

'Danny, it's Harry. I'm returning your husband's call.'

'He's asleep.'

'Can you wake him, please? It sounded important.'

'I can tell you what he wanted to tell you.'

'Okay.'

'He wanted to tell you that when he was working he used to keep copies of his active files. He kept them here in the home office.'

I didn't recall seeing an office in the house.

'Full copies?'

'I don't know. He had a filing cabinet and it was full.'

'Had?'

'His sitting room is where the office was. I had to move everything out. It's all in the garage now.'

I realized I needed to stop the flow of information from her. Too much had already been said on the phone. Paranoia was raising its ugly head again.

'I'm coming out tonight,' I said.

'No, it's too late. I'm going to bed soon.'

'I'll be there in half an hour, Danny. Wait up for me.'

I hung the phone up before she could further dispute my intentions. Without having gone further into the house than the kitchen I turned and left, this time leaving the light on.

A light rain had begun to fall in the Valley. Oil beaded on the freeway and slowed everybody down. I used all of the half hour and more to get to the house on Melba and shortly after I pulled into the driveway the garage door started to go up. Danny Cross had been watching for me. I got out of the Mercedes and entered the garage.

It was a two-car garage and it was cluttered with stacked boxes and furniture. There was an old Chevy Malibu with its hood sprung like somebody had been working on the engine and had just lowered the lid without latching it while taking a break. I think I remembered something about Lawton Cross driving a '60s muscle car as a private vehicle. But there was a thick layer of dust on the car and boxes stacked on its roof. One thing for sure was that he was never going to work on it or drive it again.

A door that connected to the house opened and Danny stood there in a long bathrobe with a belt knotted tightly around her thin waist. She had the same look of disapproval she always had on her face and that I had become quite used to. It was too bad. She was a beautiful woman. Or had been, at least.

'Danny,' I said, nodding. 'I won't be long. If you can just point me in—'

'It's all over there next to the washing machine. The file cabinets.'

She pointed to a spot in front of the Malibu where there was a laundry alcove. I walked around the car and found two double-drawer file cabinets standing next to the stacked washer and dryer. They were key-lock cabinets but the locks had been punched out on each. Lawton had probably picked them up used at a yard sale.

There was no exterior labeling on the four drawers that could help me with my search so I bent down and opened the first drawer on the left. It contained no files. Rather, it held what looked like the contents of a top of a desk. There was a Rolodex file, its phone cards yellowed, a stand-up photo frame featuring Danny and Lawton Cross at some happier moment, and double-decked in and out trays. The only thing in the tray marked 'IN' was a folded map of Griffith Park.

The next drawer contained Cross's files. I thumbed through the tabs looking at the names and hoping for connections to what I was working. Nothing. I went to the top drawer of the second cabinet and found more files. Finally, I found a file marked 'Eidolon Productions.' I pulled it and put it on top of the cabinet. I went back to thumbing through the files, knowing that often cases expanded into many folders.

I came across a file marked 'Antonio Markwell' and remembered the case because it had played hotly in the media about five or six years earlier. Markwell was a nine-year-old boy who disappeared from his backyard in Chatsworth. RHD worked the case with the FBI. It lasted a week, until they found a suspect – a pedophile with a motor home. He led Lawton Cross and his partner, Jack Dorsey, to the boy's body in Griffith Park. It had been buried up near the caves in Bronson Canyon. They would have never found it if they hadn't turned the killer. There were too many places to hide a body in those hills.

It had been a big case, the kind that made your name in the department. I imagined that both Cross and Dorsey thought that they were golden after that. They had no idea what the future was holding for them.

I closed the drawer. There were no other files that seemed connected to my investigation. The bottom drawer, the last one, was empty. I took the file I had pulled over to the Malibu. I put the file down on the hood and opened it. I should have just put it under my arm and left with it. But I was excited. I was anticipating something. A new lead maybe, a break. I wanted to see what Lawton Cross had kept in the file.

As soon as I opened it I knew the file was incomplete. Cross had copied some of the working documents of the case for use at home or on the road. The basic case reports were missing. There were no reports that specifically related to the investigation of the murder of Angella Benton. The file mostly contained reports relating to the movie set robbery and shoot-out. There were witness reports – including my own – and forensic reports. There was a DNA comparison between the blood found in the stolen movie van and the semen found on Angella Benton's body; no match. There were interview summaries and a time and location spread sheet – a document on which the locations of various players in the case are charted at different times important to the case. These T&L reports were also known as alibi sheets. It was a way of sifting through multiple players in a case and possibly coming up with a suspect.

I quickly went through the pages of this report and determined that

Cross and Dorsey had been charting eleven different people and not all of the names were familiar to me. The T&L report was a good find. I put the document to the side because I would put it at the top of the stack in the file when I was finished my review.

I moved on and had just picked up a copy of the currency report, which contained the serial numbers taken at random from the stolen money, when I heard Danny's voice behind me. She had remained in the doorway to the house watching me and I hadn't realized it.

'Find what you were looking for?'

I turned and looked back at her. The first thing I noticed was that the belt of her robe was untied and the robe had fallen open to reveal the light blue nightgown beneath.

'Uh, yes, it's here. I was just taking a quick look. I can go now if you want.'

'What's your hurry? Lawton is still asleep. He won't wake up until the morning.'

She held my eyes as she said the last line. I was trying to read what was said and what was meant. Before I could respond, the moment was broken by the sound and the lights of a car pulling quickly into the driveway.

I turned and saw a standard government car – a Crown Victoria – pulling into the light from the open garage. Two men were in the car and I recognized the one in the passenger seat. With as little noticeable movement as I could manage I lowered the currency report onto the T&L report. I then picked them both up and slid them into the crack between the Malibu's hood and fender. I heard the pages fall through the slot into the engine compartment. I then stepped back from the car, leaving the rest of the file open on the hood, and around into the open bay of the garage.

A second Crown Vic pulled into the driveway. The two men from the first car were already out and entering the garage.

'FBI,' said the man I recognized as Parenting Today.

He held up an ID case with a badge affixed to it. He just as quickly closed it and put it away.

'How are the kids?' I asked.

He seemed confused for a moment and it put a pause in his step. But then he pressed on and took a position in front of me while his partner, who had not shown a badge, stood a few feet to my right.

'Mr. Bosch, we are going to need you to come with us,' said Parenting Today.

'Well, I'm kind of busy at the moment. I'm trying to get this garage in shape.'

The agent looked over my shoulder at Danny Cross.

'Ma'am, could you return inside and close the door? We'll be out of your hair in a few moments.'

'This is my garage, my house,' Danny responded.

I knew her protest was useless but I liked that she'd made it just the same.

'Ma'am, this is FBI business. It does not concern you. Please step inside.'

'If it is in my garage it concerns me.'

'Ma'am, I won't ask you again.'

There was a pause. I kept my eyes on the agent. I heard the door close behind me and knew my witness was gone. In the same moment the agent to my right made his move. He raised both hands and charged me, pushing me into the side of the Malibu. My elbow slid across the roof and hit a box, sending it over the other side of the car and crashing to the floor. It sounded like it had glassware in it.

The agent was well practiced and I offered no resistance. I knew that would be a mistake. That would be what he wanted. He roughly pushed my chest against the car and pulled my arms behind my back. I felt the handcuffs cinch tightly around my wrists, then his hands patted me down for weapons and invaded my pockets in a routine search.

'What are you doing? What is going on?'

It was Danny. She had heard the crash.

'Ma'am,' Parenting Today said sternly, 'go back inside and close the door.'

The other agent twirled me away from the car and pushed me out of the garage toward the second car. I looked back at Danny Cross just as she was closing the door. The look of disapproval I was so used to was gone. There was a look of concern on her face now. I also saw that her bathrobe had been retied.

The silent agent opened the back door of the second car and started pushing me in.

'Watch your head,' he said just as he put his hand on my neck and pushed my head sharply into the door frame. I went sprawling across the backseat. He slammed the door, narrowly missing my ankle with it. I could almost hear a groan of disappointment from him through the glass.

He knocked his fist on the roof of the car and the driver dropped the transmission into reverse and hit the gas. The car jerked backwards and the sudden motion threw me off the seat onto the floor. I was unable to break my fall and the side of my face hit hard on the sticky floor. With my hands behind me I struggled to push myself back onto the seat. But I did it quickly, my struggle fueled by my anger and embarrassment. I sat up as the car jerked forward and I was thrown back into the seat. The car sped away from the house and through the rear window I saw Parenting Today standing in the garage and staring back at me. He held Lawton Cross's file down at his side.

I breathed heavily and watched the agent grow small in the window. I could feel crud from the floor mat on my face and could do nothing about it. My face burned. Not with pain and no longer with anger and embarrassment. It was pure helplessness that burned me now.

19

Halfway to Westwood I stopped talking to them. It was useless and I knew it but I had spent twenty minutes hitting them with questions, then veiled threats, and no matter what I said there was no response. When we finally got to the federal building the bureau car was driven down into a subterranean garage and I was pulled out and shoved into an elevator marked 'Security Transport Only.' One of the agents put a card key into a slot on the control panel and punched the '9' button. As the stainless-steel cube rose I thought about how far I had fallen from the badge. I had no juice with these men. They were agents and I was nothing. They could do with me what they wanted and we all knew it.

'I can't feel my fingers,' I said. 'The cuffs are too tight.'

'That's nice,' one of the agents said, his first words of the evening to me.

The doors opened and each one of them took an arm and pushed me into the hallway. We came to a door one of them opened with the card key, then we went down a hallway to another door, this one with a combination lock.

'Turn away,' an agent said.

'What?'

'Turn away from the door.'

I followed instructions and was turned away when the other agent tapped in the combination. We then went through and I was led into a dimly lit hallway of doors with small square windows head high. At first I thought they were interview rooms but then I realized there were too many. These were cells. I turned my head to look through some of the windows as we passed and through two of them I saw men looking back out at me. They were dark skinned and of Middle Eastern descent. They wore unkempt beards. Through a third window I saw a short man looking out, his eyes barely at the bottom level of the small window. He had bleached blond hair that had a quarter inch of black at its roots. I recognized him from the photo I had seen on the computer at the library. Mousouwa Aziz.

We stopped in front of a door marked '29,' and it was popped open electronically by some unseen hand. One of the agents stepped behind me and I heard him working a key into the handcuffs. I was beyond being able to feel it. Soon my wrists were free and I brought my hands around so that I could rub them and get the circulation going again. They were as white as soap, and a deep red welt ran around the circumference of each wrist. I had always believed that cuffing a suspect too tightly was a bullshit thing to do. Same with hitting a custody's head on the frame of the car door. Easy to do, easy to get away with. But always a bullshit move. A bully's move. The kind of thing a boy who enjoyed teasing the younger kids in the schoolyard would grow up to do.

As the tingling feeling started to work its way into my hands a burning sense of anger started building behind my eyes, edging my vision with a velvet blackness. In that darkness was a voice urging me to retaliate. I managed to ignore it. It's all about power and when to use it. These guys didn't know that yet.

A hand pushed me toward the cell and I involuntarily braced myself. I didn't want to go in there. Then a sharp kick hit me behind my left knee and my leg buckled and I was hurled forward with a stiff arm shove from behind. I crossed the small square cell to the opposite wall and put my hands up to stop my forward momentum.

'Make yourself at home, asshole,' the agent said to my back.

The door was slammed before I could get back to it. I stood there looking at the square of glass, realizing that the other prisoners I had seen in the hallway had been looking at themselves. The glass was mirrored.

Instinctively I knew the agent that had kicked and shoved me was on the other side looking at me. I nodded to him, sending the message that I would not forget him. He was probably on the other side laughing back at me.

The light in the room stayed on. I eventually stepped away from the door and looked around. There was a one-inch-thick mattress on a shelflike outcropping from the wall. Built into the opposite wall was a sink-and-toilet combination. There was nothing else except a steel box in one of the upper corners with a two-inch-square window behind which I could see a camera lens. I was being watched. Even if I used the toilet I was being watched.

I checked my wrist but there was no watch. They had somehow taken it, probably when they took off the cuffs and my wrists were so numb I could not feel the theft.

I spent what I thought was the first hour of my incarceration pacing in the small space and trying to keep my anger sharp but controlled. I walked without pattern other than that I used the entire space, and when I came to the corner where the camera was located I raised the middle finger of my left hand to the lens. Every time.

In the second hour I sat on the mattress, determined not to exhaust myself with the pacing and trying to keep track of time. On occasion I still gave the camera my finger, usually without even bothering to look up while I delivered it. I started thinking about interview room stories to pass the time. I remembered one about a guy we had brought in as a suspect in a double bagger involving a drug rip-off. Our plan was to sweat him a little before we went into the room and tried to break him down. But soon after being placed in the room he took his pants off, tied the legs around his neck and tried to hang himself from the overhead light fixture. They got to him in time and the man was saved. He protested that he would rather kill himself than spend another hour in the room. He had only been in there twenty minutes.

I started laughing to myself and then remembered another story, one that wasn't so funny. A man who was a peripheral witness to a strong-arm robbery was brought into the box and questioned about what he saw. It was late on a Friday. He was an illegal and he was scared shitless, but he wasn't a suspect and it would mean too many phone calls and too much paperwork to send him back to Mexico. All that the detective wanted was his information. But before he got it the detective was called out of the interview room. He told the man to sit tight, that he'd be back. Only he never came back. Breaking events on the case took him out into the field and soon he forgot about the witness. On Sunday morning another detective who had come in to try to catch up on his paperwork heard a knocking sound and opened the interview room door to find the witness still there. He had taken empty coffee cups out of the trash can and filled them with urine during the weekend. But as instructed he had never left the unlocked interview room.

Remembering that one made me feel morose. After a while I took off my jacket and lay back on the mattress. I put the jacket over my face to try to block out the light. I tried to give the impression I was sleeping, that I didn't care what they were doing to me. But I wasn't sleeping and they probably knew it. I'd seen it all before when I had been on the other side of the glass.

Finally, I tried to concentrate on the case, running all of the latest occurrences through my head, trying to see how they fit. Why had the bureau stepped in? Because I was getting a copy of Lawton Cross's file? It seemed unlikely. I decided that I had struck the nerve in the library when I had looked up the reports on Mousouwa Aziz. They had talked to the librarian or checked the computer – new laws allowed them to. That was what brought them out. That was what they wanted to know about.

After what I estimated to be about four hours in the cube the door snapped open with an electronic release. I pulled the jacket off my face and sat up just as an agent I had not seen before stepped in. He was carrying a file and a cup of coffee. The agent I knew as Parenting Today stood behind him with a steel chair.

'Don't get up,' the first agent said.

I stood up anyway.

'What the hell is—'

'I said don't get up. You sit back down or I'm out of here and we'll try again tomorrow.'

I hesitated a moment, holding my pose as an angry man and then sat down on the mattress. Parenting Today put the chair down just inside the door and then stepped out of the cell and closed the door. The remaining agent sat down and lowered his steaming coffee to the floor. The smell of it filled the room.

'I'm Special Agent John Peoples with the Federal Bureau of Investigation.'

'Good for you. What am I doing here?'

'You are here because you do not listen.'

He brought his eyes to mine to make sure I was doing what he just said I do not do. He was my age, maybe a little older. He had all of his hair and it was a little too long for the bureau. I guessed that it wasn't a style choice. He was just too busy to get it properly cut.

His eyes were the thing. Every face has a magnetic feature, the thing that draws you in. A nose, a scar, a cleft chin. With Peoples everything was drawn to the eyes. They were deeply set and dark. They were worried. They carried a secret burden.

'You were told to stand down, Mr. Bosch,' he said. 'You were told rather explicitly to leave things alone and yet here we are.'

'Can you answer a question?'

'I can try. If it's not classified.'

'Is my watch classified? Where's my watch? It was given to me when I retired and I want it back.'

'Mr. Bosch, forget about your watch for now. I am trying to get something through that thick skull of yours but you don't want it to get through, do you?'

He reached down for his coffee and took a sip. He grimaced as he burned his mouth. He put the cup back down on the floor.

'More important things are at work here than your private investigation and your hundred-dollar retirement watch.'

I put a look of surprise on my face.

'You really think that's all they spent on me after all those years?'

Peoples frowned and shook his head.

'You are not helping yourself here, Mr. Bosch. You are compromising an investigation that is vitally significant to this country and here all you want to do is show how clever you are.'

'This is the national security rap, right? It is, isn't it? Well, Special Agent Peoples, you can hang onto it for next time. I don't consider a murder investigation to be unimportant. There are no compromises when it comes to murder.'

Peoples stood up and stepped toward me until he was looking directly down at me. He leaned over the bed, putting his hand against the wall for support.

'*Hieronymus Bosch*,' he yelled, actually pronouncing it correctly. 'You are trespassing! You are driving the wrong way down a one-way street! Do you understand!'

He then turned and went back to his chair. I almost laughed at the theatrics and for a moment thought that he did not realize that I had spent twenty-five years working in rooms like these.

'Am I getting through to you at all?' Peoples said, his voice calm once again. 'You are not a cop. You carry no badge. You have no provenance, no case. You have no standing.'

'It used to be a free country. That used to be enough standing.'

'It's not the same country it used to be. Things have changed.'

He proffered the file held in his hand.

'The murder of this woman is important. Of course it is. But there are other things at play here. More important matters. You must step back from it, Mr. Bosch. This is the final warning. *Stand down.* Or we will stand you down. And you won't like it.'

'I bet I'll end up back here? Right? With Mouse and the others? The other enemy combatants. Isn't that what you call them? Does anyone even know about this place, Agent Peoples? Anyone outside your own little BAM squad?'

He seemed momentarily taken aback by my knowledge and use of the term.

'I recognized Mouse when they brought me in. I was window shopping.'

'And from that you think you know what goes on here?'

'You're working the guy. It's obvious and that's fine. But what if he's the one who killed Angella Benton? What if he killed the bank security man? And what if he killed an FBI agent, too? Don't you care about what happened to Martha Gessler? She was one of your own. Has the world changed that much? Is a special agent no longer special under these new rules of yours? Or does the line change according to convenience? Am I an enemy combatant, Agent Peoples?'

I could see it hurt. My words opened an old wound if not an old debate. But then a resolve came across his face. He opened the file in his hands and took out the printout I had made at the library. I could see the mugshot of Aziz.

'How did you know about this? How did you make this connection?'

'You people.'

'What are you talking about? No one here would tell you—'

'They didn't have to. I saw your man tailing me in the library. Make a note of that – he's not that good. Tell him to try *Sports Illustrated* next time. I knew something was up so I ran a search through the newspaper files and came up with that. I printed it out because I knew it might flush you people out. And it did. Your kind are very predictable.

'Anyway, then I saw Mouse when they were walking me down the hall and I sort of put things together. Money from my robbery was under the seat of his car when you arrested him. But you don't care about that or the two and maybe three murders attached to it. You just want to know where that money was going. And you don't want a little thing like justice for the dead to get in the way of that.'

Peoples slowly slid the printout back into the file. I could see his face changing, growing darker around the eyes. I had stuck my words directly into a nerve.

'You have no idea what the world is like out there or what we are doing about it in here,' he said. 'You can sit here and be smug and talk about your ideas of justice. But you have no fucking idea what is out there.'

My response to that was a smile. My words came readily.

'You can save that speech for the politicians who change the rules for you until there are no rules anymore. Until something like justice for a murdered and violated woman adds up to nothing in the equation. That's what's going on out there.'

Peoples leaned forward. He was about to spill and he wanted to make damn sure I got it.

'Do you know where Aziz was going with that money? We don't know but I can tell you where I think he was going with it. To a training camp. A terrorist training camp. And I'm not talking about in Afghanistan. I'm talking about within a hundred miles of our border. A place where they train people to kill us. In our buildings, in our planes. In our sleep. To come across that line and kill us with blind disregard for who we are and what we believe. Are you going to tell me that I'm wrong, that we should not do everything we can to find such a place if it exists? That we should not take whatever measures are necessary with that man to get the information we need from him?'

I leaned back across the mattress until my back was against the wall. If I'd had a cup of coffee I wouldn't have ignored it the way he was ignoring his.

'I'm not telling you anything,' I said. 'Everybody's got to do what they've got to do.'

'Wonderful,' he said sarcastically. 'Words of wisdom. I'm going to get a wall plaque for my office and put that right on it.'

'You know, I was in a trial once and the lawyer on the other side said something I always try to remember. She quoted a philosopher whose name I don't recall offhand – I've got it written down at the house. But this guy said that whoever is out there fighting the monsters of our society should make damn sure that they don't become monsters themselves. See, because then all is lost. Then we don't have a society. I always thought that was a good line.'

'Nietzsche. And you almost got the quote right.'

'Getting the quote right isn't what matters. It's remembering what it means.'

Peoples reached into the pocket of his coat. He pulled out my watch. He threw it to me and I started putting it on. I looked at the face. The hands of the clock were set against a gold detective's badge with the city hall on it. I noted the time and saw that I had been in the cube longer than I had thought. It was almost dawn.

'Get out of here, Bosch,' he said. 'If you cross our field of vision on this again you will find yourself back here faster than you'd think was possible. And no one will know you are here.'

The threat was obvious.

'I'll be among the disappeared then, huh?'

'Whatever you want to call it.'

Peoples raised his hand over his head so the camera would see it. He twirled a finger in the air and the electronic lock on the door clacked and the door opened a few inches. I stood up.

'Go,' Peoples said. 'Somebody will see you out. I'm cutting you a break here, Bosch. Remember that.'

I headed toward the door but hesitated when I was passing him. I looked down at him and the file he still clutched.

'I assume you cleaned me out, took my files. Lawton Cross's too.'

'You won't be getting it back.'

'Right, I understand. National security. What I was going to say is look through the photos. Find one of the photos of Angella on the tile. Look at her hands, man.'

I headed toward the open door.

'What about her hands?' he called after me.

'Just look at her hands. The way we found them. You'll know what I'm talking about then.'

In the hallway Parenting Today was waiting for me.

'This way,' he said curtly and I could tell he was disappointed that I was being cut loose.

On the way up the hallway I looked for Mousouwa Aziz in one of the square windows but didn't see him. I wondered if by chance I had looked into the face of the killer I was looking for and that it would be my only glimpse, that I would get no closer. I knew that as long as he was in here I would never get to him, literally or legally. He was gone from me. He was among the disappeared. The ultimate dead end.

We went out through two electronic doors and then I was delivered to an elevator alcove. There was no button for me to push. Parenting Today looked up at a camera in the corner of the ceiling and rolled an extended finger in the air. I heard the elevator start coming.

When the doors opened he escorted me on. We went down to the basement but not to a car. He walked me up the ramp after yelling to a garage man to open the roll-up door. As the door went up I was hit with sunlight and had to squint.

'I take it you aren't giving me a ride back to my car.'

'You can take it any way you want to. Have a good day.'

He left me there at the top of the ramp and turned around to get under the door before it reclosed on him. I watched him disappear as the steel curtain dropped. I tried to think of a clever line to throw at him but I was too damn tired and let it go.

20

The bureau had been in my house. That was expected. But the agents had been subtle about it. The place hadn't been torn apart and left for me to put back together. It had been methodically searched and most things had been left exactly in place. The dining-room table, where I had left the spread of files relating to Angella Benton's murder, had been cleared. It looked like they might have even polished the empty surface with Pledge when they were through. I had been left nothing. My notes, my files, my reports were all gone and so it seemed was the case. I didn't dwell on it. I looked at my murky reflection in the polished surface of the table for a few moments and decided I needed to sleep before making my next move.

I grabbed a bottle of water out of the refrigerator and went out through the slider to the back deck to watch the sun come up over the hills. The cushion on the lounge chair had morning dew on it so I flipped it over and sat down. I put my legs up and leaned back into the soft comfort. There was a slight chill in the air but I still had my jacket on. I put the water bottle on the arm of the chair and tucked my hands into the pockets of the jacket. It felt good to be home after the night in the cube.

The sun was just cresting the hills on the other side of the Cahuenga Pass. The sky was filled with diffused light as its rays refracted off the billions of microscopic particles that hung in the air. Soon I would need sunglasses but I was too dug in to get up to get them. I closed my eyes instead and soon fell asleep. I dreamed of Angella Benton, of her hands, of a woman I never knew in life but who came alive in my dreams and reached out to me.

I woke up a couple hours later with the sun burning through my eyelids. Soon I realized that the pounding I had thought was in my head was actually coming from the front door. I got up, knocking the unopened water bottle off the arm of the lounge chair. I made a grab for it but missed. It rolled off the deck and down into the brush below. I walked to the rail and looked down. Steel pylons held my house cantilevered over the canyon. I could not see the bottle down there.

Whoever it was out front knocked again and then I heard a muffled version of my name. I went in off the deck and crossed the living room to the front hallway. He was pounding on the door again when I finally opened it. It was Roy Lindell and he wasn't smiling.

'Rise and shine, Bosch.'

He started to push by me into the house but I put my hand on his chest and pushed him backwards. I shook my head and he picked up the vibe. He pointed in the house and put a question mark in his eyes. I nodded and stepped out through the door, pulling it closed behind me.

'Let's take my car,' he said in a low voice.

'Good. 'Cause mine's in Woodland Hills.'

His bureau car was parked illegally at the front curb. We got in and headed up Woodrow Wilson to the curve that took it around toward Mulholland. I didn't think he was taking me anywhere. We were just driving.

'What happened to you?' he asked. 'I heard through the grapevine you got picked up last night.'

'That's right. By your BAM squad. They put the bam on me, you could say.'

Lindell looked over at me and then back at the road.

'You don't look the worse for wear. You even got some color in your cheeks.'

'Thanks for noticing, Roy. Now what do you want?'

'You think they've got your house bugged?'

'Prob'ly. I haven't had time to check. What do you want? Where are we going?'

Though I guessed I knew. Mulholland wound around the hill to an overlook with views, depending on the smog ratio, from the Santa Monica Bay to the spires of downtown.

As expected, Lindell pulled into the small parking lot and stopped next to a Volkswagen van three decades out of place. The smog was heavy. For the most part the view dropped off just past the Capital Records building.

'Get to the point, huh?' Lindell said, turning in his seat toward me. 'Okay, I'll get to it. What's going on with the investigation?'

I looked at him for a long moment, trying to gauge whether he had turned up because of Marty Gessler or as a follow-up from Special Agent Peoples. As a test to determine if I was out of it. Sure Lindell and Peoples were different animals from different floors of the federal building. But they both carried the same badge. And there was no telling what kind of pressure had been brought to bear on Lindell.

'What's going on is that there is no investigation.'

'What? Are you fucking me?'

'No, I'm not fucking you. You could say I see the light. I was made to see it.'

'Then what are you going to do, just drop it?'

'That's right. I'm going to get my car and go on vacation. Vegas, I think.

I got a start on the sunburn this morning. I might as well go lose my money, too.'

Lindell smiled like he was clever.

'Fuck you,' he said. 'I know what you're doing. You think I've been sent out to test you, huh? Well, fuck you.'

'That's nice, Roy. Can you take me back now? I need to pack a bag.'

'Not until you tell me what is really going on.'

I cracked the door.

'Okay, I can walk. I need the exercise.'

I got out and started walking toward Mulholland. Lindell threw open his door, hitting the side of the old van. He came hurrying after me.

'Listen, Bosch, listen to me.'

He caught up to me and stood in front of me, very close, forcing me to stop. He put his hands into fists and held them up in front of his chest as if he was trying to break apart a chain that was binding him.

'Harry, I'm here for me. Nobody sent me, okay? Do not drop this. Those guys down there, they were probably just throwing you a scare, that's all.'

'Tell that to the people they've been holding in there. I don't feel like disappearing, Roy. You know what I mean?'

'Bullshit. You've never been the kind of guy who would—'

'Hey! Asshole!'

I turned around at the sound of the voice and saw two men piling out of the sliding door of the Volkswagen van. They were bearded longhairs who looked like they belonged on Harleys, not in a hippie van.

'You dented the shit out of the door,' the second one yelled.

'How the fuck can you tell?' Lindell shot back.

Here we go, I thought. I looked past the approaching behemoths and could see a four-inch crease in the front passenger door of the Volkswagen. Lindell's door was still open and in contact with it, the obvious culprit.

'You think it's a joke?' said the first heavy. 'How about if we put a dent in your face?'

Lindell reached behind his back and in one swift move his hand came out from under his jacket with a pistol. With his free hand he reached forward and grabbed the first heavy by the front of his shirt and pulled him forward, taking a handful of beard in the process. The gun came up and the barrel was pressed into the taller man's throat.

'How 'bout you and David Crosby get back in that piece of shit and flower power your way the fuck out of here?'

'Roy,' I said. 'Easy.'

The smell of marijuana was just now reaching us from the van. There was a long moment of silence while Lindell held eyes with the first heavy. The second stood nearby watching but unable to make a move because of the gun.

'Okay, man,' the first one finally said. 'Everything's cool. We'll just back on out of here.'

Lindell shoved him away and dropped the gun down to his side.

'Yeah, you do that, Tiny. Back on out. Go smoke the peace pipe somewhere else.'

We watched silently while they went back to the van, the second man angrily slamming Lindell's door so he could get into the front passenger seat of the van. The engine started and the van backed out and pulled out onto Mulholland. The requisite hand gestures were offered from both driver and passenger and then they were gone. I thought about myself just a few hours earlier giving the same salute to the camera in the cube. I knew how helpless the two men in the van felt.

Lindell turned his attention back to me.

'That was good, Roy,' I said to him. 'With skills like that I'm surprised they didn't tap you for a ninth-floor gig.'

'Fuck those guys.'

'Yeah, that's the way I was feeling a few hours ago.'

'So then what's it going to be, Bosch?'

He had just pulled a gun on two strangers in a near-violent collision of high-testosterone levels and already the tide had subsided. The surface was calm. The incident was off his radar screen after only one sweep. It was a trait that in the past I had most often seen in psychopaths. I wanted to give Lindell the benefit of the doubt so I chalked it up to the sort of federal arrogance I had also seen before as a genetic trait in bureau men.

'You staying or running?' he asked.

That made me angry but I tried not to show it. I cracked a smile.

'Neither,' I said. 'I'm walking.'

I turned and left him there. I started walking up Mulholland toward Woodrow Wilson and home. He threw a barrage of curses at my back but that didn't slow me down.

21

The garage door was open at Lawton Cross's house and it looked as though it might have been left that way through the night. I had the cab drop me off in the street next to my Mercedes. It didn't look like the car had been moved, though I had to assume it had been searched. I had left it unlocked and it still was. I put the small bag I had packed and brought with me into the backseat. I then got behind the wheel, started the engine and pulled the car into the open bay of the garage.

After I got out I went to the house's door and pushed a button that would either ring a bell inside or close the garage door. It closed the door. I went over to the Chevy, slid my hands beneath the hood and felt for the release latch. The steel springs yawned loudly as I raised the hood. I looked down at a dusty but clean engine with a chrome air filter cowling and fan highlighting a painted red block. Lawton had obviously babied the car and had appreciated its internal as well as exterior beauty.

The documents from the investigative file that I had slipped beneath the hood the night before had survived the FBI search. They had fallen and been cradled by the web of spark plug wires on the left side of the block. As I gathered them I noticed that the car's battery had been disconnected and I wondered when this had been done. It was a smart thing to do with a car that was not going to be used for a while. Lawton probably would have thought of doing it but would not have been able to actually do it. Maybe he had talked Danny through the procedure.

'What's going on? What are you doing, Harry?'

I turned. Danny Cross was in the doorway to the house.

'Hello, Danny. I just came back for some things I forgot. I also need to use some of Law's tools. I think something's wrong with my car.'

I gestured toward the workbench and Peg-Board that lined the wall next to the Malibu. An array of tools and automotive equipment was on display. She shook her head like I had forgotten to explain the obvious.

'What about last night? They took you. I saw the handcuffs. The agents who stayed said you wouldn't be coming back.'

'Scare tactics, Danny. That's all that was. As you can see, I'm back.'

I closed the hood with one hand, leaving it partially sprung in the way I had found it. I walked to the Mercedes and reached the documents in through the open window to the passenger seat. I then thought better about that and opened the door, raised the floor mat and put them under it. It wasn't a great hiding place but it would do for the moment. I closed the door and looked at Danny.

'How is Law?'

'Not good.'

'What's wrong?'

'They were in there with him last night. They wouldn't let me in and then they turned off the monitor so I couldn't exactly hear everything. But they scared him. And they scared me. I want you to go, Harry. I want you to go and not come back.'

'How'd they scare you? What did they say?'

She hesitated and I knew that was part of the scare.

'They told you not to talk about it, right? Not to talk to me?'

'That's right.'

'Okay, Danny, I don't want to get you in trouble. What about Law? Can I talk to him?'

'He said he doesn't want to see you anymore. That it's caused too much trouble.'

I nodded and looked over at the workbench.

'Then let me just get to my car and I'll get out of here.'

'Did they hurt you, Harry?'

I looked at her. I think she really cared about the answer.

'No, I'm all right.'

'Okay.'

'Uh, Danny, I need to get something from Law's sitting room. Should I go in or can you get it for me? What would be better?'

'What is it?'

'The clock.'

'The clock? Why? You gave it to him.'

'I know. But I need it back.'

A look of annoyance came across her face. I thought maybe the clock had been a point of argument between them, and now I was taking it back.

'I'll get it but I'm telling him you're the one taking it off the wall.'

I nodded. She went inside the house and I went around the Malibu and found a dolly leaning against the workbench. I took a pair of pliers and a screwdriver off the Peg-Board and went back to the Mercedes.

After throwing my jacket into the car I got down on the dolly and slid under the car. It took me less than a minute to find the black box. A satellite tracker about the size of a hardback book was held to the gas tank with two industrial size strip magnets. There was a twist to the setup I hadn't seen before. A wire extended from the box to the exhaust pipe where it was connected to a heat sensor. When the pipe heated up, the sensor switched on the tracker, conserving the unit's battery when the vehicle wasn't moving. The boys on the ninth floor got the good stuff.

I decided then to leave the box in place and slid out from underneath the car. Danny was standing there, holding the clock. She had taken the back off, exposing the camera.

'I thought it was too heavy for just a wall clock,' she said.

I started getting up.

'Look, Danny . . . '

'You were spying on us. You didn't believe me, did you?'

'Danny, that's not what I want it for. Those men that came here last—'

'But it *is* what you put it on that wall for. Where's the tape?'

'What?'

'The tape. Where did you watch this?'

'I didn't. It's digital. It's all right there in the clock.'

That was a mistake. As I reached for the clock she raised it up over her head and then threw it down to the concrete floor. The glass shattered and the camera broke loose from the clock shell and skittered under the Mercedes.

'Goddamnit, Danny. It isn't mine.'

'I don't care whose it is. You had no right to do that.'

'Look, Law told me you weren't treating him right. What was I supposed to do? Just take your word for it?'

I got down on the floor and looked under the car. The camera was within reach and I pulled it out. The casing was badly scratched but I could not make any judgment about its interior mechanisms. I ejected the memory card the way Andre Biggar had taught me and it looked okay to me. I stood up and held it up for Danny to see.

'This might be the only thing that keeps those men from coming back. You better hope it's not damaged.'

'I don't care. And I hope you really enjoy what you see on it. I hope you're very proud of yourself when you watch it.'

I had no response for that.

'Don't come back here ever again.'

She turned and went into the house, her hand slapping the wall button, which brought the garage door up behind me. She closed the house's door without looking back at me. I waited a moment to see if she would reappear and throw another verbal attack at me. But she didn't. I pocketed the memory card and then squatted down to gather the pieces of the broken clock.

22

At Burbank Airport I parked in the long-term lot, got my bag out and took the tram to the terminal. At the Southwest counter I used a credit card to buy a round-trip ticket to Las Vegas on a flight leaving in less than an hour. I kept the return open. I then proceeded through the security checkpoint, waiting in line like everybody else. I put my bag on the conveyor and dropped my watch, car keys and the camera's memory card into a plastic bowl so I would not set off the metal detector. I realized I had left my cell in the Mercedes and then thought, just as well, they might use it to triangulate my location.

Near the departure gate I stopped and bought a ten-dollar phone card and took it to a nearby bank of pay phones. I read the instructions on the phone card twice. Not because they were complicated but because I was hesitant. Finally, I picked up the receiver and called long distance. It was a number I knew by heart but had not called in almost a year.

She answered after only two rings but I could tell I had woken her up. I almost hung up, knowing that even if she had caller ID she would not be able to tell it had been me. But after her second hello I finally spoke.

'Eleanor, it's me, Harry. Did I wake you up?'

'It's okay. Are you all right?'

'Yeah, I'm fine. Were you playing late?'

'Till about five and then we went for breakfast. I feel like I just got to bed. What time is it?'

I told her it was after ten and she groaned. I felt the confidence go out of my plan. I also got stuck wondering who the 'we' she referred to was but didn't ask. I was supposed to be long past that.

'Harry, what is it?' she said into the silence. 'Are you sure you're all right?'

'Yeah, I'm fine. I didn't get to sleep till about the same time, too.'

More silence slipped into the wire. I noticed that they were boarding my flight.

'Is that why you called me? To tell me your sleeping habits?'

'No, I, uh ... well, I sort of need some help. Over there in Vegas.'

'Help? What do you mean? You mean like on a case? You told me you retired.'

'I did. I am. But there's this thing I'm working on . . . Anyway, I was wondering if you could meet me at the airport in about an hour. I'm flying in.'

There was silence while she registered this request and all that it might mean. As I waited my chest felt heavy and tight. I was thinking about the single-bullet theory when she finally spoke.

'I can be there. Where am I taking you?'

I realized I had been holding my breath. I exhaled. Deep down in the velvet folds I knew that would be her answer but hearing it spoken out loud, the confirmation of it, filled me immediately with my own confirmation of the feelings I still carried. I tried to picture her on the other end of the line. She was in bed, the phone on the bed table, her hair messy in a way I always found to be a turn-on, that made me want to stay in bed with her. Then I remembered that this was a cell number. She didn't have a landline, at least one that I had the number for. And then that 'we' thing came up again, intruding like a telephone solicitor. Whose bed was she in?

'Harry, you still there?'

'Yeah, I'm here. Uh, just to a car-rental place. Avis, I guess. They try harder. Supposedly.'

'Harry, they have buses that come by the airport every five minutes for that. What do you need me for? What's going on?'

'Look, I'll explain when I get there. My flight's boarding. Can you be there, Eleanor?'

'I said I'll be there,' she said in a tone I was too familiar with, as if she was relenting and reluctant at the same time.

I didn't dwell on it. I had what I needed. I left it at that.

'Thank you. How about right outside Southwest? Is it still the Taurus you had before?'

'No, Harry, it's a silver Lexus now. Four-door. And I'll have my lights on. I'll flick them if I see you first.'

'Okay, I'll see you then. Thanks, Eleanor.'

I hung up and headed for the gate. A Lexus, I thought as I moved. I had priced them before buying the used Mercedes. They weren't outrageous but they weren't cheap. Things must be changing for her. I was pretty sure I was happy about that.

By the time I got on the plane there was no room in the overhead compartments for my bag and only middle seats left for me. I squeezed in between a man in a Hawaiian shirt and thick gold neck chain and a woman so pale I thought she might detonate like a match the moment she was hit by the Nevada sun. I zoned out, kept my elbows to myself, though the Hawaiian shirt guy didn't, and managed to close my eyes and almost sleep for most of the short flight. I knew there was a lot to think about and the memory card was almost burning a hole in my pocket as I wondered about its contents, but I also instinctively knew that I needed to grab rest while I could. I wasn't expecting to get too much of it once I got back to L.A.

Less than an hour after takeoff I walked out through the terminal's automatic doors at McCarran and was hit with the oven-dry blast of heat that signaled arrival in Las Vegas. It didn't faze me. My eyes intently searched the vehicles stacked in the pickup lanes until they held on a silver car with its lights on. The sunroof was open and the driver's hand was reaching through it and waving. She was flicking the brights at me, too. It was Eleanor. I waved and trotted to the car. I opened the door, threw my bag over the seat into the back and got in.

'Hi,' I said. 'Thanks.'

After a moment's hesitation we both leaned to the middle and kissed. It was brief but good. I had not seen her in a long time and I was suddenly shocked by the realization of how fast time could slip between two people. Though we talked every year on birthdays and Christmas, it had been almost three years since I had actually seen her, touched her, been with her. And immediately it was intoxicating and depressing at the same time. For I had to go. This would be quicker than any of those birthday calls we made each year.

'Your hair's different,' I said. 'It looks good.'

It was the shortest I had ever seen it, cut cleanly at the midpoint of her neck. But it wasn't a false compliment. She looked good. But then again she would have looked good to me with hair to her ankles or even shorter than mine.

She turned from me to check traffic over her left shoulder. I could see the nape of her neck. She pulled into the through lane and we headed out. As she drove she reached up and held her finger on the button that closed the sunroof.

'Thank you, Harry. You don't look that different. But you still look good.'

I thanked her and tried not to smile too much as I got my wallet out.

'So,' she said, 'what's this big mystery that you couldn't tell me about on the phone?'

'No mystery. I just want some people to think I'm in Las Vegas.'

'You are in Las Vegas.'

'But not for long. As soon as I pick up the car I'm heading back.'

Eleanor nodded like she understood. I pulled my ATM and American Express cards out of my wallet. I kept my Visa card for the car rental and anything else that might come up.

'I want you to take these cards and use them over the next couple of days. The ATM code is oh-six-thirteen. Should be easy enough to remember.'

It had been our wedding day.

'Funny,' she said. 'You know, this year it falls on a Friday. I checked. That's bad luck, Harry.'

Friday the thirteenth somehow seemed appropriate. For a moment I wondered what it meant that she was checking on when future anniversaries of a failed marriage landed on the calendar. I dropped it and came back to the present.

'So just use them over the next few days. You know, go have dinner or something. If I were here I'd probably buy you a present for letting me stay with you. So go to the ATM and get some money and buy something you like. The AmEx still has my full name on it. You shouldn't have a problem.'

Most people don't know what gender my given name Hieronymus is. When we had been married Eleanor regularly used my credit cards without a problem. The only difficulty that would arise now would occur if an ID was requested at point of purchase. This rarely happens in restaurants anywhere and especially not in Las Vegas, a place that takes your money first and asks questions later.

I handed her the cards but she didn't take them.

'Harry, what is this? What's going on with you?'

'I told you. I want some people to think I am over here in Vegas.'

'And these are people who can monitor credit card purchases and ATM usage?'

'If they want to. I don't know if they will. This is just a pre–'

'Then you're talking about the cops or the bureau. Which is it?'

I laughed quietly.

'Well, it might be both. But as far as I know it's the bureau that's most interested.'

'Oh, Harry . . . '

She said it with a here-we-go-again tone in her voice. I thought about telling her that it involved Marty Gessler but decided I shouldn't involve her any further than I already had.

'Look, it's no big deal. I'm just working on one of my old cases and it's got an agent's nose out of joint. I want him to think he scared me off. For just a few days. Okay, Eleanor? Can you do this, please?'

I held the cards out again. After a long moment she reached up and took them without a word. We were on an airport road where all the rent-a-car complexes were lined up in a row. I wanted to say something else. Something about us and about how I wanted to come back over when all of this nastiness was finished. If she wanted me to. But she pulled into the Avis lot and put her window down to tell a security man that she was just there to drop me off.

The interruption ruined the flow of the conversation, if it even was a conversation. I lost my momentum and dropped any thought of saying anything further about us.

She pulled up to the Avis pickup office and it was time for me to get out. But I didn't. I sat there and looked at her until she finally turned and looked at me.

'Thank you for doing this, Eleanor.'

'It's not a problem. You'll get the bill.'

I smiled.

'Do you ever go back to L.A.? You know, to the card rooms or anything?'

She shook her head.

'Not in a long time. I don't like to travel anymore.'

I nodded. There didn't seem like there was anything else to say. I leaned over and kissed her, this time just on the cheek.

'I'll call you tomorrow or the next day, okay?'

'Okay, Harry. Be careful. Good-bye.'

'I will. Good-bye, Eleanor.'

I got out and watched her drive off. I wished I had been able to spend more time with her and wondered if she would have let me if I'd had the time. I then put those thoughts away and went inside. I showed my driver's license and credit card and picked up the key to my rental. It was a Ford Taurus and I had to get used to being low to the ground again. On my way out of rent-a-car row I saw a sign with an arrow pointing the way to Paradise Road. I thought that everybody needed a sign like that. I wished that it was that easy.

23

Four hours and a nonstop drive across the desert later I was in the tech lab at Biggar & Biggar. I took the memory card from my pocket and handed it to Andre. He held it up and looked at it and then looked at me as though I had just put used gum in his hand.

'Where's the case?'

'The case? You mean the clock? It's still on the wall.'

I hadn't figured out yet how to tell him that the clock was broken and probably the camera as well.

'No, the plastic case for the card. You put the spare card I gave you into the clock when you took this one out, right?'

I nodded.

'Right.'

'Well, you should have put this one into the spare card's case. This is a delicate instrument. Carrying it around with your pocket change and lint is not the proper way of—'

'Andre,' Burnett Biggar interrupted, 'let's just see if it's going to work. It was my mistake for not schooling Harry on the finer points of care and maintenance. I forgot he's such a throwback.'

Andre shook his head and walked over to a workbench with a computer set up on it. I looked at Burnett and nodded my thanks for the rescue. He winked at me and we followed Andre.

The son used a pneumatic air gun that looked like it was from a dentist's office to blast dust and debris off the memory card I had mishandled and then plugged it into a receptacle that was attached to the computer. He typed in a few commands and soon the images from Lawton Cross's sitting room were playing on the computer screen.

'Remember,' Andre said, 'we were using the motion sensor so it's going to be a bit jerky. Watch the clock in the corner and you'll be able to keep track.'

The first image on the screen was my own face. I was staring right at the camera as I adjusted the time on the clock. I then backed away, revealing Lawton Cross in his chair behind me.

'Oh, man,' Burnett said, seeing his former colleague's condition and situation. 'I don't know if I want to see this.'

'It gets worse,' I said, confident in what I thought was ahead on the surveillance.

Cross's voice croaked from the computer's speakers.

'Harry?'

'What?' I heard myself ask.

'Did you bring me some?'

'A little.'

On the screen I flipped open the toolbox to get the flask.

In the lab I said, 'Can you fast-forward this?'

Andre nodded and used the computer's mouse to click a FAST-FORWARD button on the screen. The screen blinked black for a moment, indicating the camera had gone off for lack of movement. It then came back on as Danny Cross entered the room. Andre switched the playback to real time. I checked the time and saw this was just a few minutes after I had left the room. Danny stood with her arms crossed in front of her and stared at her invalid husband as though he was a misbehaving child. She started speaking and it was hard to hear because of the television noise.

'This is amateur hour here,' Andre said. 'Why'd you put it next to the TV?'

He was right. I hadn't thought about that. The camera's microphone was picking up the voices from the television better than those in the room.

'Andre,' Burnett said, quieting his son's complaint. 'Just see if you can clean it up some.'

Andre used the mouse again to manipulate the sound. He backed the image up and played it again. The television noise was still intrusive but at least the conversation in the room was audible.

Danny Cross spoke with a sharp tone in her voice.

'I don't want him coming back here,' she said. 'He's not good for you.'

'Yes, he is. He's fine. He cares.'

'He's using you. He pours booze into you so he gets the information he needs.'

'So what's wrong with that? I think it's a good trade.'

'Yes, until the morning, when the pain comes.'

'Danny, if one of my friends comes here, you let him in.'

'What did you tell him this time, that I'm starving you? That I abandon you at night? Which lie this time?'

'I don't want to talk now.'

'Fine. Don't talk.'

'I want to dream.'

'Be my guest. At least one of us still can.'

She turned and left the room and the picture held on Lawton's motionless body. Soon his eyes closed.

'There's a sixty-second cutoff,' Andre explained. 'The camera stays on for a minute after motion ceases.'

'Fast-forward,' I said.

We spent the next ten minutes fast-forwarding and then stopping to watch mundane yet heart-ripping scenes of Lawton being fed and cleaned by Danny. At the end of the first night he was wheeled out by his wife and the camera went dark for nearly eight hours before he was wheeled back into the room. A new round of feedings and cleanings began.

It was horrible to look at, made more so because the clock was positioned just to the left of the television. Lawton Cross spent his time looking at the TV but the angle was so close it almost looked like he was staring up at the camera, looking right at us.

'This is pathetic,' Andre finally said. 'And there's nothing here. She treats him fine. Better than I would.'

'You want to see it through, Harry?' Burnett asked.

I nodded.

'I think you're right. She's clean. But there's something coming up. He had visitors last night. I want to see that. You can fast-forward if you want. It was near midnight.'

Andre worked the toggle and sure enough at 12:10 a.m. on the surveillance clock two men entered the room. I recognized Parenting Today and his partner. The first thing Parenting Today did was walk behind Lawton to turn off the baby monitor on the bureau. He then signaled his partner to close the door. Lawton's eyes were open and alert. He'd been awake before they had come into the room and the camera had activated. His eyes moved about in their sunken sockets as he tried to track the agent moving behind him.

'Mr. Cross, we need to have a little talk,' Parenting Today said.

He moved forward past Cross's chair and reached up and turned off the television.

'Thank God for that,' Andre said.

'Who are you people?' Cross rasped from the screen.

Parenting Today turned and looked at him.

'We're the FBI, Mr. Cross. Who the fuck are you?'

'What do you mean? I don't—'

'I mean who the fuck do you think you are, compromising our investigation?'

'I don't – what is this?'

'What did you tell Bosch that put the fire under his ass?'

'I don't know what you're talking about. He came to me, I didn't go to him.'

'Doesn't look like you can go anywhere now, does it?'

There was a short silence and I could see Lawton's eyes working. The man couldn't move a single limb but his eyes showed all the body language necessary.

'You're not FBI,' he said gallantly. 'Let me see badges and IDs.'

Parenting Today moved two steps toward Cross, his back blocking our view of the man in the chair.

'Badges?' he said in his best Mexican accent. 'We don't need no *steenking* badges.'

'Get out of here,' Cross said, his voice the clearest and strongest I had heard since I first visited him. 'When I tell Harry Bosch about this, you better watch your ass.'

Parenting Today turned in profile to smile at his partner.

'Harry Bosch? Don't worry about Harry Bosch. We're taking care of him. Worry about yourself, Mr. Cross.'

He leaned down now, putting his face close to Cross's. We now could see Lawton's eyes as they looked into the agent's.

'Because you are in harm's way. You are trespassing on a federal case. That is federal with a capital F. You understand?'

'Fuck you. And that is fuck you with a capital F. You understand?'

I had to smile. Lawton was doing his best to stand up to him. The bullet had taken away his body but not his spine and not his balls.

On the screen Parenting Today moved away from the chair and to the left. The camera caught his face and I could see the anger in his eyes. He leaned against the bureau, just out of the reach of Cross's view.

'Your hero, Harry Bosch, is gone and he might not be coming back,' he said. 'The question is, do you want to go where he's gone? A guy like you, in your condition, I don't know. You know what they do to guys like you in lockup? They wheel them into the corner and make them give blow jobs all day. Nothing they can do about it but sit there and take it. You into that, Cross? That what you want?'

Cross closed his eyes for a moment but then came back strong.

'You think you can pull that off, then take your best shot, Big Man.'

'Yeah?'

Parenting Today came off the bureau and up behind Cross. He leaned over his right shoulder as if to whisper in his ear. But he didn't.

'What if I take my shot here? Huh? How would that be?'

The agent brought his hands up on both sides of Cross's face. He took hold of the plastic breathing tubes that were attached to Cross's nostrils. With his fingers he crimped the tubes closed, cutting off the air supply.

'Hey, Milton . . .,' the other agent said.

'Shut up, Carney. This guy thinks he's smart. Thinks he doesn't have to cooperate with the federal government.'

Cross's eyes grew wide and he opened his mouth to gulp for air. He wasn't getting any.

'Motherfucker,' Burnett Biggar said. 'Who is this guy?'

I said nothing. I watched silently, the anger rising in me. Biggar had it right, though. In the lexicon of cop talk 'motherfucker' was the ultimate expletive, the one reserved for the worst offender, the worst enemy. I felt like saying it but my voice wouldn't come. I was too consumed by what I saw on the screen. What they had done to me was nothing compared to the humiliation and scarring they were putting on Lawton Cross.

On the screen Cross was trying to speak but couldn't get the words out with no air in his lungs. There was a sneer on the face of the agent I now knew was named Milton.

'What?' he asked. 'What's that? You want to talk to me?'

Cross tried again to talk but couldn't.

'Nod your head if you want to tell me something. Oh, that's right, you can't nod your head, can you?'

He finally let go of the tubes and Cross began to pull in air like a man coming up out of the water from fifty feet down. His chest heaved and his nostrils flared as he tried to recover.

Milton came around in front of the chair. He looked down upon his victim and nodded.

'You see? That's how easy it is. You want to cooperate now?'

'What do you want?'

'What did you tell Bosch?'

Cross's eyes flicked up toward the camera for a moment and then back to Milton. In that moment I didn't think he was checking the time. I suddenly thought that maybe Lawton knew about the camera. He'd been a good cop. Maybe he knew what I had been doing all along.

'I told him about the case. That's all. He came to me and I told him what I knew. I don't remember it all. I got hurt, you know. I got hurt and my memory isn't so good. Things are just starting to come back to me. I—'

'Why did he come here tonight?'

'Because I forgot I had some files. My wife called for me and I left him a message. He came for the files.'

'What else?'

'Nothing else. What do you want?'

'What do you know about the money that was taken?'

'Nothing. We never got that far.'

Milton reached forward and held the breathing tubes again. He didn't crimp them this time. The threat was enough.

'I'm telling you the truth,' Cross protested.

'You better be.'

The agent let go of the tubes.

'You are finished talking to Bosch, is that understood?'

'Yes.'

'Yes, what?'

'Yes, I'm finished talking to Bosch.'

'Thank you for your cooperation.'

When Milton moved away from the chair I saw Cross's eyes were downcast. As the agents were leaving, one of them – probably Milton – hit the wall switch and the room and screen dropped into darkness.

We stood there staring at the screen and in the minute before the camera cut off we could hear but not see Lawton Cross crying. They were the deep sobs of a wounded and helpless animal. I did not look at the two men with me and they didn't look at me. We just watched the dark screen and listened.

The camera finally – thankfully – cut off at the end of the minute but then the screen came alive again when the room's light was flicked back on and Danny entered the room. I checked the time on the screen and saw this was only three minutes after the agents had left the room. Her husband's face was streaked with tears. Tears he could do nothing to hide.

She crossed the room to him. Without a word she climbed onto the chair in front of him, her knees alongside his thin thighs. She lowered her hips onto his lap. She opened her bathrobe and pulled his face forward to her breasts. She held him there and he cried again. No words were spoken at first. She quietly and tenderly shushed him. And then she started to sing to him.

The song I knew and she sang it well. Her voice was as soft as a breeze, whereas the song's original voice carried the rasp of all the world's anguish in it. I didn't think anybody could ever touch Louis Armstrong but Danny Cross certainly did.

I see skies of blue
And clouds of white
The bright blessed day
The dark sacred night
And I think to myself
What a wonderful world

And that was the hardest part of the surveillance to watch. That was the part that made me feel the most like an intruder, as if I had crossed some line of decency within myself.

'Turn it off now,' I finally said.

24

The defining moment for me as a police officer did not occur on the street or while I worked a case. It occurred on March 5, 1991. It was during the afternoon and I was in the squad room in Hollywood Division ostensibly doing paperwork. But like everybody else in the squad I was waiting. When everybody started leaving their desks to gather at the televisions I got up, too. There was one in the lieutenant's office and one was mounted overhead on the wall by the burglary table. I didn't get along with the lieutenant at the time so I moved to the burglary pen to watch. We had already heard about it but few of us had actually seen the tape yet. And there it was. Grainy black-and-white but still clear enough to see and to know that things would change. Four uniform cops gathered around a man flopping on the ground. Rodney King, ex-con and now speeding scofflaw. Two of the cops were wailing on him with batons. A third kicked him while the fourth controlled the juice for the Taser gun. A second larger ring of uniforms stood around and watched. A lot of jaws dropped in the squad room as we looked up at the screen. A lot of hearts fell. We felt betrayed in some way. To a man and woman we all knew that the department would not withstand the tape. It would change. Police work in Los Angeles would change.

Of course we didn't know how or whether it would be for better or for worse. We didn't know then that political motives and racial emotions would rise up over the department like a tidal wave, that there would later be a deadly riot and complete tearing of the city's social fabric. But as we watched that grainy video we all knew something was coming. All because of that one moment of anger and frustration acted out under a streetlight in the San Fernando Valley.

As I sat in the waiting room of a downtown law office I thought about that moment. I remembered the anger I felt and I realized it had come back to me across time. The recording I had of Lawton Cross being abused was no Rodney King tape. It would not set back law enforcement and community relations decades. It would not change the way people viewed police and decided whether to back them or cooperate with them. But it had a clear kinship in its sickeningly pure depiction of the abuse of power.

It didn't have the juice to change a city but it could change a bureaucracy like the Federal Bureau of Investigation. If I wanted it to.

But I didn't. What I wanted was something else and I was going to use the recording to get it. In the short run at least. I wasn't thinking yet about what might happen with it or with me further down the road.

The law library I sat in an hour after leaving Biggar & Biggar was lined with cherry-wood paneling and bookshelves full of leather-bound volumes of law books. In the few open spaces on the walls there were lighted oil paintings depicting the law firm's partners. I stood in front of one of the paintings studying the fine brushwork. It showed a handsome man standing tall with brown hair and piercing green eyes set off by a deep tan. The gold plate on the top of the mahogany frame said his name was James Foreman. He looked like everything a successful man should be.

'Mr. Bosch?'

I turned. The matronly woman who had escorted me to the library now beckoned to me at the door. I went to her and she led me down a hall thickly carpeted in a soft green that whispered *money* with every step I took. She led me to an office where a woman I didn't recognize was waiting behind a desk. She stood up and offered her hand.

'Hello, Mr. Bosch, I'm Roxanne, Ms. Langwiser's assistant. Would you like a bottle of water or coffee or anything?'

'Uh, no, I'm fine.'

'You can go on in, then. She's waiting.'

She pointed me toward a closed door to the side of her desk and I walked to it, knocked once on it, and went in. I was carrying a briefcase I had borrowed from Burnett Biggar.

Janis Langwiser was sitting behind a desk that reminded me of a two-car garage. She also had the twelve-foot ceiling and the cherry-wood paneling and shelves. She wasn't a small woman. Rather, she was tall and slim. But the office made her look diminutive. She smiled when she saw me and I did likewise.

'They never asked me if I wanted bottled water or coffee when I came to see you at the DA's office.'

'I know, Harry. Times have certainly changed.'

She stood up and reached her hand across the desk. She had to lean forward to make it. We shook hands. I met her when she was a rookie filing deputy in downtown criminal courts. I watched her grow up and handle some of the biggest and toughest cases. She was a good prosecutor. Now she was trying to be a good criminal defense attorney. Rare was the prosecutor who made a whole career of it. The money was too good at the other table. Judging by the office I was in, Janis Langwiser was sitting pretty at that other table.

'Have a seat,' she said. 'You know I've been meaning to track you down and call you. You just turning up like this today is great.'

I was confused.

'Track me down for what? You're not repping anybody I put in the clink, are you?'

'No, no, nothing like that. I wanted to talk to you about a job.'

I raised my eyebrows. She smiled like she was offering me the keys to the city.

'I don't know what you know about us, Harry.'

'I know you were pretty hard to find. You're not listed in the phone book. I had to call a friend of mine at the DA's office and he got me the number.'

She nodded.

'That's right. We're not listed. We don't need to be. We have very few clients and we handle every legal detail that crops up in their lives.'

'And you handle the criminal details.'

She hesitated. She was trying to judge where I was coming from.

'That's right. I'm the firm's criminal expert. That's why I was meaning to call you. When I heard you retired I thought this would be perfect. Not full-time, but sometimes – depending on the case – it gets hot and heavy. We could really use somebody with your skills, Harry.'

I took a moment to compose my answer. I didn't want to offend her. I wanted to hire her. So I decided not to tell her that what she was suggesting was impossible. That I could never move to the other table, no matter what the money was. It wasn't in me. Retired or not, I had a mission in life. Working for a defense attorney wasn't part of it.

'Janis,' I said, 'I'm not looking for a job. I sort of already have one. The reason I'm here is because I want to hire you.'

She giggled.

'You're kidding,' she said. 'Are you in trouble?'

'Probably. But that's not why I want to hire you. I need a lawyer I can trust to hold something for me and take the appropriate actions with it if necessary.'

She leaned forward in her desk. She still was at least six feet away from me.

'Harry, this is getting mysterious. What is going on?'

'First off, what is your normal retainer? Let's get the client thing out of the way first.'

'Harry, our minimum retainer is twenty-five thousand dollars. So forget about that. I owe you for all of those airtight cases you brought me. Consider yourself a client.'

I pushed the surprise off my face.

'Really? Twenty-five grand just to open a file?'

'That's right.'

'Well, they got the right person for it.'

'Thank you, Harry. Now what is this thing you want me to do?'

I opened the briefcase Burnett Biggar had given me to carry the second round of equipment I borrowed from him along with the memory card and the three CDs containing copies of the clock surveillance. Andre had made the copies. I put the card and the CDs on her desk.

'This is a surveillance I took. I want you to hold the original – the memory card – in a safe place. I want you to hold an envelope with one of the CDs and a letter from me. I want your private office number. I'm going to call it every night by midnight and tell you I am okay. In the morning you come in and if the message is there, then everything is all right. If you come in and there is no message from me, then you deliver the envelope to a reporter at the *Times* named Josh Meyer.'

'Josh Meyer. That name is familiar. Is he on courts?'

'I think he used to cover local crime stuff. Now he's on terrorism. I think he works out of D.C. now.'

'Terrorism, Harry?'

'It's a long story.'

She checked her watch.

'I've got time. I've also got a computer.'

I first took fifteen minutes to tell her about my private investigation and everything that had happened since Lawton Cross had called me out of the blue and I had pulled down the box of old cases off the closet shelf. Then I let her put the CD in her computer and watch the surveillance video. She didn't recognize Lawton Cross until I told her who he was. She reacted with appropriate outrage when she viewed the section with Agents Milton and Carney. I had her turn it off before Danny Cross came into the room and comforted her husband.

'First question, were they real agents?' she asked after the computer kicked the disk out.

'Yeah, they're part of the anti-terrorism squad working out of Westwood.'

She shook her head in disgust.

'If this ever gets to the *Times* and then onto TV, then—'

'I don't want it to get there. Right now, that is the worst-case scenario.'

'Why not, Harry? Those are rogue agents. At least that one Milton is. And the other is just as guilty for standing there and letting him do it.'

She gestured toward her computer, where the surveillance video had been replaced by a screensaver that showed a bucolic scene of a house on a cliff overlooking the ocean, the waves rolling endlessly to shore.

'Do you think this is what the attorney general and the Congress of the United States wanted when they enacted legislation that changed and streamlined the bureau's rules and tools after September eleventh?'

'No, I don't,' I answered. 'But they should have known what could happen. What's the saying, absolute power corrupts absolutely? Something like that. Anyway, it's a given that this sort of thing would happen. They should have known. The difference here is that that isn't some Middle Eastern bag man on there. That's an American citizen. He's a former cop and he's a goddamn quadriplegic because he took a bullet in the line of duty.'

Langwiser nodded somberly.

'That is exactly why you should get this out. It has to be see—'

'Janis, are you working for me or should I gather all this up and just find somebody else?'

She threw her hands up in surrender.

'Yes, I'm working for you, Harry. I'm just saying that this should not be allowed to just go by.'

'I'm not talking about letting it go by. I just don't want it out yet. I need to use it as leverage first. I need to get what I want out of it first.'

'Which is what?'

'I was going to get to that but you started in like Ralph Nader.'

'Okay, I'm sorry. I'm all calmed down now. Tell me your plan, Harry.'

And so I did.

25

Kate Mantilini's on Wilshire Boulevard had a row of high-backed booths that afforded their inhabitants more interior privacy than the lap-dance cubicles in the back rooms of any of the strip clubs in town. That was why I chose the restaurant for the meeting. It was very private yet very public. I was there fifteen minutes before the appointed time, got a booth with a window fronting Wilshire and waited. Special Agent Peoples got there a little early, too. He had to walk along the row of booths and look into each one to find me. He then slipped silently and morosely into the space across from me.

'Agent Peoples, glad you could make it.'

'I didn't feel like I had much choice.'

'I guess you didn't.'

He flipped open one of the menus that were on the table.

'Never been here before. Food any good?'

'It's not bad. Good chicken pot pie on Thursdays.'

'It's not Thursday.'

'And you're not here to eat.'

He looked up from the menu and gave me his best deadeye stare but he didn't have the juice this time. We both knew I was holding the high card this time. I looked out the window and glanced up and down Wilshire.

'You have your people out there, Agent Peoples? Are they waiting for me?'

'I came alone as instructed by your attorney.'

'Well, just so you're clear. If your people grab me again or make any move against my attorney, then the consequences are that the surveillance recording you were e-mailed will go to the media and out across the Internet. There are people who will know if I disappear. They'll put it out, no hesitation.'

Peoples shook his head.

'You keep saying that. 'Disappear.' This isn't South America, Bosch. And we're not Nazis.'

I nodded in agreement.

'Sitting in this nice restaurant it sure doesn't seem so. But when I was sitting in that cube on the ninth floor and nobody knew I was there, that was a different story. Mouse Aziz and those other guys you've got up there probably don't know the difference between California and Chile right now either.'

'And you are defending them now, is that it? The men who would like to see this country burn to the ground.'

'I'm not de–'

I stopped when the waitress came to the booth. She said her name was Kathy and asked if we were ready to order. Peoples ordered coffee and I ordered coffee and an ice cream sundae with no whipped cream. After Kathy left, Peoples looked at me funny.

'I'm retired. I can have a sundae.'

'Some retirement.'

'They make good sundaes here and they're open late. That's a good combination.'

'I'll remember that.'

'Did you ever see the movie *Heat*? This is the place where Pacino the cop meets De Niro the burglar. It's where they both tell each other they won't hesitate to put the other down if it comes to that.'

Peoples nodded and we held each other's eyes for a long moment. Message delivered. I decided to get down to the business at hand.

'So what did you think of my clock camera?'

The façade dropped and Peoples suddenly looked wounded. He looked as though he had been thrown to the lions. He knew what the future held for him if that recording got out. Milton worked for him; therefore he'd take the fall, too. The Rodney King tape cut a swath through the LAPD that went all the way to the top. Peoples was smart enough to know he would get trampled if he didn't contain this problem.

'I was disgusted by what I saw. First off, I apologize to you and my plan is to go out to see that man, Lawton Cross, and apologize as well.'

'That's nice of you.'

'Don't think for a moment that that is how we operate. That it is the status quo. That I condone it. Agent Milton is gone. He's out. I knew that the moment I saw the recording. I'm not promising you he will be prosecuted, but he won't be carrying a badge for very long. Not an FBI badge. I'll see to that.'

I nodded.

'Right, you'll see to that.'

I said it with high-octane sarcasm and I could see it put some color in his cheeks. The color of anger.

'You called the meeting, Bosch. What do you want?'

There it was. The question I was waiting for.

'You know what I want. I want you people off my back. I want my files and my notes back. I want Lawton Cross's file back. I want a copy of the

LAPD murder book— which I know you must have – and I want access to Aziz and what you have on him.'

'What we have on him is classified. It's a national security matter. We can't—'

'Declassify it. I want to know how strong the connection is to my movie heist. I want to know what you have on his whereabouts on two nights. All that federal intelligence has got to be good for something and I want it. And then I want to talk to him.'

'Who? Aziz? That's not going to happen.'

I leaned across the table.

'Yes, it is. Because the alternative to that is that everybody who has a TV or America Online is going to see what your boy Milton did to a helpless man in a wheelchair. Make that a highly decorated retired cop who had the use of his limbs and fucking life taken from him while in the line of duty. You think the Rodney King tape did some damage to the LAPD? You wait and see what happens with this one. I guarantee you that Milton and you and your whole little ninth-floor BAM squad will be cut loose by the bureau and the attorney general and everybody else faster than you can say civil rights indictment. You understand, *Special* Agent Peoples?'

I gave him a moment to respond but he didn't. His eyes were fixed and staring out through the window to Wilshire.

'And if you think for one minute I won't pull the trigger on this, then you haven't done your homework on me.'

This time I waited him out and eventually his eyes came back through the window and to me. The waitress came and put down our coffees and told me my sundae was on the way. Neither Peoples nor I said thank you.

'Believe me,' Peoples said, 'I know you will pull the trigger. You are that kind of guy, Bosch. I know your kind. You will put yourself and your own interests ahead of the greater good.'

'Don't give me that 'greater good' bullshit. This isn't about that. You give me what I want and you get rid of Milton, then you get to cruise along like nothing ever happened. The recording is never seen. How's that for greater good?'

Peoples leaned forward to sip his coffee. As he had done in the cube on the ninth floor he burned his mouth and grimaced. He pushed the cup and saucer away on the table and then slid to the edge of the booth before looking back at me.

'I'll be in touch.'

'Twenty-four hours. I hear from you by this time tomorrow night or all bets are off. I go public with it.'

He stood up and remained next to the booth looking at me and still holding a napkin. He nodded his agreement.

'Let me ask you something,' he said. 'If you're here, who used your credit card tonight to buy dinner at Commander's Palace in Vegas?'

I smiled. They had been tracking me.

'A friend. Is that a nice place, Commander's Palace?'

He nodded.

'One of the best. I've been there. The shrimp in the gumbo is as soft as marshmallow.'

'That's great, I guess.'

'Expensive too. Your friend put over a hundred bucks on your AmEx. Dinner for two it looked like.'

He tossed his napkin onto the table.

'I'll be in touch.'

A moment after he was gone the waitress brought my sundae. I asked her for the check and she said she'd bring it right away.

I poked a spoon into the fudge and ice cream but I didn't taste it. I sat there thinking about what Peoples had just said. I wasn't sure if there was an implied threat in his telling me he knew somebody was using my credit card. Maybe he even knew who. But the thing I thought about the most was what he had said about it being dinner for two at Commander's Palace. That 'we' thing again. Just as with Eleanor, I couldn't let it go.

26

Since the Las Vegas ruse was no longer in play I drove out to Burbank Airport, turned in my rental and took the tram out to the long-term lot to collect my car. I had borrowed Lawton Cross's dolly and it was in the back of the Mercedes. Before driving off I got it out and slid underneath the car. I detached the satellite tracker and the heat sensor and slid under the pickup truck parked in the next space. I attached the equipment to the pickup's underside and then got into the Mercedes. As I backed out I saw that the pickup had an Arizona plate. I figured if Peoples didn't dispatch somebody soon to collect the bureau's equipment, then they'd have to chase it to the next state. That left me smiling to myself when I pulled up to the parking booth to pay.

'You must have had a nice flight,' said the woman who took my ticket.

'Yeah, I guess you could say that. I made it back alive.'

I went home and called Janis Langwiser on her cell phone as soon as I got in the door. She had changed my plan a little bit. She didn't want me leaving a message on her office line every night. She insisted I call her directly on her cell.

'How did it go?'

'Well, it went. Now I just have to wait. I gave him until tomorrow night. I guess we'll know by then.'

'And how did he take it?'

'About what we expected. Not well. But I think by the end he saw the light. I think he'll call tomorrow.'

'I hope so.'

'Everything set on your end?'

'I think so. The memory card's in the office safe and I'll wait to hear from you. If I don't, then I'll know what to do.'

'Good, Janis. Thanks.'

'Good night, Harry.'

I hung up and thought about things. Everything seemed to be in place. It was Peoples who would have to make the next move. I lifted the phone again and called Eleanor. She answered immediately, no sleep in her voice.

'Sorry, it's Harry. Are you playing?'

'Yes and no. I'm playing but I'm not doing well so I took a break. I'm standing outside the Bellagio watching the fountains.'

I nodded. I could picture her there at the railing, the dancing fountains lit up in front of her. I could hear the music and the splash of water over the phone.

'How was Commander's Palace?'

'How did you know about that?'

'Had a visit from the bureau tonight.'

'That was quick.'

'Yeah. I heard that's a good restaurant. Shrimp like marshmallow. Did you like it?'

'It's nice. I like the one in New Orleans better. The food's the same but the original is the original, you know?'

'Yeah. Plus it's probably not so great eating by yourself.'

I almost cursed out loud at how lame and transparent that was.

'I wasn't alone. I took a friend that I play with. One of the girls. You didn't tell me there was a spending limit, Harry.'

'No, I know. There wasn't.'

I needed to steer away from this. We both knew what I had been asking about and it was getting embarrassing, especially considering there might be other ears listening.

'You didn't notice anybody watching you, did you?'

There was a pause.

'No. And I hope you didn't get me into any kind of trouble, Harry.'

'No, you're fine. I'm just calling to let you know the scam is over. The bureau knows I'm still here.'

'Damn, I never got the chance to go shopping and get myself that present you promised.'

I smiled. She was kidding and I could tell.

'That's okay, you can still do that.'

'Is everything okay, Harry?'

'Yeah, fine.'

'You want to talk about it?'

Not on this line, I thought but didn't say.

'Maybe when I see you next time. I'm too tired right now.'

'Okay, then I'll let you go. What should I do with your cards? And you know you left your bag on my backseat.'

She said it like she knew I had done it on purpose.

'Um, why don't you just hold onto that stuff for now and maybe when I get past this thing I'm working on I'll come back out and get it from you.'

It was a long time before she answered.

'Just give me a little more notice than you did today,' she finally said. 'So I'm ready.'

'Sure, no problem. I will.'

'Okay, Harry, I'm going to go back in. Maybe talking to you will have changed my luck.'

'I hope so, Eleanor. Thanks for doing this for me.'

'No problem. Good night.'

'Good night.'

She disconnected.

'And good luck,' I said into the dead line.

I hung the phone up again and tried to think about the conversation and what she had meant. *Just give me a little more notice than you did today. So I'm ready.* It was like she wanted a warning before I came out. So she could do what? What did she have to get ready for?

I realized that I could drive myself nuts thinking and worrying about it. I put Eleanor and all of that aside and grabbed a beer out of the refrigerator and took it out to the back deck. It was a cool and clear night and the lights of the freeway far below seemed to sparkle like a diamond necklace. I could hear a woman's laughter carrying up the hillside from somewhere down below. I started thinking about Danny Cross and the song she had gently sung to her husband. In love and in loss the night is always sacred. It's only a wonderful world if you can make it that way. There are no street signs pointing to Paradise Road.

I decided that when all of this was over I would go to Vegas and not turn back. I would throw the dice. I would go see Eleanor and take my chances.

27

The next morning I spread the documents I had rescued from the engine compartment of Lawton Cross's muscle car across the table. I went into the kitchen to brew a pot of coffee but discovered I was out of coffee. I could go down the hill to the store but I didn't want to leave the phone. I was expecting Janis Langwiser to call early. So I sat down at the table with a bottle of water and started in on the reports Cross had copied and taken home almost four years before.

What I had was a copy of the currency report prepared by the bank which had loaned the cash to the movie company, and the time and location sheets that Lawton Cross and Jack Dorsey had been working on before their schedule became crowded with other cases.

The currency report was four pages of typed serial numbers taken from randomly selected one-hundred-dollar bills contained in the shipment to the movie set. The report was prepared by two people listed as Linus Simonson and Jocelyn Jones. It was then signed off on by a bank vice president named Gordon Scaggs.

Simonson was a name I knew. He had been one of the bank employees at the movie set on the day of the heist. He had been wounded during the shoot-out. Now I knew why he was there; he had helped prepare the money shipment and was most likely there to baby-sit it through the day of filming.

Scaggs was also a name that was familiar to me. It was among the names given to me by Alexander Taylor when I had asked the film producer who specifically knew about the cash delivery to the movie set. I no longer had the list of nine names I had collected from Taylor. The FBI had taken that during the search of my home. But I remembered the name Scaggs.

Committed to studying everything about the case I could get my hands on, I scanned the listings of currency numbers, thinking maybe something would stick out. But nothing grabbed me. The numbers were like an unbreakable code locking away the secret to the case. It was simply four pages of numbers in no particular sequence.

Finally, I put the currency report aside and took up the alibi sheets. I first checked for the names Scaggs, Simonson and Jones and saw that

Dorsey and Cross had indeed run out T&L checks on all three of the bank employees. Cross had taken Scaggs and Jones while Dorsey ran down Simonson. Their locations were checked against key times in the murder of Angella Benton and the subsequent movie set heist.

All three were cleared by alibi of physical involvement in the crimes. Simonson, of course, was at the scene of the heist, but he was there as a representative of the bank. His being shot by one of the robbers also tended to add weight to his clearance. This did not, of course, clear them of ancillary involvement. Any one of them could have been the mastermind behind the heist who had stayed in the background as the plan was carried out. Or, at the very least, any one of them could have simply been the source of information on the delivery of money to the movie set.

The same went for the other eight names in the T&L report. All were cleared by alibi of active involvement in the crimes. But I had no other files or reports to indicate what had been done to determine if they had a background connection to the crime.

I realized I was spinning my wheels. I was trying to play solitaire without a full deck. The aces were gone and there was no way I could win. I had to get all the cards. I took a swig of water and wished it was coffee. I started thinking about how important the play with Peoples was. If it didn't work, I was done. Angella Benton's outstretched hands might haunt me for the rest of my life but there wasn't anything I was going to be able to do about it.

As if on cue the telephone rang. I went into the kitchen and picked up. It was Janis Langwiser, though she didn't identify herself.

'It's me,' she said. 'We have to talk.'

'Okay, I'm in the middle of something. I'll call you right back.'

'Good.'

She hung up without a protest. I took that as a sign that she now believed what I had told her about my house and phone being bugged. I also took it as a sign that Peoples was acting in the way I had hoped he would. I grabbed my keys off the counter and went out the door.

I drove down the hill. At the place where Mulholland wraps around the other side of the hill and meets Woodrow Wilson at Cahuenga I saw a vintage yellow Corvette waiting at the light across from me. I knew the driver, sort of. Every now and then I'd see him jogging or driving the 'vette past my house. And I'd seen and spoken to him in the police station on occasion, too. He was a private eye who lived on the other side of the ridge from me. I put my arm out the window and gave him the sweeping palm-down salute. He did likewise back to me. Smooth sailing, my brother. I was going to need it. The light changed and he went south on Cahuenga while I went north.

I bought a cup of coffee in a convenience store and used a pay phone next to the Poquito Mas to call Langwiser back on her cell. She answered right away.

'They came in last night,' she said. 'Just like you predicted.'

'Did you get it on the camera?'

'Yes! It's perfect. Clear as day. It was the same guy in the first surveillance. Milton.'

I nodded to myself. The call to my house the night before in which Janis said she'd locked the memory card in her office safe had been the bait and Milton had taken it. Before leaving her office I had set up another one of Biggar & Biggar's cameras – the radio – on her desk and trained it toward the bookcase which hid the safe.

'He stumbled around looking for a while but then he found it. He took the whole safe out of the wall. It's gone.'

She had emptied everything from the safe the night before. I had put in a folded piece of paper. It said, 'Fuck you, with a capital F.' I imagined Milton unfolding it and reading it – if he had managed to get the safe open.

'Anything else hit in the offices?'

'A couple drawers pulled out here and there. The quarter jar in the coffee room. All just cover to make it look like a regular burglary.'

'Anybody call the police to report it?'

'Yes, but nobody's shown up yet. Typical.'

'Keep the surveillance out of it. For now.'

'I know. Like we said. What should I do now?'

'You still have Peoples's e-mail address?'

'Sure do.'

The night before, she had gotten the e-mail address rather easily from a former colleague who worked at the U.S. Attorney's office.

'Okay, send Peoples another e-mail. Attach the latest surveillance and tell him I've changed the deadline to noon today. I hear from him by then or he can start watching CNN for the results. Send it as soon as you can.'

'I'm on-line now.'

'Good.'

I sipped coffee while listening to her type. Andre Biggar had included in the briefcase I borrowed the computer attachment Langwiser would need to view the memory card taken from the radio camera. She could now attach a file containing the surveillance recording to an e-mail.

'It's away,' she finally said. 'Good luck, Harry.'

'I'll probably need it.'

'Remember, call me tonight by midnight or I'll follow the instructions.'

'Gotcha.'

I hung up and went back to the convenience store for a second cup of coffee. I was already wired from Langwiser's report but I figured I might be needing the spare caffeine before the day was finished.

When I got back to the house the phone was ringing. I got the door unlocked and got inside just in time to grab the phone off the kitchen counter.

'Yeah?'

'Mr. Bosch? John Peoples here.'

'Good morning.'

'Not really. When can you come in?'

'I'm on my way.'

28

Special Agent Peoples was waiting for me in the first-floor lobby of the federal building in Westwood. He was standing when I got there. Maybe he'd been standing there the whole time since he'd made the call.

'Follow me,' he said. 'We're going to make this quick.'

'Whatever works.'

After giving a uniformed guard the nod he led me through a security door using a card key and then he used it again to access the elevator I was already familiar with.

'You guys got your own elevator and everything,' I said. 'Pretty cool.'

Peoples wasn't impressed. He turned so he was looking right at me.

'I'm doing this because I have no choice. I've decided to agree to this extortion because I believe in the greater good of what I'm trying to accomplish here.'

'Is that why you sent Milton into my lawyer's office last night? Was that all part of the greater good you're talking about?'

He didn't answer.

'Look, you can hate me and that's fine. That's your option. But let's not bullshit each other. Don't hide behind that stuff, because we both know what's going on here. Your guy crossed the line and got caught. Now it's just time to pay the price. That's what this is about. It's that simple.'

'And meantime an investigation is compromised and lives may be at stake.'

'We'll see about that, won't we?'

The elevator opened on the ninth floor. He led me out without answering. The ever handy card key got us through another door and into a squad room where several agents were working at desks. As we passed through, most of them stopped what they were doing to look at me. I assumed that they had either been briefed on who I was and what I was doing or just the occurrence of a non-agent in the inner sanctum was worth noting.

When I was halfway across the room I spotted Milton sitting at a desk near the back. He was leaning back in his chair giving me his best show of being relaxed. But I could sense the anger pulsing beneath the façade. I winked at him and turned my attention away.

Peoples led me into a small room with a desk and two chairs. On the desk was a cardboard box. I looked into it and recognized my own notebook and the file I had kept on Angella Benton. There was also the file from Lawton Cross's garage and a black binder full of documents two inches thick. I assumed it was the copy of the LAPD's murder book. I got excited just looking at it. It was the full deck of cards I had been looking for.

'Where's the rest?' I asked.

Peoples walked around behind the desk and opened the middle drawer. He removed a file and dropped it on the top of the desk.

'In there you will find subject location reports covering the two dates you requested. I don't think they will help you but it's what you wanted. You can look at them here but you cannot take them with you. They will not leave this office. Do you understand that?'

I nodded, deciding not to push it.

'What about Aziz?'

'When you are ready I will put you in a room with him. But he won't talk to you. You'll be wasting your time.'

'Well, it's mine to waste.'

'Then, before you leave here, you will call your attorney and instruct her to turn over to me the original and all copies of the surveillance recordings you have from last night and the night before.'

I shook my head.

'Sorry, that's not the deal.'

'It certainly is.'

'No, I never said I would turn over the recordings. What I said was that I would not go public with them. There's a difference. I'm not going to turn over the only leverage I've got. I'm not stupid, John.'

'We had a deal,' he said, his cheeks beginning to quiver with anger.

'And I'm keeping the deal. Exactly as offered.'

I reached into my pocket and pulled out a cassette tape. I held it out to him.

'If you don't believe me you can listen for yourself. I was wearing a wire last night in the booth.'

I watched his eyes register that I now even had him directly tied in.

'Take it, John. Call it a goodwill gesture. It's the original. No copies were made.'

He slowly reached up and took the tape. I moved around behind the desk.

'Why don't I take a look at what you've got in the file while you go do whatever you have to do to get Aziz ready?'

Peoples pocketed the tape and nodded.

'I'll be back in ten minutes,' he said. 'If anyone comes in here and asks what you are doing, close that file and tell them to see me.'

'One last thing. What about the money?'

'What about it?'

'How much money from the movie set heist did Aziz have under his car seat?'

I thought I saw a small smile start to play on Peoples's face, but then it went away.

'He had a hundred bucks. One bill traced to the heist.'

He stayed long enough to see the disappointment on my face, then turned to the door.

After he left the room I sat down at the desk and opened the file. It contained two pages that had security stamps on them and had words in the middle of paragraphs and then whole paragraphs blocked out with black ink. Peoples clearly wasn't going to let me see anything I had not bargained for – or extorted from him, as he had put it.

The pages were taken from what I assumed was a larger file. There was a coding in small print at the top left corner. I reached into the cardboard box and opened my file. I took out one of the loose sheets of note paper and wrote the code number from each page down. I then read what Peoples was allowing me to read.

The first page had two dated paragraphs.

> 5-11-99 – SUBJECT confirmed in Hamburg at [redacted] in company with [redacted] and [redacted]. SUBJECT seen in restaurant by [redacted] approximately 20:00 until 23:30 hours. No further detail.
>
> 7-1-99 – SUBJECT passport scan at Heathrow at 14:40 hours. Follow up determination arrival on Lufthansa Flight 698 from Frankfurt. No further detail.

The paragraphs before and after these two were completely blacked out. What I was looking at was the log in which tabs on Aziz had been kept over the years by the feds. He was on the watch list. This is what it amounted to. Sightings by informants or agents and airport passport checks.

The two dates on the page were on either side of the murder of Angella Benton and the movie set heist. It by no means cleared Aziz of active or background involvement in the crimes. Yet, if I believed the document in front of me, he was in Europe both before and after the occurrence of the crimes I was investigating. But it was no alibi. Aziz was known, according to the *Times* article I had read, to travel with false identification. It was possible he had slipped into this country to commit the crimes and then slipped out.

I went on to the next page. This one had only one paragraph that was not blacked out. But the date was a direct hit.

> 3-19-00 – SUBJECT passport scan at LAX-CA. Arrival on Qantas Flight 88 from Manilla at 18:11 hrs. Security check and search. Questioned by [redacted], Los Angeles field office. See transcript #00-44969. Released at 21:15 hrs.

Aziz had what appeared to be a perfect alibi for the night Agent Martha Gessler disappeared. He was being questioned by an FBI agent at Los Angeles International Airport until 9:15 p.m., which put him in federal custody at the same time Gessler disappeared while on her way home from work.

I put the two sheets back in the file and put it back in the drawer. I wrote no further notes – there was nothing to write – on the page from my file. I put it back inside the file and lifted out the murder book. I was just about to start into it when the door to the room opened and there was Milton. I said nothing. I waited for him to make the first move. He stepped in and looked around the room as though it was the size of a warehouse. He finally spoke without looking at me.

'You have some balls on you, Bosch. Doing what you're doing and thinking you're going to just walk away from it. Away from me.'

'I guess I could say the same thing about you.'

'If it was me I would have called your bluff.'

'Then you would have called it wrong.'

He leaned down and put both hands on the table and looked right at me.

'You are a has-been, Bosch. The world's passed you by, but here you are, grabbing at straws, fucking with people who are trying to protect the future.'

I was unimpressed and hoped I showed it. I leaned back and looked up at him.

'Why don't you relax, man? You've got nothing to worry about as far as I can tell. You've got a boss who's more interested in a cover-up than a cleanup. You'll do okay on this, Milton. I think he's mad because you got caught, not because of what you did.'

He pointed a finger at me.

'Don't fucking go there. Don't. The day I want career advice from you is the day I turn in my badge.'

'Fine. Then what do you want?'

'I want to give you a warning. Watch out for me, Bosch. 'Cause I'm coming.'

'Then I'll be ready.'

He turned and walked out, leaving the door open. A few seconds later Peoples was back.

'You ready?'

'Been ready.'

'Where's the file I gave you?'

'It's back in the drawer.'

He leaned over the desk and slid open the drawer to make sure. He even opened the file to make sure I hadn't pulled a fast one.

'Okay, let's go. Bring your box.'

I followed him through a couple security doors and I was once again in the hallway of cells. But before we got close to the doors with the mirrored windows he used his card key to open a door and he ushered me into an interview room. There was a table and two chairs. Mousouwa Aziz was already sitting in one of them. An agent I had not seen before was leaning against the corner to the left of the door. Peoples moved into the other corner.

'Have a seat,' he said. 'You've got fifteen minutes.'

I put the box I carried down on the floor, pulled out the remaining chair and sat down across the table from Aziz. He looked weak and thin. A line of dark hair had grown in below the blond dye job. His hooded eyes were bloodshot and I wondered if they ever turned the light out in his cell. Things had certainly changed in his world. Two years ago his arrival and identification at LAX had brought a custody hold for a few hours while an agent attempted to interview him. Now a border stop got him an interminable hold in the FBI's inner sanctum.

I wasn't expecting much from the interview but felt I needed the face-to-face before proceeding or disposing of Aziz as a suspect. After viewing the intelligence reports a few minutes earlier, I was leaning toward the latter. All I had that connected the diminutive would-be terrorist to Angella Benton was the money. At the time of his arrest at the border he'd had in his possession one of the hundred-dollar bills that had come from the movie set heist. Only one. There were probably a lot of explanations for this and I was beginning to think that his involvement in the murder and heist was not one of them.

Reaching down to the cardboard box I pulled up my file on Angella Benton and opened it on my lap, where Aziz could not see it. I took out the photo of Angella that had been provided by her family. It showed her in a studio portrait taken at the time of her graduation from Ohio State, less than two years before her death. I looked up at Aziz.

'My name is Harry Bosch. I am investigating the death of Angella Benton four years ago. Does she look familiar to you?'

I slid the photo across the table and studied his face and eyes for any tell, any giveaway. His eyes moved over the photograph but I saw nothing in the way of a reaction. He said nothing.

'Did you know her?'

He didn't answer.

'She worked for a movie company that was robbed. You ended up with some of the money. How?'

Nothing.

'Where did the money come from?'

He raised his eyes from the photo to mine. He said nothing.

'Did these agents tell you not to talk to me?'

Nothing.

'Did they? Look, if you didn't know her, then tell me.'

Aziz dropped his sad eyes to the table again. He appeared to be looking at the photo again but I could tell he wasn't. He was looking at something far away. I knew it was useless, just as I had probably known before sitting down.

I got up and turned to Peoples.

'You can keep the rest of the fifteen minutes.'

He pushed off the wall and looked up at an overhead camera. He made the little swirling motion with a finger and the door's electronic lock snapped open. Without thinking I moved toward the door and pushed it open. Almost immediately I heard a banshee cry from behind me and Aziz was up and over the table. He hit me in the upper back with all his weight – maybe 130 pounds tops – and I went through the door and into the hallway.

Aziz was still on me and as I started to go down I felt his arms and legs flailing for purchase. He then jumped off and started running down the hall. Peoples and the other agent were quickly down the hall after him. As I got up I saw them corner Aziz at a dead end. Peoples held back while the other agent moved in and roughly wrestled the smaller man to the ground.

Once Aziz was controlled Peoples turned and came back to me.

'Bosch, are you all right?'

'I'm fine.'

I stood up and made a show of straightening my clothes. I was embarrassed. I had been taken by surprise by Aziz and I knew it would probably be the talk of the squad room at the other end of the hall.

'I wasn't ready for that. I guess being out of the life so long, I got rusty.'

'Yes. You never can turn your back on them.'

'My box. I forgot it.'

I went back into the interview room and got the photo off the table and the box. Just as I came back out Aziz was being walked by, his wrists cuffed behind his back.

I watched him go by and then Peoples and I followed at a safe distance.

'And so,' Peoples said, 'all of this was for naught.'

'Probably.'

'And it all could have been avoided if . . . '

He didn't finish so I did.

'Your agent hadn't committed those crimes on camera. Yeah.'

Peoples stopped in the hallway and I did, too. He waited for the other agent and Aziz to go through the door.

'I'm not comfortable with this arrangement,' he said. 'I have no guarantees. You could walk out of here and get hit by a truck. Does that mean those recordings will end up on the news?'

I thought for a moment, then nodded.

'Yeah, it does. You better hope that truck misses me.'

'I don't want to live and work under the weight of that.'

'I don't blame you. What are you going to do about Milton?'

'What I told you. He's out. He just doesn't know it yet.'

'Well, let me know when that happens. Then we can talk about the weight again.'

He looked like he was about to say something more but then thought better of it and started walking again. He led me through the security doors to the elevator. He used his card key to summon it and then to push the button for the lobby. He held his hand on the door's bumper.

'I'm not going down with you,' he said. 'I think we've said enough.'

I nodded and he stepped back through the door. He stood there and watched, maybe to make sure I didn't sneak off the elevator and try to spring the incarcerated terrorists.

Just as the door started closing I hit the bumper with the side of my hand and it slowly reopened.

'Remember, Agent Peoples, my lawyer has taken steps to secure herself and the recordings. If something happens to her it's the same as it happening to me.'

'Don't worry, Mr. Bosch. I will make no move against her or you.'

'It's not you I'm worried about.'

The door closed as we were holding each other's eyes in a pointed stare.

'I understand,' I heard him say through the doors.

29

My dance with the *federales* was not totally for naught as I had led Peoples to believe. Yes, my chasing down of the tiny terrorist may have been a false lead but in any case there are always false leads. It is part of the mission. At the end of the day what I had was the full record of the investigation and I was happy with that. I was playing with a full deck – the murder book – and it allowed me to write off in my mind all that had occurred in the two days leading up to the point I got it, including my hours in lockdown. For I knew that if I was to find Angella Benton's killer, the answer, or at least the key that would turn the case, would likely be sitting somewhere in the middle of that black plastic binder.

I got home from the federal building and came into the house like a man who thinks he may have won the lottery but needs to check the numbers in the newspaper to be sure. I went directly to the dining-room table with my cardboard box and spread out everything I carried in it. Front and center was the murder book. The Holy Grail. I sat down and started reading from page one. I didn't get up for coffee, water or beer. I didn't turn on music. I concentrated fully on the pages I was turning. On occasion I jotted notes down on my notepad. But for the most part I just read and absorbed. I got in the car with Lawton Cross and Jack Dorsey and I rode through their investigation.

Four hours later I turned the last page in the binder. I had carefully read and studied every document. Nothing struck me as the key, the obvious strand to pursue, but I wasn't discouraged. I still believed it was in there. It always was. I would just have to sift it from a different angle.

The one thing that struck me from the intense immersion into the documented part of the case was the difference in personalities of Cross and Dorsey. Dorsey was a good ten years older than Cross and had been the mentor in the relationship. But in their writing and handling of reports I sensed strong differences in their personalities. Cross was more descriptive and interpretive in his reports. Dorsey was the opposite. If three words summed up an interview or a lab report, then he went with the three words. Cross was more likely to put down the three words and then add another ten sentences of interpretation of what the lab report or the witness's demeanor meant. I preferred Cross's method. It had always been my philosophy to put everything in the book. Because sometimes cases go months and even years long and nuances can be lost in time if not set down as part of the record.

It also made me conclude that maybe the two partners had not been close. They were close now, inextricably linked in department mythology as keepers of the ultimate bad luck. But maybe if they had been close that moment in the bar, things would have been different.

Thinking about what could have been made me remember Danny Cross singing to her husband. I finally got up and went to the CD player and put in a disc of the collected works of Louis Armstrong. It had been put out in unison with the Ken Burns documentary on jazz. Most of it was the very early stuff but I knew it ended with 'What a Wonderful World,' his last hit.

Back at the table I looked at my notepad. I had written down only three things during my first read-through.

$100K
Sandor Szatmari
The money, stupid

The company that had insured the money on the movie set, Global Underwriters, had put up a $100,000 reward for an arrest and conviction in the case. I hadn't known about the reward and was surprised that Lawton Cross hadn't told me. I guessed that it was just another detail that had escaped from his mind due to trauma and the passage of time.

The fact that there was a reward was of little personal consequence to me. I assumed that since I was a former cop who at one time was involved in the case, albeit before the heist that spawned the reward, I would not be eligible for it if my efforts resulted in an arrest and conviction. I also knew that it was likely that the small print on the reward proclamation said that full recovery of the $2 million was required for collection of the $100,000, with the amount prorated according to the amount of recovery. And four years after the crime the chances of there being anything left to recover were small. Still, the reward was good to know about. It might be useful as a tool of leverage or coercion. I might not be eligible but I might encounter someone useful who would be. I was glad I found out about it.

Next on the notepad was the name Sandor Szatmari. He or she – I didn't know which – was listed as the case investigator for Global Underwriters. He or she was someone I needed to talk to. I opened the murder book to the first page, where investigators usually kept a page of most often called phone numbers. There was no listing for Szatmari but there was for Global. I went into the kitchen to get the phone, turned down Louis Armstrong on the CD player and made the call. I was transferred twice before I finally got a woman who answered with 'Investigations.'

I had trouble with Szatmari's name and she corrected me and then told me to hold. In less than a minute Szatmari picked up. The name belonged to a he. I explained my situation and asked if we could meet. He seemed skeptical, but that might have just been because he had an accent from Eastern Europe that made him hard to read. He declined to discuss the case over the phone with a stranger but ultimately agreed to meet me in person at ten o'clock the next morning at his office in Santa Monica. I told him I'd be there and hung up.

I looked at the last line I had written on the notepad. It was just a reminder of an old adage good for almost any investigation. Follow the money, stupid. It always leads to the truth. In this case the money was gone and the trail – other than blips on the radar in Phoenix and involving Mousouwa Aziz and Martha Gessler – had gone cold. I knew that left me one alternative. To go backwards. Trace the money backwards and see what came up.

To do that I needed to start at the bank. I checked the phone number page in the murder book again and called Gordon Scaggs, the vice president at BankLA who had arranged the one-day loan of $2 million to Alexander Taylor's film company.

Scaggs was a busy man, he told me. He wanted to put off meeting with me until the following week. But I was persistent and got him to squeeze me in for fifteen minutes the next afternoon at three. He asked me for a callback number so his secretary could confirm in the morning. I made up a number and gave it to him. I wasn't going to give him the opportunity to have the secretary call me back and tell me the meeting had been canceled.

I hung up and weighed my options. It was late afternoon and at the moment I was clear until ten the following morning. I wanted to take another run at the murder book but knew I didn't need to be sitting in the house to do that. I could just as easily be sitting on a plane.

I called Southwest Airlines and reserved a flight from Burbank to Las Vegas, arriving at 7:15, and a return flight leaving early the next morning and arriving at 8:30 back at Burbank.

Eleanor answered her cell phone on the second ring and seemed to be whispering.

'It's Harry. Is something wrong?'

'No.'

'Why are you whispering?'

She spoke up.

'Sorry, I didn't realize I was. What's going on?'

'I'm thinking about coming over there tonight to get my bag and my credit cards.'

When she did not respond right away, I asked, 'Are you going to be around?'

'Well, I was going to play tonight. Later.'

'My plane gets in at seven-fifteen. I could come by around eight. Maybe we could have dinner before you go to play.'

I waited and again it seemed like she was taking too long to respond.

'Dinner would be nice. Are you staying overnight?'

'Yeah, I've got an early flight out. I have some things to do over here in the morning.'

'Where are you going to stay?'

There was as clear a signal as any.

'I don't know. I didn't reserve anything yet.'

'Harry, I don't think it would be good for you to stay here.'

'Right.'

The line was as silent as the three hundred miles of desert between us.

'I know, I can get you comped at the Bellagio. They'll do it for me.'

'You sure?'

'Yes.'

'Thanks, Eleanor. You want me to come to your place after I get in?'

'No, I'll come pick you up. Are you checking luggage?'

'No. You already have my bag.'

'Then I'll be parked out in front of the terminal at seven-fifteen. I'll see you then.'

I noticed she was whispering again but I didn't say anything about it this time.

'Thanks, Eleanor.'

'Okay, Harry, I need to juggle some things to get free tonight. So I'm going to go. I'll see you at the airport. Seven-fifteen. 'Bye.'

I said good-bye but she had already hung up. It sounded as though there was another voice in the background just as she disconnected the call.

As I thought about this, Louis Armstrong started singing 'What a Wonderful World' and I turned it up.

30

At 7:15 that night Eleanor and I repeated the same airport scene. Right down to the kiss when I got into the car. Afterward, I turned awkwardly and lifted the heavy murder book I'd been carrying over the front seats to the back. I dropped it on the backseat next to my suitcase which was on the seat behind Eleanor.

'That looks like a murder book, Harry.'

'It is. I thought I might be able to go through it on the flight.'

'And?'

'I had a screaming baby in the seat behind me. Couldn't concentrate. Why would anybody bring a kid to Vegas anyway?'

'It's actually not a bad place to raise a kid. Supposedly.'

'I'm not talking about raising. I mean, why take a little kid like that on a vacation to Sin City? Take him to Disneyland or something.'

'I think you need a drink.'

'And some food. Where do you want to eat?'

'Well, remember when we were still . . . in L.A. and we'd go to Valentino on special occasions?'

'Don't tell me.'

She laughed and just being able to look at her again thrilled me. I really liked the way her hair accented her lovely neck.

'Yep, they have one here. I made a reservation.'

'They must have one of everything in Las Vegas.'

'Except you. There's absolutely no duplicating Harry Bosch.'

The smile stayed on her face as she said it and I liked that, too. We soon dropped into a silence probably as comfortable as it can get with two formerly married people. She expertly maneuvered through traffic that looked like it could easily rival anything found on Los Angeles' clogged streets and freeways.

It had been about three years since I'd been on the strip but Vegas was a place that taught that time was relative. In three years it had all seemed to change again. I saw new resorts and attractions, taxicabs with electronic ad placards on their roofs, monorails connecting the casinos.

The Las Vegas version of Valentino was in the Venetian, one of the newest jewels in the crown of high-end casinos on the strip. It was a place that didn't even exist the last time I had been in town. When Eleanor pulled into the valet parking circle I told her to pop the trunk so I could put my suitcase and the murder book in it.

'I can't. It's full.'

'I don't want to leave this stuff out, especially the murder book.'

'Well, put it in the bag and put it on the floor. It will be all right.'

'Don't you have room back there for just the book?'

'No, everything is jam-packed in there and if I open it, then it will all spill out. I don't want that to happen here.'

'What is in it?'

'Just clothes and things. Stuff I want to take to the Salvation Army but haven't had the time.'

Two valets opened our doors simultaneously and welcomed us to the resort. I got out, opened the back door and leaned in to open the carry-on bag and put the murder book inside it. After closing the bag I slid it down to the floor behind Eleanor's seat.

'You coming, Harry?' Eleanor asked from behind me.

'Yeah, I'm coming.'

As the valet was driving the car away I looked at the trunk and back end. It didn't seem particularly heavy. I looked at the license plate and silently read it three times to myself.

Valentino was Valentino. As far as I could tell, the L.A. restaurant had been perfectly cloned. It was like trying to tell the difference between one McDonald's and another – on a much different culinary level.

I didn't force the conversation while we ate. I was comfortable and happy just being with her. At first the conversation, though spare, was focused on me and my retirement or lack thereof. I told her about the case I was working, including the connection to her old friend and colleague Marty Gessler. In another lifetime Eleanor had been an FBI agent and she still had the analytical mind of an investigator. When we were together in L.A. she had often been a sounding board for me and on more than one occasion had helped with a suggestion or idea.

This time she had only one piece of advice and that was to stay clear of Peoples and Milton and even Lindell. Not that she knew them personally. She just knew the FBI culture and knew their kind. Of course, her advice came too late for me.

'I'm doing my best to do just that,' I told her. 'It would be fine with me if I never see any of them ever again.'

'But not very likely.'

I suddenly thought of something.

'You don't have your cell phone on you, do you?'

'Yes, but I don't think they like you using cells in a place like this.'

'I know. I'll go outside. I just remembered I have to make a call or the shit's going to hit the fan.'

She got her phone out of her purse and gave it to me. I left the restaurant and stood in an indoor shopping mall that had been built to look like a Venetian canal complete with gondolas. The concrete sky was painted blue with wisps of white clouds. It was phony but at least it was air-conditioned. I called Janis Langwiser's cell number and told her the coast was clear.

'I was beginning to worry because I hadn't heard from you. I've called your house twice.'

'Everything's fine. I'm in Vegas and will be back tomorrow.'

'How do I know you're not under duress? You know, being held and forced to say that.'

'You got caller ID?'

'Oh, that's right. I saw it was a seven-oh-two number. All right, Harry. Don't forget, call me tomorrow. And don't lose too much money over there.'

'I won't.'

When I got back to the table Eleanor wasn't there. I sat down and was anxious about it but she came back from the rest room in a few minutes. As I watched her approach I felt she was different but I couldn't place how. It was more than the hair and the deeper tan. It was like she carried more confidence than I remembered. Maybe she had found what she needed on the blue-felt poker tables on the strip.

I gave her back the phone and she dropped it into her purse.

'So how has it been here?' I asked. 'We've been talking about my case. Let's talk about your case for a while.'

'I don't have a case.'

'You know what I mean.'

She shrugged.

'Things are going well this year. I won a satellite and took a button. I get to play in the series.'

I knew she was talking about winning a qualifying tournament for the World Series of poker. The last time we talked about poker she had told me that her secret goal was to be the first woman to ever win the series. The winner of a qualifying tournament can take the cash prize or a so-called button, which is an entry into the series.

'This will be your first time in the series, right?'

She nodded and smiled and I could tell she was proud and excited.

'It starts pretty soon.'

'Well, good luck. Maybe I'll come over and watch.'

'Bring me luck.'

'It still must be hard, Eleanor, making a living on the turn of the cards.'

'I'm good at it, Harry. Besides, I've got backers now. It spreads the risks.'

'What do you mean?'

'That's how it works these days. I have backers. I use their money when I play. They get seventy-five percent of what I win. If I lose, they take the loss. But I don't lose too often, Harry.'

I nodded.

'Who are these people? Are they . . . you know?'

'Legitimate? Yes, Harry, very. They're businessmen. Microsoft men. From Seattle. I met them when they were out here playing. So far I've made them money. With the way the stock market's been, they'd rather invest in me. They're happy and so am I.'

'Good.'

I thought about the money Alexander Taylor had offered me. And then there was the reward offered on the heist case. If I solved it, got back some of the money and somehow qualified for the reward, I could be her backer. It was a pipe dream. I wondered if she would even take my money.

'What are you thinking about?' she asked. 'You look so concerned.'

'Nothing. I was just thinking about the case for a second. Something I want to ask the insurance investigator tomorrow.'

The waiter brought the check and I paid after getting my AmEx card back from Eleanor. We left and got the car and I checked to make sure the suitcase was still in the back. We drove over to the Bellagio, a short distance that took a long time because of the traffic. I grew nervous as we got closer because I didn't know what was going to happen when we got there. I checked my watch. It was almost ten.

'What time do you play?'

'I like to start around midnight.'

'Why do you like to play through the night? What's wrong with the day?'

'The real players come out at night. The tourists go to bed. There's more money on the table.'

We rode in silence for a little bit and she eventually continued as though there had been no pause.

'Plus, I like coming out at the end of the night and seeing the sun coming up. Something about it, like you're just happy you survived another day or something.'

Inside the Bellagio we went to the VIP desk and picked up a card key that had been left under Eleanor's name. It was that simple. She led me to the elevator like she had been in it a hundred times and we went up to a suite on the twelfth floor. It was the nicest hotel room I had ever seen, with a living room and a bedroom and a view that looked down on the signature lighted fountains in the front pond.

'This is nice. You must know some people.'

'I'm getting a rep. I play here three or four nights a week and it's starting to draw people. High rollers who want to play me. They know that here, and they don't want me to play anywhere else.'

I nodded and turned to her.

'I guess things are really going well for you.'

'I'm not complaining.'

'I guess . . . '

I didn't finish. She walked over to me and stood in front of me.

'You guess what?'

'I don't know what I was going to ask. I guess I wanted to know what was missing. Are you with somebody now, Eleanor?'

She drew closer. I could feel her breath.

'You mean am I in love with somebody? No, Harry, I'm not.'

I nodded and she spoke again before I could.

'Do you still believe in that thing you told me? About the single-bullet theory.'

I nodded without hesitation and looked into her eyes. She leaned forward, her head against my chin.

'What about you?' I asked. 'Do you still believe what that poet said, that there is no end of things in the heart?'

'Yes, I believe it. Always.'

I raised her chin with my hand and kissed her. Soon our arms were around each other and her hand was on the back of my neck pulling me toward her. I knew we were going to make love. And I knew for a moment what it meant to be the luckiest man in Las Vegas. I pulled away from her lips and just hugged her to my chest.

'All I want in this world is you,' I whispered.

'I know,' she whispered back.

31

On the flight back to Los Angeles I tried to refocus on the case. But it was a fruitless effort. I had spent a good part of the night watching Eleanor win several thousand dollars from five men at a table down in the Bellagio poker room. I had never watched her play at any length before. It is fair to say she embarrassed the other players, cleaning out all but one of them, and even he was left with only a single stack of chips by the time she cashed out five racks of her own. She was a cold, hard player who was as impressive as she was mysterious and beautiful. I spent my life learning to read people. But I never read anything off of her while she was playing. There was not a tell anywhere in her game as far as I could see.

But when she was finished with those men she was also finished with me. Outside the poker room she told me she was tired and had to go. She said I couldn't go with her. She didn't even offer me a ride to the airport. It was a short good-bye. We parted with a kiss as lacking in passion as our moments in the suite above had seemingly been full of it. We parted without promises of rejoining or of even calling each other again. We just said good-bye and I watched her walk away through the casino.

I got to the airport on my own. But once on the plane I couldn't let it go. I tried opening the murder book but it did me no good. I kept thinking about the mysteries. Not the good moments, the smiles and the memories and the making love. I thought about our abrupt departure and how she had skillfully avoided the question when I'd asked if she was with somebody. She'd said she wasn't in love but that didn't really answer the question. I thought about why she had wanted me to stay in a hotel room and why she wouldn't open her car's trunk. On the front page of the murder book I wrote down her license plate number from memory. After doing it I felt like I had in some way betrayed her and I then crossed it out. But even as I did this I knew I could not cross it out in my memory.

32

The investigative offices of Global Underwriters were in a six-story black box on Colorado about six blocks from the ocean. When I got there the secretary who guarded entrance to the office of Sandor Szatmari looked at me as though I had just ridden the elevator down from the moon.

'Didn't you get the message?'

'What message?'

'I left a message for you after getting your number from Mr. Scaggs's office. Mr. Szatmari had to cancel your appointment this morning.'

'What happened, somebody die?'

She looked slightly insulted by my brashness. Her voice took on a tone of impatience.

'No, in reviewing his schedule for the day he decided he did not have the time to fit you in.'

'So he's here?'

'He cannot see you. I'm sorry you didn't get the message. I thought there was something wrong with the number I got, but I *did* leave a message.'

'Please tell him I'm here. Tell him I didn't get the message because I was out of town. I flew in for this meeting. I'd still like to see him. It's important.'

Now she looked annoyed. She lifted the phone to make the call but then thought better of it and hung up. She got up and walked down a hallway off to the side of the waiting room so she could deliver the message in person. A few minutes later she came back and sat down. She took her time in delivering the news to me.

'I talked to Mr. Szatmari,' she said. 'He'll try to get you in as soon as he can.'

'Thank you. That's nice of him and nice of you.'

There was a couch and a coffee table with a spread of outdated magazines on it. I had brought the murder book with me, mostly as a prop, so I could impress Szatmari with it and the access it showed I had. I sat down on the couch and spent the time waiting by leafing through it and rereading some of the reports. Nothing new hit me but I was becoming well versed in the facts of the case. This was important because I knew it would help when I sifted through new information to not have to check the murder book every time.

A half hour went by and then the secretary's phone buzzed and she got the word to send me in.

Szatmari was a solidly built man in his mid-fifties. He looked more like a salesman than an investigator but the walls of his office were hung with commendations and handshake photos testifying to his success as one. He pointed me to a chair in front of his cluttered desk and spoke as he wrote something down on a report.

'I'm busy, Mr. Bosch. What can I do for you?'

'Well, like I told you yesterday on the phone, I'm working one of your cases. I thought maybe we could share some information, see if one of us has gone down a road the other hasn't.'

'Why should I share with you?'

Something was wrong. He was predisposed not to like me before I had even set foot in his office. I wondered if somehow Peoples had talked to him about me. Maybe Szatmari had called the LAPD or the bureau to check me out and got the word not to cooperate. Maybe that was why the appointment had been canceled.

'I don't get this,' I said. 'Is something wrong? It's called solving the case, that's why maybe we should share information.'

'And how about you? Would you share with me? How much of the reward do you give to me?'

I nodded. Now I got it. The reward.

'Mr. Szatmari, you have it wrong. You have me wrong.'

'Sure. Have reward, will travel. I see your kind all the time. Come in here, wanting information, maybe make some big bucks.'

His accent became more pronounced as he got worked up. I flipped open the murder book and found the black-and-white photocopies of the murder scene photos. I tore the page with Angella Benton's hands on it out of the book and slapped it down on his desk.

'That's why I'm doing this. Not the money. Her. I was there that day. I was a cop. I'm retired now but I was on this case until they took me off it. That probably cuts me out of any reward, okay?'

Szatmari studied the grainy copy of the photo. He then looked at the binder on my lap. He then finally looked at me.

'I remember you now. Your name. You were the one who hit one of the robbers with a round.'

I nodded.

'I was there that day, but since we never found the robbers it's not known for sure who hit who.'

'Come on, eight rent-a-cops and an LAPD veteran. It was you.'

'I think so.'

'You know, I tried to talk to you back then. Interview you. But the department stonewalled me.'

'How come?'

'They'd do anything they could to keep other investigations and investigators out of the picture. They're like that over there.'

'I know. I remember.'

He smiled and leaned back in his seat.

'And now here you are, wanting cooperation from me. Ironic, eh?'

'Very.'

'Is that the investigative file? Let me see it, please.'

I handed the heavy binder across his desk. He put it down and flipped back to the front section and started leafing through the reports until he came to the original offense report. The homicide. He worked a finger down the page until he came to my name in the block marked 'I/O' for investigating officer. He then closed the murder book but didn't hand it back.

'Why now? Why do you investigate this?'

'Because I just retired and it's one of the ones that won't let go.'

He nodded that he understood.

'Our investigation, you understand, was in regard to the money, not the woman.'

'It's all the same thing, you ask me.'

'Our investigation is no longer active. The money is gone by now. Split up, spent. Without the possibility of recovery. There are other cases.'

'The money's been written off,' I said, 'but she hasn't been. Not by me, not by those who knew her.'

'*Did* you know her?'

'I met her that day.'

He nodded again, seeming to understand what that meant. He straightened the corners on a stack of files on his desk.

'Did it ever go anywhere?' I asked. 'Did you get close to anything?'

He took a long time answering.

'No, not really. Only dead ends on this one.'

'When did you put it aside?'

'I don't remember. It was a long time ago.'

'Where's your file on it?'

'I cannot give you my file. It is against company policy.'

'Because of the reward thing, right? The company doesn't allow you to cooperate with unofficial investigations if there's a reward.'

'It can lead to collusion,' he said, nodding. 'Also, there is the legal jeopardy. I don't have the luxury of the protections the police have. If my investigative notes and summaries were to become public, I'd be left open to possible lawsuits.'

I tried to think for a minute about how to play this. Szatmari seemed to be holding something back and whatever it was might be in the file. I think he wanted to give it to me but wasn't sure how.

'Take a look at the photocopy again,' I said. 'Look at her hands. Are you a religious man, Mr. Szatmari?'

Szatmari looked at the photo of Angella Benton's hands again.

'Sometimes I am religious,' he said. 'Are you?'

'Not really. I mean, what is religion? I don't go to church, if that's what it is. But I think about religion and I think I have something like it inside. A code is like religion. You have to believe it. You have to practice it. The thing is, look at her hands, Mr. Szatmari. I remember when I saw her down on the tile and saw how her hands were ... I sort of took it as a sign.'

'A sign of what?'

'I don't know. A sign of something. Like religion. That's why this is one of the cases that didn't go away.'

'I understand.'

'Then pull out the file and put it on your desk,' I said as if giving instruction to someone in a hypnotic trance. 'Then go get a cup of coffee or have a smoke. And take your time. I'll wait for you right here.'

Szatmari looked at me for a long moment and then reached down to what I guess was a file drawer in the desk. He finally took his eyes off me so he could pull the right file. He brought it up – it was a thick one – and put it down on the desk. He then pushed back his chair and got up.

'I'm going to grab a cup of coffee,' he said. 'You want something?'

'I think I'll be fine. But thanks.'

He nodded and went out, closing the door behind him. The moment it clicked I was up out of my seat and moving behind the desk. I sat down and dove into the file.

For the most part, Szatmari's file was filled with documents I had already seen before. There were also copies of contracts and directives between Global and its client BankLA that were new, as well as summaries of interviews with several bank and film company employees. Szatmari had conducted interviews with every one of the security transport men who had been on the scene the day of the shoot-out and heist.

But there was no interview with me. As usual the LAPD had put up a wall. Szatmari's request to interview me never even got to me. Not that I would have accepted the request if I had seen it. I had an arrogance then that I hoped I had now lost.

I scanned the interviews and summaries as fast as I could, paying particular attention to the reports pertaining to the three bank employees I hoped to talk to later in the day, Gordon Scaggs, Linus Simonson and Jocelyn Jones. The subjects did not give Szatmari much. Scaggs was the one who handled everything and he was very specific as to the steps he had taken and the planning of the one-day loan of $2 million in cash. The interviews with Simonson and Jones depicted them as worker bees who did what they were told. They could have just as easily been putting labels on cans as counting twenty thousand hundred-dollar bills and writing down eight hundred serial numbers while they were at it.

My curiosity meter jumped when I came across documents pertaining to the financial backgrounds of Jack Dorsey, Lawton Cross and myself. Szatmari had pulled TRW reports on all of us. He had apparently called our banks and credit-card companies. He wrote short summaries on each of us, my record coming out cleanest, while Cross and Dorsey did not fare as well. According to Szatmari, both men carried huge credit-card debt, with Dorsey in the most difficult financial position because he was divorced but still supporting four children, two of whom were in college.

The door to the office opened and the secretary looked in, just about to say something to Szatmari when she saw it was me behind his desk.

'What are you doing?'

'Waiting for Mr. Szatmari. He went to get a coffee.'

She put her hands on her ample hips, the international sign of indignation.

'Did he tell you to go behind his desk and start reading that file?'

It was incumbent upon me not to leave Szatmari in a potential jam.

'He told me to wait. I'm waiting.'

'Well, you get right back around to the other side of that desk. I'll be informing Mr. Szatmari about what I saw.'

I closed the file, got up and came around the desk as instructed.

'You know, I'd really appreciate it if you didn't do that,' I said.

'I don't care what you'd appreciate, I'm telling him.'

She then disappeared, leaving the door open in her wake. A few minutes went by and Szatmari stormed in and closed the door sharply. He then lost his anger as he turned to face me. He was carrying a coffee mug with steam rising out of it.

'Thanks for playing it that way,' he said. 'I just hope you got whatever you needed because now to make good on the little fit I had out there I have to throw you out.'

'No problem,' I said, standing up. 'I've got one question, though.'

'Go ahead.'

'Was that just routine to do the background financials on the cops on the case? Me, Jack Dorsey and Lawton Cross.'

Szatmari folded his brow as he tried to remember the reason for the financial checks. Then he shrugged.

'I forgot about that. I think I just thought that with the money that was at stake I should check everybody out. Especially you, Bosch, with the coincidence of you being there at the set at the right moment.'

I nodded. It sounded like a solid investigative move.

'Are you angry about it?'

'Me? No, not mad. I was just curious about where it came from, that's all.'

'Anything else helpful?'

'Maybe, you never know.'

'Good luck then. If you don't mind, keep me informed of any progress.'

'I will. I'll let you know.'

We shook hands. On my way out I passed by the indignant secretary and told her to have a nice day. She didn't respond.

33

The interview with Gordon Scaggs went quickly and smoothly. He met me at the agreed-upon time at the BankLA tower in downtown. His forty-second-floor office faced east and had one of the best views of the city's smog I had ever seen. His recounting of his involvement in the ill-fated $2 million loan to Eidolon Productions deviated in no noticeable way from his statement in the murder book. He negotiated a $50,000 fee for the bank, the costs of security included. The money was to go out in the morning on the day of filming and come back before 6 p.m. closing time.

'I knew there was a risk,' Scaggs told me. 'But I saw a nice, quick profit for the bank. I guess you could say that clouded my vision.'

Scaggs turned the money transport issues over to Ray Vaughn, head of bank security, while he turned his attention to the chores of insuring the one-day operation through Global Underwriters and then gathering together the $2 million in cash. It would have been highly unusual for a single bank – even the downtown flagship – to have that much money in cash available on one day. So in the days before the loan took place Scaggs had to arrange for cash shipments from various BankLA branches to the downtown location. On the day of the loan the money was loaded into an armored vehicle and driven from downtown to the movie set in Hollywood. Ray Vaughn rode in a lead car. He was in constant radio contact with the driver of the armored truck and led him on a meandering course through Hollywood in an effort to determine if they were being followed.

When they arrived at the set location they were met by more armed security and Linus Simonson, one of the assistants who had helped Scaggs pull the cash together and had created the list of serial numbers the insurance company had demanded.

And, of course, the bank entourage was met by the hooded and heavily armed robbers as well.

One thing new I got from Scaggs during the initial part of the interview was that bank policy had changed since the heist. BankLA no longer engaged in what he called boutique cash loans to the movie industry.

'What is that saying?' he asked. 'Once burned is an education. Twice burned is just plain stupidity. Well, we're not stupid here, Mr. Bosch. We're not going to get burned by those people again.'

I nodded in agreement.

'So you feel confident it was 'those people' where this came from? The heist originated over there and not here within the bank?'

Scaggs looked indignant at the very thought of anything else.

'I should say so. Look at the poor girl who was murdered. She worked for them, not me.'

'True. But her murder could have been part of the plan. To throw suspicion on the movie production instead of the bank.'

'Impossible. The police have been over this place with a fine-tooth comb. Same with the insurance company. We received a clean bill of health from everyone involved. We are absolutely one-hundred-percent clean on this.'

I nodded again.

'Then I guess you won't mind if I talk to your employees, too. I'd like to speak to Linus Simonson and Jocelyn Jones.'

Scaggs realized he'd been cornered. How could he not let me speak to employees after that ringing endorsement of honesty and innocence on the bank's behalf?

'The answer is yes and no,' he said. 'Jocelyn is still with us. She's an assistant branch manager now in West Hollywood. I don't think there will be a problem talking to her.

'And Linus Simonson?'

'Linus never came back to us after that awful day. I guess you know he got shot up by those bastards. Him and Ray. Ray didn't make it but Linus did. He was in the hospital and then he was on sick leave and then he didn't want to come back at all and I can't see as I blame him.'

'He quit?'

'That's right.'

I had not seen mention of this in the murder book or even in Szatmari's records. I knew the investigation was most intense in the days and weeks after the heist. This was probably when Simonson was still recovering and still technically an employee. The investigative records generated at this time would have no reason to mention his leaving employment at the bank.

'Do you know where he went from here?'

'I used to. I don't now. But to lay it all out there for you, Linus went and got himself a lawyer who started making liability claims. You know, that the bank put Linus in harm's way and all of this nonsense. None of the claims mentioned that he volunteered to be out there that day.'

'He wanted to be there?'

'Sure. He was a young guy. He grew up in town and probably had Hollywood aspirations at one time or another. Everybody does. He thought spending the day on the set, being the guy in charge of the money, would be a good deal. He volunteered and I said fine, go. I wanted somebody from my office there anyway. Besides Ray Vaughn, I mean.'

'So did Simonson actually sue the bank or just make noise with his lawyer?'

'He made noise. But he made enough noise that legal settled him out. They gave him a chunk of cash and he went away. I heard he used it to buy a nightclub.'

'How much they give him?'

'I don't know. One time I asked our attorney, Jim Foreman, what the kid got and he wouldn't tell me. He said terms of the settlement were confidential. But from what I understand, this club he bought, it was a nice one. One of those Hollywood-type places.'

I thought of the portrait I had looked at in the legal library while waiting to see Janis Langwiser.

'Your lawyer is James Foreman?'

'Not my lawyer. The bank's lawyer. Outside counsel. They decided not to keep it in-house because of the possible conflict.'

I nodded.

'Do you know the name of the club he bought?'

'No, I don't.'

I sat there looking past Scaggs at the smog through the window behind him. I was seeing but not seeing. I had gone inside where I was feeling the first stirrings of instinct and excitement, of the state of grace that comes with my religion.

'Mr. Bosch?' Scaggs said. 'Don't disappear on me. I've got an officers' meeting in five minutes.'

I came out of it and looked at him.

'Sorry, sir. I'm done here. For now. But before your meeting can you call Jocelyn Jones and tell her I'm coming out to see her? I need to know where the branch is, too.'

'That will be no problem.'

34

On the way to the West Hollywood branch of BankLA to see Jocelyn Jones I had some time to kill so I drove west on Hollywood Boulevard. I had not been down there much since my retirement and I wanted to see the old beat. According to the newspaper it was changing and I wanted to see this for myself.

The asphalt on the boulevard still glittered in the sunlight but the storefronts and office buildings near Vine still slumbered beneath the patina of a half century of smog. No difference there. But once past Cahuenga and onto Highland I saw where the new Hollywood was springing to life. New hotels – and I'm not talking about the type with hourly rates – and theaters, people centers with popular up-style restaurant franchises anchoring them. The streets and sidewalks were crowded, the brass stars imbedded in the sidewalks were polished. It was safer and cleaner but less genuine. Still, the word that popped into my head was *hope.* There was a sense of hope and vigor. There was a definite vibe coming off the street and I guess I liked it. The idea, I knew, was that the vibe would spread from this core area and move down the boulevard like an earthquake wave, leaving renovation and reinvention in its wake. A few years ago I would have been first to say the plan had no chance. But maybe I was wrong.

Still feeling lucky from Vegas I decided to let the vibe ride and dropped down Fairfax to Third and pulled into the farmer's market to grab something to eat.

The market was another remake job I had stayed away from. There was a new parking garage and open-air people center built next to the old clapboard market with its comforting combination of good, cheap food and kitsch. I think I liked it better when you could just pull into a parking space next to the newsstand but I had to admit they had done it right. It was the old and new sitting side by side and getting along. I walked through the new section, past the department stores and the biggest bookstore I had ever seen and into the old. Bob's Donuts was still there and every other place that I remembered. It was crowded. People were happy. It was too late in the day for a doughnut so I picked up a BLT and change for a dollar at the Kokomo Café and ate the sandwich in one of the old-time phone booths that they had left in place next to the Dupar's. I called Roy Lindell first and caught him eating at his desk.

'What do you have?'

'Tuna on rye with pickles.'

'That's sick.'

'Yeah, what do you have?'

'BLT. Double-smoked bacon from Kokomo's.'

'Well, that beats me all to hell. What do you want, Bosch? Last time I saw you, you wanted nothing to do with me. In fact, I thought you went to Vegas.'

'I did go but I'm back. And things are smoothing out now. You could say I've come to an understanding with your pals on the ninth floor. You want back in on this thing or you want to pout about it?'

'You got something?'

'Maybe. Not much more than a feeling at the moment.'

'What do you want from me?'

I shoved my sandwich wrapper off the murder book and opened it to get the information I needed.

'See what you can come up with on a guy named Linus Simonson. Thirty-one-year-old white male. He owns a club in town.'

'What's it called?'

'I don't know yet.'

'That's great. You want me to pick up your dry cleaning while I'm at it?'

'Just run the name. You'll get a hit or you won't.'

I gave him Simonson's birthdate and the address listed in the murder book, although I had a feeling it was old.

'Who is he?'

I told him about Simonson's former work at BankLA and about him being shot during the movie set heist.

'The guy was a victim. You think he set it up and told his guys to shoot him in the ass?'

'I don't know.'

'And what's he got to do with Marty Gessler?'

'I don't know. Maybe nothing. *Probably* nothing. But I just want to check him out. Something doesn't seem right to me.'

'Okay, you keep having the hunches and I'll do the legwork, Bosch. Anything else?'

'Look, if you don't want to do it, just say so. I'll get somebody else to—'

'Look, I said I'll do it, and I will. Anything else?'

I hesitated but not for too long.

'Yeah, one other thing. Can you run a plate for me?'

'Give it to me.'

I gave him the number I had gotten off the car Eleanor had been driving.

It was still in my memory and I figured it would stay there until I checked it out.

'Nevada?' Lindell asked, suspicion obvious in his voice. 'This have to do with your trip to Vegas or this thing over here?'

I should have known. Lindell was a lot of things but stupid wasn't one of them. I had already opened the door. I had to step inside.

'I don't know,' I lied. 'But could you just get me the registration on it?'

If the car, as I suspected, was registered in someone other than Eleanor's name, I could make up a story about thinking I had been followed and Lindell would never know the difference.

'All right,' the FBI agent said. 'I gotta go. Call me later.'

I hung up and that was that. Guilt washed around me like the waves hitting the pylons under the pier. I might be able to fool Lindell with the request but not myself. I was running a check on my former wife. I wondered if I was capable of doing anything lower.

Trying not to dwell on it, I picked up the receiver and dumped more change into the phone. I called Janis Langwiser and realized as I waited for her to answer that I might be about to answer the question I had just posed to myself.

Langwiser's secretary said she was on a phone call and she would have to call me back. I said I wasn't reachable but would call back in fifteen minutes. I hung up and walked around the market, spending the most time in a small store that sold only hot sauce, hundreds of different brands of it. I wasn't sure when I would use it because I rarely cooked at home anymore, but I bought a bottle of Gator Squeezins because I liked the place and I needed more change for the call back.

Next stop was the bakery. Not to buy, just to look. When I was a kid and my mother was still around, she used to take me to the farmer's market on Saturday mornings. What I remember most was watching through the bakery window when the cakemaker would dress the cakes people ordered for birthdays and holidays and weddings. He would make grand designs on the top of each cake, squeezing the icing through a funnel, his thick forearms covered in flour and sugar.

My mother usually had to hold me up at the window so I could see the top of the cake being decorated. Sometimes she would think I was watching the cakemaker but I was really watching her in the reflection of the window, trying to figure out what was wrong.

When she would grow tired of holding me up she'd go grab a chair from the nearby restaurant seating area – what they now call a food court in the malls – and I would stand on that. I used to look at the cakes and imagine what parties they would go to and how many people were going to be there. It seemed like those cakes could only go to happy places. But I could tell that when the baker was icing a wedding cake, it made my mother sad.

The bakery and the cakemaker's window were still there. I stood in front of the glass with my bag of hot sauce, but there was no baker there. I knew it was too late in the day. The cakes were made early each day so they would be ready for pickup or delivery for birthday parties and weddings and anniversaries and things like that. On the rack next to the window I looked at the selection of stainless-steel funnel tips the baker could use to make various designs and flowers out of icing.

'No use waiting. He's done for the day.'

I didn't need to turn. In the reflection of the window, I saw an old lady walking by behind me. It made me think of my mother again.

'Yeah,' I said. 'I think you are right.'

The second time I went into the phone booth and called Langwiser she was available and picked up right away.

'Is everything okay?'

'Yeah, fine.'

'Good, you scared me.'

'What are you talking about?'

'You told Roxanne that you couldn't be reached. I thought maybe you were in a cell or something.'

'Oh, sorry. I didn't think about that. I'm just not using the cell phone still.'

'You think they are still listening?'

'I don't know. Just precautions.'

'So is this just your daily check-in?'

'Sort of. I've got a question, too.'

'I'm listening.'

Maybe it was because of the way I hadn't told Lindell the whole truth or because of the way checking out Eleanor made me feel, but I decided not to run a play on Langwiser. I decided to simply play the cards I had.

'A few years ago your firm handled a case. The attorney was James Foreman and the client was BankLA.'

'Yes, the bank's a client. What was the case? I wasn't here a few years ago.'

I closed the door to the phone booth even though I knew it would quickly get hot in the tiny cubicle.

'I don't know what it was called but the other party's name was Linus Simonson. He worked for the bank as an assistant to the vice-president. He took a bullet in the shoot-out during the movie set heist.'

'Okay. I remember somebody was wounded and somebody was killed but I don't remember the names.'

'He was the wounded. The dead guy was Ray Vaughn, chief of security for the bank. Simonson lived. In fact, he only took a round in the ass. Probably a ricochet, if I remember the way the shooting team worked it out.'

'So he then sued the bank?'

'I'm not sure if it went that far. The point is he was out on medical for a while and then decided he didn't want to come back. He got a lawyer and started making noise about the bank being liable for putting him in a position where he was in harm's way.'

'Sounds reasonable.'

'Even though he volunteered to be there. He had helped put the money together and then volunteered to baby-sit it during the movie shoot.'

'Well, it still was probably actionable. He could make a case for volunteering under duress or—'

'Yeah, I know all of that. I'm not worried about whether he had a case or not. He apparently did, because the bank settled and James Foreman handled it.'

'Okay, so where is this going? What is your question?'

I reopened the door of the booth so I could get some fresh air.

'I want to know what he settled for. How much did he get?'

'I'll call Jim Foreman right now. You want to hold?'

'Uh, it's not that simple. I think there was a confidentiality agreement.'

There was silence from her and I actually smiled while I waited. It had felt good to just come out with what I wanted.

'I see,' Langwiser finally said. 'So you want me to violate that by finding out what he got.'

'Well, when you put it that way . . . '

'What other way is there to put it?'

'I'm working this thing and he's come up. Simonson. And it would just help me a lot if I knew how big a chunk of cash the bank gave him. It would help me a lot, Janis.'

Again my words were met with a long silence.

'I'm not going to go snooping through files in my own firm,' she finally said. 'I'm not going to do anything that could get me in the shit. The best thing I can do is just go to Jim and ask him and see what he says.'

'Okay.'

It was better than I thought I would get.

'The wedge I have is that BankLA remains a client. If you are saying that this guy Simonson might have been part of this heist which lost the bank two million and its chief of security, then he might be inclined.'

'Hey, that's good.'

I had thought of that angle but wanted her to come to it. I started to get jazzed. I thought maybe she'd be able to get what I needed from Foreman.

'Don't get excited, Harry. Not yet.'

'Okay.'

'I'll see what I can do and then I'll call you. And don't worry, if I have to leave a message on your home number it will be in code.'

'Okay, Janis, thanks.'

I hung up and left the booth. On the way back through the market in the direction of the parking garage I passed the cake window and was surprised to see that the baker was there. I stopped for a minute and watched. It must have been a last-minute order because it looked like the cake had been taken out of one of the inside display cabinets. It was already iced. The man behind the window was just putting on flowers and lettering.

I waited until he wrote the message. It was pink writing on a field of chocolate. It said, *Happy Birthday, Callie!* I hoped it was another cake going to a happy place.

35

Jocelyn Jones worked in a branch bank on Santa Monica at San Vicente. In a county for decades known as the bank robbery capital of the world she was in about as safe a location as was possible. Her branch was right across the street from the sheriff's department's West Hollywood station.

The branch was a two-story art deco job with a curving façade with large round windows along its second level. Inside, the tellers' counter and new-accounts desks were on the first floor and the executive offices upstairs. I found Jones up there in an office with a porthole that looked over the sheriff's compound to the Pacific Design Center, known locally as the Blue Whale because from some angles its blue-sheathed façade looked like the tail of a humpback protruding from the ocean.

Jones smiled and invited me to sit down.

'Mr. Scaggs told me you would be coming by and that it was all right to talk to you. He said you were working on the robbery.'

'That's right.'

'I'm glad it hasn't been forgotten about.'

'Well, I'm glad to hear you say that.'

'What can I do for you?'

'I'm not sure. I'm sort of retracing a lot of steps that were taken before. So it might be repetitive but I'd just like to hear you talk about your part in it. I'll ask questions if I come up with any.'

'Well, there isn't a whole lot for me to tell. I mean, I wasn't there like Linus and poor Mr. Vaughn were. I was mostly around the money before it was transported. I was an assistant at that time to Mr. Scaggs. He's been my mentor with the company.'

I nodded and smiled like I thought it was all nice. I was moving slowly, the plan being to gradually steer her in the direction I wanted to go.

'So you worked on the money. You counted it, packaged it, got it ready. Where was that?'

'At the downtown center. We were in a vault the whole time. The money came in to us from the branches and we did everything right there without ever leaving. Except, you know, at the end of the day. It took about three, three and a half days to get everything ready. Mostly waiting for it to come in from the branches.'

'When you say 'us,' you mean Linus . . . '

I opened the murder book on my lap as if to check a name I didn't recall.

'Simonson,' she said for me.

'Right, Linus Simonson. You worked on this together, correct?'

'That's right.'

'Was Mr. Scaggs his mentor, too?'

She shook her head and slightly blushed, I think, but it was hard to tell because she was very dark-skinned.

'No, the mentoring program is a minority program. I should say 'was.' They suspended it a year ago. Anyway, Linus is white. He grew up in Beverly Hills. His father owned a bunch of restaurants and I don't think he needed a mentor.'

I nodded.

'Okay, so you and Linus were in there for three days putting all of this money together. You also had to record serial numbers off the bills, right?'

'Yes, we did that, too.'

'How was that done?'

She didn't answer for a moment as she tried to remember. She swiveled slowly back and forth in her chair. I watched a sheriff's helicopter land on the roof of the station across Santa Monica.

'What I remember is that it was supposed to be random,' she said. 'So we just took bills out of the bricks at random. I think we had to get about a thousand numbers and record them. That took a long time, too.'

I leafed through the murder book until I found a copy of the currency report she and Simonson had put together. I unsnapped the binder's rings and removed the report.

'According to this you recorded eight hundred of the bills.'

'Oh, okay. Eight hundred, then.'

'Is this the report?'

I handed it to her and she studied it, looking at each page and her signature at the bottom of the last page.

'It looks like it but it's been four years.'

'Yes, I know. That was the last time you saw it – when you signed it?'

'No, after the robbery I saw it. When I was questioned by the detectives. They asked if that was the report.'

'And you said it was?'

'Yes.'

'Okay, going back to when you and Linus made this report, how did that go?'

She shrugged.

'Linus and I just took turns typing the numbers into his laptop.'

'Isn't there some sort of computer scanner or copier that could have recorded the serial numbers much more easily?'

'There is but it wouldn't work for what we had to do. We had to randomly select and record bills from every pack but keep each recorded bill in its original pack. That way if the money was stolen and split up, there would be a chance of tracing every pack.'

I nodded.

'Who told you to do it that way?'

'Well, I guess it came down from Mr. Scaggs or maybe Mr. Vaughn. Mr. Vaughn was the one who dealt with security and the instructions from the insurance company.'

'Okay, so you are in the vault with Linus. How exactly did you record the money?'

'Oh, Linus thought it would take forever if we wrote down the numbers and then had to type them into a computer. So he brought his laptop in and we entered them directly. One of us would read off the number while the other typed.'

'Which one of you did which?'

'We both did. We switched. You might think sitting at a table with two million dollars in cash on it is a real thrill but it actually was boring. So we switched around. Sometimes I read and he typed, and then I'd type while he read out the numbers.'

I thought about this, trying to see how it could have worked. It might appear that having two employees put the list together would provide a double-checking system, but it didn't. Whether Simonson was reading off numbers or entering them on the laptop computer, he was controlling the data. He could have made up numbers in either position and Jones would not have known it unless she looked at either the bill or the computer screen.

'Okay,' I said. 'Then when you were finished you printed out the computer file and signed the report, right?'

'Right. I mean, I think so. It was a while back.'

'Is that your signature on there?'

She flipped to the last page of the document and checked. She nodded. 'That's it.'

I held out my hand and she gave me the document back.

'Who took the report to Mr. Scaggs?'

'Probably Linus. He printed it out. Why are all of these details so important?'

Her first suspicion of where I was going. I didn't answer. I flipped the report she had been studying to the back page and looked at the signatures myself. Her signature was below Simonson's and above Scaggs's scrawl. It had been the order of signing. Simonson, then her, then it was taken to Scaggs for final sign-off.

As I held the report up to the light from the porthole, I thought I saw something I hadn't noticed before. It was only a photocopy of the original or maybe even a copy of a copy, but even still, there were gradations in the ink in Jocelyn Jones's signature. It was something I had seen before on another case.

'What is it?' Jones asked.

I looked at her while putting the document back into the murder book.

'Excuse me?'

'You looked like you saw something important.'

'Oh, nothing. I'm just looking at everything. I have just a few more questions.'

'Good. I should get downstairs. We're closing soon.'

'I'll get out of your hair, then. Mr. Vaughn, was he part of this process in which the money was prepared and the serial numbers documented?'

She shook her head once.

'Not really. He sort of supervised us and came in a lot, especially when the money came in from the branches or the Federal Reserve. He was in charge of that, I guess.'

'Did he come in when you guys were dictating the numbers and typing them into the computer?'

'I don't remember. I think he did. Like I said, he came in a lot. I think he liked Linus so he came in a lot.'

'What do you mean, he 'liked' Linus?'

'Well, you know.'

'You mean Mr. Vaughn was gay?'

She shrugged.

'I think he was, but not in an open way. It was a secret, I guess. It was no big deal.'

'What about Linus?'

'No, he's not gay. That's why I don't think he liked Mr. Vaughn coming in so much.'

'Did he say that to you or was that just your take on it?'

'No, he sort of said something about it one day. Like he joked, saying he was going to have a sexual harassment suit if this keeps up. Something like that.'

I nodded. I didn't know if this meant anything to the case or not.

'You didn't answer my question before.'

'What was that?'

'About why you are focusing so much on all of this. The currency numbers, I mean. And Linus and Mr. Vaughn.'

'I'm not really. It just seems that way to you because that is the part of this you are familiar with. But I'm trying to be thorough about all aspects of this. Do you ever hear from Linus anymore?'

She seemed surprised by the question.

'Me? No. I visited him in the hospital once, right after the shooting. He never came back to work, so I never saw him again. We worked together but we weren't really friends. Different sides of the tracks, I guess. I always thought that was why Mr. Scaggs picked us.'

'What do you mean?'

'Well, we weren't really friends and Linus was, you know, Linus. I think Mr. Scaggs picked two people that were different and weren't friends so we wouldn't get any ideas. About the money.'

I nodded and didn't say anything. She seemed to go off into a thought and then she shook her head in a self-deprecating way.

'What?'

'Nothing. It's just that I was thinking about going to see him at one of the clubs but thought they probably wouldn't even let me in. And if I said I knew him, it might be embarrassing, you know, if they called him and he acted like he didn't remember or something.'

'Clubs? There is more than one?'

She closed her eyes to suspicious slits.

'You told me you were being thorough. But you really don't even know who he is now, do you?'

I shrugged.

'Who is he now?'

'He's Linus. Like he only uses his first name now. He's famous. He and his partners own the top clubs in Hollywood now. It's like where all the celebrities go to see and be seen. Lines out the door and velvet ropes.'

'How many clubs?'

'I think at least four or five now. I don't really keep track. They started with the one and then they kept adding.'

'How many partners are there?'

'I don't know. There was a magazine story – wait a second, I think I saved it.'

She bent down and opened a drawer at the bottom of her desk. I heard her shuffling its contents around and then she came out with a copy of *Los Angeles Magazine*, the coffee-table monthly. She started turning its pages. It was a glossy magazine that listed restaurants in the back and usually ran two or three long feature articles on living and dying in L.A. Behind the gloss was a bite, though. Twice over the years writers from the magazine had done stories on my cases. I always thought they had come closest of any media reports to the truth of a crime in terms of its effects on a family or neighborhood. The ripple effect.

'I don't know why I was holding onto this,' Jones said, a bit embarrassed after just saying she didn't keep track of her former coworker. 'I guess because I knew him. Yeah, here.'

She turned the magazine around. There was a two-page opening spread on the story under a headline that said, 'The Night Kings.' There was an accompanying photo of four young men posed side by side behind a dark mahogany bar. Behind them were shelves of colored bottles lit from beneath.

'Can I see that?'

She closed it and handed it across the desk to me.

'You can have it. Like I said, I don't think I'll ever be seeing Linus again. He has no time for me. He did what he said he was going to do and that's that.'

I looked up from the magazine to her.

'What do you mean? What did he tell you he was going to do?'

'When I saw him in the hospital. He told me the bank owed him a lot of money for getting shot in the . . . uh, you know. He said he was going to get it, quit his job and open up a bar. He said he wouldn't make the mistakes his dad made.'

'His dad?'

'I didn't know what that meant. I didn't ask. But for some reason, opening that bar was Linus's life ambition. To be king of the night, I guess. Well, he got there.'

Her voice had a mixture of longing and jealousy in it. It didn't work well with her and I wished I could tell her what I thought of her hero. But I didn't. I didn't have everything I needed yet.

Thinking I had taken the interview about as far as I could, I stood up and held up the magazine.

'Thanks for your time. Are you sure you don't mind me taking this?'

She waved me off.

'No, go ahead. I've looked at it enough. One of these nights I ought to just put on my black jeans and black T-shirt and go on down and see if I can catch Linus for a minute. We could talk about the good old days but he probably doesn't want to hear about them.'

'Nobody does, Jocelyn. Because the old days weren't that good.'

I got up. I wanted to offer her some words of encouragement. I wanted to tell her not to be jealous, that what she had and what she'd accomplished were things to be proud of. But the sheriff's helicopter took off and banked across the street and over the bank. The place shook like an earthquake and took my words with it. I left Jocelyn Jones sitting there thinking about the other side of the tracks.

36

The magazine had been published seven months earlier. The story on Linus Simonson and his partners was not a cover story but it was hyped on the cover with a line that said, 'Hollywood's After Hours Entrepreneurs.' The story was hooked to the impending opening of a sixth club in the foursome's lineup of all-star late-night establishments. The article referred to Simonson as the king of the night crawlers, the one who parlayed the whole empire out of one hole-in-the-wall bar he had bought with a legal settlement. He had taken that first club, in an alley off of Hollywood and Cahuenga, renovated it, cut the lighting in half and brought in female bartenders who were prized more for their looks and tattoos than their skills at mixing drinks and adding bar tabs. He played the music loud, charged a $20 cover and didn't let anyone in wearing a tie or a white shirt. The club had no name on the wall outside and no listing in the phone book. A flashing neon blue arrow over the front door was the only indication of a commercial venture. But soon the arrow was no longer needed and was removed because there was always a line of clubbers stretching from the door down the alley.

The article stated that Linus – he was referred to by first name through most of the article – then partnered up with three buddies from his days at Beverly Hills High School and started opening new clubs at a rate of one every six months. The entrepreneurs primarily followed the pattern that worked with the first club. Buy a rundown establishment, renovate and reopen, put the word into the pipeline and wait for it to spread through the ranks of the Hollywood cool. After the nameless bar, the lounges the group opened tended in style and name to follow a literary or musical theme.

The second bar the group bought, closed and then reopened was Nat's Day of the Locusts, a nod to Nathanael West and his classic Hollywood novel. It wasn't their name. The place had been known as simply Nat's for decades and most patrons probably believed it was named for Nat King Cole. Either way the name was cool and the group kept it.

Nat's was also the same place Dorsey and Cross had gotten shot up in. The article reported that the murder had acted to depress the sales price of the place. In fact, it was a steal. But once the bar was reopened – without a name change – and marketed to the night crawlers, the place's history only added to its mystique. It was another immediate and huge success for the high-school pals who called their burgeoning company Four Kings Incorporated.

For a long time in my life I did not believe in coincidence. I now know better. But there are coincidences and there are coincidences. Kiz Rider coming to my house and laying the high jingo on me as Art Pepper was playing it – that was coincidence. But as I sat in the Mercedes and read the magazine article, I wasn't accepting the happenstance of Linus Simonson buying the bar in which two detectives who investigated the heist of $2 million he counted and prepared for shipment were shot. I didn't think it was coincidence for a moment. I thought it was pure arrogance.

Besides the nameless bar and Nat's, the foursome also opened places called Kings' Crossing, Chet's and Cozy's Last Stand, named, according to the article, after a friend who had disappeared. The place which had occasioned the magazine story and was due to open was to be called Doghouse Reilly's, after an alias used by private eye Philip Marlowe in a Raymond Chandler novel.

The story didn't delve deeply into the financing behind the four-man operation. It was more interested in the glitz than the underpinnings of the supposed success story. It was taken and reported as a given that the first establishments supported the group's expansion in a continuing cycle. Profits from the first bar financed the second and so on.

But the picture wasn't purely positive. The article's writer ended the story with a suggestion that the four kings might become victims of their own success. The theory espoused was that the population of black-clad night crawlers was finite in Hollywood, and that opening and operating six lounges did not convincingly expand the client base. It only spread it out. The article noted that there were also many pretenders to the throne, a raft of inferior, uncool bars and lounges that had opened in recent years.

The story ended by noting that on a recent Friday night at midnight, there was no line of night crawlers waiting to get into the nameless club. It cynically suggested that it might be time to put up the blue arrow again.

I dropped the magazine into the binder and sat there thinking about things. I had the sense that things were coming together. I felt anxious because I knew instinctively I was close. I didn't have all the answers but experience told me that they would come. What I had was the direction. It had been more than four years since I had looked down on Angella Benton's body and I finally had a solid suspect.

I opened the center console and got out the cell phone. I figured there would be no harm in calling my own home number. I checked messages and found I had two. The first was from Janis Langwiser. It was short and sweet.

'It's me. Call me but use all precautions.'

I knew that meant a pay phone. The next message was from Roy Lindell. He also followed the standard of brevity.

'All right, asshole, I've got something for you. Call me.'

I looked around. I was parked in front of a post office on San Vicente. My meter was up and I was out of change for both the parking and the calls I needed to make. But I figured there would be a phone inside the post office and a machine for getting change to buy stamps from other machines. I got out and went in.

The main post office was closed but in an outer room that was open after hours I found the machine and pay phone I was looking for. I called Langwiser first because I figured that I had already moved the investigation past the information I had asked Lindell to get for me.

I got Langwiser on her cell but she was still in her office.

'What did you get from Foreman?' I asked, getting right to the point.

'This has to remain highly confidential, Harry. I did talk to Jim and when I explained the circumstances he didn't mind talking to me about it. The caveat being that this information goes into no reports and you never reveal its source.'

'No problem. I don't write reports anymore, anyway.'

'Don't be so quick and cavalier about it. You're not a cop anymore and you're no lawyer. You have no legal shield.'

'I have a private eye ticket.'

'Like I said, you have no shield. If a judge ever ordered you to reveal your source you would have to do it or face contempt. That would mean possibly going to jail. Ex-cops in jail don't do so well.'

'Tell me about it.'

'I just did.'

'Okay, I understand. It's still no problem.'

The truth was, I couldn't see how this would ever come up in a court and with a judge. I wasn't worried about the possibility of jail.

'Okay, as long as we're clear. Jim told me that Simonson settled for fifty thousand dollars.'

'That's all?'

'That's it and it really isn't that much. He was represented by a thirty-five percenter. He also had to pay filing costs.'

He'd had a lawyer who took a 35 percent cut of any settlement in exchange for working the case without hourly billing. It meant that Simonson probably cleared a little over thirty grand. It wasn't a lot when it came to quitting your day job and starting a late-night lounge empire.

The sense of anxiety I had been feeling ticked into a higher gear. I had suspected that the settlement would be low but not that low. I was beginning to convince myself.

'Did Foreman say anything else about the case?'

'Just one other thing. He said that it was Simonson who insisted on the confidentiality agreement and that the agreement itself was unusual. It required that there be not only no public announcement about the settlement but no public record of it.'

'Well, it never went to court anyway.'

'I know, but BankLA is a publicly held corporation. So what the confidentiality agreement entailed was that Simonson be carried under a pseudonym on all financial records related to the payout. He's carried, again at his request, as Mr. King.'

I didn't respond as I thought about this.

'So how did I do, Harry?'

'You did real good, Janis. Which reminds me, you've been doing a hell of a lot of work on this. Are you sure you don't want to bill me?'

'Yes, I'm sure. I still owe you.'

'Well, now I'll owe you. I want you to do one last thing for me. I just decided that tomorrow I'm going to give what I've got to the powers that be. It might be good if you were there. You know, to sort of make sure I don't step across any lines with these people.'

'I'm there. Where?'

'You want to check your calendar first?'

'I already know I have the morning free. You want to do it here or are you going into the police station?'

'No, I've got butting jurisdictions. I'd like to do it at your place. You have a room we can put about six or seven people in?'

'I'll book the conference room. What time?'

'How about nine o'clock?'

'Fine. I'll be here early if you want to come in and talk first and go over everything.'

'That would be good. I'll see you about eight-thirty.'

'I'll be here. Do you think you have it?'

I knew what she meant. Did I have the story, if not the actual evidence that would push the LAPD and FBI into running with the case again.

'It's coming together. There's maybe one more thing I can do and then I've got to give it to somebody who can get warrants and knock down doors.'

'I get it. I'll see you tomorrow. And I'm glad you made it through on this. I really am.'

'Yeah, me too. Thanks, Janis.'

After hanging up I realized I had forgotten about the parking meter. I went out to feed it but it was too late. West Hollywood Parking Enforcement had beat me there. I left the ticket on the windshield and went back inside. I got Lindell in his office just before he was leaving for the day.

'What do you got?'

'Herpes simplex five. What do you got?'

'Come on, man.'

'You're an asshole, Bosch, asking me to wash your dirty laundry.'

I realized what he was mad about.

'The plate number?'

'Yeah, the plate number. As if you didn't know. It belongs to your ex-wife, man, and I really don't appreciate being pulled into your bullshit. I mean, either kill her or get over her, you know what I mean?'

I agreed that I knew what he meant but not what he had suggested. I could tell that I had seriously put him out with the plate check.

'Roy, all I can tell you is that I didn't know. I'm sorry. You're right. I shouldn't drag you in and I am sorry I did.'

There was silence and I thought that I had placated him.

'Roy?'

'What?'

'Did you write down the address from the registration?'

'You fucking asshole.'

He vented for another minute but eventually, grudgingly gave me the address Eleanor's car was registered to. There was no apartment number with it. It looked like she had not only come up a level in wheels. She was living in a house now.

'Thanks, Roy. It's the last time on that. I promise. Anything come up on the other thing I asked about?'

'Nothing good, nothing useful. The guy's record is pretty clean. There is some juvenile stuff but it's all sealed. I didn't go any further with it.'

'Okay.'

I wondered if the juvenile stuff involved his former Beverly Hills High classmates and now partners.

'The only other thing is that he's a junior. There is another Linus Simonson on the computer. Going by the age it looks like Daddy.'

'What's he on there for?'

'He's got an IRS rap and a bankruptcy. It's all old stuff.'

'How old?'

'The IRS came first, like they usually do. That was in 'ninety-four. The old man went bankrupt two years later. Who is this guy Linus and why did you want me to check him for a tail?'

I didn't answer as I found myself looking into a Most Wanted picture on the post office wall. A serial rapist. But I wasn't really looking at him. I was looking at Linus. I was working the interior circuits as another piece fell into place. Linus said he wasn't going to make the same mistakes as his father, who had gone belly up and broke, an IRS collar around his neck. The question that poked through all of that was, how does a guy with no job and no backing from Daddy parlay the thirty grand he's got in his pocket into the purchase and major renovation of a bar? And then another, and then another.

Loans maybe – if he qualified. Or maybe with a $2 million bank withdrawal.

'Bosch, you there?'

I came out of it.

'Yeah, I'm here.'

'I asked you a question. Who is this guy? Is he on the movie deal?'

'It's looking like it, Roy. What are you doing tomorrow morning?'

'I'm doing what I'm always doing. Why?'

'If you want a piece of this be at my lawyer's office at nine. And don't be late.'

'Is this guy connected to Marty? If he's the guy I don't want a piece. I want all of it.'

'I don't know yet. But he'll get us closer, that's for sure.'

Lindell wanted to ask more questions but I cut him off. I had more calls to make. I gave him Langwiser's name and address and he finally said he would be at the law office at nine. I hung up and then called Sandor Szatmari and left a message inviting him to the same meeting.

Lastly I called Kiz Rider in the administration office at Parker Center and extended the invitation to her as well. She went from zero to sixty on the anger speedometer in about five seconds.

'Harry, I warned you about this. You are going to find yourself in a lot of trouble. You can't just work a case and then call in a gang bang when you think it's time we were made privy to your private investigations.'

'Kiz, I already did. You just have to decide if you want to be there or not. There will be a nice piece of this for somebody at the LAPD. As far as I'm thinking, it might as well be you. But if you're not interested, I'll call RHD.'

'Goddamnit, Harry.'

'In or out?'

There was a long pause.

'I'm in. But, Harry, I'm not going to protect you.'

'I wouldn't expect it.'

'Who is your lawyer?'

I gave her the information and was ready to hang up. I felt a sense of dread about the damage to our relationship. It seemed permanent to me.

'Okay, see you then,' I finally said.

'Yes, you will,' she replied sternly.

I remembered something I needed.

'Oh, and Kiz? See if you can find the original of the currency report. It should be in the murder book.'

'What currency report?'

I explained and she said she would look for it. I thanked her and hung up. I went out to my car and grabbed the parking ticket off the windshield. I got in and threw it over my shoulder into the backseat for good luck.

It was almost seven on the dashboard clock. I knew things didn't get going in the Hollywood club scene until ten or later. But I had forward momentum and didn't want it to ebb away while I just went home and waited. I sat there thinking with my hand over the top of the wheel, ticking my fingertips on the dashboard. Soon they were going through the phrasing that Quentin McKinzie had taught me, and when I realized this, I knew how I could spend the next few hours. I opened up the cell phone again.

37

Sugar Ray McK was waiting for me in his chair in his room at the Splendid Age. The only indication that he knew he was going out was the porkpie hat he was wearing. He once told me he only wore it when he went out to hear music, which meant he rarely wore it anymore. Under the brim his eyes were sharper than I had seen them in a long while.

'This is going to be fun, dog,' he said and I wondered if he'd been watching too much MTV.

'I hope they've got a decent crew for the first set. I didn't even check.'

'Don't worry. It'll be fine.'

He drew out the last word.

'Before we go can I borrow that magnifying glass you use to read the TV guide?'

'Sure can. What do you need?'

He dug the glass out of a pocket on the arm of his chair while I took the last page of the currency report out of my shirt pocket and unfolded it. Sugar Ray handed me the glass and I went over to the bed table and turned on the lamp. I held the page over the top of the shade and then studied Jocelyn Jones's signature with the magnifier. I got a confirmation of something I had seen earlier while in her office.

'What is it, Harry?' Sugar Ray asked.

I handed him the glass back and started refolding the paper.

'Just something I've been working on. Something called forger's tremor.'

'Hmmm. Man, I got tremors all over.'

I smiled at him.

'We've all got 'em, one way or the other. Come on, let's go. Let's hear some music.'

'I'm going. You turn that lamp off. That costs money.'

We headed out. As we went down the hallway I thought of Melissa Royal and wondered if she might be visiting her mother. I doubted it. A moment of dread spiked me because I knew the day was coming when I would have to sit down with Melissa and tell her I was the wrong guy.

A porter from the center helped me get Sugar Ray into the car. The

Mercedes SUV was probably too high for him to climb into. I realized I would have to think about that if I took him out on any more field trips.

We went over to the Baked Potato and had dinner and watched the first set of the first act, a quartet of journeymen called Four Squared. They were decent but maybe a little tired. They were partial to Billy Strayhorn's stuff and so am I, so it didn't matter.

It didn't matter to Sugar Ray either. His face lit up and he kept the beat in his shoulders as he listened. He never spoke while they played and he clapped with enthusiasm after every song. Reverence is what I saw in his eyes. Reverence for the sound and the form.

The players didn't recognize him. Few people would now that he was down to just skin and bones. But that didn't bother Sugar Ray. It didn't diminish our evening by one note.

After the first set, I could see him starting to flag. It was after nine and time for him to sleep and dream. He'd told me once that he still could play in his dreams. I thought we should all be so lucky.

It was also time for me to look into the face of the man who had taken Angella Benton from this world. I had no badge and no official standing. But I knew things and believed that I still stood for her. I spoke for her. In the morning they could take it all away from me, make me sit down and watch from the sidelines. But I still had until then. And I knew I was not going home just yet. I was going to confront Linus Simonson and take his measure. I was going to let him know who put the bead on him. And I was going to give him the chance to answer for Angella Benton.

When we got back to the Splendid Age I left Sugar Ray dozing in the front seat while I went in to get the porter. Getting him into the Mercedes outside the Baked Potato by myself had been a chore.

I gently shook him awake and then we got him down onto the sidewalk. We walked him in and then down the hall to his room. Sitting on his bed, trying to shake off the sleep, he asked me where I'd been.

'I've been right here with you, Sugar Ray.'

'You've been practicing?'

'Every chance I get.'

I realized that he may have already forgotten our evening's outing. He may have thought I was there for a lesson. I felt bad about him being robbed of the memory so soon.

'Sugar Ray, I've gotta go. I've got some work to do.'

'Okay, Henry.'

'It's Harry.'

'That's what I said.'

'Oh. You want me to turn on the box or are you going to go to sleep?'

'Nah, put the box on for me if you don't mind. That'd be good.'

I turned on the television that was mounted on the wall. It was on CNN and Sugar Ray said to leave it there. I went over and squeezed his shoulder and then headed for the door.

'"Lush Life,"' he said to my back.

I turned around to look at him. He was smiling. 'Lush Life' was the last song of the set we had heard. He did remember.

'I love that song,' he said.

'Yeah, me too.'

I left him to his memories of a lush life while I headed out into the night to see a king about a stolen life. I was unarmed but unafraid. I was in a state of grace. I carried the last prayer of Angella Benton with me.

38

Shortly after ten o'clock I approached the doorway to Nat's on Cherokee, a half block south of Hollywood Boulevard. It was still early but there was no line of people waiting to get in. There was no velvet rope. There was no doorman selecting who got in and who didn't. There was no collector of a cover charge. When I got inside, there also were almost no customers.

I had been in Nat's on numerous occasions in its former incarnation as a dive bar populated by a clientele as devoted to alcohol as any other aspect of life. It wasn't a pickup spot – unless you counted the prostitutes who cooled their heels at the bar. It wasn't a celebrity-watching spot. It was a drinking spot and that was the sum of its entire purpose, and as such it had an honest character. As I walked in and saw all the polished brass and rich woods I realized that what it had now was glamour and that was never the same or as long-lasting as character. It didn't matter how many people lined up on opening night. The place wasn't going to go the distance. I knew that within fifteen seconds. The place was doomed before the first citron martini was poured, shaken not stirred, into its frosted glass and placed on a black napkin.

I went right to the bar where there were three patrons who looked like tourists in from Florida after a dose of much needed California Cool. The bartender was tall and thin and wore the requisite black jeans and tight body shirt that allowed her nipples to introduce themselves to the customers. She had a black-ink snake wrapped around one bicep, its forked red tongue licking the crook of her elbow, where the needle scars were evident. Her hair was shorter than mine and on the nape of her neck a bar code was tattooed. It made me think of how much I enjoyed discovering Eleanor Wish's neck the night before.

'There's a ten-dollar cover,' the bartender said. 'What can I get you?'

I remembered from the magazine article that it used to be $20.

'What does it cover? This place is dead.'

'Stick around. That's ten dollars.'

I made no move to give her the money. I leaned on the bar and spoke quietly.

'Where's Linus?'

'He's not here tonight.'

'Then where is he? I need to talk to him.'

'He's probably at Chet's. That's where he keeps his office. He doesn't usually start bopping around to the places until after midnight. Are you going to pay the ten?'

'I don't think so. I'm leaving.'

She frowned.

'You're a cop, aren't you?'

I smiled proudly.

'Going on twenty-eight years.'

I left off the part about the twenty-eight years coming before I retired. I figured she'd get on the phone and send the word a cop was coming. That might work in my favor. I reached in my pocket and pulled out a ten. I tossed it onto the bar.

'That's not the cover. That's for you. Get a haircut.'

She put an exaggerated smile on her face, one that showed she had a nice set of dimples. She snatched the ten.

'Thanks, Dad.'

I smiled as I walked out.

It took me fifteen minutes to get over to Chet's on Santa Monica near LaBrea. I had the address thanks to *Los Angeles Magazine*, which had conveniently put a listing of all of the Four Kings establishments in a box on the last page of the story.

Again there was no line and few customers. I was beginning to think that once you are declared cool in the tourist books and magazines, then you're dead in the water. Chet's was almost a carbon copy of Nat's, right down to the sullen bartender with the not-so-subtle nipples and tattoos. The one thing I liked about the place was the music. Chet Baker's 'Cool Burnin'' was playing when I walked in and I thought maybe the kings might have some taste after all.

The bartender was déjà vu all over again – tall, thin and in black, except her bicep tattoo was Marilyn Monroe's face circa 'Happy Birthday, Mr. President.'

'You the cop?' she asked before I said a word.

'You've been talking to your sister. I guess she told you I don't pay cover.'

'She said something about that.'

'Where's Linus?'

'He's in his office. I told him you were coming.'

'That was nice of you.'

I stepped away from the bar but pointed at her tattoo.

'Your mom?'

'Hey, come here, take a look.'

I leaned back over the bar. She bent her elbow and flexed her muscles repeatedly. Marilyn's cheeks puffed up and then down as the bicep beneath expanded and contracted.

'Kind of looks like she's giving a blow job, doesn't it?' the bartender said.

'That's real cute,' I said. 'I bet you show that to all the boys.'

'Is it worth ten bucks?'

I almost told her I knew places where I could get the real thing for a ten but let it go. I left her there and found my way to a hallway behind the bar. There were doors for the rest rooms and then a door marked 'Management Only.' I didn't knock. I just went through and it only led to a continuation of the hallway and more doors. The third door down said 'Linus' on it. I opened that one without knocking, too.

Linus Simonson was sitting behind a cluttered desk. I recognized him from the magazine photo. He had a bottle of Scotch whiskey and a snifter on the desk. There was a black leather couch in the office and on it sat a man I also recognized from the magazine as one of the partners. His name was James Oliphant. He had his feet up on a coffee table and looked like he wasn't the least bit concerned by a visit from a man he'd been told was a cop.

'Hey, man, you the cop,' Simonson said as he waved me in. 'Close the door.'

I stepped in and introduced myself. I didn't say I was a cop.

'Well, I'm Linus and that there's Jim. What's up? What can we do for you?'

I held my hands out as though I had nothing to hide.

'I'm not sure what you can do for me. I just wanted to drop by and sort of introduce myself. I'm working on the Angella Benton case and of course that includes the BankLA case so . . . here I am.'

'Oh, man, BankLA. That's some serious ancient history there.'

He looked at his partner and laughed.

'That was like another lifetime ago. I don't want to go there, man. That's a bad memory.'

'Yeah, well, not as bad for you as it was for Angella Benton.'

Simonson suddenly got serious and leaned forward on his desk.

'I don't get this, man. What are you doing here? You're not a cop. Cops come in twos. If you *are* a cop, then you aren't legit. What do you want? Let me see a badge.'

'I didn't tell anybody I had a badge. I was a cop, but not now. In fact, I thought maybe you'd recognize me from that other lifetime you were talking about.'

Simonson looked at Oliphant and smirked.

'Recognize you from what?'

'I was there that day you took it in the ass. I'm talking about the bullet. But then again, you were rolling around and screaming so much you probably didn't have time to look at me.'

But Simonson's eyes widened in recognition. Maybe not physical recognition but recognition of who I was and what I had done.

'Shit, you're the guy. You're the cop that was there. You're the one who shot—'

He stopped himself from saying a name. He looked at Oliphant.

'He's the one who hit one of the robbers.'

I looked at Oliphant and I saw recognition – physical recognition – and maybe something like hate or anger in his eyes.

'That's not known for sure because we never got the robber. But, yeah, I think I hit him. That was me.'

I said it with a smile of pride. I kept it on my face as I turned back to Simonson.

'Who are you working for?' Simonson asked.

'Me? I'm working for somebody who isn't going to stop, who isn't going to let up. Not for a minute. He's going to find out who put Angella Benton down on the tile and he'll go at it until he either dies or he knows.'

Simonson smirked again arrogantly.

'Well, good luck to you and him, Mr. Bosch. I think you ought to go now. We're kind of busy here.'

I nodded to him and then looked at Oliphant, giving him the best deadeye in my repertoire.

'Then I guess I'll see you boys around.'

I went through the door and down the hallway back to the bar. Chet Baker was now singing 'My Funny Valentine.' As I headed for the main door I noticed the bartender flexing her bicep for two men sitting at the bar where I had stood. They were laughing. I recognized them as the remaining two kings from the magazine photo.

They stopped laughing when they saw me and I felt their eyes on me all the way out the door.

39

On the way home I stopped at the twenty-four-hour Ralph's on Sunset and bought a bag of coffee. I didn't expect that I'd be getting much sleep between the night and the multi-agency confab the following morning.

On the drive up the hill to my house there are too many curves to use the rearview mirror to check for a tail. But there is one sweeping curve halfway up that allows you to look to your right out the passenger window and across the drop-off to the road you just covered. It's always been my habit to slow at this spot and check for a trailer.

This night I slowed more than usual and watched a little longer. I didn't expect my visit to Chet's to be taken as anything other than a threat and I wasn't wrong. As I looked across the drop-off I saw a car with no lights on round the hill and move into the sweeping curve. I eased the gas pedal down and slowly picked up speed again. After the next curve I punched it and put a little more distance between us. I pulled all the way into the carport next to my house and quickly got out with the bag from the store. I moved into the darkest corner of the carport and waited. I heard the trail car before I saw it. Then I watched it glide by. A long Jaguar. Someone was lighting a cigarette in the backseat, and in the glow from the flame I saw the car was full. The four kings were coming for me.

After the Jag had gone by I saw the bushes across the street glow red and I knew they were stopping just past my house. I moved to the door that led into the kitchen and went inside, making sure to lock the door afterward.

This was the moment when people without badges called the police for help. It's when they desperately whispered, '*Hurry, please! They are coming!*' But badge or no badge, I knew that was not an option for me now. This was my play and I didn't care in that moment about what authority I had or didn't have.

I had not carried a gun since the night I left my badge and service pistol in a drawer at Hollywood Division and walked out. But I had a weapon. I'd bought a Glock P7 for personal protection. It was wrapped in an oil rag and in a box on the shelf of the walk-in closet in the bedroom. I put the bag from Ralph's down on the counter and moved into the hallway and down to the bedroom without turning on any lights.

When I opened the closet door I was suddenly shoved backwards with great force by a man who had been waiting in there for me. I hit the opposite wall and slid to the floor. He was on me immediately, straddling and pushing the barrel of a pistol up under my jaw. I managed to look up and in the pale light coming in through the French door leading to the deck I could see who it was.

'Milton. What the—'

'Shut up, asshole. You surprised to see me? Did you think I was going to let them wash me down the toilet without doing something about it?'

'I don't know what you're talking about. Listen, there are people—'

'I said, shut the fuck up. I want the disks, you understand? I want the original data chip.'

'Listen to me! There are people about to come in here for me. They want—'

He shoved the barrel in so deep under my jaw that I had to stop talking. The pain sent shards of red glass across my vision. Milton held the gun there and leaned down, his breath in my face as he spoke.

'I've got your gun right here, Bosch. And I'm going to turn you into another suicide statistic if you don't—'

There was a sudden crashing sound from the hallway and I knew it was the front door coming in off its hinges. Then there were footsteps. Milton jumped up off of me and stepped through the bedroom door into the hallway. Almost immediately, there was the booming thunder of a shotgun blast and Milton was slammed back against the wall, his eyes wide with the terror of knowing he was dying. He then slid down the wall, his heels pushing back the hallway rug to reveal the handle of the trapdoor that led beneath the house.

I knew they had mistaken him for me. It was a break worth a few seconds at the most. I rolled over and quickly moved to the French door. As I opened it I heard someone's panicked voice call out from the hallway.

'It's not him!'

The door squealed when I opened it, its hinges protesting from lack of use. I quickly crossed the deck and went over the railing like a cowboy mounting a stolen horse. I went down the railing until I was hanging from the deck, twenty feet above the sharply sloping ground below. In the dim moonlight I looked for one of the iron support beams that held the deck and house to the side of the hill. I was intimately familiar with the design of the house from having supervised its reconstruction from the ground up after the 'ninety-four earthquake.

I had to move six feet along the edge of the deck before I could reach in and grab hold of one of the support beams. I wrapped my arms and legs around it and slid down to the ground. As I went down I heard their footsteps on the deck above me.

'He went down there! He went down there!'

'Where? I don't see—'

'He went down there! You two go. We'll take the street.'

I was on the ground beneath the shelter of the deck. I knew if I stepped out and tried to make my way down the steep slope to one of the streets or houses in the canyon below I would be exposed to my armed pursuers. Instead I turned and climbed up the hill under the house and further into the shelter of the structure. I knew there was a trench dug into the ground up there, where the sewer main had to be replaced after the quake. Above me there would also be the trapdoor that opened in the hallway. But I had designed it during the rebuilding of the house as an escape route, not a means of ingress. It was locked from inside and no use to me at the moment.

I moved up the hill, found the trench and rolled into it. I blindly moved my hands around at the bottom, looking for a weapon. All I found were cracked pieces of the old sewer main. I found one shard that was triangular and might work as a weapon. It would have to do.

Two men moved like shadows down the support beams to the ground below the deck. The moonlight reflected off the steel of their pistols. The reflections also showed me that one had on eyeglasses and I remembered him from the magazine story and photo. His name was Bernard Banks, known as B.B. King among the night crawlers. He had been at the bar at Chet's when I had left.

The two shadows exchanged whispers and then split up, one moving down the hill and to the left, the other – Banks – maintaining his position. It was some kind of tactical strategy in which one would hopefully chase me into the waiting pistol of the other.

From my angle above him Banks was a hard target silhouetted by the lights from the canyon below. He was fifteen feet from me but I had nothing to use as a weapon except a shard of old iron pipe. Still, it was enough. I had survived more missions into the tunnels of Vietnam than I could remember. I'd once spent a whole night in the elephant grass with the enemy moving all around me. And I had lived and worked for twenty-five-plus years on the streets of this city with a badge. This kid was going to be no match for me. I knew none of them would be.

When Banks turned to look down the canyon slope, I rose up in the trench and threw the pipe shard into the brush out to his right. It made a sound like an animal moving through high grass. As he turned, tensed and raised his weapon I slid over the top of the trench and started moving down the slope toward him, all the while keeping one of the iron beams between us as a sound and visual blind.

I got to the beam and he still had not turned from the direction of the sounds in the brush. He was just putting the misdirection together and finally turning back when I got to him. My left fist hit him squarely between the eyes while my right closed over the gun and I put a finger through the trigger guard. I had actually been aiming for his mouth but the punch broke his glasses in half at the bridge and staggered him just the same. I pivoted and swung him in a 180-degree arc, gathering momentum and putting him headfirst into one of the support beams. His skull made a sound like a water balloon breaking and the iron beam hummed like a tuning fork. He dropped to the ground like a bag of wet laundry.

I put his gun into the waistband of my pants and then turned him over. The blood on his face looked black in the moonlight. I quickly propped his back against the beam, brought his knees up and folded his arms on top of them. I leaned his face down on his arms.

Soon I heard the other one call for him from further down the hillside.

'B.B., you got him? Hey, Beeb!'

I backed away from Banks and crouched in the bushes ten feet away. I pulled the gun from my pants. In the moonlight I could not tell the make. It was a black steel pistol with no safety. Probably a Glock. I then realized it was probably my own gun. It must have been the one Milton had shoved into my neck. Banks had taken it from his body.

I heard the other one approaching in the brush. He was coming from my left and would cross within five feet of me when he approached Banks. I waited until I heard him and knew he was close.

'Banks, what are you doing? You pussy, get up and—'

He shut up when he felt the barrel of the gun against his neck.

'Drop the gun or you die right here.'

I heard it hit the ground. With my free hand I reached up and grabbed the back of his collar and pulled him around and then back underneath the shelter of the deck where we couldn't be seen from above. We were both facing the lights of the canyon and the freeway below. He was the fourth king, the one in the magazine picture who had the bar towel over his shoulder. I couldn't remember his name in all of the excitement. He'd been sitting at the bar at Chet's with Banks.

'What's your name, asshole?'

'Jimmy Fazio. Look, I—'

'Shut up.'

He was quiet. I leaned forward and whispered into his ear.

'Look at the lights. You are going to die here, Jimmy Fazio. The lights are the last thing you'll ever see.'

'Please . . . '

'Please? Is that what Angella Benton said? Did she say please to you?'

'No, please, no, I mean, I wasn't even there.'

'Convince me.'

He didn't say anything.

'Or die.'

'Okay, it wasn't me. Please believe me. It was Linus and Vaughn. It was their idea and they did it without even telling the rest of us. We couldn't stop it because we didn't know about it.'

'Yeah, what else? You're only alive because you're talking.'

'That's why we shot Vaughn. Linus said we had to because he was going to take the money and pin the girl on Linus.'

'What about Linus getting shot? Was that part of the plan?'

He shook his head.

'That wasn't supposed to happen but we figured out how to make it work. Like a cover for us buying the clubs.'

'Yeah, it worked all right. What about Marty Gessler and Jack Dorsey?'

'Who?'

I jammed the gun's muzzle hard into his neck.

'Don't give me that shit. I want the whole goddamn story.'

'I don't—'

'Faz! You fucking coward!'

The voice came from above us. I looked up and saw the upper body of a man hanging down over the edge of the deck. His arms were extended, two hands on a gun. I let go of my captive and dove left just as the gunfire erupted. The shooter was Oliphant. He screamed as he fired. Just blindly screamed. The whole shelter area beneath the house lit up with the flashes. Slugs ricocheted off the iron beams. I came up on the side of one of the beams and fired three times in a quick burst at him. His shout cut off and I knew I'd hit him. I watched as he dropped his gun, lost his balance and fell the twenty feet down, making a heavy thud in the bushes.

I looked around for Fazio and found him on the ground near Banks. He'd been hit in the upper chest but was still alive. It was too dark to see his eyes but I knew they were open and panicked, looking at me for help. I grabbed his jaw and turned his face to mine.

'Can you talk?'

'Uh . . . it hurts.'

'Yeah, it does, doesn't it? Tell me about the FBI agent. Where is she? What happened to her?'

'Uh . . . '

'Who killed the cop? Was that Linus, too?'

'Linus . . . '

'Is that a yes? Did Linus do it?'

He didn't answer. I was losing him. I lightly patted his cheeks and then shook him by the collar.

'Come on, man, stay with me. Was that a yes? Fazio, did Linus Simonson kill the cop?'

Nothing. He was gone. Then a voice came from behind me.

'I think that would be a yes.'

I turned. It was Simonson. He had found the trapdoor and come down out of the house behind me. He was holding a sawed-off shotgun. I slowly stood up, leaving my gun on the ground next to Fazio's body and raising my hands. I backed away from Simonson, stepping further down the hill.

'Cops on the payroll are always a pain in the ass,' he said. 'I had to put an end to that pronto.'

I took another step backwards, but for every step I took, Simonson did likewise. The shotgun was only three feet away. I knew I'd be unable to escape its kill range if I tried to make a move. All I could do was play for time. Somebody in the neighborhood had to have heard the shots and made a call.

Simonson aimed the weapon at my heart.

'I'm going to enjoy this. This one's for Cozy.'

'Cozy?' I asked, though I had already put it together. 'Who the hell is Cozy?'

'You hit him that day. With your bullets. And he didn't make it.'

'What happened to him?'

'What do you think happened? He died in the back of the van.'

'You buried him? Where?'

'Not me. I was sort of busy that day, remember? They buried him. Cozy liked boats. They gave him a burial at sea, you could say.'

I took another step back. Simonson followed. I was walking out from beneath the deck. If the cops ever showed up they could put a bead on him from above.

'What about the FBI agent? What happened to Marty Gessler?'

'See that's the thing. When Dorsey told me about her and what the plan was, that was when I knew he had to go. I mean, he was—'

The shotgun suddenly pointed skyward as the foot Simonson had put his weight down on went out from under him. He took a classic pratfall, landing on his back. I was on him then like a wild man. We rolled and fought for control of the shotgun. He was younger and stronger and quickly was able to hold the top position. But he was an inexperienced fighter. His focus was on controlling the struggle rather than on simply overpowering his opponent.

I had my left hand wrapped around the snubbed barrel while the other was gripped at the trigger guard. I managed to squeeze my thumb into the guard behind his finger. I closed my eyes and an image came to me. Angella Benton's hands. The image from memory and dreams. I channeled all my strength into my left arm and pushed. The angle of the gun shifted. I closed my eyes and depressed the trigger with my thumb. The loudest sound I have ever heard in my life roared through my head as the shotgun discharged. My face felt like it had caught on fire. I opened my eyes and looked up at Simonson and saw that he no longer had a face.

He rolled off of me and an inhuman sound gurgled from the pulp that had been his face. His legs kicked like he was riding an invisible bicycle. He rolled back and forth as his hands balled into fists as tight as stones, and then he stopped and went still.

Slowly, I sat up, registering what had happened. I touched my own face and found it intact. I was burned from the discharge gases but otherwise I was okay. My ears were ringing and for once I couldn't hear the ever present sound of the freeway below.

I saw a glint in the brush and reached for the object. It was a water bottle. It was full, unopened. I realized that Simonson had slipped on the water bottle I had knocked off the deck a few days before. And it had saved my life. I twisted the cap off the bottle and poured water over my face, washing away the blood and the sting of the burn.

'Don't move!'

I looked up from my position and saw a man leaning over the deck railing, pointing another gun at me. The moon reflected off the badge on his uniform. The cops had finally arrived. I dropped the bottle and spread my hands wide.

'Don't worry,' I said. 'I'm not moving.'

I leaned back, my arms still spread. My head rested on the ground and I pulled great gulps of air into my lungs. The ringing in my ears was still there but I could now also hear my heart as it slowed its cadence to the normal beat of life. I looked up into the dark, sacred night, to the place where those not saved on earth wait for the rest of us above. Not yet, I thought. No, not yet.

40

While the cop on the deck above kept his gun on me his partner dropped through the trapdoor and made his way down the slope to me. He had a flashlight in one hand and a gun in the other and the wild eyes of a man who has no idea what he has stepped into.

'Roll over and put your hands behind your back,' he ordered, adrenaline drawing his voice high and tight.

I did as I was instructed and he put his flashlight down on the ground as he cuffed my wrists, thankfully not in the style of the FBI. I tried to calmly talk to him.

'Just so you know, I—'

'I don't want to know anything from you.'

'–I'm LAPD retired. Out of Hollywood. Pulled the pin last year after twenty-five-plus.'

'Good for you. Why don't you save it for the suits?'

My house was in North Hollywood Division. I knew there was no reason why they should know me or care.

'Hey,' said the one from above. 'What's his name? Put the light on him.'

The man on the ground put the light in my face from a foot away. It was blinding.

'What's your name?'

'Harry Bosch. I worked homicide.'

'Har–'

'I know who he is, Swanny. He's all right. Get the light out of his face.'

Swanny took the light away.

'Yeah, fine. But the cuffs stay on. The suits can sort it all – ah, Jesus!'

He had put his light on the faceless body in the brush to my left. Linus Simonson, or what was left of him.

'Don't puke, Swanny,' came the voice from above. 'It's a crime scene.'

'Fuck you, Hurwitz, I'm not gonna puke.'

I heard him moving around. I tried to lift my head to watch him but the brush was too tall. I could only listen. It sounded like he was moving from body to body. I was right.

'Hey, we got a live one down here! Call it in.'

That would be Banks, I assumed. I was glad to hear it. I had the feeling I was going to need a survivor to back up my account. I figured that with Banks facing the fall by himself for the whole thing, he would cut a deal to save his ass and tell the story.

I rolled over and sat up. The cop was kneeling next to Banks on the dirt below the deck. He looked over at me.

'I didn't tell you to move.'

'I couldn't breathe with my face in the dirt.'

'Don't fucking move again.'

'Hey, Swanny,' Hurwitz called down. 'The stiff in the house? He's got a badge. FBI.'

'Holy shit!'

'Yeah, holy shit.'

And they were right. It was a holy shit case. Within the hour the place was swarmed. By the LAPD. By the LAFD. By the FBI. By the media. By my count, there were six helicopters circling in the sky through most of the night, the cacophony so loud I found myself preferring the shotgun blast ringing in my ears.

The LAFD used a chopper to bring Banks up out of the canyon on a stretcher. When they were done with him I called the paramedics over and they put a clear aloe-based gel over the gas burns on my face. They gave me an aspirin and told me the injuries were minor and that there would be no scarring. It felt to me like I'd had my face laser-peeled by a blind surgeon.

I was uncuffed long enough to climb up the slope and then up through the trapdoor. In my house I was recuffed and made to sit on a couch in the living room. From there I could see Milton's legs extending from the hallway as a crime scene team hovered over him.

Once all of the suits started showing up it started getting serious. Most of them followed the same pattern. They came in, somberly studied Milton's body, then walked through the living room without looking at me and out onto the deck, where they looked down at the other three bodies. Then they came back in, looked at me without saying a word and went into the kitchen, where somebody had taken it upon himself to open up my new bag of coffee and put the percolator into heavy rotation.

This went on for at least two hours. At first I didn't know any of them because they were North Hollywood detectives. But then the command decision was made to shift the investigation – LAPD's part of it – to Robbery-Homicide Division. When the RHD dicks started showing up it started getting like old-home week. I knew many of them and had even worked side by side with some. It wasn't until Kiz Rider showed up from the chief's office that anybody thought to take the cuffs off my wrists. She angrily demanded that I be released from the bindings and when nobody made a move to do it, she did it herself.

'You okay, Harry?'

'I think I am now.'

'Your face is red and kind of puffy. You want me to call paramedics?'

'They already checked me out. Minor burns from getting too close to the wrong end of a shotgun.'

'How do you want to do this? You know the score. You want to get a lawyer or can we talk?'

'I'll talk to you, Kiz. I'll tell you the whole story. Otherwise, I'll take the lawyer.'

'I'm not in RHD anymore, Harry. You know that.'

'You should be and you know that.'

'But I'm not.'

'Well, that's the deal, Kiz. Take it or leave it. I've got a good lawyer.'

She thought about it for a few moments.

'All right, wait here for a minute and I'll be right back.'

She went out the front door to consult with the powers that be about my offer. While she was gone and I was waiting I saw Special Agent John Peoples come in and crouch next to Milton's body. He then looked over at me and held my eyes. If he was trying to send me a message I wasn't sure exactly what it was. But he knew I held something of his in the balance. His future.

Rider came back inside and over to me.

'This is the deal. It's turning into a major gang bang. We've got FBI all over this. The guy on the floor is apparently from a terrorism squad and that trumps all. They're not going to let you and me waltz off into the sunset.'

'Okay, this is what I'll do. I'll talk to you and one agent. I want it to be Roy Lindell. Wake him up and bring him in and I'll lay it all out for everybody. It's got to be you and Roy or I lawyer up and everybody can figure it out for themselves.'

She nodded and turned and went back out. I noticed that Peoples was no longer in the hallway but I hadn't seen him leave.

This time Rider was gone for a half hour. But when she came back she strode in with a command presence. I knew before she told me that the deal had been made. The case was hers, at least on the LAPD side of the ledger.

'Okay, we're going to go down the hill to North Hollywood Division. We'll use a room there and they'll tape it for us. Lindell is on his way there. This way everybody's happy and everybody's got a piece.'

That was always the way. You had to walk the gauntlet of departmental and intra-agency politics just to get the job done. I was glad I no longer had a part of it.

'You can stand up now, Harry,' Rider said. 'I'll drive.'

I stood up.

'I want to go out on the deck first. I want to look down there.'

She let me go. I walked across the deck and looked down over the railing. Below, large crime scene lights had been erected. The slope was like an anthill with crime scene techs working all over the place. Crews from the medical examiner's office were huddled over the bodies. Above it all the helicopters moved in a loud, multilevel choreography. I knew that whatever relationships I'd previously had with my neighbors were surely gone now.

'Know what, Kiz?'

'What, Harry?'

'I think it's time to sell this place.'

'Yeah, good luck with that, Harry.'

She took me by the arm and pulled me away from the railing.

41

The North Hollywood station was the newest in the city. It was built post-earthquake and Rodney King riots. On the outside it was a brick fortress designed to withstand both tectonic and social upheavals. On the inside it was state-of-the-art electronics and comfort. I was sat in the center seat of a table in a large interview room. I could not see the microphones and the camera but I knew they were there. I also knew I had to be careful. I had made a bad deal. If a quarter century in the cops had taught me anything, it was not to talk to cops without a lawyer's advice. And here I was about to do just that. I was about to open up to two people predisposed to believe me and to want to help me. But that wouldn't matter. What would matter was the tape. I had to step carefully and make sure I said nothing that could come back on me when the tape was reviewed by those who were not my friends.

Kizmin Rider started things off by entering all three of our names into the record, reporting the date, time and location, and then reading me my constitutionally guaranteed right to a lawyer and to hold my tongue if I wished. She then asked me to acknowledge both orally and in writing that I understood these rights and was willingly waiving them. I did so. I had taught her well.

She then got right to it.

'Okay, Harry, you have four people including a federal agent dead at your house, not to mention a fifth man in a coma. You want to tell us all about it?'

'I killed two of them – in self-defense. And the guy in the coma, I did that too.'

'Okay, tell us what happened.'

I began the story at the Baked Potato and took it from there. I mentioned Sugar Ray, the quartet, the porter, the bartenders and their tattoos. I even described the cashier I had bought the coffee from at Ralph's. I used as much detail as I could remember because I knew that the details would convince them once they checked it all out. I knew from experience that conversation was hearsay, it wasn't provable one way or the other. So if you were going to tell a story about what people said and how they said it – especially people who were no longer alive – then you'd best salt the story with the things that could be checked and proven. The details. Safety and salvation were in the details.

So I put everything I could remember on the tape, right down to the Marilyn Monroe tattoo. That one made Roy Lindell laugh but Rider didn't see the humor in it.

I walked them through the story, describing things as they had happened. I offered no background story because I knew that would come out in the questioning that would follow. I wanted them to have a moment-by-moment and detail-by-detail account of what had happened. I did not lie in what I told them but I didn't tell them everything. I still wasn't sure how to play the Milton angle. I would wait for a signal from Lindell on that. I was sure he had been given his orders long before he got to the station.

I held the Milton details out for Lindell. The detail I held out for myself was what I had seen when I closed my eyes before pressing the shotgun's trigger. I kept the image of Angella Benton's hands to myself.

'And that's it,' I said when I was done. 'Then the uniforms showed up and here we are.'

Rider had been jotting down notes occasionally on a legal pad. She put her pad down and looked at me. She seemed stunned by the story. She probably believed I was very lucky to have survived it.

'Thank you, Harry. That was certainly a close call for you.'

'It was about five close calls.'

'Um, I think we're going to take a break for a few minutes. Agent Lindell and I are going to step out and talk about this and then I'm sure we will come back with some questions.'

I smiled.

'I'm sure you will.'

'Can we get you anything?'

'Coffee would be nice. I've been up all night and at the house they wouldn't give me any from my own machine.'

'Coffee coming up.'

She and Lindell got up and left the room. A few minutes later a North Hollywood detective I didn't know came in with a cup of black coffee. He told me to hang in there and left.

When Rider and Lindell came back in I noticed that there were more notes on her pad. She kept the lead and started out doing the talking again.

'We need to clear up a couple things first,' she said.

'Okay.'

'You said that Agent Milton was already in your house when you came in.'

'That's right.'

I looked at Lindell and then back at Rider.

'You said you were in the process of informing him that you believed you had been followed home when the front door was kicked in by the intruders.'

'Correct.'

'He stepped into the hall to investigate and was immediately hit with a blast from a shotgun, presumably fired by Linus Simonson.'

'Right again.'

'What was Agent Milton doing in your house if you weren't there?'

Before I could speak Lindell blurted out a question.

'He did have permission to be there, didn't he?'

'Hey, how about we take one question at a time?' I said.

I looked at Lindell again and his eyes turned down to the table. He couldn't look at me. Judging by his question, which was really a statement disguised as a question, Lindell was revealing to me what he wanted me to say. I believed at that point that he was making an offer of trade. He was almost certainly in trouble with the bureau for his aid to me during my investigation. And as such, he now had his orders: keep the bureau's nose clean on this, or there would be consequences for him and possibly for me. So what Lindell was saying to me was that if I told the story in a way that helped him accomplish that objective – without legally compromising myself – then we would both be better off.

The truth was I didn't mind sparing Milton posthumous controversy and shame. As far as I was concerned he'd already gotten what he deserved and then some. Going after him now would be vindictive and I didn't need to be vindictive to a dead man. I had other things to do and wanted to preserve my ability to do them.

There was Special Agent Peoples and his BAM squad but there was too much gray between them and Milton's actions. I had Milton on tape, not Peoples. Using one to try to get to the other was a tough road to drive. I decided in that moment to let the dead man sleep and to live to drive another day.

'What was Agent Milton doing in your house if you weren't there?' Rider repeated.

I looked back at her.

'He was waiting for me.'

'To do what?'

'I had told him to meet me there but I got delayed because I went and bought the coffee on my way home.'

'Why was he meeting you so late at night?'

'Because I had information that would clear some things up for him.'

'What was that information?'

'It was about how a terrorist involved in a case he was working ended up with a hundred-dollar bill that supposedly came from the movie set heist I was investigating and had been warned off of. I told him I had put things together and found that the two cases were actually unrelated. I invited him to come to my lawyer's office in the morning when you two were going to come and I'd explain it all to everybody. But he didn't want to wait so I told him to meet me at the house.'

'And what, you left him a key?'

'No, I didn't. But I must've left the door unlocked because he was inside when I got home. I guess you could say he had permission because I invited him to the house but I didn't exactly tell him to go inside. He just sort of did that on his own when he beat me to the house.'

'Agent Milton had a number of miniaturized listening devices in the pocket of his coat. Do you know anything about that or why he had them?'

My guess was that he had removed them from my house but I didn't say this.

'No idea,' I said. 'You would've had to ask him, I guess.'

'What about his car? It was found parked about a block north of your house on Woodrow Wilson. In fact, it was further away from your house than the car the four assailants used. Any idea why Milton would park so far from your house if he was invited to be there?'

'No, not really. Like I said, I guess he's the only one who knew that.'

'Exactly.'

I could see her getting heated. Her eyes grew sharper and she seemed to be trying to read the looks I was giving Lindell. She knew there was a play on but she was smart enough not to mention anything on camera. I had taught her well.

'Okay, I'll tell you what, Harry. You told us every detail about what happened last night but not how it fits into anything. Before all the shit hit the fan you called the big meeting for this morning in order to lay it all out for us. So go ahead and do it now. Tell us what you've got.'

'You mean from the beginning?'

'From the beginning.'

I nodded.

'Okay, well, I guess you could say it all started with Ray Vaughn and Linus Simonson deciding to rip off the cash shipment to the movie set. There was some sort of connection between them. One of their former colleagues at the bank said she thought Vaughn was gay and Simonson had said he was making a move on him. Anyway, whether Simonson drew Vaughn in or it was the other way around, they decided to take the money. They planned it out and then Simonson recruited his four pals for the heavy work. It went from there.'

'What about Angella Benton?' Rider asked.

'I'm getting to that. Without telling the others, Vaughn and Linus decided they needed a device, something that would make the cops think the heist came from inside the movie company, not the bank. So they picked her. She'd come to the bank as a liaison once with documents pertaining to the loan. So they knew a case could be made that she knew about the money. They picked her and probably watched her for a couple days and then figured out when she was most vulnerable and when to do it. They killed her and one of them put the semen on her so it would look like a sex case at first and it wouldn't immediately reflect on the movie company or the plan to shoot scenes with real money. That would come later. After the heist.'

'So she was just a device is what you are saying,' Rider said dejectedly. 'Her life taken simply because she fit into the plan.'

I nodded somberly.

'What a wonderful world, right?'

'Okay, go on. Did they both do it?'

'I don't know, maybe. Simonson had an alibi for that night but it was cleared by Jack Dorsey, and we'll get to him in a minute. But my guess is that they did it together. It would take two to completely overpower her without a struggle.'

'The jizz,' Rider said. 'We can see if it matches one of them. Since Vaughn was killed during the robbery and Simonson was shot, it was never thought to type them against the semen collected at the murder scene.'

I shook my head.

'I have a feeling that it won't match either one of them.'

'Then who did it come from?'

'We may never know. Remember the spatter evidence? We decided the semen was brought to the scene and dripped onto the body. Who knows where they got it. Maybe from one of themselves but if they were smart they wouldn't have left their own. Why leave a direct tie to the crime?'

'So, what, they just go up to a stranger and ask him to jerk off in a cup for them?' Lindell asked incredulously.

'It wouldn't be that hard to get,' Rider said. 'Go into any alley in Hollywood and you'll find a loaded condom. And if Vaughn was gay, then it could have come from one of his partners and the partner might not have ever known it.'

I nodded. I had been thinking the same thing.

'Exactly. And that's probably why he was killed. Simonson double-crossed him. He told his guys to make sure they took him out during the robbery. It would mean more money for them and a link to the Benton case eliminated.'

'Jesus, these are cold-blooded fucks,' Lindell said.

I could tell he was thinking about Marty Gessler and her unknown fate.

'Simonson further secured the operation and the future use of the money by switching the currency report he and another BankLA employee had put together. You could say he unmarked the bills.'

'How?' Rider asked.

'I thought at first that he probably just put wrong currency numbers into the report he and another bank employee made in the vault. But I guess that would have been too risky because she wasn't in on it and she might have decided to double-check the numbers. So I think what he did was create a second, phony report on his computer. It listed currency numbers he just made up. He then printed it out and forged his coworker's signature on it and turned it in to the vice-president for his signature. From there it went to the insurance company and then to the cops after the heist and eventually to the FBI.'

'You told me to bring the original to the meeting we were supposed to have this morning,' Rider said. 'Why?'

'You know what forger's tremor is? It's something you can see in a signature that has been forged by tracing. He traced his coworker's signature off the original or real currency report. In the photocopy of the one he turned in I could see hesitation marks. Her signature would have been one smooth, uninterrupted scrawl. But it looks like whoever signed that page never lifted the pen but stopped and started after almost every letter. It's a tell and I think the original will show it beyond a doubt.'

'How was that missed?'

I shrugged.

'Maybe it wasn't.'

'Dorsey and Cross.'

'I think Dorsey. I don't know about Cross. Cross helped me with this. In fact, he called me and gave me the jump start on it.'

Lindell leaned forward. We were getting to the part about Marty Gessler and he wanted to get it right.

'So Simonson turns in a report with made-up numbers and then his buddies go and rip off the delivery and kill Vaughn in the process. Intentionally.'

'That's right.'

'What about Simonson? He got shot, too. Were they trying to cut him out, too?'

'No, that wasn't supposed to happen. Not according to Fazio. At least that was what he was saying to me before he got nailed last night. It sounded like Simonson getting shot was just dumb luck. A ricochet. If Banks comes out of his sleep with his brain intact maybe he can tell you about that. I have a feeling he'll want to talk. He'll want to spread the blame around.'

'Don't worry, if he comes out of it, we'll be there. But the early word from the hospital is that that's a big if.'

'The thing about that ricochet is that it actually helped them. It gave Simonson a valid out from the bank. No suspicion there. Then he hid the purchase and renovation of the bars behind a settlement from the bank. The truth was he didn't make enough off the settlement to put in a new beer cooler.'

'How do you know that?'

'I just know.'

'All right, let's get back to the heist for a minute,' Lindell said. 'So other than Simonson taking a slug in the ass, the heist goes off as planned. All the cops—'

'Not exactly,' Rider said. 'Harry was there. He nailed one of the robbers.'

I nodded.

'And he apparently died in the van during the getaway. Simonson told me the others took him out on a boat or something and buried him at sea. His name was Cozy. They named one of the bars after him.'

'Okay,' Lindell said. 'But when the dust settles from this thing, all the cops have is Angella Benton dead and a phony list of numbers that nobody knows is phony. Then nine months sail by and lo and behold one of those numbers scores a hit when Marty Gessler puts it into her computer.'

I nodded. Lindell knew where it was going.

'Wait a minute,' Rider said. 'I'm not tracking this part.'

Lindell and I took five minutes to fill her in on Marty Gessler's computer program that tracked currency numbers and what her discovery meant.

'Got it,' Rider said. 'She came up with the first inference that something was wrong. She came up with a hit that didn't work because the hundred-dollar bill in question was already in evidence lockup. It could not have been taken during the movie set heist.'

'Exactly,' I said. 'One of the numbers Simonson made up just happened to be on a bill already accounted for. The same thing would later happen when they arrested Mousouwa Aziz at the border. One of the hundreds he was carrying matched Simonson's phony list. That brought Milton and the Homeland Security heavies into it and it was all bullshit. The truth was, there was no connection between the two cases.'

Which meant I had spent the night in federal lockup for nothing and Milton had been killed while pursuing what amounted to nothing, a wild goose chase. I tried not to think about this and moved on with the story.

'When Marty Gessler got that hit, she called up Jack Dorsey because his name was on the list when it was circulated to other law enforcement agencies. It went from there.'

'You're saying that Dorsey then put two and two together and came up with Simonson,' Lindell said. 'Maybe he knew about the forgery or maybe he knew about something else. But he knew enough to know. He went to Simonson and cut himself in.'

I noticed that we were all nodding. The story worked.

'Dorsey had money problems,' I added. 'The insurance investigator on this did routine background checks on all the cops involved. Dorsey was in debt up to his neck, had two kids in college and two still to go.'

'Everybody's got money problems,' Rider said angrily. 'It's no excuse.'

That made us all silent for a long moment and then I took up the story again.

'There was just one problem at that point.'

'Agent Gessler,' Rider said. 'She knew too much. She had to disappear.'

Rider didn't know anything about Lindell's relationship with Gessler, and Lindell did little to reveal it. He just sat quietly, his eyes down. I moved the story forward.

'My guess is that Simonson and his guys played Dorsey along while they took care of the Gessler problem. Dorsey knew what they did, but what could he do or say about it? He was in too deep. Then Simonson took care of him in Nat's. Cross and the bartender were window dressing.'

Rider squinted her eyes and shook her head.

'What?' Lindell asked.

'Doesn't work for me,' she said. 'There's a disconnect there. With Gessler, she's gone without a trace. Very smooth. Three years later and who knows where the body is?'

I was cringing for Lindell's sake but tried not to show it.

'But with Dorsey, it's a shoot-out at the OK Corral. Dorsey, Cross, the bartender. Two completely different styles. One smooth as smoke, the other a blood bath.'

'Well,' I said, 'with Dorsey, they wanted it to look like a robbery gone wrong. If he just disappeared, then the obvious thing to do would be to go back over the old cases. Simonson didn't want that. So he orchestrated the big blowout so the investigators would think robbery.'

'I still don't buy it. I think they're different. Look, I don't remember all the details but didn't Marty Gessler disappear while driving home through the Sepulveda Pass?'

'That's right. Somebody bumped her and she pulled over.'

'Okay, then here's an armed and trained agent. Are you going to tell me Simonson and these guys got her to pull over by bumping her car and then they got the best of her? Uh-uh, guys. I say, no way. Not without a fight. Not without somebody seeing something. I think she stopped because she felt safe. She stopped for a cop.'

She pointed at me and nodded when she said the last line. Lindell brought a fist down hard on the table. Rider had convinced him. I had defended my theory but now saw the cracks in it. I started thinking Rider might be right.

I noticed Rider looking at Lindell. She was finally picking up the vibe.

'You really knew her, didn't you?' she asked.

Lindell just nodded to the question. Then he brought his eyes up to stare angrily at me.

'And you blew it, Bosch,' he said.

'I blew it? What are you talking about?'

'With your little stunt last night. Going in there like fucking Steve

McQueen. What did you think, that they'd be so spooked they'd march right down to Parker Center and turn themselves in?'

'Roy,' Rider said, 'I think we—'

'You wanted to provoke them, didn't you? You wanted them to come after you.'

'That's crazy,' I said calmly. 'Four against one? The only reason I'm alive right now and talking to you is because I saw them tailing me and because Milton distracted them long enough for me to get out of the house.'

'Yeah, that's just it. You saw the tail. You saw it because you were looking for it and you were looking for it because you wanted it. You blew it, Bosch. If that kid in the hospital doesn't wake up with a working brain, then we'll never know what happened to Marty or where—'

He stopped before his voice lost it. He stopped speaking but didn't stop staring at me.

'Guys,' Rider said quietly, 'let's take a break here. Let's stop questioning motives and accusing. We all want the same thing here.'

Lindell slowly and emphatically shook his head.

'No, not Harry Bosch,' he said quietly, his eyes still on mine. 'It's always just what he wants. He's always been a private investigator, even when he carried a badge.'

I looked from Lindell to Rider. She didn't say anything but her eyes dropped away from mine, and in their movement was a tell. I saw her confirmation.

42

It was dawn by the time I got back to my house. The place was still a swarm of police and media activity and the police would not let me back in. The house and canyon comprised a major crime scene and as such they had commandeered custody of it. I was told to try back in a day, maybe two. They would not even let me go back inside to get fresh clothes or any other belongings. I was strictly persona non grata. I was asked to stay away. The one concession I was able to talk my way into was my car. Two uniform cops – Hurwitz and Swanny, who had caught the precious overtime assignment – cleared room for me among the police and media vehicles and I backed the Mercedes out of the carport and took off.

The adrenaline rush that came with the near-death experience of the night before had long since ebbed away. I was exhausted but had no place to go. I drove aimlessly along Mulholland until I came to Laurel Canyon Boulevard and then took a right and drove down into the Valley.

I started getting a sense of where I was headed but knew it was too early. When I got to Ventura I took another right and pulled into the parking lot at the Dupar's. I decided that I needed some high octane, and coffee and pancakes would fit the bill. Before getting out of the car I got the cell phone out and turned it on. I called the numbers I had for Janis Langwiser and Sandor Szatmari and got no answers but left messages that the morning meeting was canceled because of circumstances beyond my control.

The phone's screen showed that I had messages waiting. I called to pick them up and listened to four messages left through the night by Keisha Russell, the *Times* reporter. She started out very cool and concerned about my well-being and wanting to talk to me at my convenience to make sure I was okay. By the third message her voice had taken on a high-pitched urgency, and in the fourth she demanded that I make good on our deal in which I promised to talk to her if anything happened with what I was working on.

'Something's obviously happened now, Harry. You've got four on the floor on Woodrow Wilson. Call me like you *promised* me you would.'

'Yes, dear,' I said as I erased the message.

The last message was from Alexander Taylor, the box office champion. There was a proprietary tone to his voice. He wanted me to know that this story was his.

'Mr. Bosch, I see you are all over the news. I am assuming that the nastiness on the hill last night is related to my heist. There were four robbers; the news says there are four dead men on your property. I want you to know that the offer I made still stands. But I'll double it. One hundred thousand as an option on the story. The back end is open to negotiation and we can talk about that when I hear back from you. I will give you my assistant's private number. Call me back. I'll be waiting.'

He gave a number but I didn't bother writing it down. I thought about the money for all of five seconds and then erased the message and closed the phone.

As I walked into the restaurant I wondered about what constituted circumstances beyond my control and what Lindell had said at the end of the interview in North Hollywood. I thought about fighting monsters and what had been said about me and to me in the past, and what I had said to Peoples in that restaurant booth just a few nights earlier. I wondered if a subtle slide into the abyss was any different from the kind of swan dive Milton had taken.

I knew I would have to think about this and the motives behind my actions of the last ten hours. But I soon decided it would have to keep. There was still a mystery to solve and as soon as I refueled I was going after it.

I sat at the counter and ordered the number two special without looking at a menu. The waitress with the wide hips poured my coffee and was about to put the order in at the kitchen window when somebody took the stool next to me and said, 'I'll have coffee, too.'

I recognized the voice and turned and saw Keisha Russell smiling at me as she put her bag down on the floor between us. She had followed me down the hill.

'I should've known.'

'Harry, if you don't want to be followed all you have to do is return your calls.'

'I just got your messages five minutes ago, Keisha.'

'Well, now you don't have to call me back.'

'I'm not talking to you. Not yet.'

'Harry, your house is like a war zone. Bodies all over. Are you all right?'

'I'm sitting here, aren't I? I'm all right. But I still can't talk to you. I don't know how this is going to play out and I'm not going to say anything that shows up in the paper and might be at odds with the official line. That's suicide.'

'You mean you don't want to tell me the truth just in case what they put out isn't.'

'Keisha, you know me. I will talk to you when I can. Why don't you let me have my coffee and eat in peace now?'

'Just answer one question. It's not even a question. Just confirm for me that whatever happened up there is related to what you called me about. About Martha Gessler.'

I shook my head in frustration. I knew I wasn't going to be able to shake her without giving her something.

'Actually, I can't confirm that, and that's the truth. But, look, if I give you something that will help you, will you let me be until there is a time I can talk about it?'

Before she answered, the waitress slid a plate in front of me. I looked down at a short stack of buttered pancakes with a fried egg and two pieces of bacon forming an X on top. She then put down a small pitcher of maple syrup. I grabbed it and started pouring syrup over everything.

'My God,' Russell said. 'You eat that and I'm not sure there will ever be a time you can talk about it. You are killing yourself, Harry.'

I looked up at the waitress, who was standing there writing up my check. I gave her a what-are-you-going-to-do smile and shrugged.

'Are you paying for her coffee?' she asked.

'Sure.'

She put the bill down on the counter and walked away. I looked at Russell.

'Why don't you say that louder next time?'

'Sorry, Harry, but I don't want you to get fat and old and ugly. You're my bud. I want you around.'

I saw through all of that. She hid her motives the way the bartenders I'd seen the night before hid their nipples.

'Do we have a deal? I give you something and you hit the road, leave me alone?'

She took a sip from her free coffee and smiled.

'Deal.'

'Go pull your clips on the Angella Benton case.'

She narrowed her eyes. She didn't remember it.

'You didn't do much with it at first, then it blew up big when it was connected to the movie set heist over on Selma. Eidolon Productions? Ring a bell?'

She almost came off her stool.

'Are you fucking kidding me?' she said a little too loud. 'The four on the floor are those guys?'

'Not quite. Three of them are those guys. Plus the one they took to the hospital.'

'Then who is the fourth?'

'I gave you what I'm giving you, Keisha. I'm going to eat now.'

I turned to my plate and started cutting my food up.

'This is so cool!' she said. 'This is going to be big.'

As if four bodies in the Cahuenga Pass wasn't already big. I took my first bite and the syrup hit me like a sugar bullet.

'Great,' I said.

She reached down to her bag and started getting up.

'I've gotta go, Harry. Thanks for the coffee.'

'One last thing.'

I took another bite and turned to her and started talking with my mouth full.

'Check out *Los Angeles Magazine* seven months ago. They did this story on these four guys who own all the hot bars in Hollywood. It called them the kings of the night crawlers. Check it out.'

Her eyes widened.

'You're kidding.'

'No, check it out.'

She leaned down and kissed me on the cheek. She had never done that before, when I carried a badge.

'Thanks, Harry. I'll call you.'

'I bet you will.'

I watched her glide quickly through the restaurant and out. I turned back to my plate. The egg had been over easy and cutting it up had made a mess of things. But at that moment it tasted like the best thing I had ever eaten.

Finally alone, I considered the question Kiz Rider had raised during the interview about how the style of the Marty Gessler disappearance was so different from the massacre at Nat's. I was now sure Rider was right. The crimes had been designed, if not carried out, by different perpetrators.

'Dorsey,' I said out loud.

Maybe too loud. A man three stools down turned and looked at me until I turned and stared him back to his coffee cup.

Most of my records and notes were in the house and not attainable. I had the murder book in the Mercedes but it contained nothing from the Gessler case. From memory I worked on the details of the FBI agent's disappearance. The car left at the airport. The use of her credit card up near the desert to buy more gas than her car could hold. I tried to fit these facts under the new heading of Dorsey. It was hard to make it work. Dorsey had been working crimes from one side of the law for nearly thirty years. He was too smart, he had seen too much, to leave a trail like that.

But by the time I finished my plate I thought I had something. Something that worked. I looked around to make sure the man three stools down and nobody else was looking at me. I poured a little more syrup onto my plate and then dipped my fork into it and ate it. I was about to dip again when the wide hips of the waitress appeared in front of me.

'Finished?'

'Uh, yes, sure. Thank you.'

'More coffee?'

'Can I get a to go cup?'

'Yes, you may.'

She took the plate and my syrup away. I thought about my next moves until she came back with the coffee and reworked my bill. I left two bucks on the counter and took the bill to the cashier, where I noticed bottles of the restaurant's syrup were on display and for sale. The cashier noticed my gaze.

'How about a bottle of syrup to go?'

I was tempted but decided to stick with the coffee.

'Nah, I think I've had enough sweetness for today. Thanks.'

'You need sweetness. It's a nasty world out there.'

I agreed with her, paid my bill and left with my cup of harsh black coffee. Back in the car I opened the phone and called Roy Lindell's cell number.

'This is Roy.'

'This is Bosch. We still talking?'

'What do you want, an apology? Fuck you, you're not getting one.'

'No, I can live without an apology from you, Roy. So fuck you, too. I want to know if you still want to find her.'

There was no need to use a name.

'What do you think, Bosch?'

'Okay, then.'

I thought for a moment about how to do this.

'Bosch, you still there?'

'Yeah, listen, I've got to go see somebody right now. Can you meet me in two hours?'

'Two hours. Where?'

'You know where Bronson Canyon is?'

'Above Hollywood, right?'

'Yeah, Griffith Park. Meet me at the end of Bronson Canyon. Two hours. If you're not there, I won't wait.'

'What's up there? What do you have?'

'Right now just a hunch. You going to meet me?'

There was a pause.

'I'll be there, Bosch. What should I bring?'

Good question. I tried to think of what we'd need.

'Bring flashlights and a bolt cutter. I guess you better bring a shovel too, Roy.'

That brought another pause before he replied.

'What are you bringing?'

'I guess just my hunch for now.'

'Where are we going up there?'
'I'll tell you when I see you. I'll show you.'
I closed the phone then.

43

The garage door at Lawton Cross's house was closed. The van was parked in the driveway but there were no other vehicles. Kiz Rider hadn't gotten there yet. Nobody had. I pulled in behind the van and got out and knocked on the front door. It didn't take too long for Danny Cross to answer it.

'Harry,' she said. 'We were just watching it on the TV. Are you all right?'

'Never better.'

'Are they the ones? The ones who did this to Law?'

She had a pleading look in her eyes. I nodded.

'It was them. The one who was in the bar that day, who shot Law, I took his face off with his own shotgun. Does that make you happy, Danny?'

She pressed her lips together in an effort to hold back tears.

'Revenge tastes sweet, doesn't it? Just like pancake syrup.'

I reached out and put my hand on her shoulder but not to comfort her. I gently pushed her to the side of the doorway and stepped in. Rather than head left toward Lawton Cross's sitting room I went to the right. I went into the kitchen and found the door to the garage. I went to the file cabinets in front of the Malibu and pulled the file on the Antonio Markwell case, the abduction murder that had made Cross and Dorsey in the department.

I returned to the house and entered the sitting room. I didn't know where Danny had gone but her husband was waiting for me.

'Harry, you're all over the tube,' he said.

I looked up at the television screen. It was a helicopter view of my house. I could see all the official cars and media vans on the street in front. I could see the black tarps covering the bodies in the back. I hit the power button with the side of my fist and the screen went blank. I turned back to Cross and dropped the Markwell file on his lap. He couldn't move. All he could do was lower his eyes to it and try to read the tab.

'How does it feel? Does it give you a hard-on watching what you did? In your case, a make-believe hard-on?'

'Harry, I—'

'Where is she, Law?'

'Where is who? Harry, I don't know what—'

‘Sure you do. You know exactly what I’m talking about. You sat there like a puppet but the whole time you were pulling the strings. My strings.’

‘Harry, please.’

‘Don’t ‘Harry, please’ me. You wanted revenge on them and I was your ticket. Well, you got it, partner. I took care of all of them, just like you thought. Like you hoped. You played me just right.’

He didn’t say anything. His eyes were cast down, away from mine.

‘Now there’s one thing I want from you. I want to know where you and Jack hid Marty Gessler. I want to bring her home.’

He remained silent, his eyes away from me. I reached down and took the file off his lap. On the bureau I opened it and started leafing through the documents.

‘You know, I didn’t see it until somebody I taught the job to saw it first,’ I said as I looked through the file. ‘She’s the one who said it had to be a cop. It was the only way Gessler could’ve been taken so easily. And she was right. Those four punks didn’t have the steel.’

I gestured toward the empty television screen.

‘I mean, look what happened when they came for me.’

I found what I was looking for in the file. A map of Griffith Park. I started unfolding it. Its creases cracked and split. It had been folded in the file for maybe five years. It was marked by the location where Antonio Markwell’s body had been found in Bronson Canyon.

‘Once I started in that direction, then I began to see it. The gas had always been a problem. Somebody used her card and they bought more gas than her car could hold. That was a mistake, Law. A big one. Not buying the gas. That was part of the misdirection. But getting so much of it. The bureau thought maybe it was a truck, that they were looking for a trucker. But now I’m thinking Crown Vic. The Police Interceptor model they make for all the departments. The cars with extra-capacity gas tanks so you don’t get caught out there on the hunt without any juice.’

I had delicately spread the map open. It depicted the many winding roads and footpaths of the huge mountain park. It showed the public road up through Bronson Canyon and then the fire road which extended further up into the rocky terrain. It showed the area of caves and tunnels left behind when the canyon had been a quarry, its rock payload crushed and used for railroad beds across the west. I laid the map across Cross’s lap and over his dead arms.

‘The way I figure it, you guys followed her from Westwood. Then in the Pass you pulled her over in one of the quiet spots. Used the blue light on your Crown Vic and she thought, *No problem, they’re cops.* But then you put her in the trunk of that big car with the big gas tank. One of you drove her car to the airport and the other followed and picked him up. Probably you backed her car into another car or a pillar or something somewhere. Nice touch. Sell the misdirection. Then you drive up to the desert and use the gas card. Again, sell that misdirection. And then you turn around and take her back to the real hiding place. Which one of you did it, Law? Which one actually took from her everything she had or would ever have?'

I didn't expect an answer and didn't get one. I pointed to the map.

'That's my bet. You guys went to a place you were familiar with, a place nobody would be looking for Marty Gessler because they'd all be looking up in the desert. You wanted her hidden but you wanted access to her, right? You wanted to know exactly where she was. She was your ace in the hole, right? You would use her to get to them. Marty and her computer. The connection was on that box. Find her and find the box, the connection would be made and there'd be a knock on Linus Simonson's door.'

I paused to give him a chance to protest, to tell me to get the hell out or call me a liar. But he didn't do any of that. He didn't say a word.

'It all seemed to work,' I said. 'And then that day at Nat's you guys were supposed to cut the deal, right? Shake hands and share the wealth? Only Linus Simonson had other ideas about that. Turned out he didn't want to share anything and he'd take his chances with Gessler's computer. That must have shocked you. There you two were, waiting in there, probably already counting your money. And he comes in and opens up on you . . .

'I think you should've seen it coming, Law.'

I leaned down and tapped the map with a finger.

'Bronson Canyon. All those tunnels, caves. Where you found the boy.'

My eyes came up from the map.

'That's my guess. They've got the roads going up there locked. But you two had a key, didn't you? From the boy's case. You kept that key and then it came in handy. Where is she?'

Cross finally brought his eyes up to mine and spoke.

'Look what they did to me,' he said. 'They deserved what they got.'

I nodded in agreement.

'And you deserved what you got. Where is she?'

His eyes turned and he looked up at the empty TV.

He said nothing. Anger bloomed inside of me. I thought of Milton squeezing the air tubes shut. Of becoming a monster, of becoming the thing I hunted. I took a step toward his chair and looked down on him with eyes dark with rage. Slowly I raised my hands toward his face.

'Tell him.'

I turned and Danny Cross was in the doorway. I didn't know how long she had been there or what she had heard. I didn't know if it was a story that was new to her or not. All I knew is that she brought me back from the edge of the abyss. I turned and looked back at Lawton Cross. His eyes were on his wife and his frozen face still somehow took on an expression of sadness and misery.

'Tell him, Lawton,' she said. 'Or I won't be there beside you.'

A look of fear immediately took over his face. Then there was pleading in his eyes.

'You promise to stay with me?'

'I promise.'

His eyes dropped to the map spread across the chair.

'You don't need this,' he said. 'Just go up there. You go in the big cave and then take the tunnel on the right. It comes to an open clearing. Somebody told us they call it The Devil's Punchbowl. Anyway, that's where we found him. She's there now.'

He could no longer hold my eyes and looked away, back down at the map.

'Where do I look, Lawton?'

'Where the kid was. That family marked the spot. You'll know when you get there.'

I nodded. I understood. Slowly I took the map from him and refolded it. I watched him as I did it. He seemed becalmed, his face now returned to expressionless. I'd seen the look a thousand times before in the eyes and faces of those who have confessed. A lifting of the burden.

There was nothing else to say. I slipped the map back into the file and took it with me as I left the room. Danny Cross remained just outside the door, looking in at her husband. I stopped as I passed her.

'He's a black hole,' I said. 'He'll suck you in and take you down. Save yourself, Danny.'

'How?'

'You know how.'

I left her there and went out. I got in my car and started driving south toward Hollywood and the secret the hills had hidden for so long.

44

It wasn't raining yet but the sky was full of the low rumbling of thunder by the time I got to Hollywood. From the freeway I took Franklin over to Bronson and then up into the hills. Bronson Canyon had been in more movies than I had probably seen in my whole life. Its rugged terrain and jagged rock outcroppings formed the backdrop of countless westerns and more than a few low-budget interplanetary explorations. I had been there as a kid and I had been there on cases. I knew that if you weren't careful you could get lost on the trails or in the caves and quarried-out spaces. The rock facings would begin to crowd you and after a while they all looked the same. You could lose your bearings. In that sameness was the danger.

I took the park road up until it terminated at the fire road. Entrance to this dirt and crushed gravel extension was blocked by a steel gate with a padlock on it. The key to that lock resided with the fire department and the city's film bureau, but thanks to Lawton Cross I knew better than that.

I got there before Lindell and I was tempted not to wait. It would be a long walk up to the caves on foot, but my anger had forged into resolve and momentum. Sitting at the locked gate was not the way to stoke those fires and keep them burning. I wanted to get up into the hills and get it over with. I pulled out the cell phone and called him to see where he was.

'Right behind you.'

I checked the mirror. He was coming around the last bend in a federal Crown Vic. It made me think about how he would react when he found out the last clue I had put together had been so close all along.

'It's about time,' I said.

I hung up and got out of the Mercedes. When Lindell pulled up I leaned into his window.

'Did you bring the bolt cutter?'

Lindell looked out the windshield at the gate.

'For that? I'm not going to cut that. They'll climb all over me if I break their lock.'

'Roy, I thought you were a big-time federal agent. Give me the cutter, I'll do it.'

'And you can take all the heat. Just tell them you had a hunch.'

I threw him a look, hoping to communicate that I was operating on more than a hunch now. He popped the trunk lid and I went back and pulled out the bolt cutter he had probably checked out of the federal equipment shed. He stayed in the car while I walked over and cut the lock and pushed the gate open.

I walked by his window on the way back to the trunk.

'By any means, Roy,' I said as I passed. 'I think I'm getting the idea why you weren't picked for the squad.'

I threw the tool in the trunk, slammed it and told him to follow me up the hill.

We drove up the winding road, the gravel crunching under our wheels sounding like the rain that was still coming. The road up took a final 180 and terminated in front of the main tunnel entrance, a fifteen-foot-high opening cut into a granite deposit the size of an office building. I parked next to Lindell and met him at the trunk. He'd brought two shovels and two flashlights. As I was reaching in for mine he put his hand on my arm.

'Okay, Bosch, what are we doing?'

'She's here. We're going to go in and find her.'

'Confirmed?'

I looked at him and nodded. In my life I have told a lot of people – too many to count – about loved ones they weren't going to see alive again. I knew Lindell had long ago given up hope for Marty Gessler, but the final confirmation is still never easy to get. Or to give.

'Yes, confirmed. Lawton Cross told me.'

Lindell nodded and turned away from the trunk. He looked up at the crest of the granite mountain. I busied myself with getting the tools from the trunk and checking to see if my cell phone was catching a signal. Over my shoulder I heard him say, 'It's going to rain.'

'Yeah,' I said. 'Let's go.'

I handed him a light and a shovel and we approached the mouth of the tunnel.

'He's going to pay for this,' Lindell said.

I nodded. I didn't bother to tell him that Lawton Cross had already been paying for it every day of his life.

The tunnel was big. Shaquille O'Neal could walk through with Wilt Chamberlain on his shoulders. It was nothing like the stale, claustrophobic systems I had crawled through thirty-five years before. The air inside was fresh. It smelled clean. Ten feet in we put on the lights, and in another fifty feet the channel curved and we were out of sight of the entrance. I remembered Cross's directions and kept to the right, moving slowly.

We came to a central cavern and stopped. There were three tributary tunnels. I focused my light on the third opening and knew it was the way. I then turned my light off and told Lindell to do the same.

'Why? What's going on?'

'Nothing. Just turn it off for a second.'

He did and I waited a moment for my eyes to adjust to the darkness. My vision and focus came back and I could pick up the outline of the rock walls and jutting surfaces. I could see the light that had followed us in.

'What is it?' Lindell asked.

'Lost light. I wanted to see the lost light.'

'What?'

'You can always find it. Even in the dark, even underground.'

I snapped my light back on, careful not to hit Lindell in the face with the beam, and headed toward the third tributary tunnel.

This time we needed to duck and proceed in single file as the tunnel grew smaller and more cramped. The channel curved to the right and soon we could see light ahead. An opening. We moved through and came out into an open bowl, a granite stadium chiseled out decades before. The Devil's Punchbowl.

Over time the bottom of the bowl had filled with a layer of run-off granite debris and dust, a layer just thick enough for brush to put down roots and for a body to be buried. It was here that Dorsey and Cross had been led to the body of Antonio Markwell and where they would come back again with Marty Gessler. I found myself wondering how long she had been alive on that night three years ago. Had she been pushed at gunpoint through the tunnel or dragged, already dead, to her final resting spot?

Neither answer was any comfort. I looked back at Lindell as he came out of the tunnel into the opening. His face was ghostly white and I guessed that he might have been considering the same thing.

'Where?' he asked.

I turned from him and scanned the bottom of the bowl and then I saw it. A tiny white cross rising in the brown-and-yellow brush line by the granite facing.

'There.'

Lindell took the lead and walked quickly to the cross. He lifted it out of the ground without a second thought and tossed it to the side. He was already putting his shovel into the ground when I got there. I looked down at the cross. It was made from an old picket fence. At its center point was a photo of a young boy. A school photo framed with popsicle sticks. Antonio Markwell was long gone from this life and this spot but his family had marked it as a holy ground. Dorsey and Cross had then used it because they knew the ground here would never be disturbed by trespassers.

I leaned down and picked the tiny cross up. I leaned it against the granite wall, and then I went to work with my borrowed shovel.

We didn't really dig with the shovels. We scraped at the surface, both of us instinctively reluctant to drive the point of the blade down too deeply.

In less than five minutes we found her. One final scrape of Lindell's shovel revealed a thick plastic tarp. We put the shovels aside and we both squatted to look. The plastic was opaque, like a shower curtain. But through it was the distinct outline of a hand. A small withered hand. A woman's hand.

'Okay, Roy, we found her. Maybe we should back out of here now. Make the calls.'

'No, I want to do this. I . . . '

He didn't finish. He put his hand on my chest and gently pushed me back away. He then crouched over the spot and started digging with his hands, his arms moving quickly, as though he thought he was in a race against time, that he was trying to save her before she suffocated.

'I'm sorry, Roy,' I said to his back but I don't think he heard me.

In a few minutes he had uncovered most of the plastic. From her face down to her hips. The plastic had apparently slowed but not stopped decay. The air in the bowl took on a musty smell. Moving back closer and peering over Lindell's shoulder I could see that Agent Martha Gessler had been wrapped and buried fully clothed, with her arms crossed in front of her. Only half of her face was dimly visible through the plastic. The rest was hidden in blackness; blood in the folds of the plastic. I guessed that they had killed her with a head shot.

'Her computer is here,' Lindell said.

I stepped further forward to see. I could make out the outline of a laptop computer. It was wrapped in its own plastic and left on her chest.

'It holds the connection to Simonson,' I said, though that was obvious by now. 'It was their edge. They wanted the body and the laptop someplace where they could get to it. They thought it would keep Simonson and the others in line. But they were wrong.'

I saw Lindell's shoulders start to shake but I knew he was no longer digging.

'Give me a minute, Harry,' he said, his voice straining.

'Sure, Roy. I'm going to make my way back to the cars and call some people. I left my cell phone.'

Whether he knew I had lied or not, he didn't object. I picked up one of the flashlights and headed back. On my way back through the smaller tunnel I could hear the big man crying behind me. The sound was somehow picked up and intensified as it came into the tunnel. It was like he was right next to me. It was like he was inside my head. I moved faster. I got to the main channel and was almost running by the time I got to the entrance. When I finally came out into the light it was raining.

45

The following afternoon I took another Southwest jet from Burbank to Las Vegas. I still wasn't allowed back into my house and wasn't sure I ever wanted to go back anyway. I was still a key part of the investigation but nobody had specifically told me not to leave town. They only say that sort of stuff in movies, anyway.

As usual the flight was full. People going to the cathedrals of greed. Bringing their stores of cash and hope. It made me think of Simonson and Dorsey and Cross and Angella Benton and what part greed and luck had played in their lives. Most of all I thought of Marty Gessler and the bad luck she had. Left to molder for more than three years in that place. She had simply made a phone call to a cop, and that had brought about her own destruction. Good intentions. Trust. What a way to go. What a wonderful world.

This time I rented a car at McCarran and I fought my own way through the traffic. The address Lindell had gotten for me off the license plate number I had given him was located on the northwest side of the city. It was out near the end of the sprawl. For now, at least. It belonged to a house that was newly built and large. It had a French Provincial style to it. I think it did, at least. I'm not that good at that sort of thing.

The two-car garage was closed but off to the side of the circular driveway was a car that wasn't the one I had been in with Eleanor. It was a Toyota, maybe five years old with a lot of miles on it. I could tell. I am good at that sort of thing.

I parked the rental at the edge of the circle and slowly got out. I don't know, maybe I thought if I took my time somebody would open the door and invite me in and all my qualms would be eased.

But it didn't happen. I got to the door and had to push the button and knew I would probably have to push my way in. Figuratively. I heard a chime sound from inside and I waited. Before I needed to ring again the door was answered by a woman, a Latina who looked to be in her sixties. She was small and had a kind but worn face. She looked like she felt bad about the shotgun burns on my face. She didn't wear a uniform of any type but I was guessing she was the maid. Eleanor with a maid. I had a hard time picturing that.

'Is Eleanor Wish here?'

'Can I say who it is, please?'

Her English was good and carried only a slight accent.

'Tell her it's her husband.'

I saw the alarm go off in her eyes and I realized that I had been stupid.

'Former husband,' I said quickly. 'Just tell her it's Harry.'

'Please wait.'

I nodded and she closed the door. I heard her lock it. As I waited I could feel the heat working through my clothes, penetrating my scalp. All around me the sun was reflecting brightly. It was almost five minutes before the door was opened again and Eleanor stood there.

'Harry, are you all right?'

'I'm fine.'

'I saw everything on TV. CNN.'

I just nodded to that.

'It's so sad about Marty Gessler.'

'Yeah.'

And then nothing for a long moment before she finally spoke.

'What are you doing here, Harry?'

'I don't know. I just wanted to see you.'

'How did you find this place?'

I shrugged.

'I'm a detective. Was, at least.'

'You should have called me first.'

'I know. I should have done a lot of things but I didn't, Eleanor. I'm sorry, okay? Sorry for everything. Are you going to let me in or should I just melt out here in the sun?'

'Before you come in I have to tell you, this is not how I wanted to do this.'

I felt a deep downward tug in my chest as she stepped back and opened the door. She raised her hand in a welcoming gesture and I stepped into a foyer area that had arched doorways leading in three different directions.

'It's not how you wanted to do what?' I asked.

'Let's go into the living room,' she said.

We took the middle arch and stepped into a large room that was neat and nicely furnished. In one corner was a baby grand piano that caught my eye. Eleanor didn't play, unless she had taken it up since she'd left me.

'You want something to drink, Harry?'

'Um, water would be good. It's hot out there.'

'It usually is. Stay here and I'll be right back.'

I nodded and she left me there. I looked around the room. I recognized none of the furniture from the apartment where I had once visited her.

Everything was different, everything was new. The rear wall of the room was comprised of sliding glass doors that looked upon a screened-in pool area. I noticed that surrounding the pool was a white plastic safety fence that people with children put up as a precaution.

Something suddenly began to click about all of Eleanor's mysteries. The obtuse answers, the car trunk that couldn't be opened. People carry fold-up strollers in their trunks. People with children.

'Harry?'

I turned. Eleanor was there. And standing next to her was a little girl with dark hair and eyes. They held hands. I looked from Eleanor to the girl and then back and forth again. The girl had Eleanor's features. The same wave in her hair, the same full lips and bobbed nose. There was something about her demeanor that was the same, too. The way she looked at me.

But the eyes weren't Eleanor's. They were the eyes I saw when I looked in the mirror. They came from me.

A sudden rush of feelings welled up in me, not all of them good. But now I could not take my eyes off the girl.

'Eleanor . . . ?'

'This is Maddie.'

'Maddie?'

'Short for Madeline.'

'Madeline. How old?'

'She's almost four now.'

My mind shifted back. I remembered the last time we'd been together before Eleanor left for good. In the house on the hill. It could have happened then. Eleanor seemed to read my thoughts.

'It was like it was supposed to be. Like something was supposed to make sure we never . . . '

She didn't finish.

'Why didn't you tell me?'

'I wanted it to be the right time.'

'When was that going to be?'

'Now, I guess. You are a detective. I guess I wanted you to find out about it.'

'That's not right.'

'What would have been right?'

Twin skyrockets were going off inside me. One left a trail of red, the other green. They were going different ways. One anger, one warmth. One led to the heart's dark abyss, a devil's punchbowl filled with recriminations and revenge I could dip my cup fully into. The other led away from all of that. To Paradise Road. To bright, blessed days and dark, sacred nights. It led to the place where lost light came from. My lost light.

I knew I could choose one path but not both. I looked up from the girl to Eleanor. She had tears on her face and yet a smile. I knew then what path to choose and that there is no end to things of the heart. I stepped forward and squatted down in front of the girl. I knew from dealing with young witnesses that it was best to approach them on their level.

'Hello, Maddie,' I said to my daughter.

She turned her face and pushed it into her mother's leg.

'I'm too shy,' she said.

'That's okay, Maddie. I'm pretty shy myself. Can I just hold your hand?'

She let go of her mother's hand and extended hers to me. I took it and she wrapped her tiny fingers around my index finger. I shifted forward until my knees were on the floor and I was sitting back on my heels. She peeked her eyes out at me. She didn't seem scared. Just cautious. I raised my other hand and she gave me her other hand, the fingers wrapping the same way around my one.

I leaned forward and raised her tiny fists and held them against my closed eyes. In that moment I knew all the mysteries were solved. That I was home. That I was saved.